Randall Thomas Davidson, William Benham

Life of Archibald Campbell Tait, Archbishop of Canterbury

Vol. I

Randall Thomas Davidson, William Benham

Life of Archibald Campbell Tait, Archbishop of Canterbury
Vol. I

ISBN/EAN: 9783743305397

Manufactured in Europe, USA, Canada, Australia, Japa

Cover: Foto ©Raphael Reischuk / pixelio.de

Manufactured and distributed by brebook publishing software
(www.brebook.com)

Randall Thomas Davidson, William Benham

Life of Archibald Campbell Tait, Archbishop of Canterbury

ARCHIBALD CAMPBELL TAIT

LIFE

OF

...HIBALD CAMPBELL TAIT

Archbishop of Canterbury

BY

RANDALL THOMAS DAVIDSON, D.D.

DEAN OF WINDSOR

AND

WILLIAM BENHAM, B.D.

HON. CANON OF CANTERBURY

IN TWO VOLS.

VOL. I.

LONDON

MACMILLAN AND CO.

AND NEW YORK

1891

PREFACE

THE position occupied by Archbishop Tait in the public view made it inevitable that some biography of him should, ere long, be published. It is now more than eight years since he died, and if it be asked why these volumes have not appeared more speedily, the answer must be found in the extent and variety of the work their preparation has involved. To give sustained attention to the subject has been at times impossible, owing to the constant pressure of duties of other kinds, and each interval in which the book was laid aside has involved fresh labour on its resumption. In place of the material on which biographers can usually rely, Archbishop Tait left behind him a mass of business correspondence, preserved with care, and in some periods well arranged. Valuable as these letters will become hereafter, as giving a picture of the Church of England of our day, they are of comparatively little service for such a book as this. His letter-files contain about 62,500 letters. Not one in a hundred of these is available for biographical purposes, but it may be confidently hoped that their perusal has at least put the writer of each chapter in touch with the circumstances of the years he is recording, and has secured him against mistakes of date, or misrepresentation of important facts.

It would be impossible to thank publicly the many correspondents who have contributed valuable reminiscences, or revised the account of episodes in which they were themselves concerned, or permitted letters in their possession to be used or read. Piquancy might doubtless have been added to some chapters had a less strict rule of reticence been observed, but mistakes in this direction, if such there be, are mistakes upon the right side. What has been attempted is the plain record of a busy and eventful life, covering a period in the history of Church and Nation the importance of which grows every year

CONTENTS

CHAPTER VII.

1852-1856.

CHAPTER VIII.

CHAPTER IX.

1856.

CHAPTER X.

EARLY YEARS OF LONDON EPISCOPATE—1856-60.

CHAPTER XI.

EVANGELISTIC WORK—1857-59.

CHAPTER XII.

1860-64.

CHAPTER XIII.

1861-66.

CHAPTER XIV.

1866-68.

CHAPTER XV.

RITUALISM—1860-1868.

CHAPTER XVI.

THE LONDON EPISCOPATE—1863-1867.

CHAPTER XVII.

THE LONDON EPISCOPATE (*continued*).

1863-1867.

CHAPTER XVIII.

THE LONDON EPISCOPATE (*continued*).

1863-1868.

THE LIFE

CHAPTER I.

1811–1827.

ON Thursday, February 11th, 1869, Archbishop Tait was presiding in the Jerusalem Chamber at Westminster over a meeting of the Ritual Commission. Dean Stanley was sitting by his side. In the course of certain works in the adjacent Abbey a search had for some time been in progress to discover, if possible, the unknown burial-place of King James I. Just as the meeting closed, a messenger entered the Jerusalem Chamber, and whispered to Dean Stanley that the coffin had been discovered in one of the vaults under Henry VII.'s chapel. The excited Dean sprang up, and, inviting the other Commissioners to accompany him, hastened to the spot. As they all drew near, the Dean motioned them back. "It is fitting," he said, "that our first Scottish Archbishop should lead the way into the tomb of our first Scottish King."

Of pure Scottish blood both on his father's and his mother's side, Archibald Campbell Tait, though he lived for more than half a century in England, retained through life his Scottish characteristics, Scottish interests, and Scottish friends ; and some account of the facts and surroundings of his earliest days is essential, in a more than ordinary degree, to the right understanding of his busy life.

It is not often that the early history of a life of three-score years and ten can, when the life is closed, be recorded in detail by a competent witness still alive and strong. The biographers of Archbishop Tait have gratefully to acknowledge the benefit of this unusual aid. The Archbishop's sister, Charlotte, Lady Wake, who was twelve years his senior, and who survived him for six years, has written in full and graphic detail her reminiscences of his early life. Many of these reminiscences had in later years the advantage of his personal correction, and such of them will be quoted as are necessary to give a sufficient picture of his home and boyhood.

"Two hundred years ago," says Lady Wake, "there dwelt in Aberdeenshire—transplanted, however, from the south of Scotland—a family valued for their worth, the Taits[1] of Ludquharn, of the class that used to be known in Scotland by the name of 'bonnet lairds,'—honest men, living on their own farms, and wearing the broad blue 'bonnet' that marked the simplicity of rural and patriarchal lives far removed from the fashions and customs of towns."

The family had many branches, and some of its members seem to have been active in other work besides the cultivation of their farms. The ample records which remain of Aberdeenshire life during the earlier Jacobite strifes picture them as the leading builders and handicraftsmen, advancing steadily in prosperity and social status in the country-side. William Tait of Ludquharn was laid to rest, as the stone over his grave records, "in the year of human salvation 1725, with Agnes Clerk his wife," and in the same grave, in the parish churchyard of Longside, Aberdeenshire, rests his son Thomas, whose merits are recorded in an elaborate Latin epitaph from the ready pen of his friend and pastor,

---

[1] "Tait" is said to be an old Norse name, signifying affection. Some curious legends connected with it are to be found in Ferguson's *English Surnames*, chapter viii.

John Skinner, famous a hundred years ago as a controversialist, an historian, a scholar, and, above all, as the author of 'Tullochgorum' and other well-known Scottish songs.[1] The district of Aberdeenshire to which Longside belongs remained faithful to Episcopacy long after Presbyterianism had been established throughout Scotland, and to this day a large proportion even of its poorest inhabitants adhere with unswerving loyalty to the Church system for which their grandfathers endured indignity and wrong. To the Episcopalians of Longside John Skinner ministered, in sunshine and storm, for no less than sixty-four years, from 1742 to 1807, and the registers and other records of his eventful pastorate, which extended right through the 'persecution period,' show that neither the imprisonment of their minister nor the burning of his chapel was able to detach any branch of the Tait family from a faithful allegiance to their Church's cause.[2] John Skinner was no Jacobite, but he and his flock had to suffer for the Jacobite sympathies of their co-religionists elsewhere, and for many years the scene of his quaint sermons and his famous catechisings was the little yard of his poverty-stricken cottage at Linshart near Longside. "There the

---

[1] The epitaph, which is engraved with singular taste and vigour on a huge sandstone slab, is as follows :—

SUB HOC LAPIDE CINERES GULIELMI TAIT CARPENTARII IN LUDQUHARN ET AGNETIS CLERK EJUS CONJUGIS ILLE HUMANAE SALUTIS 1725 AETATIS SUAE 57 ILLA 1739 AETATIS 70 ANNIS OBIERUNT NEC NON JOANNIS GULIELMI ALTERIUS GULIELMI ET AGNETIS TAIT SOBOLIS EORUM QUI IIS PRAEDECESSERUNT SEPULTI SUNT. HIC QUOQUE CONDUNTUR EXUVIAE THOMAE TAIT IN THUNDERTON FILII S. D. GULIELMI ET AGNETIS NATU MAXIMI QUI IN ARTE LAPIDARIA DUM POTUIT GNAVUS IN ALENDA FAMILIA FAELIX MORIBUS PROBUS ANIMO ÆQUUS VICINIS AMICUS TANDEM ANNORUM SATUR FIDEQUE ET SPE FULTUS AD PATRES MIGRAVIT ANNO MDCCLXX AET. LXXIX. R.I.P.

The final letters of the epitaph have a special interest, John Skinner being one of those who were at that time contending vehemently in favour of the doctrine and practice of prayer for the dead.

[2] Many members of the Tait family still live in Longside and the neighbouring parishes, and are firm adherents of the Scottish Episcopal Church.

congregation," we are told, "were obliged to sit, sometimes under a heavy rain, sometimes with their benches or stools planted in the snow, while he officiated and addressed them from the window."[1]   Among these undaunted worshippers was the large family of Thomas Tait, whose son John, on leaving Aberdeenshire to settle in Edinburgh, must have carried with him stirring memories of the Sundays of his early years.   Small was the encouragement or support which these sorely pressed and gallant Churchmen received from the great sister Church of England, and it would have startled them indeed to learn that the grandson of John Tait would be Archbishop of Canterbury.

Once settled in Edinburgh, John Tait was articled in the office of Ronald Craufurd, a well-known Writer to the Signet, in whose hands lay the legal business of many of the foremost Scottish families, and there John received the legal training of which he made good use in after life when he succeeded, on Mr. Craufurd's death, to the increasing business of the house.   There is a portrait of John Tait, by Raeburn, which well represents the calm good sense and the spirit of manly enterprise which he inherited from the ' blue bonnets ' of Aberdeen.   He married, in 1763, a lady of the singular name of Charles Murdoch, so called after Prince Charlie, the hero of Scottish imagination, in whose cause her family had suffered much.   "She was," we are told, "well born, well educated, very pretty, and very poor, and so independent was her spirit that, like many of the Stuart ladies of the day, she supported her widowed mother by the work of her own hands."   Charles Murdoch, Jacobite though she was, was a Presbyterian, and drew her husband to the Established Church of Scotland, into which their only son, Craufurd, was baptized. Craufurd Tait's mother died when he was only sixteen.

---

[1] See Walker's *Life of John Skinner*, p. 59.

"She had," says Lady Wake, "imparted to her son much of the poetry of her own mind, and a love for the many traditions of her ancestry.[1]   Perhaps it would have been better if his father's practical sense had rather been the prevailing element in his character."

The family house in Edinburgh was in Park Place, close to 'The Meadows,' on the outskirts of the Old Town.[2] It was next door to the house of Sir Ilay Campbell, Lord President of the Court of Session, the highest judicial office in Scotland.   He was a man as much beloved for the straightforward simplicity of his character as respected for his legal knowledge, and his house was one of the most popular resorts in Edinburgh.   Susan, a younger daughter of Sir Ilay Campbell, became, at the age of eighteen, the wife of Craufurd Tait.   In the year 1800, John Tait, the Archbishop's grandfather, died at the age of seventy-three.

"He had been as happy in the tender care of the young wife of his only son as if she had been his own child.   His death, though it came in the fulness of years, was a heavy misfortune to the young couple, for his calm good sense was a safer guide to his son than his own erratic genius.   He left

[1] The ravens which formed part of the armorial bearings of Archbishop Tait have their origin in the following legend :—"There dwelt in the wilds of Galloway, in the days of Robert Bruce, a lady known as the Widow of the Peak, whose three brave sons were devoted to the adventurous king.   His hiding-places among the mountains had again and again been discovered by means of three ravens who followed and hovered over the little band.   At length Murdoch, youngest son of the Widow of the Peak, brought down the traitorous ravens with his arrows, and was rewarded by the grateful king with the lands of Cumlodden."

[2] The house has now been pulled down to make way for the new buildings of the University of Edinburgh.   In the wall of these buildings a bronze bust of the Archbishop, by Raggi, stands in a sculptured niche, under which is the following inscription :—"To commemorate in his native country the piety, the virtues, and the wisdom of Archibald Campbell Tait, Archbishop of Canterbury 1868-1882, friends and admirers in Scotland have erected this monument on the site of the house in which he was born."   The monument was unveiled with public ceremonial on February 27th, 1885.

to him the estate of Harviestoun in Clackmannanshire, with a tolerably good house, and in addition to this, and to the house in Edinburgh, a beautiful property on the shores of Loch Fyne, which he had named Cumlodden, after the family place of the Murdochs. This he had purchased with the express intention of its being resold if ever the estate of Castle Campbell, adjacent to Harviestoun, should be offered for sale by its owner, the Duke of Argyll. The addition of this to Harviestoun would make a consolidated instead of a divided property. The unfortunate result was, that when his son became the proprietor, he did indeed purchase Castle Campbell, but he was so attached to the romantic shores of Loch Fyne that he could not persuade himself to part with Cumlodden, and kept the two, borrowing a large sum of money to enable him to do so."

At Cumlodden he threw himself with enthusiasm into the improvements which his imagination already saw transforming the habits and lives of the Highlanders. He devised a new order of things, building model cottages, and apportioning to each its garden and its four-acre field of arable land. Immense sums of money were thus spent in vain. The whole scheme was foreign alike to the desires and the capabilities of those whom he tried to benefit. The soil and its inhabitants successfully united their efforts to baffle his plans, and he retired discomfited and impoverished to Harviestoun. There, in like manner, but on a more congenial soil, he lavished money on 'improvements' on the largest scale. The house was half rebuilt.

"The high-road," says Lady Wake, "ran too near the house, so it was lifted, as if by magic, half a mile lower down the glen. A garden was laid out with Milton's description of Eden for the model. And surely no garden ever was like it! Of immense extent, it enclosed the lower part of the glen; a dell of green turf led right through it, while a bright and noisy burn leaping from the rocks above danced merrily through its entire length, speeding through ferns and wild-flowers till it suddenly disappeared, to emerge with a bound from a cave many yards

below. Our home was a very happy one; our father, thoroughly
enjoying the society of his children, and seeing all his dreams of
picturesque beauty assuming tangible form, had no misgivings as
to the expense which attended the gratification of his tastes. It
never crossed his wife's mind that he could err in judgment, and
thus the 'improvements' went on in rapid succession. Inventions
for farm and field, now in common use, were seen in their earliest
days at Harviestoun—machinery for chopping and steaming all
manner of food for cattle, the kitchen spit turned by water-pressure
from the mountain burns, elaborate poultry-houses, the wonder of
the country-side,[1]—these were among the least of the products
of his active brain, with which no thoughts about expense were
allowed to interfere.

. "Our father commanded the Clackmannanshire Yeomanry,
and I well remember our enthusiasm at the warlike feats of that
gallant corps as they performed a sham fight at Harviestoun on
the occasion of the jubilee of George III. in 1809. Our father,
mounted on one of the grey carriage-horses, was most magnificent
in our eyes, with his helmet adorned with a silver thistle, and
the motto, translated for us, 'For our country and our firesides.'
The whole land had been excited to a frenzy of patriotism by
Buonaparte's threatened invasion, and real as was our loyalty to
the King, our hatred for the French was more real still. Besides
the military ardour of the yeomanry, there was a quieter witness
close at hand that the French were expected, in the shape of an
immense 'caravan,' as it was then called,[2] which had been built
by our father's orders, for the purpose of carrying us all to the
other side of the hills when the French fleet should appear in

[1] "I remember them well. Story upon story of comfortable chambers
rose one above the other, reached by a series of little ladders, up which the
various inhabitants ascended with the utmost decorum, the cocks conducting
their hens to the highest story, the turkey-cocks and their ladies taking
possession of their apartment on the second floor, while the geese and ducks
waddled, well satisfied, into the lowest room. Once in the midst of one of
the absorbing and interminable arguments of which our father was so fond,
he was astonished by his brother-in-law, Lord Succoth, starting off in a race
towards the poultry-house, where he stood agape watching the ascent of a
large old turkey-cock. 'Well, if I had not seen him, I never could have
believed that Bubbly-Jock [the usual name in Scotland for a turkey-cock]
would have done such a thing,' was his speech, as he quietly turned back,
and took up the broken thread of his argument."—C. W.

[2] "It would now be more modestly termed an 'omnibus,' but it was of
gigantic size and weight."—C. W.

the Forth.   We secretly regretted that they never came, and we rather grudged, as time went on, that the 'caravan' had nothing nobler to do than perform the peaceful duty of carrying us all to church on rainy days.   Our family was Presbyterian, and our Sundays were strict indeed, and terribly irksome to us children, who were too lively to be content with reading grave books which we could not understand.   Yet we could not but receive abiding impressions from our gentle mother.   Each night, when she knew her little ones were in bed, she would bend over us, whispering the well-known verse—

> 'This night I lay me down to sleep,
> And give my soul to Christ to keep ;
> Sleep I now : wake I never,
> I give my soul to Christ for ever.'

This became so fixed a habit with us all that in after years our soldier brother used to tell that he never, even when sleeping under arms on the ground, forgot to repeat this prayer.

"It was in 1811 that a heavy trouble came into our home. We were now eight children in all,[1] the youngest being a little black-eyed boy, Ilay Campbell by name, who was just two years old.   He was the plaything of the house.   One night he was restless and ill ; in the morning it was found that in the course of that night one limb had been completely paralysed. The medical men said it was in consequence of cutting his teeth.   Our poor mother was grievously distressed.   She could not bear to think of the child's blighted life, for to her mind the restoration of the withered limb seemed impossible ; the misfortune made too deep an impression on her, and cast a shadow forwards.

---

[1] Viz. :—

John, born 11 Feb. 1796.   [Died 22 May 1877.]

Susan Murray (afterwards Lady Sitwell), born 2 March 1797.   [Died 13 May 1880.]

James Campbell, born 29 October 1798.   [Died 18 Jany. 1879.]

Charlotte Murdoch (afterwards Lady Wake), born 9 June 1800.   [Died 31 March 1888.]

Anna Mary (afterwards Mrs. Wildman), born 15 Feb. 1804.   [Died 22 Feb. 1879.]

Thomas Forsyth, born 20 Aug. 1805.   [Died 16 March 1859.]

Craufurd, born 9 Sept. 1807.   [Died 6 April 1828.]

Ilay Campbell, born 1 June 1809.   [Died 28 Feb. 1821.]

"Shortly after this we were enjoined to be very still, for that our mother was ill. The cause was soon made clear to us by the arrival of the old nurse, in whose presence we always took a mysterious pleasure. She had visited us about every two years, telling us that she had brought a new little brother or sister. Sometimes she had found it among the cabbage-beds, sometimes below a rose-bush. Whatever she chose to say we believed, for while her short reign lasted her power was absolute. By her permission alone we could see our mother, or make whispering visits to the new baby's apartment, close to her. Accordingly on the night of the 21st, or rather on the morning of the 22d, of December 1811, we perfectly understood why we were to have a holiday on the usual condition of being very quiet; but we observed in the days that immediately followed that something unusual had happened. There was some mystery in the house, for there were grave looks and shakings of the head, not only among the servants, but among the lady friends who came and went. There was not the usual gladsome tone in all that was said, though we were kept at too great a distance to hear the words spoken. At length, after some days, with the connivance of the old nurse, I crept into my mother's room, and through the darkened light saw her in earnest conversation with the family doctor, George Bell. She had been crying; he was comforting her with hopeful words. He said: 'You have been thinking too much of poor little Campbell's leg; but I hope we shall be able to set all to rights.' Catching sight of me, as though glad of a diversion, he lifted me up, and placed me on the bed. My mother gently kissed me, but told me not to stay; so I passed at once into her dressing-room, from which was heard the wailing voice of the new-born baby, and for the first time I saw my little brother. He lay on the old nurse's lap, making a complaining noise—and no wonder; for, poor little thing! instead of the lovely little feet that it had always been our delight to kiss when a new baby was brought among us, the nurse showed me a mass of bandages. He was born club-footed!

"Certainly the circumstances of his birth did not promise the noble career of usefulness with which God blessed him. Had he been born in poorer circumstances, or had his parents been either careless or faint-hearted, he must have remained a cripple all his days, for his poor little feet were found to be completely doubled inwards. However, the assurance was given that there was good hope; they could in time be brought to a proper shape. 'In time!' Alas! it was over those words that my poor mother wept, for she knew that they expressed a suffering infancy, and a childhood debarred from childhood's active enjoyment. She was full of faith and love, and perhaps God whispered to her heart that by those very means He would best form her child for the work He destined for him; for when she left her room to rejoin the little circle, which never felt right when she was absent, she brought with her the usual gentle cheerfulness; and the only outward sign of the misfortune was that the baby Archie was fondled and spoken of with an inexpressible tenderness. She was the most submissive of women, and so she found rest to the disquietude of her heart. She knew her husband to be the most energetic of men, and, thoroughly believing in him, she felt sure that all that could be done would be done. Many were the visits the baby received before he was a month old in the little apartment in which the old nurse held her court; but his first appearance in public— that is to say, his christening—was the event to which we, the younger branches of the family, looked forward with the greatest interest. At length the day appointed arrived—the 10th of February 1812. Our mother was sufficiently recovered to receive her friends, and the usual little circle was gathered round her, while all her children, except the eldest, who had gone to Harrow after the Christmas holidays, dressed in their best, gazed with a little more than the usual amount of watchfulness on the well-remembered ceremony which added a new member to the visible Church of Christ and a new name to the chorus which already filled the nursery. The mysterious large china bowl occupied once again its conspicuous place in the drawing-room, making the centre of the solemn group, where the father held up his infant, Archibald Campbell, to receive his baptism from the hands of the friendly minister of the Old Church of St. Giles', Dr. Thomas MacKnight, who had come once more to perform his loving office. The gentle mother and the seven brothers and sisters encircled him. The newly named Archibald Campbell was a lovely baby: his long robes hid the poor little feet; and if there was any difference in the welcome given to him from that which greeted his predecessors, it was only that it was more tender and loving; and as our mother passed her treasure from friend to friend, admiring smiles saluted him, and soothed the distress she had hid away in her heart.

"And thus she returned to the daily duties of her life, bringing back with her the quiet influence that had on the family all the effect of an absolute rule. On looking back to her character, there shines out this remarkable difference between her and other women,—that no one ever saw her in the slightest bustle or fuss of any kind, nor can any one remember her voice raised in anger. Her memory comes back with a sort of moonlight radiance. Clouds in her daily life there must have been; but she passed through them all, brightening them to others, and by them herself undimmed.

"I love to remember her kneeling in the large white old-fashioned chair which belonged to her bedroom. She often retired thither for private prayer; and among the memories of earliest childhood her figure shines out as in a picture, kneeling upon the cushion of the high-backed chair, her earnest face lifted up to God; but she never prayed aloud. It was only when we were very little children that she did not mind the presence of one of us when she carried her distresses to the Comforter. Everything she did was so quietly done that though we saw, when we were at Harviestoun, that she always kept in her bedroom a little bunch of daisies, carefully tended in a glass of water, not one of us knew until long afterwards that she gathered them from our little brother Willie's grave, and thus treasured them for his sake; yet he had died so long ago that few of us had the slightest recollection of his birth, and he had lived but for six months. She must have gone to the grave quite alone in the early morning, for no one ever saw her there.

"Dear mother! She was so purely and innocently good. The modern language of what is called the religious world was unknown to her, but the true spirit of religion dwelt in her, and her right hand did not know what her left hand had done. Of her self-denying deeds of charity few were known until her death caused them to be missed, and I cannot remember ever to have heard her speak unkindly of a single human being. I remember her sympathising in the remark made to her by a poor woman, to whom she had lent a volume of Blair's Sermons. To my mother's inquiry whether she liked them, the reply was: ''Deed, leddy, no that weel; for in a' that reading [turning over a number of pages] there's neither God nor Jesus Christ.'[1]   Her good-natured charity was so well understood by the poor around her country home that some of them did not hesitate to encroach on it.   I remember her amusement at the answer made to her by a pensioner, as to whether she would like to have money or oatmeal.   'Weel, leddy,' she replied, with a curtsey, 'baith's best.'

"The birth of Archibald was followed by two bright and happy years in the family circle.   The two eldest boys came and went between Harrow and Harviestoun, the eldest daughter was growing into womanhood, and the nursery was full of cheery little faces.

"The winters were spent, as usual, in the Edinburgh home, the summer and autumn at Harviestoun.   Suddenly, on January 3, 1814, our mother died, almost in a moment.   The overstrained heart had given way.   We were summoned to her room, where she lay dead upon the sofa, on the very spot where I can first remember her.   My earliest recollection is that of sitting, some ten or eleven years before, upon a little stool beside that sofa, pricking upon paper the outline of the chintz flowers on her dress, while she laid her hand upon my head, and repeated in a low voice Cowper's lines to his mother's picture.   The two scenes—the beginning and the end—are, even now, inextricably blended in my mind.   Dark and dreary were the clouds that now fell upon the happy home in Park Place.   While we children crept about the house, and remarked to each other that the snow was falling upon mother's grave, relations and friends were anxiously discussing up-stairs what could be done for the best with the nine children thus thrown suddenly upon our father's care.   Our father!   O how well I remember his constant pacing up and down, care and grief altogether changing his countenance!   For now, at this very crisis, he had come to know that to this crowning sorrow of his life were added other causes of perplexity and trouble.   While she was by his side there had been sunshine, and one difficulty after another had seemed to melt.   But now he had to face the fact that, misled by his sanguine temperament, he had embarked in, and even carried through, enterprises which, while

---

[1] The criticism is severe, but it is worth noting that more than half a century afterwards the Archbishop used frequently to describe a sermon which had dissatisfied him as "a trifle Blairy."

benefiting many, had ruined himself. The children soon came to understand that heavy trials lay ahead. The establishment was to be broken up, the servants whom we loved must go, including the dear old coachman whom we had known all our lives; his grey carriage-horses were now to work upon the farm. The schoolroom life came to an end. My younger sister and I were sent to school, and household cares of every sort devolved upon our eldest sister, Susan, who was barely seventeen years old. The constant care that little Archie required endeared him specially to us all. He soon became a well-grown child, with a touching look of appeal that went straight to the heart. He was naturally more lame than Campbell, who had only one limb affected, but both boys were unable for climbing or games, and became all in all to each other, while yet a complete contrast—the one with bright black eyes and hair, his face all rippling with fun; the other—Archie—blue-eyed and fair-haired, watching the quicker movements of his brother as though they were necessary parts of his own existence."

The nurse, Betty Morton by name, was a person so remarkable that she became almost the centre of the family life. She ruled her nursery with a strictness only equalled by her loyal devotion to the young mistress at its head. But little Archie was of course her special charge, and she was destined to take no unimportant part in his education for the work of life. She was a strict Sabbatarian, and the Sunday amusements were confined mainly to a study of the absorbing pictures in an ancient Family Bible, "dedicated to Catherine Parr, and full of such illustrations as that of a man with a beam as large as a rafter sticking straight out of his eye." To the systematic nursery study of this Bible, however, both the Archbishop and his sisters attributed in after years their unusually thorough acquaintance with the details of Scripture history. In the first three autumns after their mother's death the younger boys were taken by Betty Morton to Garscadden, a strange, weird old house, three miles from Sir Ilay Campbell's home at Garscube near Glasgow. The Archbishop frequently declared that this quaint old house, with its wonderful turreted gateway, its hideous carved faces grinning from every corner, and its trim old-fashioned garden, was the very first recollection of his life. His early reading-lessons were under the charge, not only of his eldest sister Susan, whose hands must have been more than full, but of Betty Morton, no despicable instructress, and one rigidly accurate in exacting the daily quota of lessons.

In the autumn of 1818 Susan Tait was married to Sir George Sitwell of Renishaw, near Chesterfield, and Archie began a few months later to make acquaintance with the beautiful Derbyshire home which was to be the scene of many of his holidays for thirty years to come. Soon after her marriage Lady Sitwell invited her four youngest brothers to pay a long visit to Renishaw. Slow was their method of conveyance thither. Under the faithful charge of Betty Morton they were put on board a smack at Leith. A dead calm soon came on, and seven days and eight nights were passed upon the sea before the travellers in hungry plight reached Hull, whence they had to journey up the Humber to Gainsborough, and thence post. When the visit came to an end, a plan was carried out, at Lady Sitwell's instigation, which materially affected the whole life of the future Archbishop. Time and skill had hitherto done nothing towards curing the lameness of the two little boys. Campbell's right leg was shrunk and feeble, while Archie's feet were, to all appearance, hopelessly deformed. Sir George and Lady Sitwell were bent on sending the two children to Whitworth, in Lancashire, where dwelt two doctors, famous for their general skill, but especially for their cures effected upon twisted or broken limbs. The father's consent was obtained, and to Whitworth the little boys were sent, under the guardianship of the faithful Betty.

Whitworth was then a small village—it is now a very large one—three miles from Rochdale, in a wild and hilly region. More than a century ago John Taylor, farrier and blacksmith, carried on his profession in this village, and was so successful therein that he began to practise, as he expressed it, on 'humans.' Here also he succeeded so well that his fame soon sounded throughout the neighbouring country, and his biped patients began to exceed the quadrupeds in number, though he is said always to have given the preference to the latter. His reputation in the new branch of his profession was due mainly to his real or supposed cure of cancers, and his skill in the setting of broken bones, and in straightening twisted or contracted joints. Patients came to him from all parts of England, and innumerable anecdotes testify, at the least, to his shrewd common sense, his homely skill, his rough independence, and his kindly heart. His charge was eighteenpence a week for medicine and attendance. Any further payment from his richer patients served to replenish the boxes from which the fees of those unable to pay for his help were drawn. His fame advanced so rapidly that before many years had passed he was sent for by George III. to prescribe for the Princess Elizabeth, whom he is said to have cured of some ailment which had baffled all ordinary skill.

John Taylor had died before the two little brothers were taken to Whitworth, but the business was carried on by his son James and two nephews. James Taylor, who is described as "a stout man in a blue coat, about fifty years of age, having much the appearance of a well-to-do farrier," seems to have inherited his father's eccentricities as well as his skill. "He was often to be seen walking about before the house with an old hat slung before him by a cord over his shoulders.   In this hat he had a large lump of some compound, which he rolled into pills as he walked about.   The hat was fairly saturated through and through with the drug, and appeared to have been used for that purpose for years."

His surgery is thus described by an eye-witness, who visited Whitworth in this very year, 1819 :—

"There were more than a hundred patients in the village. . . . Wretched invalids were to be seen on every side, some with patched faces, some with an arm or a leg bound fast to a board, some with splints on their arms, others moving slowly along like spectres, in the lowest stage of physical exhaustion. . . . The doctor's house was sufficiently pointed out by its large size, and by the wooden machine standing in the street before it, for fixing immovably horse patients when under their hands.   In the 'surgery' were some fifty patients waiting to be dressed or examined.   They were arranged in a row round the room, and in one corner sat James Taylor, with his surgical apparatus, consisting of the old shoeing-box of the blacksmith. In this were a few bottles and pots of the invariable remedies —'keen,' a caustic ointment to which the Taylors had given this name, 'green salve,' 'red-bottle,' some blisters and plasters ready spread, a large wooden skewer or two, and some hurds.[1] The patients came in succession before the doctor, and he rapidly examined and dismissed them, 'flirting' off the blisters when necessary with the wooden skewers, or roughly dressing with the 'keen.'   Among his patients that morning was a stalwart blacksmith, whose ill-set arm was in a primitive but effectual fashion re-broken and re-set in the space of a few moments."[2]

To John Taylor's care the little boys were now committed, and the following account of his experiences was dictated by Archbishop Tait himself fifty-two years afterwards :—

"No one but myself can give you the history of my life

---

[1] Coarse undressed tow.

[2] See *A Biographical Sketch of the Whitworth Doctors*; Rochdale, 1876.

at Whitworth in 1819. Camie and I, with dear old Betty, lived in the Red Lion, a common public-house, but the best in the place. Our sitting-room was the best parlour in the house, with a sanded floor, adjoining the bar; our bedroom, a garret up-stairs. In one large bed I slept with Betty, Camie in a smaller one close to it. We soon made acquaintance with the men who habitually frequented the house,—Jim o'Dick's and Tom o'Simon's (their names being simply their Christian names attached to their fathers')—the manners and customs of the district being too simple to admit of a universal use of family names amongst the working classes. The skittle-ground and the tap-room were our places of conversation, yet I do not remember much evil; probably we were too young to understand or observe it, and certainly Betty kept a watchful look-out on us. One great object of interest was, I remember, the courtship carried on by young Lomax, the son of a farmer in the neighbourhood, who was paying his addresses to Betty Lord, the daughter of the fat old landlady of the Red Lion. This was full of interest to us. We went to the doctor's every day early to have the tin boots in which he kept our legs encased properly arranged, and the progress of the cure attended to. These tin boots hurt us very much, and I have often marvelled how we were able to hobble about in them as we did all day long, except the short time Camie had lessons from the village schoolmaster, or read Latin with the clergyman of the parish, Mr. Porter. I cannot recollect ever doing anything in the way of lessons during the nine months I was there. I have since been told I had writing lessons from this schoolmaster, but either I have forgotten it, or he has confused me with my brother. I do not remember ever reading story-books, but I used to wander about with all sorts of mysterious thoughts, making plays to myself out of them, and fighting all sorts of imaginary enemies with my stick or whatever I could lay my hands upon. Camie and I amused ourselves very well, and dear old Betty was very kind to us, helping us in every way she could think of. During the nights we were distressed by the tin boots, in which we were obliged to sleep, but by degrees we got accustomed to them. There was scarcely any one approaching to lady or gentleman in the place, which was full of invalids of the lower middle classes, chiefly with real or supposed cases of cancer, or stiffened limbs, for the management of which the Whitworth doctors were famous. One of the brothers kept what he called a pack of hounds, which were of course a continual source of amusement. He went out with them after he had seen his patients in the early morning, and in the evening, when the sport was over, spent the hours in the midst of an admiring circle in the tap-room of the Red Lion. This was the mode of life of both the Taylors, yet to these men, under Providence, we owed our restoration to the perfect use of our limbs. Probably my brother's—dear Camie's—case was more difficult than mine, for, though much deformed in shape, my feet were possessed, I imagine, of each bone and muscle in full vigour; therefore they had only, as it were, to be formed into their proper natural shape by continual gentle force, the force that comes from constant pressure, while Campbell's limb had, from paralysis while yet a baby, been weakened to that degree that its growth had never kept pace with the rest of his body. Yet by the strange treatment of these men it was perfectly restored, and at the end of a year his lameness gradually wore off."

Returning to Edinburgh in amended health, Archibald Tait was admitted in October 1821[1] to the celebrated High School of the city. Up to the time of which we write, and for many years afterwards, it was the habit of most of the best-known families in Scotland to spend the winter half of the year in Edinburgh, or, if not themselves living there, to send their sons thither for education. It is scarcely an exaggeration to say that almost every Scotchman of literary or political eminence during the previous century and a half had received his education within the walls of the High School of Edinburgh. Of men then living it may suffice to name Walter Scott, Henry Brougham, Francis Jeffrey, and Henry Cockburn. At the banquet given to Brougham on April 25th, 1825, the future Lord Chancellor thus characteristically described his former school :—

[1] There is some little doubt about the precise date, and unfortunately the High School Registers for these years have been lost. But the above is probably accurate.

"A school like the old High School of Edinburgh is invaluable. And for what is it so? It is because men of the highest and lowest rank of society send their children to be educated together. The oldest friend I have in the world, your worthy Vice-President,[1] and myself were at the High School of Edinburgh together, and in the same class, along with others who still possess our friendship. One of them was a nobleman, now in the House of Peers, and some of them were the sons of shopkeepers in the lowest part of the Cowgate of Edinburgh—shops of the most inferior description—and one or two of them were sons of menial servants in the town. There they were, sitting side by side, giving and taking places from each other, without the slightest impression on the part of my noble friends of any superiority, on their parts, over the other boys, or any ideas of inferiority, on the part of the other boys, to them; and this is my reason for preferring the old High School of Edinburgh to other, and what may be termed more patrician, schools, however well regulated or conducted."

It was here, and under these conditions, that Archibald Tait received his first systematic education between the years of nine and twelve. The Head-master, or Rector, was Dr. Carson, and the number of boys in the school was about 700. His education until his return from Whitworth had been, as may be supposed, of the most desultory and fragmentary sort.[2] But his progress, once begun, was very rapid. An extant poetical translation of some lines from the second Æneid, done by him in Dr. Pyper's class in the early months of 1824, would do credit to a much older boy.

It was during his early school days that Archie experienced his first great sorrow. Never, to the very end of his life, was he able even to allude to it without tears. His brother Campbell, who had been from earliest

---

[1] Lord Douglas Gordon Hallyburton.

[2] An extant letter to his sister, written June 15th, 1820, is more like the handiwork of a boy of six than of eight and a half.

childhood his inseparable companion, had always longed to be a sailor.   But his lameness had been such as to render the fulfilment of the wish impossible.   Now—thanks to the Whitworth 'doctors'—the lameness was gone, and the boy, to his unspeakable delight, was passed as fit for service.   He was to go to Portsmouth for the usual training, and his departure was only delayed for a few weeks because the attention of the houschold was taken up by little Archie, who was sharply attacked with scarlet fever.   He rapidly recovered, however, and a farewell party was given by Campbell to his school-fellows before starting for Portsmouth.   That evening, when the party broke up, Campbell complained of feeling ill.   Scarlet fever in its most malignant form was upon him, and after two days' illness he died.   The shock to Archie, still weak after his fever, was terrible, and he used himself to say in later years that it had affected his whole life.   The two boys, whose strange experiences together at Whitworth had forged a link between them of no ordinary strength, had become wholly dependent on one another.   The loss of his bright-eyed active brother was therefore the more irreparable to Archie, who, unable for the rough games of his school-fellows, was now more than ever thrown in upon himself and his books for amusement and occupation.

In October 1824 Mr. Tait removed his son from the High School to the newly founded 'Edinburgh Academy,' where he took his place in the highest class.   With this important school he maintained through life so close a connection that a few sentences seem desirable to explain its origin and character.

Lord Cockburn, in the sparkling *Memorials of his Time*,[1] writes of it as follows:—

"Leonard Horner and I had often discussed the causes and

---

[1] Vol. i. p. 414.

the remedies of the decline of classical education in Scotland.
. . . So one day on the top of the Pentlands—emblematic of
the solidity of our foundation and the extent of our prospects
—we two resolved to set about the establishment of a new
school. . . . [Sir Walter] Scott took it up eagerly. . . . We were
fiercely opposed, as we expected, by the Town Council, and (but
not fiercely) by a few of the friends of the institution we were going
to encroach upon.[1] In 1823 the building was begun. It was
opened, under the title of 'The Edinburgh Academy,' on October
1st, 1824, amid a great assemblage of proprietors, pupils, and
the public. We had a good prayer by Sir Harry Moncreiff, and
speeches by Scott and old Henry Mackenzie, and an important
day for education in Scotland, in reference to the middle and
upper classes."

The school thus auspiciously founded rose at a bound
to the first rank of importance. Among its earliest
governors, or, as they were called, directors, were Sir
Walter Scott, Lord Cockburn, Francis Jeffrey, and Leonard
Horner. Its first Head-master, or Rector, was the Rev.
John Williams, Vicar of Lampeter, and afterwards, while
retaining his Scotch head-mastership, Archdeacon of
Cardigan. The character and work of the school are thus
described in a speech delivered by Principal Shairp on the
occasion of its ' Jubilee,' celebrated under the Archbishop's
presidency in 1874.

"Our founders," he said, "kept their eye on utility—little or
nothing on amenity. The situation they chose, the building they
erected, the six hours' continuous work by day, with nearly as
many more by night, required from the boys who stood near the
top, made the existence of most boys of my time somewhat too
unrejoicing. In vain you would look there for the green
'Playing-fields' of Eton by the shining Thames, or even for the
green Close of Rugby with its venerable elm-trees, and all the
pleasant associations that gather round these. These things the
Academy did not affect. But it aimed at and affected careful
grounding, sound learning, and a most laborious work. And the

---

[1] *i.e.* the High School of Edinburgh.

result has been that no Academy boy ever learned any part of scholarship there which he had afterwards to unlearn, go where he might. Ten continuous months of as faithful teaching and as hard a grind as any school in Britain ever knew,—this is my impression in looking back to four years spent within the Academy walls."

It was a day-school only. The boys lived at home or boarded with Edinburgh families, their preparation-work being carried on, in most cases, with the help of a private tutor. But Archie had no such assistance. His father's affairs were becoming more and more embarrassed, and it was thought necessary to practise the most rigid economy.

"In his earlier school-days," says Lady Wake, "the faithful Betty was his only help in learning his lessons. She used to hold the Latin books close to her eyes, diligently following each word as he repeated page after page. 'Ay, it maun be richt; it's just word for word, and it sounds like it,' was his encouragement, or else a sudden lowering of the book, with 'Na, na, it's no that ava',' would warn him that he was wrong. Of one principal part of his education she was absolute mistress, and none could have been better. She took care that he was out of bed early in the morning, and allowed no relaxation on this point. This was no unimportant help, for had he been left to himself, delicate as he was, the little fellow would hardly have had the resolution required."

The school-year lasted from the beginning of October to the end of July, and at its close the results of the year's work and examination were announced, and the prizes given by some public man, in the presence of an immense assemblage of parents and friends. It is difficult for those unacquainted with Scottish life, and especially the Scottish life of fifty years ago, to realise the importance attached, not in Edinburgh alone, but throughout Scotland, to the doings and the speeches of this annual Exhibition Day.

At the close of his first year the name of Archibald Tait
stood third in order in the school, although the average
age of the upper boys was much higher than his own.　In
his second and third years he obtained in each case the
gold medal as 'Dux' of the whole school, besides carrying off prizes innumerable for Latin, Greek, English, and
French.　The prize poems and essays, which were published at the time, attest alike the high efficiency of
the school and the vigour of the boy's own powers.
In particular, an English poem on the 'Conversion of
St. Paul,' and a set of Latin hexameters on American
Independence, are worthy of a more than ordinary prize-
poem immortality.　On the 'Exhibition Day,' August
1st, 1827, the prizes were given by Lord Cockburn,[1] whose
speech of earnest eloquence, addressed to the youthful
'Dux,' was long remembered by all who listened to it.
Tait's success on this occasion was remarkable.　He had
secured no less than six of the foremost prizes in what
was already a school of the first order,[2] and Lord Cockburn
was justified when he concluded his address in these
words : "Go forth, young man, and remember that where-
ever you go, the eyes of your country are upon you."

The pale-faced boy who stood forward as 'Dux' and
prizeman in 1827 was called upon, as Dean of Carlisle, on
an 'Exhibition Day,' twenty-five years later, to give
away the prizes in the same room.　His speech, too,
in addressing the 'Dux' of the school, was one long
remembered, but probably no one present, except the
speaker, connected together at the time the speeches of
the two men, alike in earnestness of purpose, but characteristically different in tone.　"I hope and believe that

---

[1] By this name he is best known, but he was not made a Judge till 1834,
and in 1827 he was still Mr. Henry Cockburn.

[2] The number of boys in the school in its first year was 372, in its second
year 440, and in its third year 519.

you are going forth into life, not to seek the applause which depends on the fleeting breath of your fellow-men, nor that success which ends only in this life, but that you will remember that another Eye besides that of man is upon you, and that a higher approbation is to be won than that of your fellow-creatures."

CHAPTER II.

1827–1833.

IN October 1827 Archibald Tait matriculated as a student
of the University of Glasgow. Far less change has been
wrought during the last half-century in the system of the
Scottish than of the English Universities. Now, as then,
the students in the University of Glasgow have but one
session in each year, lasting from the beginning of November to the end of April. There is little which corresponds
to the college life of an English University. The students
live in lodgings where they will, and attend the professors'
lectures, the actual classes of each lecturer being very
much larger than is at all usual in any English University.
The expenses of a student can, in such circumstances, be
easily reduced to a far smaller sum than was possible,
until quite recent years, either at Oxford or Cambridge.
Scores of lads belonging to the working classes have, from
time immemorial, become students at the Scottish Universities, earning enough money during the long summer
vacation, either by teaching or by manual labour, to pay
their way at Glasgow or Edinburgh during the six months'
session, and thus, living hard and straining every nerve,
attain their desired end—a University education, and
admission, it may be, into the Scottish ministry.

In 1827 the number of students in the University of
Glasgow was about 1200. The Principal, or resident

head, was Dr. Macfarlane, and the leading Professor was Mr. Daniel Sandford,[1] who occupied the Greek Chair. Archbishop Tait used to maintain, in after years, that Sandford was, from a professional point of view, the best teacher he had ever known :

"He possessed in a wonderful degree the power of quickening into life the latent intellect of his pupils. That he inspired and kept alive the spirit of absolute enthusiasm which stimulated a class of three hundred not very clever lads to press forward in their studies, as in a race, is no slight evidence of the ability and character of the man. To him and to Archdeacon Williams I owe more than to any other teachers. I ought to add that the Chair of Logic was held by another remarkable man, Professor Buchanan, who, without any shining abilities, had a peculiar power of developing the mind and intelligence of his pupils by perpetually requiring them to arrange their ideas in essays, which were read aloud and commented on in the presence of the whole class. Some of the other Professors were less capable, and the large classes of quite young lads were apt to become boisterous. Some of the scenes I remember in the Mathematical class would baffle description. 'Here, let off these !' Henry Page called to me one day, handing me a bundle of crackers. When I refused, he let them off himself, whereupon a student instantly fell down and pretended to be dead, to the unspeakable terror of the simple Professor."[2]

During the Glasgow sessions Tait had lodgings near the College. There he was waited upon and tended with motherly care by the faithful Betty Morton, who, having

---

[1] He is commonly remembered as Sir Daniel Sandford, but he was not knighted till 1830.

[2] Tradition avers that the same Professor used to suffer terribly from the pea-shooting propensities of his boisterous class, shouts of unmerciful laughter greeting his plaintive remonstrances, "Gentlemen, gentlemen, this is verra undignified ; besides, it's sair." Even in the more decorous University of Edinburgh the practice of pea-shooting has been not unknown on the occasion of the installation of a Lord Rector, or, strange to say, even on the occasion of the Principal's address at the opening of the session. The late Principal Sir Alexander Grant used to describe his experience as that of "peas with honour."

nursed him from his infancy, insisted upon remaining with him throughout his Glasgow course. She guarded him with keen vigilance, and his College friends had many stories to tell of inexorable repulses from his door when they ventured upon what she deemed intrusion into his hours of study.

His father, who had throughout taken the warmest interest in the precise details of his work, accompanied him to Glasgow at the beginning of his first session, and the following characteristic letter is only one among many. In others of a similar sort he remarks that "four is a desperately early hour for rising"; that he fears Archie "does not take exercise enough"; that he is to "continue the excellent resolution of writing every essay and exercise in the Logic class, for Jeffrey ascribes all his facility and power of composition to doing so when he was at Glasgow." The letters are full of shrewd and precise remarks about books, politics, and the topics of the day.

Mr. Craufurd Tait to A. C. T.

"EDINR., 22 *April* 1828,
Tuesday forenoon.

"MY DEAREST ARCHIE,—I yesterday received your letter to James of Sunday's date, with the journal annexed. I rejoice to observe that you have been continuing to go on regularly in your studies, and that there has been no indolence or falling off towards the end of the session. I am sure, my dear boy, the mode you have conducted yourself since I took you to Glasgow in October must be a source of pleasing reflection to yourself in life, and in nothing more than the great happiness which your excellent conduct has bestowed on me. The idea of your keeping so particular a journal was a lucky thought of mine, and I should advise you to continue to keep a similar one through life; at least, in all events, until your education be completely finished. All your journals I have preserved, and they should be stitched together and kept. I noticed that you are to have no exercise or reading at College after Saturday next; that the

Monday, Tuesday, and Wednesday are to be employed in adjudging the prizes;[1] and that the exhibition on Thursday the 1st of May will conclude the session. I trust your fellow-students will allot many prizes to you; but at any rate I am sure you deserve them. I agree with you that the boys are not always strictly impartial, and I am told that there are many observations on their conduct this year at the Edinburgh College. I hope, however, you have a good chance for their votes; for, independently of your attention and progress in your studies, I do not think there can be anything in your manners unkind, or which they could take offence at. You must write to me on the Thursday night, and send to me the printed list by the coach or some safe, attentive private hand. I suppose it will be printed on the Wednesday, and I trust your name will be often in it. During the three idle days at the beginning of the week, occupy your time with walking a good deal, calling upon and taking leave of the Lockharts, M'Farlanes, and all who have been kind to you, and with reading some amusing English author. Have you read Pope's Rape of the Lock, or Milton's L'Allegro or his Comus? You have them with you. . . . By the by, in little excursions which you happen to make, as well as longer journeys, always take with you some well-written, agreeable author, that you may fill up pleasantly the broken hours which occur on such occasions. It might be a good thing for you and me to make out a list with that view. By going on regularly, in taking one book after another in such a list, it is wonderful what you may accomplish without diminishing, but rather increasing, the pleasure of your journeys. These are most proper and convenient times to commit fine passages of the poets to memory.

"You know that I some time ago secured for you during the summer an hour from Marriott[2] for Greek, and one for French from Buquet.[2] I have now also secured an hour three times a week from Roberts for Elocution. The only others I wish for you are one three times a week for Mathematics, and one also three times a week for dancing. But I have not yet been able to ascertain the best masters for these branches.

"Nothing this summer will give you hard work but the Greek. Upon it, however, you must bestow great attention, and keep next

---

[1] According to the custom in the University of Glasgow, the prizes are adjudged by the votes of the students.

[2] A master in the Edinburgh Academy.

winter's Black-stone [1] in your constant view. I am determined you shall get it. I enclose a letter to Mr. Sandford, which you will immediately deliver. It is asking him what Greek authors, or parts of Greek authors, you should read during the vacation. Mr. Marriott wished me to do this, and I am sure Mr. Sandford will give me good advice. God for ever bless you, my dearest Archie, and I sincerely pray that He may enable you to proceed as you have been going on, and that you may continue to be the happiness, the pride, and the honour of your affectionate father,   CRAUFURD TAIT."

The earliest portion of the " particular journal " to which Mr. Tait alludes is not to be found, but the following extracts, taken from that of 1829, will show that the promise was faithfully kept :—

" 1829, *Nov.* 30, *Monday.*—Rose at $4\frac{1}{2}$. 5-7, Aristotle. Dressed. $7\frac{1}{2}$-$9\frac{1}{2}$, College. Breakfast, etc. Read *Spectator.* Prepared Logic notes. 11-12, Logic Class. Got ready, and went out to walk (Botanical Gardens). Returned about $2\frac{1}{2}$. Till 4 revised difficulties in Euripides. Dined. $4\frac{1}{2}$-$6\frac{1}{2}$, read Euripides. Tea, newspapers, etc. At $7\frac{1}{2}$ began again to read Euripides, but did not get much done. Bed at 10.

" *Dec. 1st, Tuesday.*—Rose at $4\frac{1}{2}$. 5-7, Greek verses. Dressed. $7\frac{1}{2}$-$9\frac{1}{2}$, College. Breakfast ; *Spectator* (Addison on Wit). Prepared for examination in Logic Class. 11-12, College. $12\frac{1}{2}$-$2\frac{1}{2}$, with $\frac{1}{4}$ hour's interruption, difficulties in Euripides. Walked till dinner. Dined at 4.10. $4\frac{1}{2}$-$6\frac{1}{2}$, Euripides with M'Kinlay. Tea, etc. Went to Greek verses at $7\frac{1}{2}$. Did not get on very well, being tired. Went to bed at 10. . . .

" *Decr. 11th, Friday.*—I have never found time to write my journal for these few days. Have been working very hard at Black-stone preparation. On Wednesday I dined with Dr. Gibb, but made amends by rising next morning at $3\frac{1}{4}$, having gone to bed by 9. This morning I rose at 20 to 5. Began to study at

---

[1] Before entering any class, each student had to undergo an examination on the subject of his last year's studies. This was called the " Black-stone " examination, the name being derived from the fact that the candidates were placed on a black stone seat. A prize was given to those who passed best. The details are now somewhat different, but the name and the seat from which it is derived are still in use.

$5\frac{1}{4}$. To $\frac{1}{4}$ to 7, Thucydides. Dressed. Prepared Herodotus. $7\frac{1}{2}$-$9\frac{1}{2}$, College. Breakfast; *Spectator*. Revised Logic notes. 11-12, College. Sat with Swinton for some time. $\frac{1}{4}$ to 2 to 25 to 4, Thucydides. Swinton came to me with my Logic notes and sat till dinner. After dinner read three or four papers of the *Spectator*. Journal. Began to read Thucydides about $5\frac{3}{4}$. Tea for half an hour at $6\frac{1}{2}$. Returned to Thucydides, and fagged till $\frac{1}{4}$ past 11 with very little interruption. . . .

"15*th Decr., Tuesday.*—Rose about 4. From, I think, $4\frac{1}{2}$ till 9, Thucydides. Dressed. Breakfast. Filled up notes. 11 to 12, Logic Class. Returned home. Studied till dinner. Studied during evening. Lay down on my bed about 10. Rose again at 12. To $5\frac{1}{2}$ read Thucydides. Went to bed. Rose at $8\frac{1}{2}$. Dressed, breakfasted.

" *Wednesday,* 16*th.*—At $10\frac{1}{4}$ returned to Thucydides. Continued till 10 to 4. Swinton sat a few minutes with me. Dined. At 20 to 5 returned to Thucydides. With 20 minutes' interruption for tea, and about 20 again in the evening for two visitors, worked till $5\frac{1}{2}$ in the morning. Went to bed."

This was obviously exceptional work, at high pressure, in immediate preparation for the coming examination. But it gives clear evidence that there was now, at least, no failure of working power.

His circle of intimate friends at Glasgow does not appear to have been a very large one. Perhaps the most intimate was Archibald Swinton, who had known him from early boyhood, and had been his competitor and friend at the Edinburgh Academy, where they were together among the prizemen of the highest class.[1] Another was Henry Selfe Page, who afterwards, as Mr.

---

[1] To Mr. Swinton, who was Professor of Civil Law in the University of Edinburgh from 1840 to 1860, and was subsequently a candidate for the representation of the University in Parliament, we are indebted for many reminiscences. The intimate friendship remained unbroken till the Archbishop's death. The first act of Bishop Tait after his appointment to the See of London was to marry his niece, Miss Sitwell, to Mr. Swinton, and twenty-two years later Mr. Swinton's nephew married the Archbishop's daughter.

Selfe, the well-known London magistrate, became the Archbishop's brother-in-law.   Among their fellow-students were Archibald Smith of Jordanhill, who graduated at Cambridge as Senior Wrangler, and a remarkable genius named James Halley, son of the guard of the Perth stage-coach,[1] who carried everything before him at Glasgow, and whom Sir Daniel Sandford used in later years to introduce as 'the man who beat Tait.'[2]

The triennial election of a Lord Rector by the votes of the students makes all Scotch University students politicians.   Political feeling ran high in Tait's Glasgow days, and he seems to have been one of the foremost among the orators and pamphleteers upon the Tory side.   The University Debating Society—the 'Athenæum'—had given full scope for the exhibition of his already considerable powers as a public speaker, and he took an active part in an ineffectual endeavour to secure the Lord Rectorship in 1829 for Lord President Hope, the Tory candidate, against Lord Lansdowne, the nominee of the Whig party, who had held undisputed possession of the field for ten years.   The minutes of the Athenæum Debating Society, of which he was Secretary, and frequently President, exhibit him as a less decided partisan.   Among the causes he advocates are Catholic Emancipation, Parliamentary Reform, the maintenance of Church Establishments, and the inex-pediency of abolishing rotten boroughs.   In 1829 he became editor, with Swinton and Page, of a successful

---

[1] See *Our Little Life*, by A. K. H. B., p. 145.

[2] Another friend, five years older than himself, was John Morell Mackenzie, an English Nonconformist of very great ability. His compositions distinguished him above all competitors in the Logic class, and were remembered by Professor Buchanan many years afterwards as standing entirely by themselves. He became in 1833 a Congregationalist minister at Poole in Dorsetshire, and subsequently held important charges elsewhere. He was drowned in the wreck of the *Pegasus* off the Northumbrian coast on July 19th, 1853. See p. 53.

'College Album,' contributing to its pages both poetry and prose.[1]

The students of the University had every opportunity of becoming acquainted with any of the residents in or near Glasgow who were disposed to show them hospitality, and Tait had a special advantage in the fact that Sir Archibald Campbell of Garscube, one of the chief landed proprietors in the neighbourhood, was his uncle and friend.[2]   His Sundays were frequently spent at Garscube, and he used himself to declare that, as a matter of fact, he owed his 'Snell Exhibition,' not to any merits of his own, but to the ready and profuse hospitality shown at Sir Archibald's table to the College Professors, in whose hands the election lay.[3]   If such was the case, it must at least be admitted that the electors were fortunate in the attainments of the nephew whom, 'to please Sir Archibald,' they decided to send to Oxford upon the foundation of John Snell.[4]   Tait's career at

[1] In a satirical account of the Debating Society which appears in the Magazine, Tait is described as "a pale-looking youth, dressed in a single-breasted drab greatcoat, black and white check pantaloons, and an oilskin cap."

[2] The somewhat confusing facts as to the Campbell family are as follows: —Mr. Ilay Campbell of Succoth and Garscube (Archbishop Tait's grandfather, see p. 5) became in 1789 Lord President of the Court of Session, and in accordance with Scottish custom took the title of ' Lord Succoth ' during the tenure of his office as a judge.   On resigning his judicial office in 1808 he was made a baronet, and, dropping the title of Lord Succoth, was known as Sir Ilay (or Islay) Campbell till his death in 1823.   In 1809 his son Archibald Campbell became a judge, and adopted the same official title (Lord Succoth) as had been held by his father.   On his father's death in 1823 he succeeded to the baronetcy, and, having resigned his judgeship in 1824, he was known as Sir Archibald Campbell till his death in 1846.

[3] In a speech at a Balliol dinner many years afterwards he referred to it as a process of "natural selection."

[4] John Snell had, in 1679, founded certain "schollarships or exhibitions for the further education, at Balliol Colledge, Oxford, of schollars borne and educated in Scotland, who shall each of them have spent three years, or two at the least, in the colledge of Glasgow."   The scholars were to be recommended to the authorities at Oxford by the Principal and Professors of Glasgow.

Glasgow had been uninterruptedly successful,[1] and with the single exception, perhaps, of James Halley, he stood foremost among the students of the University. Had it not been for this Exhibition, however, it would in all probability have been impossible for him to go to Oxford. The clouds which had long darkened his father's fortunes now burst forth in storm, and the family embarrassments were such that no further funds were available towards the expense of Archie's education.

His election as 'Snell Exhibitioner' did not relieve him of the necessity of going to Oxford to matriculate.

"How well I remember," he wrote long afterwards, "the gloomy journey through the deep snow, and my first impression of Balliol. I slept at the 'Angel,' and next morning repaired to Balliol at the hour Dr. Jenkyns, the Master of the College, had appointed. Not feeling in high feather, I waited in the rooms, afterwards so familiar, for the dreaded interview, and after a time Dr. Jenkyns appeared, a little man, faultless in his academical dress, with a manner that might be called finnikin, and speech to match, his words seeming to be clipped as they left his lips. He received me with a pompous kindness, saying, 'I will send for the Senior Proctor,' a title which was intended to and did rather overawe me, a freshman, not knowing that he meant simply the tutor of the College, who happened then to hold that University office. The Proctor shortly appeared in his black velvet sleeves. I was invited to sit on a little sofa, and a book placed in my hands. It was Lucan, a book of which I knew nothing, and I was told to construe a passage that looked to me a mass of difficulties. Catching, however, at the meaning of a few words I saw that it was an account of Cæsar in the boat

---

[1] He obtained in 1828 the first prize in the Latin Black-stone Examination; in the Senior 'Humanity' Class, first for Latin Verses, first for English Verses, second for General Excellence, and second for Weekly Exercises; in the Junior Mathematical Class, third for General Excellence. In 1829, first in the Senior Greek Class (Greek side), Lord Rector's University Medal for best Latin poem, third prize in Senior Mathematical Class. In 1830, first in Senior Greek Class (Logic side), first for Translation from Thucydides, second in the Greek Black-stone Examination, third prize in the Logic Class.

between Brundusium and Dyrrachium, and with the courage of the hero himself I dashed through the difficulties, and gave a rapid, and providentially a correct, translation of Cæsar and his fortunes. The approbation of the Master and the Proctor was very decided. 'And now, Mr. Tait,' said Dr. Jenkyns, in his peculiarly clipped rather than polished English, 'allow me to ask you with what view you come here?' This was rather a poser. I knew nothing of the man who spoke, or of his peculiarities; but by a happy inspiration made reply: 'First, in order to study, and also, I hope, to benefit by the society of the College.' I had hit upon the very answer to please him. 'Mr. Tait,' he said, with an approving smile, 'your answer is that of a very sensible young man, and I am happy to welcome you to Balliol.' From that day forward I always kept my place in the good books of the master. While this process had been going on, little Oakeley, afterwards so kind a friend, limped in to have a good look at his new pupil."

The matriculation over, Tait returned to Glasgow to complete the session, paying a visit by the way to his sister, Lady Sitwell, at Renishaw.

He was not yet nineteen years of age, and there is nothing in the extant letters to show that he had as yet announced or entertained any definite intention of taking Holy Orders. It is, therefore, curious to find, in Lady Sitwell's memorandum of this visit, that he was called upon one Sunday evening at Renishaw, when the house was full of visitors, to read prayers and give a short address. He did so, and his sister's account says, " It was a very striking sermon, and was listened to with profound attention. But he whispered to me at the close, 'I thought I should have fainted when I discovered that there was no Lord's Prayer in the book. I really feared I should break down.'"

This incident leads naturally to a short consideration of what had been, up to this time, the religious training and surroundings of the future Archbishop. For two generations the family, as we have seen, had been Presbyterian, and into the Established Church of Scotland Archibald Campbell Tait had been baptized.   His father's influence over him, admirable as it was in many ways, had never been of a distinctly religious sort, and of his mother he could have no remembrance.   His earliest education, both in religious and secular matters, had been carried on by his elder sisters, Susan and Charlotte, with the invaluable aid of the strict but faithful Betty Morton, whose nursery *régime* has already been described.   Desultory and unprofessional the teaching had necessarily been, but of the loving motherly care bestowed by his sisters on his early childhood he used all through life to speak with earnest gratitude.   Merry as he showed himself at times, there seems to have been about the little boy from the very first an almost pathetic seriousness.   Certain it is that, from whatever cause, or by whomsoever the name was first given, he used to be called ' The little Bishop ' from the time he was six years old.

There was nothing precocious about those early years.

"In his first school-days," writes Lady Wake, "he and Campbell used, during their holidays, to have some sort of lessons in my room.   They might easily have had a wiser teacher, for, with a young girl's want of judgment, I gave them the books I was most fond of myself, and was greatly disgusted to find that they could not be appreciated.   I still possess a copy of Milman's beautiful poem, 'The Fall of Jerusalem,' in which the passage beginning

> ' There have been tears from holier eyes than mine,
> Poured o'er thee, Zion ! yea, the Son of Man,
> This thy devoted hour foresaw and wept,'

is all blotted and blurred with dear little Archie's own tears, caused not because he was stupid, but because his sister, who was old enough to know better, was so foolish as to expect a little child to understand it.   When Dean Milman, long years afterwards, had become the Bishop of London's intimate friend he was much amused at hearing of the Bishop's first association with his name and works."

Neither at the High School nor at the Edinburgh Academy was any religious teaching of a denominational sort given, the theory being that the religious instruction of boys attending these day-schools would be amply cared for at home. In Mr. Tait's family all such teaching was in accordance with the doctrine and discipline of the Established Church of Scotland, and the family 'sittings' were in Old Greyfriars Church in Edinburgh, and, when the household was at Harviestoun, in the parish church of Tillicoultry.

But before his studentship at Glasgow began, an intimacy, which was to be life-long, had sprung up between Archibald Tait and his cousin and school-fellow, Ramsay Campbell, son of Sir Archibald Campbell of Garscube. Sir Archibald's house, as we have seen, was next door to Mr. Tait's in Park Place, and the children of the two households were constantly together. The Campbells were members of the Scottish Episcopal Church, and the intimacy between Archibald Tait and Ramsay Campbell had the effect of bringing the former, somewhat more markedly than would otherwise have been possible, under the influence of what then used, in Scotland, to be called 'the English Church,' and the two boys used, with Mr. Tait's entire approval, to attend together the services in St. John's Church in Edinburgh, of which the then incumbent was Bishop Sandford.[1]

The following reminiscence must be given exactly as it stands. It was found in the Archbishop's desk after his death, written upon a sheet of foolscap, and folded by itself :—

"*June* 22, 1879.—I have been preaching to-day in Lambeth Church on God's revelation of Himself in Jesus Christ, and have dwelt on His revelation to individual souls, rousing them to

---

[1] Bishop of Edinburgh, 1806 to 1830.

think of heavenly things, and attend to the continued revelation set before them in the Bible. The earliest recollection I have of a deep religious impression made on my mind has often since recurred to me with the vividness of having heard a voice from above. I suppose I must have been some ten or twelve years old. I had ridden over with my brother Craufurd from Harviestoun to Glendevon to visit old Miss Rutherford, and stayed the night in her house. I distinctly remember in the middle of the night awaking with a deep impression on my mind of the reality and nearness of the world unseen, such as, through God's mercy, has never since left me. I have fallen into many sins of omission and commission ; I have had many evil desires, and have gratified them ; but this sense of the reality of the world unseen has remained with me through God's mercy. What the value of the impression was it is difficult to say, but that it was made by God the Holy Ghost working on my soul I have no doubt. O Lord, give me grace to preserve it to the end, and may that guiding and guarding Spirit of holiness and purity, from Whom I believe it came, ever be with me to give me an unfeigned repentance for the sins which have defaced the holy image of God in my soul, and worked on my natural corruption, leading me into evil ! O Lord, keep me to the end, washing me in Christ's blood, and making me fit for that glorious and holy presence, which at that early age I faintly realised !"

Ramsay Campbell did not accompany him to Glasgow as a student, but his home, Garscube, was in the immediate neighbourhood, and Tait, as has been said, spent many of his Sundays under Sir Archibald's roof. When at Glasgow the church he usually attended was that known as the Ramshorn Church. Its minister was Dr. Welsh, who afterwards, as Moderator of the General Assembly, headed, in 1843, the great 'Free Church Secession. The Archbishop, only a few days before his death, more than fifty years later, spoke in terms of the warmest thankfulness of the help he had received, as a student, from Dr. Welsh's earnest evangelical preaching. Whether he was at this time a communicant seems doubtful. He was certainly never a communicant member of the Presbyterian Church, but it is possible that, though neither of them was yet, for some reason, confirmed, he and Ramsay Campbell may together have occasionally received the Holy Communion in the Scottish Episcopal Church both in Edinburgh and Glasgow. As soon as his residence at Balliol began, Tait applied to his tutor, Mr. Moberly, as a candidate for confirmation, and after such preparation as was deemed necessary, he was confirmed by the Bishop of Oxford.

His last session at Glasgow came to an end in May 1830, and the months which intervened before he began residence at Oxford seem to have been spent with his father, partly in the Highlands and partly in Edinburgh, where, at his father's desire, he attended lectures on Chemistry, Botany, and other subjects. The friendship between father and son had always been very close, and Mr. Tait evidently gave the most minute and painstaking attention to the details of his son's education, and looked forward to his future with characteristic confidence.

In October 1830 he went up to Balliol, furnished by his father with all the introductions which forethought could secure. On the way a week was spent in London with Leonard Horner, who was not only the kindest of friends to each and every member of the family, but whose talents and character secured him the intimacy of some of the foremost literary men of the day. The following is the Archbishop's reminiscence, half a century later, of his first introduction to London :—

"On board the steamer which carried us from Leith to London was young Adair, returning from the moors with his father, Sir Robert. We naturally made the sort of acquaintance one does under such circumstances, and were together below when the captain summoned us on deck with, 'Now, gentlemen, come up, and you will see the finest sight in the world.' We instantly followed him, and certainly it was a magnificent spectacle which we beheld on entering the Thames towards sunset,—ships from every quarter of the world, representing all nations, and the river alive with boats. We steamed into the jostling crowd of vessels of every size and description. It was quite dark when we reached the Artichoke Stairs at Blackwall. For a moment I felt very desolate, alone, and for the first time in great London. The way to Leonard Horner's house in Gower Street seemed to me interminable, but at length I found myself in the hospitable home of my kind friends, with whom I was already intimate.

"In the morning I was provided with the names of the places I ought to see, and with all necessary advice and directions; and in the next few days I lionised London far more thoroughly than I have ever done since, even pushing my researches, for the first and last time, into the ball of St. Paul's. I much enjoyed this week. I was but eighteen, but Leonard Horner treated me as a man, asking pleasant people to dinner, and introducing me to them. It was at this table that I first made the acquaintance of Herman Merivale, afterwards my life-long friend.

"Arrived at Oxford, I took possession of my rooms in the top attics of Balliol, as completely a garret as could be imagined. I was at once introduced to George Moberly, Tutor of Balliol, whose favour had been bespoken for me. He asked me to breakfast with him next morning, which was Sunday. The party consisted of Herman Merivale—whom I had already begun to know, —Manning,—whom I never did know well,—and Stephen Denison.

"Dr. Jenkyns followed up his first kindness by giving me excellent advice, cautioning me as to the young Scotchmen from Glasgow, who formed a set by themselves, not, in his fastidious opinion, of the most desirable or creditable description, and advising me to go in at once for the Balliol scholarship, which was to be given in November. This advice I followed with success, and the having obtained a scholarship after scarcely a month's residence gave me an important standing in the College; and Jenkyns looked with increased benignity on the young undergraduate, notwithstanding that he had been led to his beloved Balliol by the helping hand of John Snell, to whom he bore no good-will, looking upon his liberality in creating the Glasgow exhibitions more as an impertinence than as a good deed.

"The scholars of Balliol, when I first joined them, were ─

Payne, son of Sir Peter Payne of Bedfordshire (he had the first of the open scholarships); Grove, who became Principal of Brasenose; Whitaker Churton, afterwards Fellow of Brasenose; Charles Marriott, afterwards Fellow of Oriel; Sir John Eardley-Wilmot; Elder, afterwards Head-master of Charterhouse; and Herbert, a very clever man from Eton, strange and rough in his manner —he was accidentally drowned when on a walking tour in Switzerland. All these I found there. Blackburn was elected with me; he gained the first scholarship, I the second. The next year came Lord Cardwell and Father Tickell of the Jesuits. After them Vice-Chancellor Wickens and Dr. Holden, Head-master of Durham; a little later came Arthur Stanley and Professor James Lonsdale; then Lake, Dean of Durham, and Goulburn, Dean of Norwich; Jowett, Sir Stafford Northcote, Arthur Clough, Lord Coleridge, Chief-Justice of England, John Seymour, who died early, and James Riddell. All these were my friends and contemporaries; but the men with whom I so habitually lived that we acquired the name of 'the family party,' our rooms being on the same stairs, were Bence Jones, Joseph Salt, Alexander Hall, and dear old John William Pugh, a truly Christian friend, two years older than myself. This man, though never known in public life, was one of the most saintly characters I have ever met, and to me he was invaluable.

"I found my letters of introduction of the greatest use. One was to Mills, the Professor of Moral Philosophy, who introduced me to the acquaintance of Cramer, the head of New Inn Hall. Both Whately (at that time head of St. Alban's Hall, to whom I had a letter from Sir William Hooker, Professor of Botany at Glasgow) and Shuttleworth, afterwards Bishop of Chichester, were in the habit of inviting me to their houses. No person of any eminence ever came to Oxford without dining with Shuttleworth, and from his intimate relations with Holland House, having been tutor to General Fox, Lord Holland's son, his acquaintance was most extensive with all the intellectual lights of the day. The invitations to his house, therefore, were of the highest interest to a young undergraduate."

The Balliol scholarship won, and, his first term at Oxford ended, he spent Christmas with the Sitwells at Renishaw. The following is written thence:—

Mr. A. C. Tait to Mr. Archibald Swinton.

"RENISHAW HALL, 19 *Dec.* 1830.

"MY DEAR SWINTON,— . . . These satirical hints and insinuations of yours were rather an agreeable variety. For, to tell the truth, I am sick of letters of congratulation, written in as high-flown style as if I had been appointed Archbishop of Canterbury at once, or been invited by the Poles on account of my extraordinary merits to accept the sovereignty of their kingdom. I am sure when these letters are published in my Memoirs they will be found a thousand times more bombastical than those which I receive when promoted to the first named of these dignities. But I shall take good care that they are not published in these Memoirs, for what a picture of Scotland would be presented if it were known what a row Scotchmen made about one of their number obtaining that which Englishmen are in the habit of receiving every year. . . . Had it not been for the voice of satire which pervades your epistle, I should have sworn that you too were turned Whig with the new Ministry. . . . I have nothing to do here but vegetate, and regret extremely that my brother-in-law has given up his hounds, with which I might have had excellent fun this Christmas. . . . You need not fear for me ; I am ashamed when I think how little I have done in the way of reading this last term. I could do nothing else while I was preparing for the scholarship, though I only worked what we should have called hard at Glasgow for five or six days before the examination. And after the examination was over I felt as idly disposed as ever I did after a long essay for Buchanan. I am doing nothing but reading English while here. . . .—
Your affect. friend,   A. C. TAIT."

Strange to say, the above is far from being the only allusion in these early days to the Archbishopric of Canterbury. It is, of course, a mere congratulatory commonplace, when the rawest of youths takes Holy Orders, or 'eats his dinners' in the Temple, to remind him, as the case may be, of Lambeth Palace or the Woolsack. But in the case of Archibald Tait the allusion is so persistent as to acquire an interest of its own. At least a score of such references might be culled from the correspondence of his early years, and from the recollections of his friends. On his first visit to London, for example, of which mention has been already made, "he came in," as a letter tells, "one evening from a walk.   'Where have you been to, Archie?' he was asked, 'Walking through Lambeth,' he replied. 'Through Lambeth!' was the astonished answer; 'why, what ever possessed you to walk in Lambeth?'   'Well, I wanted to see how I shall like the place when I get there.'" A few years later his friend Mr. Hall writes :

"Ogilvie is flourishing about town, and Jones and I have agreed to pay him a visit together at your future episcopal residence next week."

(Mr. Ogilvie was chaplain to Archbishop Howley at Lambeth.)   And again, with reference to the disastrous fire which occurred in the Houses of Parliament, one of Tait's friends wrote to him as follows, on October 21st, 1834 :—

"I was seriously alarmed that I should have had to communicate to you the intelligence that your palace at Lambeth was burnt to the ground.   It gives me great pleasure, however, to be able to state that the only serious loss which you have incurred consists in the total destruction by fire of the Bishops' Bench in the House of Lords."

During his early undergraduate days, the man to whom, according to his own account, he owed most, was Frederick Oakeley, Fellow and Tutor of Balliol, afterwards the well-known Canon of the Roman Catholic Church in Islington.   Though Oakeley was ten years older than Tait, and had been a tutor long before Tait entered the College as an undergraduate, the two soon became attached personal friends, and on one occasion they spent some weeks together in Scotland during a long vacation.   "He never seemed tired," wrote the Archbishop long afterwards, "of doing me acts of kindness.

His mind was opened wide to religious impressions, and the influence of Bishop Sumner [1] and his friends had given him a strong bias to the Evangelical school. This continued more or less all through my undergraduate days, but gradually he succumbed to the then almost irresistible fascination of John Henry Newman."

As years went on, and Oakeley identified himself more and more closely with the advanced school of the Tractarians, the intimacy of his friendship with Tait was, of necessity, impaired, but neither then nor afterwards, through the course of their widely divergent lives, was there any real break in their affectionate intercourse and mutual regard. In his earlier Oxford days Tait seems to have looked constantly to Oakeley for the advice and help which were freely given. The following letter from Oakeley is one among many of like sort :—

"July 16, 1833.

"My dear Tait,— . . . I hope you have not many inducements to idleness, or rather, that you are able to withstand them. I think you ought to pay a good deal of attention to Divinity, or I should rather say, I hope you read your Bible with much attention. For I do not like the idea of reading Divinity for the Schools at Oxford. Do, my dear Tait, make the Bible the subject of your daily reading and reflection. I shall be very glad—very glad indeed—if you distinguish yourself in the Schools, but I care for nothing so much as that you should improve in religious knowledge and feeling. For that will, by God's blessing, guard you from caring too much either for success or failure, and remember that it is the one thing needful, in comparison with which all other subjects are as nothing."

It was not till several years after he had left Oxford, and become a London incumbent, that Frederick Oakeley, under the influences to which at Balliol he had begun to yield, joined the Church of Rome, and entered its

---

[1] Oakeley had been a favourite pupil of Sumner's.

priesthood.[1] To extreme old age he retained his warm affection for his former pupil, and he lost no opportunity, in speech or letter, of giving expression to his regard. When he felt himself dying[2] he said to those about him : "Let my dear friend the Archbishop of Canterbury know as soon as I am gone."

Of Tait's undergraduate days there is not very much to tell. He worked hard and successfully, but he does not seem to have been widely known beyond the walls of his own College, except for the prominent part he took from the first in the debates of the Union Society.

In place of the boyish Toryism of his Glasgow days, he was now, if we may judge from the Union records, developing into an earnest and consistent Whig, and the votes he gave in the Oxford Union were such as he would have given to the end of his life. Before he had been six months at Oxford, he stood forth, in opposition to Roundell Palmer, to defend 'the Spirit of Democracy,' and the happy results of Catholic Emancipation. In the debates which followed the passing of the great Reform Bill, his name appears regularly upon the popular side. Twice within a year he urges "that no ministry can hope to carry on the government of this country which is not framed as well upon a principle of extensive practical Reform as of preserving the established rights of property." In 1833 he succeeded Edward Cardwell as President of the Society. The last debate in which he took part was on March 28th, 1835, when he affirmed "that a legislative provision for the Roman Catholic priesthood in Ireland would be a most beneficial measure." On a division the motion was defeated by more than two to one, and upon

---

[1] He went to London in the summer of 1839, and joined the Roman Catholic Communion a few years later, being admitted to Priest's Orders in the Roman Church in 1847.

[2] On January 29, 1880. See vol. ii. p. 525.

this question he found himself in a like minority throughout his life. But he never swerved from his first opinion,
even when he stood almost alone among his friends in
supporting it thirty-four years afterwards in the Irish
Church debates in the House of Lords.[1]

His prowess as a debater is immortalised in the once
famous *Uniomachia* of 1833, which records in wondrous
dog-Greek, with corresponding Latin notes, an internal
conflict which threatened the very life of the Union Society.
The occasion of this epic was a debate upon the question
whether members of the 'Rambler' Society, which had
recently been formed in the University, should be allowed
to retain their membership in the Union Society, with
which the Ramblers were supposed to be in rivalry.[2] The
Homeric character of the poem was completed by the
publication of an English translation after the manner of
Pope. The then President of the Union was Mr. Robert
Lowe, whom the English version thus describes :—

> "In many a sable fold of honour dressed,[3]
> The great Lowides towered above the rest ;
> Before the faithful lines advancing far,
> With winged words the chief provoked the war :
> 'O friends, be men !   Be ours the noble boast
> From Union rooms to drive a traitor host ;
> Against our sovereign will they dare combine,
> Form a new club, a different club from mine :—
> Accursed crew, whose ruthless hands have gored
> Their mother's breast with parricidal sword.' "

A vehement debate follows, and at last, as one of the
champions of the Ramblers,

> "With thundering sound
> Tait shook his tasselled cap and sprang to ground

---

[1] See vol. ii. p. 33.

[2] Among the 'Ramblers' were Tait, Roundell Palmer, W. G. Ward,
Arthur Stanley, and Thomas Jackson, to whom is attributed the original
Greek *Uniomachia*, the translations and notes being subsequently added by
other hands, among them Robert Scott, the late Dean of Rochester.

[3] Mr. Lowe was already a graduate.

(The tasselled cap by Juggins' hand was made,
Or some keen brother of the London trade,
Unconscious of the stern decrees of fate
What ruthless thumps the battered trencher wait),
Dire was the clang and dreadful from afar
Of Tait indignant, rushing to the war.
In vain the Chair's dread mandate interfered,
Nor chair nor fine the angry warrior feared :
A forfeit pound the unequal contest ends,
Loud rose the clamour of condoling friends." [1]

Against the fine thus imposed "for disobedience to the order of the chair," Tait, in the following term, appealed to the House, but the decision of the future Chancellor of the Exchequer was sustained by a majority of four votes. "It is the only occasion," writes Lord Sherbrooke, "on which I ever fined an Archbishop for disorderly behaviour."

In the summer vacation of 1833, when his undergraduate days were drawing to a close, Tait was one of a reading party who spent some weeks at Seaton in Devonshire, under the tutorship of Mr. Johnson, afterwards Dean of Wells. The party attracted the notice of a dissenting minister there, who was also a local poet, and who introduced a picture of the group into a poem, which he soon afterwards published, under the title of 'Seaton Beach.' The following lines occur in the poem :—

"And if Lavater rightly has defined,
From sign external, features of the mind,

---

[1]
Ταιεῖτος δ' ἆλτο χαμᾶζε·
Καὶ πῖλον βράνδισσε, νεὸν δέ τε ῥοῦον ὅρωρεν.
Πῖλον Ἰόγγινσος ποιήσατο καὶ κάμε χερσίν
Ἦ τις Λονδεῖνου τράδσμαν· ἀλλ' οὐκ ἐνόησε
Ἐν τούτῳ ποτε κἂν πῖλον θύμψεσθαι ἀγῶνι,
Ἀδδράσσειν δ' ἐθέλοντι φίλους πρεσιδέντιος αὐτῷ
Σίγην κομμάνδει, ὅτ' ἄρ' ἰντέρρυπτε δέβατα·
Ἀλλ' ὅτι περσίστει δύστηνος φείνεται ὄνπουνδ.
Δεινὴ δ' ἦν κλαγγὴ ἰσσόντων ἤδε κλαπόντων·
Ἴστατ' ἀειρόμενός τε, καὶ αὐτῷ βούλεται αἷμα.

> He whom near yonder cliff we see recline
> A mitred prelate may hereafter shine ;
> That youth, who seems exploring Nature's laws,
> An ermined judge may win deserved applause."

The youth who was to become a ' mitred prelate ' was Archibald Tait, and the future ' ermined judge ' was Roundell Palmer, who, revisiting Seaton as Lord Chancellor of England just fifty years afterwards, was entertained by the Corporation of Exeter, and mentioned in his speech that Archbishop Tait, in writing to congratulate him on receiving the Great Seal, had reminded him of the Seaton poet's prophecy. Lord Selborne added that the poet had apparently been forgotten in his own country, for that he had in vain inquired after him and his book a few days before.

Meantime there had fallen upon the life of Archibald Tait another great sorrow—the death of his father. Mr. Tait's health had been visibly failing for some time past, and he had refused in the spring of 1832 to make his usual visit to Harviestoun. " No, I do not wish it ; I shall soon be walking in even fairer gardens with your beloved mother." His letters testify to the unabated interest which he continued to feel till the very last in the Oxford career of his youngest and favourite son. The dispositions of father and son were singularly unlike one another, but the friendship and mutual confidence which existed between them had been remarkable ever since Archie, as a little child, used to ride about the grounds of Harviestoun with his father, seated on a little pad in front of his saddle. In later days, when Archie was at school, long walks and rides with his father formed his chief holiday amusement. He used afterwards to tell how, in these rides over the Ochils, near Harviestoun, and when in Edinburgh, in the long rambles on foot over the Salisbury Crags and Arthur's Seat, he had drawn infinite stores of information on facts both past and present from the ceaseless flow of his father's conversation. Mr. Tait, whose memory was singularly retentive, had been an omnivorous reader, and he liked nothing so well as an attentive listener. Eccentric and unbusiness-like he certainly was. His son recounts, for example, how, "when my brother Tom left home for India in 1826, my father took James, Craufurd, and myself with him to accompany Tom upon the first part of his journey. Together we embarked at Leith in the London steamer. Suddenly, in the middle of the night, my father decided to go on shore at Berwick, by means of a boat which had accidentally put out with a passenger. Next day he took us for a long walk into England, and falling in with a stranger on our walk, we all accepted for a night his equally sudden hospitality, and returned next day to Edinburgh." Of course these unplanned excursions were full of charm for the boys, who immensely enjoyed their father's companionship. To Archie he specially devoted himself. His letters are a curious mixture of shrewd precision and strange fancies ; and he continued till his death to write to Archie as though he were still a little boy. He enjoins him to be sure to "wrap up well "; "to sit in the coach with his back to the horses "; "to buy a road-book, and to be sure to get a cheap one "; not to be imposed on by coachmen or guards (this is followed by a tariff of what he ought to give) ; to read some entertaining book in the coach—"perhaps the two last volumes of Chesterfield's Letters, or Hume's Essays, or Addison's papers in the *Spectator* " ; to go to bed early ; to work hard at his Greek—"for ancient Greek is not unlikely to become the living language of modern Greece, especially if a proper system of Infant and Elementary Schools be set on foot there to teach it," and there is very much more advice of similar character.

The father's tender love was as tenderly returned, and it was a heavy sorrow to the son when the old man lay quietly down to sleep on the 10th May 1832, and never rose again. He was just breathing when they came to him in the morning, but he was quite unconscious, and in a few minutes he died. A memorandum-book was afterwards found in his study, containing elaborate notes of his ideas respecting his youngest son's studies, and expressing not only his unchanged pride and joy in him, but his unabated confidence in his future greatness.

To Archie, the shock of this sudden death was terrible. A faithful biography should record, when possible, not only the deeds and words of him who is its subject, but some at least of the influences which have combined to mould his life. In such a connection the following letter from Lady Wake may find a place :—

"We have all a sad loss, but to you, my dearest Archie, I feel that it is the greatest, for he was to you both a motive for exertion and a reward to success, for what could be so stimulating as his anxious interest, and what so delightful as the gratified happiness with which each new successful effort filled his heart? But even now, though he is no longer here, his memory remains as a more sacred influence.

"In speaking of him now, many will recur to his loss of fortune, and the imprudences which perhaps caused it. But it is in your power, my Archie, to cause that in future he will only be spoken of as the father who formed a great and good man, useful to his country in that manner in which the benefits bestowed survive time, to be acknowledged in eternity. . . . We have been counting your age, and are amazed to find that you will be twenty-one next birthday. I had thought you were still a child, and behold, you are a man!"

He took his degree, November 28th, 1833, obtaining a first class in the Final Classical Schools. "I do not know," he says, "how much this success was due to my *vivâ voce* examination in Aristotle, which was conducted by William Sewell, but I know that Sewell, in consequence of this examination, recommended me to several pupils, and always had a friendly feeling towards me through his long, chequered, and sadly overclouded life."

Immediately on taking his degree he went to Scotland for Christmas. It proved a great comfort to him that he had so arranged, for he was thus enabled to repay in some measure the tender love and devotion with which old Betty Morton had watched over his infancy and boyhood. It is surely a fact worth noticing that three at least among the leading public men of our generation—Lord Shaftesbury, Lord Lawrence, and Archbishop Tait, have each of them, in recalling the main influences which contributed to mould their lives, assigned a foremost place to the nurse of their early years.[1] Maria Millis, Margaret Morse, and Betty Morton deserve one and all to be gratefully remembered by the English men and women of to-day. And, as Lord Lawrence's biographer has said, there are few ties more sacred and more indissoluble than those which unite the younger, ay, and the elder, members of a family to an old and trusted nurse. Witness it some of the most exquisite passages in all literature, from the time of Deborah the aged nurse of Rebekah, or Eurykleia the nurse and confidante alike of Telemachus and Penelope, right down to the 'Lord of the Isles' and the 'Lady of the Lake,' or, again, to Tennyson's 'Nurse of Ninety Years,' or, we may add, to Alison Cunningham, the heroine of Stevenson's touching poem.[2]

Finding herself no longer equal to the long stairs in

---

[1] See *Lord Shaftesbury's Life*, vol. i. pp. 39, etc.; *Lord Lawrence's Life*, vol. i. pp. 133, etc.

[2] Dedication of *A Child's Garden of Verses*.

the Park Place house, Betty Morton was now living in lodgings, visiting the family frequently, and interested as ever in all their concerns. One day, towards the end of December, she was taken ill. The ailment seemed slight at first, but by the time her beloved Archie arrived she was in high fever, and occasionally distressed in mind. He never left her side except once, when he went to obtain the aid of Mr. Craig, a clergyman of the Scottish Episcopal Church, in order that the old nurse and her grown-up charge might together receive the Holy Communion, which at that time was rarely, if ever, administered privately in the Presbyterian Church, of which Betty was so staunch an adherent. When the Holy Communion had been celebrated, Mr. Craig left the two alone together. All night the young man sat by the old nurse's bed, and spoke to her words of peace and comfort as she was able to bear it. She died with her hand clasped in his as the morning broke on the first day of 1834.

His Rugby journal, twelve years later, contains the following entry :—

"*31st December* 1845, $\frac{1}{4}$ *to* 12.—At this hour, twelve years ago, I sat by the bedside of almost my oldest and dearest friend. Grant that no length of years may make me forget what I owe to Thee for having given me in infancy and childhood, when motherless and helpless, so kind and good a friend."

CHAPTER III.

TAIT had now set his heart upon obtaining a Balliol fellowship, and in the meantime, being entirely dependent for income upon his own exertions, he remained at Balliol and took private pupils. It was the birth-time of the storm which was to shake the University to its centre. Cardinal Newman dates the start of the Oxford movement from Mr. Keble's 'Assize Sermon,' preached in the University pulpit on July 14th, 1833, a few months before Tait took his degree.[1]   Then came the famous Hadleigh Conference, and in September the first of the *Tracts for the Times.* It was impossible for a man of Tait's temperament to be uninterested in what was going on, but it was as yet mainly an interest from outside. His natural sympathies and his Scotch training were alike unecclesiastical, and he does not seem to have been brought at that time into personal contact with any of the leaders of the new movement.

"It was a strange experience," writes Principal Shairp, "for a young man trained anywhere, much more for one born and bred in Scotland, and brought up a Presbyterian, to enter Oxford when the religious movement was at its height.   He found himself all at once in the midst of a system of teaching which unchurched himself and all whom he had hitherto known.   In his simplicity he had believed that spiritual religion was a thing of

[1] *Apologia,* p. 100.

the heart, and that neither Episcopacy nor Presbytery availeth anything. But here were men—able, learned, devout-minded men—maintaining that outward rites and ceremonies were of the very essence, and that where these were not, there was no true Christianity. . . . Now and then it would happen that some adherent, or even leading man of the movement, more frank and outspoken than the rest, would deign to speak out his principles, and even to discuss them with undergraduates and controversial Scots. To him urging the necessity of Apostolical Succession, and the sacerdotal view of the Sacraments, some young man might venture to reply, 'Well! if all you say be true, then I never can have known a Christian. For up to this time I have lived among people who were strangers to all these things, which, you tell me, are essentials of Christianity. And I am quite sure that, if I have never known a Christian till now, I shall never know one.' The answer to this would probably be. 'There is much in what you say. No doubt high virtues, very like the Christian graces, are to be found outside of the Christian Church. But it is a remarkable thing, those best acquainted with Church history tell me, that outside of the pale of the Church the saintly character is never found.' This *naïf* reply was not likely to have much weight with the young listener. It would have taken something stronger to make him break faith with all that was most sacred in his early recollections. Beautiful examples of Presbyterian piety had stamped impressions on his memory not to be effaced by sacerdotal theories or subtleties of the schools. And the Church system which began by disowning these examples placed a barrier to its acceptance at the very outset." [1]

The following letter to his old Glasgow friend, Morell Mackenzie, who had become a Nonconformist minister at Poole, shows the bent of Tait's sympathies at this time :—

Mr. A. C. Tait to the Rev. J. Morell Mackenzie.

"27 *March* 1834.

"My DEAR MACKENZIE,— . . . I have commenced taking pupils in Oxford, which I find not at all an unpleasant employ-

[1] *Studies in Poetry and Philosophy*, pp. 240-242.

ment, as the books in which men wish to be lectured before going up for their degree are principally those which I am most fond of—the *Ethics* and *Rhetoric* of Aristotle, Butler's *Analogy*, and such like. It makes me feel very old to have so soon become an instructor of others, instead of merely a learner myself. I return to Oxford in a fortnight, and shall continue residing there till next Christmas, at least, as there will be a vacancy in the Balliol Fellowships about that time, for which I hope to be allowed to stand. Should I, by any wonderful degree of luck, contrive to be elected, I shall remain in Oxford, and probably become a College Tutor. But if the more probable alternative occurs, I shall then look about me for a country settlement. You seem to doubt whether my High Church notions, contracted in this seat of 'port and prejudice,' will allow me to hold any dealings with those without the pale. I hope I am not a bigot, but I confess myself much more of a High Churchman than I was ; nor has the Church of Scotland so much of my admiration as in former times. Have you seen the essays on the Church by Seeley the bookseller's son? I like them, though not quite so much as I expected ; but certainly I think that he gives some hard hits to Mr. James of Birmingham, who appears to be the champion of your party. I have also been reading Girdlestone's plan for altering the Liturgy, so as to embrace Dissenters. I am afraid no alterations could quite conciliate your friends, who object totally to the principle of an Establishment, but perhaps some judicious concessions might bring us nearer, though we could hardly be quite united. Your intimacy with the clergy in your neighbourhood looks well. I suppose you approve highly of the Cambridge minority petition.[1] I cannot, nor do I see what good any party would gain from such a step. You are surprised at my launching into all these topics, but I want to irritate you to an answer, that we may not forget each other, even though I may not be able at present to accept your kind invitation, nor you to trust your nonconforming person in Oxford. If you come, I will guarantee your personal safety.—Hoping to hear soon from you, I am, your very sincere friend,   ARCH. CAMPBELL TAIT."

[1] A petition signed by sixty members of the Senate of the University of Cambridge in favour of abolishing Religious Tests in that University, was presented in the House of Lords by Earl Grey on March 21, 1834, and gave occasion to an important debate.—*Hansard*, vol. xxii. pp. 497-522.

The summer vacation of 1834 brought a new experience. It was the first of a series of long vacations, in each of which he travelled abroad. His companion on this first occasion was Mr. Oakeley. They went to Holland, up the Rhine, and home by Paris. His rough diary bears evidence of the care he invariably took to pick up accurate information upon the statistics and politics of lands other than his own. It used often to be remarked in later days what an unusual interest the Archbishop took in the internal politics of Germany and France, and this may in great measure be ascribed to the basis he had early laid of accurate information upon subjects about which most Englishmen know very little.

The Fellowship election came on in November 1834. Tait believed himself to have failed in the examination, and he has often described how he was sitting in his room, in disappointed and anxious thought, listening to the bell ringing for evening chapel, when the door flew open, and his friend Tickell rushed in to drag him off to the chapel to take his place among the Fellows.

So began a new life, with many new friends. On the same day with himself was elected to a Balliol Fellowship a man who was to play no small part in the coming fortunes or misfortunes of the Church in Oxford. William George Ward at the time of his election was a strong Radical, and an admirer of Dr. Arnold, but he was destined before long to fall, like others, under the spell of John Henry Newman, and to become, in his own peculiar fashion, a leader in the fray.

No sooner did Archibald Tait enter on his Fellowship than he seems to have tried to inaugurate reforms of which, as an undergraduate, he had felt the need. But he was able to do very little in this direction until he became, a year later, a Tutor of the College. In December 1834, just after his election as Fellow, he began to keep a rough journal of an altogether different kind from that which has been quoted above. It was almost entirely devotional, and from the irregular and haphazard way in which it is written, in old half-used note-books, and the like, with pages crossed and torn, it seems at first to have been intended rather as a mode of systematising for himself at the moment his religious thoughts and prayers and resolutions, than for any future reference, even by himself. It would be unsuitable, for every reason, to quote freely from this 'journal,'[1] if so it can be called. But a few sentences from it here and there are almost essential to a faithful picture of his life.

"*Friday, Dec.* 12, 1834.—A fortnight ago I was elected a Fellow. Do I feel sufficiently the weighty responsibility which has devolved on me, to use my utmost exertions that the increased means placed in my hands may be made subservient in all things to God's glory, the good of my fellow-men, and of my own soul? O God, do Thou enable me to keep these things more in view. . . . I have now not even the poor excuse of being forced to spend so much of my time in worldly concerns. Henceforward my worldly business, as well as my Christian duty, is God's service."

"*June* 21*st*, 1835.—It is now more than six months from the time of my writing the above; I fear me that time has not been improved as it ought. . . . I must take more pains to become intimate with people if Ward's account of my stiffness be correct, for there is no good to be done in Oxford unless one is intimate with undergraduates. . . . I know I shall do nothing without fervent prayer, and I cannot have that unless my heart be touched. Let me not lose sight of my Ordination. Though there is no hurry, its approach should be a strong stimulus."

In the long vacation of 1835 he was again in France and Belgium, and kept a systematic diary. On the flyleaf is the following characteristic note :—

---

[1] He called it so, but the entries are quite irregular, and many weeks sometimes elapse between them.

"*Mem.*—To inquire about L'Université de France—Education—Cours de France—Juges—Election à la Chambre des Députés—L'Université de Paris—Qui est-ce qui nomme les pairs?—Loi de Primogéniture—Succession aux titres de la noblesse—Sorbonne."

In Paris they had some French lessons from a M. de Maison. "He gave us a wonderful rule for the genders of nouns—all with *un* are masculine, with *une* feminine."

On returning to Balliol in October 1835 he was requested by the Master to undertake the tutorship vacated by Moberly's appointment to the Head-mastership of Winchester. Looking back upon it forty years afterwards he wrote as follows:—"A totally new field of interest was opened to me in the tutorship of the foremost College in Oxford. Of course I succeeded to some eminent pupils whose time was already half over : among them Arthur Stanley, James Lonsdale, and Wickens. But my own peculiar class, with which I began my lectures, was certainly not undistinguished, including Waldegrave, Goulburn, Lake, Sir Benjamin Brodie, Jowett, and Hugh Pearson. I was established in Moberly's rooms, the best in Balliol, and I am vain enough to think that my lectures were as good as any others in the College, and that for a young man of twenty-three I found myself in a somewhat unusual position of importance and usefulness."

On Trinity Sunday, 1836, he was ordained Deacon on his College Fellowship, by Dr. Richard Bagot, Bishop of Oxford. The Ordination sermon was, to his great delight, preached by his friend Mr. Oakeley. The entry in the 'journal' is as follows :—

"*May* 28, 1836.—I have now for three terms been public Tutor, and what a field of usefulness has this opened! I trust I have not forgotten the great responsibility which has devolved upon me, but still, how little have I done! Thirteen immortal souls committed to my charge, and that at the most critical period of their lives. As far as the mere teaching goes, I believe I have done my duty, but I have not laboured for their moral and religious good as I ought. Remember that I must give account. To-morrow will see me an ordained minister of Christ, bound to labour in season and out of season for the good of souls. O God, give me strength, by Thy grace, never for one instant to lose sight of my spiritual duties to my pupils. Some of them are fitter to teach me in heavenly things than I to teach them. . . . I must live more a life of prayer. I must pray for them. . . . I rejoice in the prospect that to-morrow I shall be authorised, bound, to teach and exhort. I trust there is no presumption in saying that my dedication to the ministry is prompted by the Holy Ghost. O God, give me a greater measure of Thy Spirit ; enable me to labour in Thy service, giving myself wholly to it, for Christ's sake. Amen."

It must have been after making this entry that he was summoned to what seemed at the time to be the dying bed of his pupil, Samuel Waldegrave, with whom he remained throughout the night. Thirty-three years later, when Archbishop of Canterbury, he knelt once more by the sick-bed of Samuel Waldegrave, then Bishop of Carlisle, and was present at his death, on October 1st, 1869.[1]

Notwithstanding the large number of clergy then resident in Oxford, some of the country parishes in its immediate neighbourhood were in a terribly neglected state.

About five miles to the south-east of Oxford, on the rising ground between the Thame and the Isis, lies the district of Baldon, or, in its old form, Baudendon, a tract of sparsely populated land, once under the supervision of the monks of Dorchester. One Peter de la Mere had built and endowed a chapel there in 1341, and in process of time 'De la Mere's Baldon,' now corrupted into 'March Baldon,' passed, with its neighbouring parish of

<hr>

[1] See vol. ii. p. 46.

Toot Baldon, into the hands of the Willoughby family. In 1836 the Rev. Hugh Willoughby, Vicar of both 'the Baldons,' was resident abroad in ill-health, and the two parishes were left untended. A few months after his Ordination, Tait volunteered, to the amazement of his friends, to undertake the vacant curacy. It was not an attractive or enviable charge. The straggling cottages were occupied by agricultural labourers and a few small farmers. The two churches were in extremely bad repair, and there was neither salary nor vicarage-house available. But Tait was bent upon the task, and, with the warm approbation of the Bishop, he was duly licensed to the curacy on August 30th, 1836. He was at that time strong and active, but March Baldon is full five miles from Balliol, and he soon found that with his increasing tutorial work the efficient charge of the two parishes was more than he could compass single-handed. Accordingly he turned for help to his trusted friend and counsellor, Mr. Oakeley, who replied as follows :—

"LONDON, *Nov. 26th*, 1836.

"MY DEAR TAIT,—I am sorry to find by your letter that you have any doubts of being able to go on with your curacy. To offer you the sort of help which you say you will not allow me to offer you, is the utmost I can at present do,— I mean that of assistance to any extent, short of a positive undertaking of the curacy in conjunction with you. . . . I will say more when we meet. Do not by any means think of giving up the curacy, or entering into any other arrangement till I see you. If you find the curacy with the tutorship too much for your health you must undoubtedly give up the former; the latter is a very sufficient responsibility. . . . —Ever yours affectionately,

"FREDERICK OAKELEY."

Failing to obtain Mr. Oakeley's co-operation, he succeeded after a time in enlisting the aid of two friends, both senior to himself—Mr. Johnson, Tutor of Queen's, and Mr. C. P. Golightly of Oriel. They rendered him efficient help for several years, especially during the long vacations, but he retained the sole responsibility for the parish, riding or walking from Oxford several times a week, usually sleeping on Saturday nights in the hired cottage which served as an apology for a parsonage, and returning to Balliol in time for the College Service on Sunday afternoon. For five years he carried on this work with unremitting care, and in all the changes of his after life the recollections and the lessons of March Baldon never passed away. To the very close of his life he used to recount with a certain humorous pathos the quiet obstruction offered by the farmers to his Sunday-school, and the difficulties of a rustic congregation on a hot summer's day, and the petty quarrels and flirtations and ambitions of his village choir. When inaugurating in the diocese of London his then novel and unconventional plans of Home Mission work among the poor, he helped to justify them by a special reminiscence of his Baldon days, using these words from the pulpit of St. Paul's in his Primary Diocesan Charge :—

"I cannot but remember how, when a curate in a small village in Oxfordshire, I marvelled at the excitement raised in a quiet and dull place by the gathering of the Methodists on a fine summer's day on the Common, under the shadow of the old trees; how the voice of their preacher, sounding through the stillness of a listening crowd, and the burst of their hymns pealing far and wide through the village, seemed well suited to attract and raise the hearts of many who never entered within the Church to join in its measured devotion, and listen to its calm teaching." [1]

Assuredly no picture of his Oxford life is a true one which regards him merely as a busy college tutor, and forgets his steady and persevering work under most

[1] Charge of 1858, p. 83.

unfavourable conditions in a very unromantic country parish.

But his foremost charge, of course, was Balliol. And College duties were in the meantime multiplying fast upon his hands. Changes among the Fellows followed in rapid succession. Oakeley, though he did not finally leave Oxford and settle in London till 1839, was now very frequently absent, and felt it right to resign his tutorship. Thus before Tait had completed his twenty-sixth year he found himself the senior and most responsible of the four Balliol Tutors.

Rev. J. W. Pugh to Rev. A. C. Tait.

"MANARAVON, LLANDILO, May 23d, 1837.

"MY DEAR TAIT,—You will wonder why I have not written to you before, and I have no other excuse than that, like yourself, I have no taste for letter-writing. . . . I hope, my dear Tait, you are going on prosperously in College. I have been thinking a good deal since I saw you what a very trying situation yours must be; I mean that it must be one of considerable danger to a young man. Oakeley being gone, and you therefore the Senior Classical Tutor, the affairs of the College must be a good deal under your control. Now I do not know how it is with you, but with regard to myself I am sure the least success has a tendency, without very great watchfulness, to draw away my mind from God, and I know how the best of men have been allowed to fall when at any time they have forgotten to live in entire dependence on Him.

"If I may speak my mind to you, I should say ambition was one of your greatest snares, and I am sure there are others of your friends who think so too. Beware of it, my dear Tait, for I do not think there is anything more likely to dim the eye of faith. . . . You see I am not afraid of telling you home-truths, and one reason is that I know you too well to think you will be offended. . . . —Your affectionate friend,

"J. W. PUGH."

These were eventful years in Oxford. The spell of Mr. Newman's influence was at its height, and the Tracts *for the Times* were in full circulation. It would be out of place to discuss here the causes and character of the influence exercised by the famous Tracts. The fact of their success, however it be explained, is beyond dispute, and surprise has sometimes been expressed that no more serious attempt should have been made at the time to counteract their influence by the issue of any similar series upon the other side. The following letter would seem to show that the possibilities of such a scheme were at least under consideration, though nothing came of it :—

Mr. A. Hall Hall to the Rev. A. C. Tait.

"LONDON, *Jany.* 20*th*, 1837.

"MY DEAR TAIT,—We were very sorry not to have the pleasure of seeing you in town. . . . Jones and Oakeley are regular Newmanites, and hate moderate men, and scout your notion altogether. Oakeley says, if he writes at all, it will be for the Oxford Tracts. He is more virulent in old Jones' company than out of it. I think myself there is something in the idea. But I want you to define your *moderate* men, and give something of a plan to your work : whether is it to refute doctrinal or political dissenters, to convert antagonists, or to fortify Churchmen in their own opinions? These would require and might allow of a very different cast of arguments. . . .

"On the whole, 'Our Judgment is' that you had better mature your opinions, and try them by the test of years before you commit yourself. . . . If, however, disregarding Jones and Oakeley, who are much more decided on the subject than I am, you still determined to write, I will give you any assistance I can, or at least I will promise to buy and read. I will not promise to distribute till I know that it is sound. . . . —Believe me, very truly yours, ALEXR. HALL HALL."

The immediate cause of such a scheme coming under consideration was probably the publication of Mr. Richard Hurrell Froude's *Remains*. This book, which appeared in the last months of 1836, was a shock to many who had followed the 'movement' thus far without serious mistrust. Mr. Newman's Tract on the Breviary had been published a few months before, and it now became evident that there were two forces at work among the Tractarians, one of which, whether consciously or not, was tending definitely Romewards. For the present, however, there was no open rupture.

In the long vacation of 1837 Tait was again abroad, first with W. C. Lake, and then with Ramsay Campbell. His diary is full of notes about the systems in vogue for the support of church fabrics, the maintenance of the clergy, the various systems of elementary education, and the like. Their route comprised Antwerp, Cologne, Bonn, Frankfort, Strasburg, Berne, the Simplon, Milan, Verona, and Venice. Thence home by Innsbruck, Munich, and the Rhine. "English Protestants," he writes, "should gain a lesson from the multitude of little chapels one sees everywhere." Verona and Venice seem to have captivated him beyond all other places on this long and comprehensive tour. Monasteries and libraries he visited whenever it was possible, and described their pictures and books with curious and painstaking accuracy.

Towards the close of the year 1837, the Rev. Walter Kerr Hamilton, who was at that time Vicar of St. Peter's, Oxford,[1] appealed to Tait to exchange his pastoral work at Baldon for a curacy under him in Oxford. Tait at first welcomed the suggestion :—

"I cannot but feel that such a connection might be of the greatest use to myself as a preparation for the most important duties of my profession, and as I enjoy the blessing of very good health and strength and lungs, and have not the slightest objection to hard work, perhaps I might hope not to be an inefficient assistant to you. I feel also, what is of still greater importance,

---

[1] For an account of Mr. Hamilton's views and position at this time, see Canon Liddon's *Sketch of Walter Kerr Hamilton*, pp. 12-15.

that the views of Christian truth and practice which I know you to hold are such as I have long been, I trust, sincerely attached to, however far short I have fallen in carrying them out."

The proposal, however, came to nothing, as it was found that there would be the greatest difficulty in persuading any one to undertake the work at Baldon, and also that the duties in Balliol would clash with those in St. Peter's.

"I look upon my College duties as paramount, and I think that for many reasons I should do wrong in withdrawing from the tutorship at Balliol. For the next two terms I am positively engaged to deliver a lecture each Sunday evening in the College Chapel."

The beginning of the year 1838 seemed likely to be marked by a very important change in his life. News reached him that the Professorship of Moral Philosophy in his old University of Glasgow was about to be vacant, and his friends urged him to become a candidate. The position was one of great importance and large emolument. But there was in the forefront a religious difficulty. Certain subscriptions were required of the Glasgow Professors, and among them was one expressing adherence to the Westminster Confession of Faith. Sir Daniel Sandford, though son of the Bishop of Edinburgh, and himself a decided Episcopalian, had not found in the subscriptions any obstacle to his own tenure of the Greek Professorship, and to him accordingly, as an old friend and trusted counsellor, Tait wrote as follows:—

The Rev. A. C. Tait to Sir Daniel Sandford.

"BALLIOL COLLEGE, 30*th Jany.* 1838.

"MY DEAR SIR DANIEL,—I have lately been informed that there is likely, at no distant period, to be a contest for the Moral

Philosophy Chair in my old University. The subject of Moral Philosophy is one to which I have devoted much of my time for several years, and in which I have been engaged in lecturing in this College for the last two years. I should therefore be anxious to offer myself as a candidate if there were any reasonable hope of success, provided I could do so without at all compromising my duty to the Church of England, being, as I am, one of her clergy, and warmly attached to her doctrine and discipline. I am so ignorant on the point that I do not even know whether it is lawful for a clergyman of the Church of England to hold a Scotch Professorship, and I should feel very much obliged if you could tell me what is the state of the case. Perhaps you would be good enough to let me know what the declaration or subscription is which a Professor is called upon to make, and what is the meaning of the subscription as generally understood by the body who impose it. I am very sorry to give you so much trouble, but a Chair in my old University is a situation which I should value so much that I trust you will forgive me for trespassing on you, and will let me know what candidates are already in the field, if any have as yet declared themselves. . . . —Yours very truly,   A. C. TAIT."

This letter Sir Daniel Sandford never received. He was stricken with fever on the very day it was written, and a few days later Tait heard from his intimate friend Mr. Swinton, who announced to him Sir Daniel's death, and expressed his conviction that Tait ought now to stand, not for the Chair of Moral Philosophy, but for the still more important Professorship of Greek. Mr. Swinton mentioned at the same time three gentlemen, "all bigoted Episcopalians," who had found no difficulty in signing the Confession. The Greek Professorship was worth at least £1500 a year, with a house, and his presence in Glasgow would be required for only six months in each year. Tait, who maintained the warmest affection for his old University, determined at least to test the question of the obligatory subscription by becoming a candidate. He accordingly wrote as follows to his brother :—

The Rev. A. C. Tait to Mr. John Tait.

"BALLIOL COLLEGE, *Feb.* 9, 1838.

"MY DEAR JOHN,—Poor Sandford's death is a most sad and striking thing. It is specially striking to me, seeing that I wrote to him on the subject of the Moral Philosophy Chair about ten days ago, and had an answer from Ramsay, he being in bed. Ramsay declared there was nothing to prevent a clergyman of the Church of England holding a Chair. The Principal expressed a different opinion. Now, here is the point. I should like of all things to succeed poor Sandford, but I will on no account make any declaration whatsoever that will compromise my duty to the Church whose minister I am, and to whose doctrine I am sincerely attached. I have again looked hurriedly at the Confession of Faith. An assent to all its articles as matters of my belief I cannot see how I can give. Two doctrines in particular—that of God having foreordained a portion of His creatures to damnation, and that the Elect can be infallibly assured of their salvation in this life—are no parts of my creed; therefore to say that they were would be a lie, and however such a statement may be gulped by men in general, I could not gulp it. A mere acquiescence in the articles as the formulæ of the Church of Scotland, a declaration that I recognise that Church as the Established and lawful Church in Scotland, and that I have no objection to its worship, would be very well. The Principal, to whom I wrote on the subject of the Moral Philosophy Chair, sent me a declaration which is far too strong to be made by any clergyman of the Church of England. Must the articles of necessity be signed? What is the interpretation put by the imposing body on the signature? Is there a declaration which must of necessity be made? Might one sign under public protest? These are questions which I put to you as a lawyer. I am exceedingly anxious on the subject, and should like the situation very much, provided it can be consistently held by a clergyman continuing to act as such. I beg you to sift the matter thoroughly, and to ascertain exactly the law of the case. I shall in the meantime announce myself as a candidate conditionally, and mean to write this evening to the Principal and others. I shall state my intention of becoming a candidate if the situation can be held by a clergyman of the Church of England.—Your affectionate

"A. C. T."

In his letter to the Principal he says :—

"I shall without doubt offer myself as a candidate for the Chair, provided it shall appear on examination that I could conscientiously hold the situation, reserving to myself liberty of conscience, and the free and public exercise of my own mode of worship as a clergyman of the Church of England. . . . I hope your friendship will attribute what I say on the subject of my opinions to my anxious desire to act in perfect fairness at the very outset in proposing myself to your kind consideration. I should be proud, indeed, to return to my old University as a Professor, but could never consent to do so by a compromise of my duty to the Church of England. I am the minister of that Church, and bound to uphold publicly her doctrine and discipline."

Two days later, while the question of subscription still remained open, he writes thus to his brother :—

The Rev. A. C. Tait to Mr. John Tait.

"BALLIOL COLL., 11*th Feb.* 1838.

"MY DEAR JOHN,—I have just time before post to call your attention to what has struck me. There is a party in this University who have become somewhat famous of late (*vide* the last *Edinburgh Review*), persons who hold extremely High-Church doctrines about Episcopal authority, and who regard the Kirk of Scotland as the synagogue of Baal. With these it would be peculiarly hard if I was at all identified on the present occasion, as I have spent my breath and influence for a long time back in protesting against their (what I conceive to be) most dangerous and superstitious opinions. . . ."

With respect to the necessity of formal subscription, the answers which he received from Principal Macfarlane and Dr. M'Gill, though personally they were most encouraging and laudatory, were quite uncompromising, both in their hostility to the Episcopalian system, and in their adherence, as of necessity, to the Calvinism which Tait had declared himself unable to accept. His Scotch friends, who naturally wished to see him again settled among them, quoted to him instance after instance in which well-known Episcopalians had held Scotch Professorships (other than those of Divinity) and made the necessary subscriptions. But he remained firm, and before many days had passed withdrew finally from the contest. To his brother he wrote :—

"I will answer your letter explicitly. You ask if I will sign the Confession of Faith without qualification. To this I answer decidedly and distinctly, *No.* . . . . I have nothing to do with judging other people, but it seems to me that a man who, intending to remain an Episcopalian, sets his hand to such an unqualified declaration, does neither more nor less than write one thing and mean another. It is no use to mention instances of good people, such as ——, who have done so ; this only shows how good people may differ as to what seem plain matters of duty. . . . Again, you ask whether I would take the situation on the understanding that I was not to act publicly as an Episcopalian clergyman in Glasgow. To this I answer as distinctly and decidedly, *No.* I trust there is no situation on earth which I would accept on such terms ; certainly there is none, I think, which I could so accept without a violation of my ordination vow. You now understand my mind, I trust, perfectly. . . . The whole subject is, no doubt, beset with difficulties, but it appears to me the electors have only to choose between two fair alternatives. One is, to confine the Professorships to Presbyterians, or those who are ready to become such ; the other, openly to admit Episcopalians when they see fit, reserving in their own hands the power of enforcing subscription in the case of any dangerous appointment. . . . The Professorship would have been pleasant as a settlement among you all. I shall be sorry if they appoint an indifferent successor to Sandford. . . . Good-bye. Withdraw my name, when you see fit, and let me hear soon.—Yours ever,

"A. C. TAIT."

In a subsequent letter to the Principal he emphasises his own withdrawal by sending a testimonial in favour of another candidate, Mr. Robert Lowe.[1]

---

[1] Now Viscount Sherbrooke.

This episode over, Archibald Tait set himself once more to the hard work of his Balliol tutorship and his Baldon curacy. He does not seem to have kept a diary with any regularity, but there are spasmodic efforts now and then which recall, in the minuteness of the entries, the 'particular journal' kept for his father in the Glasgow days. From its pages it appears that, besides what was necessary for his lectures, he was engaged at this time on a wide course of general reading. The following is part of a long list of books which he seems to have studied carefully in the years 1838-39 :—Locke on Toleration, Gladstone on Church and State, Thirlwall's Greece, Adam Smith's Wealth of Nations, Strype's Memorials, South's Sermons, Whately's Lectures on Political Economy, Palmer's Origines Liturgicæ, Dugald Stewart's Philosophical Dissertations, Archbishop Secker's Lectures. Like every one else in those years, he seems to have read Newman's sermons with avidity. They appear again and again in his journal, and it is evident that he was paying the utmost attention to the development of his teaching. He was giving much thought, too, to educational questions, and in the summer of 1839 he determined to spend some months, not, as heretofore, in foreign travel, but in systematic residence and study at a German University. He selected Bonn, which he had already visited once at least, arriving there on June 22d, 1839. Various Oxford friends spent a few days with him in turn, among them W. C. Lake, Arthur Stanley, and Edward Goulburn. True to his invariable wish to combine a certain amount of pastoral work with his studies, he volunteered to be responsible for the duties of English Chaplain, and preached almost every Sunday during his three months' stay. But his object in going to Bonn, and the success with which he attained it, are best attested by the following testimonial which was given to him three years afterwards, when a candidate for the Head-mastership of Rugby:—

From Dr. F. G. Sommer, Professor at Bonn.

"The Rev. A. C. Tait came here in the year 1839, at which time I first made his personal acquaintance. His object was to inform himself more nearly concerning the state of German literature and education, especially to become acquainted with our Prussian University system and methods of instruction, and also to form lasting connections with German men of letters and Professors. This aim he accomplished with the happiest results during his residence here of three months, and afterwards by a literary journey to Germany. Intimately versed in our language, of which he became master partly by the study of our literature, partly by the personal intercourse with Germans, he was enabled to attend the lectures in our University; and I have often remarked in our discussions the great interest which he took in and his intimacy with those subjects. This practical information of the method of instruction pursued by us Mr. Tait perfected by means of his acquaintance and literary intercourse with several of our most eminent Professors, through whom he became theoretically informed of the whole system and views of our Universities. . . . He did not less turn his attention to other Institutes of Education in our country. He was introduced into the different classes of the Gymnasium, and learned in this way, by his own experience, the arrangements, method, and extent of instruction in our schools. . . .

"I hope to have shown that Mr. Tait spared neither time nor pains to become acquainted with the system of education pursued in the Prussian dominions.—I sign myself, Gentlemen, your obedient, humble servant,

"F. G. SOMMER,

"Licentiate and Docent of Protestant Divinity in the University of Bonn."

On leaving Bonn he travelled for several weeks with two German Professors, visiting their homes, and sedulously gathering and tabulating precise information as to the various systems of German education both for the upper and lower classes. In the following year he was again abroad, accompanied by Goulburn, Lake, and Stanley, and during part of the time by Sir Charles and Lady Wake.

These frequent foreign tours, and especially the prolonged residence at Bonn, obviously gave him an exceptional knowledge of the affairs both of Germany and France. They were no mere holidays, but times of hard and systematic work, and he used constantly to refer in later years to the usefulness of the particular knowledge he had acquired. The subject of Education, then a less popular topic than now, continued to absorb much of his attention. A pamphlet which he published in 1839,[1] advocating certain changes in the professorial and tutorial system at Oxford, attracted wide notice in its careful and suggestive comparisons between the English, Scottish, and Continental systems, about all of which he was now able to speak from personal experience.

With reference to his work as Tutor of Balliol, Principal Shairp writes as follows:—

"When in October 1840 I went into residence at Balliol, Tait received me as his pupil, for at that time all the undergraduates were divided among the four Tutors, as their pupils, over whom they had a special charge and responsibility. I considered myself fortunate in having Tait for my Tutor, for he was not only the senior, but by far the most influential of the then Balliol Tutors. The Master, Jenkyns, was a sort of constitutional monarch, and Tait was his Prime Minister, on whom he leant, to whom he looked for advice and support with absolute confidence. The other Tutors and the younger Fellows, several of whom had been his own pupils, might each of them be cleverer in this or that line of scholarship, but they all felt that there was in Tait a manliness and sense and a weight of character to which they could not but defer. The undergraduates all respected and liked

---

[1] *Hints on the Formation of a Plan for the Safe and Effectual Revival of the Professorial System at Oxford.* By a Resident Member of Convocation.

him. They felt that there was no getting round him. His shrewdness, his dry and not unkindly humour, were too much for them ; and if any one, more forward than the rest, tried to cross swords with him, he had in his calm presence of mind an impregnable defence. . . . He was, I think, the first man in Oxford to appreciate the as yet unrecognised genius of Arthur Hugh Clough. I remember his excitement when, in the summer of 1841, Arthur Clough, to the dismay of Balliol, got only a second class in the Final Schools. Tait was furious, and went about the University loudly denouncing the incapacity of the examiners. 'They had not only a first-rate scholar, but a man of original genius before them, and were too stupid to discover it.' He would fain have had him elected to a Balliol Fellowship, but it was ruled otherwise, and Clough went to Oriel. I remember Tait saying that a paper which Clough wrote on the character of Saul, during the competition for the Balliol Fellowship, was the best and most original thing he had ever known in any examination."

Besides his keen interest in the intellectual work of his Balliol pupils, Tait had a deep and, for that time, quite an unusual sense of personal responsibility for the quasi-pastoral charge committed to him in the College.

On November 16th, 1839, his diary contains the following entry :—

"*Mem.*—What can be done for the College servants ? what to make more of a pastoral connection between the tutors and their pupils ? What can be done for making the tutor more fully superintend his individual pupils' reading without mere reference to the Schools ? what for reviving provisions to enable the lower classes to profit by the Universities, as they did when Servitorships existed ? "

With respect to the first of these points—the pastoral care of the College servants—a formal letter was written to the Master by Tait a few months later, embodying a definite proposal made by himself and three other Fellows of the College. They promised to hand over £300 to trustees on condition that the interest should be given as an honorarium to one of the tutors, appointed by the Master, for the definite weekly instruction in chapel of such of the College servants as might be willing to attend. The names appended to the memorial, or deed of gift, are A. C. Tait, W. G. Ward, Robert Scott, and E. C. Woollcombe.

The master discovered many difficulties in the way of giving effect to this plan. But they were overcome at last, and the journal of 1841 (a few days before the publication of the Four Tutors' Protest against Tract XC.) has the following entry :—

"*Ash Wednesday*, 24 *Feby*. 1841.—I have spent much of this day in prayer, though, I fear, it has come too little from the heart. I have begun to-day a most important work in the teaching of the boys among the College servants. O God, send Thy blessing on this endeavour. Above all, lead my own heart aright, or how can I teach others? Lord, I thank Thee that Thou hast smoothed the way for carrying out this plan for the College servants. . . . Grant Thy Spirit to teacher and taught, that it may not all end in dead formality."

CHAPTER IV.

1841.

TAIT'S influence now extended beyond the limits of
Balliol. His position in the University had become a
prominent one, and his friendships, both there and elsewhere, were multiplying fast. Between him and some of
his older friends a certain degree of estrangement had
necessarily arisen. Many of them were by this time
closely identified with the school of Mr. Newman, and
Tait's sympathies were markedly, and perhaps increasingly,
leading him in an opposite direction. Among the Fellows
of Balliol, Mr. Oakeley and Mr. Ward were now enthusiastic and prominent Tractarians, and from his necessary
intimacy with them and with their friends, Tait had
ample opportunity of forming his own judgment as to the
character and probable issue of the opinions they had
embraced. What that judgment was has already been
shown in one of the letters he wrote about the Glasgow Professorship.[1]　It is not surprising, therefore, to
find, from a correspondence which took place between
Mr. Oakeley and himself in the winter of 1838, that they
now 'agreed to differ' upon matters of the highest
importance. In the course of the correspondence, which
relates to an entirely different subject, Tait remarks in-
cidentally :—

[1] See above, p. 67.

"You must be fully aware that for some time back (owing, I always supposed—I hope erroneously—to your own wish) I have not seen so much of you in private as I once did, and as I have always desired."

To this Oakeley replies :—

"As to what you say of our not meeting so much of late, I am glad you have said it, because it is open and friendly. If you have much felt it, I am sorry you have not said it before. The fact is this : It seems to me we have agreed far better since we have met less. Disputing with friends I cannot bear, and yet, as we do not quite agree on essential matters, and each feels strongly his own way, dispute we must. You have kept your opinions ; I have a good deal changed mine. . . . In one respect, our intercourse is to me far more satisfactory than of old, in that I do not think we encourage one another in our faults as we used. Anything is better than that."

With Mr. William George Ward, who was elected to a Balliol Fellowship on the same day as himself, Tait's friendship had been of a different character. Their intimacy was great, but the friendship had never been of so sacred a sort, and, perhaps for that very reason, it was less interrupted by the increasing divergence of their religious views. In Mr. Mozley's *Reminiscences* [1] Ward is described as representing

"the intellectual force, the irrefragable logic, the absolute self-confidence, and the headlong impetuosity of the Rugby school. Whatever he said or did was right. As a philosopher and a logician, it was hard to deal with him. He had been instantaneously converted to Newman by a single line in an introduction to one of his works to the effect that Protestantism could never have corrupted into Popery. . . . Ward's weight in the University was great, and that weight he brought to Newman's cause, though eventually he became a very unaccommodating and unmanageable member of the crew. Ward, I must add, was a great musical critic, knew all the operas, and was an admirable buffo singer."

[1] Vol. ii. p. 5.

Since Mr. Mozley's reminiscences were published, Mr. Ward's son has given to the world in graceful form a detailed and careful account of the life and opinions of this powerful and eccentric man.[1]

Archbishop Tait, who always appreciated and liked him, used to give an amusing picture in after years of Ward's peculiarities of appearance and manner in Oxford. Immensely stout, very careless as to his apparel, brilliant in conversation, with a restless love of argument and repartee, and fond above all things of producing startling effects—he was not a man whom those who had known him would be likely to forget, while his kindness of heart and genuine goodness made him cling to old friends, even when they differed from him most widely.

These two stood foremost among Tait's Tractarian friends. He was never on intimate terms either with Dr. Pusey or Dr. Newman; but in the wide circle of his Oxford associates he had abundant opportunity of forming a competent judgment both as to the characteristics and the results of the new Church Revival. How far he ever appreciated its best points must remain a matter of opinion on which it is not probable that his critics will agree. Principal Shairp thinks he entirely failed to do so :—

"His Scotch nature and education, his Whig principles, and, I may add, the evangelical views which he had imbibed, were wholly antipathetic to this movement; so entirely antipathetic that I do not think he ever, from first to last, caught a glimpse of the irresistible attraction which it had for younger and more ardent natures, or of the charm which encircled the leaders of it, especially the character of John Henry Newman. To his downright common sense the whole movement seemed nonsense, or at least the madness of incipient Popery. Evening by evening, in Balliol common-room, he held strenuous debate with Ward,

[1] *William George Ward and the Oxford Movement.* Macmillan, 1889.

who was a champion of the new opinions. To Tait's stout reassertion of the old Protestant fundamentals, momentum was added by his high personal character and the respect in which he was universally held."

Be this as it may, it is certain that Tait very early perceived what was the issue to which his friend's opinions must necessarily lead, and that his profound distrust of the teaching which he had seen Oakeley and Ward imbibe was based on no accidental prejudice, but on a deliberate conviction, the truth of which became apparent before many years had passed.

"Mr. Ward," his biographer tells us, "openly avowed his adherence to Newman's party in the latter part of 1838. There was, about this time, a considerable accession to the ranks of the party of able men with directly Roman sympathies. . . . Mr. Ward's party commenced its action with a new and startling programme. . . . Rome was directly looked on by them as in many respects the practical model ; the Reformation was a deadly sin ; restoration to the Papal communion the ideal—even if unattainable—aim." [1]

Dr. Newman has himself narrated how, in this very year (1840), he began to see, much more clearly than his followers yet saw, whereunto his teaching must necessarily lead :—

"People tell me that I am, whether by sermons or otherwise, exerting at St. Mary's a beneficial influence on our prospective clergy ; but what if I take to myself the credit of seeing further than they, and of having in the course of the last year discovered that what they approve so much is very likely to end in Romanism?" [2]

So he wrote to a friend in 1840. But the letter was a private one, and this, his view about his own teaching, was not made public until long afterwards. On the contrary, as Mr. Palmer, himself a contributor to the *Tracts*, has

<hr>

[1] *William George Ward and the Oxford Movement*, p. 136.
[2] *Apologia*, p. 237.

told us, many of his followers were supporting him at this time, in spite of their own misgivings, simply because, ignorant of what was really passing in his mind, they trusted him implicitly.[1]

It was in these circumstances that the crisis came. Tait was sitting quietly in his rooms in Balliol on Saturday morning, February 27, 1841, when Ward burst excitedly in. "Here," he cried, "is something worth reading!" and he threw down a pamphlet on the table. It was 'Tract XC.'

Dr. Newman has himself given us in his *Apologia* the history of that famous Essay. It had been urged both by friends and foes that so long as the Tractarians continued to accept the Thirty-nine Articles, there was, to say the least, a strong bulwark against any Romeward movement. Drawn up to maintain the Church of England's protest against Rome, the Articles had held their own for three centuries, and they held it still.

"From the time," says Dr. Newman, " that I had entered upon the duties of public Tutor at my College, when my doctrinal views were very different from what they were in 1841, I had meditated a comment upon the Articles. Then, when the movement was in its swing, friends had said to me, 'What will you make of the Articles?' But I did not share the apprehension which their question implied. Whether, as time went on, I should have been forced, by the necessities of the original theory of the movement, to put on paper the speculations which I had about them, I am not able to conjecture. The actual cause of my doing so in the beginning of 1841 was the restlessness, actual and prospective, of those who

---

[1] " Relying as I and most other Churchmen did on the honour and integrity of Newman and his associates, and aware that they were in many points maintaining the truth against its impugners, we did not openly oppose the progress of Newman's opinions, though we could not concur with many of his positions, or those of his immediate disciples, Ward, Oakeley, Robert Wilberforce, and others."—*Narrative of Events connected with the Tracts for the Times*, p. 57.

neither liked the *via media* nor my strong judgment against Rome.
I had been enjoined, I think by my Bishop, to keep these men
straight, and I wished so to do. But their tangible difficulty was
subscription to the Articles, and thus the question of the Articles
came before me."[1]

The tract was dated "Oxford, The Feast of the Conversion of St. Paul,[2] 1841." Though anonymous, there
was no real doubt as to its authorship, and hence, in large
measure, the importance attaching to it.

"The Tract," said Dr. Newman a few days later, "is grounded
on the belief that the Articles *need* not be so closed as the received
method of teaching closes them, and *ought* not to be, for the
sake of many persons. If we so close them we run the risk of
subjecting persons whom we should least like to lose or distress
to the temptation of joining the Church of Rome, or to the
necessity of withdrawing from the Church as established, or to
the misery of subscribing with doubt and hesitation."[3]

Accordingly, in the pages of this voluminous tract, he
examined in detail those Articles which, in their ordinary
acceptation, are directed against the distinctive teaching
of the Church of Rome ; and by an ingenious manipulation
of what had seemed to most people plain and straightforward words, maintained them to be capable of quite
another interpretation. A single example will show the
style of reasoning adopted. The Reformers are commonly
supposed to have protested against the doctrine of infallible Church Councils, and to have given expression to that
view in Article XXI. The following, however, is Dr. Newman's treatment of the subject :[4]—

---

[1] *Apologia*, p. 158.

[2] Although so dated, it was not published till Feb. 27th.

[3] *Letter to Dr. Jelf*, pp. 28, 29.

[4] This example is chosen because it is possible in small compass to give
the substance of Dr. Newman's argument. In none of the five cases specifically referred to by the "Four Tutors" would this be possible without an
unfair compression of the author's words. (*N.B.*—The italics in the extract
given are Dr. Newman's own.)

"§ 5.—*GENERAL COUNCILS.*

" *Article* XXI.—*General Councils may not be gathered together without the commandment and will of princes. And when they be gathered together, forasmuch as they be an assembly of men, whereof all be not governed with the Spirit and Word of God, they may err, and sometimes have erred, even in things pertaining to God.* . . .

"'That great bodies of men . . . when met together, though Christians, will not all be ruled by the Spirit or Word of God is plain from our Lord's parable of the net, and from melancholy experience. That bodies of men deficient in this respect, may err is a self-evident truth—*unless*, indeed, they be favoured with some divine superintendence, which has to be proved, before it can be admitted.

" General Councils then may err, *unless* in any case it is promised as a matter of express supernatural privilege, that they shall *not* err, a case which lies beyond the scope of this Article, or at any rate beside its determination. Such a promise, however, *does* exist, in cases when General Councils are not only gathered together according to 'the commandment and will of princes,' but *in the name of* Christ, according to our Lord's promise. The Article merely contemplates the human prince, not the King of Saints. While Councils are a thing of earth, their infallibility of course is not guaranteed : when they are a thing of heaven, their deliberations are overruled, and their decrees authoritative. . . ."

A similar mode of interpretation was adopted, *mutatis mutandis*, with regard to thirteen others of the 39 Articles —and long extracts were given from various books to show the absurd and extravagant distortions of fact and faith against which, rather than against the authoritative teaching of the Church of Rome, the 39 Articles were believed by Dr. Newman to be directed. "The Articles are not written," he said, "against the Creed of the Roman Church, but against actual existing errors in it, whether taken into its system or not."[1]

As soon as Tait had read the Tract he seems to have

---

[1] *Tract XC.* p. 61.

felt that the time had arrived when a public protest was called for. His first idea was to write himself to the Editor, and among his papers is the draft of a letter which was never sent. For he decided, after consideration, to invite the co-operation of others, and, accordingly, on March 8th, 1841, the following document was published. Its authorship is placed beyond dispute by the fact that, with the exception of about three lines, every sentence it contains is to be found in one part or another of the original draft letter, which is considerably longer than the published Protest :—

" To the Editor of the ' Tracts for the Times.'

"Sir,—Our attention having been called to No. 90 in the series of ' *Tracts for the Times*,' by Members of the University of Oxford, of which you are the Editor, the impression produced on our minds by its contents is of so painful a character that we feel it our duty to intrude ourselves briefly on your notice. This publication is entitled ' Remarks on certain Passages in the Thirty-nine Articles,' and as these Articles are appointed by the Statutes of the University to be the text-book for teachers in their theological teaching, we hope that the situations we hold in our respective Colleges will secure us from the charge of pre-sumption in thus coming forward to address you.

"The Tract has, in our apprehension, a highly dangerous tendency, from its suggesting that certain very important errors of the Church of Rome are not condemned by the Articles of the Church of England—for instance, that those Articles do not contain any condemnation of the doctrines—

"1. Of Purgatory,
"2. Of Pardons,
"3. Of the Worshipping and Adoration of Images and Relics,
"4. Of the Invocation of Saints,
"5. Of the Mass,

as they are taught authoritatively by the Church of Rome, but only of certain absurd practices and opinions which intelligent Romanists repudiate as much as we do. It is intimated, more-over, that the Declaration prefixed to the Articles, so far as it has any weight at all, sanctions this mode of interpreting them, as it is one which takes them in their 'literal and grammatical sense,' and does not 'affix any new sense' to them. The Tract would thus appear to us to have a tendency to mitigate beyond what charity requires, and to the prejudice of the pure truth of the Gospel, the very serious differences which separate the Church of Rome from our own, and to shake the confidence of the less learned members of the Church of England in the Scriptural character of her formularies and teaching.

"We readily admit the necessity of allowing that liberty in interpreting the formularies of our Church which has been advocated by many of its most learned Bishops and other eminent divines; but this Tract puts forward new and startling views as to the extent to which that liberty may be carried. For if we are right in our apprehension of the author's meaning, we are at a loss to see what security would remain, were his principles generally recognised, that the most plainly erroneous doctrines and practices of the Church of Rome might not be inculcated in the lecture-rooms of the University, and from the pulpits of our churches.

"In conclusion, we venture to call your attention to the impropriety of such questions being treated in an anonymous publication, and to express an earnest hope that you may be authorised to make known the writer's name. Considering how very grave and solemn the whole subject is, we cannot help thinking that both the Church and the University are entitled to ask that some person beside the printer and publisher of the Tract should acknowledge himself responsible for its contents.—We are, sir, your obedient and humble servants,

"T. T. CHURTON, M.A.,
Vice-Principal and Tutor of Brasenose College.

H. B. WILSON, B.D.,
Fellow and Senior Tutor of St. John's College.

JOHN GRIFFITHS, M.A.,
Sub-Warden and Tutor of Wadham College.

A. C. TAIT, M.A.,
Fellow and Senior Tutor of Balliol College.

"OXFORD, *March 8th*, 1841."

It does not fall to the biographer of Archibald Tait to recount in any detail the fiery controversies which followed upon the publication of the Protest. It is not to that document, by itself, that the conflagration can be reasonably ascribed. The four Tutors did but lay a match to the tinder which had been long preparing. Tait had, at all times, the courage of his opinions, nor was he ever afraid to become the spokesman of those who shared his views. Few impartial critics, whatever their personal opinions may be, will deny that the Protest itself is a calm and reasonable document, giving expression to apprehensions which the event showed to be well founded. To the end of his life Archibald Tait used to be taunted with having "hounded Newman out of Oxford," and the Protest has been again and again described as bigoted, narrow, and unfair. Dr. Newman himself never so regarded it. On the first page of his letter to Dr. Jelf, published five days after the Protest had been issued, he thus describes it :—

"Four gentlemen, Tutors of their respective Colleges, have published a Protest against the Tract in question. I have no cause at all to complain of their so doing, though, as I shall directly say, I think they have misunderstood me. They do not, I trust, suppose that I feel any offence or soreness at their proceeding; of course I naturally think that I am right and they are wrong; but this persuasion is quite consistent both with my honouring their zeal for Christian truth and their anxiety for the welfare of our younger members, and with my very great consciousness that, even though I be right in my principle, I may have advocated truth in a wrong way. Such acts as theirs, when done honestly, as they have done them, must benefit all parties, and draw them nearer to each other in good-will, if not in opinion." [1]

Similarly, Mr. Ward, writing in warm support of the Tract, refers to

"the remarkably temperate and Christian tone of the Paper

[1] "A Letter addressed to the Rev. R. W. Jelf, D.D., in Explanation of No. 90, by the Author," p. 5.

which began the contest: a tone which may well encourage us in sanguine hopes that, the beginning having been made in such a spirit, whatever may be said on either side may be said, on the whole, in a temper not unworthy of the grave importance of the subject."[1]

A few days after the Protest had been published, the Hebdomadal Board took up the subject. In deprecation of the censure which it was understood they would pronounce, Mr. Newman wrote to Dr. Jelf the letter of vindication from which the foregoing extract is taken. But before the letter was in type the Board passed a resolution of censure, ending with the following words:—

"Resolved that modes of interpretation, such as are suggested in the said Tract, evading rather than explaining the sense of the Thirty-nine Articles, and reconciling subscription to them with the adoption of errors which they were designed to counteract, defeat the object, and are inconsistent with the due observance of the above-mentioned Statutes."

The sequel is well known. The Bishop of Oxford conveyed to Mr. Newman his opinion that the Tract was dangerous in its tendencies, and recommended that the series should be discontinued.[2] In this recommendation Mr. Newman acquiesced, and the Tracts came to an end.

Such was the immediate consequence of the 'Four Tutors'' action. Whether that action was wise or unwise it had at least the merit of straightforwardness and courage. It has been sometimes spoken of as a bid for popularity in Oxford. The accusation betrays an absolute unacquaintance with the then state of Oxford opinion.

"At this distance of time," writes Principal Shairp in 1885, "it is not easy to realise how much courage it required in Tait to take the step he did. He might have the Protestant and No-

---

[1] "A Few Words in Support of No. 90," page 4.

[2] See "A Letter to the Lord Bishop of Oxford, on Occasion of No. 90." By J. H. Newman, March 29, 1841, p. 3.

Popery feeling of the country on his side. But in Oxford, where his life then lay, Protestantism was at a discount with all but the old fogies. Those who represented liberalism in theology, the remnants of the Whately school, Hampden, Baden-Powell, Cox, and others, were now nowhere. All that was most ardent and generous among the younger fellows and among the undergraduates went enthusiastically with the romantic devotion and the utter unworldliness of the Tractarian leaders. They had shown a new thing in Oxford and in England : had turned their backs on promotion and preferment, and given their lives to what worldlings called a hopeless enterprise." [1]

To stand up against them was to court unpopularity, misrepresentation, and attack, on the part of the very 'public' for whose good opinion Tait cared most. And the attack came unsparingly. The controversy soon waxed vehement, and on either side indignant pamphlets followed one another in rapid succession. Among those who thus defended the controverted Tract were Dr. Pusey, W. G. Ward, Frederick Oakeley, and William Palmer of Magdalen.[2] Among the pamphleteers on the other side were Professor Sewell and William Palmer of Worcester (both of whom had been friends of the Tract writers), C. P. Golightly, and Robert Lowe.

Tait, after the issue of the original Protest, seems to have taken no public part in the controversy, and although his private correspondence on the subject was considerable.

[1] Principal Shairp continues : " I remember another occasion on which he showed, though in a smaller matter, the same kind of courage. He was preaching in St. Mary's, before the University, and, having occasion to allude to the older Evangelicals, Newton, Cecil, Wilberforce, etc., he spoke of them as 'those men whom, after all, I will not hesitate to call the most truly religious section of our own Church.' That it cost him an effort to make this demonstration was shown by the sudden raising of his voice and flushing of his countenance." The sermon to which Principal Shairp alludes was afterwards published in *The Dangers and Safeguards of Modern Theology*. The words quoted above are on p. 45.

[2] Mr. Keble's Pamphlet, published by Dr. Pusey in 1866, was only *privately printed* in 1841.

there is little additional information to be gained from it. In a letter to Professor Sewell, who had published a pamphlet against the Tract,[1] he thus describes his own action :—

"I cannot tell you how strongly I feel the danger of young men's minds being altogether unsettled by the tone which characterises the Tract, and in which I have long been accustomed to hear individuals of the same sentiments with the writer express themselves in private. This danger has been forced upon my attention by several very painful instances that have fallen under my personal observation. If young men lose their confidence in that branch of the Church of Christ of which they are members, and have their attention forced to curious questions that seem only to minister strife, there seems no telling to what extent their whole religious character may be affected. It was under a strong sense of this danger that I felt bound to put myself in the invidious position of signing the letter which mainly called the attention of the University to this Tract. And I cannot tell you how glad I am to find that one who justly stands so high in public estimation as yourself has thought it necessary to enter a public protest against this unsettling spirit."

Among the following letters of thanks that he received, the following, from Dr. Arnold, has, in the light of subsequent events, a peculiar interest :—

The Rev. Dr. Arnold to the Rev. A. C. Tait.

"RUGBY, *March* 11, 1841.

"MY DEAR SIR,—I thank you much for sending me your address to the Author of the Tract.

"I am extremely glad that the Tract has been so noticed ; yet it is to me far more objectionable morally than theologically ; and especially the comment on the 21st Article, to which you have not alluded, is of such a character, that if subscription to the 21st Article, justified by such rules of interpretation, may be honestly practised, I do not see why an Unitarian may not subscribe the first Article or the second. The comparative im-

---

[1] "A Letter to the Rev. E. B. Pusey, D.D., on the Publication of No. 90. By William Sewell, Professor of Moral Philosophy in the University of Oxford."

portance of the truths subscribed to does not affect the question ; I am merely speaking of the utter perversion of language shown in the Tract, according to which a man may subscribe to an article when he holds the very opposite opinions,—believing what it denies, and denying what it affirms.—Believe me to be, dear Sir, very truly yours,   T. ARNOLD."

More than one of Tait's correspondents warns him against the temptation to put himself unduly forward. Speaking in after life of the accusation that he had done so, he used to say that it was impossible for him, holding the opinions he did, not to come forward. His position in the University required it of him. Though he was not yet thirty years old, he had for several years been the Senior Tutor in what was admittedly, by this time, the foremost College in Oxford. He was known to lay great stress upon the responsibilities of the University teachers (whether Tutors or Professors) in religious matters, and he had never scrupled to declare his distrust of the teaching which had now found expression in No. 90. "Were it all to happen again," he said in 1880, "I think I should, in the same position, do exactly as I did then."

But having, with his three colleagues, come forward where others who agreed with him held back, he was perfectly willing to leave to older, more experienced, or more authoritative men the actual conduct of the controversy. He never had any love, or any particular capacity, for the public discussion of the deeper doctrinal questions. His Protest, as he was always careful to remind his friends, had been raised rather against what he deemed a disingenuous and dangerous mode of treating formularies to which the writers had subscribed, than against the doctrinal system of the Tractarians. With that system he had always avowed his disagreement, but what he objected to still more strongly, both then and in after years, was the ingenious distortion, as he deemed it, of the meaning of plain English formularies to make them compatible with the very errors they were intended to oppose. His position in this controversy corresponded in some degree to that which he had taken three years before with regard to his own candidature for the Glasgow Professorship. It was a question of the plain and natural meaning of words, and the course which he now criticised in others was the course he had himself indignantly declined to take. But against the introduction of personalities or recriminations into the controversy he contended with all his might. There were some among his friends who would gladly have joined in the original protest, but whose co-operation, as his correspondence shows, he deliberately declined, lest the issues involved should be narrowed, and the controversy needlessly embittered. The following letter to Mr. Golightly, his Baldon colleague, was called forth by a communication sent by Mr. Golightly to the *Standard*, a few weeks after the Tract XC. explosion, accusing Mr. Ward and others of being disguised Romanists, and referring to a private visit Mr. Ward had paid to Dr. Wiseman at Oscott College :—

The Rev. A. C. Tait to the Rev. C. P. Golightly.

"BALLIOL. [*Nov.* 15, 1841].

"MY DEAR GOLIGHTLY,—I yesterday evening heard the subject of your letter canvassed, and it was the general opinion that the step was unjustifiable. . . . I disliked, as you knew, your last Tract, as transgressing the rule which it is desirable to keep up in Oxford, of not speaking, or at least not speaking any evil, of one's antagonists, and I should be extremely sorry if bitterness or harshness to individuals were to be introduced into the controversy. . . . On a matter of this kind no man's advice is worth much of whom you are not sure that he has a high personal regard for yourself. Having, however, put you in possession of what I think,—which I should not have been justified in withholding—I doubt not that

you will act rightly.   But pray remember that any appearance of
bitterness or a persecuting spirit is not only wrong in itself, but,
if shown on the right side, will be sure, in the present ticklish
state of opinion in Oxford, to drive many who are now doubtful
into the wrong.—Yours very sincerely,   A. C. TAIT."

In a similar spirit Tait invariably expressed his confidence in the personal character and high purpose of
Dr. Newman himself, and he used in later years to defend
him earnestly against those who took a lower view of his
conduct.   But he used at the same time to avow the
distrust he had always felt of his qualifications as a
religious teacher.   In the course of a discussion which
took place at Addington in 1877 he was asked to give
his then view of Dr. Newman's character.   The following
is a note of his reply :—

"I have always regarded Newman as having a strange duality
of mind.   On the one side is a wonderfully strong and subtle
reasoning faculty, on the other a blind faith, raised almost entirely by his emotions.   It seems to me that in all matters of
belief he first acts on his emotions, and then he brings the
subtlety of his reason to bear, till he has ingeniously persuaded
himself that he is logically right.   The result is a condition in
which he is practically unable to distinguish between truth and
falsehood."

But though he abstained from active controversy on
the subject, there was one element in the doctrines now
enunciated by the Tractarians which awoke in the mind
of Archibald Tait something more than a passive resistance.   In one of his letters about the Glasgow Professorship, quoted above,[1] he had referred, with some asperity,
to those "who regard the Kirk of Scotland as the
synagogue of Baal," words hardly too strong to describe
the views put forward, for example, by Mr. William Palmer
of Magdalen, in such a passage as the following :—

[1] P. 67.

"I once more . . . say Anathema to the principle of Protestantism . . . and to all its forms, sects, and denominations. . . . Likewise to all persons who, knowingly and wittingly, and understanding what they do, shall assert, either for themselves or for the Church of England, the principle of Protestantism, or maintain the Church of England to have one and the same common religion with any or all of the various forms and sects of Protestantism, or shall communicate themselves in the temples of the Protestant sects, or give communion to their members, or go about to establish any intercommunion between our Church and them otherwise than by bringing them in the first instance to renounce their errors, and promise a true obedience for the future to the entire faith and discipline of the Catholic and Apostolic Episcopate—to all such I say Anathema." [1]

Is it wonderful that, with the memories fresh in his mind of the Christian influences which had affected his boyhood, with his deep affection for the brothers and sisters to whom he owed so much, and his warm regard for a host of Scottish friends, Archibald Tait should have expressed his repugnance to a theological system which practically put almost every one north of the Tweed outside the pale of Christianity?

The following letters speak for themselves, and the subject is so important, both in its public and its personal aspect, that no apology is required for an endeavour to show how Tait's action presented itself at the time to some of his more intimate friends.

The Rev. Robert Scott[2] to the Rev. A. C. Tait.

"DULOE, *Monday night* [15*th March* 1841].

"MY DEAR TAIT,—Your packet only reached me this morning. The Protest itself, without comment, I saw on Saturday

---

[1] From a pamphlet entitled *Letter to the Rev. C. P. Golightly*, 1841, p. 13.

[2] Mr. Scott had been Tait's colleague and friend as Fellow of Balliol since 1836. He was afterwards Master of Balliol from 1854 to 1870, and Dean of Rochester from 1870 to 1888.

in a London paper: but was in entire ignorance of the Tract, except in so far as the Protest stated its tone. How painful the document itself must have been to me—whichever party proved to have been wrong—you may well suppose. And I do not fear that you will be offended at my saying that I knew not what to think. We understand one another well enough to own that your views are not mine, nor mine yours, on many subjects connected with the Tracts. In the Protest itself your name was coupled with that of one man whom I believe to hold extreme opinions, and of another who has the character of being crotchety: while I had no knowledge whatever of the views of the fourth. And I could not but ask myself why the particular *four* were left to protest by themselves, while so many of equal standing and University position remained silent, and the description of the Tract's contents themselves seemed much more like what was the impression of the mind of a hasty, nay, hostile reader, than what could be the 'literal and grammatical sense' of the writer. Such were the considerations which I could not help occurring to me, to balance my knowledge of your caution, and my persuasion that you would never have taken a step which may be, and probably will be, so momentous in its consequences, upon any slight or uncertain grounds—on any grounds which you were not confident would approve themselves to persons of more than one shade of opinion. I was left therefore in a state, I will say, of extreme and perplexing distress, until your packet arrived this morning. And certainly, if that has relieved my perplexity, it has not diminished my sorrow.

"To-day I have been reading the Tract which you were good enough to send me—hastily, indeed (for I have had other things to do also): but I do not think that the matter is so difficult as to require long study. There are some things which seem sensible enough—for instance, the remarks on the sense in which we accept the Book of Homilies. There are others which I do not know what to say of, because, though the remarks seem strange, yet I do not and cannot make out what they are aimed at, being apparently intended to meet difficulties which some individual has suggested, but which are not specified, and cannot be (by me) clearly made out. But there can be very little mistake about many of them. And especially looking at those on which you ground your Protest, I must say that I have no objection to make to any part of *it*: and that consequently the situations you hold make the course you have adopted a proper one, nay, a most necessary one.

"I think that words cannot bind a man who deals with the Church's Articles as the writer of the Tract does.

"Detailed criticism is needless, if there were time either for me to write, or you to read it. My wonder that your four names alone were appended to this Protest still continues, my other doubts being solved. I hope it was not from any hurry on your parts leaving them unconsulted; for that would have been to cast a slur on all the tutorial body in the University, with the exception of the four Colleges. I need not conceal my fears of what will be the result, grounded on my conviction of the existing want of moderation, and the prejudice of both sides, both in Oxford and elsewhere. I should be driven nearly to despair of the consequences were my confidence less strong in my own Church's share of God's promise. Doubtless it will be overruled; and that must be enough for those who have to wait, not seeing the end. To those who are of necessity engaged in it, the painful lessons of ill-feeling and human jealousies which the Hampden matter taught will be most useful now. As for yourself, my dear Tait, let me, as your contemporary, beg of you to keep steadily before you through the whole matter the recollection of your own youth, and endeavour to contend throughout with singleness of purpose *for* one side, and not *against* another. God guide you all as seems Him right, and bless Alma Mater and her sons. Pray let me hear from you soon. . . .—Ever, my dear Tait, yours most sincerely,   ROBERT SCOTT."

A yet closer friend, Arthur Stanley, had been travelling in Greece and Italy with another ex-pupil of Tait's, Hugh Pearson. They were now on their way home.

Rev. Arthur P. Stanley to Rev. A. C. Tait.

"ROME, *March* 30, 1841.

"O MY DEAR BELVEDERE,[1]—What have you been doing? Rome is only in a less state of excitement than Oxford. The Pope has just issued a Bull defending the Decrees of Trent, on the ground that they are not contradictory to the Thirty-nine

---

[1] One of the names by which Tait was known among his Oxford friends, his curly hair being said to resemble that of the statue in the Vatican.

Articles; and the Cardinals have just sate in conclave on him, and determined that he is against the usages of the Vatican. But to speak seriously: What has happened? First comes a letter from London to Pearson, intimating that a Tract on such a subject has appeared, and that you are in a state of frenzy. Next an intelligence from papers, that a Protest of five Tutors, Belvedere being one, has appeared in the *Times*. Next, the great manifesto from the Heads themselves, accompanied by a private letter from Twiss to me announcing that a 'convulsive movement' will 'not improbably take place, only equal to a moral Niagara ceasing to flow'—Pearson and I are in a state of ferment beyond bounds. Seriously, my dear Greis,[1] do not draw these Articles too tight, or they will strangle more parties than one. I assure you, when I read the monition of the Heads I felt the halter at my own throat. Of course I speak on the hypothesis that J. H. N. has maintained the patience, not the ambition, of the Articles. If he maintains the latter, then certainly it does become time to throw away the scabbard; but if the former—ah! my dear Greis, consider the great train of consequences which a resistance to such a theory involves. One consolation dawns upon me, and that is—that this convulsion will directly or indirectly lead to the subversion of the Heads and establishment of the Professors on their ruins—in what way I have not now time to explain, but I see it clearly in the distance. But my chief object in writing to you was not to give bad advice on imperfect data, but to implore a letter by return of post to Poste Restante, Genoa, where I trust to be by the end of April, to point out what is going on, and whether I am to post straight from Dover to Oxford, to give my first vote in Convocation, or whether I had better absent myself from the scene altogether. A letter from Ward, or from some defendant of No. 90, would also be in the highest degree acceptable. Pray remember me to him, and to all my suffering friends, whether in the defeated or victorious party. Take this in the light of a rush into your room before breakfast. Will you remember me most kindly to Johnson, and say that I have often reproached myself for not writing to him, and that I am often reminded of him in

---

[1] Another familiar name by which Tait was known. One day when he and Arthur Stanley were together at Bonn in 1839, the servant of a Professor on whom they called was said to have reported to her master that "ein Greis und ein Kind" had been to see him. The names adhered to them among their friends for years.

this great city, which pleases me even beyond what I had expected —beyond even Athens itself? We are off for Tivoli to-morrow, and leave Rome on Friday after Easter. I have seen the Pope, and might say much on that head, but I forbear. I am sorry to say that your prototype is very unlike you—as well as unlike all the casts of him—very ethereal, but not giving me so much pleasure as I expected.—Ever yours, in a fever,

"A. P. STANLEY.

"Remember Hampden—remember the Supra- and Sublapsarians; remember me. But are the Heads *representatives of the University*, or are they not? This is, I think, very important, and the question may throw light on a previous statement of mine.

"Even have you (which indeed I trust you have) sent a letter here, do not fail to send another to Genoa, reporting the progress of this fearful drama. Of course you understand that I write, being, as far as my knowledge goes, opposed to this demonstration of yours."

Rev. A. C. Tait to Rev. A. P. Stanley.

"BALLIOL COLL., 16 *April* 1841.

"MY DEAR CHILD,—The hurried scenes through which I have been passing, though they have prevented me from writing, have made me think daily and hourly of you. When I set my hand to that document of which you speak, your image was before me. I rejoiced that you were not in Oxford, lest you should have died of excitement; but I could not help thinking that if your nerves had allowed you to think, you would have approved of my act. If you saw our letter you must have noted this sentence: 'We readily admit the necessity of allowing that liberty in interpreting the formularies of our Church which has been advocated by many of its most learned Bishops and other eminent divines; but this Tract puts forth new and startling views as to the extent to which that liberty may be carried. For if we are right in our apprehension of the author's meaning, we are at a loss to see what security would remain, were his principles generally recognised, that the most plainly erroneous doctrines and practices of the Church of Rome might not be inculcated in the lecture-rooms of the University, and from the pulpits of our churches.' You will at once recognise the pen from which the first clause in this sentence flowed. When you read No. 90 I think you will allow that we were right. Really, it was the 'ambition,' not the 'patience,' of the Articles which, in some passages at least, seemed to be advocated, for, observe, the author actually had the effrontery to assert that his interpretation (allowing all the doctrines of Trent) was the 'literal and grammatical sense' of the Articles, and did not affix any new sense to them. Besides, I confess there was something disgusting in his declaring that he never would be a party to any attempts to relax subscription to these Articles, at the very moment that he was treating them with the most marked contempt. Surely you cannot think it was right to profess that he would never try to do that openly which he was labouring hard to do by the most strange distortion of language and every kind of half-expressed insinuation? *Er sieht, mein kind, sehr viel zu Jesuitisch aus, und wie er sieht so schreibt er.* At the same time, this I must say in justice, that I believe this appearance of Jesuitry comes, not from dishonesty, but from a natural defect, a strange bent of the genius that loves tortuous paths, perhaps partly because it requires an exercise of ingenuity to get along in them. I have been much struck with the contrast in reading Ward's pamphlet, written with the most manly, straightforward tone. At present, as you will see, the controversy is principally confined to the Bishop of Melipotamus (do you recognise Dr. Wiseman under so grand a name?) and the Newmanites. Others have only quietly to sit by till this battle is over, waiting to take up the victor, or hoping that the antagonists may swallow each other. On the whole, things are wonderfully calm. In College here the utmost good-will has prevailed. Ward is certainly, in good-humour and candour, the prince of controversialists. The result of the whole matter up to the present moment may be shortly summed up. First—as the most interesting to you—the Bishop of London's theory of a literal adherence to every iota of the formularies is blown to the winds of heaven. Secondly, the consciences of Ward and one or two others are much satisfied by having had an opportunity of utterly throwing away the false colours of Church-of-Englandism, which Pusey mounted last year in his letter to the Bishop of Oxford. Thirdly, —— has safely disengaged himself from the sinking vessel. Fourthly, Newmanism has been proclaimed from one end of the kingdom to the other by the mouth of its own prophet to be twin-sister of Popery.

"But I must interrupt my summary to hasten to a much more home subject, which for the last ten days has driven all thoughts of Newmania from my head. Alas! alas! alas! I fear I must leave Oxford. I cannot contemplate the prospect without a shudder; but it really seems as if it must come to that. Timsbury[1] seems to call me with a loud voice. The matter stands thus: Oakeley refuses it. Poor Payne, now apparently almost in a dying state, of course does the same. I go down there with my mind almost fully resolved to refuse it also; am much struck by what I see and hear of the importance of the charge, and remember that this is the second time that the place has seemed to force itself upon me. I consider that —— cannot be equal to such a charge; but Balliol is too important a post to be relinquished, and I feel resolved to refuse Timsbury, when most unexpectedly it turns out that I need not leave Balliol for three years, though I should begin to reside at Timsbury this long vacation, as my position at Balliol is deemed by the Bishop sufficient reason for granting me for that time leave of absence from Timsbury during term time, till I can settle matters in College. . . . All this seems almost arranged for me by events over which I have no control: whenever it might be my fate to leave Balliol, it seems very doubtful whether I should have it in my power to leave it in better hands than by this present leisurely retreat. Then Oxford has no situation to which I can look forward, except one which I cannot anticipate will be vacant for the next twenty years. There is no parish in our gift which seems so well suited for me, almost none so important, and next to my present occupation, which cannot last for above a certain number of years, parish work is my line. Lake, Ward, and all whom I consult here seem to agree; the real point being the importance of the charge and the impropriety of passing it down to one quite inexperienced. The emolument has no particular attraction—£450 a year. I have no wish to go, but I think, on the whole, I ought; and therefore, having tried to view the matter entirely as one of ministerial duty, I have almost resolved to write to-morrow to Chancellor Law, the Bishop's son, who manages everything for him, that if he can get mé the leave of absence of which he spoke when I was there, and the Archbishop's sanction, which is necessary, I shall be prepared to take charge of the living in the long vacation, appointing a curate, and residing during the vacations henceforward, and gradually disentangling myself from Balliol, so as to be able to begin uninterrupted residence in three years from this time.

[1] A small parish near Bath, in the patronage of Balliol College.

Three years is a long time to look forward to, and, by God's help, much may be done in Balliol and Oxford before then. Perhaps the Bishop and Archbishop may not approve the Chancellor's plan, and then the matter is at an end, for I cannot in conscience leave Balliol now. But if I am to go in three years, if I live so long, let us work heart and hand during that time. I do not think late divisions need at all prevent co-operation among those who love what is good. Indeed, Newman pledges himself in a letter to the Bishop to co-operate with religious men of all opinions. Therefore let us make the most of the time while it lasts. But we shall do nothing unless we do it in a truly religious spirit, and make the good of our University the subject of our earnest prayers. Do, my dear Stanley, let us strive, while God gives us the opportunity, to do everything in a more seriously religious spirit. I fear our plans cannot do any good unless they are more the subject of our earnest prayers. There is no doubt we love what is good, but I fear we do not seek it in a sufficiently serious, religious spirit.

"I long very much to see you back here. Best regards to Pearson.—Your affect. friend,   A. C. TAIT."

Rev. A. P. Stanley to Rev. A. C. Tait.

"GENOA, *May* 2, 1841.

"MY DEAR GREIS,—Although I have but little time to write, and shall be in England so soon after my letter, I cannot help thanking you for your account of Oxford and yourself which I found here yesterday. I hope there was nothing in my foolish letter from Rome at all tending to annoy you, as, of course, not knowing facts, neither having read No. 90, nor the 'Tutors' Protest, I had no business to say anything. From what you say I cannot be surprised at any one using any measures against the Tract who thinks it unadvisable *per se* that Roman Catholics should be members of the Church of England—still less at any one being angry at the tone which you describe as pervading No. 90—though perhaps, as I myself see no reason against Roman Catholics being Anglicans, except the impracticability of it, I should not have objected to any mode of rendering it practicable which was not on other grounds objectionable. I shall be very anxious to see Ward's pamphlet, of which your letter contains the first intimation. What, however, gave me most pleasure was your announcement of the good-will preserved through all this storm. I had hoped it would be so, and I believe it would have happened nowhere in this intolerant world except at Oxford.

"And now to pass to the second part of your letter : I don't know whether you will be glad or sorry to know what a blank fell over my face and heart on catching the words, 'I fear I must leave Oxford.' My spirits were already beginning to sink at my return to that troubled ocean, and this seemed to sink them still deeper. But after what you say I cannot complain—and although Bonn and Oxford and the professorial system may, and perhaps will, cease to exist —I believe you are right ; and as far as my commendation goes, I give it you most cordially, though most sorrowfully. Three years, as you say, is still a long time, and if [our work] is to be done at all, it is perhaps as likely to be done in that time as in any other. I do most earnestly hope we may all be enabled to look upon it in the light you urge. I trust I have endeavoured to do so, but nothing has convinced me more of the truth of what you say than the difficulty I now find in turning my thoughts again to it, as if it had been a thing taken up, not from any real wish to do good, but from a fit of foolish excitement. I hope I shall not return the worse for my travels. I have certainly derived from them far more instruction and delight than I could have conceived possible. The flood of light which my month at Rome let in upon my benighted mind was almost overwhelming. But some of the advantages which I most hoped to have attained I certainly still desiderate, and look forward to the troubles of England with much the same feelings as those with which I left them. So pray, my dear Greis, be ready to console and advise me as before—for, as before, I still want all of both that all my friends can give me. Once more, farewell, my dear Tait ; may God bless you, whether you stay to help us at Oxford, or whether you go elsewhere.—With all remembrances to Lake and Ward, and all hopes of seeing you all soon in good health of body and mind, believe me, ever yours,   A. P. STANLEY."

Though Oxford continued to be the centre of the conflict, its arena was very soon enlarged, and an attention hitherto unwonted was paid to the Charges of the Bishops, almost every one of whom spoke his mind upon the subject. A special interest attached to the Charge of

Bishop Phillpotts of Exeter, whose vigorous and uncompromising High Churchmanship had led many to identify him with the Tractarian school. He spoke before long, and as usual with no uncertain sound—

"The tone of the Tract," he said, "as respects our own Church is offensive and indecent: as regards the Reformation and our Reformers absurd, as well as incongruous and unjust. Its principles of interpreting our Articles I cannot but deem most unsound: the reasoning with which it supports its principles sophistical: the averments on which it founds its reasoning, at variance with recorded facts. . . . It is idle to argue against statements which were not designed for argument, but for scoffing. . . . It is far the most daring attempt ever yet made by a minister of the Church of England to neutralise the distinctive doctrines of our Church and to make us symbolise with Rome." [1]

Considering what has so often been said in later years about the mere ignorance, or haste, or partisan bias of the ' Four Tutors ' and their friends,[2] it is not out of place to call attention to such words as these, and to the source from which they came. Most of the Bishops spoke in similar, if less trenchant, terms. Bishop Blomfield, in some respects the foremost Bishop on the Bench, had some difficulty, as his Biography shows, in deciding clearly as to his best line of conduct; and a curious triangular correspondence took place between Tait, Oakeley, and the Bishop, with reference to a supposed remark of the Bishop's to Oakeley in favour of the Tractarians, which Tait had repeated upon Oakeley's authority. The only bearing of the letters upon the present biography is their evidence to the firm friendship subsisting between Tait and Oakeley during the controversies wherein, upon different sides, both were involved.

These controversies do not seem to have interfered

<hr>

[1] Charge, pp. 31, 32.
[2] *e.g.* by Dr. Pusey in his pamphlet on Tract xc., published in 1865.

with Tait's ordinary Oxford work. In his letter to Arthur Stanley, quoted above, he had announced, as almost certain, his acceptance of the living of Timsbury, and he even went so far as to give directions for the furnishing of the house. He decided, however, upon further consideration, that the arrangement proposed, whereby he was, while Vicar of Timsbury, to continue for a time his work in Balliol, would be good neither for the parish nor the College, and the living was therefore declined. Among the subjects to which he turned his attention in the year 1841 was the possibility of stimulating in the University a warmer zeal with regard to the Foreign Missions of the Church. Together with three other Tutors[1] (not his former colleagues) he founded a small society, the members of which were in turn to read papers on missionary subjects at meetings held fortnightly during term. He also continued to give great attention to the whole subject of Education both in England and abroad, and contributed articles to more than one periodical dealing with the question. He seems to have been half inclined to offer himself as a candidate for the Principalship of St. Mark's Training College, which had just been founded, and though, after an interview with its promoters, he abandoned this intention, he was evidently beginning to look for work elsewhere than in Oxford. His friends in Scotland had naturally made more than one endeavour to bring him back across the border, and in 1839 he was in actual negotiation with respect to the junior incumbency of St. Paul's Church, Edinburgh, a joint charge, the senior incumbent being the Rev. C. H. Terrot, who, two years afterwards, became Bishop of Edinburgh. In connection with this it may be mentioned that (to the surprise of some

---

[1] The names appended to the original draft rules are as follows:—
A. C. Tait, E. C. Woollcombe, F. A. Litton, E. M. Goulburn.

of his friends, who, even after the episode of the Glasgow professorship, had apparently failed to realise the strength of his Churchmanship), Tait was in 1842 a prominent subscriber to the foundation of Trinity College, Glenalmond, as a seminary for the Scottish Episcopal Church. Some important correspondence passed on this occasion between Bishop Terrot of Edinburgh and himself, in which Tait urged upon the Bishop the importance of securing the co-operation of others besides the High Churchmen, on whose support the promoters of the scheme had too exclusively relied.

The Rev. A. C. Tait to the Right Rev. Bishop Terrot.

.   .   .   .

"You will not misunderstand me when I say that I feel confident the great obstacle to the success of your appeal to England, under existing circumstances, is the fear lest in any way your scheme should fall into the hands of what is now very generally regarded amongst moderate men as a dangerous and revolutionary party, who are striving to break down the barriers which separate us from Rome in her fallen state. The only way to allay this apprehension must be by endeavouring to get influential names of persons of all shades of opinion in our Church, . . . and so to give the plan a more truly Catholic air. I wish it were in my power to make a large subscription, but I must be content to give what I can afford, and I trust your plan may be blest for the three great objects which it seems to me so likely to promote— the sound theological instruction of your clergy—the strict and systematic religious education of the boys who must necessarily be sent from home to attend school—and though last, still very important, the revival of a general taste for classical literature, by prolonging that study of the Greek and Latin authors which in Scotland is rendered almost useless by being generally brought at the age of 14 or 15 to a premature close. I trust that if you can suggest any way in which I may be of use in making the claims of your place more generally known, you will not scruple to apply to me.—With many apologies for having so freely spoken my mind to you, I remain yours most faithfully,   A. C. TAIT."

The following letter from Dean Lake of Durham may be appropriately inserted here.   Many of the facts to which he refers have been already recorded in these pages, but to omit these references would be to spoil the completeness of a letter which has an independent and peculiar value :—

"DEANERY, DURHAM, 23*d March* 1888.

"MY DEAR DEAN OF WINDSOR,—When you asked me to contribute my recollections of our dear friend, the late Archbishop of Canterbury, to your Memoir of his life, I could not hesitate to make some attempt to do so, for I have never ceased to feel his loss, nor have I ever had a friend whom I have known so long and so intimately, and of whom my remembrances are still so fresh.

"The first time I ever saw Archbishop Tait was when he was reading the second Lesson in chapel, as a young Probationary Fellow of Balliol, in October 1835.   I had heard of his ability, particularly as a vigorous, and sometimes a very fiery, speaker, at the Union, and as I knew he was to be my tutor, I was naturally anxious to see him.   I had expected one of the scholars to read the lesson, whose manner, I was told, was heavy and pompous, and instead of this, a young and very good-looking man walked from the Fellows' seats to the Lectern, and read rapidly, and with great animation, the second Evening Lesson.   'Who was that?' I asked Stanley, with some surprise, when chapel was over.   'Oh! that was our new Tutor, Tait.' He gave me at once that impression of strength and spirit ' which I always associated with him through life.   I soon became almost, or quite, his earliest College pupil; and felt at once his genuine kindness and interest in his pupils.   In those days at Oxford—I know not how it is now—intimacies between tutors and pupils ripened rapidly.   I was his companion in a short tour in Belgium and Germany in 1837, and again in 1839, and during my last undergraduate year in 1838 was constantly with him; and this was of course still more the case during the years we were Fellows together from 1839 to 1842.   In 1842 Dr. Arnold's death caused a vacancy in the head-mastership at Rugby, and some of Arnold's old pupils, particularly Stanley and myself, were very anxious for Tait's election to the post, believing him to be the one person who was most likely to continue the work in the spirit and with something of the power of his predecessor. Owing to accidental circumstances it was rather a difficult election, and one which left behind it some important remembrances, and made Tait's Rugby career, in some respects, the most trying period of his life.   It was also, in various ways, one of the most touching and interesting; and I cannot help hoping that you may be able to give a pretty full record of it, as it greatly developed his powers of dealing with and governing men, especially in his tact, courtesy, and respect for the feelings of those with whom he was working.

"I have ventured to give you this short outline of the earlier days of what I may call the dearest friendship of my life, as justifying me in my right to express some opinion on the character of one whom I loved so much, and whose memory is so dear. Certainly, no one out of the circle of his very nearest relations could have had greater opportunities for knowing him ; and the interest of looking back on those days is even increased by remembering that our friendship was nowise diminished by strong differences of opinion, particularly on religious subjects. It was a feature in Tait's character, and one for which he often expressed thankfulness himself, that differences of opinion, though they necessarily diminished sympathy, did not diminish affection ; few men have had, and retained through life, such warm friendships with men from whom he differed widely, and whose differences he was glad to hear frankly expressed, and from which he even believed himself to learn much.   It was the great secret of the real largeness and generosity of his character.

"My earliest acquaintance then with Tait was as my College tutor, and the first impression he gave us was of the excellence of his lectures, particularly (in fact almost exclusively) of his Aristotle and Butler Lectures.   Here he was entirely at home, very much more so than in either scholarship or history ; and 1 remember the pleasure with which Stanley, who was in the year before me, and who came in for Tait's first lecture on the Ethics, ran into my rooms to tell me what a capital one it was.   He was, however, in this, as in a good many other points, a real Scotchman ; and all Scotch scholars at Oxford were in those days—matters, I believe, have somewhat altered since—much more inclined to what they called

' *Metapheesics*' than to scholarship. Tait's great power of ready
and vigorous speech, which was afterwards one main secret of
his strength as Bishop of London, and in the House of Lords,
helped him in giving lectures where animation and clearness
were particularly required. He was indeed then, as I think he
always continued to be through life, far better in extempore
addresses than as a writer; and his power of speaking was lighted
up by a gift of humour which he could use very effectively when
it was needed: one or two *sets down* to some of our liveliest
scholars are even now hardly forgotten. He was, in fact, on
occasions, though not very often, impulsive enough; and though
his manner was always courteous and gentlemanlike, we used to
say that he was a thorough specimen of the *perfervidum Scotorum
ingenium*. Meanwhile his intellectual character as a teacher
often came out in lively hits at anything which he thought over-
poetical or mystical; he was anything but fond of Plato, very
impatient of his and Aristotle's discussions on 'Ideas,' and
was currently reported to have called one favourite writer—
I think his own countryman Brown—'a long-winded old ass,'
while we retorted by humorous criticisms on a rather weary
disquisition between the ' Fancy and the Imagination,' which he
had crammed up for our benefit out of Wordsworth and Coleridge. As to his Divinity Lectures, he was, as well as I remember,
a good deal exercised by the Calvinism of the 17th Article;
and indeed, when he was on the point of standing for a Glasgow
Professorship of Greek in 1840, where the acceptance of a Pre-
destinarian Article was then generally swallowed as a mere
matter of form, he at once, on hearing of this, declined to become a candidate.

"Such, regarded merely as a Lecturer, the first aspect in
which undergraduates would look at him, was the view which we
should mostly have taken of Tait, as vigorous, acute, fluent and
felicitous in language, and on the whole, so far as I had the
means of judging, the ablest lecturer in his day at Oxford. And
some of us soon saw far more than this; and as a certain stiffness
which hung about him during most of his earlier life gradually
thawed, we quickly began to feel the straightforwardness and
manly simplicity of his character, combined with a thorough
courtesy of mind and manner, and with a genuine warmth of
heart, a little veiled by his reserve. In all these respects it is
difficult for me to express my own sense of all that I owed him

myself in my undergraduate days, and I can hardly help feeling some surprise that while he was certainly influencing our characters, he had so little direct influence on our opinions. It must not be forgotten, however, that he was throughout life rather a man of action than of the deepest thought ; and, not to dwell here upon one or two intellectual defects in this respect, his life at Oxford was passed at a very remarkable time, which made his position there a peculiar and a very isolated one. And certainly this fact very much coloured his whole Oxford life ; for he was almost the only tutor at once of a powerful intellect, and of a high moral tone, who was hardly in the least influenced by the spirit which moved almost every young man of thought in Oxford from about 1835 to 1845, and which, at the same time, he felt that he had no power of resisting. The tale of that movement has been told us lately in very different styles by three able writers, Mr. Mozley, Mr. Mark Pattison, and Professor Shairp, as well as in the lively and interesting description of Mr. Newman's preaching by Sir F. Doyle ; but they all come back to this, that the one great power which then ruled and inspired Oxford was John Henry Newman, the influence of whose singular combination of genius and devotion has had no parallel there, either before or since ; the only persons who were left outside the charmed circle being a somewhat apathetic race, the twenty or twenty-two heads of houses, and a few tutors, of whom Tait was the only one of real power. If this statement seems to you exaggerated, I must remind you that it is scarcely so strong as the words of Professor Shairp, himself a Scotchman and a friend of Tait's, and one who, if his own genius and devotion led him keenly to appreciate Newman, was no adherent of the movement, but simply spoke of what he had seen as a matter of history. I daresay you may have mentioned this already, but it may be worth while even to repeat Shairp's own words—' The influence which Newman had gained,' he says—he was there in 1842—' apparently without setting himself to seek it, was altogether unlike anything else in our time. A mysterious veneration had by degrees gathered round him, till now it was almost as if some Ambrose or Augustine of elder days had reappeared :' and he adds, ' There was not, in Oxford at least, a reading man who was not more or less indirectly influenced by it. Only the very idle or the very frivolous were proof against it. . . . It raised the tone of average morality in Oxford to a level which perhaps it had never before reached. You may call it overwrought, and too highly strung. Perhaps it was. It was better, however, for young men to be so, than to be doubters or cynics.'

"Tait's position, both at Oxford and at Balliol, standing as he did quite outside of this great movement, was a curious, and, in some respects, a trying one. Brought up in a good Presbyterian family, he had, as may be supposed, very little sympathy with the 'High Church Party' in the English Church, and never the slightest inclination to 'Newmanism'; and indeed, -owing to a certain want of poetry in his character, he was long, if not always, unable to do full justice to the character of the great leader himself. Meanwhile he had not, like Arnold or Maurice, anything like a counter system of religious or intellectual thought, and soon felt himself incapable of resisting an influence to which he saw so many of those to whom he was most attached succumbing. Of these his old tutor, and long his dearest friend, Oakeley, was one of the first. Oakeley, the son of a former Governor of Madras, and who after passing, as was not unusual, through the phase of Evangelicalism, joined the Roman Church about the same time as Newman, had been Tait's earliest friend at Oxford, and his affection for him ended only with his life. It is touching to remember that in the last thing which the Archbishop ever wrote (a short notice of Mr. Mozley's 'Reminiscences'), he spoke of Oakeley and Ward as two of the best men he had ever known, and I well remember his saying to me on a day which they had both been spending with him at Fulham, about the year 1860, 'It would indeed be disgraceful in me, if I could ever forget all that Oakeley did for me, when I first came up as a raw young Scotchman, and with scarcely a friend, to Oxford; he was,' I think he added, 'quite a father to me.' Their friendship continued during the first years of Tait's tutorship, but Oakeley was gradually drawn into the stream of 'Newmanism'; and I have no doubt that their entire separation, though unaccompanied by any bitterness, was a heavy trial to Tait. Nor was it mended by the fact that others to whom he was much attached, his own pupils particularly, were either affected by the same influence, or of a different way of thinking from himself. He had, indeed, in Balliol a formidable counter influence in the person of his brother tutor Ward, who, having been always, as Lord Tennyson's epitaph describes him, 'the most unworldly of mankind,' had already also become 'the most generous of

Ultramontanes,' and whose powerful and thorough-going logic, not always under the control of facts, often carried most of us, who were then young 'Fellows,' off our legs; he laid himself out indeed for proselytism to an amusing extent, and Stanley and Clough were successively, rather to the annoyance of their friends, almost absorbed by him. Common rooms are said, in these later days, to have very much changed their character, but about that time one or two of the principal, such as Merton with (Cardinal) Manning, Hope-Scott, and Bruce (Lord Elgin), and Balliol with Tait and Ward, were delightful arenas of intellectual life. Many and vehement certainly were the disputes between Tait and Ward in the Balliol Common Room, where they were admirably matched, each respecting the other's acuteness and power of argument, and I never remember the slightest loss of temper on either side. I must say, on referring to a journal which I kept at that time, that Ward seems to me never to have shrunk from any extravagance, or what he called 'going the whole hog,' when his argument required it.

"As I have alluded once or twice to Tait's pupils, I may perhaps complete this picture of his tutorial life by saying that he had fallen in with a rather remarkable and active-minded set of 'scholars,' not very easy to manage intellectually. Sir John Wickens, Stanley, Goulburn, Jowett, Clough, Sir Stafford Northcote, Lord Coleridge, Temple Bishop of London, and Matthew Arnold, all followed each other as scholars in the seven years of his tutorship; and the list of names will show you that we were a set of young fellows who were very much disposed to take our own line—no doubt too much so—almost from the first days of our Oxford life. About half were Etonians, and most of the others had come fresh from Arnold, full of raw ideas, which we had got from our 'Pops,' and other debating societies, and having looked forward to Oxford as a new world of life and thought. It certainly became so to many of us, and I, for one, cannot look back to any years so full of life and enjoyment as my three undergraduate years at Balliol, when 'old Ward,' as we familiarly called him, was inducting us into John Stuart Mill, John Austin, etc., and we were ourselves vainly endeavouring to imbue *him* with Coleridge and Wordsworth—both he and Tait being at that time equally intolerant of poetry—while the successive works of Newman, and his weekly sermons, exercised a sort of sobering influence in the background. Meanwhile Tait's lectures kept us to our regular work, for they were full of character, and the very style of lecturing in those days served as a sort of moral link between him and his pupils. This old style is now, I believe, a thing of the past ; and I have no doubt that the new one, where the number of hearers amounts to one or two hundred, is of a much more learned and professorial character. But I may be allowed to doubt whether, given a really able man, the lectures in a tutor's own room to a class of some eighteen or twenty pupils, who were sure to be well *shown up* if they had not prepared their work, were not a thoroughly effective style of teaching; and I am disposed to agree with the dictum of a Conservative friend and brother Dean, whose name would carry a great deal of weight, and who is fond of saying : 'They may talk as they like about their new styles of teaching, but my notion of a good education is what we used to get from dear old Tait and Scott.'

"I don't know, my dear Dean, whether these remembrances, on which I feel I have dwelt too long with an old man's fondness, will have given you a true idea of the position which Tait had at Oxford. But putting aside, as far as I can, the feelings of a deep personal attachment, I should say that he was then a man of marked character rather than of the genius which distinctly influences others—thoroughly Scotch in its independence, its caution, and its reserve of expression, but also with a reserve of power which belonged to the man himself—a character which was sure to grow, and, in the best sense of the word, be successful. I ought to add that he left Oxford before he was thirty, and that on the only public occasion which called him forth (rightly or wrongly), the protest against No. xc., he had shown great decision. It was his quiet power, however, which I myself always felt most strongly—combined, of course, with other great moral qualities—for he always seemed to me to rise to the occasion, whatever it might be ; and I felt confident, both when he went to Rugby, and when he was made Bishop of London, that, though he would make some mistakes, his force and dignity of character, his quiet self-confidence, and his strong good sense— the great quality in which he most believed—would ensure his success. May I be excused for mentioning a conversation which I well remember with Mr. Gladstone, on Tait's appointment to London in 1856, when he was much annoyed at Tait's being preferred to Bishop Wilberforce—and of which he reminded me nearly thirty years afterwards, at the time of the Archbishop's death, by saying: 'Ah! I remember your maintaining to me at that time that his σεμνότης and his judgment would make him a great Bishop.'

"Such are some of my recollections of his earlier years.   Perhaps you will let me add in separate notices such memoranda as occur to me with reference to his life at Rugby, and as Bishop and Archbishop.—I am, my dear Dean, yours very truly,

"W. C. LAKE."

CHAPTER V.

1842–1850.

THE summer of 1842 opened a totally new and unexpected field of interest and of work. In the first week of June, Tait was spending a few days at Courteen Hall, in Northamptonshire, with Sir Charles and Lady Wake, who had just lost a beloved daughter.

"The visit over," writes Lady Wake, "Archie returned to Oxford. I had gone with him to Blisworth Station to see him off, when our attention was attracted by the sight of a multitude of boys filling the carriages of the train, all silent and sad. 'Who were they?' 'The young gentlemen from Rugby!' was the reply. Evidently it was no holiday. 'What brought them there?' 'Arnold is dead,' passed from mouth to mouth. Their hushed voices and subdued looks told evidently how suddenly the blow had fallen, and how it had affected each one of them."

Dr. Arnold died on Sunday, June 12th, 1842, and, ten days later, Archibald Tait, mainly at the instigation of Lake and Stanley, declared himself a candidate for the vacant post. His diary has the following on June 23, 1842: "O Lord, I have this day taken a step which may lead to much good or much evil. Do Thou suffer me to succeed, only if it be to the good of my own soul, and to Thy glory."

The unique position held by Dr. Arnold among schoolmasters, and indeed among Englishmen, gave an altogether exceptional interest to the question—Who was to be his successor? Among Rugbeians, and not among them alone, the excitement as to the appointment was immense ; and when, on July 28th, 1842, it was announced that Archibald Tait had been elected, his friends scarcely knew whether to congratulate him or not upon the perilous inheritance. Among the unsuccessful candidates were several whose qualifications in some particular respect were superior to his own. Mr. C. J. Vaughan, besides his high Cambridge reputation as a scholar, had been one of Dr. Arnold's foremost pupils ; while Mr. Bonamy Price had not only been his pupil at Laleham, but had successfully served under him as an assistant master ; nor could Tait lay claim to the technical and accurate scholarship of such men as Mr. Merivale, Mr. Kynaston, and Mr. Blakesley. Mr. Lake, who had been one of the first to urge him to become a candidate, and whose intimacy with Dr. Arnold gave special weight to his opinion, was fully aware of Tait's weak points. A few days before the election he writes :—

"O my dear Tait, I do not envy you if you do get it. I quite quake for the awful responsibility, putting on that giant's armour. However, I really believe you are far the best. My main fears are for your sermons being dull, and your Latin prose, and composition generally, weak, in which latter points you will have, I think, hard work. But I earnestly say, as far as we can see, 'God grant he may get it !'"

According to the account given by Lady Wake, who had special opportunities of knowledge, it was found, when the trustees met for the election after study of the testimonials, that some of them had Tait's name first upon their lists, while all the rest, without exception, had placed it second. The issue was finally narrowed, it is said, to the consideration of the relative merits of two of the youngest among the eighteen candidates, Archibald

Tait and Charles John Vaughan, and it was not till after long and anxious debate that the decision was arrived at, and Tait was elected in Arnold's room.

To realise the nature of the task to which he was thus suddenly called, it is only necessary to read the remarkable chapter in Stanley's *Life of Dr. Arnold*, which describes the great master's 'School Life at Rugby.' No other schoolmaster has ever occupied so large a place as Arnold in the attention of England, and the most self-confident of men might well have shrunk from exposing himself to the fierce light which continued to beat upon the scene of that conspicuous life, and to the necessity of being judged by the standard which Arnold had created.

On the day before the election Tait writes as follows in enclosing a testimonial to a friend :—

"It is quite a delightful interlude for me to have to put forth any one's merits but my own. As you may suppose, I feel somewhat nervous about the result of to-morrow's election. But the near approach of the day has brought so vividly before me the deeply responsible nature of the office for which I am a candidate that I shall be able to make up my mind to failure. The responsibility of such a situation seems to me every day more awful; but all situations are responsible just in proportion to their usefulness, and if it were in my power to keep up that system which Dr. Arnold has begun, I should certainly think my life well spent."

The news of his election did not reach him until July 29th, when his diary contains the following :—

"*Oxford, 29th July* 1842.—A most eventful day. . . . This day my election at Rugby has dissolved my direct connection with Balliol. O Lord, when I look back on the $7\frac{1}{2}$ years that have passed since I was elected Fellow, what mercies have I to thank Thee for! Yet how little have I improved. God, be merciful to me, a miserable sinner. . . . When entering on this new situation, let no worldly thoughts deceive me. The sudden death of him whom I succeed should be enough to prevent this.

Grant me, Lord, to live each day as I would wish to die. Let me view this event, not as success, but as the opening up of a fresh field of labour in Thy vineyard. Now I may look forward to dedicate my whole life to one object—the grand work of Christian education. Let me never forget that the first requisite for this is to be a true Christian myself. Give me a holy heart. Give me boldness and firmness in Thy service. Give me unfailing perseverance. Banish all indolence. Give me freedom from worldly ambition. O Lord, I have much labour before me—much to do of a secular character. Grant that this may never draw me from regular habits of devotion, without which the Christian life cannot be preserved within me."

As has been already said, it was largely at the instigation of Arthur Stanley that he had resolved to become a candidate for the Head-mastership. But in the weeks which followed, Stanley seems to have felt it impossible to recommend any one as really fit to take Dr. Arnold's place, and before the actual election took place he had practically ceased to support Tait's candidature.

Several characteristic letters from him followed one another in rapid succession as soon as the election was over.

The Rev. A. P. Stanley to the Rev. A. C. Tait.

"July 29, 1842.

"My dear Tait,—The awful intelligence of your election has just reached me. At any time it would have been a most serious responsibility to me—from circumstances which have transpired in the last week[1] it is absolutely overwhelming. I have not heart to say more than that I conjure you by your friendship for me, your reverence for your great predecessor, your sense of the sacredness of your office, your devotion to Him whose work you are now more than ever called upon to do, to lay aside every thought for the present except that of repairing your deficiencies.

---

[1] These 'circumstances' are explained in a subsequent letter to be the objections of some of the Rugby masters to the new appointment, but the same letter adds that he finds he has overrated the difficulties, and they are vanishing.

. . . Read Arnold's sermons. At whatever expense of orthodoxy (so called) for the time, throw yourself thoroughly into his spirit. Alter nothing at first. See all that is good and nothing that is bad in the masters and the Rugby character."

A few days later he writes :—

"I feel as if your appointment to this tremendous office without an ordination had given a shock to my tendencies to believe in Apostolical succession which they will never recover. It is of course impossible not to recur to the chasm never to be filled up when I think of your election ; but my thoughts sometimes return thence charged with the hope that God has in store great things for you also, and that the object of this whole dispensation, so far as I am concerned, has not been solely to break down my chief earthly stay, but to show me how his work may be continued by others."

And again :—

"Forgive me, if in the first agony of distress, when your election brought before me what I had lost—not only in him at Rugby, but in you at Oxford—I may have spoken too sadly. You must not expect that I could go scatheless through so terrible a convulsion as this has been."

Tait's inauguration as Head-master took place on Sunday, August 14th, when the sermon was preached by Arthur Stanley. The Head-master was deeply moved by the *sors liturgica*, which gave as the opening words of the Epistle for the day, "Such trust have we through Christ to God-ward : not that we are sufficient of ourselves to think anything as of ourselves ; but our sufficiency is of God."

Diary.

"*Sunday Evening, August 14th*, 1842.—Gracious Lord, accept my heartfelt thanks for the mercies of this day. May the words which Stanley spoke be fixed deeply in my heart, and in the hearts of all who heard them. Oh may the solemn responsibility which has this day come so fully upon me make me a man of prayer. Without incessant prayer I am lost, and, if I perish, how many souls perish with me."

"*Monday Evening, August* 15*th*.—Almighty God, give me strength of body to stand the labour of this place, and strength of mind to conduct myself in it aright. Enable me, in the midst of all, to have time for serious earnest devotion. God Almighty, bless the young souls over whom Thy Providence has placed me. Amen."

It was from the first a great satisfaction to him to know that he had the entire confidence of Dr. Arnold's own family and friends. In a letter received soon after his appointment Mr. Matthew Arnold wrote :—

"From the very beginning, when we found that Archdeacon Hare would not stand, I heartily wished for your success, as my first feeling was that the one point of paramount importance was to provide for the efficient government and firm and consistent management of the school, which seemed to me far the most necessary requisite in the election, and one that there was some danger of neglecting. I feel so confident that if you have a school wisely and firmly governed, and boys and masters alike impressed with the conviction that their main object should be to unite their efforts in making and keeping the place a Christian school, all the intellectual proficiency which is apt to be the first thing considered will be sure to follow as a matter of course."

It would be useless to give the chronological details of a life so necessarily monotonous as that of the Headmaster of a public school,[1] and a few reminiscences furnished by colleagues or contemporaries who knew him well will probably be the best mode of presenting some picture of Tait's position and work at Rugby.

The following is contributed by the Dean of Westminster :[2]—

"When the news of Dr. Tait's election came (I was

----

[1] See Stanley's *Life of Arnold*, chap. iii.

[2] Dr. Bradley was a pupil of Dr. Arnold at Rugby from 1837 to 1840.

then an undergraduate at Oxford), I remember being, on the whole, content ; and I think I am right in saying that the Rugby undergraduates, when we met in October—though the loss of Arnold absorbed us to a degree difficult to make others realise—turned with great loyalty to Tait. I was intimate with many who came up to Oxford from Rugby in the year following his appointment, and the impression I got of him was that of quite indefatigable earnestness and industry, and of his throwing himself heart and soul into the Rugby tradition. Indeed, I am not wrong, I suspect, in thinking that Tait and Cotton (though both of course with an infinite fund of humour) probably over-strained the amount of responsibility and high-strung sense of duty which Arnold had made a part of the older boys' education. Some few boys flung off from it entirely, but others came to Oxford in Tait's earlier days over-weighted. We older Rugbeians had perhaps been as bad ; but we used to think that the younger generation carried the flag of 'moral thoughtfulness' rather too high.[1] . . .

"Early in 1846 Dr. Tait appointed me an assistant master at Rugby. I remember our interview to arrange preliminaries. There was truth as well as humour in his remark (to which I cordially assented) that we had other things to do at Rugby besides exalting the Arnold tradition. The school was at that time somewhat out of gear. The influx of boys had been immense ; the houses were overcrowded ; the system of payment was inequitable, enriching the older masters, but leaving no funds for increase of staff. The Head-master's position must, I am sure on looking back, have been surrounded with difficulties and anxieties. He worked very hard : rose early and worked before first school, which was at 7 o'clock, especially

---

[1] Arthur Stanley in one of his sermons at Oxford speaks of Arnold's boys as having felt at school "the care of all the Churches." (*Sermons on the Apostolic Age*, p. 28.)

hard at his Modern History and Divinity Lectures. He was not, of course, remarkable as a scholar, and from the first he wisely had the assistance of a Composition master. But his teaching was, so far as I can say, thoroughly good in the main, better, I think, than that of many more brilliant scholars, and he always left on the mind of the Sixth the idea of conscientious and thorough work. . . . His sermons were very earnest and devout. No one could sneer at them; no one did, I think. They were sometimes really impressive. More than this I can hardly say; but I feel sure that he exercised a great deal of religious influence on the school. It was a very busy life. I probably saw more of him than almost any master except Cotton; but there was not much time for this except in occasional rides and short conversations. He was very hospitable, and fond of society, and I often dined there and met various people from the outer world. I remember Cotton summing up his position by applying to him Tertullus' words to Felix: 'Seeing that by thee we enjoy great quietness, and that many worthy deeds are done unto this nation by thy providence.' Indeed, I think that he was thoroughly respected and, in the main, appreciated. There was a sort of inflated idea that Rugby was the centre of the world, and that none but a man of genius could preside over it; but I can't recall anything more marked than this. His illness came in the spring of 1848: it was terribly severe, and one day we really walked about the quad expecting that any moment the chapel bell might toll. It of course shook him greatly, and he was long unfit for work, and never, I think, was quite at home again at Rugby, though getting better when the Deanery of Carlisle came in 1849. Then I think every one felt what a loss he would be, and the feeling of the boys especially rose to enthusiasm. He left in the middle of the year 1850, and the carriage was drawn down by the boys, and there was the greatest possible excitement. One member of the school-house, an Irishman, I found weeping so dreadfully at the station that I brought him back, and got leave from the new Head-master to let him stay with me for the remaining week or two before he left school, to save him the distress of beginning with a new Head-master. . . . His tenure of the Head-mastership was a very remarkable instance of goodness and good sense (and, I need hardly add, very good abilities), enabling a man to fill a post for which he was not specially designed. One may fairly say this of so great a Bishop of London and Archbishop of Canterbury. I try in vain to recollect any special failure which I could point out. His interest in individual boys was warm ; he never forgot them when they had left, and the school-house received infinite kindness both from him and from Mrs. Tait. I can only add that the impression he made upon myself was such, that when I heard of his being made Bishop of London I felt sure that he would succeed or die."

The following is from the pen of Principal Shairp :—

" Tait was certainly by no means a born school-master. He had not himself been at an English public school, and his sympathies and powers of influence lay more with young men than with boys. . . . Besides this, the assistant masters over whom he was to be placed had many of them been devoted pupils and friends of Arnold, and they were apt to fancy themselves exalted beyond other men by their contact with him. It was not to be expected that these men should have the same feelings towards Tait, who was an entire stranger to them, which they had towards Arnold. It may have been that some of them may have been thought, both by their friends and by themselves, fully equal to Tait. But when a successor to Arnold was wanted, it was to Oxford that men naturally looked for one. And among the Oxford Fellows and Tutors of that day they naturally turned to the chief Tutor of the best College ; and he stood out from all his compeers, if not for the finest scholarship, yet for the most substantial character and robust manhood. And it was all needed at this crisis. For of all the transitions of his eventful life, I do not believe that any so tried him as the passage from Oxford to Rugby. But he faced it with that calm meek courage so characteristic of him—a courage founded not on self-assertion, or any over-appreciation of his own power, but on the sense that this was the thing to do, and that by God's help he would do it. And, whatever difficulties there may have been at the outset, the school quickly grew and prospered under his Head-mastership. The 400 boys whom it contained at Arnold's death soon increased to 500. This was no doubt in great measure due to the reputation which Arnold had left, and to the great expansion of that reputation which followed the appearance of Stanley's famous Biography. But if this was the source whence the prosperity came, it was Tait who nurtured and garnered it. He showed his usual good sense in accepting the position to which he had been called of being the conservator of Arnold's work, and building on the foundation which he had laid.

"Dr. Tait had been Head-master for more than four years when he offered me an assistant-mastership which had become vacant. For the first week or ten days I was the guest at the school-house, where I was received with much kindness. One afternoon, the first or second day after my arrival, Dr. Tait took me into his study, and there gave me some hints about the school and its ways, and, especially, gave a slight sketch of the several masters of whom I was about to become a colleague. He said a few words about each, and when I afterwards came to know them, I found his estimate to have been wonderfully true. I especially remember the emphasis of admiration with which he dwelt on the character of Cotton, and on the way he did his work. Evidently he was a master after Dr. Tait's own heart."

Delicate as his position was with regard to the assistant masters who knew so much more than he could know of Rugby and its traditions, his relations with them were from the first of the most cordial kind. An interruption of this was at one time threatened, when, in the year 1845, a strong disagreement arose respecting the appointment of a new master to a particular form. For some days the resignation of several of the best men of the staff seemed imminent, but it was averted by a combination of firmness and gentleness on Tait's part which, as the correspondence shows, won the warm appreciation even of those who had at first felt most aggrieved. On this, as on several other occasions, he emphatically asserted his view as to the independent rights, the possession of which he, like Dr. Arnold, considered essential to the due maintenance of the Head-master's position. The only entry on the subject in his journal is as follows :—

"*Saturday, 5th April* 1845.—O Lord God, in this great difficulty as to the management of the school, grant that I may put away every thought but how I shall best regulate it as a portion of Thy Church to Thy glory and the good of souls. Suppress every angry or proud thought; may I not seek my own glory. May I be ready to make any sacrifice myself; but teach me to be bold in Thy service. May no fear of man compel me to do what is wrong, no desire of peace lead me to give up principle; but, on the other hand, may I be saved from all harshness or unkindness, and from any proud continuance in my own determinations, because I have once committed myself to them.

Lord, may I remember that Thou hast intrusted to me many souls."

The following extracts from some of his letters to his future wife during the months of their engagement show the keen interest he was feeling in his work :—

"I certainly have my time here most fully occupied, but I could not have any work more truly interesting. I find the Sixth take great interest in Plato's *Phædo*—as they ought. I consider the books they are reading with me now about the most interesting that could possibly be found. Not to mention the Acts of the Apostles—reading which carefully with them opens up new and striking features in it every day—we are reading the *Phædo* of Plato, which, as I daresay you know, contains the conversation of Socrates, on the day of his death, with his disciples on the immortality of the soul ; the sixth book of Virgil's *Æneid*, which gives the account of Æneas going down to the abode of the dead, and sets forth the belief of the ancients on the state of future retribution ; the first book of Tacitus' *Annals*, which is a noble picture of Rome in its fallen state under Tiberius ; and the *Electra* of Sophocles, about the noblest of ancient tragedies. So that you see I live in good company, having daily converse with such great men. This is really no nonsense."

And again :—

> "*Good Friday.*

"This day has been full of interest. To-night I have had a conversation—which I shall tell you about when we meet—with a boy who, having been brought up a Unitarian, is anxious, with his father's consent, to become a member of the Church of England, and receive the Communion on Easter Sunday. Many people think that a schoolmaster's is not a proper profession for a clergyman. My opinion, on the contrary, is that there is no situation of so directly pastoral a nature as mine. How very few clergy have parishioners who are so willing to be led as my boys !"

And again :—

"This afternoon has been a very melancholy one. The speeches ended at half-past two. It was altogether an interesting sight. And when it was over, the thoughts of a whole year passed in this place came upon me—the terrible responsibility—the little good that has been done—the great difficulties that lie before me—and altogether the separating from all these young faces, with the certainty that many of them I shall never see on earth again—and yet that for the good or evil they have contracted here I shall certainly have to give an account."

On Midsummer-day 1843, the Head-master of Rugby was married in Elmdon Church to Catharine Spooner, the youngest daughter of Archdeacon Spooner, vicar of Elmdon. The little volume is now well known in which Archbishop Tait has himself told the story of their wedded life of five-and-thirty years, and his biographer half shrinks from treading, however reverently, upon holy ground. But no picture of his life during any one of those eventful years would be a true one which failed to show her working in bright activity by his side, sharing and lightening every labour and every sorrow. After eagerly embracing in her earlier girlhood the best teaching of the Evangelical party, to which her father and his friends belonged, she had fallen, some years before her marriage, under the influence of the Oxford school; and, as the Archbishop has himself told us—

"She could scarcely bear that it should be opposed and spoken against. She has often told me how, when she heard that one of the four protesting tutors who helped to bring to a sudden close the series of the Oxford Tracts was a candidate for the Head-mastership of Rugby, she earnestly hoped he would not be successful. . . . It was a strange turn of fate which made her open her heart next year to the very candidate whose success she had deprecated, and become the happy partner of his life at Rugby, Carlisle, Fulham, Lambeth; sharing in all his deepest and truest interests, helping forward for thirty-five years every good work which he was called to promote; united to him in the truest fellowship of soul, while still tempering by the associations of her early Oxford bias whatever might otherwise have been harsh in his judgments of the good men from whom on principle he differed."[1]

It is a fact that among the many reminiscences of those Rugby days which have been furnished by pupils and friends, there is not one which does not record the deep impression which seems to have been made, even on the least susceptible, by the bright presence of the beautiful young wife who presided over the school-house hospitality, and entered with the keenest zest into every Rugby interest, great and small.

She had been brought up in the quietest of country homes—till she was twenty-one years old she had never seen the sea—and though her mind was richly stored with English literature of every kind, she had few friends beyond the rather wide circle of her family, and she knew little of the world outside. To show her so much that was new when the successive school holidays came round, was to her husband a very keen enjoyment.

In the summer of 1845 they undertook a journey which must have tested severely even her untiring strength. Leaving England on the last day of June, in company with his two brothers and a nephew, they posted through France and Italy, and in perhaps the seven hottest weeks of an exceptionally hot summer they drove from Paris, over Mont Cenis, to Genoa. Sailing thence, they disembarked their carriage at Naples, and after visiting Sorrento and Vesuvius—then in eruption—they drove by Rome, where they spent six days, to Perugia, Florence, Bologna, and Milan. Thence over the Splügen into Switzerland, and back to Calais.

The rough journal which Dr. Tait kept throughout this remarkable tour tells of the many difficulties which they encountered on the journey, due in part to the

____
[1] *Catharine and Craufurd Tait*, p. 6.

necessity of travelling more rapidly than their drivers and hotel-keepers approved, and in part to the suspicion which seems somehow to have attached to their party, especially in the Neapolitan and Papal dominions. This entry is thrice repeated :—

"*Mem.*—Let no man in his senses ever again introduce a carriage into the kingdom of Naples by sea."

At Naples he writes :—

"I confess the more I see of Sundays on the Continent, the more does one's opinion of the Puritans rise. Sunday cannot be a day of rest to the hard-pressed poor unless it be made a day of religious rest."

"I cannot endure Museums, but the paintings of Herculaneum and Pompeii, the rusty irons to which the skeletons of prisoners were found chained, the statues of the Balbi and of Agrippina, the Farnese Hercules—these save this from giving me the sickening feeling which a museum generally brings."

In Rome they worked day and night at sight-seeing.

"It is very well to pass a few months abroad, but the hurry and want of peace makes it by no means the best relaxation for a man who fears that during the rest of the year he has more work than is consistent with quiet thoughtfulness."

"Pope not to be seen. 'Aujourd'hui il ne sort pas. Demain il y a une procession, et il ne sort pas. Samedi il ne sort jamais. Ni dimanche.' I hope he may live through the week."

"PERUGIA, *July 29th.*—The landlord warned us that next day was to be the exhibition of the ring of the Virgin at the church close by, and that we must expect about 3 A.M. to hear thousands of poor people from the Abbruzzi and from Calabria, and from most distant parts of Neapolitan dominions pass under our windows singing Vivat Maria and Ave Maria. We were roused accordingly; and to-day, about eleven, we saw a scene the most wonderful that I ever beheld. The people of the country here, it appears, do not think very much of the relic, but its fame is great at a distance. This year there were not above 2000 pilgrims from a distance, which is a small number. They were the most abject of the peasantry,—poor, tired, ragged,—having come, some of them, hundreds of miles. One end of the church was filled with them. As soon as the relic was brought down to be exhibited to the authorities of the town who were present, these poor creatures, who were wrought to the highest pitch of excitement, shouted out their Vivat Maria. The senators retired, and then began a scene which baffles all description. We at last succeeded in getting into a gallery, immediately above the chapel where the relic was displayed. The people were admitted by an iron gate in the railing. The dense mass was crushed together in such a way as seemed to threaten that many would be stifled. As the gate was opened they shrieked and rushed, and those who got in only did so with their lives. The soldiers who shut the gates had hard work.

"One man naked, beating himself with iron chains, on his knees. The crowd treated him with the respect paid to a dervish. One woman crawled like a worm up the aisle, and received similar respect. The rest were nearly squeezed to death. Each party as they entered fell on their knees, kissed the floor, rushed to the relic, had their heads rubbed against it by the two priests, and made (most of them) some very small offering. Our friend the dervish of the iron chains we afterwards met in the streets, in a great state of excitement, though it was more of terrestrial kind than that of which he had at least assumed the appearance in church, when, in the midst of admiring groups, he clasped his hands and assumed a beatific look. Now he was very like a sturdy beggar, and his tones were anything but saintly when we passed without giving him anything.

"It is from such scenes as these, not from the elegant Monsignori of Rome, that we must judge of the evils of Rome. The scene was indeed like the worship of some heathen deity. This surely is Anti-Christ. And this is the city of an archbishop, and within the Pope's own territory."

In the opening months of this same year, 1845, he had been again in the thick of ecclesiastical strife, though rather as a moderator than as a combatant.

It is always difficult for a Head-master to interfere prominently in public affairs unconnected with his school. Dr. Arnold's position had been unique, but some of his warmest admirers maintain that he would have been an even greater Head-master had he been less prominent as a politician and a controversialist. Dr. Tait was of this opinion, and it was only on rare occasions during his eight years at Rugby that he allowed himself to take part in public controversy. But every visitor to the school-house remembers his keen interest both in home and foreign politics, and, above all, in questions of University reform. A controversialist, in the stricter sense, he had never been, but he intervened with marked effect in the exciting struggle which was waged in 1845 round the person of his old antagonist and friend, Mr. William George Ward.

Mr. Ward, whose opinions, even in the view of his best friends, had been becoming less and less consistent with any reasonable adherence to the Church of England, published in 1844 *The Ideal of a Christian Church*, an elaborate volume wherein, according to his opponents, he publicly defied the University, held himself up as an instance of the inability of her tests to exclude an avowed Roman Catholic, and proclaimed his readiness to subscribe the thirty-nine articles as often as they should be tendered to him, and, at the same time, his abhorrence of the Reformation, and his determination, in his own words, "to renounce no one Roman doctrine."

The University accepted the challenge, and a Convocation was summoned for February 13th, 1845, wherein three resolutions were to be proposed,—the first declaring Mr. Ward's book to be "utterly inconsistent with the Articles of Religion of the Church of England," and with Mr. Ward's own good faith in respect of his subscription to them ; the second annulling the degrees of B.A. and M.A. conferred on Mr. Ward on the strength of such subscription ; and the third imposing for the future on all graduates a new form of subscription to the Articles, with a view to avoiding any possibility of such interpretations as Mr. Ward and the supporters of Tract XC. had put upon them.[1]

Among the members of Convocation whose support of these propositions was deemed certain, were those who had signed or approved the 'protest' of the four tutors three years before. And accordingly Dr. Tait was confidently appealed to for the use of his name in the circulars which advocated the resolutions.

Instead of giving it, however, he published a pamphlet, in the form of a letter to the Vice-Chancellor, which greatly disconcerted many of his friends. Admitting with reluctance the apparent necessity of the proposed annulling of Mr. Ward's degrees, inasmuch as he held him to be "a Roman Catholic in everything but the name," he yet argued with all his might against the indiscriminate imposition of a test which he declared could do nothing but harm. Without referring directly to the part he had taken in the 'protest' of the four tutors, he explained the consistency of his action then with his action now. "Mr. Ward," he said, "has publicly and boldly challenged the Church and the University, . . . and unless I much mistake his character, after an intimate acquaintance with him for above ten years, I am sure that he will look with very great contempt upon the Protestantism of any who are not ready to urge the necessity of his challenge being accepted."

But "by the third proposition which they intend to bring before Convocation, [the Heads of Houses] have plunged into a new field, in which they must lose the support of those who are most able and willing to stand

---

[1] The new test was to contain the following words :—"Ego, A. B., . . . profiteor . . . me Articulis istis omnibus et singulis eo sensu subscripturum in quo eos ex animo credo et primitus editos esse, et nunc mihi ab Universitate propositos tanquam opinionum mearum certum ac indubitatum signum."

by them." Evangelicals, Anglo-Catholics, and Broad Churchmen [1] would, he maintained, be alike placed in a difficulty were the new form of subscription carried. It would operate to the exclusion of the best, because the most conscientious, men. Extreme cases like Mr. Ward's may occur from time to time. "Liberty may degenerate into licence, and in his case it has done so. . . . He has received his commission as an authorised teacher on condition of his renouncing Romish error. But let the University deal with each of such cases as it arises. There is no need of our narrowing the limits of the Church of England because some amongst us wish to make it too wide."

This pamphlet, which had an immediate and wide circulation, was a disappointment to the friends who had reckoned too hastily on Tait's partisanship in their attack. Mr. Golightly, for example, his old fellow-worker at Baldon, wrote in much wrath:—

"Your pamphlet has caused extreme concern here to many whose opinions you value. Pray, for the sake of Rugby, the interests of which it may really injure, let me entreat you to withdraw it immediately. I cannot tell you how grieved I am. . . . You were not called upon to come forward, nor justified in advising the Heads of Houses. Cramer and the Vice-Chancellor have expressed themselves strongly against your pamphlet. Let me again beseech you to withdraw it."

Mr. Lake, on the other hand, wrote:—

"I think you have acted most rightly and consistently, and although I hear that our Oxford friends attack the tone of your arguments, I really do not see under the circumstances, and in your position, what other you could adopt. . . . The Heads are one and all furious at your advice, 'My dear Mr. Vice-Chancellor' one of the most so. You have, indeed, most prudent of men, put your foot into it. I would not be you at your next visit."

---

[1] He does not use the word, indeed it had hardly yet been coined, but he describes them at some length.

From Mr. Ward himself he received the following:—

"*Jan.* 13, 1845.

"My dear Tait,—I am extremely obliged both by your kind letter and by the tone of your pamphlet. I cannot but think the latter will do great good; it is so open, honest, and plain-spoken; if you will allow me so far to express a judgment on it. I may possibly make some adverse use of it in a pamphlet of mine which I hope will be out in a few days. I must really return you my warmest thanks for your most gratifying mention of myself throughout your pamphlet.—Ever, my dear Tait, yours very sincerely,   W. G. Ward."

Partly, it would appear, in consequence of this pamphlet, partly on other grounds, the suggested 'test' resolution was withdrawn by its proposers some weeks before the Meeting of Convocation, and another Resolution was substituted for it, conveying the formal censure of the University upon the principles of interpretation adopted in Tract XC. This resolution, it was determined, at all costs, to put to the vote.

"At last," writes Dean Stanley, "came the memorable day which must be regarded as the closing scene of the conflict of the first Oxford movement. It was February 13, St. Valentine's Eve. . . . Clergy and laity of all shades and classes crowded the colleges and inns of Oxford for the great battle of Armageddon. . . . When the whole assembly of upwards of 1000 voters was crowded within the Sheldonian theatre, the Registrar of the University read out the incriminating passages of the *Ideal of a Christian Church.* The general proceedings were in Latin, but it was curious to hear the grave voice of the Registrar proclaiming in the vernacular from his high position these several sentences, 'O most joyful! O most wonderful! O most unexpected sight! we find the whole cycle of Roman doctrine gradually possessing numbers of English Churchmen.'"[1]

Mr. Ward spoke in his own defence,

"boldly, clearly, and with great self-possession, . . . but the

[1] *Edinburgh Review*, vol. cliii. p. 322.

matter seemed intended *auditores malevolos facere*.   Every statement and every inference that could offend their prejudices,
irritate their vanity, or wound their self-respect, was urged with
the zeal of a candidate for martyrdom. . . . 'The speech over,
the Vice-Chancellor put the question.   There was a roar and
counter roar of *placets* and *non-placets*.   A scrutiny was ordered,
and the first resolution—the censure of the passages from the
Ideal—was carried by 777 to 391.   The second—the degrada-
tion—by a much smaller majority, 569 to 511.'   When the third
resolution was put, every eye was fixed on the two Proctors, who,
in virtue of their office, had a constitutional veto upon every act
of the University.   'They rose, Mr. Guillemard and Mr. Church,
afterwards Dean of St. Paul's, and uttered the words which,
except on one memorable occasion [the Hampden case], no one
then living had ever heard pronounced in Convocation : *Nobis
procuratoribus non placet.*' "

In accordance with University rule a motion thus
negatived by the Proctors fell at once to the ground.   To
the satisfaction with which this result was generally
received Dr. Tait's pamphlet had materially contributed.
Ward walked back from the theatre in company with Tait,
who had voted against him on the first count.   " In the
course of this walk," we are told, " Tait warmly praised
the peroration of Ward's speech.   Ward's reply was
characteristically candid : ' I am glad you liked it.   These
rhetorical efforts are out of my line, but Stanley said there
should be something of the kind.   He wrote it for me.' "[1]

The virulence of the party spirit exhibited on each side
in this contest was to Archibald Tait a source of keen
distress.   Writing to Arthur Stanley a few days after
the Convocation, he says : " I saw you at a distance on the
black Thursday—a dreadful day, full of the most painful
thoughts of any day I have known for long, and making
me melancholy ever since."

---

[1] For an account of the whole scene and its consequences, see *W. G.
Ward and the Oxford Movement*, chap. xiii.

The above seems to have been the only instance in his Rugby life in which his name came before the outside public in any other capacity than that of a successful schoolmaster. But there were certain controversies of the time from which it was almost impossible for any prominent Oxford graduate to hold aloof. Foremost among these was the 'Hampden Controversy' of 1847.

On November 15th, 1847, Lord John Russell recommended Dr. Renn Dickson Hampden to the Queen for the vacant Bishopric of Hereford, and a commotion of the wildest kind immediately began. Eleven years had elapsed since Dr. Hampden, on his appointment by Lord Melbourne as Regius Professor of Divinity, had been practically censured by the Convocation of the University of Oxford for the supposed unsoundness of his theology as indicated by the Bampton Lectures he had delivered four years previously.[1] Under this censure Dr. Hampden had rested ever since, and it is difficult to say whether the Tractarian or the Evangelical School was the more indignant when Lord John Russell, in his desire for a liberal theologian, nominated him to the Crown for the vacant Bishopric. The history of what followed has recently been published in full detail in the Biography of Bishop Wilberforce,[2] who, foremost at first in opposition to the appointment, caused extreme surprise by a real or supposed change of front during the warfare which ensued. An attempted prosecution for heresy was vetoed by Bishop Wilberforce, but thirteen bishops and innumerable clergy joined in protesting to the Prime Minister against the nomination. A counter memorial in Dr. Hampden's

---

[1] A statute was passed, by 474 votes to 94, depriving the new Regius Professor of his share in the nomination of select preachers, on the ground that he had "so treated theological questions, that in this behalf, the University has no confidence in him." The Bampton Lectures had been delivered in 1832.   [2] Vol. i. pp. 419-514.

favour obtained the signatures of 250 members of the Oxford Convocation. Among these was Dr. Tait. He had never been intimately acquainted with Dr. Hampden, nor had he any admiration for what he termed the Professor's "frigid and somewhat shallow and uninspiring theology." But he was unable to see anything very heretical in his opinions, and he considered him to have received scant justice and much unmerited abuse.

When the election to the See of Hereford was 'confirmed' in Bow Church, Dr. Lushington, as representing the Archbishop of Canterbury, refused a hearing to the opposers, although the ceremony of confirmation includes an invitation to objectors to come forward. The opposers thereupon applied to the Court of Queen's Bench for a *mandamus* compelling the Archbishop or his representative to hear them. The case was fully argued, and, the four judges being equally divided, the *mandamus* was refused, and Dr. Hampden was soon afterwards duly consecrated in Lambeth Palace chapel.

The following letter from Dr. Tait to his brother was written when the Queen's Bench had granted a preliminary 'rule,' but before the final decision of the Court. His statement as to the scant attention which had been paid to the actual book so vigorously impugned has been curiously verified by the correspondence recently made public in Bishop Wilberforce's Life.

Rev. A. C. Tait to Mr. James Tait.

"18 DOVER STREET, LONDON,
18*th January* 1848.

"MY DEAREST JEM,— . . . What do you Scotch people say to the state of the Church of England? You see that the Queen's Bench have granted a Rule to require the objectors to be heard unless some more valid reasons for refusing to hear them can be given. I am glad of this, for, however groundless or incapable of proof the objections really are, it is monstrous that they should be smothered in the strange way which Dr. Lushington proposed. I think the opposition to Hampden quite uncalled for and wrong; but I do not see how he himself could wish the matter to be smothered in the way proposed. . . . If the law is really as Dr. Lushington expounded it, then certainly either the old forms of citation, etc., ought to be abolished, or new powers granted, to allow objections when made to be entered on. The whole matter is certainly a very grave one. Lord John would have done much better not to appoint Hampden at first. After he had done so the Bishops were strangely unwise to make their protest, knowing, as they must have done, that Lord John could not draw back with common respectability, and also being well aware that no such grave objections now lay against Hampden as the clamour of a few party men had tried to persuade the world. And now, the objections having been personally stated, I think Hampden will behave ill if he tries to stifle inquiry. The most absurd part of the matter is that almost no one has read the book objected to. To be sure, it is very long and somewhat dull, but Bishops at least ought to read it. I have re-read it on this occasion with great care,[1] and am fully of opinion that no case of heresy can be made out after the explanations in Hampden's subsequently published writings. . . . I signed the address which deprecated the original agitation in opposition to the appointment."

Two years of specially hard work followed upon the Italian tour which has been described above. Besides his absorbing duties at Rugby, which multiplied with the increasing numbers of the school, he maintained a keen interest both in Oxford affairs and in the wider public questions of the day. But the work was too much for his physical strength. His devotional journals during these years contain an ever-recurring reference to his frequent fatigue and drowsiness. He seems to have regarded it in the light of a fault to be conquered. It might better have

---

[1] This statement is amply confirmed by the pencil-marks and annotations, which may still be seen throughout his copy of the volume.

been noted as a warning that he was overtaxing his powers.

"O Lord, save me from indolence. My body becomes so wearied that I cannot pray to Thee as I ought. Forgive me, O Lord, and give me strength for Christ's sake."

And again:

"Lord, make me more constantly diligent. Forgive that indolence which at times so overcomes me in the evenings, and prevents me from having my heart and thoughts active when I would draw near to Thee."

And again:

"I have been sadly drowsy. This is the very sin which I most called to mind this morning at Thy Holy Table. Yet so weak am I that this very afternoon it has been overpowering me. Last night I felt it and deplored it deeply. O Lord, deliver me from it."

Suddenly, in February 1848, he was stricken with rheumatic fever. Both heart and lungs were affected, and the illness soon assumed so alarming a character that for several days recovery seemed hopeless. His brothers and sisters were summoned, and he took leave of them one by one. On Ash Wednesday, March 8th, it was thought that he might die at any moment. He dictated a letter of farewell to the Sixth Form, and sent special messages to many friends.[1]

"Before I left the room that evening," writes Lady Wake, "I heard him put this question to his doctor, 'In what manner will death come?' The doctor, who had given up all hope, answered, 'Either in that faintness which so frequently comes over you, or in a fit of coughing.' He listened in silence. His breathing was difficult, and he was in much suffering. Wearied in body and mind, my sister and I fell asleep in the adjoining room. A

---

[1] The message to Mr. Shairp was as follows: "Tell him I have perfect peace, from faith in the simplest of all truths, that Christ died for the ungodly."

dreadful sound as of a succession of screams in Archie's room recalled my senses. Marion was already gone. In another instant I was in his room and saw him propped up in a paroxysm of coughing—coughing is not the word for the sound. His wife and sisters stood in mute expectation of the close ; and, when the fit was over and he was gently lowered to his pillows, it was a relief to see that he still breathed. He remained perfectly still, and from that moment his breathing became regular and improvement began. One of the most dangerous conditions of his illness had been the adhesion of the pericardium to the heart. The violence of the cough had probably assisted to relieve circulation, and after this relief he slept peacefully during the remainder of the night."

On the following day he was quieter, but the doctor gave little hope of a recovery. He was much distressed about certain intricacies in the school accounts, which he thought would not be understood after his death, and to set his mind at rest his two brothers, who were both skilled and accurate men of business, tried to arrange them. They were puzzled by the intricate character of the books, and found that to unravel the complications was beyond their power. Quietly and composedly Mrs. Tait herself sat down to the task, and, with a calmness which amazed them all, made everything clear and simple, and then returned to her husband's side. There is a chorus of testimony to the remarkable power she showed in these days of trial, carrying on as usual all necessary business, and, though she had come to think recovery hopeless, retaining her composure, and exercising a quieting influence upon them all.

As he has himself written :—

"There were long days and nights of watching during that spring of 1848, when kingdoms all over Europe went down with a crash, and England itself was by many supposed to be on the brink of a Revolution. Of all these outward events I knew nothing for many days. But my young wife kept watch beside my bed. All through the worst days, and still more when I was recovering, she was ready to pray with me, and to repeat helpful texts and hymns. . . . Never shall I forget the thankfulness with which at last on Easter Day—though my health was much shattered for life, and I rose a very different man in bodily strength from what I had been when I lay down—she and I together returned thanks and received the Holy Communion amid the bright band of youthful worshippers in the dear Rugby chapel." [1]

For two years more he continued his Rugby work, and though there was no apparent lack of efficiency, and no decrease in the reputation or numbers of the school, it became clear both to himself and to his intimate friends that his physical powers were no longer equal to the strain of a schoolmaster's life. It was still uncertain what the effect of arduous work might be upon his weakened heart, and there were recurring warnings which he dared not disregard.

" Perhaps it is good for me to meet with these checks, for they make me better able to realise my entire dependence upon God. I have at times thought what a dreadful thing it would be to have some organic disease which one knew must cut one off some day in a moment without warning. But, after all, would not this enable a man only the better to realise the fact of his responsibility? . . . If it is indeed Thy good will to make me, either here or elsewhere, still useful to Thy Church on earth, may I never lose the very solemn thoughts which Thou hast brought near to me. . . . When I think of past times there are certain days which occur vividly to me—my ordination day, some Ash Wednesdays passed in Oxford of which I have a record. How solemn a day should Ash Wednesday be to me when I think how, on its last return, I lay on the very brink of the grave. May I never forget the day in which Bucknill told me after evening chapel how he expected I should die. . . . For Jesus Christ's sake, make me a faithful minister of Thy word. Lord, save me from my evil heart. Amen."

And again :

" Lord, Thou only knowest whether I can carry through my

<hr>

[1] *Catharine and Craufurd Tait*, p. 26.

duties at Rugby. May I feel no distrustful anxiety. Thou knowest what is best. Thou wilt find enough for me to do either in acting or in suffering for Thee."

These thoughts recur almost daily in the rough journal which he kept with even more than usual regularity in his two last years at Rugby. In the journals there is little or nothing except prayers, with now and then such comments as the following :—

"I still find great difficulty in fixing my thoughts for prayer unless I use the help of writing. If I use a printed form, my prayers are not sufficiently a direct approach to God. Yet if I pray without a form, it is dreadful to feel how my thoughts wander. Lord, give me the spirit of prayer; I have all my life long felt my sad want of it."

He kept manfully to his work, and some of his colleagues used to maintain that his lectures to the Sixth Form in his last year of office were the best he ever gave. But his friends grew increasingly anxious, and it was a relief both to him and to them when an opportunity was given to him of laying down a burden which undoubtedly overtaxed his strength. On October 18, 1849, he received through Lord John Russell the offer of the vacant Deanery of Carlisle, and at once accepted the post.

" Perhaps his life at Rugby," writes Dean Lake, " was the least marked period of Tait's career, though I think it greatly developed some of his best qualities. It was the happiest time of his life, when he delighted to have his intimate friends staying with him, and all varieties of opinion were discussed, almost with the animation, though with much less than the vehemence, which sometimes marked the still more interesting conversations of Arnold. It is difficult to imagine any scenes more pleasant than those of the drawing-room, or the long walks and rides at

Rugby. But as the head-master of a public school he was hardly a success. He succeeded a man of real genius and extraordinary force of character, by far the greatest teacher of his day, and who had formed a staff of able under-masters entirely devoted to him. Tait was anything but a finished scholar himself, and he had to run the gauntlet of a good deal of severe criticism. At the same time, Rugby offered him a more congenial and more independent sphere than Oxford, and gave a great scope to his tact, and his natural power of dealing with men. Another and more delicate feature in his life must also be mentioned ; for the circumstances of his most happy marriage, of which I have many touching records, brought him for the first time into a close connection with many members of the High Church party; I have still vividly before me many expressions, both in his letters and his conversations, showing that he recognised the position of the High Church party in the English Church much more distinctly than he had done before. This feeling came out strongly on the publication of a work which I have no doubt that you have fully described elsewhere, Ward's *Ideal of a Christian Church*, and of which it is needless to say more than that it created—as it was probably intended to do—a perfect uproar in Oxford. The book itself was condemned, and Mr. Ward deprived of his degree, and something of the nature of a general Test Act might, not impossibly, have passed, but for a very vigorous pamphlet written by Tait, then at Rugby, who thus drew down upon himself the distrust of the Low Church party, which he never entirely overcame. Any reader of Lord Shaftesbury's Life may see that even when he was Bishop of London, Tait did not possess the confidence of the Low Church leaders. I remember his saying to me, with a touch of

bitterness, that he had never any influence in the appointments during the Palmerston *régime*.   But the truth is,
he was never in any full sense of the word an Evangelical.
He was a Protestant, if you will, and with a strong dash
of the Presbyterian, to the end.   But, except in the sense
of believing that the early Evangelicals had greatly
revived the spirit of religion in the English Church, and
in a warm sympathy with their best members, he had
very little of the distinct opinions of the Evangelical
party about him.   'A good man, but a thorough fanatic,'
he once said to me of their greatest lay representative.
It was perhaps a part of his inveterate distrust of
enthusiasm.   'I respect an enthusiast,' he used to say,
laughingly, 'and all the more, because I could never
possibly be one myself'; and I never remember his caring
much for the Venns or Cecils, to whom, for a time at
least, many of us were attached.   His special hero in
the English Church was for long, perhaps always, Archbishop Tillotson.

" His sudden and almost fatal illness during his last
years at Rugby, which led to a weakness of health lasting
more or less through his whole life, I need not dwell
upon.   I had till then looked upon him as, on the whole,
a strong man, and I well remember the horror with which,
in March 1848, I received a very short letter from Mrs.
Tait—' If you wish to see your friend alive, come at once ';
he was then too ill to be spoken to, though I saw him, and
he only remarked to Mrs. Tait, ' Surely that was Lake
whose voice I heard.'   You will probably have mentioned
that it was long before they could even tell him of the
French Revolution, and others, which had occurred during
his illness.   While he was Dean of Carlisle I only saw him
at intervals, and it was in the spring of 1856 that, being
then engaged abroad on a Commission of Education, I

remember finding at each successive great town a letter informing me of the death of five children in succession. From this blow he could scarcely rally, and his friends doubted his ever doing so. Dr. Vaughan, then at Harrow, who first mentioned to me the report that 'Tait was not only to be made one of the new Bishops' (there were four Sees then vacant), 'but was to be Bishop of London,' remarked at the same time, 'I think it will kill him.' It was shortly afterwards that I received a note from him with the words, 'I have just been offered, and accepted, the Bishopric of London. Give me your prayers.'"

The following reminiscences, contributed by Mr. Arthur Butler, give a vivid picture of his later years at Rugby :—

"The general impression that Dr. Tait made on boys (I speak as an old member of his house during the last years of his Head-mastership) was, in the first place, that of a most dignified and courteous gentleman, with a grave manner, an impressive voice, and an occasional sparkle of deep feeling or quiet humour, which we felt lying in the background, ready either to flash out upon our faults or make allowance for our shortcomings. Everything about him was dignified, kind, and trustful. He left us very much to ourselves, rarely interfering in any house affairs, taking little apparent interest in our sports or pleasures, but yet observant and well acquainted with what was going on, and, when the occasion came, striking in with a master-hand. Yet he rarely punished. It was a favourite joke with us to say that his admonitions, beginning most seriously, ended with a twinkle of the eye and a 'Don't let it occur again.' Doubtless he knew what faults were bad and dangerous, what were only slight outbreaks of high spirits and boyish thoughtlessness. Even when a boy, whom he had locked up for the afternoon, broke out, and was found riding on one of Wombwell's elephants, all he did was to rebuke him sternly, ending with the usual twinkle, and 'Remember I won't be disobeyed, even for an elephant.'   He had in a high degree the gift of humour.   Naturally, I should think, quick of temper, with much of the '*perfervidum Scotorum ingenium*,' his humour always saved him from over-severity.   'Give him time,' we used to say on the rare occasions when he was provoked to exaggerate faults, 'and it will all come right.' And it did always come right ; and we liked him all the better for the quick flash followed by the ready forgiveness.   And this, the feeling in the house, was also the feeling in the School.   He knew exactly where to overlook and where to interfere, and when he did punish or rebuke, it was done in the best manner, with a force, dignity, and judgment which left nothing to be desired.   And the result of all this was seen in the high tone and discipline both of the house and School.   There was indeed a singular absence of the graver faults of school life ; and though this was doubtless mainly due to the traditions bequeathed by Arnold, quickened as they were by Arnold's Life, just then written by Stanley, yet the greatest credit is also due to the man who carried on these traditions, and left the School at the end still better than he had found it. Of this latter change and gradual improvement, and of the way in which Tait developed and helped it on, I may perhaps say a few words.   No one can have read Arnold's Life without being struck by his deep, perhaps excessive, feeling of the evil incident to school life, and by the part which the Præpostors were called upon to play in the moral government of the School.   This, the essential feature of Arnold's system, which has had such lasting influence for good in our great public schools, was not, however, without its dangers.   It produced strained and often hostile relations between the Sixth and the rest of the

School, and it reacted in many cases injuriously on the character of these boy-masters, making them self-important and unnatural. This condition of things Tait (whether intentionally or not I cannot tell) did much to alter. In the first place, he regulated the authority of the Sixth, fixing limits to their power of inflicting punishment, and giving a right of appeal to any lower boy who felt himself aggrieved. Secondly, he did away with certain old customs, thought by the Sixth privileges, which did no good, but only caused friction and annoyance in the School. And lastly, while impressing upon the Sixth their duties and responsibilities with weighty, and often eloquent words, he never failed also to make them see that there was a right and a wrong way of doing things, and that it was quite possible to be strict and firm without being high-flown and aggravating. And so gradually, without in any way injuring discipline, he introduced a more easy and natural relation between the Sixth and School, which was good for all. And his triumph was, that, while thus relaxing the strain of the old system, necessary at its first establishment, he preserved all that was really vital in it, and led the way to that simpler working of monitorial authority now so general in all our great schools.

" Again, I think he had something of the same object before him both in his pulpit teaching and in school lessons. More than once he protested in his sermons against introducing boys prematurely to political and religious controversies ; and in School, whenever questions of a speculative character forced themselves upon his notice, he would endeavour to lead us to more practical considerations by throwing the burden of proof on impugners of received opinions, or bidding us wait till rival controversialists had settled their difficulties, geological or

theological, among themselves.   This side of his teaching
was not, as may be imagined, satisfactory to the more
ardent minds; but in the ferment of thought which he
found existing at Rugby, he doubtless thought it well to
allay rather than excite the fever.   I can still remember
how, when one youthful and able essayist brought him an
essay of portentous length, he said in his gravest of
manners, after reading some few pages, 'Yes; there seems
a good deal of it.'   Needless to say that the performance
was not repeated.   Much may doubtless be said against
such a mode of damping enthusiasm in ordinary cases, but
in the Rugby of that day a little cold water from time to
time, kindly administered, was not without its uses.
Stanley's Life had greatly excited us, and the danger was
that boy-life would lose all naturalness and unconscious-
ness while straining prematurely after effect.   It must not
be thought, however, that he was a quencher of enthusiasm
when rightly directed.   When he heard of any boy or
boys contending against school evils, he would take
occasion to thank them earnestly and kindly, with just a
slight tremor in his deep voice, but careful not to excite
or exaggerate.   He wished boys (so at least it always
struck me) to be above all simple and natural.

"And so things went on till the time of his great illness
in 1848, his teachings, sermons, government, all good and
sensible, but somewhat cold and repressive; of a kind
rather to create respect and confidence than affection and
admiration.   And yet behind his reserve and dignity there
was, we all felt, a deep fund of power and feeling, which it
only needed the occasion to bring forth.   Even as it was,
the deeps were sometimes stirred.   Thus, for instance, I
can still remember the delight of hearing him expound
Aristotle.   For technical scholarship he had little taste,
but in the *Politics* all his instincts as a statesman and

historian found free and congenial scope. And it was the same with his sermons. In ordinary times there was little in them either to arouse or stimulate. But on touching occasions, such as the death of a boy or master, he gave the rein to his feelings, and moved us as deeply as he was himself moved. No one, I think, doubted that he was naturally an orator of no common kind. Our only regret was (as I heard it often said), that we could not remove his MS., and leave him in the pulpit to the natural eloquence of the moment. It was a great power in him, which boys thoroughly appreciate, but which for some reason he would not, or but rarely, use.

"But with his illness there came a change—a change both in him and our feeling towards him. Of the illness itself, and of the long struggle between life and death, and of the eager interest taken by us in the ever-changing bulletins of his condition, I will not speak. It is not my province. But two circumstances which happened at the time may be worth recording, as showing the influence he still exerted over us even on his sick-bed. The first was in the house. One evening, when he was at the worst, a letter dictated by him came to the head of the house, in which he begged us, as a dying man, to think seriously of the great issues of our school life, and never to go to bed at night without reading some portion of our Bibles. I have not a copy of that letter now, though at the time I made one ; but I remember well the impression made by its simple, earnest appeal to our higher nature. The response to it was general. Not only then, but for a long time after, there was an unwonted silence after evening prayers in the long schoolhouse passages, as singly, or by twos or threes, we read our Bibles. Nothing could better show his influence. There was no talking about it, no parade ; but every one at once did what 'dear old Tait' asked us to do from his seeming deathbed.

"The other circumstance happened later on, when, though still very ill, he was beginning to recover.

"I have before spoken of the hostile feeling existing between the Sixth and School. This, owing to a trifling incident, which would never have happened had he been well, gave rise to something very like a rebellion. It was, moreover, the great year of revolutions, and this possibly, in so receptive a soil as that of Rugby, was not without its effect. Anyhow, everything was arranged for an outbreak. Lists were made out, one of which by accident or design fell into our hands, assigning two, three, or even four assailants to each of the Sixth. (I well remember the comical look of our protagonist, a sturdy, short-haired son of Anak, when he heard that four picked youths, stout and fearless, were told off to grapple him.) Only the time and place were hidden from us; and even this was at last made known (as always happens) by a friendly member of the Eleven, who thought the thing absurd, and gave warning to some other members of the Eleven in his house in the Sixth, with a view to save them. It was just in time. That morning the *émeute* was to take place at 9.30 in the school-yard. The signal was to be given by an orator from the pump. Such, at least, was the information given, and immediately the whole body of the Sixth in Price's house, where the secret oozed out, moved down to the scene of action, gathering up or summoning all the other Præpostors for the expected conflict. It was a striking scene. The quadrangle was swarming with the excited Demos when we arrived, and I remember thinking how few we were—the Thirty Tyrants, as they chose to call us— and how easily they would have bowled us over if the fight had once begun. Just, however, when things looked most angry and the hubbub was loudest, there went round a sudden murmur (a φήμη the Greeks would have called it) of 'Tait, Tait!' and the thought that he would hear us, and that the knowledge of what was happening would be bad for him, acted as an instant sedative. At the same time one of the masters, brother of the present Dean of Westminster, then acting as his substitute, appeared on the scene, and ($\mu\iota\kappa\rho\grave{o}\varsigma$ $\delta\acute{\epsilon}\mu\alpha\varsigma$ $\grave{a}\lambda\lambda\grave{a}$ $\mu\alpha\chi\eta\tau\acute{\eta}\varsigma$) fearlessly charged the rebels. They, having already lost their first impulse, and awed partly by the show of present authority, partly by the thought of him who was absent, began slowly to disperse ; and when Bradley began to chase a small boy who would not *disperse* round one of the cloister-columns, the whole affair ended in merry laughter, and the *émeute* was over. But for the moment a rebellion was imminent ; and but for the sudden thought of the Head-master, lying sick and suffering close by, an outbreak probably would have followed.

"After this I remember nothing but the acclamation which greeted his return. It was on a warm summer day when we were playing cricket in the Close that his well-known, stately form was seen, supported by Mrs. Tait, walking under the elms. Instantly every bat and ball was laid aside, and such a cheer arose, again and again repeated, as may well be imagined. It was the beginning of a wholly new relation between boys and master. It was the first expression of a popularity which went on increasing till he left us, and which, I believe, has been rarely equalled at any public school. It was not that he had changed outwardly to any great extent. He was always rather the statesman than the schoolmaster, the ruler than the friend. But everything between us took a warmer tone. We had been drawn to him in his illness ; we understood him better. We felt (many a word that fell from him in his later sermons quickened the feeling) what a depth of almost passionate emotion lived under that calm and dignified exterior. And when the time came, two years after, for him to remove to Carlisle, the flood of loyalty and affection rose to its height.

"One more scene, and these reminiscences, too long already, must come to an end. It was, I think, the day before his departure when we were to present him with a testimonial. The head of the school, Goschen,[1] in a truly eloquent address, had assured him of our gratitude, our affection, and last, not least, our high hopes and expectations for him in the future, when he rose to say to us his last words. It was a perfect speech. Still, after nearly forty years, I can recall many of the tones and gestures with which he stirred and thrilled and carried us along, as he dwelt on the great work begun by Arnold, which he had striven, however imperfectly, to carry on. He could remember, he said, how often in old days he wished that he had been a Rugbeian, and what a privilege he felt it to have become one in his manhood. There was indeed a spirit in the place from which he had learned far more than he had ever taught, and from which he had derived lessons which would abide with him during his life, and after life was over. And then he bid us remember that, after all, the welfare of the school depended mainly on ourselves, not merely the welfare which is proved by large numbers and University honours, but the higher welfare, which consists in making the school a place where God is feared and loved. In comparison with this, he said in conclusion, perish the honours, perish the intellectual distinctions, which can be but the lot of few! It was the high tone and high character of the School which were its real, imperishable greatness, and which he prayed might long continue.

"Such topics were, of course, only natural on such an

____
[1] Now the Right Hon. G. J. Goschen, M.P.

occasion, but it is the manner which makes the orator ; and though afterwards I heard him speak most effectively, both at Exeter Hall and in the House of Lords, yet he never came up to the grace and fire and dignity of that last speech at Rugby. After this nothing remained but on the following day to take out the horses from his carriage and draw him to the station. I have a confused memory of much shouting, one or two short speeches, and shouting again, and then we turned sorrowfully homeward. On the way back three friends thus discoursed upon the day's proceedings. One said, 'After all, wasn't it a queer way of showing regret to drag him to the station ? It was as if you were glad to be rid of him.' And the second said, 'I wonder what he thought of it himself?' And the third answered, 'Probably he would have said' (to use his own favourite expression) 'there was a good deal to be said on both sides.' And then one of the others said, 'How shall we ever get on without him ?'--with which boylike mixture of jest and earnest, of criticism and affection, we took leave of our old Head-master."

CHAPTER VI.

DEANERY OF CARLISLE—OXFORD UNIVERSITY
COMMISSION.

1849–1853.

FORTY years ago the position of a Dean was regarded as one of dignified retirement rather than of active usefulness, and if his friends now expected any further work from Archibald Tait, it was probably only such work as could be done by a scholar whose active days had come early to a close, and who might, at the best, vary by an occasional pamphlet, or an article in some grave Review, the classical or theological researches of an uneventful life. It is not too much to say that this view of decanal responsibilities was at that time almost universal. In offering to submit his name to the Queen the Prime Minister wrote as follows :—

Lord John Russell to Rev. A. C. Tait.

"PEMBROKE LODGE, RICHMOND, *Oct.* 17, 1849.

"REV. SIR,—Your reputation for learning and sound Divinity have induced me to propose to you to recommend you to the Queen for the vacant Deanery of Carlisle. I should be unwilling to deprive Rugby of the advantage it derives from your superintendence, had I not been assured that your health is scarcely equal to the labour which the direction of a great school imposes. I trust, however, that you would pursue with greater opportunity those studies which have already made you eminent.—I have the honour to be, your obedient servant,   J. RUSSELL."

The congratulations of his friends struck the same

note. Lord Cockburn, in a characteristic letter, advises him thus—

"I see redeeming advantages in your new position. It will give you ease, consequently health, leisure, and, I trust, ambition to embalm yourself worthily in some original work. . . . I know that in point of usefulness and celebrity the crosier has no chance against the pen in the long-run. Don't doze upon the cushion, which is too often the only use that high official cushions are put to. I want you to write a great book on a good subject. Next to this—though they may be united—do, pray, distinguish yourself as the apostle and the type of that common sense which is perhaps more rare than it might be among some Churchmen, though it be the Church's only true buttress."

A somewhat different view was taken by his old friend and pupil, Samuel Waldegrave, whose hopes corresponded so closely with the facts which followed that it is interesting to quote the letter which expressed them :—

"I do hope that in your hands the post of Dean will prove not to be a completely useless office. For, indeed, it seems to me that if a man has judgment and courage, a Dean might prove an invaluable person in a Cathedral town. Not only might he take the lead in the works of mercy and in the business of education, but he might also be the foremost man in preaching the Gospel to the people. But this last will require that he should step out of the beaten path by instituting some such thing as an Evening Service, or a service at some suitable hour for the poor. Often as I walk in the nave of our Cathedral[1] do I wish that our Dean had the health and the inclination to make that large building available for the poor. . . . How good would it be for you to take the lead in such a work—good for the people and good for yourself. . . . Of course I know that you must wait and feel your way, and gain the confidence of others before you act ; but all I wish to impress upon you is the importance of attempting some such thing, and of not being deterred by the numerous lions which the slothful habits of chapters put in the way of any attempt to make Cathedrals of use. I remember well your effort to save the poor College servants, and I cannot but hope that

---

[1] Mr. Waldegrave was at this time a Canon of Salisbury.

you will prove that you have still the same mind, now that you are not a College but a Cathedral Don. Again, may I ask you to forgive me if I suggest another subject for serious thought? Cannot you as Dean be kind to some of the poorer clergy? It is quite painful to see how great people forget our Lord's command to invite those who cannot repay them. At Salisbury, if a Bible or Missionary Meeting bring the poor clergy in, they may (except in one or two cases, as when the Bishop happens to take the chair) seek refreshment at inns. Now, this ought not to be; for great luncheons are provided when the rich come in to infirmary sermons, to which they and their wives and their daughters go, while the utmost a poor clergyman can expect is a dinner for himself occasionally, while his wife and children may go anywhere. Do, my dear Tait, be kind to the poor clergy. And if the Whigs carry you up higher, and make you a Bishop, never forget the advice of a truly affectionate friend, who does long to see you breaking through the miserably unchristian customs of most Cathedral dignitaries, and proving yourself to be one who is willing, not to make a show in society, but by simple-minded preaching of the Gospel, by self-denying simplicity of habits and tastes, by self-humbling endeavours, to show kindness to the poor in all classes, to earn from your Master the name in your Deanery of a good and faithful servant."

The following from a former pupil is one among several of a like sort :[1]—

"To you, sir, more than to any one else do I owe the softening of more than one harsh prejudice against the Church of England, for in you I found a liberality towards those of other sects for which I had never given the members of that Church credit, and I cannot but rejoice that there will now be wider scope for its exercise. There would be but little enmity from Dissenters to the Church had they been treated by the ministers of that Church as you have treated me."

Before he finally resigned the charge of the School he was called upon to meet a somewhat serious attack. *The Guardian* newspaper, in reviewing a book written by Mr. Highton, one of the assistant masters, warned the public in impressive tones against the character of the religious

---

[1] The writer afterwards took Orders in the Church of England.

teaching given at Rugby.   This teaching, it was said, " has undergone of late years a development which would have shocked the celebrated man whose great name still rests upon the School"; and the accusation was expanded at some length.   The article, appearing as it did just when public attention was directed to the School by the vacancy in the Head-mastership, seemed likely to work considerable mischief, and drew from Dr. Tait an immediate and vehement reply.   If it is difficult to recognise in his somewhat fiery letter the man who in later years had a very different way of meeting such onslaughts, it must be remembered that it was less his personal opinions which were challenged than the Christian character of Rugby School.

The Dean of Carlisle to the Editor of " The Guardian."

"SCHOOLHOUSE, RUGBY, 17*th Dec.* 1849.

"SIR,—My attention has been directed to an article in your last number, in which, in terms as direct as it usually suits the purpose of an anonymous calumniator to employ, you speak of Rugby School as having become, under my superintendence, 'a refuge for heresy and latitudinarianism'; and endeavour to represent 'the spirit now paramount in the place' as that of 'a sectarian' and 'a freethinker.'

"However indifferent I and my colleagues may be to any personal attacks on ourselves, I feel that I ought not lightly to allow this great place of religious education to be vilified. . . . As to the words 'sectarian' and 'latitudinarian,' and even 'heretic,' I suppose you use them considerately ; but I believe that coming from you they will be rightly understood by the public to mean simply that the person to whom these epithets are applied differs from your particular views in interpreting the formularies of the Church of England, though he may be supported in his interpretation by the authority of many of the wisest and most pious of those whom the Church delights to honour. . . . I do not intend to enter here on any indication of Mr Highton's opinions as to the particular subject to which you allude. . . . If you really wish to know whether the charge you have made against the School is unfounded, I beg to refer you to such books as I have distinctly recommended in the School, *e.g.* to Mr. Cotton's admirable book of *Prayers and other Helps to Devotion*, or to his short work on Confirmation, or to my own writings, which last is the most obvious source whence a clear idea of the theological teaching of the School may be derived. . . . We who teach here have much to lament in our own unfitness for the difficult part assigned us in the Church : but amidst discouragements it is a great comfort to think of the abundant blessing which God has given, in enabling us to be the instruments of training many young minds in an intelligent and earnest faith.   It is a comfort to us to know how many have looked back with gratitude on their religious training at Rugby, as having been blessed to their usefulness and peace in life, and, I may add, in not a few instances to their calmness in the hour of death, when all the false supports of an artificial system must have failed them.

"Allow me, sir, to beg that you will consider the injustice you have been guilty of, and let me, as a minister of our common Master, remind you that slander of those who are labouring in His Church, if persisted in, is great wickedness.

"I need hardly say that I expect, as an act of justice, that you will publish this in your next number.—I have the honour to be, Sir, your obedient, humble servant,   A. C. TAIT."

To this letter *The Guardian* called attention in a courteous leading article, expressing its cordial admiration for "the energy of Dr. Tait's character, his manly straightforwardness in avowing such opinions as he definitely holds, his generosity, and the tone of honour and morality which he has always endeavoured to maintain both as College Tutor and as a Head-master of Rugby." It proceeded, as was natural, to justify or explain to some extent the language which had been used, urging that, whatever Dr. Tait's own views,

"the opinions of some of his fellow-workers are of the laxest kind.   Is not Germanism (to use a common word) the avowed admiration of some ; Carlylism of others ; Cobdenism of others? Is there any political or religious theory on the so-called liberal side which might not find its supporters there?   Now, this is what we call a Freethinking spirit: not that Dr. Tait is a free-thinker any more than Dr. Arnold was a freethinker, but because the tendency of a system of education conducted by either of them is to a false and irreligious liberality."

Though appointed in October to the Deanery of Carlisle, Dr. Tait acquiesced in the wish of the trustees that he should retain his Head-mastership until the following spring. He went to Carlisle, however, for his formal installation in the Cathedral. The ceremony took place on Saturday, 5th January 1850. Next day he entered in his diary, with much dismay, that though it was Sunday and the feast of the Epiphany, there were only nine or ten communicants. Some days were spent in a vigorous inspection, not only of the Cathedral precincts and all belonging to them, but of the condition generally of the various parishes in the town. He noted the want of order in one of the National Schools, the fact that there was no chaplain at the Infirmary, and many other details of Cathedral and parochial shortcomings; he issued new orders regulating the Minor Canons' interchange of duty and the attendance of the bedesmen at divine service, and returned to Rugby, having given evidence that, in Lord Cockburn's phrase, he at least did not mean to " doze on the decanal cushion."

In the early days of May 1850 they were settled with their three little children [1] in the Deanery of Carlisle. Mrs. Tait used to describe in after years the thankfulness she at this time felt that her husband had, after all, 'escaped alive' from his Rugby work, and her expectations of comparatively quiet and uneventful usefulness in the Border City.

---

[1] Catherine Anna, born March 15, 1846. Mary Susan, born June 20, 1847. Craufurd, born June 22, 1849.

Diary.

"*Carlisle, Sunday, 5th May* 1850.—This is our first Sunday in our new home. What great blessings have we received from God! How graciously has He dealt with me in providing a quiet useful retirement when the bustle and work of Rugby seemed too much for me! O Lord, enable me to use the retirement of this place for my own increase in spiritual-mindedness, by Thy Holy Spirit's help. Enable me to labour faithfully for others. Pardon my sin, and bless to my soul the Holy Communion which I have this day received. Through Jesus Christ. Amen."

At Carlisle he rapidly regained a large measure of his former strength, and though he was never again a robust man, and his heart was always irregular in its action, the work he succeeded in doing during the six Carlisle years was sufficient evidence of his physical energy. In the Cathedral itself there was much to be done ; but his reforms did not greatly commend themselves to all his colleagues, and he had an uphill fight to wage before he carried them. There was special difficulty, for example, about the establishment of an afternoon sermon in the Cathedral on Sundays, although he took the entire responsibility of it upon himself. But he was not easily daunted, and he gained his points one by one.

With returning strength came new calls for its exercise, in what was practically the opening of his public life. He had for many years been known by his Oxford friends as an advocate of wide reforms in the system of the University. His pamphlet on the subject in 1839[1] had attracted considerable attention, and he had continued while at Rugby to give expression to the same views in magazine articles and elsewhere. And the subject was now coming to the front. From his accession to the premiership in 1846 Lord John Russell had been alarming the more conservative among the clergy by his avowed sympathy with what

[1] See p. 71.

they deemed a dangerous liberalism in the Church. True, he had passed the Manchester Bishopric Act in 1847 in the teeth of Radical opposition, but then he had appointed Dr. Prince Lee, an avowed Liberal, to be its first Bishop; and, far worse, he had promoted Dr. Hampden to the See of Hereford, and now the cry was raised that the Universities were themselves to be handed over to the reformer.

On April 25th, 1850, Mr. Heywood, the Radical member for North Lancashire, moved in the House of Commons a long resolution to the effect that all systems of academical education require modification from time to time; that the ancient English and Irish Universities have not made such modifications, and therefore are not promoting as they might the interests of religious and useful learning, and requesting the issue of a Royal Commission of inquiry into the state of the Universities, " with a view to assist in the adaptation of these important institutions to the requirements of modern times."

The last thirty years have so familiarised us with inquiries of this sort that it is difficult now to realise the indignation which such a proposal called forth at the time. The debates upon the resolution were of the highest interest and importance, the motion for inquiry being strenuously resisted as unconstitutional, unnecessary, and altogether mischievous. Mr. Gladstone, Mr. Roundell Palmer, and Sir Robert Inglis were the recognised champions of the party which opposed the appointment of such a commission, and at first it was quite uncertain what course would be taken by Lord John Russell and his Government. Lord John rose early in the debate, and while disclaiming any wish to attack the Universities, and declining therefore to vote for Mr. Heywood's resolution, promised on behalf of the Government that a Royal

Commission should issue. No hint of this intention had transpired, and the announcement took the House of Commons completely by surprise. At the instance of Mr. Roundell Palmer, the debate was adjourned for some months, that the friends of the Universities might consider the situation. Lord John, however, without waiting for a formal decision of the House of Commons, wrote privately to Dean Tait, and to one or two other friends of the Universities, to ask whether they would be willing to serve on such a Commission when appointed.

Tait at once replied as follows :—

The Dean of Carlisle to Lord John Russell.

"CARLISLE, *7th June* 1850.

"MY LORD,—I shall very gladly undertake the duties which your Lordship's letter, received this morning, intimates your wish to impose upon me. The deep attachment which I feel to the University of Oxford will make me most anxious to fulfil zealously and to the utmost of my ability any of the duties that may be assigned to me. I am unwilling to conclude without expressing my conviction, if your Lordship will allow me, that the best friends of Oxford ought to feel deeply indebted to your Lordship for having undertaken and persevered in the appointment of this Commission ; and my belief that, notwithstanding the present symptoms of opposition, the wisdom of the course adopted, as conducive to the best interests of the Universities, will in time be acknowledged by all who are anxious for their welfare."

In a subsequent letter he adds :—

"I fear it is hopeless to expect to secure anything like a cordial reception for the Commission from the Heads of Houses, but I shall be very much surprised if we are not welcomed by those who have much more real influence in Oxford than they ; I mean the most active and intelligent of the College Tutors."

Meantime the opposition gathered strength and volume. The Heads of Houses at Oxford were almost unanimous in their denunciations ; pamphlets and protests were circulated broadcast among the clergy, and the Ecclesiastical and Conservative newspapers joined loudly in the cry. Prince Albert incurred some unpopularity by taking the opposite line, and it became very clear that the Commissioners, when appointed, would have no easy task.

It was a serious matter to oppose the opinion of so great a majority of those entitled to speak officially for the University, and it began to be rumoured that the Government would, at the last moment, give way, probably under the pretext of postponing action for a time. In a series of vigorous letters to *The Times*, signed 'Oxoniensis,' Mr. Goldwin Smith, who was already prominent in Oxford, tried to stimulate their drooping courage, and Dean Tait thought it well to assure Lord John privately that he, at least, was not afraid to go forward.

The Dean of Carlisle to Lord John Russell.

"DEANERY, CARLISLE, 29 *June* 1850.

"MY LORD, . . . The more I consider the state of the University, the more convinced I am that the Commission ought to lose as little time as possible in setting about and completing its work. I shall hold myself in readiness to begin at once, so soon as I hear who my colleagues are to be, and that we are authorised to proceed. The mere publication of such a Report as the Commission is sure to put forth—drawing attention to evils, many of which the several Colleges might alter any day if they pleased, must do much towards the removal of such evils. . . . I confess a careful perusal of the Debates in Parliament only confirmed my opinion as to the wisdom of issuing such a Commission, and the great benefits which the University and the nation may hope for if it rightly discharges its duties . . ."

Thus encouraged, Lord John resolved to stand to his guns. The appointment of a Royal Commission rested of course with the Government, and not with Parliament, but the question was debated at full length in the House of Commons, where Mr. Gladstone, in a long and vehement speech, appealed to the Government not thus

"to fall back upon arbitrary and undefined prerogative, and, regardless of the interests you are sacrificing or the rights you are invading, to resort to an intermeddling and inquisitorial power which is neither supported by history nor law."[1]

In the final division, which was taken on a question of adjournment, the Government were in a majority of 22, and the names of the Commissioners were soon afterwards announced. The Oxford Commissioners were as follows: Dr. Hinds, Bishop of Norwich; Dean Tait of Carlisle; Dr. Jeune, Master of Pembroke;[2] The Rev. H. G. Liddell, Head-master of Westminster;[3] Professor Baden-Powell, Mr. John Lucius Dampier, and the Rev. G. H. S. Johnson.[4] The Secretary of the Commission was the Rev. Arthur P. Stanley, afterwards Dean of Westminster, and the Assistant Secretary was Mr. Goldwin Smith.

These gentlemen were appointed a Commission "for inquiring into the State, Discipline, Studies, and Revenues of the University of Oxford, and of all and singular the Colleges in the said University."

Diary

"*June* 8, 1850.—Yesterday a new means of great usefulness was opened up to me, and a very solemn responsibility. Lord, grant me Thy grace to acquit myself as Thy faithful servant. Make me to labour in all that concerns it with a single eye to Thy glory. May it be Thy good pleasure to employ us as instruments whereby that great seat of learning to which I owe so much may be made more to fulfil its high vocation. Strengthen our hands; let us labour in love and in the spirit of prayer. And

---

[1] *Hansard*, July 18, 1850, p. 1506.
[2] Afterwards Bishop of Peterborough.
[3] Now Dean of Christ Church.
[4] Afterwards Dean of Wells.

meanwhile, Lord, enable me to redouble my efforts here [in Carlisle] for the good of souls; direct me in a wise course; assist me this day in preparing to preach to-morrow. Direct us to wise and energetic efforts amongst the poor."

The Commissioners met for the first time on October 19th, 1850. Their place of meeting was the Prime Minister's own house in Downing Street. They at once issued respectful circulars to the University authorities and others, asking for statistical information of various kinds. Most of those addressed declined absolutely to render any such assistance to a Commission of which they disapproved; but, from many of those best qualified to give information and advice, the inquiry met, as Dr. Tait had anticipated, with a civil response; and, in the opinion even of hostile critics, the Commissioners proved themselves to have steered wisely at the outset.[1] Mrs. Tait had naturally shared the almost unanimous apprehensions of those with whose opinions on Church questions she was in personal sympathy, and it was with trembling that she saw her husband enter upon so perilous a task. He writes repeatedly to reassure her :—

"DEAREST WIFE,—I have thought a great deal of what you said the last morning. I am sure we are all working here with a deep feeling of the importance of what is intrusted to us, and I cannot think that the feeling you expressed is well founded."

His Diary has daily such entries as the following :

"O Lord, bless and guide this University Commission, on which we have now fully entered. May we seek Thy glory with a single eye, through Jesus Christ our Lord. Amen."

And again :

"Grant me, O Lord, at the Commission a more quiet and conciliatory spirit; a greater desire to be kind to all; a greater feeling of the deep responsibility of the work we have in hand.

[1] See, e.g. the *Guardian*, Dec. 4, 1850.

Lord, make me more to realise that in this too I have Thy work to do. Give me more of a spiritual mind, for Jesus Christ's sake."

In his letters to Mrs. Tait he recounts step by step the progress of their work :—

"31*st October* 1850.— . . . To-day we received several important letters. A thundering one from the Bishop of Exeter,[1] declaring that he would oppose us to the death, was far outweighed by the Archbishop of Canterbury's letter promising to help us to the utmost. The Duke of Wellington merely acknowledged our letter."

During the following spring and summer they had to face incessant opposition. A fresh attempt was made to test the legality of the Commission, and four eminent lawyers[2] on a ' case ' laid before them by the University formally pronounced their opinion " that the Commission

---

[1] This letter, which may be taken as a specimen of the kind of opposition which the Commissioners had to face, is as follows :—

"BISHOPSTOWE, *October* 30, 1850.

"MY LORD,—I yesterday had the honour of receiving a letter from you 'on the part of Her Majesty's Commissioners.' . . . I had hoped to be spared the necessity of saying anything on the subject of this Commission ; but thus called upon officially to become a party in the execution of it, I should be guilty of a culpable dereliction of my duty if I were to forbear expressing my sentiments. . . . I cannot see without the deepest concern and astonishment the name of our present gracious Sovereign used by her advisers to 'authorise and empower' your Lordship and your colleagues to institute an inquisition which no precedent could justify, and which, . . . as relates to the venerable bodies which are now concerned, has had absolutely no parallel since the fatal attempt of King James II. to subject them to his unhallowed control. It is under the solemn conviction that your Lordship, and the other eminent persons who have consented to act on the Commission, have no right whatever to call before you any members of the College of which I am Visitor, . . . that I shall require the Rector, Fellows, and other members to weigh well all the injunctions of their Statutes before they can feel themselves at liberty to testify any deference to your authority. Especially I shall enjoin them, under the sacred obligation of their oaths, to beware how they permit themselves to answer any inquiries, or to accept any directions or interference whatsoever which may trench upon that visitatorial authority which their Statutes, under the known law of the land, have intrusted solely to the Bishop of this See. . . . Your Lordship's most obedient servant,   H. EXETER."

(Vide *Report*, Appendix B, p. 7.)

[2] G. J. Turner, Richard Bethell, Henry S. Keating, J. R. Kenyon. On

is not constitutional or legal, or such as the University or its members are bound to obey." In respect to this opinion a characteristic memorandum was drawn up by Dean Tait, who, while disclaiming any intention to dispute the lawyers' technical arguments, drew attention to their deliberate avoidance of the term 'illegal,' and pointed out that their expression '*not legal*' simply meant that the Commission, as all were aware, possessed no compulsory powers.

"It will be found that the much-vaunted opinion leaves the Commission where it found it. The Hebdomadal Board has now, as it has had all along, only one point to settle, namely, 'Does it choose to answer the questions of the Commissioners, though not compelled to do so? Will it act in the conciliatory spirit adopted at Cambridge, or resist? Will the Board assist a friendly Royal Commission, or will it, by throwing impediments in the way, do what it can to ensure the appointment of an unfriendly Parliamentary Commission, whose powers will be compulsory?' The Commission itself is very little interested (except for the regard which its members entertain for the University) in the way in which the Board settles this question. Nay, we should not be surprised if the Report appears before the Hebdomadal Board can make up its mind."

The Hebdomadal Board, however, invoked the aid of the Convocation of the University, and on May 21st, 1851, a petition to the Crown was adopted by 249 votes against 105, praying Her Majesty that Her Commission be "forthwith revoked and cancelled" as "unconstitutional and illegal."

The Commissioners meanwhile persevered steadily with their task, and were, as they hoped, drawing their labours to a close, when, on February 23d, 1852, Lord John Russell's Government was defeated, and Lord

the other hand, the Commission was declared by the law officers of the Crown not to be " in any respect illegal or unconstitutional." (Vide *Report*, Appendix B, pp. 25-33.)

Derby became Prime Minister. Both the friends and the foes of the Commission believed that Lord Derby's accession might very possibly be its death-blow, and, at the least, that its work must now be carried on under great disadvantages. The following are extracts from Dean Tait's letters to his wife :—

"*Friday, 27th February* 1852.—Yesterday the Bishop of Norwich called on Lord John to ask what ought to be done. He first said Lord Derby would extinguish us ; then, on consideration, that he dared not, for that he (Lord John) and his friends would be down upon him. He advised that we should not meet at Downing Street to-day, as Lord Derby would be coming into the house, and it might have an unpleasant air to take possession of his room without his leave. The Bishop wrote a note to Lord Derby requesting an interview to-morrow."

"*Saturday, 28th Feb.* 1852.—The Bishop saw Lord Derby at 2 o'clock. Lord D. had not an idea for what purpose the Bishop sought the interview ; and when the Bishop, with proper apologies for intruding at such a time, etc., said that he had come on the part of the Oxford Commission, to ask whether they might continue to hold their meetings as heretofore in Downing Street, he was a little taken aback, and said he would take time to consider. The Bishop (canny old boy) replied that he was very sorry to intrude, but what was to be done ? Here were the members of the Commission all in town—one come from Carlisle—and this by arrangements made before the change of Government was contemplated ; what were they to do ? *Lord D.*—'Where are they meeting at present ?' *The Bp.*—'Oh, they are holding no meeting ; they wait your Lordship's answer.' *Lord D.*—'Where is the room in Downing Street ?' The Bishop described it, and Lord Derby ended by saying there was no reason why we should not meet as usual. Without the Bishop's skilful diplomacy I doubt whether Lord Derby would not have put us off, and then, in the interval, have been got hold of by the Oxford people and persuaded to refuse. Now he is committed to a certain extent, and we shall hold our own. And depend upon it, there is more chance now than ever of a vigorous measure of University reform, for Lord John and his friends will urge it in opposition, which they could not have done in power. So much for our prospects.

. . . As regards the political world, last night's display on the part of Lord Derby seems to be regarded as a proof that he cannot keep his ground. He said in plain English that he would restore protection if he could get a majority in favour of it, but not propose it if he could not. This is simply to disgust both parties. The farmers will clamour and not be satisfied at his holding it back ; and the other parties—Whig, Peelite, and Radical—will be thoroughly alarmed by the prospect of his threatening protection in the distance."

"*Draper's Hotel, Sackville Street, Sunday, 29th Feby.* 1852.— . . . This afternoon I went as usual to Lincoln's Inn and heard Maurice. He is preaching a course of sermons on the Prophets —to-day on Hosea. He dwelt very forcibly on the way in which his family distress—from the misconduct of his wife—was an emblem to him of God's feelings with regard to Israel, and how the distress also was a preparation to him, as all sufferings even of the most harassing kind may be, for his great office. I walked home with Wood. . . . He is now a barrister, and tells me that he looks forward all the week to these sermons of Maurice's on the Sunday. . . . I think I hardly did justice to Lord Derby's speech in my letter yesterday—I was speaking only of its political aspect—for certainly it had a good tone in the end of it, which it is very pleasant to find in statesmen. He is too straightforward a character to assume what he does not feel, and he certainly spoke very pleasingly of the deep responsibilities which had come to him. It is a pity that so fine a fellow should have put himself at the head of so hopeless a movement, and not have stuck to his early opinions. A good man in power may do much if he understands the feelings and wants of the age, but he is simply mischievous if he is vainly trying to thwart them instead of giving them a right direction."

The following reference possesses an interest of its own. Rich additions were to be made both to the associations and to the beauty of Lambeth Palace Chapel before the close of Archibald Tait's connection with it, thirty years later.

"*March* 8, 1851.—I enjoyed dining at Lambeth yesterday. There was no one present but the family, and Johnson, who was staying in the house. The Archbishop is a very kind, unaffected old man. Before I left in the evening we all went into the chapel,—the chapel where a long line of Bishops for many hundred years has, as you know, been consecrated—and had quiet family prayers, the Archbishop himself officiating."

At last on April 27th, 1852, the Commissioners issued their Report, perhaps, from a literary point of view, the most remarkable Blue-book of our time. Arthur Stanley had thrown himself with characteristic energy into the compilation of its historical records,[1] and the result was a masterly volume of the highest public interest and importance. Dean Tait was recognised in the letters of his brother Commissioners as largely responsible for its final shape, and especially for the form of its practical recommendations. One at least of them was indignant at the 'conservative spirit' he had shown. "I am almost tempted to say that I will not consent to it. I am reduced to the difficulty of signing what I dislike . . . or of making myself an ass by not signing. It will not take much to make me give up the whole concern." He is conciliated, however, by Tait's reply, and writes again : "You know my principle is to say what I think, and so, being very angry with you, I said so. But I am sorry, and you have had an opportunity of showing your better temper, for which I thank you."

The voluminous and often argumentative character of the Report renders it singularly difficult to give a satisfactory abstract of its recommendations, dealing, as they do, with every department of the University. But the subject is connected so closely with the life of Archibald Tait that it cannot be entirely passed over. Broadly speaking, the aim of the Commissioners was to popularise the University ; first by giving to its governing

---

[1] These include an elaborate paper by Mr. Goldwin Smith on the History of the Colleges and Halls of Oxford.

body a quasi-representative character, and secondly (to quote the words of the Report) by opening the University " to a much larger and poorer class than that from which the students are at present almost entirely taken."   Dealing first with the Constitution, they recommended the revival, with certain modifications, of the ancient ' House of Congregation,' once a reality, but now for some two centuries a mere shadow,[1]—its former executive functions having long been discharged, in a more or less perfunctory manner, by the small and irresponsible Hebdomadal Board, consisting merely of the Heads of Houses and the Proctors.   Under this proposed scheme the revived ' Congregation' was again to become practically the legislative body of the University, and to consist of about one hundred members, representing the whole teaching staff at work in Oxford.

In this teaching staff they suggested large and fundamental changes.   They pointed out that the instruction of the undergraduates had practically passed from the hands of the Professors recognised by the statutes of the University into the hands of College and private tutors. Though certain individual Professors, such as Arnold, had succeeded in gathering round them large numbers of students, professorial teaching had practically ceased. The Commissioners pointed out the loss suffered both by Oxford and the country at large " from the absence of a body of learned men devoting their lives to the cultivation of science and to the direction of Academical education ; " and gave it as their opinion that " for any healthy and complete scheme of University reform it will be necessary to reconstruct the professorial system, to procure for

---

[1] The House of Congregation, as it existed in 1850, is described in the *Report*, p. 10, as meeting " only for the purpose of hearing measures proposed which it cannot discuss, of conferring degrees to which candidates are already entitled, and of granting dispensations which are never refused."

the Professors ample endowments, to raise them to an important position in the University, and to call to their aid a body of younger men under the name of Lecturers."

While recognising the importance of that connection with the Church of England to which, they said, "the University mainly owes its greatness," they stated the many obvious objections to the existing system under which holders of fellowships were obliged to take Holy Orders, and urged that this obligation should be very largely relaxed. Such a relaxation did not appear to them likely to make a very material change in the clerical character of the teaching staff; they thought it probable that "if the rule were abrogated in all the colleges, the great bulk of the resident teachers would after all remain clerical," and they claimed that the Church, no less than the nation, would be the gainer by the change. "If it be desirable that moderation and a spirit in harmony with the institutions of the country should prevail among the ministers of the English Church, it is important that the zeal of their instructors in its chief seminary should be tempered by the calmer judgment of lay colleagues, who would themselves imbibe the moral and religious tone of the clerical circle in which they lived."

In the effort to retain men of ability in the service of the University, they made an advance in the direction of more recent legislation, by recommending that the Professors and other University teachers should be allowed, though married, to share in the emoluments of College fellowships.

In addition to these important constitutional changes, the Commissioners recommended the removal of many of the restrictive conditions, local and other, which fettered the ordinary candidature for College scholarships and fellowships. They urged the total abolition of the provisions as to 'gentlemen-commoners,' 'Bible-clerks,' and others, which, by a series of artificial distinctions, had tended to emphasise differences of rank and wealth in a manner equally harmful to the rich and to the poor. But the most important, in Dean Tait's opinion, of all their recommendations was the suggestion that facilities should immediately be given for the admission to the University of a great body of 'unattached students,' who, while obtaining the advantages of an Oxford education, should yet be spared many of the expenses connected, apparently of necessity, with collegiate life.[1] On the great question of religious tests the Commissioners found themselves precluded, by the terms of their appointment, from giving any formal recommendation ; but they expressed an emphatic opinion "that the imposition of subscription, in the manner in which it is now imposed in the University of Oxford, habituates the mind to give a careless assent to truths which it has never considered, and naturally leads to sophistry in the interpretation of solemn obligations."[2]

Dean Tait had evidently desired that the Commissioners should enter more fully into the whole question of the oaths imposed by Colleges upon their members. It was precisely one of those subjects which stirred his serious and straightforward spirit, and he was unable to share the unconcern with which some of his colleagues regarded it. The Tutors' protest against Tract XC., which he had drawn up ten years before, had practically turned upon a question of subscription, and the facts which the inquiries of the Commissioners brought to light as to the imposition of College Oaths appeared to him to be of the

---

[1] Not till sixteen years later (in 1868) did this plan take practical shape in Oxford. When it did so, under the wise auspices of the present Dean of Winchester, the detailed arrangements corresponded almost precisely with the suggestions made by the Commissioners of 1852.

[2] *Report*, p. 56.

highest moral importance.   Accordingly, he drafted a careful paper for insertion in the Report, protesting vehemently against the reckless imposition of oaths, in which the solemnity of the form of invocation contrasted painfully, and even ludicrously, with their now antiquated and unmeaning substance.[1]

"Why," he asked, "should a man be forced solemnly to call the Holy Trinity to witness that he will obey statutes which he knows to be almost entirely abrogated? To require this is surely to trifle with things most sacred. Any one who reads carefully the oaths required by some of our College statutes will grant that they are relics of a barbarous and irreligious state of society, and these awful denunciations will strongly remind him of the device by which William of Normandy tried to entrap unawares the superstitious conscience of his guest whom he thought neither promise nor common oath could bind. Some at least of the College oaths seem to be constructed on this principle of terrifying into superstitious obedience those whose consciences were not to be trusted. . . . These College oaths are often profane ; they are always liable to be misunderstood, and they are apt to strain and destroy the fineness of the conscience. . . . We earnestly recommend that the Legislature declare the imposition of such oaths to be altogether illegal."

A few sentences from the Dean's paper were inserted by the Commissioners in their Report,[2] but they seem to have decided that the great question of oaths, religious tests, and subscription in all its branches, lay outside the terms of their Commission, and that any attempt on their part to deal with it would divert attention from the subjects more immediately before them. Dean Tait accordingly was forced to content himself with embodying

---

[1] As examples of such oaths the Dean instances the obligation in some Colleges upon a newly elected fellow to swear, "under the pain of anathema and the wrath of Almighty God, that he will always wear a ' lilliput ' (whatever that may be), and that he will never walk abroad in the fields without having another fellow as his companion."

[2] Pp. 146, 147.

his paper in a condensed form in an article which he contributed two years later to the *Edinburgh Review*, on the general subject of educational legislation.[1]

The whole tenor of the Report was in the direction of throwing the University doors more widely open ; and when Archbishop Tait, in 1876, rose in the House of Lords to move a resolution in favour of a yet further extension of the same principle, he was able to describe his motion as the natural and legitimate sequel of the Report for which he had himself been so largely responsible a quarter of a century before. The interest aroused by its publication was immense, and voluminous as it was,[2] the first edition was sold out in a few days. The Edinburgh Reviewer described it as "a truly remarkable document, and one which is destined, we are persuaded, to form an era in the constitutional history of this country." As soon as it was in circulation, letters poured in upon Dean Tait, congratulating him upon a result which was ascribed in no small degree to the part he had himself taken in the work of the Commission.

The constant journeys between Carlisle and London—journeys very much more tedious then than now—and the immense labour which the Commission had involved, had again told seriously upon his health, and he was glad to return to a quieter and less interrupted life. The work of inaugurating University Reforms had, for the present, passed from the hands of Royal Commissioners into those of politicians ; and Dean Tait's hope was that Mr. Gladstone, notwithstanding his objection to the mode in which the inquiry had been instituted, might now, as Member for the University, be induced to support in Parliament the recommendation of the Commissioners.

---

[1] Vol. xcix. pp. 158, etc.

[2] The actual Report, apart from its immense appendices, occupies 260 closely-printed foolscap pages.

He accordingly wrote to Mr. Coleridge,[1] asking him to use his influence with Mr. Gladstone in this direction. Mr. Gladstone replied very fully, declining to pledge himself "either in regard to University Reform or to any other subject."

"Practically," he continued, "I much doubt whether public declarations of opinion on such questions by a burgess of the University would tend to promote their own purposes : whether they would not perhaps generate a positive reaction: whether they would not most probably be found inconsistent with that respect and deference, which in the face of the world he is bound most studiously to cherish, especially towards the resident body charged with the teaching and discipline of the place. . . . I consider that, subject to the restraints imposed by the law of society, a burgess of the University becomes a confidential adviser of the resident body in particular. It is his duty to point out to them the dangers of which his position enables him to perceive the approach, and not to be content merely to deal with those which have already arrived, but to make provision, as far as he can, for the future. . . . As to my opinions, I will say at present no more than this. To the principles of Oxford education I am deeply, and I think immovably, attached, while it is my earnest and ardent desire to see all the great power and resources made available in the highest possible degree, according to these principles, for the proper purposes. I am much obliged to the Dean for the frankness with which he writes, and I hope this letter will not appear to be written with any intention of shutting the door against further inquiries."

Mr. Coleridge sent this letter to the Dean, and appended to it a request that in view of the General Election which was then approaching he would allow his name to be placed on Mr. Gladstone's Election Committee. The Dean's reply may be quoted in full, as bearing on his political and ecclesiastical position at the time.

The Dean of Carlisle to Mr. J. D. Coleridge.

"DEANERY, CARLISLE, 25*th May* 1852.

"MY DEAR COLERIDGE,—I have delayed to answer your letter

---

[1] Now Lord Chief-Justice of England.

for three days, that I might fully consider both it and Mr. Gladstone's note, which you kindly enclose. I can understand the difficulty which a person in Mr. Gladstone's position must find in speaking very explicitly as to University Reform, but I fully believe from the tone both of his note and of yours that he is not less anxious now than I have understood him to be formerly for the extension of the University, and the more efficient development of its system. I believe, myself, that with his great influence he might, with perfect propriety, and with every prospect of extensive usefulness, publicly take the initiative in those particular measures of Reform, in which I feel no doubt he would be supported by the 'Liberal' party in the University, as well as by those whose opinions more nearly resemble his own. But no one can judge for another of the difficulties which such a position as Mr. Gladstone occupies must involve. For myself, I am quite ready to vote for Mr. Gladstone again as at the last election, and to do my best to induce any friends whom I can influence to the same course, trusting that opportunities will arise when he may be able to use the weight of his influence to advance an efficient improvement of the University system, and feeling confident also, that in the ordinary political topics of the day he will more adequately represent the opinions held by myself, and those with whom I am in the habit of acting, than any candidate who is likely to be brought forward against him. These feelings are quite enough to justify me in giving my vote for a candidate whom, however much I differ from him, I acknowledge to be so great an ornament to the University. But it would be going a good deal further to have my name placed on his committee. I think on mature consideration that I could not with propriety do this, feeling that on principles of the greatest importance I differ so very widely from him.

"You may therefore reckon on my vote if there is a contest, and are at liberty to say so to any one whom it may concern; but my name on the committee would be out of place, and, seeing the many other points on which I differ, could only have been justified by some more public declaration of approval of our scheme of University Reform than circumstances allowed Mr. Gladstone to make.—Believe me to be, my dear Coleridge, yours most truly,   "A. C. Tait."

The election took place in July, and after a sharp contest Mr. Gladstone was returned.[1]   A few months later he accepted office as Chancellor of the Exchequer in Lord Aberdeen's 'Coalition Ministry,' and his re-election was fiercely opposed by many of his former friends, who distrusted and feared his Whig colleagues, especially Lord John Russell and Lord Lansdowne.   His opponent, Mr. Dudley Perceval, was proposed by Archdeacon Denison, who had six months before been a member of Mr. Gladstone's committee.[2]   Dean Tait, on the other hand, wrote as follows :—

The Dean of Carlisle to Mr. G. Portal.

"DEANERY, CARLISLE, *8th January* 1853.

"MY DEAR PORTAL,—I fully intend to go up to Oxford and vote for Mr. Gladstone : I have only delayed from the impossibility of my leaving this place during the earlier days of the poll. In answer to your request that my name may appear on the committee, I beg to state that if the committee think my name can be of any use it is at their service, as I consider Mr. Gladstone's having joined a Liberal Government with Lord John Russell and Lord Lansdowne as a sufficient guarantee for the principles on which he is to act in office.   I must request that this letter be read to the committee before my name is added to the list.—I remain, yours faithfully,   A. C. TAIT."

His hope that Mr. Gladstone, notwithstanding his opposition to the appointment of the Royal Commissioners, would in the end support their recommendations, was amply justified in the result.   Lord Aberdeen's Government, in its second year of office, introduced a sweeping measure of University Reform, based almost entirely upon the Report of the Royal Commission, and its champion and spokesman in the House of Commons was Mr.

---

[1] The numbers were as follows :—Sir R. Inglis, 1368 ; Mr. Gladstone, 1108 ; Dr. Marsham, 758.

[2] See the account given in Archdeacon Denison's *Notes of My Life*, pp. 101, etc.

Gladstone. One incident in the debate, though unconnected with the subject of this book, may be worth recalling upon other grounds, at a time when the two men concerned in it have been the alternate Prime Ministers of England. The brilliant maiden speech of Lord Robert Cecil, in fiery opposition to the Bill, drew the following eulogy from Mr. Gladstone :—

"It has been no common gratification to me to listen to-night to the noble Lord, whose first efforts, rich with future promise, indicate that there still issue forth from the maternal bosom of that University men who in the first days of their career give earnest of what they may afterwards accomplish for their country."[1]

After a somewhat stormy passage through Parliament, the Bill passed into law on the 7th August 1854, to the infinite satisfaction of Dean Tait, who had never wavered for an hour in its support.

[1] *Hansard*, April 7, 1854, page 754.

CHAPTER VII.

HIS constant journeys to London as a University Commissioner had hitherto interfered greatly with the due progress of all the work he had planned at Carlisle. Now that he was released from these interruptions he threw himself into his local duties with characteristic energy.

Besides such efforts as have been already referred to for infusing new life into the somewhat sleepy parishes and schools of Carlisle, and for promoting a better attendance at the Cathedral services, he was intent upon two larger undertakings—the entire re-organisation of the Capitular revenues under the scheme which had just been approved in Parliament, and the 'restoration' of the fabric of the Cathedral itself. With reference to each of these a few words seem to be necessary.

It would be difficult, without sacrificing either accuracy or clearness, to describe the complicated and technical legislation which was at that time transforming the whole tenure of Church property in England. It is scarcely too much to say that the system upon which the lands belonging to Cathedral bodies, and other ecclesiastical corporations, had for many generations been managed, was one which would not have been tolerated in any other institution. The estates were usually leased by these corporations either for terms of years, or for a certain number of 'lives,' whose duration was of course uncertain. The rents paid under these leases were, in most cases, of merely nominal amount, but the conditions of tenure involved the payment by the lessees from time to time, and at necessarily uncertain dates, of a 'fine,' which sometimes amounted to several thousands of pounds; such fines going into the pockets of the then members of the Capitular bodies, and constituting one of the main sources of their revenue. Neither owners nor tenants were able, under this mischievous and complicated system, to calculate with any accuracy their future income or probable outgoings. And yet it was practically impossible for them, in the absence of powers of sale and purchase, to bring the wasteful process to a close.

The great 'Cathedral Acts,' the first of which was passed in 1840, provided for the gradual transfer to the Ecclesiastical Commission of portions at least of the estates hitherto belonging to the Cathedral bodies. The Commissioners steadfastly refused to renew 'on fine' the beneficial lease of any property which thus came under their control, and in 1851 another Act of Parliament was passed,[1] the outcome of much discussion, "to facilitate the management and improvement of Episcopal and Capitular estates." It would be impossible, without wearisome and technical details, to enter fully into the origin and results of that important Act. Suffice it to say that it afforded a process whereby the property belonging to the Cathedral Corporations could be economically and advantageously administered for the benefit alike of the tenants, the chapters, and the Church at large. But the changes involved in adopting the new system were considerable, and could not be applied without difficulty. They involved much laborious, responsible, and costly work on the part of the chapters, and, like other measures of Church reform,

---

[1] 14 and 15 Vict. cap. 104.

they were from the first keenly opposed by not a few of those concerned. It thus happened that many Cathedrals hesitated long before taking the voluntary steps necessary for subjecting themselves to the new arrangements. Dean Tait felt no such timidity. In 1852—within a year, that is, after the passing of the Act—the example of forward movement was set by the two Cathedrals of Carlisle and York, and it has since then been generally followed. The estates were transferred *en bloc* to the Ecclesiastical Commission, which was to hold them for a time, and to give a fixed annuity to the Cathedral body. It thus became practicable for the Commissioners to apply to the transferred estates a process of enfranchisement (whether by sale or purchase) which would substitute for the baneful system of leaseholds renewable on fine a new and un-fettered freehold tenure. In other words, either the Commissioners or the leaseholders might thus become the absolute owners of the property, the other party receiving in each case the money-equivalent of his interest. It is obvious how much responsible and difficult work was involved in the effecting of such arrangements. In the case of Carlisle, the negotiations were intricate and of portentous length ; and although the Dean found them extremely irksome at the time, he used to maintain that the experience he had gained proved afterwards to be of the greatest service to him when, as Bishop of London, he became one of the members of the Estates Committee of the Ecclesiastical Commissioners, and had to take part in similar transactions with respect to some thirteen other Cathedrals.

In the Chapter of Carlisle strong opposition was raised to the "innovation" of substituting a fixed payment for the former system of fines upon renewal, and the Dean had great difficulty in effecting his purpose.

Diary.

"This day in Chapter I was betrayed into unseemly anger. O Lord, forgive me! I will not let the sun go down upon my anger. O Lord, give me self-denial as a Christian, and more regard for the feelings of others, through Jesus Christ."

And again, a few days later :

"At times I feel greatly depressed here by the uncongenial spirits amongst whom I am thrown. But, O Lord, give me to understand that nothing great was ever done without effort, and amidst much opposition. Lord, give me wisdom, zeal, love, and make me faithful in every work. This day we have been engaged in very important business as to the transfer of our estates to the Commissioners. Guide us, O Lord. May all the matter redound to Thy glory. We hope to rebuild our Cathedral, and thus infuse a love for the outward house of God."

In this hope he was not disappointed. Under the direction of Mr. Christian as architect, the restoration of the very dilapidated Cathedral was taken in hand at once. The Ecclesiastical Commissioners had arranged, in connection with the transfer of the estates, that £15,000 should be expended on the Cathedral fabric. The roof was entirely rebuilt ; a new and rich doorway was opened in the south transept ; and the east wall and windows, which had been in a disgraceful state, were renewed at great cost ; while other necessary changes of structure and arrangement were effected in various parts of the building. During the progress of these works he was able, to his great satisfaction, to reside more continuously than had at first been possible, and the record of his multifarious labour, in matters great and small, for the good of Carlisle and its inhabitants, stands in strange contrast to what would at that time have been usually deemed appropriate to the position of a Cathedral dignitary. The home was a very bright and happy one, and there seems by universal testimony to have been something strangely attractive—not to their parents only, but even to the least emotional of guests or strangers—in the group of little daughters who made music and sunshine in the old Deanery.

At the same time it may be doubted whether either the Dean or Mrs. Tait ever thoroughly enjoyed their Carlisle life. To a mind like his, which at all times found its pleasure rather in the action and intercourse of life than in close study or retirement, Carlisle presented a very marked contrast to either Rugby or Oxford. Had he anticipated after his Rugby illness that his health would ever again be what it soon became, it is probable that he would have declined the Deanery. But once there he set himself with determination to face the task before him. A few extracts, taken almost at random from the diaries and letters of those years, will perhaps give a truer picture than even the reminiscences of friends can furnish.

Diary.

"*Saturday Evening*, 31*st August* 1850.—To-day is the meeting of Rugby. Seeing Shairp pass in the express, I have thought much of that dear place. O, my God, grant a blessing on it, and on all who labour in it. How strange it seems to be sitting here while so many are hurrying up there. The place that knew me knows me no more. . . . Chalmers' Life, which I have been reading to-night, reminded me forcibly of the great and holy work that lies upon me here. Arnold's, which I have also been reading, recalls how little I was able to do at Rugby as he did it. But, without greater vigour than for the last two years I have possessed, I could not have hoped to improve the system there, and therefore I must think that my work there was better ended. Certainly in this place, if God give me grace, and I work in the spirit of prayer, I am able to do what has not been done before. Lord, strengthen me for this great work. This Cathedral has never been what it ought to be. At Rugby I came to a system which had been fully and ably and energetically worked for many years. Here I come to a system which is dead and powerless, but where there is every facility for revivification, if only I am regular and faithful. By my sermons, by schools, by visiting the poor—especially the sick and dying—by being earnest and energetic in assisting those around to undertake any good works. Lord, give me grace so to labour."

"*Saturday, 21st Dec.* 1850.—My birthday; I am 39. How very long a portion of my life have I lived. How little have I done, especially in that greatest of all works for me, that which goes on within my own soul. How overwhelming is the thought of the deep responsibilities through which I have passed. How many scenes of my life are gone like dreams in the night—each bearing with it a thousand opportunities of serving God which can never return; each having its recollection of persons into whose society I was thrown, whom I can never meet again this side the grave, or whom circumstances have made it now very difficult for me to influence.

"My life at school, at Glasgow, as an undergraduate, as a Fellow, at Rugby—what thoughts of God's mercy and of my neglect crowd into each; and, at Rugby especially, what wonderful interests and what great warnings from God. The time of the year is fast approaching which brings back the recollection of my terrible illness. O Lord, how great was Thy mercy in that judgment. And now what duties are there here. Teach me, Lord, to labour in them faithfully. Keep me near to Thee through Jesus Christ."

"*Sunday Afternoon, Decr.* 22, 1850.—I have preached twice, and visited the workhouse. I have been very busy for others. Lord grant that the growth of holiness in my own soul may keep pace with my activity for others. The difficulty for such a character as mine is inward holiness. Outward activity comes naturally. Lord replenish me with the grace of Thy Holy Spirit. O Lord, give me holy thoughts. May I have no desire but to glorify Thee."

"*Christmas Eve,* 1850.—Preparation for the Lord's Supper to-morrow. . . .

"O Lord, help me by Thy Holy Sacrament, for Christ's sake."

"*Saturday, 28th Decr.*—This day I have had pain in the heart, evidently intended to remind me that my health is still precarious. Lord, bless to my soul the thoughts which this calls up. . . . Am I growing more meet for Thy presence? . . . I am visiting what seem to be three deathbeds. What a difference between the three! . . . O God, save me from the danger of being made callous by the sight of so much misery as is brought before me in this town."

And again :

"I have been summoned to-day to attend a man apparently dying; one of our Cathedral almsmen, very ignorant and self-satisfied. What am I to do to get a better hold over those who are thus united to the Church?"

"*Angel Inn, Oxford, Sunday Evening, Feb.* 9, 1851.—How greatly I enjoy these visits to Oxford. At this very time of year, twenty-one years ago, I stood in this inn when I came up to enter as a freshman. Lord, with what mercies hast Thou surrounded me since then. This Sunday has passed, not without serious thought, but yet with too little. I have heard Dr. Pusey preach. The exhortation to calmness and love with which he ended was very good." . . .

"*Ash Wednesday, 5th March* 1851.—Ash Wednesday has been a solemn day to me now for many years. I began to mark it distinctly at Oxford, and tried there to spend it in recollection and prayer. Six years ago Mary[1] was buried on Ash Wednesday. Three years ago I lay at the point of death on Ash Wednesday. I have to-day been talking with my dearest wife of that solemn time. No one had any hope that I could live. O Lord, Thou hast been exceeding gracious to me. And now let me ask myself very solemnly whether my soul has received a blessing. I will consider my besetting sins. . . . I will now go through the Penitential Liturgy from Jeremy Taylor. O Lord, solemnise my mind in these prayers. Keep me from wandering, for Jesus Christ's sake. . . ."

"*Sunday Evening, Feb.* 20 [1853].—I have been reading one of Arnold's travelling journals, and was much touched by the description of the towers, and old trees, and green turf of Rugby as he whirled past from Fox How to Dover. . . . In this town where my lot is now cast, there is enough of the ruggedness of life in the misery of the wretched classes round me to fill me

---

[1] Mrs. John Tait, sister-in-law of A. C. T.

with melancholy views of life. It would be pleasing, doubtless, to have some home embosomed in trees, with beautiful mountain views, where my children might grow up; and such a place to rest in for a few months in each year would be a great blessing. But though there is no beauty to soothe, there is something good for the soul in the stern reality of life which such a town as this presents; poverty and vice are here before me in their naked deformity. This sight can only be good for us if we look at it with real Christian feelings. Otherwise it only hardens and debases."

"*Wednesday, 9th March* 1853.—I have not been well for the last day or two. To-night while Mr. Page[1] was with me I fainted quite away. I was standing, and knew nothing till, after about a minute's insensibility, I found myself lying on the floor with Mr. Page unloosing my neckcloth. In the midst of life how near is death; for syncope, while it lasts, is death. O God, make me ready. My dear mother died in a faint. She was as little expecting death as I this evening. I do not fear death, I trust, because I know that my Redeemer liveth."

"*Sept.* 16, 1853.—I have visited the districts of the town to-day in anticipation of the cholera breaking out.[2] Lord make us ready for any sudden call."

"*Sunday, Sept. 18th.* — In the midst of the quiet of this time of waiting, expecting daily that pestilence will visit us, O Lord teach us to improve the time. Thou knowest what is best for us."

"*Sunday Evening, 9th Oct.* 1853.—I am here [Deanery] to-day alone. I have been reading, since church, Goulburn's sermon, 'The swelling of the Jordan.' . . . The fact that our first case of Asiatic cholera has proved fatal, and that the man was buried early this morning in St. Cuthbert's Churchyard, calls us with loud voice to be ready."

"*Sunday, 16th Oct.*—I have preached three times to-day. Lord impress the truths I have preached on my own soul. . . . I have often in my thoughts the idea that I may soon die. My many bodily ailments—though not perhaps serious—seem to show a very weakly constitution shattered by illness. Whether Thou callest me soon or late, make me ready; and bless, O bless my dear wife and children."

----

[1] The Doctor.   [2] It was raging at Newcastle and elsewhere.

It may be well to quote one or two letters of this period, showing his disinclination to identify himself with some of the religious movements then rife, movements undertaken with the view of uniting in a common cause the scattered efforts of various denominations, but tending, as he thought, to limit practically the legitimate width of the Church of England, and to narrow the sympathies of her members.

The strange agitation raised in 1850 and 1851 by what was known as 'The Papal Aggression' took shape, not only in Lord John Russell's panic-stricken 'Ecclesiastical Titles Act,' but in the formation of various societies of an anti-Roman character, for the enforcement or exposition of this or that department of Protestantism.   At an enthusiastic and influential meeting held in June 1851, 'The Protestant Alliance' was founded, under the presidency of Lord Shaftesbury—

"Not only," as its prospectus stated, "to oppose the recent aggression of the Pope . . . but 'to maintain and defend, against all the encroachments of Popery, the Scriptural doctrines of the Reformation.'   This was to be effected (1) 'by awakening British Christians of various classes . . . to regard the interests of Protestantism as the paramount object of their concern; (2) by uniting the Protestants of the Empire in a firm and persevering demand that the national support and encouragement given to Popery of late years shall be discontinued . . . and (3) by extending as far as may be practicable the sympathy and support of British Christians to those in foreign countries who may be suffering oppression for the cause of the Gospel.'"

The new Alliance at once received a wide support, and its first list of members included scores of the foremost clergymen in England.   Dean Tait's known sympathy with Evangelical opinion led to his being early invited to become a member of the Alliance.   His answer to the invitation was as follows :—

The Dean of Carlisle to Mr. W. Browne.

"*26th Jan.* 1852.

"DEAR MR. BROWNE,—Your letter has been forwarded to me. In the 'statement of objects' of the Protestant Alliance are some with which I certainly cannot sympathise. I have always been decidedly in favour of the Maynooth Grant, and should consider its withdrawal, except on the ground of proved abuse, to be unjust. I do not see how one holding this opinion could co-operate in such an Association as you say it is intended to form. Generally, also, my opinion, as far as I am yet informed, is strong that Popery in this country is better met by every Protestant clergyman and layman zealously doing his duty in the position God has assigned him than by the agitation which seems implied in the formation of a Society for the defence of Protestantism. If Government could be strengthened so as to enable them to interfere on behalf of Protestants abroad, this were indeed much to be desired.—Yours sincerely,

"A. C. TAIT."

Similarly, in reply to a request that he would allow his name to be added to a widely supported 'Sabbath Observance Society,' he writes as follows:—

The Dean of Carlisle to Mr. J. Simpson.

"*12th March* 1853.

"MY DEAR SIR,—I have attentively perused the Rules of the Sabbath Observance Society. I do not feel that I can join it. I think I shall better promote the great object of urging men to the observance, not only of the Fourth Commandment, but of all God's commandments, the rules of a Christian life, through the regularly appointed agency of Christ's Church, than by means of this Society. The Church of Christ Universal, represented for each individual Christian by that branch of it to which he himself belongs, appears to me to open up for each, in its regular ministrations, the best means through which he may, by God's help, promote such great objects.—Yours very faithfully,

"A. C. TAIT."

The following is Lady Wake's account of a visit to Carlisle, in the last year of the Dean's residence there:—

"In the autumn of 1855 we, on our way north, spent a delightful week at the Deanery, repeating the visit a month later as we returned home, and by this means had the opportunity of thoroughly understanding the extent and variety of the Dean's work, while at the same time we had the full enjoyment of his family life, which was delightful. There were now six children, and only one, the third, was a boy; the five little girls, from the eldest to the youngest, were full of life, and had such a share in all that was done that an additional spirit and animation was imparted to everything. Mrs. Tait had the talent of thus blending the children's life with that of their parents and their friends without making them little bores. In her charities and various ministrations among the poor the three eldest, Catty, May, and little Chatty (a peculiarly lovely child), were taught to be a real help, winning the affections and cheering the sadness of numbers whose various needs brought them under the influence of the Deanery, while their active little fingers performed wonders in the clothing club. Ah! who could foresee the coming storm? We were there one Sunday, and that I might understand all that he was doing, with the Dean's permission, I remained with him the whole day (so far as I could without getting up into the pulpit). Besides the two services in the Cathedral, at one of which he preached, he found time for a most touching meeting in his night schoolroom with a number of old people and invalids who were not able for a Cathedral service. He sat among them like a young apostle, making choice of such portions of Scripture as brought comfort, and hope, and strength to their failing powers; pointing out to them the bright Beyond to which the Saviour was beckoning them, and praying with them, no printed formula of prayer, but the very voice of their hearts, taking to God all their infirmities and wants. Later in the day there was a similar gathering of young women, most of them mothers, to whom he spoke so earnestly that they evidently hung upon his words. Later still there was a children's class examined by him, and quite late in the evening, when, exceedingly fatigued, I thought the duties of the day entirely over, I found a most interesting gathering of young men in the Dean's study, to whom he gave instruction more like that given to the Sixth Form at Rugby, recognising in them the craving for knowledge felt by thoughtful and educated minds. That he secured their attention so as deeply to interest them was evident, and the influence obtained must have been real over those young minds, by God's blessing expanding under the warm sunshine of His word of truth.

"And this was the work of every seventh day, that of the six intervening being in keeping with it.

"It was a bright scene that enlivened the old Deanery. Cheerful young voices sounded merrily as we gathered in the mornings in the picturesque old drawing-room to obey the solemn injunction that had been carved centuries before on the ceiling, 'That here prayer should every day be made.' The golden heads and cherub faces of the little ones, the gentle, serious calm of the two elder girls, as they knelt, recalled the groups in the pictures of the old masters, wherein some opening scene in heaven is attempted to be delineated."

Early in the year 1856, it seemed more than likely that he might be appointed to the Bishopric of Carlisle. On Shrove Tuesday, February 5th, Bishop Percy, when apparently in his usual health, was seized with sudden faintness, "and as it was growing dark that evening," wrote Dr. Tait, "Mr. Page waited on me at the Deanery to announce that the Bishop's long episcopate was over. An hour after hearing of his death I received a letter from him written in his usual health. O my God, make us to live in readiness, through Jesus Christ."

"*Sunday, Feb.* 10th.—I have preached to-day on the Bishop's death. O teach me, Lord, to imitate those qualities in which he excelled, and which my character sorely needs. Not a man-pleaser, not a dissembler, not hesitating in his principles. O Lord, strengthen me by Thy Holy Spirit."

"*Tuesday, Feb.* 12th (56).—To-day we laid our kind old Bishop in the grave. . . . We shall never see again his upright form and reverend grey head, and watch his elastic step. This cannot but be a time of much natural anxiety; but I trust, Lord, that my heart is fixed on Thee, and, like my dear wife, I trust I have no wishes but that Thy Holy Will may be fulfilled, and Thy Church may prosper, through Jesus Christ."

This last entry requires explanation. Ever since the recovery of his health in 1850, and his work upon the Oxford Commission, he had been aware of the favour with which he was regarded by some of the leaders of the Liberal party.   Lord John Russell, indeed, had made no secret of his intention to recommend him for a Bishopric on the first opportunity. The knowledge of this fact had often disquieted him, and again and again in his journal he prays against the temptation to desire such preferment.   He could not, however, pretend to be unaware of the special aptitude he possessed for certain departments of the work he longed to see done in the Church of England; and now that the See of Carlisle had fallen vacant after the accession of the Whigs to office, it seemed to his friends almost certain that his name would be submitted to Her Majesty, especially as George Moore, a Liberal to the backbone and a man all-powerful in Cumberland, was exerting himself to the utmost on his behalf.   But the Premier was Lord Palmerston, not Lord John Russell; and, on the advice of Lord Shaftesbury, Dr. Montagu Villiers, the Evangelical Rector of Bloomsbury, was appointed to the vacant See.

"*Deanery, Carlisle, 11th Feb.* 1856, 10.35 P.M.—To-day has ended a week of great anxiety, and seems to have fixed my residence here for a considerable time, if not for life. I have great cause to thank my friends who had made exertions to promote me to a greater sphere in this neighbourhood, but such things are too important for the Church of God not to be distinctly overruled by Him, and He knows what is best both for me and His Church. O Lord, if there be in my lot here some discouragements, let me think of the far greater comforts and blessings. Truly Thou hast caused my cup to overflow,—a loving wife and dear children, competent health, means sufficient far beyond most of my contemporaries, a good house, ample leisure, and great means of usefulness, blessed with the hearty good-will of the poor around me.   O help me daily more and more to do my work here as in Thy sight.

"I have felt anxious during the past week; yet have I felt able also to submit myself entirely to Thy will. This night, after the first excitement has passed—a feeling of some dissatisfaction has been creeping over me. . . . O Lord, give me a holy, contented frame; make me to desire nothing but how best to fulfil Thy holy will. O Lord, in life and in death may I be Thine: save me from worldly, ambitious thoughts: give me a holy frame, for Jesus Christ's sake. . . ."

"*Sunday Evening, 24th Feby.* 1856.—This day I have felt much how unformed is my Christian character, how great have been my past sins, and how little fitted, therefore, I am for great position in the Church of Christ. O Lord, deepen my sense of my own unworthiness, through Jesus Christ. Amen."

"*Sunday Evening, 2d March* 1856.—O Lord, regulate my mind by Thy Holy Spirit. . . . Give me a more spiritual frame. This Holy Communion in which I joined this day, may it be blest to my soul, that I may be less conformed to the world, and more transformed by the renewing of my mind. Bless my wife and dear children, through Jesus Christ. Amen."

CHAPTER VIII.

THIS chapter must be the shortest in the volume. In vain would any biographer try to describe again the storm which broke upon the Carlisle Deanery in that sad spring. The mother's own hand has given to the world a sacred record which will live in English literature, and which is already known and reverenced in every land. It stands exactly as she wrote it in the very hours of darkness and loneliness which followed upon the storm, and the impress of its birth-time is stamped upon its every page. Not for more than twenty years afterwards—not until she too had passed from earth—was the record seen by any outside the immediate circle of her friends, and the occasion of its ultimate publication was of a piece with the occasion of its birth. To that record, which can neither be abridged nor paraphrased, those must turn who desire to realise what the brightness of the Carlisle home had been, and to know the details of a sorrow, the successive shocks of which were felt, it may almost be said, throughout England.

Scarlet fever in its most virulent form appeared in Carlisle, and of the six little daughters whose presence had brought radiance to the Deanery, the heart-broken parents were called, within the space of a few weeks, to part with all except the infant who had just been born. One by one, between the 10th of March and the 10th of April, they were laid in the single grave in Stanwix

Churchyard.[1] Is it wonderful that when the parents came forth from the awful cloud of those spring days their life was lived thenceforward under wholly new conditions, and that through all the chequered and busy years that followed, whether at Fulham or at Lambeth, they carried consciously upon them the consecration-mark of the holy sorrow they had known?

The last entry which has been quoted from the diary was dated March 2, 1856. The entry which immediately succeeds it is as follows :—

"HALLSTEADS, *Thursday, 8th May* 1856.—I have not had the heart to make any entry in my journal now for above nine weeks. When last I wrote I had six daughters on earth ; now I have one, an infant. O God, Thou hast dealt very mysteriously with us. We have been passing through deep waters: our feet were wellnigh gone. But though Thou slay us, yet will we trust in Thee. . . . They are gone from us, all but my beloved Craufurd and the babe. Thou hast re-claimed the lent jewels. Yet, O Lord, shall I not thank Thee now? I will thank Thee not only for the children Thou hast left to us, but for those Thou hast re-claimed. I thank Thee for the blessing of the last ten years, and for all the sweet memories of their little lives—memories how fragrant with every blissful, happy thought. I thank Thee for the full assurance that each has gone to the arms of the Good Shepherd, whom each loved according to the capacity of her years. I thank Thee for the bright hopes of a happy reunion, when we shall meet to part no more. O Lord, for Jesus Christ's sake, comfort our desolate hearts. May we be a united family still in heart through the communion of saints — through Jesus Christ our Lord."

[1] The names and ages of the children were as follows :—
> Catharine Anna ("Catty"), born Mar. 15, 1846, died Mar. 25, 1856.
> Mary Susan (" May "), .   „   June 20, 1847, „   April 8, „
> Craufurd, .   .   .   „   June 22, 1849, „   May 29, 1878.
> Charlotte (" Chatty "), .   „   Sept. 7, 1850, „   Mar. 6, 1856.
> Frances Alice Marion, .   „   June 29, 1852, „   Mar. 20, „
> Susan Elizabeth Campbell,   „   Aug. 1, 1854, „   Mar. 11, „
> Lucy Sydney Murray, .   „   Feb. 11, 1856.

For the whole narrative, see *Catharine and Craufurd Tait*, pp. 159-243.

CHAPTER IX.

1856.

THE summer of 1856 was spent by the bereaved parents at Hallsteads, a beautiful house on Ullswater, lent to them by friends, and near enough to Carlisle to enable the Dean to resume his work in the Cathedral and elsewhere. To this work he set himself with unabated courage, and his diary is full of such entries as the following :

"*Sunday, July 27th.*—In Carlisle all day. Preached in the afternoon. Lecture 5-6. Bible-class 8.30-9.30."

"*Monday, July* 28.—10 A.M. Cathedral service. Visited Cathedral School. Administered Holy Communion to dying man. Returned late to Hallsteads."

They had not again occupied the Deanery, but the question of their return thither had become imminent, when, on September 17th, the Dean received the following letter from the Prime Minister :—

Viscount Palmerston to the Dean of Carlisle.

"94 PICCADILLY, 15 *September* 1856.

"MY DEAR SIR,—I have much pleasure in informing you that I have received the Queen's commands to offer you the See of London, which is about to become vacant by the resignation of the present Bishop on the 30th of this month ; but subject to two conditions. The first is that you should hold the See subject to a future division of the Diocese if Parliament should pass an Act for the purpose, and subject, of course, to any arrangement as to endowments or otherwise which may be consequent upon such a division, and, secondly, that the Estates of the See shall be placed under the management of the Ecclesiastical Commissioners.

"If, as I hope, you should be willing to accept the offer, you will perhaps have the goodness to place yourself without delay in communication with the present Bishop with a view to settle with him such arrangements as may be necessary for the transfer of the duties of the Diocese.—I am, my dear Sir, yours faithfully,   PALMERSTON."

Diary.

"*Wednesday, Sept. 17th*, 1856.—I have this morning received a letter from Lord Palmerston saying that he has the Queen's command to offer me the See of London. I am now (11 A.M.) about to take an hour of prayer. The subjects on which to pray are these—That I may not act rashly, seeing that I have no doubt of accepting the offer—That I may have the grace of the Holy Spirit of God abundantly poured down upon me during the time of my holding this office—That I may be kept from worldliness in every form—That I may have a single eye to the glory of God and the good of His Church—That I may have such health as is requisite for so great a post.

"O Lord! grant that thy Church may take no injury through my fault. Give me vigilance over myself first, next over others. Enable me to arrange my days and all my time so as to have ample time for prayer and the study of Thy Word. Give me wisdom—give me holiness—give me strength of mind and body—give me kind consideration for the feelings of all around me—give me boldness—give me decision. This is certainly not the post which I should ever have dreamed of for myself. The preparation which Thou hast given me for it has been deep affliction. May the memory of these afflictions help to sanctify my heart . . . May I undertake this office in the spirit of a missionary. Soon I shall be called to give account. Teach me to live in simplicity and in Thy fear, through Jesus Christ. Amen.

"I think I am not rash in accepting it, God knows I have not sought it. I trust to use it while life lasts for God's glory, and to go about my work simply in God's faith and fear . . . . As in God's sight I accept it, praying to Him heartily to help me in all my ways."

The exact influences which led to the nomination of Archibald Tait to the See of London are not now ascertainable. The position he had filled for several years in the eyes of Liberal Ministers, as one who had not been afraid to handle the thorny question of University Reform, and who was credited with the successful issue of the Royal Commission on the subject ; the influence of Lord Shaftesbury, who, as he afterwards wrote to Lady Wake, had regarded Dean Tait as "by very much the best" of the dangerous Arnoldian school ; the esteem in which he was known to be held by the Liberals, both of Oxford and of Cumberland ; and, last, but perhaps not least, the widespread sympathy and interest which had been aroused, from the Throne downwards, by the tragic illness in the Carlisle Deanery ; all these causes contributed to make it probable that he would be nominated by Lord Palmerston to fill one of the four vacant Sees. Lord Shaftesbury frankly wrote, a few months later, that his own wish had been that Mr. Pelham should be nominated to London and Dean Tait to Norwich or elsewhere. On this point the Prime Minister took his own line ; but it was indeed a bold step on his part to send Dean Tait to London. Only once during the previous two hundred years had any man, not already a Bishop, been appointed to that diocese, and, in the case of Dean Tait, the experiment must to many people have seemed rash in the extreme. It would not, perhaps, be possible to find another instance in the last half century in which a man with so little previous training of a technical sort has been placed at one step in a position at once so responsible and so independent. Oxford, Rugby, Carlisle, had each of them been the scene of hard work well done, and each had left an impress upon his life and character. But his duties as tutor and headmaster had lain outside the groove of ecclesiastical organisation, and even at Carlisle he had had little opportunity of taking part in the solution of the wider Church problems, or the general ordering of Church affairs. Of duties strictly pastoral he had had ample experience in his voluntary work, first at Baldon and then at Carlisle, and as a preacher, thoughtful and earnest rather than brilliant, he had already some reputation. But he was unknown upon religious platforms, either in London or elsewhere ; he had scarcely ever attended a clerical meeting ; he had never sat in Convocation ; and he found himself regarded with a certain suspicion by many of his clerical friends, who looked askance upon his association with the 'sacrilegious Whigs.' About strictly Episcopal work he knew absolutely nothing, and it was startling therefore to others besides himself to see him placed quite suddenly at the head of the largest diocese in the world, as the successor of one of the most remarkable Bishops of our time. To succeed Bishop Blomfield would have been a formidable task for any man. His indomitable energy, his penetrating intelligence, and his ready eloquence and wit, added to his keen business habits and his organising genius, had gone far to change men's view of the English Episcopate, and Churchmen were now wondering who could be found to take up his mantle, and to occupy his commanding place.

Public attention had been directed to the subject by the important debates in both Houses of Parliament upon the question of Bishop Blomfield's resignation. No arrangement had up to that time been in existence whereby an aged or infirm Bishop could suitably resign his See ; and a special Act of Parliament was passed in 1856 to authorise the retirement, on a suitable pension, of the Bishops of London and

Durham.[1] The Bill was hotly opposed, not only by the
Radicals, as represented by Mr. Hadfield, Mr. Roebuck,
and others of the same school, but also, on totally
different grounds, by such Churchmen as the Bishops
of Oxford and Exeter, Mr. Gladstone, Lord Robert Cecil,
and Sir William Heathcote.

Their opposition was, however, fruitless, and the Bill
became law on July 26th. The long discussions on the
subject had called public notice to the importance of the
Bishop of London's position, both in the Church and in
the country, and had greatly enhanced the interest of the
question who was to be the new Bishop. When Dean
Tait's nomination was announced, public criticism was, to
a large extent, mere guesswork, so little was the Bishop-
designate known in an ecclesiastical aspect outside the
comparatively limited circle of his Oxford and Rugby
friends, and of those interested in University Reform.
But if he was at a disadvantage in thus entering upon a
great position without any of the prestige attaching to
previous successes in a similar field, there was something,
too, to be said upon the other side. He was entirely
untrammelled by any partisan allegiance. Critics who
tried to label the new Bishop with the name of some
party in the Church found themselves able to go no
further than to say that he was certainly not a High
Churchman. Indeed, if he had had himself to choose a
leader from among the Bishops, it is hard to say to whom
he would have been willing to turn. The Episcopal
Bench was on the whole far better manned than it had
been a few years before. Several distinct types of work
and thought were now apparent. The piety and evan-

---

[1] Bishop Blomfield was seventy years old, and had been a Bishop for
thirty-three years. Bishop Maltby was eighty-six years old, and had been a
Bishop for twenty-five years.

gelical fervour of the brothers Sumner, the incomparable energy, versatility, and devotion of Bishop Wilberforce, and the masterly thoroughness and accuracy of Bishop Blomfield's constructive talent, were each of them potent to recall the Church of England into life, and the redoubtable Bishop Phillpotts of Exeter, already seventy-eight years old, had lost nothing of the ability, the pugnacity, and the shrewd and caustic wit, which made him for half a century the champion of every cause that he supported, and the sturdiest enemy of liberalism in whatever form. Tait perhaps lacked the power, even if he had had the will, to tread in the footsteps of any of these leaders. The line he was to follow was a line of his own, which, whether better or worse than any of those laid down by others, at least differed widely from them all. The Evangelical Bishops and their followers had made it impossible any longer to describe the Church of England as " dead to the spiritual hunger of human souls," but, with a few notable exceptions, they had failed to gain touch with the intellectual and critical side of the life and conversation of educated men. Literature, Science, Philosophy, Art, were by them regarded as things altogether apart from Religion. Their view of the antagonism between the Church and the world led them to a strange distrust of the higher forms of human usefulness and activity. These belonged to the world, and the main business of the religious man was with religion as a personal matter between himself and his God.

Bishop Blomfield and Bishop Wilberforce had each of them taken a view of the Church's duties very different from that of the Evangelical Bishops. It is generally admitted to have been the capacity and vigour of the former which, in the years succeeding the Reform Bill, had saved the Church from the destructive zeal of those who wished to represent her as doomed on account of her obvious abuse of trust and her cumbrous mismanagement.

Bishop Blomfield, early in his clerical life, speaking of the then disorganised and torpid condition of the Church, had said, "It is not too late for us to put fresh incense into our censers, and to stand between the dead and the living";[1] and no man ever more fully acted up to the spirit of his own words. After a thorough overhauling of her finances, he had successfully endeavoured, with the constant encouragement and support of the gentler Archbishop Howley, to settle the Church firmly down on good orthodox lines, free, so far as possible, from the taint either of Tractarian bigotry or of Arnoldian laxity of belief. Tait came to London to find an increasing likelihood that the Church of England, with all her high claims, her unquestionable orthodoxy, and her admirable business habits, might become merely the richest, best-managed, and most powerful of the English sects. The capacity of her leaders, and especially, perhaps, the restless earnestness of Bishop Wilberforce, had placed her in a new position before the eyes of men. But strong as was the growth of her new-found life, it was one of even increasing isolation from the kindred influences around. She was not attempting to sweep into her stream or to utilise for the nation's good the various Christian forces which were actively at work independently of her system or her support. Bishop Tait's training and temperament combined to lead him to take a view of the Church's life, less ecclesiastical, more national and comprehensive. From the moment of his appointment he seems to have set before himself this national position, as the one which needed all the emphasis he could give to it. Bishop

---

[1] *Memoirs*, vol. ii. p. 280.

Wilberforce in a brilliant account of Bishop Blomfield's life and work describes him as making it "clear to all that his sole object was to increase the moral and spiritual efficiency of the Church of England."[1]   Bishop Tait regarded the Church of England's efficiency rather as a means than an end, a means of raising the Christian tone of the whole nation, whether in her legislature, her jurisprudence, or her social life.   It was his aim to make the Church, in fact as well as in theory, a National Church, in a sense quite other than as embodying or expressing the Official Creed.   He was not, in any full sense, an adherent of Dr. Arnold and his school, differing almost as widely from them upon the one hand as he did from Bishop Wilberforce and the High Church Bishops on the other.   But his words and actions must speak for themselves, and it is necessary to return to the facts of 1856.

From among the letters he received, as soon as the appointment was announced, a few extracts may perhaps be given, selected, so far as possible, to show the opinion which had been formed of his powers and qualifications by those who had had the best opportunity of judging. From former pupils and friends came the following :—

Canon Arthur Stanley to the Bishop-designate of London.

" Accept, my dear friend, my best wishes—hopes. All is before you : new scenes, new work, a place where you can speak and act with the greatest effect for all that you—may I not say for all that you and I and the best friends of the Church of England —think most important. God grant you health to fulfil all your highest wishes, and may the mournful past bear its true fruits in a happy and useful future. Carlisle, Rugby, Oxford, Scotland, must all find their proper place in London. . . . I will say no more, except to express my profound conviction of the immense services which you may render to the Church. Your appointment may, under God, be a new era for us all. . . . O that they

---

[1] *Quarterly Review*, Oct. 1863, p. 556.

would make Vaughan your coadjutor at Westminster! The Church of London would then be indeed *tota, teres, atque rotunda.* —Ever affectionately yours,   A. P. STANLEY."

Rev. B. Jowett to the Bishop-designate of London.

" . . . Such a great event is almost above congratulation. I rejoice heartily in it for your sake and that of the Church of England. I think you will succeed, because you have succeeded at Balliol, at Rugby, and at Carlisle; because you are tolerant, and keep your eyes open to what is passing around you; because I believe you will not suffer yourself to be surrounded with inferior men.

"Twenty years hence the Church of England will probably have changed considerably for better or for worse, and you will have had great influence on its changes. The *Times* of yesterday addresses you a homily on your new duties. The only advice I should venture to offer is that you should do as little as possible : I mean, seriously, that you should keep yourself up to the work by getting rid in every possible way of matters of routine.—Most sincerely yours,   B. JOWETT.

" Will you tell Mrs. Tait that ' Latitudinarian ' is a tremendous long name to call a fellow ? "

Mr. Ralph Lingen[1] to the Bishop-designate of London.

". . . Our pleasure at your appointment is the pleasure of a crew who love their ship and admire good seamanship—and who in a trying time find a man in whom they have confidence called to the helm. The care and the difficulty are the very reasons why they rejoice that one man was selected rather than another, both for his sake and their own. Great as are the labours and the perils, I, for one, look forward with confidence to your surmounting them in the same spirit that has hitherto carried success with it, and I anticipate benefits in large measure both to the Church and country."

Mr. J. D. Coleridge[2] to the Bishop-designate of London.

" . . . London so much wants a vigorous man, and, above all, a just one, that I entirely rejoice that you are to come there.

---

[1] Now Lord Lingen.   [2] Now Lord Chief Justice.

You must have changed very much if any one ever gets anything but kind and generous treatment at your hands."

From the Rugby Masters as a body he received a letter of warmest congratulation and confident encouragement. In his reply, he said :—

"No man could possibly undertake such a burden as must devolve on the Bishop of London without a sense of his insufficiency, and there are many reasons why I, in undertaking it, must feel almost overwhelmed. It does therefore greatly tend to strengthen me when I learn that those who have known me long, and are kindly interested in my personal welfare, at the same time that they are anxious to see the Church of Christ fulfil its great vocation, are thus ready to bid me God-speed."

One after another among his oldest friends refers to the memories of Betty Morton, and to the joy which his appointment would have given her. His brother James, for example, writes :—

"I have been hourly thinking : What would my dear Father —and Betty—have said? John Russell, in congratulating me yesterday, asked if your old nurse was still alive : and Horner, in a letter to-day from Berlin, says—'What would Betty have thought ? ' "

On grounds public rather than personal Dr. Hook of Leeds wrote :—

"I should not offer my congratulations, if I did not believe that your appointment meets with the approbation of the Church of England generally. I have heard but one opinion expressed on the subject, and that is, of great thankfulness. . . . I believe the thankfulness at your appointment to arise from the conviction that you are a just man. *The* virtue which we require in a Bishop, in these days of party violence, is justice : we require a just and impartial Ruler, and as you have never been a partisan, and are known to possess all the other qualifications of a good Bishop, such we expect you to be."

In reply to a letter from Mr. Golightly, the Bishop-designate wrote :—

"HALLSTEADS, *29th September* 1856.

"MY DEAR GOLIGHTLY,—Yours is the sort of letter which it is well for a man in my circumstances to receive. Your advice as to the first hour of the day is, I truly believe, the only rule for passing safely through the very many temptations which are before me, and I shall strive to follow it. God's dealings with me and mine during the last six months have been deeply mysterious, and, suffering deeply as we do in our hearts from the grievous loss of children who promised to be everything to us, we cannot but feel ourselves distinctly in God's hands. If I could tell you the story of our grief you would see what a call we have to look upon this world as the merest pilgrimage. But all these softening and holy impressions may in time wear away through the pressure of business and the deep interest of the continued cycle of great employments that seems to be before me. I therefore, my dear friend, greatly need your prayers, and you will not fail to offer them. I know very well that I am exposed to the dangers you point out. In these difficult days it is certainly my desire not to drive parties to extremes, but this I trust I may be able to do without any compromise of truth. . . . Still I do love a comprehensive toleration. The Bishop of Gloucester I do not know—the Bishop of Oxford I do. Our own Bishop of Carlisle I highly regard as a heartily and truly religious man. To the Archbishop I look with the deepest veneration, and he kindly welcomes me as a friend.—Yours very sincerely,

"A. C. TAIT.

"We have still one boy and a little baby—a great comfort to our hearts."

Lord Palmerston's letter, it will be remembered, had alluded to the possible division of the See of London into two. In June 1855 a Royal Commission on Cathedrals had reported in favour of the formation of nine new Sees in England, one of them being 'Westminster,' to be separated from the See of London. The project had been at first received with considerable favour, and the Archbishop of Canterbury, in writing to Dean Tait on his appointment, said :—

"I hope that there is no doubt of the intention to divide the jurisdiction. More duty has fallen upon the retiring Bishop than any strength could safely venture to undertake."

But, on further consideration, it was felt to be undesirable to proceed with the proposed division ; and when the relief ultimately came, it was effected in a different manner altogether.

Some extracts from his Diary will best show how the next few weeks were spent, and what were the main thoughts in his mind.

Diary.

"*Sunday Evening*, 5*th October*.—I have come to the close of my ministry in Carlisle. In the morning we visited with Craufurd the dear spot. It was the first time the dear child had seen it. Some kind friend had strewed it with fresh flowers. . . . Bid farewell to the Central School at half-past ten, and tried to urge some plain lessons on the children. Holy Communion at the Cathedral ; 72 communicants, far more than I ever saw before. . . . In the afternoon I preached my farewell sermon—trying to speak faithfully, and commending many things in which I feel greatly interested to the Christian sympathy of those who crowded to hear me for the last time. O Lord, I thank Thee for the encouragement which this day has given me as to my ministry here, though I feel how weak and remiss I have been. Visited the dear girls' schoolroom for the last time, with many tears. . . . *October 8th.*—Went to Fulham ; most kindly received by the Blomfields. Stayed till Monday 13th, when went to Broadlands to Lord Palmerston. . . . [1]

"*Brighton, Sunday Evening*, 26*th October*. . . . I have been reading Trench's Introduction to *Sacred Poems for Mourners*. His analysis of the Burial Service is very striking. I have read one of F. Robertson's sermons ; full of thought, but not much of religious thought. . . . Catharine and I together received the

---

[1] Page after page of the Diary is filled with tender references to the children "safe with the Lord, now their life's brief day is past."

Holy Communion at Mr. Henry Elliott's church. The calm time during that long Communion enabled me to call up in prayer the long succession of the many friends whom I feel a desire to remember now before the Throne of Grace. This quiet time of waiting till the day of my consecration comes is a great privilege. O Lord, give me strength and spirituality to use it as I ought. . . . Give me strength to conquer my temptations. How difficult do I find it to secure proper time in the morning ! This really is one of my great difficulties. Lord, give me energy for this, or the most precious time for my soul's improvement— for bracing it to meet the trials of the day—will be frittered away. And now at the close of another week let me dedicate myself afresh, O Lord, to Thee. . . . In this new sphere give me more than ever

> The spirit of prayer,
> The spirit of holy meditation,
> The spirit of holy zeal,
> The spirit of right judgment,
> The spirit of Christian boldness,
> The spirit of Christian meekness. . . .

Grant that the insidious temptations of the trappings of worldly greatness may not impede my heavenward course. I feel the danger. Raise my soul heavenwards through Jesus Christ our Lord. . . .

" *Sunday Evening, November 9th.* . . . I have to-day read a very striking sermon of F. Robertson's 'Sleep on now, and take your rest.' The thought is how opportunities lost cannot be recalled—especially opportunities of prayer, and thus a man enters unprepared on the temptations before him. Lord, enable me so to use this quiet time that I may be braced by prayer for the great work before me and its many trials. . . . I have been read- ing some more of Blunt's *Duties of the Parish Priest.* In what I have read to-day, 'on the reading of the parish priest,' there is too much of the old *via media*—Scripture, tradition, fathers, reformers—sort of theology ; but the advice to consult original sources is good, and no doubt it is very useful for young men to have pointed out to them how great and interesting a field of reading their profession opens up.

" *Monday, November* 17.—Yesterday I heard the Bishop of Rupertsland preach twice. Strange that he and his three boys and sister should have been kept safe during these seven years in the wilderness and on the great ocean, and that five little weeks should have made such a change in our little home society! O Lord, keep me from the hurry of business. The solemn time of my consecration is fast approaching. I would be much in prayer. . . .

"*20th November*, 37 *Lowndes Square.*—This day my election was confirmed in Bow Church. The empty forms have this reality connected with them—First, that we began with the Litany; secondly, that oaths were taken full of meaning. O Lord, grant, I humbly beseech Thee, that this day's solemnities may not have been in vain—though they have been mixed up with unmeaning forms.[1] To me at least it is a great reality, as the third step in placing me in this great post, great from the boundless influence it may exercise for good or evil on so many thousands. . . . Let me resolve to live in prayer. As in old days at Balliol let me have regular intervals of prayer, however short, in the midst of the business of the day, as each hour passes, when I can be disengaged for a few moments.

"*November* 22.—I sit down to-day, in the quiet time secured, to think of the great duties which are to devolve upon me, and of the solemn vows by which I am to be bound. O Lord, my God and Saviour, who hast watched over me from my earliest years till now, who hast brought me through great prosperity, and in the midst of sad suffering to this hour, be with me, I beseech Thee. Lord, solemnise my mind, through Jesus Christ. . . . I have re-read the Service of Consecration, having read it many times before during the last two months. To be diligent in the study of the Scriptures; zealous in the attempt to practise what they teach; to be careful to drive away strange doctrine; to be kind to the poor; to be very careful in giving Holy Orders; to rule my own household well; above all, to live in prayer—O God, give me grace, for Jesus Christ's sake.

"11.30 P.M.—I have now looked through the Office for Ordering Priests and Deacons. Twenty years have passed since I was ordained deacon on Trinity Sunday 1836. How eventful a time! Balliol, Rugby, Carlisle, and now London. . . . Grant that what remains of my life may be dedicated entirely to Thee.

---

[1] In later years he was accustomed, as Archbishop, to impress upon others, who thus criticised the old 'Confirmation' ceremonial, that the forms in question were full of meaning, historical and practical.

What wisdom will be required; what kindliness; what deep conviction of Christian truth !   Lord, who is sufficient for these things ?"

On November 23, 1856,[1] he was consecrated [2] in the Chapel-Royal, Whitehall, together with Dr. Cotterill, a former Senior Wrangler, who had been appointed to the See of Grahamstown.[3]   In the reviving interest which was beginning to be felt in such services, a wish had been widely expressed that the Consecration should take place in St. Paul's Cathedral.   But ecclesiastical usage required, it was strangely said, that the Bishop should not appear in his Cathedral before the day of his enthronement.   The preacher, appointed at his request, was his dear friend George Lynch Cotton, his former colleague at Rugby, who had now for four years been headmaster of Marlborough. The sermon set forth in striking words the comprehensive character of the Church of England, and the greatness of the issues before her in the conflict against sin and unbelief.   The preacher dwelt with special emphasis on the growing 'secularism'[4] of the great towns, a fact which dwarfed into insignificance, by its very magnitude, the petty disputations about smaller things.

The Diary that night reiterates the prayers of the previous days, and the chequered memories of Rugby and Carlisle.

"Cotton's sermon was excellent.   O Lord, make me to realise the greatness of the office which has devolved on me.   Hear me, and guide me, weak and stained with sin as I am, through Jesus Christ our Lord."

[1] Twenty-seventh Sunday after Trinity.

[2] The consecrating bishops were Archbishop Sumner of Canterbury, Bishop Gilbert of Chichester, Bishop Jackson of Lincoln, and Bishop Villiers of Carlisle.

[3] He held that See from 1856 to 1871, and was Bishop of Edinburgh from 1871 to his death in 1886.

[4] He used the word 'secularism' apologetically, as one just coming into use.

"*November* 24, 11.30 P.M.—I now sit down to record my first day's Episcopal experience. I feel my weakness. To-day in my interview with Mr. Lowder, I feel that I did not produce on him the impression I desired, and when he asked me for my blessing, I was so taken aback that I only gave him half the blessing. Also I felt awkward at the meetings of Church Building Commission, etc., but perhaps there my wisdom was silence. With my ordination candidates I was more at home, and I trust that, by the short prayer offered up with each, some good may have been done. Lord, I would remember them now in prayer. . . ."

On the following Sunday he preached, in St. James's, Piccadilly, his first sermon as Bishop of London. The church was reopened on that day with the addition of 150 'free and unappropriated' seats, and an opportunity was thus given to the Bishop of striking at the outset of his Episcopate the note which was to ring through it all—the call for a better provision for bringing home the Gospel message to the poor.

On December 4th he was enthroned in his Cathedral, and next day he went to Windsor to do homage to the Queen. His Diary says :—

"The ceremony was imposing, and I felt that to her kind heart I owed much. She spoke very kindly to me after the homage. . . . [I was] conducted by Sir George Grey into the Queen's closet—a very small room—where I found the Queen and Prince Albert. Having been presented by Sir George, I kneeled down on both knees before the Queen, just like a little boy at his mother's knee. I placed my joined hands between hers, while she stooped her head so as almost to bend over mine, and I repeated slowly and solemnly the very impressive words of the oath which constitutes the Act of Homage. Longley, the new Bishop of Durham, who had accompanied me, then went through the same ceremony. He had not escaped so quietly from the ceremonial when he was consecrated Bishop of Ripon. His oath was then taken to William IV., and no sooner had he risen from his knees than the King suddenly addressed him in a loud voice thus :—' Bishop of Ripon, I charge you, as you shall answer before Almighty God, that you never by word or deed give encouragement to those d——d Whigs who would upset the Church of England.' . . . I was afterwards sworn of the Privy Council, where met and was introduced to most of the Ministers.   Lord Lansdowne said he had known my mother."

Almost his first aim on appointment to the See had been to secure the help of a thoroughly efficient body of chaplains, and to this end he took counsel far and near. In the light of subsequent events, the following letter is too remarkable to be omitted :—

Canon A. P. Stanley to the Bishop of London.

"*Oct.* 12, 1856.

" . . . I am very glad you have applied to Temple.   I am sure that he is the best choice, and now, in case he should fail you at Christmas or any other time, I shall be very happy to supply his place.

" —— has many qualifications ; active, learned, and liberal. He is over-Maurician, and has some of the savage qualities of Cantabrigians.   He has also eccentricities of his own. . . . If you cannot think of any one else, you might go further and fare worse.   I cannot call to mind any younger Cambridge pupils.   By far the best Cambridge man of fit age and the like that occurs to me is *Benson*, Fellow of Trinity, now at Rugby. He has very pleasing manners, is a very good scholar and divine, preaches well, and is a thoroughly religious man.   I think he might be worth inquiring after.   He must be about twenty-eight or thirty.   A man of the same kind, but I don't know much about him personally, is *Westcott* of Harrow.   They are both more agreeable in manner than ——.

" One other Cambridge name occurs to me—*Lightfoot*, Fellow and, I think, Tutor of Trinity—of the same stamp as Westcott and Benson, but with the advantage of having a more independent position.   All I know of him is an article in the *Cambridge Philological Review*, which contained an attack on the scholarship and accents of my book on the Corinthians, but was written with great candour and kindness, as was also a correspondence consequent thereon.   And I have heard that he is a good man. . . .—Ever yours,   A. P. STANLEY."

Mr. Temple, on account of other work, declined the post, and those appointed were—Arthur Penrhyn Stanley, Frederick Gell, George Lynch Cotton, Frederick Blomfield, William Knight, and Ramsay Campbell, with Edward Parry as domestic chaplain and secretary. Dr. Lightfoot became an examining chaplain a few years later. But these appointments were not made, as the following letters show, without the murmurs of a storm :—

The Earl of Shaftesbury to Lady Wake.

"St. Giles' House, Cranbourne, *Nov.* 12, 1856.

"My dear Lady Wake,—You spoke to me about your brother, and it was in no slight measure owing to your representation of what was in him, that I urged his name upon the consideration of the Prime Minister. I had my fears—I do not disguise it—of the Arnold school, but I felt sure then, as I feel sure now, that he was by very much the best of that section. Now I will tell you what has alarmed me. Pray read this extract from a letter :

"'Dr. Tait has appointed A. P. Stanley to be his examining chaplain.'

"The letter proceeds thus : 'The views of Mr. Stanley on Inspiration are startling. He is, moreover, much inclined to combine ritualism with latitudinarianism, and this appointment will effectually dim the lustre of the choice made by Lord Palmerston.' Hear me, I myself could have appointed Stanley a dean. I like much that he has written, but as for examining chaplain, avert it for heaven's sake! The writer of the letter I quote adds, 'Mr. Stanley takes it to oblige the Bishop.' Pray let me say that the Bishop knows not the gulf that he is opening for himself, the distrust, the suspicions, the covert, the manifest opposition, I fear, that he is preparing for himself among his clergy, ay, and his laity. Can you interfere as a guardian angel ?—Yours truly,   SHAFTESBURY."

The Bishop of London to Lady Wake.

"37 Lowndes Square, *Nov.* 26, 1856.

"My dearest Chattie,—I have this moment received your letter of yesterday, and am truly sorry to hear of Lord Shaftesbury's fears with regard to Arthur Stanley's appointment as my examining chaplain. I am sure, however, that he will soon be convinced that they are groundless. I have known Stanley now for twenty years and more, and that very intimately. He is a man against whom efforts have at times been made to excite prejudice, but you know as well as I do how admirable is the Christian simplicity of his character. As to what was said in the *Record* of his being inclined to unite ritualism with latitu-dinarianism, it is to any one who knows him simply ridiculous, and about as correct as the absurd unfounded statement in the same paper, that he is the head of St. Augustine's College in Canterbury, in which he holds no office whatever.

"'That he will be invaluable in testing the literary qualification of the candidates, no one of those who most differ from him will doubt, and those who have a distrust of him otherwise still know that the examinations will, of course, always be conducted under my own eye, if God gives me strength. I am sure Lord Shaftesbury, and those who think with him, will have no reason to regret Stanley's appointment, and the whole list of my five chaplains, as it shows my own real leanings, will, I trust and believe, very generally approve itself to earnestly religious men throughout the country.—I am, with much love, yours affec-tionately,   A. C. LONDON."

The Earl of Shaftesbury to Lady Wake.

"December 1, 1856.

"MY DEAR LADY WAKE,—It is all quite right. I have no more apprehensions. I met your brother, the Bishop, who treated me with the greatest kindness, smoothed away my fears, and showed no displeasure that I had presumed to interfere.

"I attended his first sermon yesterday, and was much grati-fied. I had not expected to hear the second and personal advent of our blessed Lord preached by the Metropolitan Bishop in the pulpit of St. James's. May God give him grace and strength, and abundant success in his spiritual warfare!—Yours sincerely,   SHAFTESBURY.

"*P.S.*—A short conversation with himself has produced this reassuring conviction."

CHAPTER X.

DIVORCE ACT—RITUALISM—CONFESSION—
ST. GEORGE'S IN THE EAST.

THE Parliament of 1857 was signalised, among other things, by the passing of the Act for the establishment of the Divorce Court, and it has been not unusual to describe Bishop Tait as one of the foremost promoters or supporters of the change. The facts do not bear out this theory. Though the Bishop very early acquired an influence in the House of Lords, and took part from the first in its debates, the Law of Marriage was not a subject on which he ever came prominently to the front. The 'Divorce and Matrimonial Causes Bill' had now been thrice introduced as a Government measure. A Royal Commission had in 1853 reported—with only one dissentient—in favour of the substitution of a court of law for the parliamentary discussion and vote which had hitherto been the only legal means of procuring a divorce. The cost of these special Acts of Parliament was enormous, and the scandals incident to such a process had been long a subject of complaint. It had become customary never to refuse the divorce if sufficient cause could be shown, and if the applicant were rich enough to pay the necessary expenses of a special Act of Parliament. The principle had thus been long admitted, but the 'relief' was of necessity confined to the richest class of the community—a fact which became the subject of constant criticism both in the Law Courts and in Parliament.

In a case, for example, tried before Mr. Justice Maule, the prisoner, a poor man, being convicted of bigamy, was called upon to say why sentence should not be passed upon him. He said, " My wife was unfaithful : she robbed me, and ran away with another man, and I thought I might take another wife." The reply of the learned judge was : " Prisoner at the bar, you were entirely mistaken. The law in its wisdom points out a means by which you might have rid yourself from further association with a woman who had dishonoured you. But you did not think proper to adopt it. I will tell you what that process is. You ought to have brought an action for ' criminal conversation.' That action would have been tried before one of Her Majesty's judges at the assizes. That might have cost you money, and you say that you are a poor working man. But that is not the fault of the law. You might perhaps have obtained a verdict with damages against the defendant, who was not unlikely to turn out a pauper. But so jealous is the law (which you ought to know is the perfection of reason) of the sanctity of the marriage tie, that in accomplishing all this you would only have fulfilled the lighter portion of your duty. With your verdict in your hand you should have instituted a suit in the Ecclesiastical Court for a divorce '*a mensâ et thoro.*' Having got that divorce, you should have petitioned the House of Lords for a divorce '*a vinculo,*' and should have appeared by counsel at the bar of their Lordships' House. Then, if the Bill passed, it would have gone down to the House of Commons ; the same evidence would possibly be repeated there : and if the Royal assent had been given, after that you might have married again. The whole proceeding would probably not have cost you more than £1000, and you do not seem to be worth a thousand pence. But it is the boast of the law that it is impartial, and makes no difference between the rich and the poor. The richest man in the kingdom would have had to pay no less than that sum for the same means of obtaining freedom from the marriage tie. The sentence of the Court is, that you be imprisoned for the term of one day, and, the assize being now two days old, you are at liberty to quit the dock."

Such a system, it was argued, could no longer be defended. Hence the Royal Commission of 1850 and the consequent legislation, Lord Chancellor Cranworth being responsible in two successive Governments for the introduction of a Bill. In 1854, and again in 1856, the Bill obtained a second reading in the House of Lords, and in the latter year it was further reported on by a Select Committee. But it was in each case crowded out in the House of Commons. In 1857 Lord Cranworth introduced it for the third time, and the Government announced a firm intention of carrying it at all costs. The minority against the Bill, though comparatively weak in numbers, were strong in determination, and met the measure with stern opposition at every stage. Bishop Wilberforce in the Lords, and Mr. Gladstone in the Commons, used every weapon to defeat the plan. The difficulty of the subject was proved by the fact that each of these leaders had changed his mind during the course of the discussions. Mr. Gladstone, as Chancellor of the Exchequer in 1854. had shared the responsibility of introducing the very Bill which he was to oppose so bitterly three years later,[1] and Bishop Wilberforce publicly modified in 1857 the opinions he had himself expressed ten months before.[2]

---

[1] *Hansard*, August 4, 1857, p. 1051.
[2] *Ibid.*, May 10, 1857, p. 523.

The Archbishop of Canterbury supported the Bill, and was followed into the lobby by nine other Bishops, including Bishop Tait, who had spoken briefly in support of it, "because in his conscience he believed the time was come when the haphazard legislation of the last 150 years ought to be done away with."[1]   Haphazard indeed it was. More than 250 such 'Divorce Bills' had been passed, for the most part unopposed, and at the very time this debate was in progress, there were four such private Bills upon the table of the House.[2]   No one even suggested that these Bills should be opposed, and the principle had thus been long conceded for all who could afford to pay.   This was the argument which 'told' both in the House and in the country, and, in spite of the earnest and eloquent opposition of High Churchmen, secured the final passage of the Bill.

The Bishop refers thus to the subject in his Diary :—

"*Sunday*, *August* 30.—On Divorce Bill in House of Lords last Monday I gave my votes in favour of the Ministerial propositions as the Bill was brought back from the Commons.   I spoke, in answer to Lord St. Leonards and the Bishop of Salisbury, in favour of accepting the compromise conferring on the clergy the liberty of refusing to celebrate the remarriage of the guilty party, and *per contra* allowing such marriage to be celebrated in the parish church by another clergyman who did not disapprove. My reasons for this course will be found in my speech.[3] . . . I was convinced that the clergy would not obtain such good terms if the Bill were sent back and the discussion opened up again and extended to another session.   I felt also the [evil] of the further continuation of these Divorce discussions. . . . On full reflection now for many months I believe this Bill right, and the clergy have gained a far greater concession to their wishes than could have been anticipated in the provision leaving it to their option to celebrate the remarriage

[1] *Hansard*, May 19, 1857, p. 533.
[2] *Ibid.*, July 31, 1857, p. 861.
[3] *Ibid.*, August 24, 1857, p. 2058.

of guilty parties or not. . . . I fear my votes on this Bill have given great offence to many, but I have acted according to my conscience, and I pray God that all may go right."

A prominent share in another controversy, destined to arouse a fiercer and more lasting blaze, he inherited whether he would or no. It was certainly from no personal inclination that he became a party to the Ritual strife which had begun to agitate the public mind, and which was to be prolonged with intermittent vigour throughout his whole Episcopate. The facts of its origin have recently been told with care in books accessible to every one,[1] and the briefest summary will here be enough.

The famous 'Gorham judgment' of 1850[2] had seemed to give a signal triumph to the Evangelical party. But in the reaction against that judgment, the pendulum swung far the other way. Old-fashioned Churchmen who had no liking for the 'Oxford Tracts,' or for Dr. Pusey, were shocked at a sentence which seemed to them a flat contradiction of the plain language of the Prayer-Book, and the result among High Churchmen was a wider tolerance for the vehemence, and even the vagaries, of men who now set themselves to emphasise by outward act as well as spoken word the Sacramental doctrines which had, as they thought, been unjustly assailed. With this encouragement there took place an advance in outward ritual, which had been discouraged

---

[1] See especially Canon Perry's *Student's English Church History*, Period III., chapters xvii. xxii. xxiii. See also *Memoir of Bishop Blomfield*, vol. ii. chapter vii.

[2] The judgment turned upon the point whether Mr. Gorham's published opinions upon the subject of Baptismal Regeneration were or were not so heterodox as to justify the Bishop of Exeter's refusal to institute him to the Vicarage of Brampford Speke. The Privy Council decided, upon appeal, "that the doctrine held by Mr. Gorham is not contrary or repugnant to the declared doctrine of the Church of England, and that Mr. Gorham ought not, by reason of the doctrine held by him, to have been refused admission to the Vicarage of Brampford Speke."

as unnecessary or inexpedient by the earlier Tractarians, but which commended itself to some at least among their followers as the necessary and logical outcome of what had gone before. Foremost among these 'Ritualists,' as they now began for the first time to be called, was the Rev. W. J. E. Bennett, Vicar of St. Paul's Church, Knightsbridge. He was indefatigable as a preacher and a pastor, and the result of his appeals to a wealthy congregation was the erection of the district Church of St. Barnabas, Pimlico, which was consecrated by Bishop Blomfield on June 11, 1850. Mr. Bennett's ritual in the parish church had been of so 'advanced' a type as to call for several remonstrances from the Bishop, but St. Barnabas', it was evident, was to be the scene of much more development, and the storm soon began in earnest. It was the year of the 'Papal Aggression,' and when Lord John Russell, in his famous 'Durham Letter,' fanned the anti-Papal fury by denouncing the "unworthy sons of the Church of England" who were "forward in leading their flocks step by step to the very verge of the precipice," he gave the signal for a clamorous outcry against Mr. Bennett, to whom he was known to be referring, and a series of disgraceful disturbances began.

"The Protestant cause," says Bishop Blomfield's biographer, "was taken up by those to whom all religions were equally indifferent, and all excuses for a riot equally acceptable, and every Sunday saw the Church doors besieged by a mob of disorderly supporters of the Reformation, and the services interrupted by their groans or hisses."[1]

Far from yielding to this clamour, Mr. Bennett became firmer than ever in his resistance, not only to the mob, but to the Bishop, and he formally signified his intention of taking

---

[1] *Memoir of Bishop Blomfield*, vol. ii. p. 146.

"three standards to guide him in the ritual of St. Barnabas: first, whatever was practised in any other churches in the Diocese, and as yet undetected by the Bishop; secondly, whatever had been done in the Bishop's presence at the consecration of the church; and thirdly, whatever he could find practised in any of the English Cathedrals. To such rules of ritual observance the Bishop, of course, was not likely to give his consent, and finding no other way of ending a controversy, the protracting of which only increased the agitation, he at length accepted an offer, made more than once by Mr. Bennett, of resigning his living."[1]

After a short interval of comparative quiet the controversy began again. Mr. Bennett had been succeeded at St. Paul's by the Hon. and Rev. Robert Liddell, whose ritual in both the churches under his control soon formed the subject of a fresh complaint. In December 1855 judgment was delivered in the Consistory Court of the London Diocese directing certain changes in the ritual complained of. The Court of Arches confirmed this sentence on appeal, and Mr. Liddell at once appealed further to the Privy Council. Matters had reached this stage when Bishop Tait's Episcopate began, and he thus found himself the inheritor of a controversy with the origin of which he had nothing to do. Within a few months of his consecration he had to sit as a Privy Council Assessor to hear Mr. Liddell's appeal, and he took part in formulating the ultimate Judgment which was delivered by Lord Kingsdown on March 21, 1857. It was the first of what is now a long series of ritual judgments. The questions raised were comparatively new, and some of the statements contained in the judgment have since been seriously impugned in the light of historical evidence, subsequently unearthed, upon a subject which is admittedly both intricate and obscure. It was evident, however, that,

---

[1] *Memoir of Bishop Blomfield*, vol. ii. p. 140.

on the basis of such information as was then available,
no effort had been spared to make the judgment both
accurate and complete.   Some of the decisions of the
Courts below were affirmed, others were reversed, the
net result being that Mr. Liddell was directed to remove
the stone Altar from St. Barnabas' Church, and to substitute a wooden table, with or without the re-table or
super-altar belonging to it ; that he was also to remove
as illegal the cross attached to the Communion Table, and
was to discontinue the use of certain embroidered altar
linen which had been objected to ; while, on the other
hand, in reversal of the decision of the Courts below, he
was permitted to retain the various coloured frontals and
hangings for the Holy Table, a credence table for the
bread and wine, and, finally, crosses of whatever material,
when erected as 'architectural ornaments' not attached
to the Holy Table, or intended to be objects of superstitious reverence.   The judgment concludes by expressing
the " satisfaction of their Lordships that both the Archbishop of Canterbury and the Bishop of London (the two
Assessors who had heard the case) concur in the judgment which has just been delivered."   The result of the
appeal was, on the whole, distinctly favourable to Mr.
Liddell and his party, and the injunctions of the Court
of Appeal were immediately complied with.   A few weeks
after the judgment was delivered, the Bishop, whose
personal relations with Mr. Liddell continued to be of the
most friendly kind, preached in St. Paul's Church at his
request, and took occasion, while plainly expressing his
disapproval of some of he services at St. Barnabas, to
defend Mr. Liddell from the charge of intentional lawlessness, and to bear testimony to the zeal and efficiency of
his work. A technical question was raised as to the
interpretation to be put upon the Privy Council direction

with respect to the cross as an 'architectural ornament.'
The Privy Council had distinctly refused to condemn
such a cross when on the chancel screen, and Mr. Liddell
now asked the Bishop whether he might interpret the
decision as applying also to the reredos.

The Bishop replied as follows :—

The Bishop of London to the Hon. and Rev. Robert Liddell.

"LONDON HOUSE, *6th April* 1857.

"MY DEAR SIR,—I should be truly glad if I could think it
consistent with my duty to yield to the request you have preferred. I am sure you will believe me when I say that I am
most unwilling to do anything which may have an appearance
of want of sympathy with good and earnest persons such as
those whose charitable and pious labours you speak of. But
having taken part in the deliberations on which the decision of
the Judicial Committee of the Privy Council was founded, I
feel that I should be departing widely from its spirit if I allowed
the wooden cross when removed from the Communion Table to
be replaced by another of stone in the 'architectural structure
of the reredos.' Such a change could scarcely be regarded
otherwise than as an evasion of the decision, and I cannot but
think that the calmer judgment of your people will, on reflection, see that I could not with any propriety accede to this
request.[1]

"Trusting and believing that the attachment of your flock to
the Church of England is far deeper than to be liable to be
shaken by such a cause as this plain discharge of my duty, I
would conclude with an earnest prayer that at this sacred season
the doctrine of the Cross and of our close union in Him who
suffered thereon, whether represented or not in our churches by
the presence of its outward symbol, may be present to all our
hearts.—I am, my dear Sir, faithfully yours,

"A. C. LONDON."

---

[1] The technical point with which this letter deals came again before the
Privy Council a few years later (on June 22, 1860) in the second suit of
Liddell *v.* Beal, when it was decided that such a cross in such a position
had not been declared by the previous judgment to be illegal.

Soon after the judgment in the case of Liddell *v.* Westerton was made public, the Bishop received complaints from several other parishes in his diocese. Most of these he was able to allay by his personal intervention and authority, and even when this was unsuccessful he was strongly averse to bringing the questions at issue before a court of law, although such litigation was at that time advocated as the proper course by the Ritualistic clergy themselves.

A single example will make this clear. One of the charges against Mr. Liddell was that he had placed candlesticks and candles, presumably for ceremonial purposes, upon the Altar of St. Paul's Church. In giving judgment upon this point in the Diocesan Court on December 5, 1855, the judge, Dr. Lushington, spoke as follows :—

"I hold that all lighted candles on the Communion Table are contrary to law, except when they are lighted for the purpose of giving necessary light."

The candlesticks and candles therefore, to which exception had been taken, were declared not to be in themselves illegal ornaments of the Altar, but the ceremonial lighting of them was in Dr. Lushington's opinion contrary to law. Against this judgment no appeal was raised when Mr. Liddell brought his case before the Privy Council, and, so far as Mr. Liddell was concerned, the judgment was not disobeyed. But other clergy took a different line, as is shown by the following correspondence between the Bishop and the Rev. Edward Stuart, a well-known and representative clergyman of the 'advanced' school, and one of the original founders of the English Church Union.

The Bishop of London to the Rev. E. Stuart.

"FULHAM PALACE, *5th March* 1858.

"MY DEAR SIR,—I have very carefully considered what passed at my interview with you yesterday in London House, and I feel myself obliged to adhere to the opinion I then expressed. I must, therefore, lay my commands upon you to discontinue the practice you have introduced without any authority in St. Mary Magdalene, Munster Square, of lighting the candles on the Communion Table in broad daylight, except when they may reasonably be considered necessary or convenient for purpose of light. I cannot hold it to be a good reason for lighting them at the celebration of the Holy Communion in our Reformed Church, that lighted candles were, in Roman Catholic times, or even during the short period of transition before the Reformation was fully settled in England, placed before the Sacrament on the high altar at the celebration of the Mass. I earnestly trust that on reflection you will see the extreme impropriety of an individual clergyman, on the authority of his own private judgment or that of his friends, as to what he considers an admissible return to ancient usage, disregarding the distinct commands of those who are set over him in the Lord. To a person like yourself, I need not urge further that this obligation is rendered if possible stronger by the oath you have taken to obey your Diocesan in all things lawful and honest.

"You will, I am sure, believe that I fully sympathise in the self-denying efforts which I know you have made and are making for the flock committed to you. And I think our conversation yesterday must have convinced you that I am anxious to allow you as great liberty as possible in so applying the services of our Church as you deem most likely to affect your people's hearts, but you will grant that a heavy responsibility devolves on me not to sanction the introduction of innovations or returns to old usages of the unreformed Church which I believe likely to break down the barriers which mark in the minds of simple people the distinction between our worship and that of Rome. The point beyond which a private clergyman must not go, in following his own private judgment in the forms of public worship must surely, in the very lowest view of Episcopal authority, be settled by the Bishop, and I cannot but hope that when your Diocesan, having given his best attention to the law and customs of the Church, forbids an innovation, you will drop the practice objected to, even though you may think it right for your own justification to place on record that you do so merely out of deference to an authority which you feel bound to respect, and to which, indeed, the Prayer-Book distinctly refers you in all points which admit of any doubt. I have told you that I have no intention at present of bringing such matters into a court of justice, believing that I best consult the well-being of the Church, already too much disturbed by the agitation of questions of ceremonial, by endeavouring to rule as long as I can by the quiet and private exercise of that power of godly admonition with which I am intrusted. Let me call to your mind that if, notwithstanding the legal grounds I have stated to you, you still suppose my exposition of the law to be erroneous, your dutiful acquiescence in my decision does in nowise prejudice the general question, while I believe you will, on calm consideration, find such acquiescence satisfactory to your own conscience, and far more likely than a contrary course to further the great object you have in view—viz., your gaining and retaining a wholesome spiritual influence over your people's souls. Such influence, I cannot doubt, would be likely to be lessened by the unseemly spectacle of your setting me at defiance.

"I know that I write to one whose life shows that he feels deeply the ministerial responsibilities, and, therefore, I am the more hopeful of your acquiescence.—Believe me to be, my dear Sir, faithfully yours,   A. C. LONDON."

The Rev. E. Stuart to the Bishop of London.

"1 MUNSTER SQUARE,
Monday, March 8, 1858.

"MY LORD,—I write to acknowledge the receipt of your letter of the 5th instant, containing a command to me to discontinue the use of lights at the celebration of the Sacrament.

"I must respectfully decline to obey this command, as I believe that in issuing it you have (unintentionally, of course) transgressed the limits of that authority which the Church of England has committed to her Bishops.

"I believe that you have done this by forbidding what the law of the Church distinctly authorises, for the Rubric (which is our law in this matter) distinctly authorises 'such ornaments of the

Church, and of the ministers thereof, as were in use in the Church of England, by authority of Parliament, in the second year of Edward VI.' Now I have no doubt whatever that lights were generally used at the celebration of the Sacrament throughout the Church of England, by authority of Parliament, in that year. If I am wrong in this belief I am, of course, subject to correction.

"I must deprecate the use of such a phrase as that of 'setting you at defiance.' It is simply impossible for a priest of the Church of England to set at defiance any lawful exercise of the authority of his Diocesan, since the Church has given abundant power to her Bishops to compel obedience in such a case; but a matter of advice implies of necessity a discretionary power in the person advised. . . .—I remain, my Lord, your obedient servant,   EDWARD STUART."

The Bishop of London to the Rev. E. Stuart.

"FULHAM PALACE, *March* [10], 1858.

"MY DEAR SIR,—I greatly regret that you should think it right to disobey my command on your own private interpretation of what you deem to be the law. Had you read the judgment of the Privy Council in the Knightsbridge case, and Dr. Lushington's previous judgment on the same, with the care that they deserve, you would, I doubt not, have seen your error as to the point of law. Your view of the obedience due to a Bishop and of the interpretation of your oath seems to resolve itself into a claim of right to resist all his admonitions unless he thinks it for the good of the Church to enforce them by penalties in a court of justice.

"I most deeply regret that one whom I believe to be so much in earnest in his endeavours to labour among his flock should be so far misled, and I earnestly trust that you will one day see how wrong is the course you are pursuing. I shall not fail to be ready to assist you in any way that may be consistent with the unfortunate position in which you have, to my great sorrow, placed yourself.—Believe me to be, my dear Sir, yours faithfully,   "A. C. LONDON."

Grave difficulties had in the meantime arisen upon a totally different subject; and again the arena of the strife was the parish of St. Paul's, Knightsbridge. The Rev. Alfred Poole, one of the curates of the parish, was accused, at the instance of several parishioners, of habitually asking outrageous questions from persons who came to him in Confession. The Bishop investigated the matter, and came to the conclusion that the accusation which had been made was unsupported by the evidence, and ought to be dismissed. It was elicited, however, that Mr. Poole's views on the subject of the Confessional had led him to adopt practices which the Bishop regarded as at variance with the teaching of the Church of England on the subject. The Bishop accordingly wrote to Mr. Poole as follows :—

"While I fully admit that the statements you have made to me tend to make me look with much suspicion upon the particular evidence laid before me, I regret to say that, quite independently of that evidence, I am led by your own admission to regard the course you are in the habit of pursuing in reference to Confession as likely to cause scandal and injury to the Church. . . . Under the circumstances I feel I ought to mark my sense of the impropriety of what you describe as your practice, and I shall therefore feel myself bound, though with great pain, to withdraw your licence as curate of St. Barnabas, and shall send you formal notice accordingly. I earnestly pray that this solemn protest on my part against a course in which I believe you have departed from the spirit and practice of the Church of England, and assimilated your mode of dealing with your people too much to the system of the Church of Rome, may cause you to pause and reflect on the dangers to which such a course of action as you have adopted may expose both yourself and those over whom you exercise influence ; and I trust you will allow me to add that I shall at any time be glad to give you my best advice and assistance in the difficulties in which you are involved.—I remain, reverend and dear Sir, yours faithfully,   A. C. London."

Mr. Poole replied in a long and perfectly temperate protest against the Bishop's action. He asked for a specific statement of the particular charges on the strength of which the licence was withdrawn, and solemnly asserted that he had "never put any questions of a nature, or in a manner, or in language 'calculated to bring scandal on the Church,' or otherwise than was calculated to assist the penitent, and to enable him or her to receive more effectually the consolation or advice which, as the minister of the Church, it was his duty to impart."

But the Bishop declined to give way. He testified strongly to his own belief that Mr. Poole was "a conscientious and upright man," for whom he had "a most sincere personal regard," and he showed that he was not unwilling to license him afresh in some other parish where party feeling did not run so high. But he deemed it necessary, on public grounds, to give this emphatic expression to his views about the teaching at St. Barnabas', and the licence was accordingly withdrawn. Mr. Poole, with the Bishop's entire approval, and even encouragement, appealed to the Archbishop of Canterbury, by whom, after a full hearing, it was formally decided[1] that there was "good and reasonable cause for the revocation of this licence, and that the Bishop of London has exercised a sound discretion in revoking the same."

Mr. Poole then carried his appeal to the Judicial Committee of the Privy Council, who, after hearing the fullest legal arguments upon either side, decided that there was no such right of appeal from the Archbishop's decision, and that they must therefore decline to enter into the merits of the case. This decision, however, was not given till March 13, 1861, three years after the com-

---

[1] The Archbishop had at first given judgment upon the case *in camerâ*, but on Mr. Poole's request a *mandamus* issued from the Court of Queen's Bench commanding the Archbishop to hear the appeal in Court. He did so, and gave formal judgment as above.

mencement of the dispute, and the general question had in the meantime been under vehement discussion on every side. The Bishop had taken pains to show from the first that it was on no grounds personal to Mr. Poole that the licence had been revoked. It was intended to be a distinct and public declaration of his opinion—an opinion to which he adhered to the end of his life—that the inculcation of the practice of habitual auricular confession was contrary to the doctrine and practice of the Church of England. Accepting this as the issue, Mr. Liddell and other London clergymen espoused with the utmost zeal the cause of Mr. Poole, while pamphlets and letters not less vehement poured forth upon the Bishop's side. While the strife was at its height the time came for the Bishop's primary Charge. Its general purport and the remarkable facts of its delivery are described elsewhere.[1] But the importance of this particular question, and the care with which it was treated in the Charge,[2] seem to require that a few extracts should be given.

"In pointing," he said, "to the difficulties which beset a young pastor, I would especially refer, as an example, to questions as to the authority and claims of the ministerial office, which have in these days grown to an importance such as has scarcely ever before attached to them in our Church since the Reformation.

"On this matter I must be explicit. First, then, let us not forget in approaching such questions that nothing can exceed the solemnity of the words in which it has been thought proper in the Church of England to confer the full rights of the office of the Presbyter. Also let us not forget that these words of ordination have always in our Church been interpreted by a large and influential body—by many, indeed, of our most honoured divines—as conferring the right, derived from Christ Himself, not only to administer His Holy Sacraments and preach His Holy Word

---

[1] See p. 265.

[2] Twenty-five pages of the Charge are devoted to this subject alone.

in the congregation, but also to speak of pardon with authority in Christ's name in the Church's service in a way in which other men cannot speak, for the comfort of distressed souls. . . . The claim, I say, of such authority for Presbyters of the Church of England has hitherto been usually expressed with guarded moderation even by those who thought most highly of it. Isolated passages may be adduced from our great divines upholding the Priest's absolving power ; but any dangerous application of such passages is guarded against by the whole tenor of those more moderate sentiments which we find breathing through the works quoted when we view them as a whole.

"At the risk of being tedious, I think it right to enter somewhat at length into this matter. The silence of the Church of England Formularies, as compared with the fulness of the Church of Rome, in treating of systematic Confession is itself, to my mind, an irrefragable argument to show that the mind of our Church is quite against the practices now sought to be introduced.[1] . . .

"Moreover, I would observe, for myself, that it is no wish of mine to insist on other people adopting my own opinions as to the exact nature of the Presbyter's office, and thus to narrow those bounds of a wise comprehensiveness, according to which the Church of England has always allowed her children, if they chose, to believe that some very especial blessing and comfort to the penitent soul is to be derived from listening to the promises of God's mercy, pronounced by his minister on those limited occasions where alone the Formularies have authorised him officially to pronounce them as Absolution. What I do utterly disapprove of, and what I feel constrained most strongly to protest against, is something very different from the common pastoral intercourse which is indicated in the three passages of the Prayer-Book I have cited, and which the Church always must uphold. It has been said that I have not explained myself when I have spoken against a systematic introduction of the practice of Confession as opposed to such common pastoral intercourse. But I really believe even those who make this objection will, when they reflect, allow—all men of common discernment must know and distinctly recognise—the difference between the pastoral intercourse I have spoken of and that

---

[1] The Charge contains at this point sixteen printed pages of elaborate reference to authorities, ancient and modern, on the subject of Confession.

which is now endeavoured to be set up amongst us under the name of the Confessional.   If any clergyman so preaches to his people as to lead them to suppose that the proper and authorised way of a sinner's reconciliation with God is through confession to a priest, and by receiving priestly absolution ; if he leads them to believe (I use the illustration I have found employed by an advocate of the Confessional) that, as the Greek Church has erred by neglecting preaching, and the Church of Rome by not encouraging the reading of the Scriptures, so our Church has hitherto been much to blame for not leading her people more habitually to private auricular confession ; if he thus stirs up the imagination of ardent and confiding spirits to have recourse to him as a mediator between their souls and God, and when they come to seek his aid receives them with all the elaborate preparation which is so likely unduly to excite their feelings, and for which there is no authority in the Church's rules of worship—taking them into the vestry of his church, securing the door, putting on the sacred vestments, causing them to kneel before the cross, to address him as their ghostly father, asking a string of questions as to sins of deed, word, and thought, and imposing penance before he confers absolution ; the man who thus acts, or — even if some of these particular circumstances are wanting—of whose general practice this is no exaggerated picture, is, in my judgment, unfaithful to the whole spirit of the Church of which he is a minister. . . . But if any will not be stayed by mild remonstrance and affectionate warning, those invested with authority in the Church must use the other means of influence which they find their position gives them to prevent evil.   How that influence shall be wielded in particular cases it must rest with the Bishop's own discretion to decide, whether in some less penal form, or necessarily by severe examples of discipline, such as it has greatly pained me of late to feel myself constrained to use against a zealous and pious and truly well-meaning but mistaken brother.   All I can distinctly intimate on this public occasion is that if what I deem a dangerous systematic invitation and admission of his people to Confession is endeavoured to be maintained by any clergyman in this diocese, I shall feel myself bound to watch his proceedings very carefully, and shall hold him most deeply responsible for any evils that ensue ; considering carefully in each particular case what power the law gives me to correct what is amiss.   One thing I wish to add, that if I have abstained hitherto from giving in any church distinct directions on this subject, it has been because I have received no assurance that my directions are likely to be obeyed.   Clergymen who seek to introduce this bad system may indeed express a general readiness to follow my advice as to the mode in which they will carry it into practice, thus endeavouring to gain for it the aid of my authority.   On such terms I am not likely to give advice. What I do advise and urge is that they abstain altogether from seeking to introduce amongst their people any systematic and habitual Confession such as I have described.   Believe me, my reverend brethren, our Church has not erred in being so guarded and cautious in this matter.   There is within the limits of her calm and reverent piety full opportunity to satisfy all the really spiritual longings of the faithful soul, while she leads it to direct personal intercourse with the Lord Jesus Christ.   Other longings which her system has made no provision to satisfy we shall be right to scrutinise very carefully before we think well of them ; putting on the guise of religion, they may be but some subtle form of the yearnings of the unregenerate heart.   Be it yours in such matters gently to restrain and guide the morbidly sensi- tive, and to teach your people daily better to understand and appreciate the blessings offered in the authorised system of our own Reformed Church."

Whether in consequence of this Charge or for other reasons, the 'Confession Controversy,' as it was called, passed almost out of sight for many years.   Its vehement revival when Bishop Tait had become Primate will form the subject of a later chapter.[1]

A few weeks after the Charge had been delivered, new troubles arose, in a different part of the diocese from that which had been disturbed before.   The riots of St. George's in the East are still remembered as a remarkable episode in the public life of the Metropolis.   Of the various mission centres for the Church's work among the poor of London, none has earned a worthier claim to a place in history than

---

[1] Chapter XXIII.

that which was set on foot by Mr. Charles Lowder and his colleagues in the great riverside parish of St. George's in the East. How much of the success which attended the efforts of these devoted men is to be attributed to the personal power and magnetism of Mr. Lowder's presence, and how much to the system he adopted, is a question on which opinions will continue to differ. It may also be fairly questioned whether Mr. Lowder's work, during its earlier years, gained or lost by its association with the scenes of excitement and controversy which, for some months, were witnessed week by week in the great Parish Church from which his mission was an offshoot. Painful and mischievous as were the riots of St. George's in the East, discreditable as their continuance undoubtedly was both to the civil authorities and to the partisan wire-pullers who instigated the controversialists on either side, the prominence which was thus given in the public mind to the devoted work which was going on in St. George's mission for the civilisation of one of the roughest neighbourhoods in London, was not without its very practical advantages both to the mission itself and to the Church at large.[1] Examples of such work were less common then than now, and the enlistment of sympathy for the Church's self-denying workers was a frequent, though unintentional, result of the endeavours to put them down by force of law, and even by personal violence.

The keepers of the dens of drink and infamy, who reap their nightly harvest from the sailors and others in the neighbourhood of London Docks, were doubtless ranged, to a man, under the so-called 'Protestant' banner during the St. George's riots of 1859. But it would be a simple error of fact to confound the mission work of Mr. Lowder

---

[1] For emphatic testimony to this advantage, see Charles Lowder's *Life*, pp. 150, etc.

with the 'movement,' such as it was, which produced these disturbances. Mr. Lowder, as he has himself recounted in a volume of the highest interest,[1] was appointed in 1856 to take charge of a separate mission district, now the parish of St. Peter's, London Docks. The work was carried on from the first upon the lines of the 'Catholic Revival,' of which Mr. Lowder had become a warm adherent. But although he encountered the usual amount of opposition from the disorderly and degraded, there seems to have been little if any attempt during his first three years of progress to enlist against him the sympathies of 'Protestants' as such. Those who knew anything about his work must have seen that the evils with which he was endeavouring to grapple were not of a kind to make men critical as to the precise means adopted for the fight. He was even assisted from time to time by such men as Arthur Stanley, Frederick Maurice, and Thomas Hughes, and had the parish been in his hands as Rector its history might have been very different.

The Rector was the Rev. Bryan King, a man of intense earnestness, high courage, and unflinching principle, but unsuited, in a singular degree, for the charge of such a parish as St. George's in the East.

He had been appointed to the Rectory in 1842, the very year in which Bishop Blomfield's famous Charge to the clergy of London, enjoining the use of the surplice in the pulpit, and the prayer for the Church Militant, had aroused the fears and the hostility of the Evangelical party. Mr. King not only made these changes, as in duty bound, but endeavoured in many other ways to give a different character to the slovenly services which had prevailed before his time. Some of his friends subscribed to the support of a paid choir, and the Psalms and Canticles, and, before long, the

---

[1] *Twenty-one Years in S. George's Mission*, pp. 18-50.

Litany, were chanted, to the great dislike of the old-fashioned members of the congregation. Unfortunately, Mr. King, with all his earnestness, had not the gift, in introducing such changes as he thought necessary, of doing it in a conciliatory manner. His congregation, partly from the removal of the richer parishioners into the suburbs, partly from other causes, grew steadily smaller, and when in 1856 he announced his intention of adopting the then almost unheard-of Eucharistic Vestments, a more widespread dissatisfaction began. The dissatisfied, how-ever, contented themselves with grumbling and absenting themselves more and more from the unpopular services. Outside the Church's walls, in the meantime, Mr. King's influence and authority were yet further on the wane. He has himself described his position as follows :—

"The number of souls nominally intrusted to my charge was about 38,000. . . . When I allude to the amount of the merely ordinary routine of clerical duties, in the celebration of the daily services and the occasional religious offices, . . . [as well as] the merely secular duties which devolved upon me as Chairman of the Vestry, . . . it will not be a matter of any surprise if I now confess that, beyond the exercise of something like discipline in regard to a few extreme cases—such as the refusal to give Christian burial to unbaptized children, or to permit the bodies of some who had died in open sin to be taken into the Church for that portion of the Burial Service, and the refusal to communi-cate one or two notorious evil livers—I was never able even to make *any attempt* at anything like active aggression upon the seething mass of evil and sin by which I was encompassed." [1]

The examples of discipline here instanced by Mr. King himself as his sole attempts at active aggression upon the evil around him serve well to illustrate the character of his earnest but ineffectual ministry at St.

---

[1] Letter from Mr. Bryan King in Mr. Lowder's *Twenty-one Years in St. George's Mission*, p. 227. The italics are Mr. King's.

George's in the East. It would be easy to name clergy of views similar to his who might have made far more sweeping changes in the services of the Church than any that were made by Mr. King, and who would yet have retained the enthusiastic support of at least a large section of their parishioners. It was the misfortune of Mr. King that his efforts after ritual improvement had the result of irritating beyond endurance many of the old-fashioned parishioners, chiefly of the middle class, who still continued to attend their parish church ; while he had, as he himself says, no such agencies among the poor as might have served to attract them by degrees within the Church's walls. One of the memorials to the Bishop of London, adopted in open vestry without a dissentient voice, states that "on account of the religious difference between the Rector and his parishioners there had not been a single charity sermon in the church for sixteen years, either for the National Schools or for the local and medical charities, although these sermons were frequent before that time."

It is essential to bear these facts in mind for the proper understanding of what followed.

From the beginning of his Episcopate Bishop Tait had been receiving periodical complaints and memorials from one or other of the parties in the distracted parish, and the following letter shows that even before his consecration he had been in communication with Mr. Lowder upon the difficulties of his work.

The Bishop-elect of London to the Rev. Charles Lowder.

"BRIGHTON, *Nov.* 13*th*, 1856.

"MY DEAR SIR,—Let me thank you for sending me the earnest expression of the feelings with which you have undertaken your difficult post in St. George's in the East.

" I sincerely trust that God may bless all earnest and single-hearted efforts to spread the Gospel of His Son through the masses of the metropolis.   You certainly may rely on my readiness to give what aid my guidance and advice afford.

" I doubt not that God will so direct the zeal of those who seek Him earnestly in prayer, as to save them from any dangerous errors in doctrine or practice.   And though there may be many zealous men in the diocese to which God has called me, from whom I must greatly differ, I still trust that I may be a fellow-worker with all who love the Lord Jesus Christ in sincerity.   Mr. King has communicated with me respecting the chapel to be opened.   I have put him in communication with Mr. Lee, of Dean's Yard, and I hope all the legal difficulties may speedily be arranged, when I shall be very glad to see the chapel secured as a chapel-of-ease.— Yours faithfully,

" A. C. LONDON (Elect)."

Matters came to a point in the autumn of 1858, when the Bishop's attention was called to certain books and tracts in circulation in the parish,[1] as well as to the ritualistic 'innovations' of the Rector.   A long interview between the Bishop and Mr. Bryan King resulted in the following letter :—

---

[1] Among these was a Catechism from which the following are extracts :—

Q. Are all the Bishops equal ?

A. All are equal in their office, but some are higher in honour than others, as Archbishops, Metropolitans, and Patriarchs, of whom the first is the Bishop of Rome, the Patriarch of the West.

.   .   .   .

Q. What is the fourth commandment of the Church ?

A. To confess our sins to our pastor or some of the priests whenever they trouble us.

Q. At what time may children begin to go to Confession ?

A. When they come to the use of reason, so as to be capable of mortal sin, which is generally supposed to be about the age of seven years.

.   .   .   .

Q. What is the Holy Eucharist ?

A. It is the true Body and Blood of Christ, under the appearance of bread and wine.

Q. How do the bread and wine become the Body and Blood of Christ ?

A. By the power of God, to whom nothing is impossible or difficult.

The Bishop of London to the Rev. Bryan King.

"FULHAM PALACE, *Dec.* 3, 1858.

"MY DEAR SIR,—I think I ought to commit to paper the result of our interview yesterday, for, indeed, in such interviews it is difficult to keep the main points in view ; and I am sure it is due to your standing in the Diocese, as well as to many personal qualities which have secured you the respect of all who know you, that I should state my opinion and wishes for your calm consideration apart from any of those unpleasant feelings which an interview to investigate complaints may call up.

"With respect to what has been laid before me by the churchwardens, I am glad to be assured by you that the candles are not lighted at the celebration of the Holy Communion except for purposes of light.

" As to the green vestments, stoles, or whatever they may have been, which it appears you yourself and Mr. Burn wore on the occasion of the anniversary, I very deeply regret that you should think it right to assume the unusual garments you described to me. I am convinced there is no sufficient warrant for it, and if you continue this, it is against my express order. Surely, if in any matters a Bishop is entitled to require the canonical obedience of his clergy it is in such a case as this. You cannot believe that there is any legal obligation on you to depart in this respect from the usage of our Church, as explained and enforced by all her living authorities. The very utmost point to which you can go must be to consider that the law of the land does not positively forbid you to use such vestments (as, indeed, there are many other strange things which it has never contemplated, and therefore does not forbid), and that, by giving an order for their disuse, I am abridging your liberty. Surely your regard for the office I hold, and the rubric enjoining upon you to refer to the Ordinary, must suggest that in such matters your own private opinion ought to be waived in deference to those set over you ; especially when I urge upon you to give up your own wishes out of regard for the 30,000 souls committed to you, to your usefulness among whom I feel convinced these excessive ritual observances are a great hindrance, as is found, it pains me to think, in the emptiness of your great church.

" As to Mr. Burn's wearing such garments, I am glad to have

been assured yesterday both by you and him that he will discontinue them, and I shall be truly glad if you will resolve to do the same yourself. I have only allowed him to officiate on his probation under very peculiar circumstances, and require obedience as one of the conditions of his probation.

"The same objections that apply to the garments apply also, though perhaps in a lesser degree, to other matters which I pointed out to you in the written description which the churchwardens have given of your service on the occasion of the anniversary, and which I am certain have raised and kept alive a grievous prejudice against your ministry in the minds of your parishioners. I know that you are anxious for the good of their souls. I pray you to consider whether you cannot sacrifice your own peculiar tastes in such matters to promote your spiritual usefulness.

"As to matters brought before me by others, and not by the churchwardens, it was very satisfactory to me to be assured by you that the Catechism complained of as teaching Romish doctrine had never been distributed in the parish, or used in the school, with your knowledge or sanction. I understand your curate, Mr. Lowder, to have given me before the same assurance as to his district of your parish. I take leave to advise that you should let your people understand that you disapprove of this Catechism, if it is still circulating among them through any dishonest influence of those two of your curates who lately joined the Church of Rome. . . .

"And now allow me, my dear sir, to conclude by repeating, what I endeavoured to express to you at the close of our interview, how gladly I would endeavour to strengthen your hands if you could bring yourself to alter your course. I do beg you to give up the matters complained of, which are, I believe, a grievous impediment to your usefulness. In carrying out the simple Scriptural system of our own Church, you will receive, I assure you, all sympathy and assistance from me ; and I cannot but think that the high opinion of your high and gentlemanlike bearing under trying circumstances which I have heard expressed, even by those of your people who are strongly opposed to you, if you showed willingness to act differently in the matters complained of, would not be without its proper weight in enabling you to do our common Master's work in the fearfully responsible position in which you are placed.

"One word more. You seem to have felt aggrieved yesterday that I should lay my commands upon Mr. Burn not to follow your example as to these (you must excuse me for calling them) foolish vestments. But I think, on reflection, you will see that a Bishop, in such a case, must exercise his power to guide and control a curate, where he conscientiously believes an incumbent is leading him astray; and Mr. Burn is not even your curate, he is simply a gentleman on his probation, assisting you by special favour.

"I have thought the simplest way of answering the present ment, if I may so consider it, of the churchwardens is to send them a copy of this letter.

"I wish to draw your attention to their statement that the congregation at the parish church is less than 150 at the most, while the number of regular attendants in the pews and free seats together is only about 40, and that in the mission chapels the united congregation altogether consists of only about 35 adults.—Believe me to be, my dear sir, yours faithfully,

"A. C. LONDON."

By an Act of Parliament passed in George II.'s reign, the Vestry possessed the right of nominating a lecturer for the parish Church, who should " be admitted by the Rector to have the use of the pulpit from time to time." And the Vestry of St. George's in the East now proceeded to elect to that office the Rev. Hugh Allen, already distinguished for the vehemence of his 'no Popery' tenets. Mr. Allen's testimonials and other papers were presented in due form, and although the consequences were not difficult to foresee, the Bishop found he had no power to intervene, and Mr. Allen was duly licensed on May 17, 1859. On the following Sunday, according to Mr. Lowder's biographer—

"Mr. Allen entered the pulpit triumphantly brandishing the Bishop's licence in his hand, and was greeted with shouts of applause. He had a band of devoted and noisy adherents who filled the Church with uproar, and, elated by their success, invaded it on the next Sunday during the usual service, the clamour and violence reaching such a pitch, that the clergy and choir were with difficulty extricated from the mob by the police."[1]

It would be tedious as well as painful, to recount the repetition, Sunday after Sunday, of these disgraceful scenes. The riot, disorder, and buffoonery grew worse instead of better, and the civil authorities believed themselves unable to interfere. In August the churchwardens appealed to the Bishop. It seems right to reproduce the Bishop's reply in full, notwithstanding its length, as it gives expression to his opinions not only on the particular points at issue, but on some of the principles which underlay both this and other strifes.

The Bishop of London to the Senior Churchwarden of St. George's in the East.

"LLANDUDNO, 5 *September* 1859.

"SIR,—I beg to acknowledge 'your official letter of the 2d instant, respecting the late disgraceful proceedings in the parish of St. George's in the East. It reached me yesterday (Sunday), and I also beg to acknowledge the copy of a report made to the vestry of St. George in the East by a Committee appointed by that body.

"In answering your letter, I think it necessary to draw your attention to a distinction as to Episcopal authority, very commonly lost sight of in such disputes. A Bishop's authority is of two kinds. Within a certain range defined by law, he has power to give orders and enforce obedience to them by penalty of law. Over a much wider range, he has authority from the good feeling of all well-disposed members of the Church, who voluntarily accept his paternal advice and guidance. It is not too much to say that by far the greater part of a Bishop's government of his Diocese is carried on through the willing deference which good Christian feeling suggests to the members of his Church, both lay and clerical, that he is entitled to claim on account of the very nature of his office.

---

[1] *Biography of Charles Lowder*, p. 173.

"Now, a difficulty arises in answering your letter, from your not distinctly intimating in which of these two capacities it is that the aid of my authority is now invoked.

"I. I shall consider the matter brought before me in reference to that authority which I can enforce by legal penalties.

"You are aware that two parties in this dispute have invoked my aid.

"(1) I am informed, on the part of the Rector, that the parish Church is desecrated by disorderly persons, the public worship of God interrupted, and the Rector, or other officiating minister, with the choristers, habitually insulted during or after Divine Service. No language can be too strong to express the abhorrence with which all persons of any true Christian feeling must regard such outrages, if they really take place, as is not denied. It is the grossest self-deceit to suppose that they can be justified by any provocation which the Rector's choral service or unusual habiliments may have given. But what is the legal remedy for these disturbances? It is that to which I have had recourse. I have required the Churchwardens to be present at the service in which the riotous proceedings complained of are alleged to take place, and to exercise the powers inherent in their office, for the suppression of disorder. These powers are well defined by Statute 1 William and Mary, cap. 18, clause 18—

"'If any person maliciously or contemptuously come into any Church and disquiet or disturb the congregation, or misuse any preacher or teacher, such person, upon proof thereof before any justice of the peace, by two or more sufficient witnesses, shall find two sureties, bound by recognisance, in the penal sum of £50, and in default of such sureties, shall be committed to prison, there to remain till the next general or quarter sessions, and upon correction, shall forfeit £20 to the use of the Crown.'

"At common law, a person disturbing Divine service may be removed by any other person there present, but the duty of maintaining order lies especially on the churchwardens. If they are absent, or being present do not repress disorder, they neglect their duty. I grant that the performance of their duty, in the present instance, is difficult, but the law seems to point out with sufficient distinctness how they ought to act. The Rector, as I learned from the report of the Committee of Vestry, has formally intimated to the churchwardens that he will hold them responsible to an Ecclesiastical Court for the performance of their duty above described, and they are certainly so responsible.   The Committee of Vestry is of opinion that they are most assiduous in the performance of their duty, and I shall be truly glad to find that this is so.

"This is the strict legal aspect of the case, as regards the complaint on the Rector's part respecting the alleged disturbance of public worship, and as regards the remedy which ought to be applied.

"(2) The complaint of the Vestry, which you forward to me, has reference to the alleged exciting cause of such disturbance. You state, as I understand you, that these disturbances arose from the exasperation of feeling caused by the objectionable mode in which you allege that the Rev. Bryan King, the Rector, and those appointed by him, celebrate Divine Service in the Parish Church, and also by the inconvenience of the hour appointed by the Rector for the afternoon lecture.

"You therefore request me to restore the afternoon (lecture) service to the hour of 3 or 3.30, and to prohibit the use of unaccustomed vestments by the officiating clergy.   I gather from your letter, and the report enclosed, that there are other matters in the ceremonial of the parish Church, which you consider to be causes of dissension, and, in particular, you bring under my notice the mode in which the morning service was conducted on Sunday, August 28, by a strange clergyman designated the Rev. Frederick George Lee.

"(a) As to the hour of the afternoon (lecture) service, you are aware that the arrangements respecting this lecture were very lately made the subject of proceedings before a Court of Law, and my understanding of the decision of the learned judge in the case is, that it was left to the Rector to fix such hour as he deemed fit and proper for the lecture.   I write at a distance from the means of verifying this impression, but, subject to correction and better information, I am of opinion that I have no legal authority to order the hour to be changed.   Your request on this subject must, I apprehend, be addressed to the Rector, and not to me.

"(b) With regard to the mode of celebrating Divine Worship in the parish Church, I understand you to complain that at 4 o'clock on Sundays the Litany is used as a separate Choral service.

"If your objection be to the celebration in the parish Church of any additional Divine Service beyond the ordinary morning service, the afternoon (lecture) service, and the evening service, I have no power to prevent such additional use of the Church, and certainly I should not employ such power if I had it. In a parish so vast as that of St. George's in the East, the more services there are the better, and the incumbent has a legal right to use his Church as often in the day as possible, and I highly approve of his multiplying the opportunities of public worship.

"Again, if your objection is to this additional service being choral, the law allows the incumbent to have a choral rather than a read service if he pleases ; and though I may highly disapprove, as I do, of forcing a choral service on an unwilling parish, I can only remonstrate. I have, by law, no power of forbidding, or, if I forbid, of enforcing obedience to my mandate.

" Again, if your objection be to this additional service being the Litany and not a third regular evening service, I must point out to you that there is a very commonly expressed desire, to which utterance has been given in Parliament and elsewhere, to have the ordinary morning service of the Church of England shortened, and I have myself, in my place in Parliament, stated that an obvious way of legally attaining this object is by separating, as the law allows, the Litany from the ordinary morning service. It is an open question whether the clergyman has not the power of effecting such a separation in strict accordance with the rubric, even without any sanction from his Bishop. If from my common authority as Ordinary, I have legal power to forbid this practice, I should be very unwilling to do so, unless I was satisfied in this instance, that it was the fact of this service being the Litany, rather than an additional repetition of the common evening service, that is the cause of the exasperation that you allege.

"But the chief real objection to this 4 o'clock service, I presume, arises from its being supposed to interfere with the (lecture) afternoon service. I have already stated to you, how, as I apprehend, the case stands regarding any legal power to regulate the hour of that lecture service. I can only point out to you, further, that I fear the parish would scarcely be satisfied, if the Rector so far gave way as to incorporate Mr. Allen's lecture into an afternoon choral service of his own, conducted according to the model of his own usual services. And if he so far gave way as to admit the lecturer to his pulpit at his usual after-

noon service, he would, I apprehend, have the legal right to
make that service choral. I confess I think it is on the whole
better that these two gentlemen (the lecturer and the rector of
the parish) should have their hours of ministration in the parish
church separate.

"I now come to the only other point you mention—the use
of unaccustomed vestments by the officiating clergy. It is well
known that I have announced my determination to put a stop to
such follies when I can do so by my summary jurisdiction over
those who are placed more immediately under my personal control; and such jurisdiction I have already exercised at St. George's,
and I hereby require the churchwardens to give me immediate
information if any clergyman so officiate in the Church, as to
give reasonable offence by this childish mimicry of antiquated
garments, or by so dressing himself up that he may resemble as
much as possible a Roman Catholic priest. Even if it be proved
that such foolish practices are not a distinct violation of the
letter of the law, they may indicate such a wrong-headed and
self-willed determination, for the sake of foolish theory, to
endanger the success of his ministrations among the souls committed to him, as to justify the Bishop in summarily withdrawing a curate's licence for the good of the parish. I need not,
however, point out to you that the law does not give the Bishop
any such power in dealing summarily with an incumbent, and in
the case of the Rector of your parish, with whom I had some
lengthened communication last winter on the subject of these
very garments, you are probably aware that on mature consideration, I determined to trust rather to my conviction that common
sense will in the end prevail, and not to go into a court of
justice on a matter which appears to me to be so foolish in itself,
and the issue in the legal prosecution of which, through all the
several courts, must, after all, be uncertain from the very nature
of a controversy turning on the shape and pattern of the clothes
worn at the time of the Reformation, and their points of resem-
blance to, and divergence from, the garments made for us in the
present day.

" But though I entertain this opinion myself that prosecutions
on what may be called the vestment question, in a court of law,
are inexpedient and indeed derogatory to the character of our
Church, I by no means wish to bind others by my opinion in
this matter, against their will; and if it is the deliberate desire

of those whom you represent to prosecute the Rector for wearing garments which (I grant not unnaturally) offend his parishioners, I shall be ready when called upon to afford you all due facilities for the commencement of your lawsuit as far as my authority extends.

"I need scarcely say further that if you have any charge to bring forward of unsoundness of doctrine, or any distinct violation of the law of the Church which you think you can substantiate, I shall be ready at once to hear and investigate it.

"With respect to the Rev. F. G. Lee, of whom you complain, that gentleman has no leave to minister in my diocese, and I have required intimation to be sent to him to desist from so officiating till he obtains my formal authority. I have written to Mr. Mackonochie, who is a licensed curate in the parish, desiring him to take the service in the parish Church till the Rector's return.

"I have thus stated to you what is the legal power I possess of interfering by my authority personally to enforce obedience on both sides of this miserable controversy, and I shall now sum up my decision as respects this legal power. On the one hand, I call on the churchwardens, at their peril, to do their duty in preserving order in the church, and bringing offenders to justice, according to the Statute. On the other hand, I prohibit all unusual vestments, such as you complain of, in the celebration of Divine service. I am ready, when I can, summarily to enforce their disuse, and if you desire it, I am ready to further your prosecution, in a court of law, of those whom I cannot myself reach summarily. Any other complaint of violation of the Church's law I am ready at once to investigate, on its being distinctly pointed out. I do not consider myself entitled in law to order the alteration of the hour of service which you may desire.

"You may feel at first surprised that my power as Bishop should go no further than I have notified, but on the whole, for my own part, I do not consider it an evil in the Church of England, that incumbents of parishes are invested with so independent a responsibility, which, I am bound to say, in most cases they exercise wisely for the good of their parishioners, and which it would not be consistent with our manly English spirit to see suspended by an arbitrary extension of episcopal dominion. As I have said, it is not by compulsory force of law, but by authority of a gentler kind that a Bishop most effectively works; and I would now shortly consider, in the second place, how such authority may avail us, in the present miserable dispute.

"II. If the Rector on the one hand and those who oppose him on the other, have any right Christian spirit, they must be thoroughly ashamed of the state into which the parish is now brought.   If the allegations which have reached me are to be depended upon, bad men have availed themselves of the irritation which has been excited to bring dishonour on the worship of God, and the name of our holy religion.   Under such circumstances sincere members of our Church cannot, I should think, hesitate as to the duty of submitting their causes of quarrel for arbitration to him whom God has placed over them in the Church for the very purpose of healing differences.   Up to this time, however, I have received no distinct intimation from either party of their willingness thus to be guided by me as their Bishop ; on the contrary, indications have not been wanting, at least on one side, that my advice will not be listened to, unless it can be legally enforced.   If the case were thus voluntarily placed in my hands, by both parties, for friendly adjustment—if the clergy of the parish, on one hand, consented to follow my directions as to the ordering of the services, and if the vestry and the churchwardens, on the other hand, were equally willing to be guided by my advice as to the best way of allaying the unseemly tumults which have arisen, I am very hopeful that all might yet go well.   There has, I doubt not, been no lack of conscientiousness on both sides, but so far as I can at present judge, there has, I am bound to say, been a sad lack of kindly Christian consideration for each other's feelings.   I earnestly beseech all concerned, for the sake of the many ignorant and thoughtless souls in this parish of St. George's, not to allow another day to pass without taking such steps towards Christian reconciliation as may by God's blessing end the present miserable disturbances.   Depend upon it, none can feel any satisfaction in these church riots but those who are the enemies of the Lord Jesus Christ and of all true religion.

" My advice to the Vestry is, formally to request the Rector to join with them in submitting the whole case to my episcopal arbitration—both parties binding themselves to act as I direct. If this offer is not made, or if, being made, it is not acceded to, I do not see how I can aid the parish in any other way than by such strictly legal interference as I have indicated.—I have the honour to be, sir, your most obedient faithful servant,

"A. C. LONDON."

The Bishop's correspondence with Mr. Mackonochie, which is alluded to in the foregoing document, was of the most cordial and friendly kind. Mr. Mackonochie, whose name was afterwards to become so famous in connection with ritual matters, was curate in charge during Mr. King's temporary absence, and had a most difficult task to discharge.

On September 15th, 1859, the Bishop writes to him—

"MY DEAR MR. MACKONOCHIE,—Let me thank you for your interesting letter. I trust that by God's blessing the efforts you have made will not fail to produce their effect, and that this disgraceful state of things will soon be ended. I am sure that the manifestation of the kindly Christian spirit of conciliation, at the same time that you show your determination not to be intimidated, must have its effect. . . . I cannot but feel much for the very difficult position in which you are placed."

But it was with Mr. King, and not with Mr. Lowder or Mr. Mackonochie, that the Bishop had to deal, and the suggested arbitration proved a matter of the utmost difficulty. For a long time it was impossible to bring about any agreement between the Rector and the Vestry as to the points on which the Bishop was to arbitrate, and so serious had the riots become, that it was found necessary for the public safety to close the Church entirely for some weeks. After endless correspondence, the Bishop succeeded in obtaining a quasi-promise, limited, however, by many provisos, that the controversialists would accept his decision; but no sooner was it pronounced, and the Church re-opened, than the rioting was renewed with greater fury than before. The presence of a large force of police for some Sundays put a curb upon the violence of the mob, but on January 1st, 1860, this assistance was suddenly withdrawn, and once again, as soon as the Choral Service was attempted, the Church became a scene of the wildest tumult.

"The whole service," wrote Mr. Bryan King,[1] "was interrupted by hissing, whistling, and shouting. Songs were roared out by many united voices during the reading of the lessons and the preaching of the sermon; hassocks were thrown down from the galleries, and after the service, cushions, hassocks, and books were hurled at the altar and its furniture. I myself, and the other officiating clergy, had been spat upon, hustled, and kicked within the Church, and had only been protected from greater outrages, for several Sundays past, by the zealous devotion of some sixty or eighty gentlemen who attended from different parts of London."

For more than half a year these disturbances continued almost without abatement. The matter came before Parliament again and again. In the session of 1860, it was discussed on six several occasions in the House of Lords, and advantage was taken of the passing of an unimportant Ecclesiastical Courts Jurisdiction Bill to introduce new provisions for the summary correction and punishment of Church 'brawlers.' Bishop Tait explained on several occasions, in the House of Lords, the difficulty in which he found himself, owing, on the one hand, to the Rector's determination to continue the obnoxious ritual, and, on the other, to the apparent inability or unwillingness of the police authorities to prevent the misconduct of the mob.

"As to the miserable state of things," he said, "in the distracted parish of St. George in the East, he regretted it as much, or more, than any man, for he had more cause to regret it, but although much abuse had been bandied about on every side, and

---

[1] The quotation is from Mr. King's pamphlet *Sacrilege and its Encouragement*, page 23.

everything that was done by anybody was wrong in the estimation of everybody else, yet no charge of which he could take legal cognisance had been brought before him. He believed that this was simply one of those miserable cases to be found in all parts of society, in which, if men would stand on their legal rights, there was no amount of disturbance they might not cause. In the domestic relation, for instance, suppose two persons determined to make themselves as disagreeable as they could, each to the other, without infringing the law, what a state of things would result in the family! He believed it was the same thing with those most sacred relations between the pastor and his flock; it was possible for a pastor to make himself very disagreeable to his flock without violating the law, and for the flock to make themselves very disagreeable to the pastor; and it was very difficult for those who wished to set them right to find by what means they could do so. . . . He had said, and he believed, that if the matter were placed in his hands it could be arranged, but it must be an unconditional surrender to the Ordinary. He must be called in to settle these disturbances, and he hoped he was not thinking too much of himself or his office, when he said he had full confidence that there was so much good feeling among Englishmen, that whenever they had no doubt as to where the authority lay, they would be quite ready to give way to it. If the Rector of that parish would do what he ought to have done months ago, and say 'I am unable to manage this parish, I beg the Bishop of the Diocese to manage it for me,' all the mischief might be put an end to."[1]

For a time the police were again introduced into the church, but although they were able to stop actual violence, they were powerless to prevent the noises and interruptions with which the service was accompanied, these last offences, as the Home Secretary explained, falling short, in his opinion, of what could technically be called an 'outrage.' At length, on the intervention of Arthur Stanley and Thomas Hughes, Mr. Bryan King was persuaded to go abroad for a year, and the parish was intrusted to the care of the Rev. Septimus Hansard, whom

---

[1] *Hansard*, May 22, 1860, p. 1600.

Mr. Hughes described as a man "without an equal for dealing with the roughest part of a London population." This arrangement had the Bishop's entire approval, and it was hoped that peace would follow. Mr. Hansard, however, had promised Mr. Bryan King that he would maintain certain of his usages unimpaired, and it soon became evident that, in the temper which had been aroused among the parishioners, even Mr. Hansard would fail to bring the strife to an end unless the choral services were discontinued. The Bishop and Mr. Hansard made a joint effort to obtain Mr. King's sanction for such alterations as seemed necessary, but Mr. King, who was residing at Bruges, declined to consent, and Mr. Hansard resigned the charge. The position was now most difficult. It was easy to point out the mischief of yielding to the demands of a disorderly mob, but it had become impossible to allow the weekly scenes of noisy irreverence to continue, and no amount of energy on the part of the police could restrain the congregation of a crowded church from the profane amusement of shouting the psalms and canticles so as to drown the choir, from shuffling with their feet and coughing, or from banging the pew-doors at intervals. The choice lay between again closing the church (a mere temporary expedient at the best) and re-arranging the services under a new curate in charge. The Bishop after repeated conferences with those best able to advise him decided upon the latter alternative. Mr. Bryan King having declined any further responsibility in the matter, the Bishop undertook to provide, at his own cost, for the charge of the parish. A new curate was accordingly licensed, and the services were so arranged as to correspond with what was then customary in London churches. This re-arrangement was in entire accordance with the advice of many, even High Churchmen, who had been concerned in the controversy,[1] and whatever its disadvantages, it resulted in the speedy restoration of peace. After a few months a memorial was presented to the Bishop, signed by 2176 of the parishioners, including churchwardens, overseers, trustees, guardians, vestrymen, and, it is said, every resident member of the legal and medical profession, with one exception. "We desire," they said, "to convey to your lordship our deep sense of the obligation we are under for the restoration of peace to this long distracted parish, through your lordship's instrumentality." In the following year Mr. Bryan King was appointed to a country parish in the diocese of Salisbury. He left behind him in the mission districts of St. George's parish devoted men who maintained in a more excellent way, and with an earnestness equal to his own, the principles for which he had perseveringly contended, and Mr. Lowder and Mr. Mackonochie, before many years had passed, found themselves loved and reverenced in their daily work by those who had once been eager to " throw them over the Dock head."

One other point is perhaps worth noticing. The curious misuse of the name of Dr. Pusey in connection with such controversies has seldom been better illustrated than in the riots of St. George's in the East. 'Down with the Puseyites!' seems to have been the usual war-cry of the mob, and the 'Society' which promoted the agitation was 'the Anti-Puseyite League.' It so happened that the Bishop of London was at that time in correspondence with Dr. Pusey in connection with the evening sermons in

---

[1] A well-known High Churchman, who as 'Eye-witness' had, in a series of letters to the *Guardian*, described the scenes all through the riots, advised, in his last letter, that the points at issue should be conceded. "It is worse than useless," he said, " to insist, for the sake of so small a difference, on the maintenance of a service of which the only result is such frightful desecration."

Westminster Abbey and St. Paul's, and Dr. Pusey, on April 26, 1860, thus refers to the ritual controversy :—

"In regard to my 'friends,' perhaps I regret the acts to which your Lordship alludes as deeply as you do.   I am in this strange position, that my name is made a byword for that with which I never had any sympathy, that which the writers of the Tracts, with whom in early days I was associated, always deprecated, any innovations in the way of conducting the service, anything of ritualism, or especially any revival of disused vestments. I have had no office in the Church which would entitle me to speak publicly.   If I had spoken it would have been to assume the character of one of the leaders of a party, which I would not do.   Of late years, when ritualism has become more prominent, I have looked out for a natural opportunity of dissociating myself from it, but have not found one.   I have been obliged, therefore, to confine myself to private protests which have been unlistened to, or to a warning to the young clergy from the University pulpit, against self-willed changes in ritual.   Altogether I have looked with sorrow at the crude way in which some doctrines have been put forward, without due pains to prevent misunderstanding, and ritual has been forced upon the people, unexplained and without their consent.   I soon regretted the attempt which the late Bishop made, and which was defeated. Had I been listened to, these miserable disturbances in St. George's in the East would have been saved. . . . May God prosper your Lordship's plans for the conversion of these long-neglected souls.[1]   From what I have seen and heard I believe that He has ' much people in that place.'—I am your Lordship's faithful servant,   E. B. PUSEY."

[1] This refers to the special evangelistic efforts which the Bishop was then inaugurating.   See p. 255.

CHAPTER XI.

EVANGELISTIC WORK.

1857-59.

IMPORTANT as these controversies were, and deep as was the mark they left upon his whole Episcopate, it would be a simple mistake to suppose that they occupied in other than a subordinate degree either the interest or the energies of Bishop Tait. On the contrary, he was frequently accused in those early years of his Episcopate of devoting too little time to the *governance* of his Diocese, and too much time to the Evangelistic work, which the critics of that day regarded as belonging rather to 'the inferior clergy' than to a Bishop. He had throughout his life an excessive dread of what he described as 'over-much machinery.' He used to complain, both at Balliol and Carlisle, that more time was spent in discussing, arranging, and systematising the work of the Foundation than in doing it ; and when he came to London the same difficulty, as he thought, confronted him in another form.

Bishop Blomfield had set himself with untiring zeal, and with the largest personal generosity,[1] to the task of Church-building in and around London, so as to overtake, if possible, the gigantic increase of population. Although

---

[1] His own contributions to the 'Metropolis Churches Fund' and other agencies amounted to at least £25,000.

he consecrated, during his tenure of the See, some two
hundred new churches, there were still, when Bishop Tait
succeeded him, a very large number of overgrown and unwieldy parishes provided only with a single church.   Nor
had the provision of new buildings realised, speaking
generally, the intentions of their founders.   It had been
too often assumed that the erection of a commodious
church in a populous locality would of itself, as a matter
of course, attract a full supply of worshippers, and the
snbscribers were puzzled and disappointed to find that
many of the new churches were standing almost empty.[1]
The machinery was there, but no grist came to the mill.
Some fresh impulse, some new enthusiasm seemed to be
wanted, and Bishop Tait bestirred himself to supply the
need.   It is difficult for those familiar with the multifarious agencies by which Church work is now diversified
in crowded parishes to realise the suspicion and even
hostility with which the authorities, forty years ago,
regarded any other ministrations of religion than those
carried on in regular course within the Church's walls.
What Bishop Blomfield had urged was that churches
should be so multiplied as "to bring home to the very
doors and hearths of the most ignorant and neglected of
the population the ordinances, the solemnities, the decen-
cies, and the charities of our Apostolical Church."   But
the encouragement of anything like mission preaching,
out-door services, or other 'irregular' evangelistic efforts,
accorded neither with his theories nor his example.   Ready
speaker as he was, he never, save on one memorable occasion, preached an unwritten sermon, and, in his earlier
years at least, he objected to an address on week-days,

---

[1] Bishop Blomfield had indeed, in his Charge of 1846, anticipated something of this difficulty, and pointed out the need of waiting patiently for
results which might be long of coming.

even if delivered in the church itself, "as leading the people to over-value preaching and under-value prayers." Where there were two full services on Sundays, such week-day services were, in his opinion, not required.[1] It is easy to conjecture, therefore, what his attitude would have been had 'revivalism' and other movements of the kind been started under his Episcopate. Bishop Tait's view was altogether different. In a sermon in St. James's, Piccadilly, on the Sunday after his consecration, he emphasised with all his might the need of more evangelistic work. At his first ordination, held a few weeks later, he was himself the preacher, and he took occasion to reiterate the same opinion with the same earnestness, beseeching the clergy to "go forth into the highways and hedges, and to proclaim in the simplest words at their command the Gospel of a living Saviour." Before he had been a month in office he presided at a great meeting held in Islington to launch a scheme for building twelve new churches at a cost of £50,000, and his speech on the occasion gave occasion to vigorous and, in some quarters, unfriendly comment.

"It will be," he said, "a source of deep consolation to my venerated predecessor, Bishop Blomfield, in the affliction which it has pleased God to lay upon him, to reflect that he has been instrumental in building and consecrating within this Diocese upwards of two hundred churches. But it is impossible to read the public prints, and to think seriously upon the subject as it presents itself to us throughout the whole Kingdom, without acknowledging that there is a good deal to be said in favour of the arguments of those who maintain that these schemes of Church Extension had better, for a little time at least, be allowed to stand still. It is often urged, and with great plausibility, that building churches throughout the kingdom is something like the occupation of a conquered land; and there is an example ready

---

[1] See *Life*, vol. i. p. 110.

at hand in the case of Ireland.   Garrisons were in former times stationed at intervals throughout that land, and fortresses were built for them to reside in ; and yet no real conquest took place, for the inhabitants only retired to their fastnesses, and there remained unsubdued.   And so it may be with the Church : additional churches may be merely the towers which contain the garrison, and the people whom we wish to bring within the pale may remain at a distance.   It will therefore be wrong if we mistake the erection of churches for the spread of the Gospel throughout the land.   It will, above all, be necessary to place in the churches faithful ministers of God's Word.   And we must be very careful to use every means to bring in the poor.   It is the upper and the middle classes who form the church-goers throughout this country ; and a vast mass of the population are estranged, not only from the Church of England, but from the Gospel itself.   Both in our crowded cities and in our remote country districts there is a very numerous body of the poor who cannot, and another who will not, enter the churches.   Under these circumstances, when asked to preside at this meeting, I inquired, first of all, whether the churches are, as much as possible, made available, whether there are as many services in them as can well be performed, and also whether attempts are made to build up the Church spiritually as well as materially."

He went on to press the need of local sympathy and co-operation in the new endeavour, and promised to subscribe £600 as a pledge of his anxiety for its success.[1]

His next public act involved him in some controversy. It was announced by the Vicar of St. Alban's, Wood Street, that on New Year's Day, 1857, the Holy Communion would be celebrated at a quarter before seven in the morning, and the Bishop of London would deliver an address to the members of the Young Men's Christian Association. The Bishop immediately received letters from clergy and others, urging him to refrain from attend-

---

[1] The amount of this subscription to the local fund for a particular parish was of course exceptional, being more than one-tenth of his total income for the year, while he was at the same time encouraging many other efforts with almost equal liberality.

ing such a service, as many members of the association were Nonconformists, or, at all events, were unconfirmed, and could not therefore present themselves at the Lord's Table. The Bishop, however, adhered to his engagement, and spoke as follows in the course of his address :—

"If there are any here who are not members of the Church of England, I rejoice that they should show their friendly feeling by being present to hear the Word preached by her ministers, and to join in her Scriptural prayers, and in hearing those portions of the Word of God which our Prayer Book sets before us at this time. As to any such approaching the most sacred rite of Communion in our Church, that is a matter which they must weigh well with themselves. We invite those to approach who are baptized, confirmed, or ready to be confirmed. I can well understand those who are members of some other National Church rejoicing to communicate with the Church of England while they sojourn amongst us, without forsaking the Church of their country and home. I can understand, also, that many of our own countrymen, who from their early training have been kept apart from our Church, may, as years advance, feel a growing desire to unite with her as the great safeguard of Scriptural Christianity in the land, though they cannot resolve entirely to separate themselves from some other body with which they have many tender associations of kindred and of spiritual privilege enjoyed in times past. Still, I am bound to say, that that seems to me an unsound state in which a man of mature age and independent position hangs doubtful between one communion and another, not feeling himself really united with the Church, and ready to cast in his lot with it, though he loves its services, or feels that they do his heart good. There is always some danger of hanging loose between two systems, and thus failing of the helps which either, according to its means, endeavours to afford for the building up of the soul. But enough of these matters. We are met together to-day to worship in the Church of England, and we, her ministers, invite you in her name to this holy feast of love, as believing you to be anxious, through her teaching and her time-honoured Scriptural forms, to seek closer union with the Lord she serves. Her zeal in spreading the Gospel is her highest claim on your allegiance. We meet in our

National Church to-day to devote ourselves for the New Year to do what we can as citizens of this great nation, that we may advance the cause of Christ and goodness amongst our fellow-citizens; and we seek grace through the Lord's Ordinance that our hearts may be right while we attempt to guide others."

His efforts in these early weeks of his Episcopate had the effect of scandalising not a few of his more old-fashioned friends, who made no scruple of expressing their disbelief in what were described by one of them as " the Bishop's undignified and almost Methodist proceedings." Worse than all, he now began to set the example of open-air preaching in the streets. In the spring and summer of 1857 he gave such addresses in almost every part of London. Those who remembered his ill-health were amazed at the ceaseless pressure of the work he undertook. His diary shows him going off from the House of Lords to speak to a shipload of emigrants in the Docks, from the Convocation discussions on Church Discipline to address the Ragged School children in Golden Lane, or the omnibus-drivers in their great yard at Islington. He preached to the costermongers in Covent Garden Market; to railway porters from the platform of a locomotive; to a colony of gypsies upon the Common at Shepherd's Bush, and this without in any way relaxing the accustomed round of confirmations and sermons and committees which must always occupy a bishop's time in addition to his huge business correspondence. The very novelty of his work seemed to inspire him for a time with a physical strength and toughness which surprised his friends.

It was owing probably to the impetus thus given by the Bishop to evangelistic work that Lord Shaftesbury and some of his friends opened in 1857 a new religious campaign, which was destined to cause no small stir in

London. It was arranged that services should be held on Sunday evenings in Exeter Hall, and some of the foremost evangelical clergymen in England consented to give the addresses, which were intended mainly for those unaccustomed to church-going.[1] Bishop Tait gave his sanction to the scheme, and was himself present at one of the services. The hall was crowded every Sunday evening, but a vigorous outcry soon arose in the Church newspapers and elsewhere. It was stated that the audience consisted largely of worshippers drawn from church and chapel, and the incumbent of the parish in which Exeter Hall stands, the Rev. A. G. Edouart, was induced in November 1857 to assert his legal right, and to issue a formal veto against the continuance of these ministrations. He wrote fully to the Bishop explaining his reasons.

"I am setting my face," he said, "against a proceeding altogether irregular, which, if permitted, would prove thoroughly subversive of all discipline and order in the Church, and would tend beyond all conception to destroy that form of sound words so essential to the purity and power of our branch of Christ's Church."

By the Bishop's advice the services were thereupon discontinued for a time, but Lord Shaftesbury immediately introduced a Bill into the House of Lords to deprive an incumbent of any such right of veto. Bishop Wilberforce protested successfully against what he called the 'indecent haste' with which Lord Shaftesbury tried to force his Bill through Parliament. More than one debate took place, and, in the end, Lord Shaftesbury, much against his will, found himself compelled to withdraw his measure in favour of an alternative Bill of a less stringent character introduced by the Archbishop of Canterbury

---

[1] The first list of preachers included Bishop Villiers, Bishop Bickersteth, Dean Close, and Dr. M'Neile.

with the support of Bishop Tait. In the course of these discussions Bishop Tait had occasion to refer, very fully, to the Exeter Hall services, and, unpopular as they were among most of his hearers, he gave them his unstinted commendation.

"He should be sorry," he said, "if any expression which had fallen from his lips could be construed into a charge against Mr. Edouart. That clergyman had acted most conscientiously, and he (the Bishop of London) should deeply regret it if he were held up to opprobrium. When, however, so great a movement as this—which he, as the Bishop of the diocese, esteemed to be one of the best works that had been undertaken since he entered upon his office—was stopped by a single incumbent, he did feel that the gentleman who had put his veto upon it did not exercise a sound discretion. He desired to thank the noble Earl (Lord Shaftesbury) and those who had acted with him for the good work which had been done, and he was happy to think that there was a prospect, a near prospect, that the example which had been so worthily set by these gentlemen would be followed by our great cathedrals. He rejoiced to be able to announce that Westminster Abbey would be open for Divine service on the evening of the 3d of January, and he could express no better wish for the services to be conducted there and in St. Paul's Cathedral than that they might be attended by as great and hearty a body of worshippers as were found at the services in Exeter Hall. Even although the cathedrals should be thrown open, there would still be room for other services, and he hoped that so long as he occupied a position of responsibility he should encourage every good work, whether it was carried on in a cathedral or elsewhere."[1]

With the Bishop of London's recommendation, the Bishops' Bill passed through the House of Lords ; but it was withdrawn in the Commons, and in the meantime Lord Shaftesbury and his friends recommenced the Exeter Hall services, having been advised that by avoiding the use of liturgical forms, they would deprive Mr. Edouart of

---

[1] *Hansard*, Dec. 8, 1857, pp. 343-344.

his legal power of veto. This opinion was disputed by
Mr. Edouart's advisers, but he decided to abstain from any
formal veto, and to throw upon the Bishop, as he said, all
the responsibility for the mischief which must inevitably
follow :—

"But though I thus retire," he wrote, "yet I continue to
object to these services, and again appeal to your Lordship as
my Diocesan to maintain the order and constitution of the
Church."

The correspondence was made public at the time, and
the Bishop's final reply, dated July 30, 1858, was the subject of much criticism among the more timid or old-
fashioned of his friends.

" I think," he said, " that you have come to a wise determination in resolving not to move further in the question of the
Exeter Hall services. You are aware that I have all along been
of opinion that it was only in a technical sense that a great building like Exeter Hall—intended for the use of London generally—could be held, in its character of a place of public meeting,
to be included in the Parish of St. Michael's, Burleigh Street,
and therefore subject to you. . . . I readily concur in the
opinion of your friends that you can in no way be held responsible for these services, and need have no apprehension lest you
be compromised by ceasing to take any further steps against
them. . . . On me must devolve the responsibility, if zealous
efforts on the part of my clergy to enable the Church to do missionary work in the midst of our overwhelming population, be
allowed to interfere with sound doctrine or the due discipline of
the Church. . . . I do, indeed, most earnestly desire that the
Gospel may be preached to the poor, and that the clergy of our
Church may be the means of preaching it ; but I am not insensible, on the other hand, to possible dangers of disorder, and am
quite ready to interfere, if in the exercise of my discretion in the
discharge of the duties of my office I come to think that any
interference on my part is desirable."

The excitement aroused by the Exeter Hall addresses
had at least one happy result: it strengthened the Bishop's

hands in his determination to secure the opening of Westminster Abbey and St. Paul's Cathedral for Sunday Evening Services for the people. From the very day of his consecration he had been in communication upon the subject with his friend, Dean Trench of Westminster, and it was by their joint effort that one by one the many ' lions in the path ' were conquered, and at last on January 3, 1858, the first great Sunday Evening Service was held in the Abbey, in the presence of an overflowing congregation.

The Westminster difficulties overcome, the Bishop had to face obstacles still graver at St. Paul's. It was at first in vain that he pressed upon Dean Milman and his colleagues the imperative necessity of utilising the great space at their command. The ' impossibilities ' were endless. "The want of such services," wrote Dean Milman, "is not felt in the City, where so many churches are available, and it is extremely doubtful whether a sufficient congregation would attend to justify so costly an experiment ;" and, further, "there is no Fabric Fund to provide for the expenses." The Bishop replied by issuing an appeal to the public for subscriptions, heading the list himself with a donation of £100. The funds were soon forthcoming, and, after further correspondence, the space under the Dome was at last thrown open to the public on the evening of Advent Sunday, 1858, when the Bishop was himself the preacher. The excitement of the occasion was immense, and Ludgate Hill was for some time completely blocked by the crowd. An hour before the time of service every seat was occupied, and enormous numbers (variously estimated in the newspapers at from 10,000 to 100,000) were turned away for want of room. The services were well attended throughout the winter, and the Bishop exhausted every effort in the endeavour to persuade the Chapter of St. Paul's to continue them in spring and summer. He promised to make a further appeal for funds, and to undertake, if desired, the entire responsibility of finding preachers for the Sunday evenings; but the Chapter, to his openly-expressed disappointment, unanimously declined to accede to his request, and it was not till long afterwards that the services were maintained throughout the year.

While these Cathedral negotiations were still incomplete, the Bishop set himself to promote in the Parish Churches of North and East London—most of which were pew-rented—a series of Sunday Evening Services for working people. The experiment, strange as it now sounds to say so, was altogether novel, and therein perhaps in part lay the secret both of its success and of the opposition offered to it. The following is one of the placards which were issued in Bethnal Green :—

"SPECIAL SERVICES FOR THE PEOPLE.—BETHNAL GREEN.

(All seats to be perfectly open to all.)

" To the Working People of Bethnal Green.

" MY FRIENDS,—Nearly a year has now passed since my appointment to the Bishopric of London, and though I have visited Bethnal Green, and heard much of its churches, no opportunity has as yet been given me of meeting many of you in the House of God or elsewhere. I now propose, if God will, to begin next Sunday evening a course of special services, to be continued till Christmas, in which I trust we may meet each other. Let me affectionately beg of you to give me the opportunity of thus joining with you in worship, and to come, that you may hear the message which I and the other clergy who will assist me are commissioned to deliver to you on Christ's behalf, in preparation for the approaching season of Christmas.—Believe me to be, my friends, your faithful servant in Jesus Christ,

" A. C. LONDON.

" LONDON HOUSE, 17*th Nov.* 1857."

Describing one of these Bethnal Green Services, the *Times*[1] wrote :—

"Long before eight o'clock, the time appointed for the commencement of the service, the spacious church was densely crowded by such an auditory as it is quite safe to say was never before seen in any church in England. The people who assembled were of the poorest possible classes—men with fustian jackets and unshaven faces; women whose faces betokened the sad privations they are called upon to endure, and many in absolute rags. . . . The church was crowded to suffocation, and hundreds of persons who had vainly struggled to obtain admission assembled in the adjacent streets, and occupied themselves in discussing the nature of this new movement for their edification."

The *Guardian*[2] thus described the first sermon of the course :—

"Three-fourths probably of the audience were men—a very considerable proportion of them being weavers of the district. . . . The Bishop's sermon was entirely extemporaneous, and the striking earnestness and sincerity which characterised his affectionate and eloquent discourse appeared to sustain throughout the attention of every member of the congregation. This first service was thoroughly successful, was unmistakably attended by the working classes, and is one of the first fruits of the newly-established London Diocesan Home Mission."

A few words are necessary to explain the origin and character of the last-named organisation. At the close of his first year of Episcopal work, Bishop Tait convened a meeting of the incumbents of the most populous London parishes, and propounded to them his plan for a 'Diocesan Home Mission' organisation, which should arrange periodically for such special services as have been described above, and should also employ a certain number of clergy, under the Bishop's direction, for distinctly evangelistic or 'aggressive' work in crowded districts,

---

[1] Dec. 10, 1857.   [2] Nov. 25, 1857, p. 910.

with a view in most cases to the ultimate formation of new parishes. This organisation, the first of its kind, has been the precursor of many others, more or less like it, in the various English Dioceses; and it is at this moment, after more than thirty years of vigorous though unobtrusive work, employing some twenty-eight missionary clergymen in London, and has an income of about £6000 a year.

It would be tedious to recount in detail the various evangelistic efforts, sometimes combined, sometimes isolated, to which the Bishop gave his encouragement in those early years.

"I wish to be very explicit," he said in his primary Charge, "as to the general principle I have followed in permitting or sanctioning these various efforts. . . . When persons have come to me to propose any work of Christian usefulness in the diocese, which has commended itself to the hearty approval of any considerable number of earnest and honest members of our Church —if it has seemed to me to aim, on the whole, at good ends, and to be undertaken zealously and in good faith, and to have some fair prospect of advancing Christ's work, I have not hesitated to give my sanction to it, though its arrangements and mode of action might be very different from what I should myself have suggested. . . . I have thought that it was the duty of my office to present no obstacle to the fair development of each man's zeal, provided I believed him sincerely desirous of dedicating it to the service of the Church, in which I am intrusted with authority; and if persons, differing widely from myself, through respect for my office, have thus requested me to allow them to put themselves under my protection, and professed their willingness in turn to have their peculiarities restrained by my authority, I have not thought myself at liberty to decline. I believe this to be the spirit of St. Paul's rule. . . . This Metropolitan Diocese is a world in itself, and its schemes of Christian usefulness must suit all tastes. Let all zealous efforts, honestly undertaken with the view of advancing our Church's means of reaching souls, be fairly tried. Properly watched and guarded, they will soon show whether or not they are likely to advance

God's glory. Do what we will, some things, which, as individuals, we do not like, cannot be stopped from working, and they
had better work under proper control. They may be blessed of
God ; if they are not of Him, they will come to naught."[1]

One such endeavour, neither authorised nor forbidden by
the Bishop, was the plan for utilising the London theatres
for Sunday evening services. At a 'Conference of Christians of all Evangelical Denominations,' held November
22, 1859, Mr. Arthur Kinnaird named seven theatres, besides other public buildings, which were open to them, and
stated that "the Bishop of London was in cordial harmony with them, and cared not whether Churchmen or
Nonconformists conducted the services." This, however,
was rashly spoken. The Bishop wrote, in answer to a
correspondent, that he had grave doubts as to the wisdom
of the movement, though he explained that his attitude
must for the time be one of watchful neutrality. These
services in theatres became, in 1860, the subject of prolonged debate in the House of Lords, when the Bishop, in
answer to a widely-supported remonstrance or challenge
from Lord Dungannon, expressed his determination not
to interfere with an effort which, however irregular, had
undoubtedly been productive of much good. Lord
Shaftesbury, in a long and eloquent speech, described the
impressive and orderly character of the services which had
been held in the theatres each Sunday evening, in the
presence of immense multitudes of the poorest classes.
Bishop Tait followed :—

"It had been supposed," he said, "that this was a public
movement which the heads of the Church were officially
sanctioning. The facts were altogether different. It was a
movement of certain private individuals, who, feeling deeply the
responsibility cast on them as Christian men, determined to try

<hr>

[1] Charge of 1858, pp. 89-91.

an experiment, not perhaps consonant with the general feeling of the Church, but yet one which they thought might result in great good. No doubt Episcopal disapproval might have induced the clergy of London to cease to take part in these services, but he felt that the responsibility would have been grave indeed of expressing such disapproval in the face of a mass of human beings whom either they or their forefathers had hitherto sorely neglected. Could they—dare they—call upon the clergy, either by inhibitions or by other means, to refrain from ministering to these persons? He was not prepared to say that he went entirely with the movement. There were some things in it which he did not like, but as regards the objection which was entertained to using places of theatrical entertainment, he did not know whether one result of this movement might not be that theatres would themselves become something better than they had ever been before. He begged their Lordships not to go away with the impression that, because this great experiment was being tried, no other efforts were being made in the same direction. True, they must wait long before sufficient churches could be built, but they need not despair on that account; and meanwhile, it would be well if those who felt strongly against this movement would see that the churches we already had were thrown open to the poor as freely as possible. It might be very difficult to lure them in, but at present they were not lured in, but locked out. No idea seemed to be more deeply ingrained in the minds of many officials of our parishes than that the abject poor had no right to accommodation in our churches. In this and other ways perhaps important results might flow from this movement. They were not to accept it as the best which could be imagined; but that it had been productive of good few could doubt, and he hoped that many other efforts of a kindred nature might be made."[1]

One subject with which the Bishop set himself to grapple in 1858 was the question of Sunday labour. The time had come, he thought, for a distinct and outspoken protest on the part of the clergy and laity of the Church against the increase of Sunday work in the Metropolis. He

---

[1] See *Hansard*, Feb. 24, 1860, p. 1692, etc.

arranged for simultaneous sermons on the subject in almost all the London churches, upon a particular Sunday, and he himself undertook the responsibility of pressing upon the great Omnibus Companies of London, in a remarkable letter which was made public at the time, the duty of a relaxation of the hours of Sunday labour for their servants.

On November 17, 1858, just two years after his consecration to the See, he delivered in St. Paul's Cathedral his primary Charge—to which more than one allusion has been already made.   That Charge remains, in the memory of all who knew him, one of the greatest achievements of his life.   It practically inaugurated a new order of Episcopal utterances, and, for a few days at least, all London sang his praises.   Even the outward delivery of the Charge was a remarkable feat.   For nearly five hours he held the attention of his hearers, under the dome of St. Paul's, his steady, sonorous voice reaching every ear from the beginning to the end.   Eye-witnesses have often described how the short November day sank into twilight, then into darkness, and still, in clear, quiet, earnest tones he went on, the only object visible in the great building (for the dome was then unlighted), turning his pages by the light of two small lamps upon the temporary desk from which he spoke.

Rightly to estimate the significance of this Charge, it is only necessary to turn, in an Ecclesiastical Library, to a volume of the Episcopal Charges which had till then been usual.   With a few noteworthy exceptions,[1] they were stilted, conventional, and jejune to the last degree ; and, so far as the average layman was concerned, they might

---

[1] Among the exceptions were such Charges as those of Bishop Phillpotts, Bishop Wilberforce, Bishop Thirlwall.   Each of these had its own vigorous characteristics, but not one of them was in any way similar either in matter or manner to this Charge of Bishop Tait.

as well have been left unspoken.   The reception accorded to the Charge of Bishop Tait gave, by its very warmth, abundant evidence of what the public view of such utterances had hitherto been.

"The day on which the Charge was to be delivered," wrote the *Guardian* in a critical and cautious article, " was looked for with extraordinary interest and even anxiety. There are said to have been nearly a thousand London clergy gathered on that day under the dome of St. Paul's—an ecclesiastical army, for it was nothing less, impressive if not unparalleled in mere numbers ; but to a Churchman especially suggestive from the place where it was for the first time held, and very solemn from the thought of the vast and unspeakably important interests which depended under God upon the men there gathered under one roof. Amongst such reflections one of the foremost must be the awful responsibility of him in whom spiritual agencies, so many and powerful, centre for direction. It was evident that the Bishop keenly felt the importance of the occasion, not only from the earnestness and emphasis of his delivery, but from the elaborate completeness and finish bestowed on the Charge both in matter and composition. . . . Truly now, if ever, the mitre is lined with thorns, and to draw up a Charge, such as was delivered on Wednesday last, is as delicate and difficult an undertaking of its kind as a man can have laid upon him."

Other newspapers, not usually giving much attention to matters ecclesiastical, devoted articles and correspondence columns to the subject for several weeks after the delivery of the Charge.

" A Christian, a gentleman, and a man of sense, is the Bishop of London, and the ample, unreserved view which he has taken of church questions in this country, in the metropolis, and in certain parishes, abounds with evidence to the qualities which he possesses for the post assigned to him."

Again :

"Bishop Tait has well won his first laurels. Had words as free from ambiguity, had plain outspoken designation of the things condemned, marked bygone Charges delivered in the same Cathedral, many of the evils of to-day might never have been."

Among the letters which he immediately received from men of weight was the following from the aged Arch-bishop Whately, who had known him years before in his undergraduate days at Oxford :—

The Archbishop of Dublin to the Bishop of London.

"DUBLIN, 30 *Nov.* 1858.

"MY DEAR LORD,—I have delayed acknowledging the excellent Charge which your Lordship kindly sent me, till I could present a little tract containing the substance of two of mine.

"Your Lordship's Charge presents a striking contrast—as all must admit—to the prevailing idea of an Episcopal Charge, viz., an elaborate and studied inanity, carefully avoiding everything that might be displeasing to any of the clergy, and accordingly keeping clear of everything on which there may be two opinions among them ; thence dealing only in vague and barren generalities, as unprofitable as they are unobjectionable.

"I am glad to see a Bishop (especially of the greatest Diocese of the world, and which I have always thought ought to be made two) determined to show that he has at least something to say, and is resolved to say it.—Believe me to be, your Lordship's faithfully,   RD. DUBLIN."

The controversial portions of the Charge have been already referred to, but it was not to these that the main interest attached.   It was rather to the record and the promise of the new and larger work by which he was trying, in the spirit not less of a Christian statesman than of an Ecclesiastic, to throw fresh life into the Church of England, to popularise it, and to make it altogether national.   He called attention, in the very forefront of his Charge, to the position and duties assigned to him in the

National Legislature,[1] and to the influence of London upon the country as a whole :—

"To provide," he said, "for the spiritual wants of the metropolis would be conferring a boon on the whole kingdom of which this metropolis is the heart ; as, on the other hand, to neglect the masses of the metropolis is to work ruin in the State. . . . The Church as a spiritual institution, the Church of Christ, can never perish ; and this our own national development of the Church of Christ—with its own peculiar institutions, dear to true-hearted Englishmen from the historical associations of the centuries of England's most real greatness ; which has been bound up with so many crises of the nation's history in times past ; which men love because it maintains the faith in which their fathers lived and died, and in which they desire to rear their children ; to which all the Protestant nations of the earth look as the great bulwark of that at once reasonable and loving Christianity which commends itself only the more to right-minded men, the more they love freedom and the more they are educated —this, our great national development of the Church of Christ, is in no danger if we, its ministers, are what we ought to be."

Upon these lines he proceeded to consider in copious (his critics said over-copious) detail the training of candidates for Holy Orders, the duties of a licensed curate in his earlier ministry, and then of the parish clergy in their maturer years, diverging to discuss the incidental questions of Ritualism and the Confessional upon one side, and of a sceptical 'intellectualism' upon the other. The respective difficulties of town and country parishes, the peculiar problem presented by the empty churches of the rich city parishes from which the population had moved away, and, above all, as has been already said, the need of more vigorous and 'aggressive' work for those who had, for one reason or another, become alienated from the Church's ministrations : such was the comprehensive theme of this remarkable Charge. Some of the

[1] Charge, p. 8.

questions (the incidence of Church rates for example) are now of merely antiquarian importance. Others, such as the 'City Churches' problem, remain still unsolved—perhaps insoluble, considering how various are the conditions to be satisfied. But on each and all of these questions—old or new—he gave abundant food for thought, and the Charge retains its practical interest to this hour.

The effort exhausted him completely, and he went to Brighton to recruit. There, six days later, his diary has the following :—

"*Nov.* 23, 1858.—This day two years I was consecrated Bishop of London. God's mercy has been great since then. Health : strength : the society of my wife and my boy, with our dear little L. : a daily increasing interest in my work. I would fain hope that by God's blessing I have done somewhat to make this Church more truly the Church of the nation. Lord, pardon my great shortcomings."

The years that immediately followed were not, so far as the Diocese was concerned, eventful, though they were full of unremitting work. The diaries give evidence of his anxiety—an anxiety inspired by frequent warnings of ill-health—to strengthen the broad foundations he had laid, and to arrange the plans of future effort. Such entries as the following occur more than once :—

"FULHAM, *Sunday Evening, 20th July* 1862.—To-day and yesterday I have been again laid up. Very unpleasant symptoms : fainting and the like. Obliged to stay in bed all yesterday, and to get the Bishop of Worcester to preach for me to-day. It is good for me to have the nearness of death thus brought before me. I trust, if God is pleased to call me, I am ready. . . . O God, watch over me this night, and if it be Thy good pleasure let this illness pass. But Thou knowest what is best for us, for my wife, my darling children. I place them, O Lord, in Thy hands : keep them, I beseech Thee. I have had, as usual, a very busy week, and have been much in God's House. How great the privilege of thus ministering continually! . . . I pray for the Diocese. Prosper the works undertaken in Thy name. Make them conduce to the good of souls. To-day I have had an hour's conversation with Hugh, the under-butler, about his confirmation. How many am I privileged to address at these confirmations! . . . My dear boy comes home, I hope, from school in ten days. It would be a great pleasure to live to see him grow up. But God knoweth what is best for him and me. . . ."

The fainting-fits proved difficult to cure, and he went to Scotland for a holiday.

On September 6th, 1862, Archbishop Sumner died at Addington, and three weeks later Archbishop Longley was translated from York to Canterbury. Bishop Tait was in the Highlands when he received the following letter :—

Viscount Palmerston to the Bishop of London.

"BROADLANDS, 27*th Sept.* 1862.

"MY DEAR LORD,—I have been authorised by the Queen to propose to you to take charge of the Archbishopric of York, which will become vacant by the transfer of the present Archbishop to the See of Canterbury; and I hope that this proposal may be agreeable to you.—Yours faithfully,   PALMERSTON."

The Bishop asked for a few days in which to consider the proposal. He consulted some three or four trusted friends, and although their advice was, on the whole, in favour of the move, he was unable to persuade himself that it would be right to leave London, and on October 5th he wrote to Lord Palmerston declining the Archbishopric. The following letters ensued :—

Viscount Palmerston to the Bishop of London.

"BROADLANDS, 6*th Oct.* 1862.

"MY DEAR LORD,—I have received your letter of yesterday, and I cannot refrain from asking you to reconsider your decision.

It is of course for yourself alone to determine the relative dignity of the post which I have proposed to you and that which you now hold, and as to the means of doing good which those posts respectively afford; but I should certainly not have made the proposal to you, if I had not thought the balance was in favour of York. There is, however, another consideration which I should wish earnestly to press upon you, and that is a regard for your own health. I may have been misinformed, but I have been told that your health has been very much affected by the labours of your present post, and I am very sure that as long as you hold that post, you will not slacken in the amount of labour which you may think that a due performance of your duties may require. But if your health should break down under the continued pressure to which it is exposed, a great part of those duties would necessarily remain unperformed, or would be inadequately performed by others, and you would have your personal discomfort embittered by the reflection that interests which you have at heart were suffering. The duties of the Archbishopric of York, though more commanding and extensive in their range and nature, are nevertheless not so personally harassing, and you would be able to perform them with less strain upon your health, and with still greater advantage to the interests of the Church. My dear Lord, yours faithfully,   PALMERSTON."

The Bishop of London to Viscount Palmerston.

"CROMER, NORFOLK, 8th October 1862.

" MY DEAR LORD,—Accept my best thanks for your letter of the 6th. I assure you that if I had not, since receiving your first letter, weighed your very considerate proposal most anxiously, and viewed it in every aspect before arriving at my decision, I should have been shaken by your renewed kindness. As it is, however, I feel that I have already given very full weight to what you so considerately urge. I fully appreciated the kind motive which offered me, in the Archbishopric of York, the opportunity of removing to a post at once of greater dignity, and of less work. The question of my health was very seriously considered, and I arrived at the conclusion—in which my usual medical adviser's opinion confirms me—that, humanly speaking, it is likely to be as good in the See of London as in that of York. I do not profess to be a strong man, and at times I am obliged to take great care; but certainly I am much stronger than I was six years ago, when I first entered on the duties of the London diocese, and from my peculiar temperament I have no particular reason to think that the work does me any harm. On the other hand, I have had to consider that a very great assistance to me in the performance of my present duties is derived from the complete knowledge of the details of my work in London, which six years' experience of the diocese has secured—that I might find the distant and untried work of York less congenial, and, though less pressing, more difficult for me—that, without some very strong counterbalancing reason, it is not desirable that I should leave plans which I have begun, but scarcely matured, in London.

"I am sure, when your Lordship reads this, you will not think that I have lightly set aside the offer made and renewed to me, or that I should be justified in now altering my decision. Believe me to be, with renewed thanks, my dear Lord, your faithful and obliged servant, A. C. LONDON."

He was encouraged and cheered by the chorus of approval with which his decision was greeted in London. Men of all sorts wrote to him to express their satisfaction.

"Our great fear," wrote one friend, "was that some who might succeed you in London would be drawn more and more by the pressing calls of parochial activity, meetings, etc., away from the more difficult work of influencing public opinion, whether legislation, or religion, or theology."

"For you to give up London for York," wrote Lady Wake, "would have seemed to me like a man making a second marriage while the first wife and family were not only yet living, but possessed all the husband's thoughts and affections."

The following extracts from his journal give a picture of what had passed in his own mind :—

"DOUGLAS HOTEL, EDINBURGH, 11*th Sept.* 1862. The Lord Advocate and Sir Harry Moncreiff to dinner, discussing the accounts of the dear Archbishop's death. Good old man! 'Well done, thou good and faithful servant, enter thou into the joy of thy Lord.' After 60 years of faithful ministerial service, he is freed from its burdens and cares, and has quietly fallen asleep in Jesus. A great loss. For all who knew the good old man venerated him. Every newspaper I have since read speaks of him with respect. An anxious time for the Church. The office indeed a difficult one. O Lord, whosoever is appointed to it, guide him by Thy Holy Spirit."

"WEEM, PERTHSHIRE, *Sunday*, 28*th Sept.* 1862.—Last night brought the announcement of Longley's appointment. . . . My anxiety is lest the Evangelical and Liberal sections of the Church may lose what they have gained of late years. But all my thoughts have been turned in another channel by the most unexpected receipt, before afternoon service, of a letter from Palmerston, offering me the Archbishopric of York. I should have at once declined to leave my great post in London for this quieter sphere had it not been that I have some fears as to my health, and the difficulties which beset the final settlement of what are to be the limits of the London diocese."

" PALACE, NORWICH, *Sunday night, 5th October* 1862.—An anxious week ended. From Weem to Lochearnhead. From Lochearnhead to Drummond Castle, where we spent two evenings. Most interesting and peculiar old place. From Drummond Castle to Harviestoun, where, on Thursday morning, consecrated the dear old burial ground. A solemn thing thus to stand and pray over so many of our dead. . . . On Thursday night to York. Friday, inspected Bishopthorpe and came on to Peterborough. On Saturday to this place. At the Ely station wrote to Palmerston declining the Archbishopric of York, and as we drove through the streets of Norwich stopped and posted the letter. I had scarcely written it, at Ely, when Mr. Walpole came from the train to ask whether he was to congratulate me. He seemed quite taken aback on hearing that I had declined, and so has every one ; but I feel satisfied that it was the right course. No doubt the decision has been very difficult. Everywhere the news of the offer having been made has preceded us, and all friends have thought we would accept. We have sought God's guidance. On Friday night at Peterborough I suffered great anxiety and could scarcely sleep. But the fact is this : there could be no reason for the change except on the plea of health ; and an inspection of Bishopthorpe, and full consideration of the nature of the duties and the sort of life, convinced us both that it was doubtful whether my health would really be likely to be stronger in that more Northern climate. And if this was doubtful, no other argument of sufficient weight remained to lead me to break off all my London work in its imperfect state, withdraw myself from the command of what must ever be the key of the Church of England—a post second only in importance to Canterbury—and separate myself also from all the many fellow-workers who helped me and expected to be helped by me. O Lord, in Thy hands are the issues. Guide all aright. I have desired all through to place myself under that guidance."

"CROMER, *Sunday, 19th October* 1862.—A very busy week. Six days' hard work brought me, by dinner-time yesterday, to the close of the rough draft of my Charge. Every day also I have had many letters : some, of common business, in which Hassard, who has been here, greatly helped me ; others in which no one could help me. One from F. Maurice, announcing his intention of resigning his Charge. . . . I wrote a careful answer, anxious if possible to preserve so holy a man to the active service of the Church.[1] Many of the letters I have received within these few days seem to show that I have a place in the Church in connection with men of unsettled minds, which no other of our present Bishops can occupy. And this, amongst other signs, seems to tell me more clearly that I have been right in deciding to remain in London.

"During the week we have been reading in the evenings the third volume of Carlyle's *Frederick the Great*. A vast improvement in style and perhaps also in matter over the two first. To-day twice at Church. Our three little girls very engaging. Baby has taken to insisting on saying her little prayer to me before she goes to bed. Little Edith came to us on the sands, saying, 'God can't see me, can He? He is in Heaven ; how can He? He can't see me when I am in bed. Where is He then?' It was the continuation of an argument with Lucy. I repeated to her the words of her hymn about 'One I cannot see who loves and cares for me.'"

The decision as to York made, he returned with renewed zest to face what were perhaps the busiest and certainly the most stormy years of his London life.

[1] See p. 512.

CHAPTER XII.

1860-64.

A CONTROVERSY had already been for some time in progress, more important perhaps than any other in Tait's public life, a conflict in which he was to stand from the first between two fires, and to run a risk of alienating the very friends in whose cause he was suffering reproach.

In his primary Charge, to which reference has been already made, he had expressed himself as follows in speaking of the temptations and dangers of the younger clergy :—

"It is not to be denied that there is, in this age, a great danger of what we may call intellectualism, as contradistinguished from a sound and vigorous exercise of the intellect. Students in our Universities, wearied of the dogmatism which ruled unchecked there some years ago, are very apt now to regard every maxim of theology or philosophy as an open question. Difficult questions there undoubtedly are, connected principally with the exact limits and nature of inspiration, which cannot in this age be avoided by men of inquiring minds. But I have no fear of such questions if they are approached in a reverential, truth-loving, prayerful spirit. There are exceptions of minds peculiarly formed ; but, as a general rule, I have no fear of a man becoming sceptical, if he has not a secret love of the independence of scepticism and a sort of self-sufficient appreciation of the supposed superiority to the prejudices of ordinary mortals which an enlightened scepticism seems to imply. If a young clergyman is a man of prayer, . . . if, having a reverential sense of God's presence, he seeks to be taught of God, I cannot myself fear that he will be beguiled by the dangerous temptations of a sceptical and would-be intellectual age. . . . But let him beware in his early days how he trifles with intellectualism, lest his whole nature be corrupted, and a shallow half-belief come to be all that he has to offer, either to his people or his own soul, instead of deep-rooted love and faith." [1]

This was the position he maintained from first to last during the stormy controversies of the next few years. But it was a position taken, at that time, by comparatively few. The science of reverent Biblical criticism was, to most people, absolutely unknown, and it is difficult now, a quarter of a century afterwards, to realise the vague terror with which much of what is to-day the general belief of Christian men was lumped together as 'Rationalism,' and thereupon condemned as an abomination. The mob who in their jealousy for Protestantism hooted and reviled the Ritualists at St. George's in the East, although more ignorant and noisy, were scarcely more violent in spirit than many of the earnest and well-meaning men and women who, week after week, cried aloud for vengeance against the traitorous 'Rationalists' who held 'free-thinking' ideas about the six days of Creation, or expressed an honest doubt whether the Deluge covered the Himalayas. But, as in the analogous case, the outcry was not all unreasonable. If the one found occasional justification in the fact that a good many Ritualists joined the Church of Rome, the other was able to point out with truth that the school of free inquiry led some of its scholars into sheer negation and unbelief. In no controversy was there graver need for a calm sobriety of judgment on the part of the rulers and leaders of the Church.

---

[1] Charge of 1858, pp. 66-67.

Although the echoes of this particular battle have now for many years been silent, the area of the strife was at the time so wide, and Bishop Tait's position in it was so peculiar and so prominent, that it is necessary to tell the story at some length.

In February 1860 a volume of theological Essays by different authors was published under the colourless title of *Essays and Reviews*. The character and purpose of the volume were made clear in its short preface or "advertisement," which ran as follows :—

" It will readily be understood that the Authors of the ensuing Essays are responsible for their respective articles only. They have written in entire independence of each other, and without concert or comparison.

"The Volume, it is hoped, will be received as an attempt to illustrate the advantage derivable to the cause of religious and moral truth, from a free handling, in a becoming spirit, of subjects peculiarly liable to suffer by the repetition of conventional language, and from traditional methods of treatment."

The Essays were seven in number. The first was by Dr. Temple, Head Master of Rugby, its title being *The Education of the World*. The seventh was by Professor Jowett, *On the Interpretation of Scripture*. The other essayists were Dr. Rowland Williams, Professor Baden Powell, the Rev. H. B. Wilson, Mr. C. W. Goodwin, and the Rev. Mark Pattison.

The volume awakened at first no very absorbing interest. In April a severe but discriminating review appeared in the *Guardian*, condemning the book as a whole, but drawing a marked distinction between the different essayists, and specially exonerating Dr. Temple's essay from having given any just grounds of offence. Other criticisms which followed in less guarded terms [1] served chiefly to

---

[1] Among these was a long and vigorous article in the *Westminster Review*, which attracted great attention at the time. It has been commonly attributed to the pen of Mr. Frederic Harrison.

stimulate curiosity as to what the book contained, and when, in his autumn Charge, Bishop Wilberforce went out of his way to denounce its teaching in unmeasured tones, its celebrity and circulation increased at a bound. In January, Bishop Wilberforce returned to the attack in an elaborate and weighty article which he contributed to the *Quarterly Review*, wherein he arraigned the seven essays collectively and severally, and declared his distinct conviction that their writers could not "with moral honesty maintain their posts as clergymen of the Established Church."[1]

So little are the details now remembered, that it may be well to say something, however briefly, upon the nature of the volume and of the attacks upon it. The preface quoted above stated distinctly that the seven authors had written "in entire independence of each other, and without concert or comparison," but it was vehemently urged that the next sentence of the preface practically admitted "a unity from which joint responsibility cannot be severed. Any one who undertook to unite in the free handling of such subjects in a common volume made himself responsible for the common effect of all the essays as a whole."[2]

This, however, was the extremest point to which the theory of their joint responsibility could be fairly carried. Every unbiassed reader was forced to admit that the two essays which opened and closed the volume—the handiwork of Dr. Temple and Mr. Jowett—were, in reverence of tone, earnestness of purpose, and ability of construction, as different as possible from those which formed the centre of the book, the contemptuous argument of Mr. Baden Powell, for example, upon the credibility of miracles, or

---

[1] *Quarterly Review*, Jan. 1861, p. 302.
[2] *Ibid.* p. 250.

the rude flippancy of Dr. Williams with respect to the Divine claims of the Old Testament.[1]

The author of the fourth essay, the Rev. H. B. Wilson, had in 1841 been one of the four tutors who, with Tait as their leader, protested against Tract XC. ; and his views as to the meaning of honest subscription to the articles had evidently undergone a startling change in the twenty years that had elapsed, for he was now able to argue in favour of the very mode of interpretation which he had then denounced, and some pages of his essay upon the National Church gave more pain perhaps to devout minds than any others in the volume.[2]

But if the essayists had, to say the least, blindly committed themselves to rash and ill-considered statements in one direction, it cannot be denied that those who stood forth to answer or impugn them used language on the other side which would nowadays be generally regarded as scarcely less open to objection. In the judgment of Bishop Tait, and of others who felt with him, the strain of denunciation in which the champions of orthodoxy indulged, and their dogmatic assertions as to what is essential to the faith, contributed not a little to the harmfulness of the whole controversy.[3] An agitation of the wildest sort immediately began. Addresses to the Archbishops came up from Rural Deaneries on every side, calling attention to the mischievous tendency of the

---

[1] Even Arthur Stanley in his fiery article in the *Edinburgh Review* in defence of the essayists condemns Dr. Williams's 'flippant and contemptuous tone' and the 'unbecoming' character of his remarks.—*Edin. Rev.*, April 1861, p. 479.

[2] See *Essays and Reviews*, pp. 180-183, 186, etc.

[3] Even Bishop Wilberforce, for example, who was by no means the hottest of the controversialists, described men as in danger of being "robbed unawares of the *very foundations of the Faith*," if they should be persuaded to "accept allegorically, or as parable, or poetry, or legend, the story of a serpent tempter, of an ass speaking with man's voice, of an arresting of the earth's motion, or of a reversal of its motion."—Charge of 1860, pp. 69, 70.

volume, and entreating that some action might be taken against its authors, who were regarded and sometimes described as traitors to their sacred calling—traitors, too, whose position—to quote the words of some of the memorialists—gave them " opportunities favourable in no ordinary degree for the diffusion of error."   This it was which mainly excited the public mind. As in the case of Bishop Colenso, a few years later, it was not so much the ' what ' as the ' who says it,' which aroused general attention.

" If other men," wrote Bishop Wilberforce, " had put forth the suggestions contained in this volume it would not, with one or two marked exceptions, have been found to possess either the depth, or the originality, or the power, or the liveliness which could have prevented its falling still-born from the press. It has been read, because to all it is new and startling—to some delightful and to others shocking—that men holding such posts should advocate such doctrines : that the clerical head of one of our great schools . . . two Professors in our famous University of Oxford, . . . the Vice-Principal of the College at Lampeter for training the clergy of the principality, and a country clergyman famed in his day for special efforts on behalf of orthodoxy—that such men as these should be the putters forth of doctrines which seem at least to be altogether incom-patible with the Bible and the Christian Faith as the Church of England has hitherto received it—this has been a paradox so rare and so startling as to wake up for the time the English mind to the distasteful subject of a set of sceptical metaphysical speculations regarding many long-received fundamental truths. . . . We hold that the attempt of the essayists to combine their advocacy of such doctrines with the retention of the status and emolument of Church of England clergymen is simply moral dishonesty." [1]

While the excitement was growing to its height both Dr. Temple and Mr. Jowett visited Bishop Tait at Fulham.

[1] *Quarterly Review*, Jan. 1861, pp. 250-274.

On January 20th, 1861, the Bishop's Journal has the following entry :—

" Jowett has been with me for two days. The unsatisfactory part of his system seems to be that there is an obscurity over what he believes of the centre of Christianity. As to the outworks, the conflict there is of comparatively little importance ; but the Central Figure of the Lord Jesus, the central doctrine of the efficacy of His Sacrifice—in fact St. Paul's Christianity—is this distinctly recognised by the writers of his school ? I have urged both on him and Temple, who has also been with me, that they are bound to state for their own sakes and for the sake of those whom they are likely to influence what is the *positive* Christianity which they hold. It is a poor thing to be pulling down. Let them build up.

" Lord, fix my own heart and soul on the great Christian Verities. Thou knowest my failures. Breathe into my heart Thy Holy Spirit, through Jesus Christ. Amen."

Early in February, while the addresses and memorials in various forms were still flowing in, the Bishops met in force at Lambeth, and decided on replying to one of these addresses in a joint letter, which might serve when published as a virtual answer to all the remonstrants, whatever the form of their respective appeals. The particular address to which they thus replied was one which emanated from a Rural Deanery in Dorsetshire. It will be observed that its objection to rationalistic teaching is couched in general terms, and that there is no express reference to the obnoxious volume :—

" We wish," said the memorialists, " to make known to .your Grace and to all the Bishops the alarm we feel at some late indications of the spread of rationalistic and semi-infidel doctrines among the beneficed clergy of the realm. We allude especially to the denial of the atoning efficacy of the Death and Passion of our Blessed Saviour Jesus Christ, both God and Man, for us men and for our salvation, and to the denial also of a Divine Inspiration, peculiar to themselves alone, of the Canonical Scriptures of the Old and New Testament.

" We would earnestly beseech your Grace and your Lordships, as faithful stewards over the House of God, to discourage by all means in your power the spread of speculations which would rob our countrymen, more especially the poor and unlearned, of their only sure stay and comfort for time and for eternity. And to this end we would more especially and most earnestly beseech you, in your Ordinations, to ' lay hands suddenly on no man ' till you have convinced yourselves (as far as human precaution can secure it) that each Deacon who in reply to the question, ' Do you unfeignedly believe all the Canonical Scriptures of the Old and New Testament ? ' answers ' I do believe them,' *speaks the truth* as in the sight of God."

To this address Archbishop Sumner replied as follows :—

"LAMBETH, *February* 12, 1861.

" REVEREND SIR,[1]—I have taken the opportunity of meeting many of my Episcopal brethren in London to lay your address before them.

"They unanimously agree with me in expressing the pain it has given them that any clergyman of our Church should have published such opinions as those concerning which you have addressed us.

" We cannot understand how these opinions can be held consistently with an honest subscription to the formularies of our Church, with many of the fundamental doctrines of which they appear to us essentially at variance.

" Whether the language in which these views are expressed is such as to make the publication an act which could be visited in the Ecclesiastical Courts, or to justify the Synodical condemnation of the book which contains them, is still under our gravest consideration. But our main hope is our reliance on the blessing of God, in the continued and increasing earnestness with which we trust that we and the clergy of our several dioceses may be enabled to teach and preach that good deposit of sound doctrine which our Church teaches in its fulness, and which we pray that she may, by God's grace, ever set forth as the uncorrupted Gospel of our Lord Jesus Christ.—I remain, reverend Sir, your faithful servant,   J. B. CANTUAR.

---

[1] The reply is addressed to the Rev. H. B. Williams, whose name stood at the head of this particular memorial.

" I am authorised to append the following names :—

C. T. EBOR.	R. D. HEREFORD.
A. C. LONDON.	J. CHESTER.
H. M. DURHAM.	A. LLANDAFF.
C. R. WINTON.	R. J. BATH AND WELLS.
H. EXETER.	J. LINCOLN.
G. PETERBOROUGH.	C. GLOUCESTER and BRISTOL.
C. ST. DAVIDS.	W. SARUM.
A. T. CHICHESTER.	R. RIPON.
J. LICHFIELD.	J. T. NORWICH.
S. OXON.	J. C. BANGOR.
T. ELY.	J. ROCHESTER.
T. V. ST. ASAPH.	S. CARLISLE."
J. P. MANCHESTER.	

It had not been without debate that this answer was
agreed to. Bishop Tait's close friendship with two at
least of the Essayists made his own position a somewhat
difficult one. But he seems from the first to have taken
the line to which he adhered to the end, drawing a marked
distinction between the different essays, while he joined in
his brethren's censure of the rash and harmful character
of the volume regarded as a whole.[1]

---

[1] The biographer of Bishop Wilberforce has in this case, as in many others,
published the Bishop's recollection of what took place at the private meetings of the Bishops (vol. iii. p. 3). These meetings being regarded as
entirely confidential, no official record is kept of the discussions or rather
conversations which take place. During the years covered by Bishop Wilberforce's Biography there was not even a rough minute-book of the proceedings. The confidential character of these conversations would obviously be
at an end if the death of any single Bishop were to be regarded as justifying
the immediate publication of his memoranda of what had passed. Whatever
the personal interest of the Bishop's memoranda, as recording the impression
left upon his own mind, they can in no sense be regarded as authoritative
history, and any one who has had the opportunity of comparing them with other
sources of information upon the subject must have been struck by the wide
but perhaps not unnatural dissimilarity which occasionally exists between
the Bishop's recollection of what was said, especially by those who differed
from him, and the recollection of others. No evidence has been given to the
world that Bishop Wilberforce intended, or would have sanctioned, the

When the formal letter of the Bishops was first published in the newspapers, it was unfortunately not accompanied by a copy of the particular address to which it was a reply, and to this mistake may be traced not a little of the misunderstanding evidenced in some parts of the following correspondence.[1]   The omission was soon rectified, but the mischief had been done.

Canon A. P. Stanley to the Bishop of London.

"CH. CH., OXFORD, *Feb.* 16, 1861.

"MY DEAR BISHOP,—I do not know when I have been more startled than in seeing your name appended to the document which this morning appeared in the *Times.*

"You have yourself expressed to me in a manner so decided as to allow me to repeat your opinion in various places, that you saw nothing seriously to condemn in Jowett's Essay and hardly anything in Temple's.

"You also gave me to understand when I was at Fulham (and thus effectually prevented me from taking any active step in the matter) that no measure could be taken by the Bishops except a general recommendation to the clergy to preach the truth more actively.   This second communication I considered confidential till now.

"I consider that the subscription of your name to this document (especially paragraph 3) is in direct contradiction to what you have said to me on the occasion to which I refer.   How can I explain this?   What can I say in your defence?—Ever yours,

"A. P. STANLEY."

publication of these reminiscences of proceedings which he has himself described as "most confidential" (*Life*, iii. 114).   Strange to say, they have been incorporated, as though they were authoritative records, in at least one popular "History of the Church of England."

[1] It may be thought that this correspondence is reproduced at unnecessary length, and that the more personal part of the controversy might well have been omitted.   But after consultation with the Bishop of London, and with the biographer of Dean Stanley, it has seemed to all to be the fairest and wisest course that the whole correspondence should be left intact, as serving to throw light upon the private and personal, as well as the official, side of the character which this Biography endeavours to portray.

The Bishop of London to Canon A. P. Stanley.

"LONDON HOUSE, *February* 18, 1861.

"MY DEAR STANLEY,—In paragraph 3 of the Archbishop's letter, as given in the *Times*, there is a typographical error which materially alters its tone. The word 'their' is substituted for 'these.' This shall be publicly corrected.

"If you read the letter with this alteration, you will see that the paper in question contains simply what I stated to you in the garden at Fulham as likely to appear. No allusion is made in the paper to any individual writer, and it is open for each to show that he is not responsible for what others have written, or for the general system which the public has put together from comparing the seven essays.

"Trust me that I have done in this matter what is best, and what was absolutely necessary.

"As to Temple's essay, I mentioned to you, that, in my judgment, there is nothing in it, taken by itself, to which such a condemnation as that of the Archbishop's letter can apply. The same must be said of Pattison's. Jowett's has a deeply earnest tone about it. Those who are acquainted with his other writings will find far less to object to in this essay than in the Dissertations or Commentary.

"The book of the Essays and Reviews as a whole is what has excited so much feeling. Cannot the copartnery be dissolved? Surely it is wrong to allow new editions of it as a whole to be appearing. The variety of names in that list of the whole Bench appended to the Archbishop's letter ought to convince you of the gravity of the occasion, of which no one but ourselves (the Bishops) can judge. I am confident that the course pursued has been the right one, and the kindest to the writers. I urged on both Jowett and Temple the duty of their each publishing something of a positive character, which would show that they are not to be confounded, say, with Baden Powell. I wish you could bring this about. Temple at least would have no difficulty in doing so.—Yours ever.   "A. C. LONDON."

Canon A. P. Stanley to the Bishop of London.

"CH. CH., OXFORD, *Feb.* 19, 1861.

"MY DEAR BISHOP,—Thanks for your letter. The typographical correction makes grammar, where before there was none, but unfortunately makes the sense (at least till the world is allowed to see the specification of the opinions thus denounced) worse than before.

"I had hoped that you would have been able to remove the contradiction between your acquittal of three of the Essayists to me in private and the sweeping censure of them in public. I am deeply grieved for your sake that this contradiction should remain.

"I cannot understand any popular panic justifying such a course. Of course I am quite aware that Bishops have the opportunity of hearing what does not reach the ears of ordinary persons. But ordinary persons hear much which does not reach the ears of Bishops, and I have unfortunately the means of knowing quite enough to assure me that, unless this call upon such men as Temple, Jowett, and Pattison to leave the Church of England turn out a mere *brutum fulmen*, which I trust in Heaven that it may be, you could not have adopted a measure more calculated to injure the cause of Christianity or of the Church in this country.

"With regard to what passed between you and myself about the Episcopal meeting, as it only concerns my own course in the matter, I need say no more of it. Of your general opinion of the book, I shall, however, consider myself free to speak, on all fitting occasions. Indeed it must be sufficiently apparent from what is known of your own views on these matters.

"I am sure that you will agree with me, that 'until this tyranny is overpast,' we had better have no more communication on this subject, at least none of a confidential nature. It can only lead to misunderstandings.

"It would have been far better that, under the circumstances, you had not invited me to Fulham on that occasion.

"I do not doubt that you acted with reluctance and with kind intentions. I have every hope that the catastrophe, which the Episcopal letter endeavours to precipitate, may, by God's help and man's courage, be averted.—Yours ever,

"A. P. STANLEY."

The Bishop of London to Canon A. P. Stanley.

"LONDON HOUSE, *Feby. 20th,* 1861.

" MY DEAR STANLEY,—I agree with you that there is no use in continuing a discussion, in which each of us must necessarily take our own view from the data brought under our particular notice.   I feel perfectly confident of the rightness and wisdom of what has been done, and I expect you to view the matter as I do in three months.

" I will only say two things : *First,* that there is really no inconsistency between the censure of certain opinions contained in the book, which give it its general tone in the estimate of those who regard it as a whole, and what I stated to you yesterday, and have often stated publicly, to be my opinion of certain of the Essays and Essayists.

" *Second,* That your visit to Fulham at the time of the Episcopal Meeting was arranged weeks before, and that I had no means whatever of knowing till after you had been with us for at least half of your visit, how things were likely to go as to this matter.   I believe it is best, as you say, that the matter should drop for the present between us.   I hope to be with you on the 22d of March to stay till the morning of the 25th.   By that time I almost expect that you will be of my mind in the matter : but if not, we can agree to differ.—Ever yours,·

" A. C. LONDON.

" You are of course quite at liberty to repeat what I have said respecting Temple's, Pattison's, and Jowett's Essays.   My opinions respecting them have been stated continually without reserve.   Would that their Essays were freed from the company of Powell, Williams, and Wilson."

The Rev. Dr. Temple to the Bishop of London.

"RUGBY, 21*st Feb.* 1861.

" MY LORD,—I have just obtained a copy of the Address presented to the Archbishop of Canterbury by a number of the clergy of the United Church of England and Ireland, to which

His Grace's letter to the Rev. H. B. Williams, signed by yourself and the other Bishops, was a reply.

"I find among the other extracts which are given as containing opinions against which the Address protests, a passage from my own Essay, on the Education of the World.

"In His Grace's reply, these opinions are declared to appear to him and His Right Reverend Brethren to be essentially at variance with the fundamental doctrines of our Church.

"I hope your Lordship will not think me to be asking more than I have a fair right to claim if I request you to be so kind as to inform me with what fundamental doctrines that extract from my Essay appears to you to be at variance.

"Your Lordship will not, I think, object to my making a public use of your answer.—Your obedient servant,

"F. TEMPLE."

The Bishop of London to the Rev. Dr. Temple.

"LONDON HOUSE, *Feb.* 22d, 1861.

"MY DEAR TEMPLE,—I have received yours of yesterday's date.

"You must have made some mistake respecting the Address to which you suppose the Archbishop of Canterbury's letter, signed by the Bishops, to be a reply. No extracts from your Essay on the 'Education of the World' were contained in, or appended to, any address either of the Rev. H. B. Williams or any other brought under my notice or laid before the Bishops by His Grace.

"For my own part I draw a marked distinction between the tone and substance of the several contributions to the book called *Essays and Reviews.* I shall be ready to state publicly, if you desire it, what is my opinion of your essay, taken by itself. But the public appears, I must say not unnaturally, resolved to regard the volume as one whole.

"Without entering on other points to which I object, I will say that, when taken as a whole, the teaching of the volume is, in my judgment, not consistent with the true doctrine maintained by our Church as to the office of Holy Scripture.

"I feel convinced that there is much in this volume of which you, as well as others of the contributors, disapprove ; and I therefore the more regret that your high character and deserved influence should, as matters stand at present, seem to give weight to the volume as a whole. I shall rejoice if the mode in which attention is now directed to this subject enables each author to stand by himself as responsible only for his own opinions, and influencing the public only by the force of his own arguments and the authority which attaches to his own name.

"I shall be obliged by your making this letter public, and remain, my dear Temple, ever yours sincerely,

"A. C. LONDON."

The Rev. Dr. Temple to the Bishop of London.

"RUGBY, 22*d Feb*. 1861.

"MY LORD,—I have to apologise for having given you needless trouble. I find I was supplied, not with the Address presented to the Archbishop, but with one now in course of signature. With the Address really presented I find that I have no concern whatever.—Your obedient Servant, F. TEMPLE."

The Bishop of London to the Rev. Dr. Temple.

"LONDON HOUSE, *Feb.* 23, 1861.

"MY DEAR TEMPLE,—I have your letter of the 22d, whereby it appears that before receiving my answer to yours of the 21st, you had become aware of your mistake as to the Address laid before the Bishops.

"It is still my wish that our correspondence should be made public, for I think it of great importance to the Church, that the opportunity should not be lost, which your letter of the 21st afforded me, of calling upon the contributors to the volume of *Essays and Reviews* (and especially on yourself) to declare more emphatically than they have done hitherto, that they claim to have their several contributions judged separately, and not as parts of a connected whole.

"It may have escaped your attention that the short preface to the volume is ambiguous and unsatisfactory. It consists but of two sentences, the first of which indeed disclaims any united responsibility; but the second speaks of the contributors as having one common object, and as approving collectively of the spirit in which each has endeavoured to promote that object.

"As circumstances stand, I hold that those especially of the contributors who, like yourself, occupy important public posts, are now solemnly bound to explain publicly, and with as little delay as possible, their relation to this book in duty to themselves, and in fairness to the many who are likely to be influenced unduly by an apparent combination of much respected names with others less known.

"The *Essays and Reviews* have, I understand, passed through several editions in consequence of the attention which has been directed to them. It seems to me that, considering the light in which this volume has been regarded, and the feeling which it has elicited, whoever undertakes the task of editor ought, on the commonest principles of right, before now to have been authorised, or rather charged, to satisfy the anxiety of the public on the subject I have brought before you.—Believe me to be, ever yours sincerely,   A. C. LONDON."

The Rev. Dr. Temple to the Bishop of London.

" *Private and Confidential.*]

"RUGBY, 25 *February* 1861.

"MY LORD,—I regret that I cannot accede to your wish that our correspondence should be published; and although in my first letter I asked for an answer of which I might make a public use, yet considering that the whole correspondence arose from a mere mistake, I can hardly think that you can insist upon publishing it without my consent.

"I do not think the short preface to the book ambiguous. The first sentence states an exact fact. So completely was the volume put together without concert or comparison that I never knew what any other writer was writing, nor even what he was writing about, till the book came to me from the Publisher's. The second sentence states the tacit understanding with which the book was undertaken, namely, that it was to treat of Biblical subjects, and that each was to write in a becoming spirit, but to say exactly what he thought. I do not see what is to be gained by any repetition of this. And in the present state of the public mind it would be understood as sanctioning the popular clamour, and that I do not suppose any other of the six writers is prepared to do ; certainly I am not myself.

"I cannot understand your fear that many will be influenced by the apparent combination of much respected names with others less known. That argument might have had weight six months ago. But surely now it is out of place. Surely the whole Bench of Bishops is enough to save the many from such influence without calling on the six contributors to give their aid. The danger seems to me to be quite on the other side.

"Many years ago you urged us from the University pulpit to undertake the critical study of the Bible. You said that it was a dangerous study, but indispensable. You described its difficulties, and those who listened must have felt a confidence (as I assuredly did, for I was there) that if they took your advice and entered on the task, you at any rate would never join in treating them unjustly if their study had brought with it the difficulties you described. Such a study, so full of difficulties, imperatively demands freedom for its condition. To tell a man to study, and yet bid him, under heavy penalties, come to the same conclusions with those who have not studied, is to mock him. If the conclusions are prescribed, the study is precluded.

"Freedom plainly implies the widest possible toleration. I admit that toleration must have limits or the Church would fall to pieces. But the student has a right to claim, *first*, that those limits should be known beforehand, and contained in formularies within his own reach ; not locked up in the breasts of certain of his brethren ; *secondly*, that his having transgressed them should be decided after fair, open trial by men practised in such decisions.

"Instead of that what do we see? A set of men publish a book containing the results of their study and thought, which, rightly or wrongly, they believe to be within the limits traced out by the formularies. Suddenly, without any warning to them that they are on their trial, without any opportunity given for explanation or defence, assuredly without any proof that they have really transgressed the limits prescribed, the whole Bench of Bishops join in inflicting a severe censure, and in insinuating that they are dishonest men. And so utterly reckless are their Lordships how much or how little penalty they inflict, that the censure is drawn in terms that are not intelligible without the production of another document which is not produced, and thus has the added force which in these cases always accompanies a vague denunciation.   How on earth is any study to be pursued under such treatment as this?

"You complain that young men of ability will not take orders. How can you expect it when this is what befalls whoever does not think just as you do?

"I know what can be said against a wide toleration.   It may be said that it would issue in wild and extravagant speculations. So it would, in a few instances.   But you know perfectly well that there is not the most distant chance of the great mass of sober Englishmen running into anything of the sort.   If therefore you tolerate extreme opinions, their very existence in the Church is a guarantee that the moderate opinions are held from conviction, not from fear of consequences.   But if you drive extreme men out of the ministry, the inevitable result is to poison the minds of the laity with the suspicion that the clergymen who remain teach what they do, not because they believe it, but because they fear the fate of their brethren.

"I for one joined in writing this book in the hope of breaking through that mischievous reticence which, go where I would, I perpetually found destroying the truthfulness of religion.   I wished to encourage men to speak out.   I believed that many doubts and difficulties only lived because they were hunted into the dark, and would die in the light.

"I believed that all opinions of the sort contained in the book would be better if tolerated and discussed, than if censured and maintained in secret.   And though there was much error mixed up in these opinions, yet certainly not more than in what was allowed, and even encouraged.   What can be a grosser superstition than the theory of literal inspiration?   But because that has a regular footing it is to be treated as a good man's mistake, while the courage to speak the truth about the first chapter of the Book of Genesis is a wanton piece of wickedness.   A wide toleration would in time set all these matters in their true relation : for if neology has strong defenders, certainly the commonly received opinions have no lack of able men to maintain them. But censures, even on the right side, will only do what you said more than fourteen years ago,—gain you the aid of some treacherous waiters upon fortune.

" In conclusion, I must say a few words personal to you and myself.

" If you do not wish to alienate your friends, do not treat them as you have treated me.   Do not, if one of them seem to you to have done a foolish, or even a wrong thing, ask him to your house, speak of the subject kindly, condemn in such a tone as to imply no severe reprobation ; and then, in deference to a popular clamour, join in an act of unexampled severity.   You might have spoken severely if you had thought severely.   Having spoken leniently, you were pledged to deal leniently.   Nothing would have been easier than to imply to me what you were going to do, if you then had thoughts of doing it.   And surely if your quiet perusal of the book had given you no such thoughts, the mere cry of this mob ought not to have influenced your judgment.

" What you did had not the intention, but it had all the effect, of treachery.

" You will not keep friends if you compel them to feel that in every crisis of life they must be on their guard against trusting you.—Yours faithfully,   F. TEMPLE."

From one of the Rugby Masters Bishop Tait had in the meantime received the following letter :—

"Since your lordship's answer to the Address has appeared, we have been placed in a very difficult position at Rugby.   As the Address itself has not yet been published, no one can say exactly who or what has been censured.   Most of us think that Dr. Temple's essay is not included in the general censure.   I am one of the few who hope that your lordships have only agreed in condemning certain specified opinions not maintained by Dr. Temple.

"Under these circumstances, would you pardon my writing to beg that the Address and the Answer should be published together?   You will be sorry to hear that Dr. Temple was very far from well when the school met.   As he is still in a very weak and nervous state we are very anxious about him.

" He has determined, for the sake of the boys, to disconnect himself in some way or other from the other essayists.   Indeed, the parents are in such an uneasy state that something must be done to reassure them."

Bishop Tait immediately replied (Feb. 23)—

"You will see in the last *Guardian* an Address from Dorchester, to which the Archbishops' letter, signed by the Bishops, was sent by His Grace as an answer.   You will observe that in that address there is no allusion to Dr. Temple, nor to any opinion which his essay, as I understand it, maintains."

His correspondent next day wrote—

"I must thank you for your prompt reply to my letter.   It has removed a very general misunderstanding at Rugby, and has been a great relief to Dr. Temple's own mind.   To-day he is ill in bed. . . ."

The writer goes on to describe a meeting of the Rugby masters, which had been held on the previous day, when Dr. Temple spoke to them about his connection with the Essays, and showed, in the opinion of the writer, how deeply he was distressed by much that the volume contained, and how conscious he was of the pain which it had caused to parents of the Rugby boys.   The letter was confidential, and, as will be seen below, Dr. Temple did not accept the detailed account it contained as an accurate record of what had passed.   It is evident, however, that the letter made a deep impression upon Bishop Tait, who wrote again as follows :—

The Bishop of London to the Rev. Dr. Temple.

"*Private and Confidential.*]

"LONDON HOUSE, *Feb.* 27, 1861.

"MY DEAR TEMPLE,—It was impossible for me yesterday to answer yours of the 25th owing to ceaseless engagements.

"Of course, if you wish it, the idea that I had entertained, that your circular to me and the other Bishops afforded an opportunity for your explaining to the public your real position towards the volume of Essays and Reviews must drop.   I was

in hopes that you would have felt with me that the Archbishops'
and Bishops' letter had so changed the state of the case that
you, and not you only, but the other essayists also, might have
publicly reiterated their demand to be judged each by his own
essay alone, and explained how far you approved or disapproved
of each other's essays. In the judgment of most thinking men,
though they might disapprove of what you had written, you
would, I believe, have been judged to have yourself kept within
the fair limits of the Church's liberty, while, perhaps, all the
writers, certainly three, including yourself, having vindicated
themselves from having their writings explained by a reference to
a gloss derived from the writings of others, would have stood
somewhat better in the estimate of those whose opinions are
worth considering. I can see nothing in such a declaration that
could have been fairly considered as ungenerous; and indeed I
believe it is called for by the present aspect of things. Seven
persons write without concert in one volume. For a long time
the volume is silently disliked; at last the feeling against it becomes very strong. The public insists upon judging it as one
whole, interpreting the words of each writer by reference to each
of the other six. Addresses pour in upon the Archbishops and
Bishops, stating the strong feeling against the general teaching of
the book considered as a whole. You will not, I trust, on
reflection justify yourself in calling those who thus memorialised
the Bishops a 'mob.' Many of them were thoughtful and pious
men, whose best feelings were deeply wounded, and were filled
with not unnatural anxiety.

"Certain opinions, quite inadmissible within the Church of
England, are asserted in some of these addresses to be distinctly
advocated by the book, while other addresses assert that the
teaching, taken as a whole, though it may not distinctly advocate,
implies these dangerous opinions. The Bishops feel themselves
bound to declare their condemnation of these opinions. What
more natural then for any of the writers who can, now to state
that the opinions in question are not advocated by them? that
they have been misunderstood; and to demand to be judged
each by his own statements, and not by the general teaching of
a book, the tone and aggregate effect of which you, at least in
your conscience, disapprove, and which you are anxious shall
not, as a whole, be regarded as an exposition of your opinions.

"It is in vain to say that the disclaimer in the preface was sufficient. Experience has shown that it was not. Something more distinct is required. And if from the way in which the Archbishops' letter was published (I presume before his authority had been obtained for its publication) there was an ambiguity as to what was condemned, it would have been very natural for each writer to request His Grace, or any other Bishop, to specify the teaching gathered from the book of which the Bishops had expressed their strong disapproval.

"I am not without hope that you may still think the proper course for yourself and others to be such as I have pointed out. And now as to your complaint of what the Bishops have done. They have spoken of certain opinions which the public suppose to be derivable from the teaching of the book as a whole, and which, it is scarcely possible to deny, are implied if not taught by it. They have announced their belief that these opinions go beyond the fair latitude allowed in the Church. Appealed to, I cannot see how they could do otherwise. As to calling upon individuals to defend themselves, this would have given the letter the character of a judgment of individuals, which I, for one, was most anxious to avoid. What was issued was a condemnation of the book as one whole, leaving individuals each to speak for himself in exculpation.

"I was convinced at the time, and I am convinced now, that this was a wiser, better, and kinder course than any other which was proposed. Other courses were urged—I thought this most free from any appearance of persecuting or endeavouring to put down individuals by authority.

"We said, in effect, of the book, to those who addressed us— We disapprove of it—of the opinions laid before us by you, we think they go beyond any fair latitude, and we cannot deny that they are, or appear to be, in the book; but as to molesting individuals, or saying how far any one of the authors whom you consider as united to teach these opinions—we can at present say nothing of them; how far they are responsible is a matter for grave consideration, as is also how far any of them who are responsible have distinctly committed themselves to anything which the law could visit. It is in vain to say, as you do, that such a declaration makes the exhortation to encourage Biblical studies a mockery. You grant that there must be limits to the freedom of the conclusions at which clergymen arrive, and which they teach. Suppose a man unfortunately to arrive at the opinion, as the result of his Biblical studies, that there is no God, and that the Bible is from the beginning to the end a lie. Am I to allow him to teach this as a clergyman of the Church of England? Or if I condemn the result of his studies, am I to be said to discourage all study? Is not this a *reductio ad absurdum*? You say that he might be dealt with in a court of law; I think it may be better to announce strong disapproval without seeking for pains and penalties. Up to the present point this is what has been done.

 " And now, my dear Temple, as to your feeling with regard to me personally—it is not just. I solemnly assure you that in all I have done I have endeavoured to act with a full remembrance of all that has passed between us, and especially of your visit to me a fortnight before the Bishops met to consider the subject. It is the misery of an official position that if a man is determined that his private friendships and his public acts shall never appear to come into collision, he must give up his private friendships. Most men, I believe, adopt this course. They confine themselves to the society and friendship of those with whom they are sure to agree. They escape thereby much danger of being misunderstood, but they rob life of what makes it of value. Remember that in Balliol in old times there was many a painful difficulty of the same kind with Oakeley and Ward. It was understood between us that private friendship should not be interfered with by the necessity for public acts. I do not speak of your connection with the Church of England as at all resembling theirs. What I said to you at Fulham I say now—and I believe what in my public capacity I have done now is not inconsistent with what I then and now say of yourself and of Jowett's essay. I think you judge amiss. If you had been in my place, I believe you would have done as I have.—Believe me to be, my dear Temple, yours very sincerely,

" A. C. London."

The Rev. Dr. Temple to the Bishop of London.

" *Private and Confidential.*]

" Rugby, 1 *March* 1861.

 " My Lord,—I am much obliged to you for taking the trouble to write me so long a letter.

"I do not think anything will be gained by my attempting to discuss these matters in detail any longer.

"Indeed, I have little to say, if you can really think that in reply to a demand on behalf of Biblical students for trial by fixed law after full argument in open court, it is enough to say that you have given something wiser, kinder, and better. Such is the doctrine of the Bishop of London. Such was not the doctrine of that Tutor of Balliol whose lecture I still remember—on the difference between government by νόμος and government by ψηφίσματα.

"With regard to my own conduct, I can only say that nothing on earth will induce me to do what you propose. I do not judge for others, but in me it would be base and untrue.

"For the personal question between us, I cannot do more than say what I said before, that such conduct has the effect (I expressly said—not the intention) of treachery. You did not like my essay. Why did you not say so? You were ready to join in this denunciation. Why did you not imply it? You ought not to make it impossible for a friend to calculate on what you will do. I do not care for your severity. I do care for being cheated.

"The greatest kindness you can now do me is to forget till all this is over that any friendship ever existed between us. That will at any rate save me from such mischief as your speech in Convocation [1] yesterday is certain to do me.—Yours faithfully,

"F. TEMPLE."

The Bishop of London to the Rev. Dr. Temple.

"LONDON HOUSE, *March* 2, '61.

"MY DEAR TEMPLE,—I am quite ready to acquiesce in your wish that after this note the subject of your essay should drop between us. But I must just take the liberty of saying to you that I am totally at a loss to understand the consistency, and propriety —I will not use any other word—of making such a statement as I know, not only from confidential communications, but openly from a quarter where no confidence or secrecy is implied—you have made to your assembled masters, and what you now write

---

[1] See page 302.

to me. Indeed, when you were at Fulham, you told me distinctly that you meant to publish, as I believe and say you ought.

"Personally, also, I must say that you quite misrepresent what passed between us at Fulham. I said then what I say now and said always respecting your essay, and it is my full belief that I said the same in distinct words to yourself.

"I am happy to think that others who have a deep regard for you and Jowett take a very different view from that which you have taken, you must allow me to say, from a somewhat arrogant over-estimate of the infallibility of your own opinion.—Believe me to be, my dear Temple, yours very sincerely,

"A. C. LONDON."

The Rev. Dr. Temple to the Bishop of London.

"RUGBY, 3*d March* 1861.

"MY LORD,—I should not have answered your letter if it did not seem to be necessary to mention two matters of fact.

"I was quite aware that in speaking to the masters I ran a considerable risk of being misrepresented by half-statements of what I said. But I thought their relation to me made openness their due in spite of the risk. Such a half statement, however, as I feared, seems to have reached you. For I do not think that whoever told you of what I said can have told you that my last words to the masters were: 'You will see that if any public statement of my disapproval of the other writers in the volume is made, I shall probably find it my duty to contradict it.' I think you could neither have been told this, nor what, you can see from its tenor, preceded it.

"I wish I could feel that I had misrepresented what passed between us at Fulham. But I have a very distinct recollection of what was said. You expressed disapproval of what I had done in joining the other writers in the volume. You quoted Dean Milman's remark about solidarity. You advised me to publish. But not one word did you say in my hearing of disapproval of my essay. Even your disapproval of the whole book was not in such a tone as would have conveyed to any ordinary listener that you were prepared to do what you have since done. Jowett came immediately after I left. Naturally enough, when we met, I asked him what sort of conversation you had had with him.

His reply was (I give his words), 'Tait was very kind, and on the whole even gave me the impression that he agreed with me.'

"I do not think you can be quite aware of the pain that you give in this way. You evidently fancy that you convey one impression when you mean to convey another. The result is that your friends complain that they cannot count on you: your enemies say that they can, and that you will always do what is popular with the Low Church party.

"I am very sorry if I have been arrogant. I was not conscious of it. I cannot honestly say that I am conscious of it now. But a man smarting under a sense of having been unfairly treated by a friend is not a fair judge of his own temper. At any rate, I am honestly grateful to you for telling me. That at least is straightforward and friendly. I will try to be on my guard against the fault.

"I owe you very much: more than I can ever repay. My heart swells sometimes when I think of lessons learned from your lips twenty years ago, and of kindnesses which perhaps were hardly thought of by you who did them, but were more than I can tell to me who received them. And you can hardly imagine the wound it gave me to see your name under the Archbishops' letter, not so much because I thought it wrong in you to sign if you really wish to condemn so severely, but because my visit to Fulham had made me feel sure that you would join in no such act. Forgive me if I have written hotly, and believe at any rate as much as this, that I am acting to the best of the light that God has given me in a very difficult time.— Yours faithfully.   F. TEMPLE."

The Bishop of London to the Rev. Dr. Temple.

"LONDON HOUSE, *4th March* 1861.

"MY DEAR TEMPLE,—I am very unwilling to add to your trouble by writing again, but I cannot refrain from saying how thankful I am for the more kindly tone of your yesterday's letter, so much more like yourself. You will not, I trust, be sorry for the trouble of reading another letter if it tends to clear up misunderstandings with one who has known and esteemed you so long as I have.

"As you say it, I must concede that I appear, when you were

at Fulham, to have left on your mind and on Jowett's an impression different from what I intended, though perhaps this difference between us may arise from your judging differently of the Bishops' protest to what I do. Remember that the protest was directed against the general teaching of the book, viewed as a whole, and against certain doctrines stated in the addresses to be extracted from it, and I do not for my life see how, when appealed to, the Bishops could have failed to speak as they did. Remember also that no one without can judge of the responsibilities under which Bishops are placed. Let me say further that in my note-book of the 20th January I find this entry, which expresses my feelings at the time of your and Jowett's visits :—

'Jowett has been with me for two days. The unsatisfactory part of his system seems to be that there is an obscurity over what he believes of the centre of Christianity. As to the outworks, the conflict there is of comparatively little importance. But the central figure of the Lord Jesus, the central doctrine of the efficacy of His sacrifice,—in fact St. Paul's Christianity—is this distinctly recognised by the writers of his school? I have urged both on him and Temple, who has also been with me, that they are bound to state for their own sakes, and for the sake of those whom they are likely to influence, what is the positive Christianity which they hold. It is a poor thing to be pulling down ; let them build up.'

"If I failed to give you the impression that such were my thoughts, I am sorry for it. The position in which a man in so responsible an office as mine is placed is, you will allow, a very difficult one, if he wishes on the one hand to retain the intimacy of his old friendships, and on the other, in his public capacity, to act exactly as he thinks right. I am convinced you will not, on reflection, judge harshly of the difficulties of such a position. One word more. I had no information of the closing words of your address to the masters. I should add that I do not now see that they are wise or right. And now I leave the subject, humbly trusting and praying that you may have wisdom to do what is right in your very trying circumstances.—Ever yours,

" A. C. London."

While this private correspondence was going on, the whole subject had been formally debated in the Convocation of Canterbury.   In the Lower House some of the speakers gave expression to their wrath or their alarm in language of the wildest kind.   Archdeacon Denison called upon the House to act with rigour "for the sake of the young, who are tainted and corrupted and thrust almost to Hell by the action of this book ";[1] adding, on another occasion, "In my judgment, of all books in any language, which I ever laid my hands on, it is incomparably the worst.   It contains all the poison which is to be found in Tom Paine's *Age of Reason*, while it has the additional disadvantage of having been written by clergymen."[2]

In the Upper House, on February 28th, Bishop Tait spoke as follows :—

"I am not in the position of the Bishop of Salisbury, for none of the writers of this book are within my diocese.   But I am in this position—that I have been, and am at this moment, the intimate personal friend of two of the clergymen whose names appear in *Essays and Reviews*, and I wish to say with regard to both of them that from my present friendship and intercourse with them for more than twenty years, I entertain for them the very liveliest affection and regard ; and in proportion as that affection and regard is strong, the more do I desire that an opportunity should be given to them of doing what I trust they will do, namely make a declaration satisfactory to the country that they are not responsible for every word that appears in this unfortunate volume. . . . I must say that I am greatly pained, that I am ashamed of those who have characterised the writers of this book, by a miserable joke, as *Septem contra Christum*.   It seems to me to be a joke as ill-suited to the solemnity of the occasion as it is unworthy of any serious person who is dealing with the characters of his brother clergymen. . . . I have known Dr. Temple, as I have said, for many years in the intimacy of private friendship. The particular essay which he has written certainly does not express my views.   I believe it was first preached as a University Sermon in St. Mary's Church, Oxford.   I dislike it, but, in my

---

[1] *Chronicle of Convocation*, Feb. 26, 1861, p. 394.
[2] *Ibid.* p. 809.

estimation, it is totally different in character from other passages which occur in this volume; and I cannot conceive by what motive the author could be restrained—if it should prove that he is restrained—from publicly declaring that he does not approve of various things which are to be found in this unfortunate book. . . . I think myself bound to say that if my right rev. brother would enter into a full examination of the passages he has quoted, he will find that the extracts which he has read do not really imply what to his mind they appear to imply. This is only an exemplification of what the history of the Church in every age confirms, that if you give isolated extracts from the book of any writer you are almost certain to give a false impression of what his opinion is. I am unwilling to rake up old stories or go back to the history of the University of Oxford at the time when I resided in it, but there were books of extracts then published which were regarded as very unfair indeed.[1] With the utmost fairness of intention it is almost impossible to give by extracts a real statement of what a man's opinion is when he has the misfortune to be writing on the dangerous confines between what is truth and what is error. . . . With regard to the two essays to which I allude, if any man would make up his mind upon them, he must read them from beginning to end. . . . I must say that I regret very much the tone of what the Bishop of Oxford has said; I regret it deeply and I also regret what the Bishop of St. David's has said, because it seems to me that those two speeches will make it very difficult for these writers to do what I believe it is their bounden duty to do. . . . Let it be distinctly understood that we, the Bishops of the Church of England, looking at the book as a whole, believe that it is likely to do great and grievous harm; but separating, as I trust I shall ever be able to do throughout my whole life, the individuals from their opinions, hoping even against hope that these individuals may return, however far they may have gone astray, I shall be indeed rejoiced if an opportunity is afforded to all these writers to make a public declaration of their belief in the great truths of Christianity. I shall be truly pleased if they can make such a declaration. I for one shall not permit myself to doubt of their honesty, and I shall not trouble myself about their consistency."[2]

---

[1] The reference is, of course, to the series of isolated extracts from Dr. Newman's writings which were constantly quoted against him by some of his opponents.   [2] *Chronicle of Conv.* Feb. 28, 1861, pp. 461, 467.

The animadversions which this speech drew upon Bishop Tait are significant of the tone and temper in which the controversy was carried on. He was accused of having " compromised and even vilified the faith he was appointed to maintain," of having allowed his private friendship to take the place of fidelity to truth, and of having "linked himself without shame to the heresiarchs of the Church." His "uncertain and dangerous tone" was contrasted with the noble outspokenness of Bishop Wilberforce, who " without conferring with flesh and blood, or any personal interest, real or supposed, has not hesitated to declare the truth of God to be dearer than all personal affection." The religious papers, both High-Church and Low-Church, were full of such comments. On the other hand he received such letters as the following, which came from one now prominent in the Church :—

"Will you forgive me for writing a letter, which needs no acknowledgment, to thank you very earnestly, and I think many must be wishing to thank you, for what you said in Convocation yesterday. I have been reading it in the *Times*, and it has been a real relief to me. . . . To say even what you said yesterday when public opinion is setting so very strongly in one direction, and when, to a very great extent, one goes along with it, requires a courage and an effort that few of us would be equal to. I cannot help writing to thank you, not for saying what you felt it to be your duty to say—that would be impertinent in me—but for the relief that I personally have felt ever since I read the report this morning."

All that had, so far, been done by Convocation was an expression of the concurrence of the Lower House in what the Bishops' letter had declared. But a few weeks later, when Convocation met again, the whole subject was re-opened, and after warm debate the Bishops resolved, by eight votes to four, that a Committee of the Lower House should examine the book and report whether there were sufficient grounds for a "synodical judgment" upon it. Bishop Tait opposed this step with all his might. After the joint Episcopal Letter already published, any further attempt at solemn condemnation would, he believed, defeat its own end by giving the book an undue importance.

"A grave and weighty document," he said, "has already gone forth to the whole country, and in my judgment it has as much authority as any document bearing upon this subject is ever likely to have. An unusual concurrence of opinion among the whole of the Bishops of both Provinces has declared the danger which is apprehended to the Church of Christ from the rash and irreverent promulgation of doctrines likely to do harm to young and thoughtless minds. What more would you do? . . . If it is the clergy you are considering,—well, I do not think they are likely to be much misled by the book, and they have naturally and properly a very high estimate of Convocation ; but in my intercourse with the laity I do not find that there is such high and reverent regard for Convocation as is, no doubt, to be desired. I own I should be surprised, for example, if the many barristers in London among whom this book has circulated, were to consider that the book was one whit worse than they thought it before, because it had been solemnly condemned by Convocation. . . . Even the protest we Bishops have already made has had the effect of causing this book to be much more generally read than if we had let it alone. When one of the Popes was asked to recommend a certain book, 'No,' said he, 'I will not recommend it, but I will do for it what will have a greater effect,—I will condemn it.' . . . I believe we are of the same mind still as we were when we signed your Grace's letter, namely that the book as a whole is full of error. But I do not wish by appointing this Committee to prolong needless discussion or to induce the Lower House to engage in a profitless and mischievous altercation."[1]

The Bishop was, however, in a minority. The Committee was appointed, and in due time the Bishops received from the Lower House a formal Resolution, " that there are sufficient grounds for proceeding to a synodical judgment

<hr>

Chronicle of Convocation, March 14, 1861, pp. 555-559.

upon the Book entitled Essays and Reviews."[1]   But a prosecution had in the meantime been set on foot in the Court of Arches against two of the essayists, Dr. Williams and Mr. Wilson.   The Archbishop of Canterbury and the Bishop of London would have to be judges in the case if an appeal should be made to the Privy Council, and any further discussion by the Bishops was therefore out of the question until the Courts of Law should have pronounced their decision.

The following scattered extracts from the Bishop's Diary, which at that time dealt mainly with other matters, give occasional glimpses of what he felt upon the subjects in dispute.

Diary.

" BRIGHTON, 18*th Nov.* 1860.—I have been reading the Bishop of St. David's' pamphlet on Rowland Williams.[2]   Very clever, but not, I think, what a Bishop ought to write.   It is a captious answer to the eccentric professor, when what the Church desires is a bold and clear positive statement.   But the invaluable part of it is the virtual declaration—'I have for many years studied these difficulties attentively, I have felt their full force.   I know all that has been written about them in Germany.   I believe they are vanity and folly.'"

" LONDON HOUSE, 6*th Jan.* 1861.—I have taken in hand to publish a new and revised edition of my 'Suggestions,' with reference to the *Essays and Reviews*.   This takes a good deal of time.

"O Lord, grant me for this new year—a more earnest faith, a greater spirit of prayer, a heart and imagination more pure, through Jesus Christ.   Amen."

---

[1] The Resolution was carried by thirty-one votes against eight.—*Chronicle of Convocation*, June 20, 1861, pp. 743-814.

[2] A volume of sermons published by Dr. Rowland Williams had been criticised and censured by Bishop Thirlwall in his Charge of 1857.   Dr. Williams had replied in a vehement pamphlet, and the Bishop thereupon in a further pamphlet reviewed the whole case and dealt with Dr. Williams' theories in detail.   It is this last pamphlet which is here alluded to.

"*24th February* 1861.—Anxiety as to the judgment of the Bishops on *Essays and Reviews*. Fear of misunderstandings with old friends."

"*3d March* 1861.—This week has been one of great trial. Temple's letters respecting the declaration of the Bishops have greatly pained me."

"*7th March* 1861.—How difficult is my position. ——'s letter speaks the truth. 'For once,' he says, 'I have no desire to be a Bishop.' We have had a great duty,—to express our disapproval: a great duty also, I think, to guard the accused from ill-usage: a great duty to the Church to guard its doctrine: and also to watch for its children likely to be led astray by any appearance of persecution. O Lord, grant me wisdom to help, even in spite of themselves, those whom I so greatly regard.

"*24th March*, CHRIST CHURCH, OXFORD.—Came here on Friday to preach at St. Mary's the last of the Mission Lent Sermons. Attentive congregation. Many undergraduates, though term is over. Yesterday, sad memory of old friends. I am staying with Stanley, who had a great gathering yesterday to meet us at dinner, wishing to unite all parties. Jowett and Dr. Jelf, accused and accuser, very nearly sat side by side.

"'To-day, St. Peter's Church, morning. Good practical sermon from an old pupil, Capel Cure. In St. Mary's heard another pupil —— (dull). The Vice-Chancellor classifies four characteristics of University Sermons: Altitude, Latitude, Platitude, Longitude. All tolerated but the last."

"LONDON HOUSE, *Sunday, 21st April* 1861—11.30 P.M.—Read to-day four of Temple's sermons. They convince me more than ever how great a mistake he made in stepping entirely out of his own line to join such people as Williams, etc. etc., in the *Essays and Reviews*. Read over again the article in the *Edinburgh* on Essays and Reviews.[1] Its logic is very poor—the writing forcible. It would be a good defence of Temple and perhaps of Jowett, if they stood alone or only with Pattison. As a defence of the book generally, it is quite powerless.

"And now I lie down commending myself and Thy Church, O Lord, to Thee."

---

[1] The article was by Dean Stanley, see p. 310.

Canon A. P. Stanley to the Bishop of London.

"6 GROSVENOR CRESCENT, *July* 6, 1861.

"MY DEAR BISHOP,—I do not like to leave London without a few words on our late controversy.

"You told me in February that in three months I should recognise the wisdom and propriety of the Episcopal signatures to the condemnation of the opinions of the Essayists. I need hardly say that anything which has happened since has only confirmed my original impression. The Episcopal censure instead of allaying has immensely aggravated it. Convocation has not only not been prevented from debating, but has disgraced the Church by the most extravagant folly in the course which it has pursued ; legal proceedings have not only not been prevented, but have been promoted on the express ground of the Episcopal letter. The only gainers have been the publishers and the extreme section of the Essayists, who have reaped the greatest advantage from the indiscriminate character of the censure, and from the moral impossibility which it has created of a dissolution of companionship between the different authors.

"I only refer to these consequences of what has been done as a reason for hoping better things in what remains to be done.

"I am quite unable to see why those Bishops who see no grave cause of complaint against the doctrines of the book (whatever they may think of its prudence) should not say so. Those with whom you have talked freely on these matters know perfectly well what your opinions were at the beginning of this year. Temple, Jowett, and Pattison you have, in private communication with me, entirely acquitted (so far as their essays are concerned) of any grave error ; of the others (with the exception of Powell, if interpreted according to the unfavourable construction) there is none whose opinions (I am not now speaking of their style and temper, which are irrelevant) you can think more untenable within the Church than what you know of Arnold, Julius Hare, or the Bishop of St. David's.

"And yet up to this time no Bishop, except the Bishop of Lincoln, has ventured to say publicly that the opinions of any one of the essayists are compatible with the position of an English clergyman.

"I will not add anything more. You know that I, and those

who feel with me, will be driven, however reluctantly, by the continued reticence of the Bishops who agree with us, and the calumnies of those who do not, to express on every possible occasion our points of agreement with men whom we regard as treated so unjustly. . . . Ever yours truly,   A. P. STANLEY."

The Bishop of London to Canon A. P. Stanley.

"FULHAM PALACE, S.W., *8th July* 1861.

" MY DEAR STANLEY,—I am obliged to regard your letter of the 6th as a proof that you are ignorant of the opinions of any but a very narrow clique on the subject on which you write.

" Of course I am disappointed that three months have not, as I expected, brought you to see the Episcopal protest as I do ; but I believe the great body of intelligent men throughout the kingdom differs from you entirely in the matter. My own impression as to the Protest is only strengthened by time. I believe —*first*, that it was inevitable and due to the Church under the peculiar circumstances ; *second*, that it has done a great deal of good.

" As to my opinion of the Essays, it is exactly now what it was at first, and is, as clearly as the circumstances allowed, stated in what I have written, signed, and said in public, which I believe to be in strict accordance with all I have said in private. Temple has found no impossibility in separating himself from the extreme section of the Essayists by his semi-public declarations to the masters, boys, and trustees. It is much to be regretted that he should have imagined for himself any impossibility in saying publicly what he has thus said semi-publicly.

" It seems to me little short of infatuation to fancy any identity between the deeply religious tone of the writings of Arnold and Hare and the flippant and reckless assault on things universally venerated, which has roused public indignation against the ill-starred volume in question. It was against the characteristics of some of the Essayists, imparting a colour to the volume, that the Bishops felt they were called upon to protest as presenting a whole apparently hostile to any generally received and intelligent view of Christianity. The particular opinions of individual writers in the book were not touched in the Protest. To examine the opinions in detail, disentangle what belongs to one and not to another, and settle in the several essays how much is insinuation or repeated guess, and how much the author's own opinion, and afterwards to pronounce as to each opinion how much in it is true, and how much false, and then go through the teaching of each, would be a very difficult and very long business. You seem to expect individual Bishops to do this.

" As far as I am capable of doing anything of the kind amidst my many avocations, I have done something towards it in my published volume.   Meanwhile I do not think you need alarm or irritate yourself about Convocation.   About the courts of law, I must be silent,—being a Privy Councillor.

" To turn the tables on yourself, I think I might say a good deal as to the mode in which a great opportunity was thrown away by the writer of the article in the *Edinburgh*.   Will you forgive me if I strongly advise you in all such difficult matters to take counsel with friends who can view the case impartially?

" But we must not quarrel about this matter.   I have been told you are going to Mount Athos.   Is this so?   I trust you will come back safe and sound.   Very many thanks for the kind expressions at the end of your letter. . . . Ever yours,   A. C. LONDON."

Canon A. P. Stanley to the Bishop of London.

"6 GROSVENOR CRESCENT, *July* 10*th*, '61.

" MY DEAR BISHOP,—Many thanks for your kind letter, which I have found here on my return.   I shall hope to be off by the beginning of August.

" I will not re-open the controversy which I shall hope to find closed on my return.   I will only say that, had the Episcopal letter contained anything like what you express in your present letter (which is exactly what I have expressed in my article in the *Edinburgh Review*), neither I nor the intelligent public would have had any just cause of complaint.—Believe me to be, ever yours,   A. P. STANLEY."

A note from Stanley to the Bishop, on the last day of the year (1861), enclosed the following Memorandum :—

" In the earlier part of this year I left a memorandum to be read in case anything befell me.   Now that the end of the year is come I may as well report to the person whom it chiefly concerns. It was to the effect that if, in an article in the *Edinburgh Review*, or elsewhere, I had said anything which caused needless pain to the Bishop of London, I deeply regret it and hope for his forgiveness. His conduct with regard to the Episcopal letter caused me at the time deep grief. But he acted, I have no doubt, for what he thought the best, and for his kindness to me since I shall always feel grateful."

The Bishop of London to Canon A. P. Stanley.

"FULHAM PALACE, S.W., *6th January* 1862.

"MY DEAREST STANLEY,—I dare say you will excuse me for having allowed some days to pass without writing to answer your most kind note. You know how routine letters crowd upon me, and prevent my having time to sit down quietly to write to a friend.

"So much has passed to agitate and distress you during the last two years that I think it very kind in you to have made the Memorandum of which you enclose a copy, and thus given me the assurance that amidst all trials your friendship for me remains unaltered. But indeed I did not need the assurance, feeling certain that it was so. I know that as life passes and one loved friend after another passes before us into the world unseen, we both of us feel more and more that the remaining friendship of those who have been long intimately associated with us becomes more precious. I am sure I feel this as to old friends, and I know that you feel it also. It has been certainly one of the greatest enjoyments of my life to have been so intimately associated with you.

"And now as to the particular matter to which your Memorandum alludes, feeling perfectly confident, as I have done, of my own desire to do right in reference to the painful state of things which has arisen since the publication of the *Essays and Reviews*, you may be sure I have been ready in my turn to feel and allow that you have acted in all you have done from nothing but a constraining sense of duty. Since however you give me the opportunity, I will tell you that you scarcely estimate aright how much you have irritated many, who have the most friendly feelings, by something in your way of treating these subjects.

Men feel that there are great principles at stake and that there is a very important difference between their way of thinking and feeling about many of the highest Christian truths, and the method, say, of Jowett's theology, and they are greatly irritated by being continually told by you that they all mean the same thing. They feel sure that Jowett would disclaim an identity of sentiment in such matters, say with Bishop Pearson, and they are irritated by what they suppose to be your attempts to show that they are fools for supposing they differ from the so-called negative theology, when they, according to your showing, in truth agree with it.

" My belief is that a great deal of bitterness was infused into the controversy in this way (quite unintentionally on your part) by the article in the *Edinburgh*, and, if I may venture to say so, I think the same sort of irritation is kept alive by your quietly quoting, in the preface of your sermons, Jowett and Temple (without any sort of expression of the possibility of other people disagreeing from your estimate) as two of our best divines.

" People are always made angry when their feelings on important matters are ignored or passed over as childish and not worth considering. I wish you would take this matter into your thoughts. Nothing can be more desirable than the attempt to show, by a straightforward sound argument, how much more of real agreement there is than people suppose in those who materially differ : but the proof of this is not helped by ignoring the real points of difference. I know you wish to know my real feelings on these matters, and so I write freely. Again let me say how thankful I am for all your friendship, and how earnestly I trust that all the bitterness which late events have engendered may pass away.—Yours ever affectionately, A. C. LONDON."

It is not necessary, for the purposes of this book, to give the history of the prosecution and trial of the two Essayists, Dr. Williams and Mr. Wilson. The former was prosecuted by his Diocesan, the Bishop of Salisbury, the latter by a private clergyman, the Rev. James Fendall. After prolonged and elaborate consideration, and many wearisome adjournments, the Dean of Arches (Dr. Lushington) pronounced judgment on December 15, 1862, holding certain of the articles of charge to have been proved, and sentencing each of the accused clergymen to a year's suspension.

From the sentence thus given the two accused clergymen appealed, as had been expected, to the Queen in Council. The appeals were heard in June 1863 before a Judicial Committee of seven members, including the Lord Chancellor (Westbury) ; the two Archbishops, and the Bishop of London.[1]   The appellants in person argued their respective cases, the same counsel appearing for both respondents.

Stated in the briefest possible form, and omitting subsidiary and rejected charges, both Essayists were accused of denying, either directly or by implication, the Inspiration of Holy Scripture, and Mr. Wilson was accused, in addition, of denying the eternity of future punishment.   These were the accusations which the Dean of Arches held to have been proved, and the judgment of the Court of Appeal was awaited with not a little interest.

Bishop Tait took the utmost pains during the whole course of the trial, and a comparison of the judgment as finally pronounced, with the printed memorandum of opinion which he, like the other judges, had circulated beforehand among his colleagues, shows how large a share he had in giving shape to the decision.

Although the case was heard in June, the judgment was not delivered until nearly eight months had elapsed.[2] They were anxious months. The sounds of the ' Colenso ' strife were waxing louder every day, as the Bishop of Natal put forth one by one the successive instalments of his work, and frightened Churchmen began sadly to complain that they were being robbed of their faith by those

[1] The other members of the Judicial Committee present were Lords Cranworth, Chelmsford, and Kingsdown.

[2] Feb. 8, 1864.

who should have been its champions, and that the Bishops at home were apathetic and indifferent at the least.

As the time for delivering judgment drew near, the Bishop of London received a series of long and earnest letters from Dr. Pusey, pointing out the evil consequences that must follow should the essayists be acquitted :—

" I am afraid of lawyers," he said, "and so I have ventured to write to your Lordship in what is a great crisis of the Church. . . . Day by day, since I heard the rumour of the impending judgment, the thought of it has haunted me. It is the greatest crisis the Church of England has ever gone through. For I, at least, see no way out of it, except that the Court must either affirm what has been a part of the faith from the first, or, if it makes the doctrines an open question, must tamper with words in a way which will throw uncertainty on every man's meaning, and sanction unbounded hypocrisy. Your Lordship remembers well the general indignation when Mr. Ward proclaimed that he held the Articles in ' non-natural ' senses—and justly. For there is an end of all faith in each other, of all trust in man, if our hearts do not believe what in their plain meaning our tongues profess. . . . If the highest Court of Appeal allows our clergy to take the word ' everlasting ' in a sense contrary to its known English meaning, . . . how can our people believe that we mean anything which we say ? . . . I do not see what would be left us. And it would be the highest Court of Jurisdiction which would be teaching the clergy and people to be thus dishonest with words. . . . Your Lordship will, I know, forgive my troubling you with this. I know how many are praying in regard to the issue, and I yet hope that God will hear us, and that He will incline the hearts of the judges not to allow His truth to be denied, or our people to be taught to mistrust all which we teach in His name for their salvation."

As one of those before whom the case was heard, the Bishop could say no more in reply than that a most careful and deliberate decision would be given by the Court upon the facts before it.

"At last," to quote the words of Dean Stanley, " the

judgment, to which the Church, not of England only, but of foreign nations also, had been looking forward with intense expectation, was pronounced. No one who was present can forget the interest with which the audience in that crowded Council Chamber listened to sentence after sentence as they rolled along from the smooth and silvery tongue of the Lord Chancellor, enunciating with a lucidity which made it seem impossible that any other statement of the case was conceivable, and with a studied moderation of language which, at times, seemed to border on irony—first the principles on which the judgment was to proceed, and then the examination, part by part, and word by word, of each of the three charges that remained, till, at the close, not one was left, and the appellants remained in possession of the field."

In judging the case, the Court declared its own powers to be strictly limited :—

"It is no part of the duty of this Tribunal," said the Lord Chancellor, "to pronounce any opinion on the character, effect, or tendency of the publications known by the name of Essays and Reviews. Nor are we at liberty to take into consideration for the purposes of the prosecution the whole of the essay of Dr. Williams or of the essay of Mr. Wilson. A few short extracts only are before us, and our judgment must be by law confined to the matter which is therein contained. If, therefore, the book, or these two essays, or either of them as a whole, be of a mischievous and baneful tendency, as weakening the foundations of Christian belief, and likely to cause many to offend, they will retain that character and be liable to that condemnation notwithstanding this our judgment." . . . "On matters on which the Church has prescribed no rule, there is so far freedom of opinion that they may be discussed without penal consequences."

Proceeding to the charges in detail, and arguing each separately with the utmost care, the Court declared itself "unable to say that the passages extracted from the essays" on the subject of the Inspiration of the Bible

" . . . are contradicted by, or plainly inconsistent with, the Articles or Formularies to which the charges refer." With respect to the further charge against Mr. Wilson, that he denied the doctrine of eternal punishment, the judgment ran as follows :—

"We are not required, or at liberty, to express any opinion upon the mysterious question of the eternity of future punishment, further than to say that we do not find in the Formularies to which this article refers any such distinct declaration of our Church upon the subject as to require us to condemn as penal the expression of a hope by a clergyman that even the ultimate pardon of the wicked who are condemned in the day of judgment may be consistent with the will of Almighty God." . . . "On the short extracts before us, our judgment is that the charges are not proved."

From this judgment, so far as the doctrine of inspiration was concerned, the two Archbishops dissented, but Bishop Tait and the lay judges were unanimous, and Dr. Williams and Mr. Wilson were accordingly acquitted.

The immediate result of this decision was a widespread and not unnatural panic. Hundreds of the clergy, who felt that the book was mischievous and was likely to corrupt the faith of their people, failed to see, or declined to see, that the court had emphatically refused to adjudicate upon the general character of the book, and had insisted upon dealing merely with specific extracts in their strict grammatical construction. For them it was enough that the essayists were unpunished, and thus, as they believed, a grievous wrong committed, and, worse than all, with the apparent approval of one of the Bishops of the Church. A defensive alliance was immediately cemented between the High Church and the Low Church leaders, and within a fortnight from the publication of the judgment, the following declaration was sent by post to every clergyman in England and Ireland, with a letter entreating him, "for the love of God," to append his name without delay :—

"We, the undersigned presbyters and deacons in holy orders of the Church of England and Ireland, hold it to be our bounden duty to the Church of England and Ireland and to the souls of men to declare our firm belief that the Church of England and Ireland, in common with the whole Catholic Church, maintains without reserve or qualification the inspiration and Divine authority of the whole canonical Scriptures, as not only containing, but being, the Word of God, and further teaches, in the words of our blessed Lord, that the 'punishment' of the 'cursed' equally with the 'life' of the 'righteous' is 'everlasting.'

"Signatures to be sent to the Secretary, Committee-room, 3 St. Aldate's, Oxford.

"Names of Committee :—C. C. Clarke, D.D., Archdeacon of Oxford ; R. L. Cotton, D.D., Provost of Worcester College ; G. A. Denison, M.A., Archdeacon of Taunton ; W. E. Fremantle, M.A., Rector of Claydon : F. K. Leighton, D.D., Warden of All Souls' College ; J. C. Miller, D.D., St. Martin's, Birmingham ; E. B. Pusey, D.D., Regius Professor of Hebrew."

The signatures of 11,000 clergymen were obtained to this document in the course of a few weeks. The Archbishops, who had formally dissented from the judgment, published each of them a Pastoral Letter explaining his position in the matter, and the wrath both of clergy and laity was expended chiefly upon Bishop Tait.

"Had the judgment," it was said, "proceeded from the lay lords alone it would have been more easy to prove that they had been misled by their inexperience in theology. . . . But they are able to shield themselves behind the authority of an Ecclesiastical judge, a Ruler in the Church, one of those whose 'lips should keep knowledge.'"

And again :

"The course taken by the Bishop of London is disastrous to his own reputation. It has awakened mingled shame and indignation, not only among the dignitaries and clergy of the Church, but, we may add, the laity, always excepting the minority of the clergy, who may be called latitudinarians, and that section of the laity who may be termed freethinkers."[1]

On March 16th a deputation waited on the two Archbishops at Lambeth Palace to present an address signed, it was said, by 137,000 lay members of the Church of England, who desired to thank the primates for the course they had pursued.

No small number of the promoters of this "thank-offering," as it was called, wrote at the same time to Bishop Tait; some in wrathful remonstrance, some in "sadness of heart," and some in earnest entreaty that he would "even now" express his repudiation of what Dr. Pusey called the "soul-destroying judgment" in which he had concurred.

In the course of a correspondence with Mr. Gladstone, arising out of the Bishop's published sermons, he explained his position with some care:—

The Bishop of London to the Right Hon. W. E. Gladstone.

"LONDON HOUSE, *April 28th,* 1864.

"MY DEAR MR. GLADSTONE, . . . I feel greatly obliged to you for writing to me so fully and candidly your opinion on the judgment of the Privy Council. Notwithstanding what you say, however, I almost feel that had you been on the Court, considering the nature of the issue ultimately referred to us, you could scarcely have come yourself to any other decision. . . . The fact is, that when such works as *Essays and Reviews* come before a Court of Law they must be judged not according to their 'general tenor,' but by the force of particular extracts, and when these extracts are exhibited in their naked legal aspect they assume a very different character from that which they perhaps presented when, viewing them in a popular and general

---

[1] This sentence from the *Record* is adopted with approval by the *Quarterly Review,* April 1864, p. 561.

way, we thought of their tendency rather than their strict logical force.

"Hence the folly of such prosecutions. Nobody agreed with Mr. Gorham, but when his opinions were exhibited nakedly before a Court of Law it was found that to declare them inadmissible within the pale of the Church of England would be to condemn by implication, if not directly, the acknowledged and publicly recognised sentiments of very many who were most sincerely attached to the Church and had shaped all their teaching by its articles. It is ever so. Extreme men insinuate or enunciate vaguely dangerous opinions ; when these are subjected to the sieve of a legal prosecution, the least objectionable part remains for the Court to judge of.

"Meanwhile, if we may look to results, it is satisfactory to feel that the Church of England, as it is more comprehensive, is stronger for the Gorham decision, the escape of Archdeacon Denison, and the recent judgment ; and as I believe that in all these cases the Court decided justly, I do not think that, notwithstanding all alarms of 1850, 1857, and 1864, truth has at all suffered by the maintenance of justice. . . . I remain, my dear Mr. Gladstone, yours very truly,   A. C. LONDON."

In the months of somewhat wearisome debate which followed upon the judgment the critics of Bishop Tait grew louder and louder in their denunciations.

"To the defection of the Bishop of London," it was said, "may be justly ascribed all the mischiefs which are likely to follow from the disastrous conclusion of [the trial]. . . . It is very melancholy that the Bishop of London should thus give occasion to the enemies to blaspheme. We earnestly pray that he may be led to pause . . . [for] it is hardly possible to exaggerate the evils which may arise from the fact that an infidel party, both in the Church and out of it, supposes that its members may now shelter themselves under the Episcopal mantle of the Bishop of this vast Metropolis."[1]

Bishop Wilberforce undertook to bring the matter again before Convocation, and formally moved, on April 20th,

---

[1] *Record*, April 25th, 1864.

that inasmuch as the suit before the Privy Council was now concluded, the consideration of the subject, which had for three years been discontinued, pending the judicial decision, should be resumed, and a committee appointed to report upon the volume as a whole. This motion gave rise to a memorable debate, and in particular to a weighty and learned speech from Bishop Thirlwall of St. David's, who opposed with all his might, as did the Bishop of London, the reopening of the discussions in Convocation. Referring to the above-quoted 'declaration,' which was then in process of signature among the clergy, Bishop Thirlwall pointed out that the document was so worded as to declare, not merely what those who appended their names to it believed, but what was, and always had been, the doctrine of the Church of England on the subject.

"Am I to suppose," he said, "that the framers of this declaration believe that the youngest 'literate'—or illiterate, they often mean nearly the same thing—who has been last admitted into Deacon's Orders is competent to express an opinion upon the subject which has occupied some of the ablest and most intellectual minds for the last two years? And the young deacon is adjured 'by the love of God,' and as a part of his bounden duty to souls, to do what? . . . If Dr. Pusey is not able to satisfy us with his authority on such a question, will the name of this young deacon do anything towards it? Will any number of men signing it? If they are the names of persons of equal learning, equally competent to judge on such a very difficult question, I admit they will, but otherwise I cannot consider these names, whatever be their numbers,—they are said to have exceeded 12,000—I cannot consider them in the light of so many ciphers, which add to the value of the figures which they follow; but I consider them in the light of a row of figures preceded by a decimal point, so that however far the series may be prolonged, it never can rise to the value of a single unit."[1]

---

[1] *Chronicle of Convocation*, April 21, 1864, p. 1532.

Not a little indignation was aroused by this somewhat contemptuous estimate of the solemn declaration of the clergy, and by the Bishop of London's angry denunciation—no milder word is possible—of the form of the condemnatory 'schedule' drawn up by Archdeacon Denison's committee three years before, and now resuscitated by Bishop Wilberforce.

"I deeply regret," said Bishop Tait, "that such a paper should ever have seen the light of day. If the book entitled *Essays and Reviews* is likely to do harm to the Christian faith . . . [this particular answer] is a document which, I undertake to say, would be received with contempt and ridicule by every impartial person who understands what the subject is which has been brought before us. Of all the foolish publications which it has been the misfortune of these controversies to call out, if there be one which, more than another, is likely to injure the Christian faith, it is this. . . . I will put it to any intelligent layman or clergyman who is not already committed on the subject, to read this paper, and I would ask him whether, in the name of the Church of Christ, he would not request that it should, as soon as possible, be committed to the flames."[1]

The Bishop of Oxford spoke with equal warmth upon the other side, and in the end his motion for the appointment of a committee to re-open the consideration of the subject was carried by the casting vote of the President, and two months later the Committee reported in favour of the synodical condemnation of the book. Bishop Tait, undaunted by the immense preponderance of clerical opinion against him, adhered to his opposition to such a course. In the final debates upon the subject he again referred to the famous declaration of the 12,000:—

"No one will, I hope, suppose," he said, "that I think there is no cause for alarm. It has been my belief for many years

---

[1] *Chronicle of Convocation*, April 21, 1864, p. 1549. The 'schedule' to which reference is made will be found in the *Chronicle of Convocation* for June 18, 1861, pp. 673-687.

that there is ; but the greater the cause for alarm from the spread of dangerous opinions, the greater the calmness and wisdom required in selecting the proper mode of meeting them. One great danger of the rise of erroneous opinions in all ages has been that they have produced statements equally and sometimes more erroneous than the statements which originally caused the alarm. . . . Reference has been made to the Declaration of the clergy, addressed to your Grace and to the Bishops generally. Having looked at the document very carefully, and considered the great number of signatures attached to it, I cannot help coming to the conclusion that a very undesirable amount of excitement has been raised. . . . I think it most undesirable that persons should append their names to any document unless they fully and entirely agree with it—at all events to such a document as this. Now I understand that document to state nothing less than this—that it has been the Doctrine of the Universal Church in all ages that Holy Scripture is not only our guide of life, and the lamp that is to enlighten our path—not only our infallible guide as to faith and doctrine, but that in matters which have no connection with either faith or doctrine—as, for example, matters of physical science, every single syllable of Holy Scripture is to be considered as infallible. If that is not the meaning, and if the words of the Declaration have any meaning at all other than to express the agitation and unwise alarm into which those who signed the Declaration were thrown, I should be glad to hear what that meaning is."[1]

In the end, after prolonged and vehement debate, a resolution was formally carried by a large majority in both Houses,[2] synodically condemning the volume "as containing teaching contrary to the doctrine received by the United Church of England and Ireland in common with the whole Catholic Church of Christ."

A remarkable scene followed in the House of Lords a

---

[1] *Chronicle of Convocation*, June 21, 1864, pp. 1660-64.

[2] In the Upper House it was carried by 8 votes to 2. The minority consisted of the Bishops of London and Lincoln, the Bishop of St. David's being absent. In the Lower House it was carried by 39 to 19.—*Chron. of Conv.* pp. 1683 and 1830.

few days later. Lord Houghton in a carefully prepared speech, bristling with precedents, asked the Lord Chancellor (Westbury) whether Convocation had not exceeded its rights and exposed itself to penalties by this Act of Condemnation. The Lord Chancellor in his reply referred contemptuously to the condemnation as illegal, but not worth noticing, and took the opportunity to make a personal attack upon Bishop Wilberforce as its principal author :—

"The judgment," he said, "is simply a series of well-lubricated terms, a sentence so oily and saponaceous that no one could grasp it—like an eel it slips through your fingers, and is simply nothing."

Bishop Wilberforce retorted in a scathing speech, delivered at white heat, and while opinions differed as to its Episcopal character, he was universally felt to have come off victor in the combat. Bishop Tait, strongly as he had in Convocation opposed the action of his colleagues, now firmly supported the privileges of the sacred synod, and his frank and helpful speech in defence of the rights of the majority which had outvoted him drew the warmest thanks from the gentle Archbishop Longley, whose proverbial courtesy and kindliness were never more severely tested than during the progress of this tempestuous controversy.

Very little additional light is thrown by the Bishop's diaries upon the closing episodes of these long discussions. The following are among the occasional allusions to the subject :—

Diary.

"*7th February*, 1864.—To-morrow comes the final judgment on the Essays and Reviews. The two Archbishops will dissent from the judgment as to the first charge against Williams and the first against Wilson. All the four law lords and myself agree. It is no doubt a most important matter for the Church. O Lord, grant that all may be overruled for good, that no stumbling-block may be thrown in the way of earnest Christians, and that Thy blessing may watch over and guard Thy Church."

"*Sunday*, 17*th April.*—Next Tuesday comes Convocation. O Lord, watch over Thy Church. Guide, calm, and settle all our minds. Lead us to speak the truth in love."

"*Sunday*, 24*th April.*—In the midst of the turmoils, and the attempts by the *Record* to separate me from my clergy, this is satisfactory. Yesterday I was waited on by Champneys, Bayley, and Thorold, three of the best men in my diocese, all of whom have signed the declaration which I so strongly denounced in Convocation and in my Preface.[1] They came to express their anxious desire that no unfriendly feeling should spring up, and to explain, more or less, their views in signing the declaration. I do not think that any evil, but rather good, will spring from my so plainly stating my opinion. Lord, watch over Thy Church. Calm and support us all under present difficulties. Lead our souls to Thee, through Jesus Christ."

"SCHOOL HOUSE, RUGBY, *May* 15, 1864.—I am sitting in our old bedroom. The room in which Catty, May, Craufurd, were all born. The room in which I lay for so many weeks in helpless sickness. All the old familiar sights are round me, as fourteen years ago. But what changes in the living souls. . . . I am going to preach for the first time in that chapel for fourteen years and more. This morning I administered the Holy Communion to above 230 boys. A noble, cheering sight. O Lord, bless the work here. Bless Temple in his vigorous honest course. Deepen every religious impression of his teaching. Last night he addressed the communicants in chapel with great earnestness and plainness."

In the following sentences from a private memorandum, written during the height of the storm, Bishop Tait gives expression to his own views of what was needed, whether

[1] The Preface to Part II. of *The Word of God the Ground of Faith.*

for safety or honest advance, during these heated disputations :—

" The folly of the publication of *Essays and Reviews*, and, still more, of Stanley's ill-judged defence of them in the *Edinburgh Review*, and then the madness of Bishop Colenso ; these things have so effectually frightened the clergy that I think there is scarcely a Bishop on the Bench, unless it be the Bishop of St. David's, that is not useless for the purpose of preventing the widespread alienation of intelligent men. . . . Meanwhile I feel my own vocation clear, greatly as I sympathise with the Evangelicals, not to allow them to tyrannise over the Broad Churchmen ; and to resist that tendency which is at present strong in them to coalesce with the High Church party for the mere purpose of exterminating those against whom the cry is now loudest. I deeply deplore, and indeed execrate, the spirit of much of the *Essays and Reviews*. I have lately read over again with the utmost care Wilson's and Williams' essays before writing my memorandum for the judgment of their cases before the Privy Council. Williams' spirit seems to me even worse than I thought it on the former perusal. I do not wonder at the outcry and alarm, but what are bishops appointed for except to direct the clergy in times of alarm ? I pray that I may never fall into the snare of following rather than leading the clergy of my diocese. . . . What is wanted is a deeply religious liberal party, and almost all who might have formed it have, in the alarm, deserted. . . . The great evil is that the liberals are deficient in religion, and the religious are deficient in liberality. Let us pray for an outpouring of the very Spirit of Truth."

CHAPTER XIII.

THE COLONIAL CHURCH—BISHOP COLENSO.

1861-66.

BISHOP TAIT had from early years been prominent in the cause of Foreign Missions. It will be remembered that as fellow and tutor of Balliol, he joined with three others in founding a private society in Oxford for the discussion of missionary questions, and, both at Rugby and Carlisle, he did all in his power to awaken and stimulate an interest in the subject. His one and only appearance as a speaker upon a London platform, before he became Bishop, was at the Church Missionary Society's Annual Meeting in Exeter Hall in 1855. The following letter to his sister belongs to the same year :—

"CARLISLE, *6th Aug.* 1855.

" . . . Have you read Sydney Smith's Life? There is a strange mixture in his character of earnest common-sense and fun. On the whole I think he will be thought more highly of in consequence of the publication of the Life, though it may be doubted whether his religion was not injured by his strong sense of the ludicrous. I cannot forgive him for his anti-missionary articles in the *Edinburgh Review*. By the way, have you read a charming little book of Miss Tucker's, *The Southern Cross and Crown*, giving an account of the wonderful progress of Christianity in New Zealand? I think it does one good to see the way in which Christianity presents itself in its simplicity to those who have never heard of it before. Its great features stand out in bold relief. And this is the way in which it best secures the mind from being worried by little matters—to dwell on its grand doctrines, which are so full of comfort for those who are sincere."

In the early years of his London Episcopate he lost no opportunity of expressing his interest in the subject, speaking three times in Exeter Hall in the course of a single year, besides preaching the great C.M.S. sermon at St. Bride's, and concerning himself actively in the ordinary business of the Society for the Propagation of the Gospel. It was in those years that the complicated and difficult question of Missionary Bishoprics came to the front, and Bishop Tait took an active, and for the time an unpopular, part in the discussions in Convocation and elsewhere.

The controversies which raged over the person and office of Bishop Colenso were soon to force into prominence the whole question of the Colonial Episcopate : who ought to appoint the Bishops—how and through whom were they to derive jurisdiction—and to what disciplinary authority were they subject. Already the importance and the difficulty of these problems had become almost painfully apparent. Up to that time (with the unique exception of the so-called Bishopric of Jerusalem, which was provided for by a special Act of Parliament) no Bishop had anywhere been consecrated in connection with the Church of England to exercise his functions altogether outside the Queen's dominions.[1] The Bishops for India and the Colonies were, one and all, appointed by the Crown, and furnished with Letters Patent defining their jurisdiction. As missionary work extended—especially in countries like South Africa—where the heathen mission-field bordered upon the Colonial Dioceses, it became necessary to provide for the Episcopal oversight of such regions, and the question arose, By what legal process could such Bishops be consecrated ? Clearly the English

---

[1] Even Bishop M'Dougall, consecrated at Calcutta, under Royal Letters Patent in 1855, for missionary work in the island of Borneo, preserved the semblance of a Colonial Bishop by taking his title from the little island of Labuan, a dependency of the English Crown.

sovereign could not give Letters Patent, or confer a juris-diction ; but, on the other hand, it was absolutely without precedent in the Church of England that Bishops should be appointed without any control or intervention on the part of the State, and it was clear that the question, in whatever way it might be settled, must seriously affect the relation of the whole Colonial Church to the Church at home. So keenly was this difficulty felt that it was even suggested in debate that the Missionary Bishops might be consecrated as Suffragans under the Act of Henry VIII., and enter upon their missionary work as Bishops of " Bedford," " Dover," " Colchester," and so forth.[1] In 1859 and 1860 the subject was debated very fully in Convocation, and each House drew up a careful Report.   The opinion of the law-officers of the Crown was obtained to the effect that, much as such a " novel proceeding " was to be " deprecated and discouraged," they were " unaware of any statute or rule of common law by virtue of which the Archbishops or their Suffragans would incur any penalty from consecrating in this country a Bishop among the heathen." The debates which fol-lowed were long and sometimes heated, and in order to understand their drift it is necessary to bear constantly in mind that, in varying degree, there was in those years a quasi 'Establishment' of the Church of England throughout the Colonial Empire, and that in Australia, for example, the bishops and clergy were above all things anxious that no step should inadvertently be taken at home which might have the effect of loosening that tie.[2] Bishop Tait, eager as he had always been in the missionary cause, was so impressed with the importance of maintaining the Royal Supremacy as a bond of union,

---

[1] See *Chronicle of Convocation*, June 7, 1860, p. 285.

[2] See, *e.g.* the petitions from the Australian Church, printed in the *Chronicle of Convocation* for 1867, pp. 914-16.

and even in some sense a guarantee of orthodoxy, among the scattered Colonial Churches, that he repeatedly urged the need of caution in accepting the bold proposals which were made by Bishop Gray of Capetown and others. He was, in consequence, held up to frequent obloquy as an opponent of missionary progress, and it may be well therefore to quote his own words in explanation of his attitude. Speaking in Convocation on June 22, 1859—

"I have expressed my opinion," he said, "as to the many difficulties which lie in the way of the scheme, as I understood it was to be launched without any very competent authority, but this by no means would prevent me from giving my cordial assent if it should, after careful consideration, prove to be a desirable thing. . . . The plan, as I understand it, is this—that under the Metropolitan of the African division of our Colonial Church a Bishop should be consecrated for missionary work by himself and his two Suffragans, the person so to be consecrated being nominated by the Metropolitan, a very serious change in what has hitherto been the universal practice of the Church of England, whether colonial or at home. It is further proposed, as I understand, that these Bishops should be consecrated without the Royal Mandate, the reading of the Royal Mandate, according to the order of the Book of Common Prayer, being at present a part of the Consecration Service. . . . These difficulties occur to me as very serious. I have thought also that there has not been a sufficient consideration of this very important point— whether, after all, this plan of appointing Bishops at the head of merely inchoate churches is authorised by any ancient ecclesiastical usage, whether the system of the universal Church has not from the earliest times been this—that the Church shall be formed first and the Bishop shall come afterwards. . . . The great missionaries who spread Christianity in this country—St. Augustine, for example—did not come as Bishops, but as presbyters. There are difficult questions connected with the history and the laws of the Church, respecting which it would be most important to have a full inquiry." [1]

---

[1] *Chronicle of Convocation*, June 22, 1859, p. 15.

And again, on June 21st, 1861 :—

"What we desire to do," he said, "is to strengthen, by the bonds of love and of mutual kindness, the connection subsisting between the several branches of the Church. . . . When this matter concerning missionary Bishops first came before us, I felt in their full force all the difficulties which now present themselves to my mind, and one of those difficulties which I always felt was that a missionary Bishop stood so much by himself, that if in the course of time he happened to be a man of eccentric modes of proceeding, he might, upon his own responsibility, compromise both the Church at home and the Church in the Colonies, and yet have no authority to represent the one or the other. At the same time, neither the Church of England nor the Colonial Church near which he was labouring would have the power of applying to him any sort of restraint ; and, in point of fact, you might in the course of time have Bishops of the most unsound opinions representing the Church of England, and carrying on in apostolic succession, it might even be, an altogether heretical Church. Such a thing exists at the present moment in the corrupt Churches of Asia, and might come to exist in other parts of the world—namely, an heretical sect, headed by the Bishop or Bishops who derived their consecration from the Church of England. That is an evil which I felt to be so great that I was very anxious that we should pause before we took any steps in the matter. . . . I look with a little alarm to the time when these Australian and African Churches may on important matters get into a different position from that which they now occupy, and when that unity of the Church, which we all desire to see maintained in every branch of the Church of England, may be impaired. . . . I can conceive a provincial Synod throwing itself so completely into a mediæval view of the Church as to make it very different from that wide and tolerant and wise system which we have inherited from our forefathers. I can conceive that difficulty increased by the circumstances in which these Churches find themselves. . . . I therefore am very desirous that no rules should be adopted by these Churches in the Colonies which should alter them so as to make them different from our Church at home, either on the side of greater exclusiveness or greater reliance on mediæval traditions, and so on. Nor, on the other hand, do I wish that any change should be made on the other side.   I think that the more they remain like ourselves the better —that a Bishop of the Church of England going into one of these Colonies ought to endeavour to make himself the representative of English Christianity, and that anything that confines his sympathies to a small section of those among whom he finds himself will do infinite harm both to the Church of which he is the head, and, what is of more importance, to Christianity." [1]

Such was Bishop Tait's view, and to it he adhered through evil report and good report for several years.

"By all means let us have Missionary Bishops," he wrote, "but all in good time.   *Festina lente.*   The autonomy of the Colonial Churches is growing fast—too fast ; and this demand, like others, will be easily met before many years have passed. Hurry the matter rashly forward now—in defiance or scorn of State rules and aid—and you will cut these Churches adrift before they are old enough or strong enough to be trusted."

But events moved quickly, and the growth of synodal action in the Colonial Church, and the withdrawal, step by step, of Crown authority in the selection and consecration of Bishops, completely changed the conditions of the problem. [2]   It will be necessary to return to the subject in a later chapter : enough has been said to explain one part of the Bishop's action in the controversy which has now to be narrated.

[1] *Chronicle of Convocation*, June 21, 1861, pp. 775-8.

[2] Many years afterwards (in 1876) the *Church Times*, in reviewing Bishop Gray's biography, wrote :—"Dr. Gray was in England again in 1858, and found bitter opposition to his plans from the Shaftesbury Bishops, and the first appearance of that enemy of God's truth, Dr. Tait, was as the opponent of any scheme for sending out Missionary Bishops, which he was pleased to denounce as unscriptural."

A correspondent wrote to ask Archbishop Tait to authorise him to contradict this statement.   The Archbishop replied:—"I think you will see that it would be quite inconsistent with self-respect for me to authorise any contradiction of such a paragraph.   My views respecting Missionary Bishops were always very different from those of the late Bishop Gray, and they remain now pretty nearly what they were in 1858.   I should be glad on any suitable occasion to state again what these views are, and I believe you will find them best illustrated by the part which I am now taking in actively promoting the appointment of Missionary Bishops in India."

For a long succession of years the name of Bishop Colenso was on everybody's lips, and the interest, indignation, and alarm which it excited were shared by thousands who had no real knowledge whatever of what the supposed arch-heretic had said. Ample material has been given to the world for learning from opposite points of view every detail of the long and painful strife,[1] and only such parts need be recounted here as will explain Bishop Tait's relation to the controversy. As the issues, however, were somewhat intricate, it is necessary to record these facts with care.

In 1853 the Rev. John William Colenso was appointed first Bishop of the newly established diocese of Natal. He was selected for the See by Bishop Gray of Capetown, from whose unwieldy diocese it was severed. The technical steps necessary to effect this severance involved consequences unsuspected at the time. Bishop Gray had been appointed to his larger diocesan jurisdiction under Royal Letters Patent in the year 1847. As these Letters Patent, describing the original geographical boundaries, could not, it was said, be altered, Bishop Gray now *pro formâ* resigned his See, and was immediately reappointed under new Letters Patent, dated December 8th, 1853. This new document declared him to be Bishop of the now reduced diocese, and to possess, in addition, metropolitan jurisdiction over the subordinate bishoprics of Grahamstown and Natal. Bishop Colenso also received Letters Patent declaring him Bishop of the Diocese of Natal, "subject and subordinate" to the Bishop of Capetown, to whom he was to take an oath of due obedience. Under these Letters Patent Dr. Colenso was duly consecrated, and took the required

---

[1] The published Biography of Bishop Gray extends to 1198 pages; that of Bishop Colenso to 1431 pages; and no small part of the four volumes is devoted to this particular controversy.

oath, and no one at the time suspected that anything informal had been done. As it afterwards turned out, however, these whole proceedings, so far as the jurisdiction conferred by the new Letters Patent was concerned, were in point of law null and void, for the following reason :—In the year 1850 a Constitutional Government was established in the Cape of Good Hope, including a Parliament, " with authority to make laws for the peace, welfare, and good government of the settlement." And from that moment the Crown ceased to have the power of conferring by Letters Patent any such coercive jurisdiction, ecclesiastical or civil, within the Colony, as the new Letters Patent professed to give to Bishop Gray. Strange to say, this point seems to have been simply overlooked by the lawyers who drew the documents of 1853 ; nor was it discovered till nearly ten years afterwards.

For several years after Bishop Colenso's consecration he was on terms of intimate personal friendship with his Metropolitan, who fully recognised the remarkable efficiency of his missionary work in the difficult diocese of Natal. But his opinions, after a time, began to cause anxiety to his ecclesiastical friends, and matters reached a crisis in the autumn of 1861 by the publication of his *Commentary on the Epistle to the Romans*, which was immediately denounced by Bishop Gray as "full of the most objectionable views, and entirely substituting a new scheme for the received system of Christianity."[1] It was admitted by Bishop Colenso's friends at the time, and to some extent by his biographer twenty years later, that in discussing subjects so momentous as the nature of our Lord's Atonement and the Eternity of Future Punishment, the Commentary set the popular theology altogether at defiance ; and it is in no

---

[1] Bishop Gray's *Life*, vol. ii. p. 22.

way wonderful that, proceeding from a Bishop of the Church, such a book should have awakened a loud outcry.

Bishop Tait, in common with others in responsible positions, was gravely anxious, and thought it wise to write an immediate letter of inquiry to Bishop M'Dougall of Labuan, Bishop Colenso's brother-in-law, who replied as follows :—

Bishop M'Dougall of Labuan to the Bishop of London.

"SARAWAK, *June* 30*th*, 1862.

"MY DEAR BISHOP,—Thank you very much for your kind note about the Bishop of Natal. I almost fear, from a note I lately had from him, that he is not only disposed to stick by what he has written, but even to go further in the 'free handling of Holy Scripture.' He has in hand a work of which he sent me the first part for my opinion, and which I could do nothing but utterly disagree from, and entreat him not to publish ;—it is an attack upon the Pentateuch, denying its inspiration, or that it was written by Moses. I have only seen the Introduction and the first chapter or two. His mathematical notions and Western mode of viewing things have plainly led him astray. He says, in short, that he can believe a miracle, but cannot believe in a bad sum and false arithmetical statements, and so he falls foul of the Book of Numbers especially, and points out what he conceives to be no end of numerical mis-statements as regards the numbers of the people at the Exodus, the number of priests, the im-possibility of their making the journey to the Red Sea in the time stated, etc. etc. In fact, it is an utter denial of any truth or authority in that part of the Bible, all owing, as it seems to me, to his arithmetical and matter-of-fact way of looking at the Eastern language and Oriental statements and descriptions in which these facts have been conveyed to us. He tells me he has been lately working up his Hebrew, and thus the thing has grown upon him. I used, I know, to be the better Hebraist of the two, and since then I have had a great deal to do with Arabic and the languages of these parts, and I find that the more I know of Eastern minds and thought, its luxuriance and inexactness in the commonest statements, the less disposed I am to find difficulties and food for doubt in the things that seem to have thrown poor dear Colenso into a sea of mental trouble and difficulty. May God grant him to see his way out of it! I love him much as a brother and a friend. I know him to be a noble, brave-hearted, loving man, but I can in no way agree with him in theology. If he has published this new work you will know more of it than I do; but as he said he wanted my opinion and that of his friends in England before he published, I hope and trust these opinions may have prevented his doing so. In that case, please let what I have said on the subject be *entre nous*, but I felt bound to let you know, after your kindness about the former book on the Romans. Poor J. W. N., he is much in my thoughts. I hope his coming to England will dispel the fogs Natal seems to have generated in his mind. If he had been here in my place, instead of in Natal, he would not have had time for encouraging these doubts and mists, and perhaps intercourse with Eastern people would have been a good corrective. . . .—Very sincerely yours,   F. T. Labuan."

When the first part of Bishop Colenso's book on the Pentateuch appeared, it was immediately seen that there was good ground for the alarm expressed in the above letter. The volume contained a series of elaborate arguments to show the difficulties surrounding the numerical and other details in the Scriptural account of the Exodus. These arguments, as Bishop M'Dougall had said, were largely arithmetical,[1] and to most readers it would appear that they did not greatly affect the sacred or historical character of the Pentateuch as a whole. But the importance of the volume lay in its Preface, in which the Bishop proclaimed the general result to which his investigations had led him; namely, a conviction that the early books of the Bible were so 'unhistorical' that he could no longer

---

[1] *e.g.* a calculation as to the number of men who could stand before the end of the Tabernacle—supposing each man to occupy a space 2 feet wide, and the width of the Tabernacle to be 8 cubits of 1·824 feet each— was solemnly elaborated to prove the 'unhistorical' character of Lev. viii. 3, "Gather thou all the congregation unto the door of the tabernacle."—(Part I. pp. 31-34.)

use the Ordination Service of the Church of England, in which the truth of the Bible is assumed. He admitted in a footnote that the decision just delivered in the Court of Arches upon *Essays and Reviews* had led him to modify his original resolve that he must resign his Episcopal office, but the general tenor of his Preface remained the same.[1] " I appeal," he said, " to the strong, practical love of truth in my fellow-countrymen, whether clergy or laity," for the promotion of such measures of reform in the system of the Church, that it may not become " necessary for me, or for those who think with me, to leave the Church of England voluntarily, and abandon the work to which we have devoted ourselves for life."[2] The volume containing this Preface was published in October 1862, and was followed, three months afterwards, by a second volume with a further Preface, in which the Bishop declared it to be impossible for him conscientiously to use the Baptismal Service on account of its clear allusion to the Deluge.[3]

Already the alarm was beginning to spread. At one of the private meetings of the Bishops in May 1862, when only the Commentary on the Romans had been published, it had been proposed, on the strength of a letter from Bishop Gray, then on his way to England, that the Bishops should discuss the question of a synodical condemnation of the book. According to the account given

---

[1] The passage in question is as follows :—" For myself, if I cannot find the means of doing away with my present difficulties, I do not see how I can retain my Episcopal office, in the discharge of which I must require from others a solemn declaration that they ' unfeignedly believe all the Canonical Scriptures of the Old and New Testament,' which, with the evidence now before me, it is impossible wholly to believe."—(Part I. p. xii.) In a footnote he adds :—" This was written before the recent decision in the Court of Arches, by which, of course, the above conclusion is materially affected." But in subsequent pages of the Preface (pp. xxiv-xxxv) he reiterates his first contention, " notwithstanding Dr. Lushington's recent judgment."   [2] *Ib.* pp. xviii-xxxv.   [3] Part II. p. xxi.

by Bishop Wilberforce,[1] it was only by Bishop Tait's refusal to join in any corporate condemnation of an absent brother Bishop, who had not even been heard in defence or explanation, that Bishop Wilberforce was prevented from carrying a resolution which would have prohibited Bishop Colenso from officiating in England. Bishop Tait was clear that such a proceeding would be, at the least, premature, and probably most unwise ; and there the matter rested for the time. Bishop Gray and Bishop Colenso were now both of them in England, and the appearance of the two volumes on the Pentateuch, during the winter of 1862-63, brought the whole question once more to the front.

Two letters to the Bishop may be quoted as showing the different hopes and fears which were stirring the various sections of the Church :—

Rev. Dr. Pusey to the Bishop of London.

"CHRIST CHURCH, *Dec.* 17, 1862.

"MY DEAR LORD,— . . . Will your Lordship bear with me while I write on a very painful subject? I fear that your Lordship's Charge is construed as intending to shield such a case as Bishop Colenso's, while yet he is using his office of Bishop to propagate among our mechanics disbelief in the authority of our Lord and of God's Word. Had he been *Mr.* Colenso still, his book would have been still-born. Now it is read by tens of thousands because he is a Bishop. It is his office of Bishop which propagates infidelity. Unbounded toleration to the laity is very different from allowing Bishops and Priests to teach publicly grave errors, destructive of all faith. Up to a certain point a latitude has always been allowed. But if such teaching as now claims to be recognised as allowed teaching of the English Church is admitted, I fear that the Church of England will lose the devout while she retains the indevout. People wait patiently to see what the result of this struggle is. Dr. Manning is using it very successfully to detach people from the Church, and your

<hr>

[1] *Life,* vol. iii. p. 115.

Lordship will be probably surprised, as I was, to learn that among our intellectual but sceptical young men there are not a few who will probably ultimately escape from scepticism by taking refuge in the Church of Rome. But the class of whom I am thinking is not this, but those who think that a Church, if she allow such deadly denial of truth as is now claiming to become part of the recognised teaching of the Church of England, forfeits all blessing from God, and is disowned by Him. They would gladly give their lives for her, but will not dare to stay in her if it should become recognised by continual sufferance that all truth or falsehood alike may be taught by her ministers.

"I have trespassed upon your Lordship's time, but I thought that I might mention to you facts of which I am more likely to be cognisant than your Lordship.—I beg to remain, your Lordship's humble servant,   E. B. PUSEY."

Rev. Dr. Lightfoot to the Bishop of London.

"TRIN. COLL., CAMBRIDGE,
Nov. 19*th*, 1862.

"MY DEAR LORD,— . . . We were much rejoiced here to learn that Mr. Maurice had recalled his resignation. I am sure it would have been a very grave calamity for the Church at such a time as the present if he had persisted.[1]

"I fear Bishop Colenso's book, poor as it is, will do a vast deal of harm among unthinking well-intentioned people. The result, I am afraid, must be to discredit reasonable inquiry with reverent spirits, and to divide men into two extreme parties, who will wage fierce war against each other and trample the truth under foot between them. I have tried in vain to extract a grain of comfort from the publication of the book. I feel very strongly, however, that it is a warning against overmuch caution in handling such subjects, for a more frank and liberal treatment of the difficulties of the Old Testament, if it had been general, would have drawn the sting of Bishop Colenso's criticism, even if it had not rendered the publication altogether impossible. . . . —I am, my dear Lord, most sincerely and faithfully yours,

"J. B. LIGHTFOOT."

The Society for the Propagation of the Gospel felt a

<hr>

[1] See p. 516.

not unnatural hesitation about placing its block-grant for the diocese of Natal in the hands of a Bishop whose Metropolitan was already denouncing him as a heretic, and whose successive books were exciting general consternation.　Archbishop Longley, who had a few weeks before succeeded to the Primacy, was disposed to support the Society in handing its Natal grants to the Archdeacons instead of to the Diocesan, but before doing so he consulted Bishop Tait, who, consistently with his previous line, replied as follows:—

The Bishop of London to the Archbishop of Canterbury.

"*Dec.* 22, 1862.

"My dear Lord Archbishop,— . . . I take it for granted that it is a principle of the Society to pay all respect to those who are at the head of the several Colonial Sees, simply in virtue of their office, and that it is only in obedience to this principle that the Society has hitherto acted in any way through the Bishop of Natal.　I know not who the persons are who now call on the Society in this distressing case to set aside its principle in reference to Bishop Colenso, while in all other respects he is recognised in undisturbed possession of his office as Diocesan of Natal; neither do I know how far such persons express the sentiments of any large body of the friends of the Society.　But I do not think the Society will act rightly in following the advice indicated.　I do not think the Society can, as matters stand at present, properly transfer to any other than the Bishop of the diocese of Natal that official position, whatever it be, which, according to its rules, a Colonial Bishop holds in reference to the Society's funds.— I am, very truly and dutifully yours,　　　A. C. London."

Bishop Gray and his friends in England were now eager to take formal action against Bishop Colenso, and in a characteristic letter to the Dean of Capetown Bishop Gray described his plan as follows:—

"*Jan.* 2, 1863.

"I have been thinking a great deal about this trial, and I have to-day had a talk with S. Oxon.　He quite agrees with my view. I am satisfied on these points :—1. The Bishops, even though only Grahamstown and I should be present, meet as the Synod of the Province, and also as a Court to try the comprovincial. 2. As a Synod they may declare what the faith of the Church is, and as a Court condemn. I will not be bound by the narrow limits, as to the Church's faith, laid down by Dr. Lushington or Privy Council. I will not recognise them as an authority as to what are the doctrines which the Church of England allows to be taught. . . ."[1]

At the usual Bishops' meeting held before the opening of Parliament, on February 4th, 1863, the position of Bishop Colenso was again under discussion. From the accounts of the meeting made public in the Biographies of Bishop Gray and Bishop Wilberforce,[2] it appears that the Bishops resolved by a large majority—(1) to advise the Society for the Propagation of the Gospel to "withhold its confidence from the Bishop of Natal until he has been cleared from the charges notoriously incurred by him"; (2) to inhibit the Bishop for the present from preaching in their dioceses. The following letter shows what was the Bishop of London's view as to the second of these resolutions :—

The Bishop of London to the Archbishop of Canterbury.

"LONDON HOUSE, *Feb.* 4, 1863.

" MY DEAR LORD,—The decision arrived at this day by a large body of the Bishops, to adopt the Bishop of Oxford's motion, and publish a formal document binding the subscribers to inhibit the Bishop of Natal from officiating in their several dioceses, makes

---

[1] Bishop Gray's *Life*, vol. ii. p. 32. It will be observed that the Metropolitan is as little ready to be guided by the Archbishop's Court of Arches as by the Privy Council.

[2] See above, p. 283. It is hardly necessary to caution those who may investigate the details of this controversy against accepting the long account of these meetings given in Bishop Gray's Biography, as other than the personal recollections and impressions of one of the parties in a sharp dispute.

it necessary for me to state publicly to your Grace the reasons on which I have felt it incumbent on me to dissent from a large majority of my brethren.

" Individual Bishops may, I conceive, properly enough prevent the Bishop of Natal from officiating in their dioceses if they think he is likely to do so, and that evil will arise ; but such an inhibition publicly announced as proceeding from the united body of so many Bishops, whatever distinctions may be attempted to be drawn, cannot, in my view, be regarded otherwise than as a sentence, and that of a very severe character. The Bishop of Oxford's motion has therefore appeared to me unwise, and, to say the least, nearly approaching injustice. Unwise, because by inflicting a highly penal sentence on the Bishop of Natal's person as the very first step in dealing with his book, it must in all probability enlist a large amount of sympathy on his side. Unwise indeed, because it has so much the appearance of being unjust. It must, I fear, degrade the sacred office of a judge, supposed to be held in this case by your Grace and the Metropolitan of Capetown, if not by others of our body. For it will appear as if the judges either desire to close the case prematurely by inflicting a very severe punishment without any *bona fide* intention of having their decision revised through further legal proceedings, or are preparing to enter on their further judicial functions pledged to a sentence of condemnation, not only against the book, but the person of its author.

" My opinion is that at present the wisest course would have been for each Bishop to deal with the existing scandal according to his own discretion, having regard to the circumstances of his own diocese, though I should have been ready also, had it appeared well to my brethren, to adopt and publish such a united resolution as that proposed by the Bishop of Winchester, to the purport that, having regard to the judicial character of several of their body, the Bishops, while deeply deploring the Bishop of Natal's conduct, felt precluded, under the peculiar circumstances of the case, from pronouncing at this stage of the proceedings an opinion which could be construed into a sentence.

" Looking then with as much disfavour as any of my brethren on what I am fain to call the rash and arrogant speculations of the Bishop of Natal, and being ready to take any legitimate opportunity of refuting his arguments to the best of my ability, and of warning the people committed to my care against his errors, and what appears to me the very unbecoming spirit in which they are urged, I greatly regret the decision at which a majority of my brethren has arrived, as likely, in my estimation, to extend the influence of the publication of which we all disapprove, and place many of those who disapprove of it in an altogether false position.—I remain, my dear Lord, yours faithfully and dutifully,   A. C. LONDON."

In consequence of this letter two further meetings of the Bishops were held, and after long and heated discussion the Bishop of London succeeded in securing the adoption by the assembled Bishops of a joint address to Bishop Colenso, instead of the collective inhibition which had been at first proposed. The address was drawn up by Bishop Tait,[1] and, after a few verbal changes, was made public in the following form, and signed by forty-one Bishops, English, Irish, and Colonial, the only dissentient being the Bishop of St. David's :—

" To the Right Reverend J. W. Colenso, D.D.,
Lord Bishop of Natal.

" We, the undersigned Archbishops and Bishops of the United Church of England and Ireland, address you with deep brotherly anxiety, as one who shares with us the grave responsibilities of the Episcopal Office.

" It is impossible for us to enter here into argument with you as to your method of handling that Bible which we believe to be the Word of God, and on the truth of which rest all our hopes for eternity.   Nor do we here raise the question, whether you are legally entitled to retain your present office and position in the Church, complicated, moreover, as that question is by the fact of your being a Bishop of the Church in South Africa, now at a distance from your diocese and province.

" But we feel bound to put before you another view of the case. We understand you to say (Part II. p. xxiii of your *Pentateuch*

---

[1] Bishop Wilberforce's biographer is in error in attributing its authorship to that Bishop.   The original MS. exists as drafted by Bishop Tait.

and Book of Joshua critically Examined), that you do not now believe that which you voluntarily professed to believe, as the indispensable condition of your being intrusted with your present office.   We understand you also to say that you have entertained, and have not abandoned, the conviction that you could not use the Ordination Service, inasmuch as in it you ' must require from others a solemn declaration that they "unfeignedly believe all the Canonical Scriptures of the Old and New Testament " ; which, with the evidence now before ' you, ' it is impossible wholly to believe in.'—(Part I. p. xii.)   And we understand you further to intimate that those who think with you are precluded from using the Baptismal Service, and consequently (as we must infer) other offices of the Prayer-Book, unless they omit all such passages as assume the truth of the Mosaic history.—(Part II. p. xxii.)

" Now it cannot have escaped you that the inconsistency between the office you hold and the opinions you avow is causing great pain and grievous scandal to the Church.   And we solemnly ask you to consider once more, with the most serious attention, whether you can, without harm to your own conscience, retain your position, when you can no longer discharge its duties or use the formularies to which you have subscribed.   We will not abandon the hope, that, through earnest prayer and deeper study of God's Word, you may, under the guidance of the Holy Spirit, be restored to a state of belief in which you may be able with a clear conscience again to discharge the duties of our sacred office ; a result which, from regard to your highest interests, we should welcome with the most unfeigned satisfaction.—We are, your faithful brethren in Christ,

> [*Here follow the signatures of forty-one Bishops.*]

" *February* 9, 1863."

Bishop Colenso's answer was to the effect that he was unable to comply with the suggestion made to him.   "To resign my office," he said, " would be to admit that my conduct has been legally or morally wrong, which I am very far from feeling."   In the meantime a discussion was raised upon the subject in both Houses of Canterbury Convocation.   The Lower House, on the motion once again of

Archdeacon Denison, requested the Upper House to direct the appointment of a committee to examine the obnoxious volumes. The suggestion was earnestly opposed by Bishop Tait. In the course of a long speech, in which he pointed out the legal and other complications which surrounded the question,

" No one," he said, "can over-estimate the difficulty of the position of those who are called upon at this moment, as Bishops of the Church, more or less to guide public opinion in these matters. . . . The clergy consider themselves properly bound to drive away all erroneous and strange doctrine, and none, of course, are more bound to do so than those who hold our office. We ourselves, with the great responsibility which falls upon us, holding a position which is looked up to as a very important one, not only by the Church, but by the whole country, may be supposed to be likely to treat of such matters with great calmness, and after mature consideration. But the clergy generally, some of them at least, may be not unlikely—I say it with the deepest respect—to allow their zeal to get the better of their discretion in their desire to drive away all erroneous and strange doctrines. . . . It was only yesterday that I received a packet containing a number of advertisements selected from the newspapers, of sermons against Bishop Colenso's book, which were to be had for a moderate sum, to be preached in the various pulpits throughout the kingdom. Of course this is a mere insult to the clergy, and very probably the advertisements were inserted in the newspapers by some person who had no such sermons to dispose of, but who wished to represent the clergy in an invidious light. But still it points to an obvious danger, that persons not well qualified for the office may think it necessary to step forth from the ranks, when their strength is not equal to the office of champion which they choose for themselves. . . . I think we might find other means of expressing our calm feelings on the subject than by engaging in such discussions [as are invited by the Lower House], and I feel confident, without wishing in any degree to magnify the office which we hold, that it is to us, in our capacity as Bishops of the Church, rather than to any discussions which shall be carried on in this or the other House of Convocation, that the country looks for quiet guidance

in these matters.   Now I would wish to speak, of course, with
the deepest respect of this body, the Convocation at this moment
assembled.   Yet it is a simple fact that it does not command (so
much, perhaps, as we might desire—at all events, as many of our
body desire) the unhesitating respect of the whole of the Church.
. . . I do not apprehend that its decisions on this question
would carry so much weight as the calm decision, whatever it
might be, of the united Bishops of the Church.   Now, on the
former occasion — the publication of *Essays and Reviews*—
though we were unable to take part in the discussion,[1] a committee of the Lower House was nevertheless appointed ; and of
this I am perfectly certain, that the publication of the book or
report, or whatever it was which originated from that committee,
was more calculated to damage the Church than any publication
I have seen for a long time.   It appeared to me to bring together in one short compendium all the objectionable statements
of the book it condemned, and then, side by side with them, to
put a number of the most meagre answers that could possibly
be conceived.   Of course, i that document has received the
approval of the Lower House, it must be treated with the greatest possible respect ; but it was not treated with respect by the
country, and the impression was that that document was anything but favourable to the cause it was intended to advance.
. . . Bearing in mind that the country does expect us—the
Bishops — to guide it in this difficult matter, . . . I think it
may be right for the heads of the Church, as they did by
their answer to an address in the case of *Essays and Reviews*,
temperately and quietly to intimate that they are alive to
the great dangers which the book may cause.   But on the
other hand, being anxious to discourage all unnecessary excitement, all rash treatment of the questions at issue, and above
all, any petty and vexatious annoyance of the author of the
book, which can only result in justly enlisting the sympathies
of the country on his side ; deprecating the slightest appearance
of persecution, and still more of injustice—I think in this case,
as I thought in the case of *Essays and Reviews*, that the appointment of such a committee as is demanded would be unwise,
and do more harm than good.   I wish to express an anxious
hope and expectation that whatever is done may be so done as
to tend to allay the natural anxiety of the country—that we

[1] See above, p. 319.

shall consider tenderly the feelings of devout men who find their old and most cherished opinions rudely assailed; while, on the other hand, we by no means overlook or undervalue the anxious longings of persons of unsettled minds. I do not see my way to agreeing to the proposal of the Lower House."[1]

Strange to say, only six Bishops were present at this discussion, and as the President did not vote, the motion for the appointment of a Committee was carried by three votes against two, the Bishops of London and St. David's forming the minority.

Bishop Tait's speech attracted much attention, and was vehemently denounced by Bishop Gray and his friends. Arthur Stanley, on the other hand, wrote :—

Canon A. P. Stanley to the Bishop of London.

"CH. CH., OXFORD, *Feb.* 20, 1863.

"MY DEAR BISHOP,—I have read your speech with great care and great pleasure. I think that it will have the best effect, and (though I should have thought a more explicit statement as to the liberty allowed in the Church on the matter in discussion would have been not only right but prudent), I consider that it takes away almost all my case against you in the matter of *Essays and Reviews.* . . . Farewell. Many thanks. I can hardly express to you the pleasure given to me by these better relations between us.—Ever yours,	A. P. STANLEY."

Hearing that Bishop Colenso was pained at the personal coldness with which he had been received in England, Bishop Tait wrote to him as follows :—

"*March* 3, 1863.

"I have heard this morning from Mr. T. D. Acland that you had expressed a wish to see me. I shall gladly hold myself in readiness at any time you might name. . . . Had it not been for the circumstance of my never having met you in former times, I should have made a point of asking to see you before now."

[1] *Chronicle of Convocation*, February 13, 1863, pp. 1092-1101.

The interview took place next day.   Bishop Tait thus records it in his Diary :—

" *5th March* 1863.—Yesterday I had a long conference with Bishop Colenso, from which I gained no hope.   He seems fanatically convinced that he has a great mission to save the theology and religion of England from a great collision with Science.   He seemed to me very wild, and to be likely to go very far in discarding the old faith."

Bishop Colenso, writing to Sir Charles Lyell of the same interview, says :—

" I had half an hour's talk with the Bishop of London by appointment on Wednesday last, about which I will talk to you on Wednesday next, if I have not the pleasure of meeting you before.   He then spoke of your book as lying on the table, and seemed to think that it was quite possible to hold both it and the Bible story as true in some sense." [1]

A few weeks later he again writes :—

" You will see that the Bishop of London does not act with the other Bishops.   *They*, headed by the Bishop of Oxford, have cut me dead.   But I met him in Pall Mall a few days ago, where he was walking arm in arm with another Bishop, and I was going to pass him with a salutation.   But he made a point of shaking me heartily by the hand, and stopping to ask me some friendly question, the other standing mute all the while.   I could not see who it was : perhaps he did not know me." [2]

Meantime the excitement grew, as the English Bishops, one after another, responded to the addresses of their Rural Deaneries by inhibiting Bishop Colenso from officiating in their dioceses.   The Bishop of London issued no such inhibition, contenting himself with the reiterated request to his clergy " to supply the antidote which is most wanted, by upholding the positive proofs of the genuineness and inspiration of the Sacred Volume, which

____

[1] Bishop Colenso's *Life*, vol. i. p. 237.   [2] *Ibid.* p. 239.

may well be brought forward without much controversy, and without the slightest mention of the book against which the arguments are directed."[1]

When the Convocation of Canterbury met in May, Archdeacon Denison carried through the House, almost without discussion, the Report of his Committee upon Bishop Colenso's book. Warned, it may be, by the reception accorded to his Report upon *Essays and Reviews* two years before, and especially by the reference made to it by Bishop Tait, the Archdeacon had couched this Report in very different terms, merely analysing the contents of Dr. Colenso's volumes, as in apparent contradiction to statements both in the Bible and the Prayer-Book, and involving, therefore, "errors of the gravest and most dangerous character." At the same time the Committee emphatically desired "not to be understood as expressing any opinion opposed to the free exercise of patient thought and reverent inquiry in the study of the Word of God."[2]

When the Report came before the Upper House, each of the leading Bishops adhered to the line he had previously taken. Bishop Wilberforce pleaded earnestly for immediate action :—

"It seems to me," he said, "that one means by which we can bear our witness against error is by setting solemnly the mark of this body, meeting synodically, upon such erroneous teaching by one of ourselves, and declaring that it is, in our judgment, false and dangerous."[3]

The Bishop of London repeated his objections to any such formal action while the whole matter was still *sub judice*. Bishop Gray had already returned to Capetown

<hr>

[1] *Chronicle of Convocation*, February 13, 1863, p. 1094.
[2] *Ibid.* May 19, 1863, pp. 1175-1184.
[3] *Ibid.* May 19, 1863, p. 1164.

and was about to bring his Suffragan to trial. From the decision to be arrived at in that trial, some appeal, urged Bishop Tait, must surely lie, and the Archbishop, he thought, was now being called upon to take part in prejudging the very issue he might hereafter have to try.

"I will never believe," he continued, "that it was the intention of the letters patent, or whatever it is that clothes the Bishop of Capetown with authority, to make him so irresponsible that there should be no earthly appeal from his decision. . . . The Bishop of Oxford has very properly said that Bishops cannot be silent and express no opinion about the grievous errors that are brought before them. Of course we must express our opinion, but there is a very great difference between expressing opinions on matters of doctrine, in fulfilling our common Episcopal functions by preaching the Word of Truth and pointing it out to our clergy, and, on the other hand, sitting here in a judicial, or something very like a judicial, capacity. . . . If in our desire to warn people we hurry into any ' decision ' now, we may perhaps destroy our ability to afford them that future and most effectual warning which it may be in our power to give them if we wait till the matter is brought before a properly constituted tribunal." [1]

The debate was adjourned, and next day, in the Bishop of London's absence, a long resolution was proposed by Bishop Sumner of Winchester, and carried, to the effect that while the book did, in the judgment of the Bishops, "involve errors of the gravest and most dangerous character," they declined to take further action in the matter, inasmuch as the book was "shortly to be submitted to the judgment of an Ecclesiastical Court." [2]

It was already in process of being so submitted. On April 11th, 1863, Bishop Gray landed at Capetown, and immediately announced that he was ready to do his duty by citing the Bishop of Natal to appear before him for trial. Formal ' Articles of Accusation ' were in the next

---

[1] *Chronicle of Convocation*, May 19, 1863, p. 1166.
[2] *Ibid.* May 20, 1863, p. 1205.

few weeks drawn up by the Dean of Capetown and two others. Bishop Colenso remained in England, where he received, on July 1st, the formal citation of his Metropolitan to appear for trial in the Cathedral of Capetown in the following November.[1] He took no notice of the summons, and in the meantime Bishop Gray's authority received a somewhat serious check. On June 24, 1863, the Privy Council gave decision in the case of *Long* v. *The Bishop of Capetown*, reversing a sentence of deposition which Bishop Gray had pronounced against the Rev. William Long, an incumbent in Capetown, for refusing to recognise the authority of the Bishop's Synod. The Privy Council judgment entered elaborately into the whole history of Bishop Gray's position.[2] It expressly declared that he would have been entitled to deprive a clergyman for any cause which would authorise a deprivation in England, but that this was not such a cause, the Synod being a voluntary association of Churchmen, whose decrees can only bind those who have already agreed, as in the case of any other contract, to be so bound. All this was important, as running directly in the teeth of Bishop Gray's diocesan action ; but, what concerned the Colenso case more closely, the judges declared the Bishop's Letters Patent, formally given him by the Crown in 1853, to be practically worthless, and to convey no such coercive jurisdiction as they professed to give.[3]

Bishop Gray did not greatly regard this judgment, as he had always determined to rest his case less upon the jurisdiction conferred by Letters Patent, than upon what he believed to be his inherent rights as Metropolitan.

---

[1] These various documents may be seen in full in the Appendices to Bishop Gray's *Life*, vol. ii. pp. 591-618.

[2] The full text appears in Bishop Gray's *Life*, vol. ii. pp. 577-591. The judges were Lord Kingsdown, the Dean of the Arches, Sir Edward Ryan, and Sir John T. Coleridge.

[3] See above, page 333.

But it gave fresh strength to Bishop Colenso in his resolve to protest altogether against the jurisdiction claimed by Bishop Gray.

The trial took place, as arranged, in the Cathedral Church of Capetown, in November 1863. The Bishop of Capetown sat in person as judge, with Bishop Cotterill of Grahamstown and Bishop Twells of Orange Free State as his assessors. It is easy to criticise, and even to ridicule, the proceedings at this quasi-trial, conducted in a manner, to say the least, unusual, and unaided by the presence of any legal assessor or lay judge. But it is impossible to read the voluminous record of what passed without recognising the extreme difficulty of the position in which Bishop Gray and those who felt with him had been placed. Their strongest religious convictions had been roughly or contemptuously assaulted by a brother Bishop, whose undisputed oath of canonical obedience seemed certainly to put him in some sense under Bishop Gray's jurisdiction. The case was altogether new in the history of the Colonial Church. Every successive decision in the law courts seemed to increase the confusion surrounding the whole position of Colonial Bishops in the growing autonomy of Colonial government. What was the value of their Letters Patent? Were such Bishops amenable to the ecclesiastical law of England? If so, with whom did it rest to try them in case of offence? If not, to what law were they amenable? What was the real value and extent of a Metropolitan's authority? What appeal, if any, lay from his decision? On all these questions, and a score of others, the lawyers were hopelessly at sea, and gave contradictory advice at every turn.

"It would not have been greatly to be wondered at," wrote Bishop Gray, "if a few clergy in a distant land, without any great amount of learning or ability, and without the opportunity of consulting any whose opinion ought to guide them, should have made mistakes with regard to questions which have troubled and perplexed the wisest and most learned, though I am not aware that we have made any of moment. It may be said, perhaps, that, foreseeing what was coming, I should have fortified myself on such questions as I should have to consider, by counsel with the Fathers of the Church, and of eminent men learned in the law. But this was precisely what I endeavoured to do, though without any great results. Men shrank, amid the uncertainties of the case, and the absence of precedents, from giving any clear, definite advice, and I left England, after every effort to obtain authoritative and decided counsel, with the conviction that I must act upon my own responsibility; that I must decide the questions which I, at least, could not avoid, as best I might, and carve out a course for myself."[1]

The difficulties and complications were certainly immense. The misfortune was that the strong, brave man who was called upon to face them was, alike by his natural temperament and by the opinions to which he had committed himself, unfitted in a singular degree for this particular task. When Mr. Keble extolled Bishop Gray's celebrated Charge as looking "like a fragment of the fourth century recovered for the use of the nineteenth,"[2] he very fairly described the position adopted by the Bishop. The complications and safeguards, resulting, for good or evil, from the conditions of modern Church life, Bishop Gray swept scornfully aside, absolutely sure of the truth of his own opinions, and determined, so far as in him lay, to smite his opponents, hip and thigh, whatever the law courts or the civil power might have to say to the contrary. His published Biography gives abundant instances of his outspoken denunciation, beforehand, both of the writer whom he was about to try, and of the Courts which might be called upon to revise his decision. It was to the actual prosecutor in the approaching trial that he

---

[1] *Life*, vol. ii. p. 73.   [2] *Ib.* vol. ii. p. 133.

had written about the "condemnation" of the accused.[1] To another he had written : " If he [Bishop Colenso] is tolerated, the Church has no faith, is not a true witness to her Lord ":[2] and to a third, " The Church of England is no true branch of the Church of Christ, nor is her South African daughter, if either allows one of her Bishops to teach what Natal teaches, and to ordain others to teach the same. If the Faith is committed to us as a deposit, we must keep it at all hazards ; and if the world and the Courts of the world tell us we have no power, we must use the power which Christ has given us, and cut off from Him and from His Church avowed heretics, and call upon the faithful to hold no communion with them."[3]

The full vehemence of his opinions, his intolerance of opposition, or even criticism, and his scorn of the 'time-servers' who showed respect to the existing Courts and modes of procedure, became more manifest, if not more earnest, in the years that followed, when even his staunchest friends in England felt bound to deprecate the steps he took, with a fiery disregard of consequences, in promoting what he believed to be the cause of truth. The far-reaching character of his Metropolitan rights, as interpreted by himself, had long been a source of combined irritation and amusement to his suffragans,[4] and in the delivery of his Capetown judgment he gave himself a licence of criticism and comment not usually regarded as judicial. Before such a judge Bishop Colenso declined, not unnaturally, to appear. He remained in England, and contented himself with putting in a protest against the whole proceedings, and refusing to admit their legality. " For further explanation of his meaning " he referred to a letter which he had written to Bishop Gray two years before.

<hr>

[1] See above, page 340 ; and Bishop Gray's *Life*, vol. ii. p. 32.
[2] *Life*, vol. ii. p. 63.   [3] *Ibid.* vol. ii. p. 64.
[4] See Bishop Colenso's *Life*, vol. i. p. 341, etc.

But he offered no 'defence' of any kind, and admitted without reserve the publication of the incriminated passages. The speeches of the prosecutors lasted for five days,[1] and on December 16th Bishop Gray delivered formal judgment, deposing the Bishop of Natal from his office as such Bishop, and prohibiting him from the exercise of any divine office within any part of the Metropolitical Province of Capetown. On a further protest by Bishop Colenso's agent against the legality of the proceedings, Bishop Gray replied, "I cannot recognise any appeal, except to his Grace the Archbishop of Canterbury, and I must require that appeal to be made within fifteen days from the present time."

This was exactly what Bishop Tait had anticipated might happen. The only appeal recognised was to the Archbishop in his personal capacity, not in his Court, and Archbishop Longley had already, by his formal inhibition, prejudged the case. Bishop Colenso, accordingly, refused to have recourse to a tribunal, fell back upon the law, and claimed to be put in the same position as any other accused clergyman.

Looking back upon the controversy now, after the lapse of a quarter of a century, most critics who are at the pains to examine what it was that Dr. Colenso really said, will doubt whether to marvel more at the alarm his words aroused, or at the arguments employed in answer to them,[2] either in the 'Capetown Judgment' or elsewhere. But it would be a simple anachronism were we to criticise Bishop Gray's action in the light of what would now be the general opinion of Churchmen. Whatever men's views as to the fairness or wisdom shown by the Metropolitan, there were few, of any party, who did not join in the desire

---

[1] Nov. 17-21, 1863.

[2] Some amazing specimens of these are collected by Bishop Colenso in the Preface to the Second Part of his *Pentateuch*, pp. xii, xix, etc.

that, at all events, Dr. Colenso should cease to be a Bishop of the Church.

Men like Frederick Maurice felt this perhaps as strongly as either the High Churchmen or the Evangelicals. Mr. Maurice, as will be seen,[1] thought a protest against Colenso's teaching so necessary that he contemplated, on grounds not very easy to understand, the resignation of his own incumbency :—

"'The pain which Colenso's book has caused me," he said in a letter to a friend, "is more than I can tell you. I used nearly your words, 'It is the most purely negative criticism I ever read,' in writing to him. Our correspondence has been frequent but perfectly unavailing. He seems to imagine himself a great critic and discoverer, and I am afraid he has met with an encouragement which will do him unspeakable mischief. . . . His idea of history is that it is a branch of arithmetic. I agree with you that it is very difficult to say to what point of mischief he may go, but it seems to me just as likely, with his tolerance of pious frauds, that he may end in Romanism, and accept everything."[2]

In pronouncing sentence, Bishop Gray gave the incriminated Bishop four months' 'grace,' within which time he might make " full, unconditional, and absolute retractation " of his opinions. Bishop Colenso, of course, took no action, and Bishop Gray, the day after delivering judgment, wrote home as follows :—

" We are prepared, if there is to be a struggle with the world, to do what we believe our duty to our Lord requires us to do. If Civil Courts interfere and send Colenso back, God helping, I will excommunicate, and, if my brethren will join, will (if the Church at home is afraid to do so) consecrate an orthodox Bishop. I know that this will provoke the vengeance of the civil power, but I am prepared to brave everything in this case. If ever there was a heretic, Colenso is one. If we allow him to

<hr>

[1] See below, p. 511.   [2] *Life of F. D. Maurice*, vol. ii. p. 423.

act in the name of the Church the sin is ours, and the punishment will be ours. What would our Lord have us do in this case? What would the early Bishops and martyrs have done? They would have said, 'To whom we gave place by subjection, no, not for an hour.' . . . It is through Civil Courts that the world in these days seeks to crush the Church. They represent the world's feelings, and give judgment accordingly."[1]

And again, a few weeks later, on hearing of the criticisms made at home upon his action :—

"The line of the press and of Churchmen sickens me. . . . I write by this mail to the Archbishop, and pray him, if Civil Courts reinstate Colenso, and prevent him from consecrating a successor, to write and encourage me to do my duty to our Lord and to the Church, for which He gave Himself, and to elect out here and consecrate one without letters patent or other idle formalities.[2]

And again :—

"I fully anticipate an appeal to the temporal Courts . . . perhaps a verdict in Colenso's favour—return to Natal—resumption of spiritual functions—excommunication—and then the real struggle. Will the diocese place the appointment of another Bishop in my hands, to be consecrated in the teeth of the Crown without letters patent? . . . Upon these topics my mind is dwelling. Nothing has more discouraged me or weakened my hands than the low, worldly, servile view which nearly everybody in England takes of these questions. Well, say they, you have done your duty, whatever the result of an appeal to the Privy Council. What would a Christian of the first three centuries have said to such a notion? And whatever your state in England may be, ours is that of the three first centuries."[3]

April 16th was the day up to which it was in Bishop Colenso's power to retract, and express his repentance, and on that very day the indomitable Metropolitan took ship for Natal.

<hr>

[1] Bishop Gray's *Life*, vol. ii. p. 108.
[2] *Ibid.* vol. ii. p. 119.   [3] *Ibid.* vol. ii. p. 136.

"I start to-morrow," he wrote, "to take charge of the diocese, and, if I can, guide it into a right path. . . . Keble writes me most loving letters, and Pusey too, and Denison, in the tone of the shield, the sword, and the battle. . . . The real struggle is now coming on—hitherto it has been skirmishing. Now it is with the world clothed in ermine. God defend the right."[1]

On May 18th Bishop Gray delivered in the Cathedral of the Diocese of Natal the fiery Charge which has already been alluded to :—

He had come, he said, to "a widowed diocese. The whole flock is without its pastor. The clergy without their guide, counsellor, friend. The Church without its ruler. The duty of my office compels me, *sede vacante*, to take charge of this diocese. I have come among you for the express purpose of doing so. During the vacancy the clergy will hold themselves responsible to me."[2]

He recapitulated in vigorous language the sum of Bishop Colenso's errors—"theories destructive of all Revelation—of Christianity itself— . . . put forth with the reckless arrogance which marked the infidels of the preceding century."[3] He recounted the process of deposition which had taken place, and announced his intention, if need be, to proceed to a solemn excommunication in accordance with the command of Christ and the injunctions laid down in the Canons of the early Church :—

"Your late Bishop," he said, "led captive of the Evil One, has parted with the Truth of God, and now seeks to destroy that faith which once he upheld. If the Church were willing to keep him company . . . she would be a dead branch of the living vine, would wither away, die out. She would be destroyed, and ought to be destroyed."[4]

Bishop Colenso, who was still in England, replied to

---

[1] Bishop Gray's *Life*, vol. ii. p. 138.

[2] Charge, p. 35.

[3] Charge, p. 20.

[4] *Ibid.* p. 33.

this attack in a copious pamphlet.[1] He had already declared his readiness to appear for trial before any competent Court, whose proceedings should be conducted in accordance with English law, and he had undertaken, in such case, to raise no merely technical objection. He now appealed to the Queen in Council as to whether the deposition which had been pronounced was valid, and on March 20th, 1865, the Lord Chancellor pronounced judgment in his favour, on grounds similar to those which had governed the decision in the *Long* case,[2] namely, that the Letters Patent had exceeded their power in professing to confer coercive jurisdiction upon the Bishop of Capetown, and that, accordingly, " the proceedings taken by the Bishop of Capetown, and the judgment or sentence pronounced by him against the Bishop of Natal, are null and void in law."

Bishop Colenso's alleged errors of doctrine had not, of course, come, in any shape, before the Court.[3] The question referred to the judges was merely whether there had or had not been a legal trial and a legal deposition. They decided that there had not, and the Bishop of Natal immediately returned to his diocese, reiterating his claim to be tried, if at all, by some process known to English law, either ecclesiastical or civil. He landed at Durban on November 6th, 1865, and, in spite of opposition, resumed his ministerial work. Thereupon "in accordance with the decision of the Bishops of the Province in Synod

---

[1] *Remarks upon the Proceedings and Charge of the Bishop of Capetown.*

[2] See above, p. 350.

[3] It is perhaps necessary to point out that the Judicial Committee of the Privy Council, which had adjudicated upon Bishop Colenso's petition, was not the much impugned Judicial Committee, "constituted as a Court for hearing Ecclesiastical Appeals." The matter came before the Court as a purely civil case. The Court had to decide whether a certain citizen of the British Empire had or had not been wronged. The judges were the Lord Chancellor, Lord Cranworth, Lord Kingsdown, the Dean of Arches, and the Master of the Rolls.

assembled, Bishop Gray, true to his word, pronounced a solemn sentence of "the greater excommunication," and required it to be publicly read and "promulged" in the Cathedral of the Diocese of Natal. This document declared John William Colenso "separated from the communion of the Church of Christ," and "to be taken of the whole multitude of the faithful as a heathen man and a publican."[1]

Bishop Colenso replied in a long and careful letter to the excommunication and the documents which accompanied it, and again offered to submit his writings,

"in accordance with the provision in your own letters patent, to the Archbishop of Canterbury—not, of course, to the Archbishop in person, for that would be a mere idle form, since his Grace has repeatedly condemned me unheard—but to the Archbishop of Canterbury sitting in his Ecclesiastical Court, before which the case of any clergyman of his province, and of every dignitary below a bishop, might be brought by appeal."

Clearly, Bishop Gray could not admit such a reference to the Court of Arches without stultifying what he had already done as Metropolitan, and he decided rather to strengthen his position, if possible, by obtaining the authoritative sanction of the Church at home to the steps he had taken against his recalcitrant or impassive suffragan. In the previous year, before Bishop Colenso's return to Natal, the Convocation of Canterbury had passed a guarded resolution expressing personal admiration of the "courage, firmness, and love of truth" which had been shown by the Bishops of South Africa in their "stand against heretical and false doctrine."[2]　But this fell far short of the definite

---

[1] For the full text, see Bishop Gray's *Life*, vol. ii. p. 248.

[2] For an explanation of the real character and purport of this resolution, which was carried without previous notice, and almost without debate, in the absence of Bishop Tait and others, see the speeches of the Bishops of Oxford and Ely a year afterwards (*Chronicle of Convocation*, June 28, 1866, pp. 488-490).

indorsement of his action which Bishop Gray desired, and now that his last step had been taken, and the excommunication formally pronounced, he felt it to be more important than ever that he should obtain specific and authoritative answers to the questions he had officially asked with respect to his own and Bishop Colenso's relations to the Church at home. These questions were reduced, for purposes of debate, to three :—

1. "Whether the Church of England holds communion with the Right Rev. Dr. Colenso and the heretical Church which he is seeking to establish in Natal, or whether it is in communion with the orthodox Bishops who in Synod have declared him to be *ipso facto* excommunicate?"

2. (From the Dean of Maritzburg.) "Whether the acceptance of a new Bishop on our part, whilst Dr. Colenso still retains the letters patent of the Crown, would in any way sever us from the Mother Church of England?"

3. "Supposing the reply to the last question to be that they would not be in any way severed, what are the proper steps for us to take to obtain a new Bishop?"

These questions obviously covered the whole ground, and, as full notice of their discussion in Convocation had on this occasion been given,[1] it was seen that the Bishops must necessarily make a public declaration of their several opinions. A debate of the utmost importance accordingly took place. Bishop Wilberforce urged upon the House the solemn duty of indorsing the Bishop of Capetown's action by a formal declaration that the Church of England is not in communion with Bishop Colenso, but is in communion with Bishop Gray. On the latter proposition there was no difference of opinion ; but Bishops Tait, Thirlwall, Harold Browne, and Jackson, succeeded in preventing any such formal pronouncement of non-com-

[1] As contrasted with the previous year, when the subject had come forward without notice.

munion with the Bishop of Natal as should seem to admit the validity of the excommunication. A few sentences from Bishop Tait's speech will make his position clear:—

"I should have been very glad," he said, "if in some mode that would have avoided the appearance of difference of opinion, we could have communicated to the Bishop of Capetown our impression that the questions addressed to us were couched in such a form that it was almost impossible for us to return the answer which he desires. . . . Of course, in times of excitement, it requires great caution and considerable courage to endeavour to stem the tide of opinion, especially as the common sense which the English people generally show in all such matters decides that the cause maintained by the Bishop of Capetown is the right cause, however he has erred in his manner of advancing it. None of us have the slightest doubt that Bishop Colenso has published most dangerous books—books of the tendency of which I doubt whether he was fully aware when he published them. Whether it be the case, as has been stated in the public papers, that he is about to proceed further with these dangerous publications, I know not; but what he has already done is sufficient to convince us that he is quite unfit to exercise the office of a Bishop of the Church of England. I only wish he had followed the judicious advice which we have given him. I do not think he can, with any satisfaction to himself, any more than to the satisfaction of the Church, continue to perform the duties of the office which he holds. But, however that may be, he would not accept our advice, and we must take the matter as we find it. We are for the moment placed in the painful position of appearing to sympathise with Bishop Colenso, and not with Bishop Gray. I think it most desirable to state how far I sympathise with the Bishop of Capetown. I have great respect for him as a man of courage, as a man of undoubted zeal in carrying out what he believes to be true, and as a man honestly desirous of extending the Church of Christ according to his own views. But I hope I am not saying anything uncourteous if I say that on every occasion on which he has come before the public, his conduct has made me suspicious of his own opinions. I consider him to hold very strong opinions on one side, differing from myself and more than one-half the Bishops of the Church of England. He is fully entitled to hold these opinions, but I think there is this fault in his character, that he is not content with merely holding these opinions, but that he wishes to make every other person hold them too. And, therefore, I do not wish to endow him with anything like absolute authority over the Church in the colony in which he presides. . . . He asks,—Is the Church of England in communion with Bishop Colenso and the heretical Church which he is endeavouring to establish? Now, is Bishop Colenso establishing a heretical Church? . . . Suppose we granted for a moment—which I do not —that Bishop Gray had acted rightly and lawfully in excommunicating, where is the proof that if a clergyman, after taking an oath of obedience to one Bishop, refuses to concede that another Bishop has the power to excommunicate him, he is thereby guilty of heresy? No such definition of heresy has been given by any writer on the subject. . . . The whole matter turns, as the Bishop of Salisbury has remarked, upon the validity of this excommunication. And that is a very difficult question. What is Bishop Colenso excommunicated for? Because he disobeyed a certain sentence. It was not for holding heretical opinions, but for disobeying a sentence condemning him on account of his opinions. ·He disobeyed that sentence, and appealed to a high Court in England, and that Court pronounced . . . that the Bishop of Capetown had no jurisdiction whatever over Bishop Colenso, and, therefore, that the proceedings against him were null and void in law. . . . I think it would be the right course for the Bishop of Capetown, instead of adhering with extraordinary tenacity to the step which has been declared null and void, to reconsider the matter, and endeavour to institute such proceedings as may be sustained by law ; and I do not believe that any difficulty stands in the way of his pursuing such a course." [1]

The last paragraph gives Bishop Tait's answer to the question frequently asked of him both then and afterwards. It used to be said—" You have shown your objections to what was done, but what do you consider ought to have been done?" In later years he frequently expressed his opinion that, if Bishop Gray had thought well to accept Bishop Colenso's invitation to submit the question of his

<hr>

[1] *Chronicle of Convocation*, June 28, 1866, pp. 505-509.

heresy to an Ecclesiastical Court in England, a conviction would almost certainly have been obtained, not probably on the ground of the Bishop's Old Testament criticism, but of his teaching as to the Person of Our Lord.   But it was impossible for Bishop Tait, before whom the case might have come in the Court of Appeal, to express at the time any opinion as to the probable issue of a new trial. Nor could the Bishop of Capetown, without stultifying his previous management of the matter, have listened for a moment to such a suggestion. He had, on his own responsibility, taken an independent and, as Bishop Tait thought, an irregular course, and it was now impossible for the Church at home to extricate him from the position in which he found himself.

Bishop Wilberforce's motion[1] was lost on a division, and the House contented itself with affirming, what was indeed undisputed, that the Church of England continued in communion with Bishop Gray.   Even Bishop Wilberforce declined to recognise the excommunication as fully valid.[2] He had, a year before, deprecated so extreme a step ;[3] but Bishop Gray was not to be restrained, and his contemptuous carelessness as to what the English Courts, either Ecclesiastical or Civil, might say, placed his friends at home in a rather uncomfortable plight. He was now, very naturally, disappointed and irritated by the marked refusal of the Upper House of Convocation to indorse what he had done. And he was in no way pacified by a further resolution carried in that House, to the effect that neither by electing nor by refusing to elect a new Bishop would the Church in Natal sever itself from communion with the Church of England. Archbishop Longley de-

---

[1] See above, page 360.

[2] *Chronicle of Convocation*, June 28, 1866, pp. 520-521, and February 21, 1868, p. 1292.

[3] Bishop Wilberforce's *Life*, vol. iii. p. 128.

clared from the chair that while he "could never vote for
a resolution which could be construed as being a recommendation to the Church to consecrate a new Bishop" in
Dr. Colenso's place, he thought the general expression of
sympathy and fellowship was "a harmless resolution, and
calculated to give much comfort." [1]   Bishop Gray, however,
thought the comfort rather cold, to say the least, and
wrote home protesting passionately against the whole tone
of the discussion :—

He had read it, he said, "with exquisite pain and humilia-
tion. . . . The Synod of the Church, expressly and deliberately,
after long time for consideration, refuses to say that the Church
of England is not in communion with the heresiarch. . . . What
a position does this place the Church of England in ! If she
refuses to cast him off, is she not implicated in his heresy ?   I
confess that her act fills me with the deepest alarm lest her
candlestick should be removed. . . . She must, I believe, repent
of that her act, or perish. . . . This surely is the secret cause of
this sad act of the Bishops of the Church : they are not prepared
to witness for Christ, or to reject this new manifestation of anti-
Christ." [2]

[1] *Chronicle of Convocation*, June 29, 1866, p. 595.
[2] *Life*, vol. ii. p. 278.

CHAPTER XIV.

1866-68.

THE controversy now entered upon a new phase, and
Bishop Colenso ceased to be its prominent figure. In
the opinion of Bishop Gray and his supporters, the
heretical Bishop had been duly deposed and excommunicated, and the Metropolitan now regarded it as his immediate duty to secure the election and consecration of
an orthodox successor for the Diocese of Natal. From
the first he had made no secret of this intention, and
Bishop Tait and Archbishop Longley had for some time
been in correspondence on the subject.

The Bishop of London to the Archbishop of Canterbury.

"*20th April* 1866.

"MY DEAR LORD, . . . I much wish something could be
done to induce the Bishop of Capetown to pause before he
proceeds to the consecration of a Bishop to act in Natal. From
what I know of the feelings of a large body of churchmen, I feel
confident that if he takes this step without waiting for the decision
of the Master of the Rolls, and for the Ministerial Colonial
Bishoprics Bill,[1] he will be held guilty of taking the law into his
own hands, and having separated himself from the Church of
England, and the Bishop whom he consecrates will be treated
as a schismatic. This feeling extends amongst a large number
of persons who hold Bishop Colenso's errors in abhorrence, but

____
[1] See below, p. 369.

highly disapprove of any violation of the law in dealing with him.
. . . —Yours faithfully and dutifully,   A. C. LONDON."

The Archbishop replied at some length, and Bishop Tait again wrote as follows :—

The Bishop of London to the Archbishop of Canterbury.

"*1st May* 1866.

"MY DEAR LORD,—Let me thank you for so kindly and fully stating your views respecting the Bishop of Capetown's proposal to consecrate a new Bishop to act in Natal.   My anxious desire is that your Grace should know all the circumstances, and the whole bearing of the case on the various parties in the Church, before anything is done.   I have just heard of letters received from 'Dr. Callaway and two or three of the sounder clergy,' amongst the ten who are said to compose the whole Diocese of Natal, 'expressing distress and apprehension under the pressure placed upon them to elect a second Bishop.'   It would, I think, be very important if your Grace could see Mr. Bullock of S.P.G. and ask him what he knows of such a feeling in Natal.

"I am very glad to hear that the Bishop of Capetown is not likely to proceed before the Government Bill is brought into Parliament and the case before the Master of the Rolls decided.

"The future position of the Colonial Church cannot be said to be known till the Bill becomes law, and, unless I am misinformed, it will contain a clause, insisted on by Mr. Venn and the Evangelical party, that missionaries and other clergy, as well as laity of the Church of England in the Colonies, who do not wish to subject themselves to the arbitrary rule of such Churches as that of South Africa, shall be recognised in their complete independence of any authority but that of the Church of England at home.   This seems to show how likely we are, if any false step is made, to exhibit in the Colony of Natal, *e.g.* in the face of the serried ranks of Roman Catholics, the spectacle of three Churches, one headed by a Bishop commonly regarded as heretical, another by a Bishop largely regarded as schismatical, a third paying no attention to either Bishop, and professing no allegiance except to the Church at home. . . .

"Lastly, I think this point is very important : let it be granted for argument's sake that the Church in South Africa is perfectly free of all connection with the Royal Supremacy. A dispute has arisen in that Church, which has found its way to the highest civil courts, just as a dispute between Wesleyan Methodists might, and the Supreme Court, while repudiating all coercive jurisdiction on the part of the Bishop of Capetown over the Bishop of Natal, has also given judgment on the terms of the voluntary compact which existed between them, just as it would on the compact between various parties in a dispute of Methodists, and this judgment has been to the effect that no such power as that claimed by the Bishop of Capetown, of deposing his suffragan, existed by compact. The case in this view is like that of a Free Church minister who lately appealed in Scotland to the Civil Courts to say whether the compact by which he entered the Free Church has been violated by his deposition.

"Certainly this view of the Natal Privy Council judgment is widely taken, and any who take it would consider the consecration of a new Bishop, without some fresh legal authority to do so, a flying in the face of the law.

"I know you will excuse my writing so fully and freely, and attribute it to my wish that your Grace should be fully informed of the views of various bodies of attached churchmen who have no sympathy with Colenso, but deprecate hasty steps against him as likely to injure the Church.—Yours faithfully and dutifully,

"A. C. LONDON."

The Archbishop, however, took a different view. He seems, at this stage, to have encouraged rather than dissuaded Bishop Gray, and the arrangements for a fresh election in Natal went briskly forward. A conference of those clergy and laity of the diocese who supported the Metropolitan was held on October 25th, 1866, and the Rev. William Butler, Vicar of Wantage,[1] was elected to be "Bishop over the Church in Natal." The Bishop-elect consulted the Archbishop of Canterbury and the Bishop of Oxford as to whether he should accept the nomination. These prelates recommended caution and delay and further inquiry.

[1] Now Dean of Lincoln.

"We perceive," they said, "(1) That the electing clergy were a decided minority of the clergy of the Diocese ; (2) That an equal number voted for and against the proceeding to an election ; (3) That some of those who opposed proceeding to an election recorded their refusal to receive a Bishop if he were consecrated as the result of so nearly balanced a vote. These considerations suggest to us the doubt whether there is, as yet, the proof which you have a right to require—(1) That the canonicity of the election is certain ; (2) That it will be recognised by the Metropolitan and Suffragans of the Province as canonical ; (3) That it will be so recognised by the Church at home.

"We further notice that though a large majority of the lay communicants present voted for the election, yet that they amounted only to twenty-nine, so small a proportion of the whole number of lay communicants in the Diocese that we doubt whether their vote can properly be taken as expressing ' the assent of the laity,' more especially as we do not perceive that they pledged their order to make the needful provision for their Bishop. We advise you, therefore, to suspend your decision until these important questions concerning your election shall have been completely answered.—With earnest prayers to God to lead you in this matter to see and do His will, we remain, ever yours,   C. T. CANTUAR.

                                                   S. OXON."

After further inquiry, however, the doubts of Archbishop Longley and Bishop Wilberforce seem to have been set at rest,[1] but, owing probably to the approaching Lambeth Conference, any actual decision in the matter was postponed.

In the meantime Bishop Colenso had brought an action at law to secure the continuance of the income hitherto paid to him as Bishop of Natal by the Council of the Colonial Bishoprics Fund, and now withheld in consequence of his deposition. On November 6, 1866, Lord Romilly (Master of the Rolls) gave judgment in Bishop Colenso's favour, and in the course of it controverted some parts of the

---

[1] Bishop Gray's *Life*, vol. ii. p. 304.

legal decision given by Lord Westbury a year before as to the status of Colonial Churches and their Bishoprics. The prevailing confusion was thus worse confounded, and a fresh maze of complication was opened for the sorely tried but undaunted Metropolitan of Capetown, who arraigned the judgment, *more suo*, as "a most impudent judgment, artfully framed to crush out all life and liberty from our Churches."[1]

The troubles of the Colonial Church came before Parliament on several occasions during the session of 1866. On May 16th Mr. Cardwell, as Colonial Secretary, introduced a 'simplifying' Bill, which might possibly have become law but for the change of Government, which took place a few weeks later. He was succeeded at the Colonial Office by Lord Carnarvon, who promised to attempt legislation in the following year. The debates which had taken place—whatever else their issue—showed, at least, the ignorance and confusion that prevailed, even on the part of those who had given attention to the subject. One speaker after another referred in general terms to the opinion of Colonial churchmen, and this was usually represented as being markedly upon what may be called Bishop Gray's side.[2] The Bishop of London believed the opinion of the Colonies to be often misrepresented in such references, and, in order to obtain definite information, he asked the Archbishop of Canterbury to issue a circular letter to the different dioceses. The Archbishop, after consulting Bishop Wilberforce, replied that there was, in his opinion, no particular need for such an inquiry. Thereupon Bishop Tait determined to act for himself. On October 13th, 1866, he wrote in circular form to all the Colonial Bishops, Deans, and Archdeacons of

---

[1] Bishop Gray's *Life*, vol. ii. p. 306.

[2] See, for example, the speeches of Lord St. Leonards and others in the House of Lords on July 13, 1866.

the Anglican Communion, asking for specific information upon the disputed questions. His letter was as follows :—

" FULHAM PALACE,
13th October 1866.

"MY DEAR [LORD],—It is probable that the connexion of the Colonial Church with the Mother Church at home will next session come under the serious consideration of Parliament. As circumstances have very closely connected me with the difficult questions likely to arise, I am desirous to be in possession of accurate information as to the feelings of the members of the Colonial Church direct from themselves. I trust, therefore, that you will excuse me for asking you kindly to send me information on some points.

"I desire very much to know what is your feeling, and what you believe to be the feeling both of the clergy and of the laity in your diocese, on the following points :—

"*First*—The desirableness, or otherwise, of all Bishops in British Colonies receiving their mission from the See of Canterbury, and taking the oath of canonical obedience to the Archbishop.

"*Second*—Whether it is desirable that there should be an appeal in graver cases from the judgments of Church Courts, or decisions of Bishops or Synods in the Colonies, to any authority at home; and, if so, (1) to what authority, (2) under what restrictions?

"*Third*—How far the Royal Supremacy, as acknowledged by the United Church of England and Ireland, can be maintained in our Colonial Churches.

"*Fourth*—What seems the best guarantee for maintaining unity of doctrine and discipline between the different scattered branches of our Church in the Colonies.

"If you are kind enough to answer this letter, may I request you to do so on thick paper, and in such form as will best enable me to circulate the answers amongst my episcopal brethren at home.

"I should be glad to do this, if possible, before or early in the next session of Parliament.—Your faithful brother in Christ,

" A. C. LONDON."

In the course of the next few months the Bishop

received about eighty replies to his inquiry. The writers for the most part thanked him in cordial terms for the interest he was taking in these knotty problems, and sent him copious and statistical information.[1]

Bishop Gray, on the other hand, was indignant at the action of Bishop Tait. Writing to a friend, he refers to the matter as follows :—

"The Bishop of London has been very impertinently addressing not only all Colonial Bishops, but their clergy, on questions at issue. He will get well snubbed, for the clergy are very indignant, and say that they should have been addressed by the Archbishop through their own Bishops. I have sent copies of my replies to him to the Archbishops, and to S. Oxon., and have written, in the name of the Synod of the Church, fully and formally to Lord Carnarvon." [2]

A few sentences may be quoted from his formal reply to Bishop Tait's circular of inquiry :—

"Your Lordship will, I trust, pardon me for saying that some dissatisfaction has been expressed to me, chiefly through the Dean and Archdeacon of another Diocese, at the course adopted by you with a view to obtain information on matters relating to the internal condition of this Church. While ready and anxious to afford any information in their power, the feeling of the clergy is, that that information should have been sought through His Grace the Archbishop of Canterbury, with whom this Church is connected, rather than by official communications from the Bishop of a diocese with which we have no immediate connection ; and that if the views of the clergy of these dioceses were desired on delicate matters affecting their internal state, they should have been approached through their Bishops. Colonial Churches are sensitive on the subject of Church Order, and feel aggrieved if they are dealt with differently from what one Bishop

---

[1] "I cannot sufficiently thank your Lordship," wrote the Bishop of Guiana, "for the interest you are taking in the Colonial Church. That God in His goodness may give you strength equal to what is required of you, is our very sincere prayer."

[2] Bishop Gray's *Life*, vol. ii. p. 316.

in England would deal with the Bishop of another diocese there. With these few remarks I proceed to answer your Lordship's questions :—

"I. The Canons of the Church require that all Bishops of a Province shall, before consecration, be confirmed in their election by the Metropolitan and Bishops of that Province. They are bound by the same Canons to take the oath of Canonical obedience to the Metropolitan of the Province. And this has hitherto been the practice wherever there are Provinces and Metropolitans in the Colonies. If by 'receiving their mission from the See of Canterbury' be meant a departure from this practice, there can be no doubt that it would be most objectionable, inasmuch as it would be a violation of the customs and Canons of the Church as received and acted upon in the Church of England. . . .

"II. I think that all the Bishops of this Province, nearly all the Clergy, and the most intelligent and earnest of the laity, would, if asked, desire that the question of the Final Court of Appeal for Colonial Churches should be referred to, and decided by, a National Synod, in which the Colonial Churches should be represented. . . . Neither the Bishops nor the Clergy of this Province would ever consent to be subjected to the Final Court of Appeal as now constituted for the Church of England. . . .

"III. I object to the form of this question, and think it calculated to mislead. It implies that the Royal Supremacy, as acknowledged by the United Church of England and Ireland, is not acknowledged by the Colonial Church; and appears to appeal to their loyalty to acknowledge it; whereas the real object of the question is to learn—and it appears to me that it had better have been put in that form—whether the Colonial Churches are prepared to submit the ultimate decision of questions affecting the faith to the Judicial Committee of Privy Council, which the Church of England cannot be considered to have acknowledged ; and, if not, whether to any other Court constituted by the British Parliament. I have already stated my opinion on that point. . . .

"IV. Nothing, in my belief, but the speedy assembling of a National Synod can bind the Churches of our Communion in one, or prevent wide dissensions and probably separations. . . .

"In conclusion, I beg to enter my solemn protest against legislation for this Church by the British Parliament. . . ."

A few weeks later Bishop Gray wrote sending further information, and added :—

"I must again express my regret that your Lordship should have forced upon the consideration of parties not very well able to understand the questions at issue, matters of very great moment to the future welfare of the Church."

Bishop Tait replied :—

" I am sorry that you should feel aggrieved by anything which I have thought it my duty to say or do in reference to the very grave and anxious questions which, arising at the Cape and in Natal, have threatened seriously to affect the Church at home, and alter its whole position as we have received it from past times. I feel sure that if I saw you I could remove from your mind any unpleasant impressions which late events have made upon you in reference to the line adopted by myself and a very large and influential portion of the Church at home. It is important that we should each remember how very grave are the points at issue, and give each other full credit for conscientious adherence to principle. I am in full hopes that I may see you at Fulham in September, and I believe the discussions at Lambeth will, by God's blessing, lead to good results."

It was only from South Africa that the Bishop received other than friendly replies, and even from the Diocese of Capetown some of the clergy wrote to him a joint letter in opposition to the views of their Diocesan :—

"We are fully persuaded," they said, "that it is most desirable, as a means of keeping up the unity of the Church, that all her Bishops in the Colonies, without exception, should receive mission from, and take the oath of Canonical obedience to, the See of Canterbury. If the claim put forward by the Bishop of Capetown, to have his decisions as Metropolitan regarded as final, be allowed,—if, in other words, as he affirms, there is no appeal to any court on earth from a judgment which he may pronounce as Metropolitan, it is evident that the Suffragan Bishops of the Province are in a far worse position than the humblest Priest in pre-Reformation times : he at least had an appeal to the Roman Pontiff, whilst they are subject without appeal to the sentence, however arbitrary, of the Metropolitan."

It would of course be impossible to summarise here the voluminous answers which Bishop Tait received. Enough to say that they confirmed him in his belief that there was a great preponderance of opinion in the Colonial Church adverse to the policy of Bishop Gray, and that they furnished him, in preparation for the events of 1867, with a mine of varied and valuable information.[1]

The affairs of the South African Church were by this time exciting attention all the world over, and one consequence resulting from what was oddly described in Parliament as their 'red-hot tangle' was the summoning by Archbishop Longley of the first 'Lambeth Conference.' The suggestion emanated, not from South Africa, but from North America, but it was admittedly the Natal troubles that prompted and strengthened the appeal for such a gathering.

On February 22, 1867, Archbishop Longley issued his invitation to the whole Anglican Episcopate, which (including the Bishops of the United States) numbered at that time 144. The venerable Bishop of St. David's had at first opposed the issue of such an invitation, believing the intention of its promoters to be nothing less than to outvote, by the voices of Bishops from America and the Colonies, the more cautious resolutions of the Home Episcopate. The influence of such a meeting, he said, would evidently be brought to bear on the disputed question in order "to modify the Constitution and Government of our Church." This view was shared by the Archbishop of

---

[1] The letters in question, although shown at the time to such Bishops and others as desired to see them, have never been published. They are of great historical interest to students of Colonial Church History.

York and the Bishops of Durham, Carlisle, Ripon, Peterborough, and Manchester, who all resolved upon declining
to attend the Conference. Bishop Tait had been expected
to join them, but he took a bolder course, and expressed
his cordial approval of such a gathering, provided its nature
and the limits of its authority should be carefully specified
beforehand.[1]   Archbishop Longley consented to this
course, and his letter of invitation stated clearly that "such
a meeting as is proposed would not be competent to make
declarations or lay down definitions on points of doctrine."[2]
To allay the fears of the Bishop of St. David's, and to
gain for the Conference the weight of his presence, the
Archbishop gave him privately a further undertaking that
the question of Bishop Colenso's position should not be
one of those debated at Lambeth. On these conditions
Bishop Thirlwall consented to attend. But whatever the
value of these ' understandings,' it was certain that the
conflict must be sharp between those who still desired, so
far as possible, to preserve in the Colonies the same degree
of liberty and discipline as are characteristic of the Church
of England, and those who aimed at the virtual independence of each Colonial Church, and the authoritative
recognition of its acts throughout the Anglican Communion,
whatever the Civil Courts might say to the contrary.
Bishop Gray was naturally regarded as the champion of
the latter party, and he had the warm sympathy of several
Colonial Bishops, and of some of those belonging to the
United States. His whole mind was set, with characteristic enthusiasm, upon securing that Mr. Butler should
be summoned as Bishop-elect to the Conference in place
of Bishop Colenso, who had received no invitation, and
that thus Bishop Colenso's deposition should be officially

---

[1] See *Chronicle of Convocation*, February 15, 1867, p. 807.
[2] See *The Lambeth Conferences of* 1867, 1878, *and* 1888 (S.P.C.K.), p. 12.

recognised even before the meeting of the Conference. He even wrote to Bishop Wilberforce as follows :—

"If the English Bishops . . . will not give the right hand of fellowship to him who has been elected, . . . but ignore the act of deposition and separation from the Church, . . . they involve the Church of which they are Bishops in formal heresy, and—forgive me for speaking what I feel—are unfaithful to Christ, and betray His cause. God forgive me and teach me otherwise if I am wrong. I shall be the greatest sufferer if I be in error; but believing this, I do not see what other course is open to us, if that came to pass which appears too probable, but for me to resign my present position, and with it communion with the Church of England." [1]

Bishop Wilberforce's Biography records his half successful efforts to restrain the fiery Metropolitan, whose attitude—clear, outspoken, and indomitable—has been so far as possible described above in order the better to explain what follows,—Bishop Tait's scarcely less vehement opposition to a system and course of action which were in his opinion intensely harmful both to the Church at home and to her growing offshoots in the Colonies. To the general question it will be necessary to return hereafter. Bishop Tait's own Diary will best describe what occurred in the Conference itself with reference to the 'burning subject' of Natal :—

Diary.

"WOODSIDE, WINDSOR FOREST, 18*th Sept.* 1867.—Yesterday we held, at 5 Park Place, in the rooms of the S.P.G., the preliminary meeting for the purpose of arranging proceedings, and it may be well to make a note of what took place.

"Met at 12. I travelled up in the train with the Bishop of Quebec—not inclined to be communicative. I introduced myself, and he did the same. I took the opportunity of expressing to him my views as to Lord Carnarvon's conduct in dispens-

---

[1] Bishop Gray's *Life*, vol. ii. p. 330.

ing with the Royal Mandate at the election of the Bishop of Niagara, as explained in Parliament at the beginning of last session.   Also I took the opportunity of showing how an appeal to the Crown could not be avoided, even by Churches not established, as shown in the recent decision of Lord Westbury in the Privy Council with reference to a minister of the Dutch Reformed Church at the Cape, deposed by their Synod or Presbytery for denying the personality of the Evil Spirit.

"I reached 5 Park Place in good time.   A large assembly of Bishops, many of whom I had never seen before, and some of whom were so much changed since I last saw them that I could scarcely recognise the new faces.   Of the latter were New Zealand, Perth in Australia—even Nova Scotia.   The others were chiefly Americans from the United States.   There were present, besides those named—Montreal, Capetown, Grahamstown, Orange-River, Huron, Quebec, Ontario, Coadjutor of Newfoundland, Bishop Smith, Bishop Trower, and a large body of Americans, including old Vermont, the presiding Bishop, a jolly old man with white beard and wideawake hat; Potter of New York, like a very respectable English clergyman; Iowa and Louisiana.

"At this preliminary meeting there cropped up, as might be expected, all the difficulties of Natal and Church-and-State.   I thought it well to let it be distinctly understood that I thought the Romeward tendency more dangerous for our clergy than the tendency towards freethought, and stated that if the Natal question were introduced, the Bishop of St. David's and others would find themselves in a great difficulty, having agreed to attend on the distinct understanding that the subject would not be entered on.   I pointed out to the Bishop of Capetown that it would be much better for him privately to take counsel with the English Bishops at home, especially those who differed from him in opinion, and with some of his Colonial brethren, than to bring the subject before a mixed body of English, American, and Scottish Bishops, many of whom could not enter into the difficulties arising from English law and the connection of the Church with the State.   The Archbishop of Canterbury entirely concurred with me, but Capetown intimated that he would certainly bring the matter forward.

"We came to Fulham on Friday the 20th, to be ready to entertain, and from the 23d to 27th inclusive kept almost open house.[1] Craufurd read a lesson in Chapel daily till Thursday, when he left us for Eton; and the little girls 'presided at the organ.' Our American brethren were much touched by the presence of Craufurd and the children, and the part they took.

"On the 24th the whole party started from Fulham in carriages, some to the station, and some to go with me. We had Holy Communion in the chapel at Lambeth at 11. A goodly array gathered from all parts of the earth. The only English Bishops absent on principle:—York, Carlisle, Durham, Ripon, Peterboro', Manchester. The Bishops of Exeter, Chichester, Bath and Wells, and Hereford are all ill. The sermon by the Bishop of Illinois was wordy, but not devoid of a certain kind of impressiveness. The subject was not clear—'We fill up what is behind in the sufferings of Christ.' The characteristics of the Episcopal work, θλιψεῖς. The Bishop of Oxford was very much afraid of ridicule attaching to us all if the sermon were published, as the hospitalities of the week were not very like afflictions. There certainly was an unreality in the sermon. The best part of it, one American Bishop pointed out, was a passage contrasting the world and the Church.

" I like the Bishop of Illinois, and though certainly it appeared to me that he was too fluent, I do not know that I should have thought more of his wordiness if our American brethren had not spoken of it as they did, telling the story of a great speech which he made in their Convention. The speech ended, the Bishops retired, and in the room in which several were spending the evening was a new Dictionary. 'What is it?' 'You will see on the title-page that it professes to contain 4000 new words.' ' Let us begin by returning thanks that our brother of Illinois had not seen it, or he would have gone on for ever.'

"After the first day we did not meet again in Lambeth Chapel. In the great dining-hall in which we sat, surrounded by the pictures of the Archbishops, we had a few prayers at the commencement of each of the four sittings, and those who were our guests assembled each morning and evening in Fulham Chapel.

" As to our discussions, it is impossible now to recall them all. The Conference decided not to admit the Press,—to have only

<hr>

[1] Most of the Bishops who were living in or near London, including Bishop Gray, were invited to dine daily at Fulham during the Conference, and fifteen Bishops spent the week there as the Bishop of London's guests.

two reporters, who would make out a fair copy of their short-hand notes, and place them in the Archbishop's custody, to be deposited in Lambeth Library. The Pastoral and the resolutions adopted are alone published. The great discussions were, as might naturally be expected, on the following points :—1st, Whether or no the Natal question was to be introduced. Its introduction most strongly opposed by St. David's, who declared that he came there on the faith of the Archbishop's programme, and ended his appeal, ' I throw myself on your Grace's honour and good faith.' I wish I could have had a photograph of the old man as he pronounced these words with the utmost vehemence and solemnity of manner and voice. Old Vermont proposed a very strong resolution pronouncing Colenso ex-communicated, but he got no backers. New Zealand committed the great mistake of attacking the Bishop of St. David's for his charge reflecting on Capetown. This produced a storm, and let the Americans and Colonials understand that St. David's was looked on as a sacro-sanct. I first rose to the rescue, and then the Bishop of Ely (Harold Browne) in great emotion reproved New Zealand, declaring St. David's to be not only the most learned prelate in Europe, but probably the most learned prelate who had ever presided over any See. The Archbishop ended the matter by declaring that he did not think it competent to introduce the Natal question except in the guarded way adopted in a resolution which appointed a committee to go into the question of the scandal existing in that diocese. But this decision was very much against the feelings of the more ardent spirits, and attempts were made each day to reintroduce the dangerous subject. A paper was drawn up by the Bishop of Oxford, and circulated privately for signatures, declaring that those who subscribed acknowledged the spiritual force of Bishop Gray's sentence against Colenso. I of course refused to sign this, on the ground that I believed the sentence had been pronounced null and void by the highest Court of the realm. Harold Browne of Ely refused, on the ground that a Metropolitan had not power to depose a Bishop in the way Bishop Gray had done, even by the purely ecclesiastical law. It was insisted on that this paper, if it did receive signatures, should in no way be connected with the Lambeth Conference, but be considered the private act of those who signed it.

"To the Bishop of New Zealand we were indebted for a

closing warm discussion. It was late on the fourth day, and thanks were expressed (I think by the Archbishop of Armagh) for the tone which had animated the meeting, and every one seemed pleased. New Zealand rose to second the resolution of Armagh, and to our surprise poured forth his regrets and disapproval in a way that shocked us. He spoke bitterly of Stanley having declined to give the Abbey, reproached the Established Church for trusting to an arm of flesh, and altogether spoke in such a spirit—holding up his Colonial Church as our model—that I could not contain myself, and spoke in severe rebuke, and think I expressed myself as I ought. I believe the meeting generally approved. Wordsworth of St. Andrews fully indorsed what I said of the Established Church, and Oxford made an apologetic speech for New Zealand.

"Thus far all had gone well. There had been ebullitions, but the general tone was good. It was late on the fourth day—the time when we were all expected at St. James's Hall for the great S. P. G. meeting was long past; some, as the Archbishop of Dublin, had left—when the Bishop of Capetown suddenly proposed that the Conference should adopt the resolution of Convocation respecting Natal. The greatest confusion ensued. He declared that he would resign his Bishopric unless his proposal was adopted. No one knew what the resolution which he proposed we should adopt was. It was with great difficulty that we could get what he wanted read. I got from him the Chronicle of Convocation, from which he was reading, and found that he had omitted the first clause of a hypothetical sentence—'*If* it be decided that a new Bishop for Natal should be consecrated.' I insisted on these words being inserted. A vote was hurried on, and began to be taken. The Bishop of Winchester moved that the subject be referred to the committee on the Natal question. Capetown's friends became greatly excited. Oxford protested that the question had been put, and that it was not competent now to introduce an amendment. Capetown tried to get both the resolutions passed by Convocation adopted by us. The Archbishop (who ought, after his previous decision, to have prevented this new question from being raised at the last moment) thought that the Bishop of Winchester's amendment was too late and could not be put. I besought them not to carry so important a resolution by a 'ruse,' but in vain.

"Then Gloucester (our admirable Secretary) insisted that the one resolution only, viz., the hypothetical one, should be put. It was put, and carried almost unanimously ;[1] and I thought that after all no great harm was done, as it was only a hypothetical proposition. Great therefore was my astonishment when we reached St. James's Hall to hear the Bishop of Capetown, as I understood him, announce that the last act of the Synod had been to give its approval to the consecration of a new Bishop for Natal. This made my blood boil, but I restrained myself in the room. I went out, and seeing the danger more clearly, as I thought of what had happened, I went to the Athenæum, where I consulted the Bishop of Limerick, and was hurrying back to the hall with a note requesting the Bishop of Capetown to explain to the meeting, when I met Argyll and others, who told me the proceedings were all ended and the hall cleared. I confess to having been made very angry, and to having spoken in the strongest terms to various persons at my dinner-table of the inaccuracy of what appeared to have been announced. I wish I had not used such strong language, as it is not right.

"Next morning I wrote a note to the *Times*, which I submitted to Lincoln, Chester, Argyll, and others, and which, with their approval, I published in all the papers.[2]

"On Saturday we met again for Communion and Sermon in Lambeth Church. I had a note handed to the Bishop of Capetown, telling him of my letter to the *Times*.

"But notwithstanding this sad incident at the close, I feel that

---

[1] The words of the Resolution as adopted by the Conference were as follows :—

Resolution vii.—"That we who are here present do acquiesce in the Resolution of the Convocation of Canterbury, passed on June 29, 1866, relating to the Diocese of Natal, to wit—

"If it be decided that a new Bishop should be consecrated,—As to the proper steps to be taken by the members of the Church in the province of Natal for obtaining a new Bishop, it is the opinion of this House,—*first*, that a formal instrument," etc.

See *Resolutions of the Conference*, published by authority (Rivingtons, 1867), page 16.

[2] The letter was as follows :—"SIR,—As the Bishop of Capetown was by some understood to say, in his speech at St. James' Hall yesterday, that the Conference of Bishops at Lambeth had given its approval to the appointment of a new Bishop of Natal, I beg leave to refer all your readers who are interested in this subject to the carefully guarded words of the resolution actually adopted by the Conference, which will, I believe, soon be published. —Yours, etc.   A. C. LONDON."

the tone of the Conference generally was very good.   And as the Bishop of Argyll said, we must consider that the poor Bishop of Capetown has had a most difficult position—that it is very difficult to know what any one would have done with such a Suffragan as Colenso.   On the whole, let us be thankful for the kindly spirit of the Conference—for the essential amity.

"'The Pastoral, though severely criticised, is the expression of essential agreement, and a repudiation of infidelity and Romanism.

"May God direct all to the good of His Church!'"

The Conference broke up on September 28th, and was adjourned until December 10th, when a few of its members met to receive the Reports which had been drawn up in the interim by its Committees.   In the deliberations of these Committees Bishop Tait took an active part, and he has left elaborate memoranda of his opinions. The adjourned Session lasted for a few hours only.   Of the eight Reports received, seven were " commended to the careful consideration of the Bishops of the Anglican Communion."   But these words were omitted in the resolution respecting the eighth Report, which " accepted the spiritual validity " of Bishop Colenso's deposition, and judged the See to be "spiritually vacant."   The Report therefore received no further indorsement than that of the Committee which drew it up.[1]

Although Bishop Gray had not attained within the Conference walls to the success he had anticipated, his presence at clerical meetings and congresses throughout the country was the signal for immense enthusiasm, and he was encouraged on all sides to go forward without more ado to Mr. Butler's consecration.   As usual, he could see

---

[1] The resolution was as follows :—" That the Report be received and printed, that the thanks of this meeting be given to the Committee for their labours, and that His Grace be requested to communicate the Report to the Council of the Colonial Bishoprics Fund."—See *The Lambeth Conferences of 1867, 1878, and 1888*, pp. 19 and 137.

no difficulties, but for this purpose he required the co-operation of the Archbishop, on whom the Lambeth debates had had anything but a reassuring effect. Indeed, Archbishop Longley had now, it would seem, come round to a view not very different in some respects from that of Bishop Tait, and a few weeks after the Conference he wrote to Mr. Butler dissuading him in decided terms from accepting the Bishopric,[1] although he retained his opinion that some orthodox diocesan must sooner or later be appointed.   Mr. Butler accordingly declined to go further, and Bishop Gray, disappointed and indignant, but not disheartened, set to work to find a substitute.   One clergyman after another was offered the post in vain, but at last, on January 13, 1868, Bishop Gray wrote to the *Guardian* that the nomination had been accepted by the Rev. W. K. Macrorie, Vicar of St. James', Accrington. " The place and time for the Consecration," he said, "have not yet been definitely fixed."   It became known, however, in a few days, that arrangements were being privately made for the consecration to take place at the earliest possible date, and that there was no intention of asking for, or waiting for, the usual mandate from the Crown.   It would have been the only consecration that had ever taken place in England without such mandate, and the new departure might have had serious results.

Had Bishop Gray been content to return to Capetown and consecrate the new Bishop there, no further difficulty would have arisen.   But he was naturally bent upon hold-ing the consecration in England, so as to secure the appa-

---

[1] " I have come to the conclusion," he said, " that I ought to dissuade you from availing yourself of your election to the See of Pieter Maritzburg.   To my mind, the appointment of any one of very marked opinions to the See would be open to serious objections, and it would be better to select some one more calculated to meet the various shades of religious opinion that exist among the faithful members of the Church of England in the Colony of Natal."—Bishop Gray's *Life*, vol. ii. p. 368.

rent *imprimatur* of the Home Church upon all that had been done. Archbishop Longley was puzzled how to act. He seems at first to have consented to allow the consecration, notwithstanding its irregular character, to be held in the Province of Canterbury, and various Churches were in turn suggested by Bishop Wilberforce and others. Failing these, it was thought that the consecration might be in Edinburgh, in accordance with an invitation from the Scottish Bishops. But everything was kept profoundly secret, and Bishop Tait's information as to what was passing was derived from a series of unauthentic and unsolicited letters and telegrams, which kept arriving from various parts of the country, announcing different and contradictory reports and plans, and begging for his advice or action. Most of these he preserved, and they give a curious picture of the excitement, the mystery, and the confusion :—

"It will be January 25th, in Chapel of St. Augustine's College. This is secret, but certain."

"It is said that the consecration will take place in St. Mary's, Oxford."

"It has been proposed to have the consecration in Wantage Church next Sunday. Bishops of Capetown and Grahamstown, and some third Bishop, to consecrate."

"The consecration will be here in Edinburgh. Can nothing be done to arrest this injudicious step?"

And so forth.

Bishop Tait at once wrote a letter to the Primus of the Scottish Episcopal Church, pointing out the gravity of the step the Scotch Bishops had proposed :—

"I venture to urge on yourself and your brethren," he said, "to be very careful on the subject. You remember what passed at the Lambeth Conference, and how many of the English Bishops feel that such a consecration is unlawful. . . . You may rest assured that the feeling on the subject is very strong in the whole evangelical and the whole so-called liberal sections of the Church of England, and that nothing but a strong feeling of the injustice and wrongness of the proposed course would induce men like myself, and the Bishops of Ely, Lincoln, and St. David's, to have appeared, by opposing it, to favour Bishop Colenso, of whose proceedings and of whose modes of thinking and writing we so strongly disapprove.   Under these circumstances I feel that the Scottish Episcopal Church will take a very false and wrong step if they thus interfere in a matter with which very important legal interests in the Church of England are bound up. . . . Do not suppose that we are insensible to the difficulties of the Bishop of Capetown's position, or the evil done by Bishop Colenso, but we think that Bishop Colenso's cause, like that of any other accused man, must be tried on its merits, and decided against him by a competent tribunal before another can be lawfully or canonically substituted in his place."

He enclosed a copy of this letter, by the same post, to the Bishop-designate, Mr. Macrorie, who had formerly been a clergyman in his diocese, and for whom he had the warmest possible regard.

The Scottish Bishops met, and it was decided that the consecration should take place in England.   Thereupon Bishop Tait published the following letter in the *Times* :—

The Bishop of London to the Bishop of Capetown.

"FULHAM PALACE, *Jan.* 20, 1868.

"MY DEAR LORD,—I feel myself constrained by a sense of duty, much against my inclination, to address your Lordship publicly on the subject of a letter which you sent to the newspapers last week.   You announce, as I understand you, that it is your intention forthwith to consecrate a new Bishop for Natal. Had Parliament or Convocation been sitting, I should have asked in my place for an answer to the following :—

"1. Whether, considering the words of the 26th of George III. cap. 84, and other Statutes, the law officers of the Crown, having been consulted by the Government, have declared such consecration to be lawful?

" 2. If you are not acting on the authority of the law officers of the Crown, has a legal opinion been taken justifying the step you propose? by whom has it been given? and what are its express terms?

" 3. When and where is it proposed that the consecration is to take place, and who are to be the officiating Bishops?

" But neither Parliament nor Convocation is in session ; and, as it seems there is no time to lose, I take the only means open to me for asking you, before you proceed further in this matter, to give a public answer to these questions. It was only last week that I learnt accidentally, but from the most undoubted authority, that you proposed to hold the consecration on the 25th inst., and in Scotland. A vigorous protest against this proceeding has been made by persons who are among the most attached members of the Scottish Episcopal Church. The Scottish plan is, I now learn, abandoned ; and it is stated that, on Saturday next, you propose to consecrate in England.

" Meanwhile your brother Bishops in England may well be thrown into perplexity. We know not in which of our dioceses an act, which, to say the least, is of most doubtful legality, is to take place. We may read in the newspapers any morning that the thing has been already done ; and we may be left in the disagreeable position of being called upon by others, as well as moved by our sense of public duty, to visit some of our clergy for taking part in proceedings contrary to the law of the Church and realm ; when, had we been properly informed beforehand, and the matter formally investigated, we might have prevented them from committing themselves.

" I am sure you will see, my dear Lord, that the Church of England is entitled to a plain and immediate answer to the questions I have asked.

" You remember, from your recent presence at the Lambeth Conference—

" 1. That the assembled Bishops, under the direction of the Archbishop of Canterbury, deliberately abstained from affirming that Bishop Colenso's deposition was valid, either spiritually or in any other way.

" 2. That at the adjourned meeting of the Conference the Report of the Committee recommending the consecration of a new Bishop, was, by the wish of the Archbishop of Canterbury, as well as of the Bishops of Lincoln, Ely, Chester, and myself, with others, deliberately not approved, but only received.

"3. That many of the English Bishops, feeling strongly, like myself, how dangerous is the teaching of Bishop Colenso, still hold that his See is not vacant, since his deposition has been pronounced null and void in law by the highest Courts of the realm.

"4. That some also of our body, whose authority is very great in such matters, believe that (quite independently of questions of English law) the deposition is uncanonical.

"You will remember also—

"5. That, whereas the words of 26 George III. cap. 84, declare that by the laws of this realm no person can be consecrated to the office of Bishop without the Royal authority, if any doubt exists as to the applicability of these words to your case, that Consecration Service which alone can be lawfully used within the Church of England prescribes that the Royal mandate shall be produced before the consecration is proceeded with; and, moreover, the Bishop-elect is called upon to declare, in the face of the congregation, that he is persuaded he is truly called to his ministration in the office of a Bishop, not only according to the will of our Lord Jesus Christ, but also 'according to the order of this realm.'

"To many it seems inconceivable that any man will be found to make this solemn declaration, in the midst of all these doubts, before the legality of his consecration has been publicly established by some competent authority.

"Under these circumstances I venture to call upon you, my dear Lord, not to go further without the most perfect openness, and the most complete examination by the authorities of Church and State as to the legality and propriety of what you are doing. You surely will allow that you ought not otherwise to proceed to a step which must be fraught with the gravest consequences for the Church, both at home and in the Colonies, and for which certainly there is no precedent since the schism of the Non-jurors.

"Let me remind you that what I ask implies no long delay as to the authoritative settlement of whether or no you are right in your view of your duty. Parliament and Convocation both meet early next month; and it surely would be unbecoming, in the face of statutes and of ecclesiastical precedent, to hurry on this step before either authority has had an opportunity of expressing its opinion.—Believe me to be, my dear Lord, yours very faithfully,   A. C. LONDON."

This letter rendered the prosecution of Bishop Gray's plan impossible. His Biography gives a vivid picture of the hurried consultations which took place—the telegrams and journeys between Cuddesdon and London — the resolution arrived at to revert, if possible, to the plan of consecrating in Scotland—the successive consent, reconsideration, and refusal by the Scottish Bishops—the unsuccessful endeavour to obtain after all a mandate from the Crown — and the ultimate resolve that there was nothing for it but to hold the consecration in South Africa.[1]   The following extracts from the innumerable letters which have been preserved, and from the Convocation Debates, will give a sufficient idea of the line adhered to by Bishop Tait throughout the stormy and complicated controversy. He received from Bishop Gray a long reply[2] to the public letter of January 20th, quoted above.   In the course of it Bishop Gray wrote :—

"You have asked me, in the name of the Church of England, a question, to which in this letter I give my answer. In return I venture, in the name of the same Church, and in my own, as Metropolitan of a province which you have deeply and grievously wounded by your whole course of proceedings in this matter, as I have shown in my published 'Statement,' to ask you whether you do hold communion with Dr. Colenso, or not? Whether you regard him as the representative Bishop of the Church of England in Natal, or not? Whether he is entitled, in his character of teacher, to speak in the name of this great and ancient Church, or not? Vague phrases about disapproving of his teaching evade the question, and do not meet the necessities of this crisis. The issue at stake is simply this :—Have we received

---

[1] Bishop Gray's *Life*, vol. ii. pp. 384-443.

[2] This letter, which afterwards formed the body of a pamphlet, was the joint handiwork of Bishops Gray, Hamilton, Wilberforce, Cotterill, and others. See Bishop Gray's *Life*, vol. ii. p. 385.

a revelation from God, of which the Scriptures are a written and infallible record?   Or have we not received any such revelation? Is Christianity, as it has been delivered to us from the first, true, or is it a lie?   Are we to exchange it for a new religion or not? Nothing less than these are the questions raised by Dr. Colenso's writings.   We must take our sides on these great questions; we cannot be neutrals.   The African Church has taken its side, and rejected from its communion this false teacher, and resolved to send forth another in his place.   It is for the Bishops of the Church of England to decide to which party in this great contest they will commit the Church which they rule.   The real question, which has yet to be decided, is this, Will the Church of England incur the guilt of complicity with heresy, by not openly separating from her communion one of whom she has declared in her Synod, that he teaches doctrine full of dangerous error, and subversive of the faith?   The whole Christian world is waiting anxiously till she shall stand clear in the sight of God and man in this matter."

The Bishop of London to the Bishop of Capetown.

"LONDON HOUSE, 6th *February* 1868.

"MY DEAR LORD,—I received yesterday afternoon your letter of the 28th ult., and have since read it in the *Guardian* newspaper in connection with the rest of your correspondence with the Archbishops of Canterbury and York in reference to the consecration of a new Bishop for Natal.

"You will not expect me to enter on all the matters to which your letter alludes.   I would only express my thankfulness that you have, as I understand you, abandoned the intention of consecrating a new Bishop in England or Scotland; also I cannot refrain from assuring you how much, considering the respect which I entertain for you, I regret that you should misunderstand the motives under which, from an imperative sense of duty, I have felt obliged on several occasions to oppose the course which approves itself to you in reference to the affairs of Natal.

"But you ask me a question which it would be uncourteous not to answer.   You remember that a similar question was addressed by you to the Upper House of the Convocation of Canterbury, and that the Bishops there assembled deliberately refrained from answering that they were not in communion with Bishop Colenso, feeling that such an answer would be equivalent to a public declaration of the validity of your act of excommunication, respecting which grave legal difficulties existed and still exist.   It is only natural for me to meet your question in the same manner, by telling you that I cannot say I am not in communion with Bishop Colenso till I am convinced, which I am not at present, that the proceedings taken against him, which resulted in your pronouncing him excommunicate, are valid. You seem to think that because, in common with very many of my brethren, I thought it right that you should take proceedings against Bishop Colenso, therefore I am bound to approve of the mode in which these proceedings were taken, and to acquiesce in their validity notwithstanding the adverse decision of courts of law.

"I understand you to ask me whether I hold Bishop Colenso to be not only the titular, but the actual Bishop of Natal, notwithstanding your deposition of him.   I should have thought there could be no doubt as to my opinion on this subject, after what I have already publicly stated.   The words in which you mention that I couched a circular letter sent in 1866 to Bishop Colenso, together with all the Colonial Bishops and other dignitaries, show the same thing : viz., that, seeing that Bishop Colenso has refused to resign his post when requested to do so by the Archbishops and myself, and the great body of the home Episcopate, I must, till the legal difficulties declaring his deposition to be null and void are removed, however much I may regret it, regard him as still holding his office.   I cannot, as at present advised, recognise the force of the arguments which lead you and many others entitled to the highest respect to look upon him as spiritually deposed, when the proceedings by which he is said to have been deposed are granted to be null and void in law, and when very grave doubts exist, in the minds of those whom I regard as best informed, as to their regularity even according to ancient ecclesiastical precedent.

"You seem also to ask me whether I am prepared to assist you and others in opposing Bishop Colenso's errors.   I might fairly refer you in answer to my published utterances, but it is only courteous to assure you again, as I most gladly do, that in every lawful and proper way I desire to assist you and others in maintaining the great doctrine of the paramount and Divine authority of Holy Scripture. But my experience has led me to believe, with respect to Bishop Colenso and all others who teach what I believe to be dangerous error, that nothing is so likely to give them influence as any appearance of unfairness in the mode of treating them, or any endeavour, through zeal against them and their errors, to override the law.—Believe me, my dear Lord, yours very faithfully, A. C. LONDON."

Archbishop Longley had in the meantime taken a more decided line, and had written to Bishop Gray as follows:—

The Archbishop of Canterbury to the Bishop of Capetown.

"ADDINGTON PARK, CROYDON,
January 27th, 1868.

"MY DEAR LORD,—I think it is only fair I should inform you that I have received letters from Bishops of every shade of opinion in our Church, some deprecating any consecration at all for the colony of Natal, others deprecating it till the meeting of Convocation, when the opinion of the Church may be in some measure ascertained.

"You may remember that when Mr. Butler consulted the Bishop of Oxford and myself as to the offer made to him by the Church in Natal, we advised that he should certify himself—

" 1. That the canonicity of his election was certain.

" 2. That it would be recognised by the Metropolitan and Suffragans as canonical.

" 3. That it would be so recognised by the Church at home.

"Mr. Macrorie may have satisfied himself upon the two first points, but the above-named communications abundantly show that he can have no certainty as to the third. In the interest, then, of Mr. Macrorie himself, as well as of the Church in Natal, it is of the utmost importance that no final step should be taken before all doubt on this point is removed. Mr. Macrorie's position would be a most painful one if after his consecration he should find that the canonicity of his election was not recognised by the Church in this country.

"With reference to the proposed consecration of Mr. Macrorie—while, as I have already intimated, I must withhold my consent to its being performed in my diocese or province, I still adhere to the opinion expressed in the letter addressed by the Bishop of Oxford and myself to Mr. Butler, that there is nothing in Dr. Colenso's legal position to prevent the election of a Bishop to preside over them, by those of our communion in South Africa who, with myself, hold him to have been canonically deposed from his spiritual office.—Believe me, my dear Lord, yours sincerely,   C. T. CANTUAR."

Disappointed in his endeavour to obtain the support of the Home Episcopate, Bishop Gray fell back upon the Lower House of Convocation, where he had good ground for expecting more encouragement. After two days of vigorous debate, the Lower House, on February 20, 1868. passed a long resolution accepting as valid both the deposition and excommunication of Bishop Colenso, and praying for a synodical declaration from the Upper House to the like effect.[1]   On the following day Bishop Wilberforce, who was now less certain than formerly as to the validity of what had been done, moved that the Upper House should postpone taking any action in answer to the prayer, and, while thanking the members of the Lower House for the zeal exhibited in their protest against false teaching, should appoint a Committee to consider the whole subject.   To the general surprise this resolution[2] was seconded by Bishop Tait:—

"I join most heartily," he said, "in admiring, if I may venture to say so, the unselfish courage and devotedness which the Bishop of Capetown has shown in this matter.   I am sure that he has acted throughout under a deep sense of his duty, as a Christian man should, and has shown an example in not swerving from that duty which is worthy of all praise ; but I have ventured at various times to express an opinion that I cannot approve of many of the individual acts to which he has considered that his duty required him to have recourse in the very

---

[1] For the words of this *articulus cleri* see *Chronicle of Convocation*, Feb. 20, 1868, p. 1275-6.

[2] See *Chronicle of Convocation*, Feb. 21, 1868, p. 1296.

difficult conjunctures he had to deal with ; and therefore, if it should appear that any phrases in this resolution are stronger than would naturally have been used by me as conveying my known opinions, I beg it to be understood that I concur in the general expressions of admiration for that courage and goodness, whilst I reserve to myself the right of criticising such acts. . . . We are, and have been always, anxious that these difficulties should be settled, but we feel they are so great that a rash step would do more harm than it would possibly do good. These difficulties are, as has been stated by the Bishop of Oxford, even connected with the canonicity of the proceedings themselves ; they are also complicated by being mixed up with a number of legal constitutional questions. We, of course, are bound by our office, even more than the members of the Lower House, to weigh all these difficulties. We are bound not to take steps which shall in any way conflict either with the law of the Church or that of the State. . . . Therefore that slowness which the outer world has been disposed to interpret as marking a want of sufficient care and anxiety on this matter, has really arisen from the greatness of our desire to take no wrong step on a matter of such importance to the interests of the Church." [1]

The Committee was appointed, with the Bishop of London as its Chairman. On June 30th, 1868, the Committee presented a report, which concluded as follows :—

"With regard, however, to the whole case, with its extreme difficulty, the various complications, the grave doubts in reference to points of law yet unsettled, and the apparent impossibility of any other mode of action, we are of opinion—(1) That substantial justice was done to the accused ; (2) That, though the sentence, having been pronounced by a tribunal not acknowledged by the Queen's Courts, whether civil or ecclesiastical, can claim no legal effect, the Church as a spiritual body may rightly accept its validity."

Bishop Tait dissented from this conclusion, and presented a separate report.

"Independently," it said, "of my views as to the general

<hr>

[1] See *Chronicle of Convocation*, Feb. 21, 1868, p. 1295.

invalidity of the trial, I entertain grave doubts whether, in conducting the proceedings, Bishop Gray did not, in several important points, so far depart from the principles recognised in English Courts of Justice as to make it highly probable that, if the trial had been valid, and had become the subject of appeal on the merits of the case to any well-constituted Court Ecclesiastical, the sentence would have been set aside. These difficulties have all along made me feel that the case of Bishop Colenso cannot be satisfactorily disposed of without fresh proceedings, in lieu of those which I understand to have entirely failed."

In his speech upon the subject he said :—

"The report is valuable, inasmuch as it states all the difficulties of the case, and the three different opinions that have been expressed upon it—the opinion, first, of those who thought the trial was canonical ; secondly, of those who think it was not canonical ; and, lastly, of myself, who think the trial might have been canonical or not, if it had not been of a character which was totally illegal. . . . One word as to the conclusion arrived at in the report, that 'substantial justice' was done to the accused. A man is tried for an offence, and he is either guilty or not, the trial is either valid or not. But, though you may say in conversation that the accused richly deserves the sentence, which I take to be the meaning of the phrase that 'substantial justice' has been done, I do not think a grave body like Convocation should record its opinion in this way. The trial failed, according to the opinion of one large section, because it was not canonical. It failed, in my opinion, because it was null and void in law. . . . The Committee believes that nothing more can be done than to declare we think Bishop Colenso has acted very wrongly, in order to satisfy the minds of our brethren that we have no sympathy with his writings. Any declaration by which that can be made apparent seems to have been made over and over again already, but I have no objection to our repeating it now. If it will be any consolation to anybody, by all means let it be done. I do not think it can be said that this report declares in any way that the Bishop of Capetown has conducted himself properly in all respects. It is obvious that, according to the views of those who signed half the report, he did not. So far as our sympathies are concerned, we have expressed them a hundred times over, and I am only glad that we have opportunity of expressing them again."[1]

The Bishop of Capetown was present during these debates, and was very far from satisfied with the conclusion arrived at :—

"It is not what I should have prepared," he writes, "and is, I think, a feeble production, but it saves the Church of England from complicity with heresy."

On October 10th he left England, after bitterly reproaching the Government for the lack of support accorded to him, and on January 25th, 1869, a few weeks after Bishop Tait's accession to the Primacy, Mr. Macrorie was consecrated in the Cathedral of Capetown, where no Royal Mandate or Licence was required, and became responsible, as Bishop of Maritzburg, for the charge of what Bishop Gray had termed the "widowed diocese" of Natal.

The seven years' controversy was thus ended for a time, so far as the Home Church was concerned. To some it may appear that the issues which had been at stake were of a local and temporary, perhaps even of a personal, character. Such had never been Bishop Tait's opinion. He saw, or thought he saw, in Bishop Gray's action, if it should receive the support of the authorities at home, a very grave peril. Large sums of money had been given for the endowment of Colonial Churches on the understanding, hitherto undisputed, that the doctrinal and disciplinary system of the Mother Church of England should be observed (so far as legal conditions allowed of

---

[1] *Chronicle of Convocation*, July 1, 1868, pp. 1404-1408. The resolutions carried in the Upper House were as follows :—1. That the Report of the Committee be adopted and communicated to the Lower House ; 2. That the remarks thereon of the Lord Bishop of London be also sent to the Lower House.

it) in her daughter Churches in every part of the empire. Difficult as it was to define the manner in which the Royal supremacy was to operate in the varying conditions of Colonial life, Bishop Tait was determined to maintain, so far as in him lay, the rules and liberties which he believed that supremacy to guarantee. The principle for which he and others were contending was well expressed by Mr. Maurice in a letter which he published during the controversy:[1]—

"If the notion [is sanctioned]," he said, "that the jurisdiction of the Queen is a mere vulgar, secular jurisdiction, which must give way, in all graver questions, to the jurisdiction of a Bishop or Metropolitan, I believe the minds of the Colonists will be perplexed as to their political allegiance; and, as to their moral duties, I believe the minds of the natives will be still more perplexed; that there will be no continuance of faith among the first, and no spread of faith among the second. . . . [Bishop Gray] seeks to establish in his colony one law for the clergy and one for the laity—the first to be administered in the name and by the authority of the Metropolitan; the second to be administered in the name and by the officers of the Queen. I do not say that these two laws will be equally administered. I believe the Queen's officers will struggle, under great obstructions, to follow some standard of justice. They will be said to obey a secular instinct. The other tribunal will be what such tribunals have been in other countries; what they have already proved themselves to be in South Africa. Those who are zealous for the well-being of their own countrymen, and of the heathen among whom they dwell, should ask themselves whether they will be parties to so fatal a contradiction. If they are, they may expect to see the example which has been afforded by the Colonies copied here: in England a jurisdiction will be restored which neither we nor our fathers have been able to bear."

No one knew better than Bishop Tait that the time must come when the link would be loosened which united the Colonial dioceses to the Church at home but

---

[1] *Times*, Oct. 4, 1864.

he desired to postpone the change as long as possible, in order that these young Churches might have time to settle themselves firmly upon the lines of English law before they should be called upon to stand alone. He had made it clear from the first that he had no sympathy with Bishop Colenso's opinions, and that his resistance to what he deemed the perilous highhandedness of Bishop Gray was no isolated act of merely personal or local significance. It was part of a definite and well-considered policy. The ecclesiastical despotism which he dreaded and opposed might take one form in South Africa, and some other form, not less mischievous, elsewhere ; and it was his deliberate opinion in later years that the restraints successfully imposed by himself and others upon the impetuous Metropolitan of Capetown had had a wholesome and reassuring effect upon Colonial Churchmanship in every quarter of the globe.

CHAPTER XV.

RITUALISM.

1860-1868.

ALTHOUGH the controversies which turned upon *Essays and Reviews*, and upon the writings of Bishop Colenso, had for some years diverted public attention from Ritual disputations, it is necessary to remember that the Ritual movement was all the while in full swing, and that the Bishop of London, from the necessity of his position, stood at the very centre of the strife, for in those years it was to London—with a few noteworthy exceptions—that Ritual difficulties were confined.   In May 1860, Lord Shaftesbury introduced a Bill into Parliament to restrain Ritualistic novelties,[1] but it perished without even the dignity of a debate, and his intolerance of High Church innovations was tempered for a time by his alliance with Dr. Pusey and others against what was regarded as the yet more dangerous rationalistic school.   Dr. Pusey, on February 17, 1864, wrote to the *Record* what was described in its leading article as "an admirable and faithful letter,"

---

[1] It provided that the Queen in Council might, on the advice of any three of the four Archbishops of England and Ireland, issue orders to regulate the furniture and ornaments of Churches and the vestments of the Clergy.

advocating a union of High and Low Churchmen to resist "the common enemy—unbelief." "The recent miserable, soul-destroying judgment,"[1] he said, "surely requires one united action on the part of every clergyman and lay member of the Church to repudiate it."

Notwithstanding this, the Ritual question came again before the House of Lords on several occasions during the next few years, on the motion of Lord Ebury, Lord Westmeath, and others, and although there was no serious attempt at legislation, Bishop Tait had frequently to answer questions, and even to debate the points at issue. His position at that time was one of singular difficulty. If ultra-Protestant opinion has of recent years taken a more active and organised shape, it is only because, thirty years ago, the Ritualistic movement was supposed by the average British Protestant to be too puny to call for the use of weapons so strong and stern. The public mind, as represented in the daily press, treated the whole thing with sovereign contempt, and the earnest advocates and the hot opponents of the Ritual advance—say, Mr. Bryan King and Lord Westmeath—were impartially ridiculed or impartially ignored. Bishop Tait had better reasons than any other man to know that the force of the movement was altogether underrated by these humorous or supercilious critics. How much of the new departure was doctrinal, and how much was æsthetic, might with him or others be an open question, but the reality of the change that was taking place became more apparent every week. It was in his diocese that the battalions were being armed and organised both for the defence and the attack, and his daily correspondence bore ample evidence to the widening area of the contest. On May 2nd, 1860, was held the first meeting of the English Church Union, with Mr. Colin

---

[1] *i.e.* on *Essays and Reviews.*

Lindsay as its President. On February 7th, 1863, the first number of the *Church Times* appeared, and by the time the Church Association, in November 1865, rallied the militant forces upon the other side, the number of London churches was considerable in which an elaborate and significant ritual was coming into use, as distinguished from what was, comparatively speaking, the mere æstheticism of 'restored' churches, choral services, surpliced choirs, and other orderly and reverent arrangements.[1]

Considering the objections which have in recent years been felt by moderate men of every school to litigation upon these ritual matters, it is curious to notice how general at that time was the opinion of High Churchmen that the questions in dispute might be, and indeed ought to be, set at rest by obtaining fresh decisions in the Courts of Law. It would be easy to multiply examples of this advice being given. The Rev. C. W. Furse, for example, then Vicar of Staines and Rural Dean, a prominent and trusted High Churchman, wrote as follows in a published letter on February 5, 1866 :—

"There is only one efficient mode of settling the vexed question at issue between the extreme Ritualists and the Moderates of the Church of England, and that is the course which was taken in the case of stone altars, crosses on chancel screens, etc. Until the legal question be decided, it is utterly futile to ask Bishops to take steps to suppress, by moral persuasion, such and such practices. We may as well provoke them to preach to the wind. . . . The silence of the law, if continued, may provoke priests to claim licence instead of liberty, and Bishops to mistake irritable impatience for a firm administration of the Church's law."[2]

---

[1] On the æsthetic rather than doctrinal character of these changes, see an important letter written by Bishop Wilberforce to Archbishop Longley on Dec. 16, 1865 (*Wilberforce's Life*, vol. iii. p. 188). See also the speech of Lord Nelson in the House of Lords on May 14, 1867 (*Hansard*, p. 506).

[2] *Guardian*, Feb. 7, 1866, p. 123.

The Ritual question, as has been said, was occasionally mooted in the House of Lords, but so far as this book is concerned, the Parliamentary discussions were of little moment until the year 1867, when Lord Shaftesbury, as will be seen below, made a vigorous attempt to procure coercive legislation in the direction he desired. And, strange to say, Convocation had been silent on the subject. During the eleven years that had elapsed since its revival in 1854, not a single debate of any importance had taken place upon the Ritual question. But the prominence which the movement had assumed in 1865, both in Parliament and outside, rendered that silence no longer possible. On February 1, 1866, weighty deputations were received by the Archbishop of Canterbury and the Prime Minister, and Archbishop Longley's replies excited wide attention. Archdeacon Wordsworth [1] headed the first and most important of these deputations, and presented a memorial "in reference to the recent introduction into the celebration of Divine Service of practices which, by their diversity, and by their deviation from law and from long-established usage, are disturbing the peace and impairing the efficiency of the Church." The spirit of the innovators, he said, in his speech, "seems to be sectarian in its character, and schismatical in its practices, inasmuch as it divides the Church into parties, wastes her energies, and casts stumbling-blocks in the way of souls for which Christ died." [2]

To a subsequent deputation from members of the English Church Union and others, who deprecated "any alteration being made in the Book of Common Prayer, respecting the ornaments of the Church and of the ministers thereof," the Archbishop said :—

"I have already declared my determination never to consent

[1] Afterwards Bishop of Lincoln.   [2] *Guardian*, Feb. 7, 1866, p. 138.

to any alteration in any part of the Book of Common Prayer, without the full concurrence of Convocation. I could not, however, concur in giving countenance to the extreme ritualism that has been adopted in some churches. I cannot but feel that those who have violated a compromise and settlement which has existed for three hundred years, and are introducing vestments and ceremonies of very doubtful legality, are really, though I am sure quite unconsciously, doing the work of the worst enemies of the Church. . . . I confess I have witnessed with feelings of deep sorrow the tone of defiance with which the recently introduced practices have in some instances been supported. I fear that such advocates know not what spirit they are of, and I would fain hope that they may still learn to adopt something more of Christian moderation and Christian humility, that, with S. Paul, they may be ready to acknowledge that there are many things which may be lawful and yet not expedient, and that they may be more ready to lend a willing ear to the pastoral and paternal counsels of those who are set over them in the Lord."

Convocation was to meet in a few days, and it was evident that the thorny Ritual problem would at last be handled in the proper quarter. In a clear and weighty speech, the Dean of Ely, Dr. Harvey Goodwin, introduced, on February 8, 1866, a series of resolutions upon the subject, and, at the request of Archdeacon Denison, a Committee of the Lower House was appointed—the first of its kind— to consider and report upon "such measures as may seem fit for clearing the doubts and allaying the anxieties" to which copious allusion had been made. In the course of the discussion which, in the Upper House, preceded the appointment of the Committee, Bishop Tait spoke as follows :—

"Of course we naturally view these subjects from different standpoints. The Church of England is very wide, embracing persons of very various opinions within the limits of our common faith, and the Episcopal Bench would not be a true representation of the Church, if within our own body there was not that variance of sentiment in minor matters which exists in the Church itself. But there are limits beyond which the practices in question cannot be allowed to go, and if men's differences are so expressed that they are practically obtruding themselves on the public in our worship, and interfering with the liberty of the Christian community, I am sure that there is not one of our body who will not desire, by persuasion or any other means, to induce those persons who infringe the liberty of the Christian community to desist from the practices we condemn. Whether or not the persons attached to this excessive ritualism have a Rome-ward tendency I do not pretend to decide. I trust they have not ; but that they have the ill-luck to be extremely like persons who have a Rome-ward tendency I think cannot be denied. That persons well acquainted with theology, persons of the calmest minds, persons willing to admit perfect liberty in the Church of England, are assured of the Rome-ward tendencies of these practices none of us can doubt. I have heard of a distinguished divine of very calm mind[1] being present at one of the churches where these practices were resorted to, with a view of satisfying himself as to what was going on, and being so shocked that he felt he could not, without a compromise of all that was dear to him, partake of the Lord's Supper at the hands of the persons who were officiating, so like was it to the Roman fashion. . . . I see nothing, I read nothing, which is brought before the public, which has the slightest chance of inducing persons who believe them to be inclined towards the errors of Rome to alter that opinion. On the contrary, I contend that works which they circulate amongst their flocks, which seem to favour the worst errors of the Church of Rome, and the general appearance which they make of sympathy with Rome, deserve the serious consideration of the leaders of this movement. . . .

" It is a serious thing that the time of the Bishops should be occupied so much as it is by complaints from parishes in their dioceses ; and if it is a serious evil that the time of the Bishops should be so occupied, what must be the evil in the parishes themselves, when a Christian community is agitated about the shape of tunicles, or the number of candles to be lighted during the day—while the ministers of the Gospel exhibit to the careless and the worldly the unseemly spectacle of contention about matters which worldly men regard as contemptible. . . . How is this evil to be dealt with ? The most satisfactory way of

---

[1] The " divine " alluded to was Archbishop Trench, who had been in communication with Bishop Tait upon the subject.

dealing with it will certainly be by good and intelligent men, who have sympathy with these innovations, coming to the rational and right conclusion that they ought to be guided by their Bishops in this matter, and if they did not desire to be guided by the opinion of a single Bishop, they might be content to be guided by the expression of your Grace's opinion, and by what they might ascertain to be the universal sentiment of the whole of the Bishops of England. That would be a highly satisfactory way of dealing with the subject, for men would be doing what they should have done long ago : namely, submit themselves to the decision of those whom God had placed over them in His Church. We are told that we ought to enforce the law, and if need be we must enforce the law, but what an unpleasant position would that place us in—a position from which any one would shrink, inasmuch as we should be involved in the prosecution of some of the best men in our dioceses. I deprecate following such cases from court to court for many reasons, not the least because I cannot bear that one whose title in the Church is that of a Father in God should prosecute the very persons for whom he has a deep respect. . . . If the laity feel that their liberty is infringed in this matter, they have a very plain course before them ; namely, to strengthen the hands of the executive of the Church. But if any mode of strengthening the hands of the Ordinary be adopted, I should greatly desire that it should be done with many safeguards. I should wish that the individual Bishop should be assisted by whatever counsellors might be thought desirable in treating of these questions, and I believe that if such power were exercised by the Ordinary, subject to the proper appeal pointed out by law, it would tend to calm many dissensions in the Church. My own experience is that many of these disputes do not arise from disputed law so much as from matters of disputed discretion, and that persons who are unwilling to submit themselves perhaps to a newly ordained priest will submit themselves to the Church of which he is the minister—to the Bishop of the diocese, calmly deciding after full consultation, subject to an appeal to the Archbishop of the province."[1]

---

[1] *Chronicle of Convocation*, Feb. 9, 1866, pp. 156, etc. It is noteworthy that the suggestion here made in general terms for the solution of ritual difficulties is precisely that to which he tried eight years afterwards to give effect when drafting the Public Worship Regulation Bill of 1874.

A strong Committee of the Lower House was appointed, and its meetings were prolonged and anxious, for it was obvious that weighty consequences might depend on its report. The Dean of Ely was its chairman, and Archdeacon Denison presided when he was absent. A special interest belongs to its Report, as the first of many documents of a similar kind. It is dated June 5, 1866, and it treats in detail of the various Ritual points at issue —Vestments ; Altar Lights ; Incense ; Elevation of the Elements ; the encouragement of non-communicating attendance, and the use of wafer bread. After full debate in the Lower House, the Report was adopted in its entirety, with scarcely a dissentient voice, "as a temperate statement on the subject of Ritual practice in the Church of England," and its conclusions may best be summarised by quoting the resolution, adopted without a division, on the motion of Archdeacon Denison himself :—

"That with regard to the six points of ritual which have been specially discussed in the Report, the judgment of the House is as follows :—1. That the use in parish churches of the surplice is a sufficient compliance with the directions of the Church. 2. That without pronouncing on the legality of the vestments prescribed in the First Book of King Edward vi., or of altar lights, the House considers that they should not be introduced into any parish church without reference to the Bishop, and that a similar reference should be made with regard to the introduction of incense in the simpler manner described in the Report. 3. That the House expresses its entire disapproval of the practice of censing persons and things, and of all elevation of the elements after consecration, and considers that the presence of non-communicants, excepting in special cases, during the celebration of the Holy Communion, and the use of wafer bread, are to be discouraged."[1]

This important resolution, the deliberate outcome of no small debate, was communicated to the Upper House on June 29th, too late for any discussion by the Bishops

---

[1] *Chronicle of Convocation*, June 28, 1866, p. 562.

in that session.   Ample time was thus given for its consideration, and on the House assembling in the following February (1867), the Bishops, after two days of debate, agreed unanimously upon a long resolution, which was moved by Bishop Wilberforce, and seconded by Bishop Tait.   After setting forth in careful terms the dangers attaching to an undue Ritualism, the Bishops' resolution ended with the following words : " Our judgment is that no alterations from long-sanctioned and usual ritual ought to be made in our churches, until the sanction of the Bishop of the diocese has been obtained thereto." [1]

In this 'judgment' the Lower House was formally invited to concur, and again there was an ample debate. In the end the Lower House resolved, with only three dissentients,

"That this House, having regard to the Ritual observances treated of in the Report presented to the House on the 26th June 1866, do concur in the judgment of the Upper House, that no alteration from the long-sanctioned and usual ritual ought to be made in our churches until the sanction of the Bishop of the diocese has been obtained thereto." [2]

It has seemed worth while to record these facts with care, as the first occasion on which the revived Provincial Synod of Canterbury came to a deliberate resolution upon the Ritual questions which were agitating the Church. Some two hundred and forty-five closely-printed pages of the Chronicle of Convocation are occupied with these particular debates, and the ultimate unanimity, after so much discussion, is almost, if not quite, without a parallel.   But the judgment, important as it was, could have no coercive force without State aid, and the scene was now shifted from the Jerusalem Chamber to the House of Lords.

[1] *Chronicle of Convocation*, Feb. 13, 1867, p. 711.
[2] *Ibid.* Feb. 15, 1867, p. 843.

In that assembly three peers, Lord Ebury, Lord Westmeath, and Lord Shaftesbury, had been long maintaining,
each from his own point of view, that the rubrics of the
Church required reform.　Lord Ebury had been the most
persistent of the three, and it was not in his opinion a
question of Ritualism alone.　His principal gravamen,
indeed, was the compulsory use of the Burial Service, and
on this subject he had for years been urging that a Royal
Commission should be issued.　His case was now
strengthened by the new and larger Rubrical difficulties
that had arisen, and many who had hitherto opposed his
annual motion were now ranged upon his side in asking
for a Royal Commission to consider not the Burial Service
only, but the whole rubrics of the Prayer Book.

Lord Shaftesbury was not among these.　He was all
in favour of immediate legislation to set at rest the question of the Eucharistic vestments, and he obtained a half
promise of support from Archbishop Longley, and from
many other Bishops, for a bill which he proposed to introduce to that effect.　The Archbishop, on further consideration, preferred to introduce a bill of his own ; but
this plan was abandoned, at the instigation of Bishop
Wilberforce, on the Government's announcing that a
Royal Commission would be issued.[1]　Lord Shaftesbury
was thereupon pressed by Bishop Tait and others, including the Archbishop himself, to postpone his action for a
time, and to await the first Report of the Commission, but
he stoutly and bluntly refused to do anything of the sort,
and on May 14, 1867, he moved the second reading of
his ' Clerical Vestments Bill.'　The bill as proposed gave
the force of law to Canon 58, which enjoins " that every
minister saying the public prayers, or ministering the

---

[1] The story of what passed is told in Bishop Wilberforce's *Life*, vol. iii.
pp. 205-212.

sacraments or other rites of the Church, shall wear a decent and comely surplice, with sleeves, to be provided at the charge of the parish."

Lord Shaftesbury's speech was an elaborate and weighty indictment of the extremer ritualistic practices and books. He was armed with abundant quotations from such sources, and although his own words were unusually temperate and calm the speech gave great offence to High Churchmen.

Archbishop Longley, "while expressing his full agreement with the greater part of the noble earl's powerful address, and his sympathy with the indignation he had expressed, urged the advantage of waiting for the action of the Royal Commission about to be appointed, and moved the postponement of the second reading."

Bishop Tait followed :—

"I should be very sorry," he said, "were an erroneous impression to prevail in the country as to the feelings of those who sit on this bench with regard to the noble earl's bill. I believe I speak the sentiments of this bench generally when I say that we are obliged to the noble earl for the clear and temperate manner in which he has laid this matter before the House to-night. We are all agreed with him in believing that a very great evil exists, and that it is our duty to endeavour to remedy this evil. . . . But I am not sanguine enough to suppose that either by the carrying of his or of any other bill, or by the most mature deliberations of any Commission, the evils the noble earl deplores will suddenly disappear. . . . Believing, as I do, that the time has now arrived for action, if the noble earl perseveres with his bill, I shall be prepared to fulfil my promise, and to support it. Still, I do not believe that mere Acts of Parliament, however carefully prepared, can cure the evil : and one important defect in the present bill is that it proposes to deal with one branch only of the subject. My impression is we must go thoroughly into the whole matter, and this can only be done by such a Commission as the noble earl at the head of Her Majesty's Government has promised we shall have. That Commission must extend its investigations to a wide range of subjects. I do not wish that it should touch doctrine; but whatever bears upon public worship must come within its sphere. One thing, it appears, would be a necessary result of the deliberations of such a Commission—the law must be made clear. I do not mean that liberty should be altogether restrained, but that liberty shall be legally secured, not licence seized by individuals in the hope that they may escape in immunity from the consequences of their licence. . . . Any legislation which is to be complete, having settled what the law is, must also strengthen the hands of the central authority, whatever it is to be—whether we refer to the Bishop called on by appeal from the laity, or the Bishop subject to the Archbishop, the central authority must be strengthened. . . . Depend upon it, if this nation once loses its Protestant character, it will suffer very greatly in the position it occupies. I believe that the Church of England has before it at this moment as great a work as ever lay before any Church. It is a time, I think, for anxiety, but not a time for alarm, still less for despondency. Even in these very eccentricities there is some proof of zeal, and zeal is a good thing. This Church more than any other has power to deal with the civilisation of this age—to deal with the very dangers civilisation causes—it is the Church's duty not to thwart the course of events; but while it follows, at the same time to lead and guide the men of the nineteenth century, and this I believe our Church can do beyond any other body, either of our Protestant or Roman Catholic brethren." [1]

On a division being taken, Lord Shaftesbury's bill was thrown out by sixty-one votes to forty-six. Seven Bishops voted in the majority, and eleven (including Bishop Tait) in the minority. A fortnight later [2] the Royal Commission was appointed to inquire into " the varying interpretations put upon the rubrics, orders, and directions for regulating the course and conduct of public worship, the administration of the sacraments, and the other services contained in the Book of Common Prayer . . . with a view of explaining or amending the said rubrics . . . so

---

[1] *Hansard*, May 14, 1867, p. 507, etc.

[2] The Commission is dated June 3, 1867.

as to secure general uniformity of practice in such matters as may be deemed essential."

Among the Commissioners were the Archbishop of Canterbury, the Bishops of London and Oxford, the Deans of Ely and Westminster, Lord Beauchamp, Sir Robert Phillimore, Mr. Beresford Hope, Mr. J. G. Hubbard, Canon Gregory, and nineteen others—twenty-nine in all. Lord Shaftesbury was invited, but declined to serve. The Commissioners began their sittings on June 17th, and issued their first Report on August 19th. This Report was confined to the ' burning question ' of the Eucharistic vestments, and the Commissioners' recommendation was practically unanimous :—

"We find," they said, "that whilst these vestments are regarded by some witnesses as symbolical of doctrine, and by others as a distinctive vesture, whereby they desire to do honour to the Holy Communion as the highest act of Christian worship, they are by none regarded as essential, and they give grave offence to many.

"We are of opinion that it is expedient to restrain in the public services of the United Church of England and Ireland all variations in respect of vesture from that which has long been the established usage of the said United Church, and we think that this may be best secured by providing aggrieved parishioners with an easy and effectual process for complaint and redress."

Five weeks after the issue of this Report came the meeting of the first Lambeth Conference, or " Pan-Anglican Synod," and the unwonted muster of American and Colonial Bishops, together with the Colenso controversies narrated in the last chapter, once more diverted the attention of churchmen from the Ritual question. But only for a time. When Convocation met in February 1868, the Bishop of London, at Archbishop Longley's request, re-opened the discussions in the Upper House, by moving the following resolution :—

"That this House, viewing with anxious concern the increasing diversity of practice in regard to ritual observances, as causing additional disquietude and contention, and perceiving with deep regret that the resolutions adopted by the Convocations of Canterbury and York have failed to secure unity, deems it expedient for the peace of the Church—1st, That the limits of ritual observance should not be left to the uncontrolled discretion of individual churchmen, and therefore ought to be defined by rightful authority ; 2d, That some easy and inexpensive process should be provided whereby, while the liberties of the officiating clergymen and their parishioners are protected, the evils of unrestrained licence in such matters may be checked."

In making this motion, the Bishop called attention to the evidence given before the Ritual Commission and published in the Blue Book, as showing that the recommendations of Convocation in the previous spring had fallen upon deaf ears.

"I am afraid," he said, "that with regard to certain persons who are promoters of these observances we must take it for granted, through their own declarations in their evidence, that they do not regard the decision which this House arrived at as in any way binding. They apparently are unwilling to be guided by their individual Bishops ; they are unwilling to be guided by the collective voice of the Bishops expressed in their visitations : they are unwilling to be guided by the decision of the Provincial Synod of Canterbury, or of the Provincial Synod of York, or by the united opinion of those two Synods when their decisions are compared together, . . . and I cannot really understand by what they would be guided except by their own individual will. True, it is stated that persons who think it right to act in this way would be guided by a General Council. Well, I do not know that a General Council is exactly the body which is to settle the ritual of a particular National Church : I think one of our Articles seems to imply that each National Church has to settle these matters for itself, and not that we are to wait till a General Council settles them. I mention this to show that the kindly intended advice which we gave in our collective and individual capacities has not succeeded. . . . Our efforts have proved a failure : this evil, be it what it may, exists unchecked, the disquietude in the public mind is increasing, and the contentions also, I am sorry to say, are increasing, and the question now arises whether anything further can be done by us to bring matters to a better state. . . . Now, for my own part, I think I may say that I have always endeavoured to act in a large and kindly spirit towards those who are advocates of these practices. I desire that my own conscience shall be respected, and I desire also that the consciences of others shall be respected, and whether in matters of doctrine, or in allowable matters of practice, I think that within due limits in the National Church we ought, as completely as we possibly can, to act upon that principle. I certainly have had very kindly intercourse during the time of my Episcopate with persons of almost every shade of opinion in my diocese, and I believe that if any blame is to be attached to me in these matters, it is rather the blame of having allowed people to act for themselves than of having interfered where I might have been expected to interfere, to restrain and curb their liberty. . . . It may be the case that certain of the points in dispute can be settled without fresh legislation—it may be the case that the courts of justice may settle some of these questions. I shall be very glad if they are so settled, provided they are settled speedily ; but I do not think we should allow a long time to pass now while these matters are the sport of the advocates in various courts ; and my experience of the ecclesiastical courts is that, with many virtues, they do not possess the virtue of speed. . . . Whatever is the mode which is adopted, I think we cannot be wrong in saying there ought to be some easy and inexpensive process whereby ‘ the evils of unrestrained ‘ licence in such matters may be checked.’ The only other point on which I ought to say a word is, ‘ Do you really think that your declaration will have any effect?’ I think it will. . . . If it be said that after all there is no binding power in these resolutions, I am afraid we must allow that that is a condition under which a Synod such as this exists. We cannot bind people by laws made by ourselves, but we can express our opinion in condemnation of these practices, and express our earnest hope that the ambiguity which betrays our brethren into these excesses may be removed. We are bound to do this for the sake of our brethren, and for the sake of the law of this country, and the authorities in ecclesiastical matters are to blame in allowing that ambiguity to exist which betrays the unwary. Men are very willing to obey laws when they understand what they are, but when you make them such that no human being can say what they mean, those who have the power of making the laws plain are much to blame in permitting that ambiguity to remain."[1]

After a long and memorable debate Bishop Tait's resolution in a modified form was adopted by the Bishops, with only one dissentient, and was sent to the Lower House for its concurrence. The debate which there arose upon it was not concluded when the prorogation took place. When Convocation reassembled on June 30th. the Ritual Commissioners had issued their second Report, and the debate — by request of the Archbishop—was accordingly allowed to drop.[2]

It will be observed that in the foregoing speech the Bishop claimed that he had always "acted in a large and kindly spirit" towards the Ritualistic clergy in his diocese. It may be right to see how far his statement is borne out by facts. The events and arguments which this chapter has hitherto chronicled were of a general and public sort, and it has sometimes been maintained that while the Bishop spoke smooth things and claimed a tolerant spirit in his utterances to the world at large, he was all the while worrying and even persecuting those of his own clergy who adopted an elaborate ritual in their churches.

Correspondents of the Church newspapers in those years were constantly reiterating such a charge. The Bishop is described, for example, as "a tyrant to the weak and a sycophant to the strong "; or again, as "that ecclesiastical bully, the Presbyterian-minded Bishop of London, who with all his professions of large-heartedness and toleration, has shown himself to be as narrow-minded

<hr>

[1] *Chronicle of Convocation*, 18th February 1868, pp. 1056, etc.

[2] *Ibid.* 30th June 1868, p. 1374.

a bigot and as un-Christian a gentleman as ever disgraced a Bishopric "; and there is much more to the same effect.[1] To this mere abuse he attached no great importance, but the difficulties of the position are illustrated by such a correspondence as the following :—

The Rev. —— —— *to the Bishop of London.*

"*5th Feb.* 1866.

" MY DEAR LORD,—Almost every post brings me some circular or form of address to somebody on the subject of Ritual. One says boldly that it wants to put down Tractarianism ; another mysteriously hints at 'certain practices' contrary to the custom of the Church, and so on. I suppose that all these are attacks on clergymen who like myself have what is called high ritual, and even hope that in time they may peacefully and profitably have more of it. Now nothing could better serve our purpose than what wears the appearance of an inconsiderate and uncharitable agitation, were it not that it helps us *too fast*. For instance, in my own church, vestments and high ritualistic practices, which six months ago would have offended very many, grieved not a few who are too good to take offence, and pleased hardly any one, are now calmly talked about, instruction sought in their meaning and use, and the things themselves asked for by many. . . . The feeling of appreciation of high ritual is very much more widely spread than is generally supposed : it is in many cases very intent, and, more than that, very bent upon being gratified. . . . I am one of the Council of the English Church Union, and I signed their memorial to the Archbishop against altering the Rubrics or touching the Prayer Book in any way ; but I desire nothing *less* for myself and for my party than to be left to carry out these rubrics unregulated and unadvised by the Ordinary, guided only by individual taste, notion, or discretion, or driven on by lay pressure. The feeling that one is regarded as lawless has a tendency to beget lawlessness ; besides, it exposes us to the influence of those who *are* lawless and want to make us so. Then the effect on the High Church laity is

---

[1] See, for example, letters in the *Church Times*, 1867, pp. 282, 283, etc., and (in milder language) in the *Guardian* of 1865, pp. 715, 739, etc.

very injurious. While *we* may invariably deplore our position and be in heart and spirit most desirous of submitting to authority (however openly we seem to act without it), *they* come to have no such feeling, and presently are developed into despisers of Bishops. . . . But if being left to act by our own discretion did no other harm, it would be intolerable as presenting the unseemly spectacle of anarchy and self-rule in a Church which in theory is a model of order. Conceive, my dear Lord, our misery—for we would be loyal as well as honest men—in *fearing* that the Bishop should visit our Churches or hear of our doings.

"Some would say that I have made out a good case against high ritual, and shown how much evil attends it. I admit it, but then, as I need not point out to your Lordship who has frankly and generously owned it, very great spiritual good has been done under it, not to say by means of it. Besides, high ritual is an established fact ; we cannot do away with it. This is what I very humbly and respectfully ask the Bishops to consider, and so to take us in hand as those who have, it may be, odd ways of their own, but who yet may be regulated and influenced as they need to be by their spiritual fathers. . . . Do not let us alone as those hopelessly beyond the pale of approval. In the beginning of any revival it is well perhaps that the visible and audible workers should be those who have comparatively little official responsibility resting upon them ; but when the revival has established for itself a footing, it must be guided in its further progress by those in authority. It may be that if we were left alone, in a few years the movement would regulate itself and settle down soberly and satisfactorily, but in the meantime a miserable school, that of the *Church Times*, is being formed and stereotyped to the spiritual injury of its disciples, and the offence, the grievous offence of all good sober Christians. It is *authority* only that can help us, and authority I am sure will be duly respected if it will cautiously take us in hand.—I am, my dear Lord, your Lordship's very obedient servant,   ——— ———."

The Bishop of London to the Rev. —— ——.

"LONDON HOUSE, *Feby.* 10th, 1866.

"MY DEAR MR. ——,—I have read your letter of the 5th very carefully. I certainly should advise any Bishop who consulted me, and I should be ready myself to act on the rule, that where any of his clergy intimate their readiness to be guided by the Ordinary in matters of Ritual, the Ordinary should show himself willing to give such guidance. But on the other hand, I do not think that it is wise in a Bishop to undertake to offer advice where he is made to understand that, unless what he says coincides with the preconceived opinion of the person seeking advice, it will be treated as of no value. I have, of course, examined and considered all or most of the questions now agitating the Church respecting Ritual, and I fully believe that I am well qualified by this fact, as well as by my office, to give proper guidance. If, therefore, you or any other of the clergy will ask for such guidance with a *bona fide* intention of being guided, I am at your service. But I do not think it would be well, by interfering unduly, to run the risk of appearing to sanction practices which there is no intention of altering whether I disapprove of them or no. I shall be very glad indeed to hear that such guidance as I have indicated is sought.—Believe me to be, my dear Mr. ——, yours very truly,   A. C. LONDON."

These letters suggest some of the difficulties which beset the Bishop's action in those disturbed years, but it is important that the facts should be made quite clear, and this can best be done by looking in detail at some typical instances of his dealings with parishes in which an 'advanced' Ritual was in use. Something has been said in a former chapter about his relations to St. Paul's, Knightsbridge, St. Mary Magdalene's, Munster Square, and the old parish of St. George's in the East.[1] A few other examples may now be given.

The Church of All Saints, Margaret Street, was consecrated on May 28th, 1859. It had formerly, as a proprietary chapel, been under the charge of Mr. Frederick Oakeley, Bishop Tait's old tutor and friend, who has left a graphic picture of the character and circumstances of his ministry, from 1839 to 1845, in this the first outpost of the

---

[1] See pp. 215-249.

Tractarians in London.[1]   Mr. Oakeley was received in 1845 into the Church of Rome, and in 1849, Mr. Upton Richards, who had been Mr. Oakeley's curate, was appointed incumbent of the Chapel, to which a district was now for the first time assigned.   In the opening years of Bishop Tait's Episcopate, the Chapel of All Saints was, so to speak, the *propugnaculum* of the extreme High Churchmen in London, and complaints (often vague and foolish) against its ritual and doctrine were incessantly arriving.   To most of these the Bishop paid no heed, but in November 1858, a correspondence passed between him and Mr. Richards, to which it is necessary to allude.   One of Mr. Richards' curates, the son of an incumbent in the diocese, joined the Church of Rome.   The father complained bitterly to the Bishop, who wrote at once to Mr. Richards, and took occasion at the same time to remonstrate against the continued use of Altar Lights at All Saints, notwithstanding the judgment delivered by Dr. Lushington in the Consistorial Court of the Diocese.[2]   Mr. Richards was dissatisfied with Dr. Lushington's *dictum*, and thought the question ought, by fresh litigation, to be carried to the Privy Council for decision. Bishop Tait, on the other hand, retained his opinion that litigation on such points was eminently undesirable.   The importance attaching, from an historical point of view, to this difference of opinion will perhaps justify the reproduction of the following letters :—

The Rev. W. Upton Richards to the Bishop of London.

"ALBANY ST., 18 *Nov.* 1858.

"MY LORD,— . . . I beg to renew my assurance to your Lordship of my desire to yield to you not only a canonical, but

---

[1] *Historical Notes on the Tractarian Movement*, Part iii. pp. 58-82.

[2] See p. 219.

a hearty and loving obedience in all things in which I am not called upon to give up my own principles. . . . Your Lordship will, I trust, pardon me for reminding you that there have always been in the Church of England, as there now are, two distinct views held by different parties within her pale, and I believe that the great object of the compilers of the Liturgy was so to frame it, that room might be given for the expression of the views of both. The Liturgy and Articles ought, I think, to be regarded as a great compromise, in which the middle course between the two contending parties was adopted, and so while both are at liberty to hold their own opinions, so are they at liberty to carry them out as they please, provided they keep within the letter of the law, the one party not exceeding, the other not falling short of, the terms agreed upon. This I believe to be the spirit of the law which governs the Church, and I conceive it to be of the last importance that this spirit should be maintained. It is, as I believe, one great office of the constituted authorities of the Church to maintain this principle inviolate, and I cannot think that, in asserting my right of appeal to the laws of the Church, I am in any way setting myself against these authorities. It is the privilege of every suitor to appeal in all cases in which he believes himself to have a fair ground to do so, and I am not aware that in any appeal to the highest tribunal the appellant is ever considered to show any disrespect to the judge from whose decision he appeals. On the contrary, it is, so far as my observation goes, always a matter of satisfaction to the Judge that any error he may have committed may be redressed by the higher tribunal.

"Your Lordship says that the interpretation of the law given in your Consistorial Court has no weight with me. My Lord, I beg most respectfully to deny having written any such thing. To speak disrespectfully of your Consistory Court would be an offence; to express any want of confidence in the individual who exercises the office of the Judge is, I submit, quite another thing, and is my undoubted right. . . .

"Of course, I do not mean to assert that the use of the lights is in any way essential, or has in itself any virtue, but I do believe that this is one of the outworks of the Church's citadel, and that in contending for this, as for every other rite which the law of the Church permits, I am only contending for those protections which the piety and wisdom of our forefathers have thrown around sacred things. The ceremonies which the Church of England has retained are few and simple enough, if all were conceded for which I and those who think with me contend, and I believe that in proportion as we refrain from the use of them, we shall encourage and propagate the laxity which prevails among us.

"These, my Lord, are some of the reasons which induce me to think that it would not be right for me to discontinue the use of lights at the Holy Communion, and I trust that they will be such as to induce you to withdraw the requirement contained in your letter.   But if not, then I must still hope that your Lordship will allow the question to be placed in such a form as may enable us to ascertain what the law really is.   If I am wrong in this (which it is my conscientious belief I am not) I assure your Lordship I shall readily and dutifully submit myself; but entertaining the very strong conviction which I have endeavoured to express to you, I can only hope that I shall not be accused of maintaining an unlawful practice against the commands of constituted authority, or of asserting that your authority is nothing unless it be enforced in a Court of Law, if, in the spirit of S. Paul I appeal to the highest judicial authority in this realm.—I am, my Lord, your Lordship's faithful servant,

"W. UPTON RICHARDS."

The Bishop of London to the Rev. W. Upton Richards.

"LONDON HOUSE, *Dec.* 15, 1858.

"REV. AND DEAR SIR,— . . . I gather from your letter of the 18th Nov. that you altogether decline to pay obedience to my advice, given in accordance with the exposition of the law made in the Consistorial Court of the Diocese, that the candles shall not be lighted on the Communion Table at the celebration of the Lord's Supper in broad daylight, unless I enforce obedience by process of law.   Now, giving due weight to all you have said on this point, I cannot look upon the course you have the intention of following as one consistent with the regard due to my office and your canonical obligations.   I may not deem it right to agitate the public mind by a lawsuit on the subject of candles, and yet I think I may fairly require you to desist from a practice which, after very mature consideration, I have satisfied myself cannot be regarded as consistent with the law, especially as you have adduced no proof that the practice was introduced at first into your church otherwise than by your own private authority. I am quite sure that any of your people who now attach importance to the practice will be quite satisfied that you should give it up if you explain to them that you do so from not wishing to put yourself into the painful position of disobeying your Diocesan. . . . Sincerely regretting that these painful difficulties should exist.—I remain, Rev. and dear Sir, yours faithfully,

"A. C. LONDON."

The beautiful and costly church erected in 1858 by the munificence of Mr. Beresford Hope and others[1] to replace the very unecclesiastical edifice in which Mr. Oakeley and Mr. Richards had ministered was duly consecrated on May 28, 1859. Appeals were made to the Bishop that he would use the occasion of his sermon on that day to protest against the 'Popish mummeries' of its ornaments and services, and there was excitement on both sides as to what he was likely to say. Taking as his text 1 Cor. viii. 9, "Take heed lest by any means this liberty of yours become a stumbling-block to them that are weak," he described the circumstances of the Corinthian Church and the practice of St. Paul :—

"We see," he said, "that St. Paul had one rule, though his practice might appear to vary. He had no objection to innocent liberty and the indulgence of old associations, if they did not interfere with the purity and simplicity of the Gospel of Jesus Christ. He had no objection to men following the bent of their own tastes in matters indifferent, if they did not endeavour to force those things indifferent as commands of God upon their brethren. He gladly showed by his own practice that he thought those points indifferent, as well by complying with them when he could do so, in furtherance of the Gospel, as by resisting them when Christian truth required it. Would, my brethren, that we

---

[1] Mr. Beresford Hope's contribution, including the gift of the site, is said to have amounted to about £70,000. One anonymous donor gave about £30,000, and another £4000, towards the cost of the building. See *Guardian*, 1869, p. 461.

could at all times approach similar questions in St. Paul's spirit, free from all strife and uncharitableness, yet never flinching from maintaining the paramount majesty of Christian truth. . . . This building which we are met to consecrate to-day, during its time of erection, has been a sort of rallying-point for two sorts of persons, who have sought—the one to exaggerate every point in its ornamental details, as if the richness of its ornaments was necessarily connected with unsound doctrines and a dereliction of the pure Gospel of the Lord Jesus Christ; the other, as if this beautiful and expensive adornment secured a holier worship and more lasting impression of spiritual truths on wavering human souls. My friends, I appeal to all of you, as you shall answer to God, in soberness to consider that the costly beauty of this house in which you worship does neither of itself secure nor endanger your Christian faith. . . . There are, of course, two kinds of minds within our pale, one of which takes great pleasure in such costly ornaments as now surround us; the other, which finds in them no help to its earnest aspirations after spiritual truth. The latter class, I presume, are not likely to be found often amongst the worshippers in this place. To the former I would say, in all affectionateness, while you thankfully acknowledge the munificence with which this church has been prepared to suit your peculiar tastes, be very careful, I beseech you, that in all your worship here, you surround yourselves, through the Lord Jesus Christ's help, with a beauty far above that of outward adornment —the beauty of a pure Gospel faith, and of a simple, earnest, self-denying Christian life. I truly believe that in these days, both amongst High Church and Low Church, there are persons who are tired of the miserable controversies that have long divided Christendom, and who simply desire, while using the liberty allowed them to follow their own tastes in things indifferent, to worship the Lord Jesus Christ faithfully, and to follow Him in their lives. God grant that the church opened this day may be no cause of any fresh dissensions, but a fresh help to those whose tastes it gratifies to serve the Lord faithfully according to the form they love. . . . Beware also lest, in your zeal for antiquity, you be not ancient enough—going back to the wavering followers of the Apostles, and not to the Apostles themselves. Alas! we must speak in this language of warning, for the age in which we live has produced many sad examples of very many persons, trained in the pure Gospel teaching of our Apostolic Church, led away by excited feelings to the miserable worship of human saints and the Lord's human Mother, into which in their calmer moments they never would have believed that they could have fallen. God grant that those who teach and those who worship in this church may ever be kept by the Spirit of God safe from these and from all delusions—that their abundant labours of self-denying love may never be tainted by an unscriptural dependence on human ministrations or human traditions in preference to the Word of God. Ah, my friends, however different may be our opinions, there is great and abundant work before all of us, to labour heartily, simply, and prayerfully in the midst of a world and of a city lying in wickedness, to advance the kingdom of Him who died to save poor human erring souls. God grant that we may all labour in that work heartily, faithfully, and in a loving spirit, as in the sight of the Lord Jesus Christ."

Similar in some respects to All Saints, Margaret Street, was the still more notable case of St. Alban's, Holborn. This church, too, was the gift of a wealthy layman, Mr. J. G. Hubbard (afterwards Lord Addington), who not only erected the building at his own cost,[1] but gave £5000 as endowment, and for some time £100 a year for each of two curates. The church was not completed till 1863, but a year previously the Rev. A. H. Mackonochie was nominated by Mr. Hubbard as the first vicar of the newly constituted parish,—a parish consisting of some of the worst streets and alleys to be found in London. Mr. Mackonochie, it will be remembered, had long been known and respected by Bishop Tait as one of the successful pioneers of the Riverside Mission in St. George's in the East.[2] While the beautiful church of St. Alban's was being built Mr. Mackonochie held his services in a room over a fish-shop in Baldwin's Gardens, and in the cellar of a house in Greville Street. As the new church approached completion the Bishop received many letters

---

[1] The site was given by Lord Leigh.
[2] See p. 243.

beseeching him not to consecrate it.   One of these, from a neighbouring incumbent, was as follows :—

The Rev. —— —— to the Bishop of London

"*Feb.* 18, 1863.

" MY LORD,—I cannot suppress my sorrow that your Lordship *will* consecrate St. Alban's with its present clergy. . . . I entreat your Lordship to consider the fearful responsibility that you, a Bishop of the Protestant Church, are incurring.   These are their doctrines : Auricular Confession, Prayers for the Dead, Absolution (opus operatum), Invocation of the Virgin, Extreme Unction, Corporal Presence.

" It was my duty, I feel, to have called upon the Primate 'with all faithful diligence to banish and drive away all erroneous and strange doctrine contrary to God's Word ' from his Province of Canterbury.   But I cannot bring myself to offer this obvious slight to your Lordship, and therefore I trust I shall be held harmless in this matter, and that your Lordship will write and state the same to me for the relief of my conscience, since I almost feel that I ought to have called together a meeting of Presbyters when the leaders of the Church neglect their duty, and certainly ought to have laid the matter before the Primate. With deep regret that your Lordship's rule over London should be instrumental to such doctrines, I remain your Lordship's faithful servant,   —— ——."

The Consecration Service took place on February 21, 1863, and Bishop Tait's sermon on the occasion was full of kindly sympathy and encouragement as to the difficulty and the hopefulness of the new work thus begun among those squalid streets.

But there was already friction between the founder, High Churchman as he was, and the new Vicar.   Within a few days of the Consecration Mr. Hubbard, as church-warden, wrote to ask the Bishop's counsel :—

" As Altar lights were not used," he said, " on the day of Consecration, I beg to know your mind upon the subject.   If your Lordship does not object to the use of lights as an accessory of Holy Communion, I shall not object.   If your Lordship does object to their use I shall express to Mr. Mackonochie my intention to act in conformity with your opinion in this matter."

The Bishop at once saw Mr. Mackonochie, and Mr. Hubbard's letter is indorsed thus :—" M. has since agreed to give up the lights."   Three weeks later the Church-warden-founder wrote in renewed distress, that Mr. Mackonochie had changed his mind as to the lights.

"His desisting from lighting the candles applied only to the day following the one on which he wrote. . . . I cannot but feel deeply disappointed at the resolve he has taken."

And again—

"I have been quite beaten down by the shock which Mr. Mackonochie's decision occasioned me . . . and I feel much uncertainty as to the best course to be taken.   I shrink from the position of having to carry out by compulsion under your Lordship's mandate a change which ought not to need such a pressure."

The Bishop cordially agreed with Mr. Hubbard in deprecating any resort to compulsion, and through all the disputes that followed, his personal relations with Mr. Mackonochie continued to be of the most friendly kind. A correspondence, for example, took place in the summer of 1863 about a sermon which had been preached by one of the curates of St. Alban's, and Mr. Mackonochie again and again thanked the Bishop for his "uninterrupted kindness" in the matter.   The final letter was as follows :—

The Rev. A. H. Mackonochie to the Bishop of London.

"ST. ALBAN'S CLERGY HOUSE,
June 29, 1863.

"MY DEAR LORD BISHOP,—I found your Lordship's letter awaiting me when I came home on Saturday night, having been absent the whole day. I cannot too strongly express my entire concurrence in your Lordship's opinion of the extreme importance of preventing any recurrence of so painful an event as the preaching of the sermon in question. I desire to assure you, my Lord, that no negligence on my part shall be wanting for that purpose.—Believe me, my dear Lord Bishop, yours most truly and respectfully, ALEX. HERIOT MACKONOCHIE."

The ritual troubles increased, and in December 1863 the Bishop offered, in accordance with the direction given in the Preface to the Book of Common Prayer, to investigate carefully, with Mr. Mackonochie and Mr. Hubbard, the various points upon which they differed, and to give his direction respecting each, transmitting any questions which might still remain doubtful "for the formal decision of the Archbishop of the Province."

"I shall," he added, "be glad, before I enter on the questions at issue, to be assured on the part of the Incumbent and Churchwardens that there is a *bona fide* agreement to abide by the decision to be pronounced. I understand it to be the desire of both parties that the questions at issue should be decided in the quietest way possible without giving occasion for needless offence and scandal, and I am of opinion that the mode of settlement thus prescribed by the Church is at once the most likely to avoid any such evil consequences, and that in which earnest and loyal members of the Church of England may most suitably bind themselves to acquiesce."

Mr. Mackonochie, however, declined to give any such assurance, and the proposed reference came to naught.

It would be impossible to follow in detail the history of St. Alban's during the next few years. Mr. Mackonochie introduced coloured vestments in 1864, and incense in 1866. Mr. Hubbard complained in each case to the Bishop that he had done so "without the consent of either of the Churchwardens." On the second occasion the Bishop replied :—

"LONDON HOUSE, *Feb.* 8, 1866.

"MY DEAR MR. HUBBARD,—If you and your brother Church-warden will submit to me a formal memorial stating that you believe unlawful practices have been introduced into the services at St. Alban's, and calling upon me to regulate the services, this will enable me to go to my Chancellor at once for full considera-tion of the case, with a view to action.—Believe me, yours very faithfully,   A. C. LONDON."

It was thought better, however, not to proceed to liti-gation, and the Bishop and Mr. Mackonochie had several interviews upon the subject. After one of these the Bishop wrote :—

"LONDON HOUSE, *Feb.* 20, 1866.

"MY DEAR MR. MACKONOCHIE,—I cannot allow the night to close after our very serious conversation of to-day without saying how earnestly I trust and pray that you may be guided to submit your own judgment and that of your friends to some authority set over you in the Lord. I cannot ask you or any man to set aside the dictates of conscience, but I pray that your conscience may be guided to see that in the outward ordering of the Church service you are not justified in acting without refer-ence to the Bishop.—Sincerely yours,   A. C. LONDON."

The following is the Bishop's reply to Mr. Spiller, one of the Churchwardens of St. Alban's, who had written in praise of Mr. Mackonochie's self-denying work among the poor, and of the beauty and attractiveness of the church services :—

The Bishop of London to Mr. C. C. Spiller.

"BRIGHTON, *Dec.* 20, 1866.

"MY DEAR SIR,—I have read your very interesting testimony to the zeal of Mr. Mackonochie and the other clergy of St. Alban's, Holborn, and if there were no other proof but their having so favourably impressed yourself, it would be much in their favour. Let me say, however, that I am sure the same amount of influence might be gained, and would be free from the objections so commonly urged against it, if the services of the Church were restrained within those limits of which, as Diocesan, I could heartily approve. It is not the heartiness of the services that any one objects to, but certain peculiarities, the effect of which is to break down the distinction between the reformed service of the Church of England and the unreformed service of the Church of Rome.

"I have heard Mr. Hubbard speak in the highest terms of you, and, if you are continued in the office of Churchwarden, I trust you may be able, in co-operation with him, to suggest such an alteration of the services as may avoid the offence at present given, while the hearty and cheering character of the whole is preserved. . . . —I am, your faithful servant,

"A. C. LONDON."

On January 4, 1867, Mr. Mackonochie wrote to the Bishop to say that in consequence of the remonstrance contained in the Bishop's Charge, which had been published a few weeks before,[1] and in consequence also of the opinions expressed by the Lower House of Convocation in the previous summer,[2] he had decided to modify the ritual of St. Alban's in certain important particulars. He enclosed at the same time a printed address to his parishioners explaining his views upon ritual symbolism generally. The Bishop replied as follows :—

The Bishop of London to the Rev. A. H. Mackonochie.

"BRIGHTON, *8th Jan.* 1867.

"My dear Mr. Mackonochie,—I have to thank you for your letter of the 4th, and for sending me the printed paper. I hail the desire which you express in your letter to make the service at St. Alban's more accordant with my wishes, and with what I feel convinced are the requirements of the Church of England, and I shall be glad to learn that the changes which

---

[1] See page 441.　　　[2] See page 405.

you, on full consideration, make in the service, go so far as to remove what is a serious stumbling-block to so many attached members of our Church. I shall at all times be ready to give you my best advice in this or any other matter. With regard to the printed paper, I should not be dealing candidly with you if I did not say that I fear its statements are very difficult to reconcile with the 29th Article, and certainly go beyond anything which I believe to be warranted by the general teaching of our formularies. I cannot but think that you make a great mistake in supposing that these (which I must hold to be) exaggerated statements are at all conducive to real devotion. The acknowledged Spiritual Presence of Our Blessed Lord with faithful worshippers, in the Sacrament of His death, must call forth all healthy reverential feelings; and I think your statements of doctrine, like certain parts of the ceremonial which you have been in the habit of using to symbolise your doctrine, are rather impediments in the way of the Spiritual worship which the Lord loves, and have a tendency to substitute for it a morbid excitement of the feelings. My belief is that the acknowledged earnestness and devotion of your congregation spring, not from the peculiarities of the ceremonial you have used or the doctrines you have preached, but, in spite of these, from God's blessing on the deep sense of the real Christian verities, and the anxious love to save souls, which are daily shown in the preaching and lives of yourself and others who co-operate with you. It is my earnest prayer that God may more and more enable you to dwell on these verities, and cause your zealous conviction of them to shine forth more and more, to the complete emancipation of yourself and your people from the errors with which I so much regret to think they are at present mixed.—Believe me to be, my dear Mr. Mackonochie, yours very truly,

" A. C. LONDON."

A few months later the long controversy entered upon a new phase. A prosecution of Mr. Mackonochie was set on foot by the Church Association, with the view, as the promoters stated, of obtaining a definite decision upon the disputed points of law. The 'promoter' was Mr. John Martin, who, as treasurer and manager of the schools in Baldwin's Gardens, had for more than thirty

years taken a keen personal interest in all that concerned
the district, although his actual residence was in another
part of London.   The case was sent by letters of request
to the Court of Arches, where it was heard in December
1867 before the newly appointed Dean of Arches, Sir
Robert Phillimore.   On March 28, 1868, in a long and
elaborate judgment, the Dean of Arches decided, *inter
alia*, in favour of the legality of the Altar Lights, but
against the (ceremonially) mixed Chalice, and the censing
of persons and things.   Immediately on the delivery of
this judgment Mr. Mackonochie wrote to Bishop Tait
as follows :—

The Rev. A. H. Mackonochie to the Bishop of London.
"St. Alban's Clergy House,
March 31, 1868.

" My dear Lord Bishop,— It is due to your Lordship that
I should communicate to you, as soon as possible, my intentions
with regard to the judgment of the Arches Court in the case sent
to it by your Lordship by letters of request.   According to the
account of that judgment in the public papers, which I assume
to be correct, I am admonished to abstain for the future from
the use of incense and from mixing water with the wine, as
pleaded in these Articles ; and further, not to recur to the
practice, which I have abandoned under protest, with regard to
the elevation of the Blessed Sacrament, and the censing persons
and things.   I have taken a few days to consider what course it
is my duty to take under this judgment, and have decided to
abide by it without appeal to the Higher Court, unless compelled
to do so by any act on the part of the promoter.   It will I know
be most satisfactory to many of my friends that I should thus
accept the decision of the Highest Court which claims Spiritual
Authority, rather than appeal to a civil tribunal.   At the same
time I cannot but feel the deepest thankfulness that a judgment
conceived in such a spirit of deep and true Catholicity should
have been pronounced at this time.   It will do more than anything to calm the minds of those who have been much troubled
by many past events.—Believe me, my dear Lord Bishop, yours
very truly and respectfully,   Alex. Heriot Mackonochie."

The Bishop of London to the Rev. A. H. Mackonochie.

"LONDON HOUSE, *6th April* 1868.

"MY DEAR MR. MACKONOCHIE,—I have delayed for some days my answer to your letter of the 31st ult., in the hope that I might know with certainty whether there is likely to be an appeal on the part of the promoters of the suit against you. I have, however, no information on the subject, and therefore delay no longer to write to you.

"I could not doubt that you would at once drop any practices in the celebration of Divine Service which were formally decided by a competent tribunal to be contrary to the law of the Church, and I gladly receive your assurance in respect of the points which you specify. Most earnestly do I trust that your hearty zeal for the spiritual welfare of the people committed to your pastoral charge may be directed aright, and that, both in point of doctrine and of ceremonial, being kept safe from dangerous extremes, you and the clergy who work with you in so self-denying a spirit may find your usefulness daily increased by being more and more enabled to give yourselves to spread among your flock the simple Gospel of our Lord Jesus Christ.—Yours very faithfully and truly,   A. C. LONDON."

On May 22, 1868, Mr. Hubbard wrote a long letter to the Bishop of London, explaining his own position with respect to the difficulties at St. Alban's. In the course of this letter, which was published at the time, he says :—

"It is now five years since I had the painful duty of presenting to you at some length the complaints which I had to urge against the proceedings at St. Alban's. You received them with the utmost kindness and consideration, you submitted them to the perusal of Mr. Mackonochie, and you invited us to leave to your decision (by which we should engage to abide) the matters in contention, including several of those which I have just noticed. Mr. Mackonochie, however, declined the reference to your Lordship, and he declined also, at successive periods, as I proposed them, references to any ecclesiastical lawyer (whom he should choose)—to his best friend, and to his own brother. Unable to accomplish a private and friendly reference, you intimated your readiness to receive a formal presentment from my co-church-warden and myself.   Mr. Spiller, having first agreed, subsequently declined to join in a formal presentment, upon the plea that Mr. Mackonochie had published his intention to abide by the decision of Convocation upon the points under contention.

"After the publication of the resolutions on Ritual passed by the two Houses of Convocation, I again proposed to Mr. Mackonochie a reference to your Lordship for a decision which should be based upon those resolutions, but Mr. Mackonochie replied that, a suit having been commenced against him in the Arches Court, he preferred awaiting its result.

"The judgment of the Dean of Arches, by condemning the ceremonial use of incense, has removed one of the causes of my dissatisfaction.   Incense is no longer used in the services at St. Alban's, but I find no pretence for delaying my petition that you will take into consideration the other matters which I have offered to your Lordship's notice. . . .

" During all these years, although I privately made known my dissatisfaction to your Lordship, I shrank from giving it any overt expression, for I was especially jealous for Mr. Mackonochie's influence, and was satisfied rather to bear the penalty of being personally misunderstood than to occasion any distrust of him or of his office in the estimation of his people.

" You, my Lord, who know the distress my difference of opinion with Mr. Mackonochie has occasioned me, know also the sincere admiration I entertain for his zeal and untiring devotion.   I gratefully acknowledge the disinterested, the abundant, and efficacious labours of himself and his curates, especially among the young, the aged, and the afflicted of his district, but I see no connection between these, his meritorious services, and the persistent introduction of strange and obsolete practices.

" In these days it would be as impolitic as unjust to narrow the liberty of either the clergy or the laity of our Church, but liberty must not degenerate into licence.   No Church, no corporation, no society, can exist without order and without law, and it must be decided whether, consistently with order, law, and the uniformity which results from them, individuals can be permitted to act independently of all authority and opinion but their own.

" I may not now claim your Lordship's hearing in any official capacity, for I hold none; yet, as founder and patron of St.

Alban's, I venture to challenge your sympathy and assistance. The law, by vesting in me the patronage of the benefice, makes me a trustee for the Church of England in general, and for the inhabitants of the district in particular, and in that character I approach your Lordship. . . ."

The Bishop's reply was as follows :—

The Bishop of London to Mr. J. G. Hubbard.

"FULHAM PALACE, *July 18th*, 1868.

"MY DEAR MR. HUBBARD,—I have very carefully perused your letter bearing the date of the 22d of May, but the finally revised copy of which, as you are aware, only reached me within the last few days.

"You scarcely require to be again assured, after all that has passed between us privately, of the sympathy which I feel with your disappointment that the services of St. Alban's Church, Holborn, have been conducted in a manner so different from what you approve of, or my regret that Mr. Mackonochie, on the various occasions on which you have appealed to him to submit the points of difference to the decision of myself as his Diocesan, or to the arbitration of some other third party, has uniformly declined any such reference. The natural result has been that the mode of conducting divine service at St. Alban's has become the subject of litigation in the Courts, and though the Dean of Arches has pronounced judgment, the parties who have moved in the prosecution of Mr. Mackonochie are not satisfied with that judgment, and have appealed to the highest Court of the Church and realm.

"Under these circumstances, you will not be surprised that I prefer, in reference to the points which you have brought before me, to wait for the ultimate decision of this case. I have for some time past been of opinion, and have taken public occasion to express my opinion, that the evils of excessive ritualism, which at present give so much distress to many attached members of the Church of England, cannot be remedied unless, either by the decision of the Courts or by fresh legislation, some new method is secured for the exercise of controlling power on the part of the Ordinary.—Believe me to be, yours very faithfully,

"A. C. LONDON."

In the year 1868 other difficulties arose, connected only indirectly with the Ritual question, and the following letters passed between the Bishop and Mr. Mackonochie :—

The Bishop of London to the Rev. A. H. Mackonochie.

"LONDON HOUSE, *Oct.* 29, 1868.

"MY DEAR MR. MACKONOCHIE,—There has been laid before me a *Catechism of Private Prayer for Children*, professing in its title-page to be compiled by you this year. I confess myself grieved at the mode in which this Catechism inculcates habitual confession and prayers for the dead. I will not undertake to say that a clergyman teaching his people to comply with these practices, as set forth in this little book, would be liable to punishment if his case were brought before a legal tribunal, and if the alleged silence of our Church were pleaded in his defence ; but I am sure that this Catechism oversteps anything to which the formularies of the Church of England have given their sanction.

"Again, I consider the teaching on the subject of the inter-cession of the Blessed Virgin, though the same defence might perhaps be set up in case of legal proceedings, to be not only unwarranted by Holy Scripture, but distinctly contrary to the mind of our Church. I deeply deplore that such a book is circulated in my diocese, and I cannot but fear that it must prepare the unformed minds of children for the gradual recep-tion of distinctly Romish error. I must warn you very earnestly of the danger of circulating this book as a Church of England Catechism amongst the children of your flock.[1]

---

[1] Among the passages which the Bishop has marked in the little Cate-chism are the following :—

Q. What do you say next ?

A. I say next a prayer to my dear LORD, to ask for the prayers of Mary and of all the Saints.

Q. Repeat this prayer.

A. The prayer is this : "Most Blessed JESUS, grant of THY mercy that Holy Mary, THY Mother, and all THY Saints may pray for us both now and at the hour of our death. Amen."

  .   .   .   .   .

[Prayer.] Bless, O Lord, my father, mother, brothers, sisters, relations, and friends. . . . Bless the clergy of this parish, especially my own ghostly Father, and our Bishop. . . . Bless THY whole Church, and make it one in

"It deeply pains me to be obliged to write thus, but I should otherwise neglect a plain duty.—Believe me to be, dear Mr. Mackonochie, yours faithfully,   A. C. LONDON."

The Rev. A. H. Mackonochie to the Bishop of London.

"S. ALBAN'S CLERGY HOUSE,
November 3, 1868.

"MY DEAR LORD BISHOP,—I have to thank your Lordship very sincerely for the great kindness of your letter. I hope I am not doing wrong in saying that it is but one more of those many acts of friendliness on the part of your Lordship which make it personally so very grievous to me that I should be paining you by acting under the supreme obligation of obeying my own fullest and most carefully formed convictions as to the teaching of the Church of England, of the whole Church Catholic, and, above all, of the Gospel of Christ. I do not presume to obtrude upon your Lordship the reasons of my conviction. They have been so often urged most ably in various quarters, that for me to reiterate them would be very unseemly; but I venture to think that your Lordship is one of the last men in England to wish me to act contrary to my convictions, or to withhold any part of that which I conceive to be the Gospel of Christ from those whom I have to teach. I cannot be ignorant that the full assertion of that which I am convinced is the truth may lead me into serious inconveniences, but I hope that the same God who has revealed it will, by His grace, carry me through any difficulties which He may suffer to come in my way.—Believe me, my dear Lord Bishop, yours very truly and respectfully,

"ALEX. HERIOT MACKONOCHIE."

In the meantime the Church Association had appealed to the Privy Council against the recent judgment of the

Faith and Love, and give eternal rest to the faithful departed, through JESUS CHRIST. Amen.
   Q. Who do you mean by your "ghostly Father"?
   A. I mean by my "ghostly Father" the priest who hears my confession.
   .   .   .   .
   Q. Do you think that your Prayers help [the dead]?
   A. Yes; I think they will get for them from GOD more grace and peace.

Dean of Arches, so far as it was in favour of Mr. Mackonochie. The case was again argued, Mr. Mackonochie appearing by counsel, and on December 23, 1868, the Privy Council reversed the Dean of Arches' decision, and declared the Altar Lights to be illegal. Bishop Tait had a few weeks before been nominated to the Primacy, and on December 29th, as the last act of his London Episcopate, he wrote to Mr. Mackonochie as follows :—

The Bishop of London to the Rev. A. H. Mackonochie.

"FULHAM PALACE, 29 *Dec.* 1868.

"MY DEAR MR. MACKONOCHIE,—I have received from the Privy Council Office a copy of the judgment which has now with authority explained the law on the various points of ritual observance in the service at St. Alban's, Holborn, respecting which there has been so much contention. I expect that this will be the last day of my tenure of the See of London ; otherwise I should have invited you, at a personal interview, to arrange with me what is the best mode of giving effect to such changes in your service as will at once bring it into conformity with the simplicity enjoined by the Rubrics, and at the same time be the least distasteful to a congregation like yours, which has been accustomed to a form of worship more ornate than, it is now ascertained, the law of the Church has sanctioned. Probably before you receive formal notification of what is now required of you, through the proper officers of the Bishop's and Archbishop's Court, I shall have ceased to be your Diocesan. But I will take upon myself, as my last act in that capacity, to advise you and all others of the London clergy who may now feel themselves placed in a difficulty by their having conscientiously, though I believe unwisely, thought it their duty hitherto to act against the advice and judgment, I believe I may say, of all the Bishops, in introducing novelties of worship, to do now what I believe all the Church principles must suggest, viz., to take counsel with those directly set over them in the Lord as to the mode in which their services are henceforward to be conducted in conformity with the ascertained law of the Church.

"Some weeks must elapse before my successor has entered

fully on the duties of his office, but I can have no doubt he will
be ready to give you his best advice at once, and to approach the
subject of your present difficulties with the same appreciation of
your devotedness and zeal which I have ever myself entertained.
You are quite at liberty to make any use you please of this letter,
which I shall myself make public.—I am, yours very faithfully,

"A. C. LONDON."

*The Rev. A. H. Mackonochie to the Archbishop of
Canterbury.*

"ST. ALBAN'S CLERGY HOUSE,
Feast of the Circumcision, 1869.

"MY DEAR LORD ARCHBISHOP,—I beg to acknowledge with
many thanks your Grace's very kind letter of Dec. 29, which has
since appeared in the *Times* newspaper. The subject of it is one
which deeply concerns many, both clergy and laity, and not myself alone. It is, moreover, at this time the matter of their most
serious deliberation. Under these circumstances, I feel sure that
your Grace will excuse me from entering into any detailed discussion of the question. I cannot, however, close this letter
without specially thanking you for the great personal kindness
and consideration which I have received from your Grace during
the last ten years.—Believe me, my dear Lord Archbishop, yours
very truly and respectfully,

"ALEX. HERIOT MACKONOCHIE."

A score of other instances might easily be given, to
show the Bishop's difficulties in various parts of London,
with respect to the practice of an ' advanced ' and advancing Ritual. The records of St. Matthias, Stoke Newing-
ton, under its successive incumbents, have recently been
given to the world, from a partisan point of view, in the
interesting and vigorous biography of Mr. Robert Brett,
the most stalwart and polemical of churchwardens, and
the champion of what he believed to be Catholic practices
of every sort and kind.[1] In matters of opinion, whether

---

[1] *Robert Brett: his Life and Work.* By Dr. T. W. Belcher. 1890.

ecclesiastical, educational, or even political, Bishop Tait
and Mr. Brett were in frequent and sometimes stormy
opposition to one other, but Mr. Brett never lost an opportunity of expressing the respect and regard which, through
all these controversies, he entertained for his Diocesan.
In a rousing speech, for example, which he delivered to
the English Church Union on June 20th, 1865, he refers
as follows to Bishop Tait :—

"I wish it to be distinctly understood that I intend no
personal reflections whatever on our Diocesan. I have had some
very earnest contentions with him on matters of principle, but I
must say he has always met me as a Christian man should do.
He has maintained his opinions, and I have maintained mine,
and when he has found that the principle which I have contended for has been right, he has yielded up his own opinion. I
feel great respect for him, not only for his office, but personally
for the many great efforts which he displays in advancing the cause
of the Church, and also for acts of personal kindness to myself,
and especially for tender sympathy in times of bitter trial. . .
Therefore, whatever I say must not be taken personally to his
Lordship." [1]

The consecration in 1866 of St. Peter's, London Docks,
the enduring outcome of Mr. Lowder's energy and faith,
was an important day in the history of the Ritualist movement. Strained as his relations had for a time been with
the Rector of the Mother Church,[2] Bishop Tait had never
ceased to encourage and support the devoted workers in
Mr. Lowder's mission district, now formed into a separate
parish. The magnetism of Mr. Lowder's personal influence, not less than his untiring devotion to the people
committed to his care, had lived down active opposition
even in the worst purlieus which he was trying to reclaim,
and on June 30, 1866, the friendly feeling which he had

[1] *Life of Robert Brett*, p. 153.
[2] St. George's in the East, see pp. 232-249.

inspired found enthusiastic utterance among those who were assembled for the consecration of his Church. In Mr. Lowder's words :

"It was a day ever to be remembered in the history of the Mission, whether for the fulfilment of long-indulged anticipations in the sight of a duly consecrated church, the beauty and solemn character of St. Peter's, the full attendance of clergy and friends, or, above all, for the hearty sympathy of the Bishop in the work of the Mission, and the warm applause which his encouraging words elicited from the large gathering of friends (about three hundred) at the luncheon."

The Bishop's speech, as reported in the *Guardian*,[1] was as follows :—

"He had had an intimate connection with the work for more than ten years, for it was before his consecration that Mr. Lowder first brought it under his notice. He was of opinion that it would not do for the Bishop of London, or the Bishop of any other place, to agree with everybody, for in that case he believed he would agree with nobody. What a Bishop was bound to have was a real sympathy with goodness wherever he found it. He would be unworthy of the office he held if he did not sympathise with the clergy and the noble-minded ladies who had worked so hard in this district, which had at one time enjoyed a world-wide reputation for the bad character of its people, but which, he was glad to say, was fast losing that stigma. . . . He then alluded to the high character and worth of Mr. Lowder, whom he looked upon as one of the principal agents in effecting that union of the East and West of which he had spoken.

"Mr. Lowder, in reply, alluded with great feeling to the manner in which the Bishop had recognised the honesty of their purpose, and said that he should indeed have felt humiliated if he had not always conducted himself as he ought to his spiritual superior. He had always met with kindness from the Bishop, even when they differed from each other, and when he had felt it his duty to bow to his Lordship's authority, he had done so in the spirit of love."

[1] See *Guardian*, July 4, 1866, p. 688.

It was not wonderful that, in the excited state of public opinion upon the Ritual question, many exaggerated stories as to the Bishop's action obtained currency. It is still commonly asserted, for example, that on one occasion the Bishop, addressing a large body of clergy, many of whom were wearing coloured stoles, bid them in a stern voice—"Take off these ribbons, gentlemen." The foundation for this story seems to be as follows [1] :—

On August 24, 1865, the Church of St. Michael's, Shoreditch, was consecrated by Bishop Tait. There was a large gathering of clergy in the Vestry. Most of them belonged to the advanced school in Ritual matters, and the occasion was taken for wearing the then very unusual coloured stoles, as well as other ornaments. Twice during the previous year the Bishop had been told, on remonstrating with clergy for Ritual innovations, that it was unfair to find such fault, seeing that he had consecrated such and such a Church without objecting to the then use of these accessories. The Bishop, as he said to a friend, felt bound on this occasion to bear these facts in mind :—

"One of the clergy at the St. Michael's consecration," says a gentleman who was present, "had on a very narrow stole which he said was copied from that of the Venerable Bede. It looked exactly like a strip of ribbon. The Bishop noticed it, and said to him, 'Oh, Mr. ——, do take this off.' He did so, and the Bishop then added, 'I must ask the clergy of my diocese who are here to-day, to wear the simple dress of clergymen of the Church of England.' Thereupon, those of the clergy present who were wearing coloured stoles took them off and laid them in the Vestry, replacing them by black stoles, which they wore during the service. While the service was proceeding, a newspaper reporter was admitted to the Vestry, and on inquiring, note-book in hand, what the stoles lying there were, was told by a very

---

[1] The facts are communicated by a very careful witness, who was present on the occasion.

unritualistic legal functionary who was waiting there, 'Oh, these are the ribbons which the Bishop made the clergy take off.' Next day appeared the story of the Bishop's stern command— 'Take off these ribbons, gentlemen.'"

On the same occasion, the Bishop required, before proceeding with the consecration service, certain other changes in the ornaments of the chancel to make it correspond with what it had been when the usual inspection prior to consecration took place. The story of what was called, in a Church newspaper at the time, "the Bishop's disgusting and irreverent conduct at St. Michael's, Shoreditch," grew to large dimensions, but seems to have been treated with deserved contempt by the clergy of St. Michael's. Indeed, Mr. Nihill, the incumbent, at a Dedication Festival of the Church in a subsequent year, in proposing the health of the Bishop of the Diocese, expressed his "firm conviction that the Bishop was placed over that Diocese by Providence for the special purpose of allowing Catholics to obtain, under his truly liberal government, a position which would be unassailable"—a testimony, by the way, which brought the Bishop no small trouble from the opposite quarter, where he used frequently to be denounced for his inactivity in the suppression of 'Popery and Popish ways.' "The Bishop of London," said the *Record*, "is, to a qualified extent, decidedly Anti-Ritualistic, but he is one of those who have planted new ritualistic churches in his diocese, and who would widen the platform of the Church of England, and does not fully go with the Evangelical school in following the old Reformers of the Church."

We have now passed in review the Bishop's relation to most of the prominent Churches of the 'advanced' school in his diocese. His personal friendship with such men as Mr. Lowder and Mr. Mackonochie was knit yet closer when he and they were toiling side by side in the cholera visitation of 1866, elsewhere described, the epidemic reaching its height a few weeks after the consecration of St. Peter's, London Docks.[1]

But it would be altogether a mistake to suppose that his growing appreciation of the character and work of these devoted men led the Bishop to change the opinion he had formed as to the errors of their ecclesiastical system, or as to the mischief arising from their disregard of duly constituted Courts of Law. Quotations have already been given in this chapter, perhaps too copiously, from his public speeches upon the subject, both in Parliament and in Convocation. These utterances were intended, of necessity, for the Church at large. But the warnings he addressed to his own Diocese were even more emphatic and detailed.

In February 1866, the Archdeacon and Rural Deans of Middlesex presented a petition to the Bishop, praying him to discountenance the Ritualistic practices which were here and there coming into use, "and, so far as they are illegal, to suppress them." The Bishop in a few days published a long and careful answer for circulation among the clergy of the diocese, and he incorporated the greater part of it in his third Diocesan Charge, published in December 1866. A few paragraphs may be quoted :—

"The phrase 'excessive Ritualism,'" he said, "requires to be explained, for, as commonly employed, it bears two meanings.

"(1) Sometimes the phrase is used for the introduction into Parish Churches of a form of worship always sanctioned and maintained in our Cathedrals, and in many of our College Chapels. . . . No doubt the spirit in which these efforts originated has done very much of late years to invest our houses of God with a more seemly dignity, and to give a liveliness to our outward worship which has been found very attractive, especially

---

[1] See p. 470.

to the young. Such changes, in my judgment, are only to be deprecated if they be introduced without proper regard to the feelings and wishes of the Parishioners, and without due reference, if need be, to the controlling authority of the Ordinary. . . .

(2) But there is an excessive ritualism of another kind, to which I suppose in your address you especially refer, and which, within the last year, has caused a very wide-spread alarm in the Church. Certain persons have taken upon themselves so to alter the whole external appearance of the celebration of the Lord's Supper as to make it scarcely distinguishable from the Roman Mass, and they endeavour on all occasions to introduce into the other services some change of vestment or ornament quite alien to the established English usage of 300 years.

" . . . The number of those who are so committed is, I am confident, very small. The Church of England from the Reformation has allowed great liberty as to the doctrine of the Sacraments ; and though I fear it cannot be denied that a few are engaged in a conspiracy to bring back our Church to the state in which it was before the Reformation, I fully believe that most of those who advocate what we deem an excessive ritual would indignantly deny that they had any such purpose. . . .

" I trust that the good sense and good feeling of the Clergy and the kindly admonitions of authority will prevail, without making it necessary to defend the Church from the innovations of a few, either by painful legal prosecutions or by a declaratory enactment of Parliament and Convocation. If admonitions fail, then at last an enactment must explain how and under what safeguards that controlling influence, which the Church has ever contemplated as vested in its chief officers, shall be made to bear on the discretion of individual clergymen.

" I feel strongly on this important question, but I would not have you, my Reverend Brethren, to suppose that I have any great anxiety as to the future of our beloved Church. As with evils of a totally different kind which alarmed us two or three years ago, so with these—in quietness and confidence is our strength. I believe our Church to be growing steadily in the affections of our people, through the self-denying lives of our Clergy, and every year to be more distinctly assuming its place, as at once expressing and guiding the religious sentiments of this great nation, and as the chief witness in the world for a zealous, loving, and intelligent Christianity.

"Commending you and all your labours and our brethren in the ministry to the intercession of our common Lord and the guidance of the Holy Spirit, I am, my dear Mr. Archdeacon and Reverend Brethren, your faithful friend and servant,

" A. C. LONDON."

1860-68] LETTER ON RITUALISM 443

"Commending you and all your labours and our brethren in the ministry to the intercession of our common Lord and the guidance of the Holy Spirit, I am, my dear Mr. Archdeacon and Reverend Brethren, your faithful friend and servant,

" A. C. LONDON."

CHAPTER XVI.

THE BISHOP OF LONDON'S FUND—THE LADIES' DIOCESAN ASSOCIA-
TION—SISTERHOODS—CHOLERA EPIDEMIC OF 1866—ST. PETE
ORPHANAGE—BISHOP'S ILLNESS—THIRD DIOCESAN CHARGE.

1863-1867.

NOTHING has yet been said about what is popularly
regarded, and not without reason, as the greatest and most
memorable act of Tait's London Episcopate—the inception and foundation of 'The Bishop of London's Fund.'
In his Charge of 1862, delivered immediately on his return
to London, after declining the Archbishopric of York, he
described, with many careful statistics, the spiritual desti-
tution of vast regions of the Metropolis. The population
of London, as he pointed out, was annually increased y
about 40,000 souls, and all the efforts which had been
made were inadequate to overtake these steadily advancing needs. Between 1851 and 1861, sixty-six permanent and twenty-one temporary Churches had been
opened, providing accommodation for about one-sixth of
the increased population.

"The appalling fact accordingly transpires," said Bishop Tait,
"that, whatever were our spiritual wants in this respect in 1851,
all our great exertions have not lessened them, but have at best
prevented the evil from growing worse."[1]

He pointed out that there were three parishes in the

[1] Charge of 1862, p. 62.

diocese with a population of more than 30,000, and only a single Church; eleven parishes with more than 20,000 for one Church; fourteen with more than 15,000.

"Let it not be supposed," he said, "that I am speaking as if the sole way to remedy the social evils of an overwhelming population, and propagate true religion, was to multiply churches, or even clergymen. We well know that neither the buildings nor the men will avail without the mighty Spirit of God. We are not insensible to self-denying labours of Dissenters and Roman Catholics, and we grant the value of many other appliances for promoting Christian civilisation used by our own Church. Yet are we deeply convinced that our own parochial system, carrying with it, besides churches and clergy, schools and a hundred arrangements of charity and philanthropy, gives the best hope of aiding our people for time and for eternity. It is difficult to conceive what a city of between two and three millions of inhabitants must become if it be not broken up into manageable districts, each placed under the superintendence of men whose mission it is to labour in every way for the social and religious improvement of the people."[1]

He went on to suggest, in considerable detail, the modes of carrying this counsel into practice, and, above all, the need of greater liberality on the part of the richer citizens of London.

This Charge, like that which preceded it, aroused wide attention.

"Its whole tone and temper," said the *Guardian*, "are such as to command respect and confidence. It is candid, earnest, and impartial, and the rules the Bishop suggests are often most wise and practical."

"We do not know," said the writer of an unfriendly and even vituperative article in *John Bull*, "why our daily contemporaries accord to the Bishop of London's *concio ad clerum* an importance so far beyond that which they attach to the authoritative enunciations even of our Primates. Yet so it is, . . . the Charge has formed the subject of comment in every paper, and, in several, food for more than one article."

<hr>

[1] Charge of 1862, p. 65.

Taking advantage of the interest awakened by his words, the Bishop, a few months later,[1] summoned in London House a large meeting of some of the weightiest and most influential men in London, and propounded to them his plan for raising a huge 'Bishop of London's Fund' of half a million sterling, wherewith to strengthen and enlarge his diocesan work in all its forms. So great was the enthusiasm he had kindled, that an amendment was carried by acclamation in the room, that they should set themselves to raise in ten years, not half a million, but a million sterling. The Bishop himself subscribed £2000, and promised to issue a Pastoral Letter to the laity of the diocese. On June 20th, 1863, his letter appeared, recounting what had taken place, and calling upon all Londoners for aid.

"It is my desire," he said, "that our scheme be as elastic as possible. . . . Each year may suggest new means for advancing the great work we are undertaking; and it is my desire that no approved agency in connection with our National Church should be excluded from our field of operations. . . . It may seem a poor thing for a Bishop to be addressing his diocese on the old question of our need of funds, but the command of ample funds is an indispensable condition of the great effort which the exigency of the times requires. . . . Consider what our Metropolis is—its vast population—its boundless influence on the whole kingdom—the certainty that as evil breeds evil wherever men do congregate, such a mass of population must demoralise the country, and disorder our whole social system, unless it be leavened by a civilising Christian influence."

"Each donor," he explained, "should state whether he wishes his money to go to a general fund or to be applied specifically to any one" of nine different objects.[2]

---

[1] April 29, 1863.

[2] The nine objects were as follows:—1. Missionary clergy or additional curates (a) to labour in the diocese generally under the Bishop's control, or (b) to be confined in their operations to particular parishes; 2. Scripture readers; 3. mission women; 4. clergymen's residences; 5. schools; 6.

At the head of the list stood the provision of missionary clergy to work in crowded parishes; the building of churches being the last of the nine objects.

The response to this bold appeal was such as to amaze and silence the opponents of the plan. The first subscription list amounted to £60,000. Before six months had passed the sum was £94,000, and in March 1864, —nine months, that is, after the issue of his letter,— the Bishop was able to announce the actual receipt of £100,456, 13s. 6d., and the promise of £92,000 more.

It would be out of place to recount here in detail the subsequent progress of the Bishop of London's fund.[1] Bishop Tait was never tired of expressing his obligation to the great body of laymen who had from the first administered its grants :—

"It has required," he said in his third diocesan Charge, "such an amount of patient and laborious attention, not only to the general condition of the diocese, but to the minute details of its parishes, and such an amount of communication, oral and written, with incumbents and others, as would fully employ the energies of the whole staff of any great public office. . . . To the laymen who have thus aided us the thanks of all of us, the clergy, are especially due. Men of all ranks, with a thousand other claims, have made time to work for us diligently, day by day, in the office, and have visited all parts of the diocese, that, by personal inspection of poverty-stricken districts, and personal intercourse with incumbents and other residents, they might better understand what it was wise to undertake in each neighbourhood."

He used always to maintain in later years that, great

mission rooms or school churches ; 7. endowment of old or new districts ; 8. endowment of curacies ; 9. building of churches.

[1] When, in 1873, the decennial period, which was originally intended to be the limit of the fund's duration, came to an end, it was reconstructed by Bishop Jackson as a permanent diocesan institution. It had then expended £497,910, and its present income is about £23,000 a year. Two of the four original trustees, Sir Walter Farquhar and Mr. John Murray, are still in office.

as was the direct work of the fund, its indirect results had proved incomparably greater, in the intelligent sympathies that were awakened, and the opportunity that was given for their active exercise.

While the energies and sympathies of the laymen of the diocese were thus enlisted, a totally new endeavour was also made to organise, in a manner till then unheard of, the scattered and disjointed work of such ladies as should be willing to make themselves useful for a longer or shorter period of the year in the poorer parishes of London.   The plan was Mrs. Tait's.

"I remember distinctly," wrote the Archbishop, fifteen years afterwards, "her awakening me one night in our room in London House, and unfolding the scheme of the Ladies' Diocesan Association, which had become impressed upon her mind ; and she quickly set herself to work to have the scheme matured.   I must leave to others to describe the labour for which the maturing of her conception called.   Her idea was that the great number of ladies who, in London, are anxious to do distinct work for Christ beyond the limits of their own families—in workhouse visitation, and in hospitals, and in ministering to the wants of the poor in their own houses—might have their efforts better systematised if they met together in one centre under their Diocesan."

The chaplains of hospitals, penitentiaries, and houses of charity, and the clerks of Boards of Guardians were communicated with and asked if ladies would be allowed to visit their respective institutions.   The movement was at once successful.   The special needs of particular parishes in East London and elsewhere were by this means brought to the notice of those able to give help, and the ladies met for a religious service once a week in London House, where the Bishop frequently addressed them.[1]   The Association, modified to suit new circum-

---

[1] The first chaplain was the Rev. T. J. Rowsell, who was succeeded by the Rev. W. D. Maclagan, now Bishop of Lichfield.

stances, is still at work ; and, in its general lines of action, it has been copied in many other dioceses.

This account of the Ladies' Diocesan Association leads naturally to the consideration of a kindred but much larger subject, the establishment of sisterhoods in the Church of England.

When the time hereafter comes for estimating and comparing the various Church movements of this century in England, it is probable that the first place, as regards utility and strength, will be assigned to the revival of sisterhood life as an active constituent in the Church's work. As with other changes, so with this, the motive force behind has been complex. Although the re-established sisterhoods have for the most part been associated with the so-called ' Oxford School ' within the Church, that school cannot rightly be credited with the entire responsibility for the new and admirable departure. Little as the fact is recognised by some of the friends of these communities, the movement forms part of a far wider change affecting the position, the independence, the training, and the responsibilities of educated Englishwomen.

So far, however, as this book is concerned, the sisterhood question may be regarded as an inherent part of the High Church revival. It was in this connection that its difficulties arose in each of the three dioceses in which the new attempt was made—Exeter, Oxford. and London. Although their aim was practically one, these various revivals were independent in their origin. A small community of women, desirous of living under rule, had for some years been established, under Dr. Pusey's care and influence, at Park Village, near Regent's Park. But their object was mainly a devotional one, and the settlement was scarcely known beyond its own borders.   In 1848 Miss Sellon began her remarkable work at Devonport, where she was at first supported by the Bishop of Exeter, in the face of a loud outcry from the ultra-Protestants, and though the Bishop found it necessary, upon other grounds, to withdraw his support, the excellent results of the labours of Miss Sellon's Sisters among the rough population of the seaport became before long her best defence.   Within the next few years, but again independently of one another, two Sisterhoods were founded in the Diocese of Oxford—at Wantage, under Mr. Butler, now Dean of Lincoln, and at Clewer, under the Rev. T. T. Carter.   The first Superior of the Clewer Sisterhood—dedicated to St. John the Baptist— was Harriet Monsell, widow of the Rev. Charles Monsell, and cousin to Mrs. Tait.[1]   Canon Carter has drawn a graphic record of the inception of her devoted work, and of the spirit and power with which she guided it.[2]   The intimacy of her friendship with Mrs. Tait, and so with the Bishop of London, must have helped him not a little in appreciating the value of the new enterprise, when his own diocese, to its great advantage, became the workfield of so many Sisterhoods.   And such help was needed, for it is hardly too much to say that at first the 'Community Life,' the Sisters' special dress, and the very notion of living under rule, were " everywhere spoken against."   It is difficult, in days when Sisterhoods have won their way, not to tolerance only but to enthusiastic support from almost every section of the Church, to realise the unpopularity, the suspicion, and even the open denunciation which had thirty years ago to be faced by any Bishop who threw over them the help of his official sanction.   The Bishops of Exeter and of Oxford were regarded by many

---

[1] See vol. ii. p. 275.
[2] *Life of Harriet Monsell*, by the Rev. T. T. Carter.

Protestant critics as deplorably tainted with Romanism by reason of the countenance they had given to the 'nunneries' at Devonport, Wantage, and Clewer, and better things were confidently hoped and prophesied of Bishop Tait. But from the first he took a larger view, and expressed his readiness—provided only the conditions he deemed essential were complied with—to become the Visitor of any Anglican Sisterhood which asked for his support. But it was not at first—not till he had learned by experience the value of their work—that he can be said to have definitely encouraged them. With Mrs. Lancaster, whose name will ever be remembered as one of the foremost promoters in England of such work as has been done by Sisterhoods, he was in active correspondence from his first accession to the See. Mrs. Lancaster seems to have shared not a few of his anxieties upon the subject, and she was never tired of urging upon him the advantage which would accrue from the controlling influence of the Diocesan.

"I do indeed trust," she writes in November 1858, "that nothing will prevent your Lordship from remaining at the head of All Saints Sisterhood. The work is very real and substantial, but unless the Bishop of the diocese is practically its visitor, I do not see how parents can possibly give up their daughters to such institutions, or feel confident as to the prosperity or continued soundness of such work."

In the course of the Bishop's reply, he says :—

"I am anxious you should understand my position with reference to All Saints Home. I was requested to become its Visitor as Bishop of the diocese, and, feeling that it was an earnest effort to serve God within our Church, which, unless submitted to some such controlling hand as that of the Bishop, might lead imaginative persons of deep piety to what was contrary to the rules and spirit of our Church, I consented to become Visitor, being thereby intrusted with power to see that nothing took place in the Institution which our Church condemns. I felt that if ladies, members of our Church, desire to live together and cultivate good works for Christ's sake under rules which separate them outwardly from worldly people, they will be enabled to do this most safely if they subject themselves to such restraints as the Visitorship of the Bishop of the diocese implies. It would be a great mistake to suppose that I myself personally think the mode of serving God which these ladies have chosen the best or the most accordant with the simple spirit of the Gospel ; but I conceive it to be my duty in my position to be ready to guide and, so far as I can, to save from error many who are working heartily for God, though not in the way which I myself think the best. . . . One point I was most strongly impressed with the importance of, and endeavoured to incorporate distinctly in the rules of the Institution : that no lady was to join it without the full consent of those who had a right to guide her actions in domestic life ; and that every one who joined it should be made to feel that she is perfectly free to leave it when she pleases, and also that there would be no sin in her doing so if at any time she conscientiously thought she would serve God better, and better fulfil her duties in life, elsewhere.

"Of course there is always danger lest persons (especially females) of strong imagination may persuade themselves that there is some peculiar sanctity in the life these ladies lead, not to be found in the quiet discharge of domestic duties. I have endeavoured to impress upon all who have applied to me respecting this Institution that such is not my view. . . . My office of Visitor will enable me to check any abuses which may be brought to my notice, and it makes me ready to give directions to Miss Byron and the other ladies as to the best mode of conducting the Institution according to the rules of the Church of England when I am requested to do so.—I am, my dear Mrs. Lancaster, yours very truly,   A. C. London."

There were many points, both of doctrine and of practice, on which Bishop Tait and Bishop Wilberforce were at variance, but, as Bishop Tait used frequently to say, they were absolutely at one with respect to Sisterhoods. The principles upon which they insisted as a condition of their acceptance of the office of Visitor were the same, and, allowing for their natural differences of style, there is a quite curious identity, even of language, in some of the letters which passed between each of these Bishops and the heads of the different communities in their dioceses.

The principal question at issue then, and ever since, has had reference to the imposition of vows of a binding character. Some twenty years later this subject was examined with characteristic learning and moderation in a well-known pamphlet by Bishop Christopher Wordsworth,[1] and his practical conclusions were entirely corroborative of the line which had been taken in earlier days by Bishop Wilberforce and Bishop Tait :—

"When you ask me," wrote Bishop Wilberforce to a clergyman in the diocese, "to give [a sister] the Apostolic benediction on her 'public resolution of chastity and devotion to Christ,' you ask me to do what, with my sense of the certain danger and probable unlawfulness of vows which Christ has not appointed, it is quite impossible for me to do. Such a *resolution* made *publicly*, and in appearance and intention confirmed by a Bishop's act is, whatever distinction may be discovered by an ingenious mind, really and *bona fide* a *vow*. . . . No one has, without God's express appointment, a right, in my judgment, to bind themselves for the future in such matters. Let them follow the guiding hand of God from day to day and rely for persevering in a course of right or service on His daily gifts of guiding, enlightening, strengthening grace, and not on the strength or effect of any past vow or resolution. As, then, such a benediction as you ask would, in my judgment, seem to confirm by a dangerous vow an unwarranted resolution, I must of course, with real regret, decline your request."[2]

And similarly with regard to another much-debated

---

[1] See Bishop Wordsworth's *Miscellanies, Literary and Religious*, vol. iii. pp. 267-289. While these pages are passing through the press, the subject is again under discussion, with no small modification of former opinions, by the Bishops of the Province of Canterbury.

[2] *Life of Bishop Wilberforce*, vol. iii. pp. 331-2.

point in connection with Sisterhoods—the systematic and ordinary practice of auricular confession—Bishop Wilberforce wrote in 1854, with reference to the Sisterhood at Clewer:—

"As to the disputed question of Confession, we must make provision that those whose consciences are burdened with any weighty matter may be able, before communicating, to open their grief to some discreet minister of God's Word and Sacraments, that by his ministry they may receive the benefit of absolution, together with ghostly counsel and advice. But we must not provide that what the Church of England so manifestly treats as an occasional remedy for exceptional cases should become the established rule of their ordinary spiritual life. . . . We cannot allow the Sisters to practise continual confession to, or erect into directors, the Warden or Chaplains of our house."[1]

Similar principles were adopted by Bishop Tait with respect to the conditions on which he consented to become the Visitor of Sisterhoods in his diocese. On February 14, 1862, the subject was debated in the Convocation of Canterbury, when Bishop Tait and Bishop Wilberforce both explained their views. The Lower House requested that a Committee might be appointed to "consider the modes and limitations under which encouragement and guidance might be given" to the movement. The Bishop of London supported the request for a Committee.

"As nothing but good," he said, "can arise from these individuals devoting themselves for Christ's sake, if their labours are judicious, so it is desirable that we should consider what advice can be given, and what checks can be put upon any tendency towards a want of that judiciousness which is necessary in such matters. . . . Though their efforts have naturally been viewed with some jealousy, I have great reason, in my own diocese, to be thankful for the amount of self-denial and goodness

---

[1] *Life of Bishop Wilberforce*, vol. iii. p. 362. In order fully to understand the attitude of Bishop Wilberforce in this matter, the whole letter from which the above extract is taken ought to be read.

of every kind which has been evinced by those who have devoted themselves to the work, and I must say that I think we ought not to be too critical in judging of the precise way in which they perform this work."

Bishop Wilberforce followed :—

"I think," he said, "that after what has fallen from the Bishop of London, it would scarcely be wise to act on the suggestion of the Lower House. There is a certain shrinking delicacy in such movements, and I think it would be better to leave those in London under his care, and those in other dioceses under the care of their spiritual guides, than to establish any formal rules, or to take any formal steps in Convocation."

He accordingly moved a resolution to the effect that it was expedient that the guidance asked for " should be sought directly from the parochial clergy and the bishops of the districts in which such devoted women labour."

The resolution was carried, and in the course of the debate the Bishop of London called attention to the ambiguity of the word ' devoted ' :—

"Etymologically," he said, "it might be supposed to have some reference to 'vows.' . . . Now, anything like a vow on the part of individuals to devote themselves to this work is the last thing we should recommend. It is most desirable that this should be clearly understood."

"In my diocese," added the Bishop of Oxford, "I have uniformly made it the condition of my connection with these institutions, that their statutes shall state explicitly that they are bound only so long as they please to continue in the Society." [1]

The following letters explain themselves :—

Mr. ——— ——— to the Bishop of London.

"*December* 26, 1865.

"My Lord,—I have to ask your Lordship's forgiveness, being personally an entire stranger to your Lordship, for troubling you

[1] *Chronicle of Convocation*, Feb. 14, 1862, pp. 963-968.

with the inquiry contained in this letter. The urgency of the
cause, and the importance of the issue, which may greatly depend
upon your Lordship's kind reply, are my only excuse.

"A very near and dear relative of ours, a young lady,
unmarried, extremely attractive in every way, and possessed of
considerable property in her own right, is very strongly minded
to enter the St. George's Mission in London, situate within your
Lordship's diocese, as a Postulant, with a pre-determination, if
the life is what she hopes to find it, to accept the Perpetual Vows
which are there administered to ladies disposed to undertake
them. She is considerably confirmed in that intention by a
belief that the system of Sisterhoods, as practised and maintained
in that Institution, is approved and countenanced by your Lordship. We are not aware of her precise warrant for this belief, but
a search, so far as one is open to us, in your Lordship's published
opinions, has failed to discover any valid reason why such an
opinion should be attributed to your Lordship. I therefore take
the liberty to ask if your Lordship will be so very good as to
inform me if my sister's belief in your opinion is well founded,
since I know that your Lordship's reply, whatever it may be, will
have the very greatest weight with her.

"No person whatever, I apprehend, could take any exception
to the great work which is undoubtedly being carried on by the
St. George's Mission—we all respect and admire that ;—it is only
to the system of administering perpetual vows, and thereby forming exclusive Sisterhoods in connection with the Church of
England, that we object so strongly, and from which we are so
painfully striving to save our sister. Still we would not take upon
ourselves to say that we are perfectly right, and our sister entirely
wrong. God forbid that we should blindly and unknowingly
strive against Him ; we only desire to find the truth of the matter,
and a knowledge of your Lordship's belief respecting it will
greatly aid us in that behalf.

"If I might be so bold as to venture still further, I would ask
another and almost greater favour. If your Lordship does disapprove of the system of perpetual Sisterhoods, and would write a
word or two tending to dissuade ladies from entering them, I
believe that it would influence my sister more perhaps than anything else in the world—certainly more than the words of any
other man in the world—so deep is her veneration for your Lord-

ship's character, which feeling, if I may be permitted to say it, is entirely shared by us all.

"With many and renewed apologies, I have the honour to be your Lordship's most obedient, humble servant,

"———— ————."

The Bishop of London to Mr. ——— ———.

"FULHAM PALACE, LONDON, S.W.,
Dec. 27, 1865.

"DEAR SIR,—I beg to acknowledge your letter of yesterday's date. There is no warrant for supposing that I in any way approve of Sisterhoods in which perpetual vows are administered. I have on more than one occasion stated publicly my belief that all vows or oaths administered under the circumstances you describe, not being sanctioned by the legislature, and being taken by persons not authorised to receive them, are of the nature of illegal oaths. It is a grave question whether a clergyman of the Church of England, administering such an oath, does not make himself amenable to prosecution before the magistrates. Certainly he acts in a most improper manner.[1] In all sisterhoods or associations of ladies, members of the Church of England, to which I have given my approval, I have been most careful to impress upon the associates that neither must any such oath be taken, nor is there any sort of obligation binding on the conscience, without an oath, to dedicate any larger time than is found conveniently compatible with other duties, to the work which the sisterhood or association promotes. I do fully approve of ladies who have no home duties, and who think they are fitted for such work, associating themselves together for the care of the poor and the sick. Such an institution, under my presidency, is St. John's

---

[1] Surprise and even amusement have sometimes been excited by the Bishop's frequent reference to the *legal* question involved in the imposition of a binding vow or oath. It is, therefore, noteworthy (as has been pointed out to the writer of this chapter by one of the foremost living authorities upon English Sisterhoods) that, whatever the cogency of the Bishop's argument, its importance has received a curious illustration during the last few years. It is understood that since, in Roman Catholic countries, the State has withdrawn its support from religious communities, modifications as to the use of permanent life-vows have been made, their legal enforcement being no longer possible.

House of Nurses in Northumberland St., Strand, and St. Peter's House, Brompton Square, and the Deaconesses' House in Burton Crescent,—in all three of which institutions arrangements are made whereby, I believe, anything I objected to as to dress, mode of life, or any other point, would at once be altered. There is also the All Saints Home, Margaret Street, with which I am connected as diocesan. Over this institution I have not the same direct control, but I cannot but admire the self-denying spirit in which Miss Byron and her ladies have undertaken their difficult work in the hospitals and among the destitute. When, however, I carried out what I understood to be Bishop Blomfield's intention of becoming Visitor of that institution, I insisted, in the most explicit terms, on the repudiation of the system of vows by the inmates, and had a clause inserted in the rules with this object. I have also taken means to prevent young persons attaching themselves to such institutions without the full consent of their parents or guardians, as I believe no blessing will ever come on work, however self-denying, which is undertaken to the neglect of those higher duties which belong to home life, and which are imposed directly by God Himself.—I am, my dear sir, very truly yours,

"A. C. LONDON."

The early days of Sisterhoods in London were for the most part uneventful days, the Sisters winning their slow way into public favour by the unchallenged excellence of the Christian service they were able to render to the sick and poor. If friction here and there arose between the ladies of the Community and their Episcopal Visitor, it must be remembered that the difficulties attending such a revival of corporate life were neither few nor small. The Sisters, as their numbers grew, had step by step to move along what was, in the Church of England at least, an almost untried path, and the Bishop had on the one hand to encourage and support them in their devoted work, and on the other to prevent them from impairing their own usefulness by a rash defiance of the popular religious sentiment, or still more by what he deemed an unauthorised departure from the principles of the Reformed Church.

The differences which arose were occasional and rare, but they did occur at times. A voluminous correspondence, for example, passed in 1867 between the Bishop and one of the Sisterhoods named above. It seems undesirable, either in this case or in any other, to make public the particulars of a controversy which was necessarily of a semi-private character. Only such letters therefore are reproduced as will serve to make clear the Bishop's attitude upon the general questions at issue. The Sisters had been dissatisfied with the ministrations of their Chaplain, whose views were not quite in harmony with those which they had themselves come to adopt. On a vacancy occurring they requested the Bishop to sanction the appointment of another gentleman whom they named to him, and to whom the Bishop wrote as follows :—

The Bishop of London to the Rev. —— ——.

"WOODSIDE, WINDSOR FOREST,
28th Aug. 1867.

"MY DEAR SIR,—The Lady Superior of —— —— tells me that you are willing to undertake the gratuitous office of Chaplain to the House as a temporary arrangement. I shall be glad to sanction this plan if you see your way to agree to the following conditions :—

"1st. That habitual Confession shall not be urged upon the Sisters or any inmates of the House.

"2d. That no vows whatsoever shall be administered or sanctioned by the Chaplain. I have expressed my views fully on the subject of these points, as connected with Sisterhoods, in my Charge of last December.

"Feeling no doubt that you will understand my feelings on these two points, and thanking you for your willingness to be of use to the ladies of ——.—I am, my dear Sir, yours very truly,

"A. C. LONDON."

The Rev. —— —— to the Bishop of London.

"*3d Sept.* 1867.

"MY LORD,—The Mother and Sisters of —— being equally if not more interested than myself in the conditions proposed by your Lordship, as those under which you would be pleased to sanction my acceptance of the chaplaincy of their House, I communicated to them your Lordship's letter. As regards myself, I feel I could not undertake to minister to them or to any other in my priestly office under restrictions not contained in the office itself. In accepting the chaplaincy under the conditions proposed, I should also find myself in regard to the Sisters in the following strange position, namely, that instead of being able as their Chaplain to do more, I should in fact be restricted to do less for them than any other Priest not their Chaplain could do; whilst I myself should be able to do more for any persons not inmates of —— who might apply to me, than I should be able to do for the Sisters, who would be *sure* to require from me the exercise of every possible function of the Priesthood. I think I may also say for them that they would be as unwilling to receive a Chaplain under the conditions proposed, as I should be to accept of the Chaplaincy. I think I may also include them with myself in expressing a hope that on consideration your Lordship will be pleased not to insist upon the proposed conditions.—I have the honour to be your Lordship's very obedient servant,   —— ——."

The Bishop of London to the Rev. —— ——.

"WOODSIDE, WINDSOR FOREST,
5th Sept. 1867.

"MY DEAR SIR,—I am obliged, in answer to your letter of the 3d, this day received, to say that I cannot sanction the practices which I understand you to wish to introduce amongst the Sisters of —— ——, viz., the urging on them the duty of habitual confession and the administering to them of vows. Both practices I consider to be quite alien to the spirit of the Church of England, and it is at least doubtful whether the latter of the two is not in violation of the law of the land. Great care has been taken by the law of the land to guard the administration of oaths, and besides all other objections, this consideration ought in my judgment to prevent a clergyman of the Church of England from administering them except where the law empowers him so to do. I fear the view you take of these matters makes it impossible for you to act as Chaplain. Though this letter is marked 'private,' you are fully at liberty to show it to [the Mother Superior], and indeed, unless I hear from you to the contrary, I shall take it for granted that you have done so, and not move further in the matter of a Chaplain at present till I am applied to.—Believe me, my dear Sir, yours very truly,   A. C. LONDON."

The Bishop of London to the Mother Superior of —— ——.

"WOODSIDE, WINDSOR FOREST,
10th Sept. 1867.

"MY DEAR —— —— . . . . I presume you are aware that in the best regulated Sisterhoods connected with the English Church precautions are taken against the Sisters binding themselves by vows. It is felt that such vows are not warranted by anything in the teaching of our Church, and are rash, as binding the conscience not to follow the leadings of God's providence in case of a change of circumstances. If, notwithstanding this, any ladies choose to bind themselves by vows, I do not see what can be done to prevent their acting in a way unwarranted by the Church, and rash, from a mistaken notion that real devotion of life to Christ's service is strengthened by this attempt to forecast the events of our changeful life which God retains in His own keeping. The Church of Rome, in sanctioning such vows, sanctions also a power of dispensing with them ; but the claim to such dispensing power is rightly repudiated by us—so that a vow for life may be an entanglement of the conscience, when God plainly, in our changing relations, prescribes for us a change of duty. The only vows which the Church of England sanctions are such as the Formularies recognise as based on the teaching of God's Word, and for these the law of the land provides by giving its additional sanction to the Formularies. . . .

"As to habitual Confession, the rule of the Church of England is almost equally plain. There is no provision for it whatsoever made in the Formularies. And it is to be noted that no form of private absolution is provided, except in the Visitation of the

Sick, in which the Confession and Absolution are treated as exceptional: 'If he feel his conscience troubled with any weighty matter.' The words in the Exhortation for the Holy Communion are the nearest approach to any sanction for habitual Confession. Yet there also the case is treated as exceptional : 'If there be any of you who by this means cannot quiet his own conscience, but requireth further comfort or counsel.'   Now, if any one feels or declares that he or she is always in this exceptional state, of course there is nothing further to be said, except that 'a discreet and learned minister of God's Word' will try to correct anything that is morbid in such feelings, but a Bishop will not be justified in authorising any of his clergy to treat as habitually required what the Church thus regards as exceptional.

" Hence the necessity of my having written to Mr. ⸺ on the subject as I did. I believe I have before referred you for your guidance in these matters to my two Charges for 1858 and 1866, where both these questions are treated at some length.   I must request you to read this letter to the Sisters, in case they may be misled by erroneous views, which some seem to entertain. I trust in this and in all other matters God may guide you to that calm understanding of the truth, and that wise deference to the authorities set over you in the Lord, which will be most consistent with the faithful and humble discharge of the great duties which you have undertaken in obedience to the call of Christ. . . .— Believe me to be, my dear   ⸺, very faithfully and truly yours,   A. C. LONDON."

The Mother Superior of ⸺ ⸺ *to the Bishop of London.*

"*12th October* 1867.

" MY LORD BISHOP,—I have taken the opportunity offered by all the Sisters being together in London at the beginning of this week, to lay before them your Lordship's letters to myself, relating to the appointment of a Chaplain for the Sisterhood, in order that we might together, prayerfully and calmly, consider all which your Lordship has kindly written to us, on a subject of such vital importance to our reality and well-being as a religious community.

"The conclusion at which we unanimously arrived was that, deeply painful and distressing as it is to us to differ, even in this one respect, from our Bishop (and God only can know how really and acutely painful it is), we yet feel so strongly, and as one, that we could not conscientiously accept the guidance of any priest who would consent to be restricted in the exercise of his ministry among us by conditions over and beyond his own ordination vow, that it would only be giving your Lordship needless trouble for us to nominate another priest under the circumstances which your Lordship judges necessary to his appointment. . . . We therefore conclude that our only right course now is to sever entirely our connection with [the Council over which your Lordship presides], and I have this day written to ——, acquainting him with this final decision.—With grateful thanks to your Lordship for many and great kindnesses, I remain, my Lord Bishop, your very faithful, humble servant, in our blessed Lord.

Although the Bishop's official relation to this Sisterhood came thus to an end, he did not allow the severance to interrupt his personal friendship with the Sisters. Writing a few months later to the same lady on another subject, he says :—

"I trust you and the rest of the ladies lately connected with —— —— will not fail to remember that I entertain a grateful sense of the services rendered by all of you.

"Much as I deplore the determination of yourself and the other ladies to separate yourselves from us, and unable as I am to justify that step, I feel it my duty to be ready at all times to give you personally any advice or assistance in my power, and I trust I shall never forget what you have done during so many years in the diocese of London."

Two other letters from the Bishop must be quoted, as showing his readiness to afford such indirect help as might be possible, even to a community whose usages he was unable officially to sanction :—

The Bishop of London to the Rev. A. H. Mackonochie.

"FULHAM PALACE, S.W., *Aug.* 16*th*, 1867.

"MY DEAR MR. MACKONOCHIE,—I take the first moment that I can command, in the midst of the work of closing the session, to write to you on a subject brought before me within the last few days. I have been told that the division of the East Grinstead Sisters who are established at Ash Grove, Hackney, are at present in much perplexity from the secession to the Church of Rome of Mr. Tuke, who has been their clerical adviser for some time, and that they are anxious to avail themselves of your assistance and advice.

"I have carefully inquired into the circumstances, and am most anxious that everything possible and right should be done to prevent these ladies from being unsettled in their allegiance to the Church of England by what has happened, and that they should have whatever assistance and advice you are able to give them consistently with your maintenance of what you believe to be right.

"My own views as to Sisterhoods in the Church of England have been clearly expressed in my Charge of December last, and I could earnestly desire that these ladies would conform to what I have thus sketched out. I have reason to believe, independently of other matters in which they dissent from the model I approve, that they have a custom in reference to the reservation of the Elements in the Holy Communion which I am certain that you disapprove of, and also that in the private Oratory there are signs of a devotion to the Blessed Virgin, going far beyond what the Church of England approves as due to her who is blessed amongst women. It would be useless for me to request any clergyman, whose sentiments are quite at variance with their own, to endeavour to influence these ladies. I understand that they have confidence in you and are more likely to listen to you than to any one else. Their practice of the reservation of the Elements in the Holy Communion alone must prevent me, and I should suppose must prevent any Bishop of the Church of England, from becoming Visitor of their Institution. I trust they may be induced to give it up.

"Meanwhile, I hear from undoubted testimony how great is their self-denial in nursing the sick, and in exposing themselves to many dangers for Christ's sake. I cannot therefore withhold the expression of my sympathy with their ceaseless labours for the poor and the afflicted. I pray God to guide them to a sober view of their duties as members of the Church of England, and I should rejoice to hear that they can bring their Sisterhood in all things to the model which I approve.

"If by kindly advice and guidance and such help as you can afford, you can be of use to them at this crisis, and afterwards in the midst of their self-denying labours, I shall be well pleased. You know how many points in your own system of doctrine and worship I disapprove ; but I have full confidence in your conscientious desire, according to your own views, to uphold the Church of England as against the slavery of the Church of Rome ; and I think it is right you should give what assistance you can to these ladies, and especially endeavour to save them from following the example of Mr. Tuke, and taking a step which I fear could never be retraced, and would be found most injurious to their souls' health. —Believe me to be, my dear Mr. Mackonochie, yours sincerely,   A. C. LONDON."

To the Superior of another Sisterhood, the members of which felt themselves unable to meet his wishes, he wrote :—

"My decision is to decline the office of Visitor. . . . Let me however say that I decline from no lack of sympathy with your self-denying labours. Indeed, I do feel that, giving yourselves to such a work in such a district, you deserve all sympathy and encouragement from those who are interested in the welfare of the poor and the advancement of Christ's kingdom. I do earnestly trust that the Lord may bless your labours to the rescuing of many from sin and misery. At any time my counsel is at your service as completely as if I were Visitor. But I am not prepared to take upon myself an office which would assign to me a greater nominal responsibility than I could properly incur, without much real power of guiding your movements. . . . At any time I shall be very glad to hear from you."

Again and again, both as Bishop and Archbishop, he was applied to by Sisters who had taken a permanent vow, from which they asked him to dispense them. He considered each such application upon its merits, and (at all events when Archbishop) took a different course according to the circumstances of the case. On the first such request which came before him, very soon after his consecration to the See of London, he wrote the following memorandum :—

"My opinion is asked on the case of a young lady who at the age of eighteen had a vow of celibacy administered to her by a clergyman of the Church of England. . . . She is now desirous of being released from the vow, on the plea : *first*, that it was presumptuous, and therefore sinful to take such a vow ; *secondly*, that when she took it she was mistaken in supposing that to lead a life of celibacy was her vocation ; *thirdly*, that she now feels that she will, by God's grace, be as holy and pure when married as she is now, and as able to do God's work in the world.

"My judgment is :—

"1. That the law of England is very jealous in respect of the administration of oaths. That any clergyman administering such a vow as is described above was highly culpable. That he who administers an oath not allowed by law is guilty of an illegal act and may be liable to be indicted. That the law holds oaths administered illegally to be void.

"2. That the whole spirit of the teaching of the Church of England condemns such vows. That whereas the Thirty-Ninth Article, while maintaining that oaths required by the magistrate, 'in a cause of faith and charity,' may lawfully be taken, 'if all be done according to the Prophet's teaching, in justice, judgment, and truth,' has yet expressly declared that 'vain and rash swearing is forbidden Christian men by our Lord Jesus Christ and James His Apostle.'

"I hold this decision of the Church to include in its condemnation such rash vows as that now under discussion, and I pronounce the taking of such a vow to have been a sinful act.

"3. I decide that the young lady in question is at liberty to marry, if, opening her heart to God in prayer, she is convinced in her conscience of the sinfulness of the rash vow, and is prepared to enter upon the holy state of matrimony in a prayerful spirit of dependence upon God, feeling humbled at the thought of the great difficulty in which her presumption has involved her."

The letters which have been recorded above contain more than one reference to what the Bishop said about Sisterhoods in his Diocesan Charge of 1866, and it may therefore be well, before passing from the subject, to quote a few sentences from that Charge. In urging upon the clergy the duty of multiplying and extending their parochial and pastoral agencies,—

"The wants of our people," he said, "are so many and so complicated, that if we are wise we shall ever be devising or borrowing fresh plans of usefulness. It will be with our spiritual as with that old secular warfare, in which the masters of the world rose to their pre-eminence by never being too wise or proud to learn from any quarter."

Bidding his hearers "not be too prejudiced to learn either from Rome," or from foreign Protestants, he went on to say :—

"Time was, and not long ago, when Roman Catholics were supposed to have a monopoly of Sisters of Mercy : when Protestants all held that women might work as true Sisters of Mercy (and, thank God, they can), one by one, from their own homes, visiting amongst the poor and desolate in their own neighbourhood ; but that the system of our Church forbade any organisation for a combined effort to use the services of women. The fearful emergency of the Crimean War dispelled this theory. Other efforts were doubtless being made before, but that melancholy time changed public opinion. The heroic spirit who stood forth to guide, and those no less brave who seconded her efforts, told the world that English Churchwomen were ready to combine, where combination was needed, for any great Christian work ; and our hospitals will probably always henceforward bear more and more, the better they are administered, the impress of that great example.

"Now I should be false to all good feeling if I did not publicly testify to the great help which London received during the late appalling sickness from the self-denying efforts of Christian women—some acting alone, on the impulse of their own individual generous nature, some living in communities, of which it is the common bond to be ready, for Christ's sake, to tend the poor, at whatever risk. Our cholera hospitals, the crowded streets and squalid homes of our East End parishes, were cheered and blessed by the presence of many true Sisters of Mercy of the Church of England, without whom it is certain that in those desolate regions the suffering would have been far worse than it was. . . . No doubt those Christian women who work in communities are still viewed by the great majority of the clergy with considerable suspicion. Would to God they would abstain from all practices which make these suspicions reasonable. . . . The time has, I think, come when the clergy generally and the heads of the Church must enter fully into the question how the help of Christian women living in community, and holding themselves ready to act amongst the sick and poor, is to be best arranged. We have amongst us a large body earnestly desirous of giving themselves to such work. I for one, seeing the vastness of the flock committed to me—knowing by experience how they can alleviate the sufferings of the poor—have not the heart, if I had the will, to discourage the zeal, which it is ours not to extinguish but to direct. God knows we need their help, if they will give it in the way which our Church approves.

"'The rules which I have myself laid down as most necessary in my dealings with such communities have been the following :—

"'To point out that the first of all duties are those which we owe to our family. Family ties are imposed direct by God. If family duties are overlooked, God's blessing can never be expected on any efforts which we make for His Church. Every community, therefore, of Sisters or Deaconesses ought to consist of persons who have fully satisfied all family obligations.

" Again, all who enter such communities must be at full liberty to leave them so soon as the leadings of God's providence point to another sphere of Christian duty. Hence all vows of continuing in the community, actually taken or mentally implied, are wrong.

" Again, the rules of the community must be simple and carefully guarded, so as to check all imperiousness in the higher, and all unworthy and unchristian servile submission in the lower, members.

" Again, great care must be taken to guard against morbid religious feelings and opinions, which all experience shows such communities have a tendency to foster. There must be no encouragement to a self-righteous estimate of the life embraced, as if it were more perfect than that of the family. Each life has its own privileges and its own trials. The only way to live as a Christian in that sphere which God from time to time assigns us is to do our work humbly as in His sight. And, indeed, the highest life, if we may venture to compare the privileges which God assigns, is that of the truly Christian head of a family. Care must be taken also that the worship of the community shall not encourage exaggerated views of doctrine, such as every narrow clique is prone to adopt; and that tendency must be steadily resisted which women often show to hang unduly on the guidance of some priestly adviser, to be making confession to him, and to become in fact his slaves.

"I cannot but hope that the great difficulties which confessedly beset the proper regulation of such communities may be grappled with. I am sure it is the part of us, the clergy, to make the attempt, that we may secure the assistance of Sisters or Deaconesses in work which in many of our parishes it is scarcely possible to accomplish without their aid. And I cannot but trust also that, as time goes on, many of these excellent women, who at present adhere somewhat tenaciously to their own peculiarities, will be ready to drop them—learning in their labour of love the infinite value of that simpler and purer Christianity which alone sustains souls on the deathbeds to which they so often minister—becoming willing to sacrifice their own opinions, from a growing truer devotion to our Reformed Church, and prizing as they ought that larger field of usefulness which formal hearty recognition, under proper rules by the clergy and authorities of the Church, would at once open to them. . . .

"Certainly, brethren, we in London have need of every help. We stand in the forefront of the battle. To us is committed the most important position in that National Church which God has chosen, that He may delegate to it the most difficult of His works—to resist the barbarism which, in the overflowing population of a vast people, is apt to spring up side by side with the highest refinement; while in its labours amongst all classes, battling against worldliness and infidelity and superstition, it does what it can to guide the religious thought of a great and intelligent nation, and to advance thereby the Christian civilisation of the world."[1]

The reference above made to the cholera epidemic of

[1] Charge of 1866, pp. 83-89.

1866 demands a somewhat fuller notice. The Bishop, who had been seriously ill in spring, was preparing in July, when he was again unwell, to leave London for his autumn holiday. Suddenly it became known, almost without warning, that Asiatic cholera in a virulent form had appeared in East London. It had been raging at Alexandria, whence a ship's crew had brought it to Southampton. From Southampton, in a manner afterwards traced, it was conveyed to Woodford, in Essex, and thence down the valley of the Lea into East London. In a few days there were many hundreds of cases in Bethnal Green alone. The Bishop, ill as he was, decided immediately that he must remain in London, and take the lead in whatever measures were necessary to inspire confidence and to organise relief.[1] He has himself, in his Memoir of Mrs. Tait, given a reminiscence of those stirring days of anxiety and even peril :—

"The state of things in the East of London," he says, "became very bad indeed. The whole district which had any connexion with the river Lea was infected. I summoned a meeting of the clergy of Bethnal Green, Stepney, and Spitalfields, and we endeavoured to make arrangements which might aid the sanitary authorities. From that time my dear wife accompanied me regularly in the visits which I made to the infected districts. . . . I can see her now standing in one of the large wards of the hospital for Wapping and St. George's-in-the-East, quietly soothing the sufferers, while one poor little girl seemed to be seized with the last agonies, and the Rev. C. F. Lowder, who attended us, stepped quietly to the bed of the poor patient, and gave her such help as, by God's blessing, resulted in her final recovery. I can see her in the well-ordered hospital extemporised by Miss Sellon, near Shoreditch, encouraging the sisters who had ventured their lives from the pure air of Ascot into that infected district ; and in the Middlesex Hospital, where other well-known ladies had undertaken to assist the permanent staff. I remember the real

---

[1] A letter from him in the *Times* elicited £3000 within twenty-four hours. The total amount subscribed was about £70,000.

danger to which I thought she was exposed near Ratcliff High-way, when, unexpectedly, she was summoned to try and guide the somewhat irregular efforts of the clergymen of the parish to distribute relief amongst a miscellaneous crowd of those whose families were suffering from the plague. I remember also how, when the evil began to abate, she helped Miss Twining, by her support and advice, in the temporary building secured for con-valescents on a spot south of the Thames.

"This visitation of the cholera led to the crowning labour of her life. Mrs. Gladstone, Miss Marsh, and herself—the 'three Catharines,' as some newspaper called them—had each of them her spirit stirred to undertake the charge of some of those many orphans whom the cholera left destitute ; and institutions, still vigorously at work, were the result. Mrs. Gladstone, I believe, undertook to provide for the boys. My wife hired a house at Fulham for the girls, and, by the aid of Mr. and Mrs. Lancaster, and the sisters of their 'Home,' soon established St. Peter's Orphanage, which has continued growing ever since. It cannot be doubted that the ever-present thought of her own children, whom she had lost, was an incentive to her care for these destitute little girls."[1]

The Orphanage, which at first contained thirty girls, remained at Fulham for about five years. In 1871 it was transferred to the Isle of Thanet, where a large building, capable of holding eighty children, was, by Mrs. Tait's exertions, erected in the parish of St. Peter's, upon a site given by the Archbishop. The 'St. Peter's Orphan and Convalescent Homes,' now established upon a secure and permanent basis, owe their origin to the Cholera Visitation of 1866.

The epidemic over, he left London in September for his sorely needed holiday. But the strain had been too great. On September 24, while walking with his brother upon North Berwick sands, he suddenly fell down in great pain. He was carried to his bed. The ancient mischief in the region of the heart had returned, and with it other

---

[1] *Catharine and Crawfurd Tait*, pp. 47-8.

internal complications, and for some weeks his life again hung in the balance. Early in November he was able to be moved to Edinburgh, and soon afterwards to Brighton, but he was greatly shattered, and not a few of his friends were convinced that his active days were over. It was the year of his third Diocesan Visitation, and he had already, when his illness began, been busy upon his Charge. He was now able to complete it for publication, but the doctors peremptorily refused to allow him to deliver it in person, and would not even consent to his being present at the visitation. The Charge was read for him in St. Paul's Cathedral by his Chancellor, Dr. Twiss. Elaborated as it was in the quiet of his sick-room, it is perhaps, in style and diction, the most careful of all his public utterances, and its publication evoked such letters as the following:—

Dean Stanley wrote :—

"I do thank you in every sense for your Charge. In my humble opinion it is quite the best that you have delivered. I do not agree with all of it, but I am sure that even the parts with which I do not agree will do good, and the whole result ought indeed to be a *sursum corda.*"

Dean Hook wrote from Chichester :—

"It does one good to read such words of wisdom in this day of rebuke and blasphemy. If any of your spiritual children were inclined to follow the example of the sons of Sophocles, you have, like Sophocles, convinced the world that under the depression of illness, your mind is, I should say, even more vigorous than before. You have never written more powerfully. I have particularly to thank you for what you have said of sisterhoods. It has settled my mind upon the subject. . . . You occupy so very important and peculiar a position at the present time, that you are in duty bound to take warning from your predecessor, and to let others do those *details* of work which they can do as well as their Principal, reserving yourself for that which pertains to your character as a man as well as of a bishop. Mrs. Tait will give her sanction to this sermon, however unbecoming it may be on the part of a Presbyter when writing to a Bishop. You will value what I say the more when I add that, highly as I esteem your judgment, and delighting as I do in the straightforward, downright, honest, English manliness of your character, I do by no means concur in all your opinions, though if I lived in London, I should back you as my Bishop and merge all differences.

"Oh! as the end approaches how consolatory is the thought that the future to which we look forward is not in the Church militant, but in the Church triumphant.   And oh, the blessedness of knowing that the great Captain of our Salvation judges us, not by what we had power *to do*, but by what we had grace to intend !"

Similarly Dr. Lightfoot wrote :—

"Independently of personal attachment, I feel very strongly that your life is of the first importance to the Church of England at the present crisis, and that it is therefore a duty you owe to the Church, as well as to your family and friends, to spare yourself as much as possible.   For once I believe in the sacred principle of delegation."

From one of the foremost and most representative of his London clergy, a man from whom he had prominently differed in some matters, came the following :—

"I shall never forget the wonderful kindness with which you have always treated me, nor the confidence which has been at once so encouraging and so stimulating.   You cannot know to what a great extent your clergy love and value you, and how many prayers are offered up for you that you may speedily recover your health, and for many years yet glorify God and bless them in your laborious but grand diocese."

Not till the middle of January (1867) was he allowed to return to Fulham and to active work, and his attacks, though in a milder form, recurred at intervals throughout the year.   It is impossible to give full value to the persistent vigour of his London work, unless we remember how often he was battling, even on his busiest days, with such ill-health and bodily pain as would have daunted and disheartened any less determined man.

CHAPTER XVII.

DEFINITENESS OF BELIEF—DIOCESAN CHARGES—SUBSCRIPTION
TO FORMULARIES.

1863-1867.

AN endeavour has been made in the preceding chapters
to describe the Bishop's relation to the two dangers—
Rationalism on the one side, and Superstition on the other
—which were supposed, thirty years ago, to be threatening the life of the Church of England. It is possible that
some reader of these chapters, unfamiliar otherwise with
the facts, may have been led to picture to himself the
Bishop of London as a strong but unattractive man,
reserved and cautious in his opinions and policy, just and
considerate no doubt, as should become a Christian
gentleman, but eager to repress in other men the enthusiasm of which he had himself no trace, and tolerant
of the religious opinions of all sorts of people, mainly
because he had no very precise or definite opinions of
his own.

If such a picture of Bishop Tait should present itself
to any, the fault must lie with his biographer. It may
safely be said that no one of those who knew him personally
either then or afterwards, would, from such a description,
recognise the man whom he remembers. It is true that
throughout his public years he was at a frequent disadvan-

tage when compared with the picturesque figures by whom he was surrounded. In every battle the popular gaze will fix itself upon the fiery champions at the front, rather than on the generals in the background ;—and, upon the one side, the impetuous pioneers of reform, and, upon the other, the immoveable defenders of the ancient ways, must always have a vivid and peculiar interest of their own. The names of Pusey and Maurice and Selwyn, of Charles Lowder and Arthur Stanley, of Shaftesbury and Wilberforce, of Walter Hook and Thomas Carter, will continue no doubt for years to come to awaken the plaudits they deserve, not from their partisans only, but from the Church at large. They, and others like them, were champions in various battles, and upon various sides, and each of them in turn stood at one time or other in active opposition to Bishop Tait. And yet most of them, as their own words show, felt at times, amid the strife of tongues, the advantage to the Church, in anxious days, of the presence, at the centre of affairs, of the calm, strong man who differed sometimes from them all, and who was able, not once or twice, by weighty and well-timed words, to arrest the storm which his more impetuous friends had raised.

> " Jamque faces et saxa volant (furor arma ministrat) ;
> Tum, pietate gravem ac meritis si forte virum quem
> Conspexere, silent, arrectisque auribus adstant ;
> Ille regit dictis animos et pectora mulcet."

It is difficult to estimate what might have been the evil consequences to the Church had the occupant of Fulham and of Lambeth, in those years of flux and change, been an intolerant or one-sided man. But if Archibald Tait, as Bishop and Archbishop, had a singular tolerance, and even sympathy, for those whose views and action differed widely from his own, it was certainly from no cold-blooded disregard of the religious questions in dispute. If he refused to join his brethren, for example, in inhibiting Bishop Colenso, and retained his friendship for the writers of *Essays and Reviews*, he was not for that reason a whit the less emphatic in enunciating his own positive opinions upon the Divine authority of Holy Scripture. It would certainly have been easier for him, in the heat of a conflict which cost him so much, and which exposed him, as we have seen, to a double fire, to have avoided any special utterance of a doctrinal sort upon the difficult subject which was setting men at variance. Such silence would have been easy to defend. But he took the opposite line. Besides referring to the subject at full length in two Diocesan Charges, he published in those years three separate volumes of sermons dealing specially with the question of the Inspiration of Holy Scripture. In the preface to the first of these, which contained a reprint of addresses delivered at Oxford fifteen years before, he makes this reference to the personal experiences of his life :—

"It may seem unlikely in these changing days that what was written for 1846 can be suitable for 1861. Most men change or greatly modify their opinions and sentiments in fifteen years. The rude test of experiment is continually making shipwreck of many skilfully constructed theories ; and even he whose views of religion and society are from the bent of his mind most practical, continually finds, as life goes on, that there is something unreal in his opinions, which requires, if not to be given up, at least to be carefully revised and altered. The trials of life greatly affect our mental vision : rightly used, they make us more sympathising, more considerate, more tolerant ; but they also more deeply convince us of the priceless value of truths which have been our soul's only stay in terrible emergencies. Few mortals pass any great length of time without sickness and sorrow, and if a man has looked death in the face, or, while well in his own bodily health, has been stunned in mind by seeing fond hopes vanish, he will naturally cling with a firmer tenacity to the great religious truths which bore him up when all else failed, and will be more jealous of any attempts to tamper with these truths, than he was when he defended them in earlier life on grounds of mere speculative orthodoxy, having not yet learned to prize and love them through —what must be to each practically the surest test—their tried value to his own spirit. . . . It would not, therefore, have been surprising if the author of the following discourses had found, in 1861, that he could neither himself indorse what he had written fifteen years ago, nor, if it did still retain its hold on his convictions, look upon it as applicable to the circumstances of a greatly changed age. He has not, however, met with this difficulty. Re-perusing what he then put forth, he finds it to be as true an exponent as ever of his real sentiments, and he thinks that, by God's blessing, the statements he long ago deliberately published may tend to quiet men's hearts even now. . . . Men need to be told now, as much as they ever did, that controversy, to be Christian, must be conducted in a Christian spirit of forbearing love. . . . Men need to be told now, as much as ever, that the truths of a living Christian faith cannot be made to find their way into reluctant minds through mere protest and negation. . . . To warn us against what is not true is very different from giving us the truth. The Holy Spirit of God can indeed alone mould the convictions, but the human advocate of truth will not do his part in upholding it, unless he tries to clothe it in the living form of an embodied and intelligible teaching, capable of warming the sympathies and attracting the affections, at the same time that it appeals, as the case may be, either to the understanding or the highest reason." [1]

Such a "living form of embodied and intelligible teaching" the Bishop endeavours throughout the volume to supply, and the twenty-five sermons it contains are, whatever else they be, neither ambiguous, nor timorous, nor vague. From very various quarters he received thanks for what were described as his "outspoken words of reassurance, hopefulness, and faith," and especially for the pains he had taken to face and not evade the exact points in dispute.

---

[1] *Dangers and Safeguards of Modern Theology*; Introduction, pp. 1-3.

"I have been fortunate enough," wrote Mr. Gladstone, "to hear some of the sermons, and I have read with cordial admiration the powerful arguments and exhortations contained in others."

"I thank you very much," wrote Professor Lightfoot, "for distinguishing what is essential and what is non-essential in Scripture. If the public mind were once impressed with that distinction, I should not fear the effect of such books as Bishop Colenso's. But I fear the great mass of religious people in England have it yet to learn."

In regard to the accusation already referred to, of a studied indefiniteness in the Bishop's expression of his own religious opinions, such an episode as the following may be of interest. An important benefice in Crown Patronage was vacant. The Bishop was not directly concerned in the matter, but a leading member of the Government asked his advice about a clergyman whose name was under consideration, and quite a voluminous theological correspondence ensued. The Bishop's final letter was as follows :—

"My dear ——,— . . . I have carefully read the sermons in question. It appears to me that, carried away by his desire to protest against certain statements derogatory to the perfect justice and infinite mercy of Almighty God, he has in these sermons lost sight of what I believe to be a most important truth. I believe that the sacrifice of Christ, consummated in His death, removed certain mysterious obstacles which stood in the way of man's pardon ; and this sacrifice was designed by infinite love as the instrument whereby God and man were again to be brought together after the disruption caused by the Fall. I dare not explain the mysterious effect of the Sacrifice of Christ simply by its reconciling the soul to God through the powerful motives called up by so wonderful an exhibition of infinite love and of infinite sympathy with the human race. I believe the Atonement to have had effects in altering the abstract relation between an offended God and fallen man, besides its power of drawing the soul of man back to that holiness and faithful waiting upon God from which it had fallen. Whether Mr. A. holds this or not, I cannot distinctly ascertain. You seemed to think, in what you said to me, that his teaching confounds man's justification with his sanctification. If there be any tendency towards this in the teaching of the sermons, I believe its evil effect is quite guarded against by the strong statements Mr. A. has made respecting the absolute freedom of the pardon won by Christ's Cross. There seems to me to be nothing in his teaching to imply our being only so far forth justified as we are by the power of the Cross sanctified. I do not therefore apprehend that in his practical application of the doctrine of free pardon through the blood of Christ, there would be any difference between him and others who more distinctly set forth what I believe to be implied in the doctrine of Christ's sacrifice being a ' ransom ' and a ' propitiation.'

"On the whole, if I had resolved on other grounds to appoint Mr. A. to a post such as you have mentioned, from conceiving him to be, as he certainly is, a self-denying, laborious, conscientious, able clergyman, of deeply religious mind, I should not be deterred from fulfilling my intention by these sermons, though I should myself have stated many things of which they treat very differently.—Believe me to be, my dear ——, yours very truly,   A. C. LONDON."

It was, however, in his Visitation Charges that he expressed himself most effectively upon such subjects. Both as Bishop and Archbishop he used his recurring Visitations as opportunities for speaking his mind upon the larger questions of the day. It was necessary, he said, for the Bishop of London to do so,

"for the Metropolis stands in the forefront of the Church's battle, and we have to grapple personally with difficulties the very rumour of which alarms our brethren in quieter places." [1]

And again :—

" London, above all other dioceses, must be indissolubly connected with the whole national Church. We do not ignore those powerful elements of the softening influences of country life, not found amongst ourselves ; nor the effect of the position, so different from ours, in which the country clergy stand to their

---

[1] Charge of 1862, p. 2.

flocks; nor the vast power of University life, moulding the thoughts of our rising youth. But still, London is the centre: to London flows yearly, in a steady tide, a large body of persons of all classes from every country; from London the stream of influence, however unobserved, sets in irresistibly, through news-papers, books, letters, the converse of friends, to hall, parsonage, farmhouse, and cottage in the remotest country districts. If we in London are faithless, all England suffers. If London could but become the really Christian centre of the nation, how would our national Christianity grow!"[1]

With the sense of this responsibility upon his shoulders he set himself in his three London Charges to make a solid contribution to the discussion of whatever questions were stirring the National Church. An account has already been given of the purport and effect of his primary Charge in 1858. It was a trumpet call to larger efforts of an aggressive sort against the sin and misery of London. The Charges of 1862 and 1866 had reference rather to the ecclesiastical questions of the hour: the scare of Ritualism on the one side, and Rationalism on the other; the desire for corporate union with those out-side the Church of England; the history and character of the Church's Courts; and the promotion of clerical efficiency and preaching power. It would be impossible to quote largely from these Charges, but a few typical extracts may perhaps be given, with special reference to the strength and definiteness of his contention for the Faith. In the Charge of 1862, he refers at length to

"the difficulties that spring from that unrestrained spirit of free inquiry, which claims the right to sift and test all theories, and bows to no authority, however venerable, which cannot make good by argument its claim on our allegiance."

"As to free inquiry," he says, "what shall we do with it? Shall we frown upon it, denounce it, try to stifle it? This will do no good even if it be right. But after all we are Protestants.

<hr>

[1] Charge of 1866, pp. 2, 3.

We have been accustomed to speak a good deal of the right and
duty of private judgment. It was by the exercise of this right
and the discharge of this duty that our fathers freed their and
our souls from Rome's time-honoured falsehoods. Are we to be
scared from those great principles which opened the closed door
of truth in the sixteenth century, because some men, using our
instruments of investigation, arrive at false and dangerous conclusions? As well might Luther have turned against the Reformation because of the eccentricities of the Anabaptists, or our
own divines have thought it best to make common cause with
the Jesuits because of the spread of Unitarianism. Am I convinced of the heavenly origin of those great truths for which the
Church of England has been appointed by the Lord Jesus as
the chief witness upon earth? And shall I, from a craven fear
lest these truths be shaken, disparage the use of that great
instrument of reason which God has given to man for the
investigation and defence of truth? If I am wise I will not
ask my people to give to the Church's teaching an unreason-
ing and stolid assent. I will set myself to work, as being
conscious of the value of that priceless gift of reason, to discipline myself, and help others, that we may use it as God directs.
. . . For example, am I the pastor of a parish, and do I
know that some intelligent and promising young man of my
flock is distressing the old-fashioned piety of his parents by giving
utterance to speculations which sound to them like blasphemy?
How shall I deal with him? . . . He has been, say, to the
University, and has heard questions freely discussed there, of
which he never dreamed in childhood; questions as to the nature
and limits of inspiration, as to the difficulties which stand in the
way of an unquestioning assent to the perfect historical accuracy
of the Bible narrative; questions as to the possibility of reconciling
a belief in miraculous interpositions with the maintenance of
unchanging laws; questions as to how far the discoveries of
modern science agree with the teaching of the sacred books; or
(after the general truth of the Bible scheme is admitted), intricate
metaphysical questions still may be raised as to the particular
mode in which the life and death of Christ avail for man's
salvation, and how far the exact truth on this momentous subject
is expressed in the Church's formularies. A man need neither
be conceited, nor shallow, nor rash, nor irreverent, to have had
his thoughts exercised on any one of these subjects. . . . You

must be able to say to him whom you would influence :—I know what these perplexities mean. I can point the way to solve them. Let us talk of those things quietly and reverently together, invoking the Divine blessing, and by the Divine guidance we shall certainly emerge into the light. We believe with the Church of all ages that the Bible is the Word of God ; that through it God speaks to each separate soul, and through it also God's voice is heard century after century proclaiming truth aloud to a world wandering in error. We believe that the eternal Son of God visited, in human guise, the earth He had created ; that His advent was heralded and His presence attested by many miracles, and that when the men he came to save slew Him, His power over death, as the Prince of Life, was shown by His rising, the greatest of all miracles. We believe that through His death the barrier was thrown down, which, as the effect of sin once entering into our nature, kept God and man asunder—that thus God was reconciled to man once for all—as, through the spectacle of His death and rising again set forth to human souls age after age, they are one by one reconciled to God." [1]

And similarly, in 1866 :—

" The Church of England," he says, " does allow amongst its people great diversity of opinion in non-essentials. This is a necessary characteristic of a Protestant branch of the Church Catholic. Sects of all kinds, whether Protestant or so-called Catholic, are narrow and unwarrantably dogmatic—venturing to define where God's word has not defined ; eager to exclude from their pale all who will not allow their minds to be forced into one groove. Such the Church of England has never been through any continuous period of its history, though at certain epochs vigorous efforts have been made—and, for a time, even successfully—to narrow it to the dimensions of a sect. . . . But then it is urged, and truly, that there must be limits to this variety, or the Church will lose all unity. It may be well that Arnold and Keble and Daniel Wilson, trained in one university, lived and died, with all their many peculiar differences, ministers of one Church. But how far is this liberty to go ? The answer is plain. It can go no further than is consistent with a common belief in the essentials of the Church's faith, and these are plainly stated

---

[1] Charge of 1862, pp. 6-11.

in the formularies as in the Bible. The mind that repudiates
these essentials may hesitate for a time (and God forbid that any
rash upbraidings should add fresh pain to the anxieties of doubt,
or precipitate by unkindness a separation which we deplore) ; but
still, if the mind repudiates these plainly-written essentials, it can
find no lasting peace in the English Church. Is it true that there
are men who even desire to act as Christ's ministers amongst
us, without believing in the resurrection of Jesus Christ ? I can
scarcely credit the assertion. The Church of England, from the
beginning to the end of its formularies, proclaims with St. Paul
that if Christ be not risen, our preaching and faith is vain, there
is no Gospel. For those who do not believe in the resurrection
of Christ we have no place, as we have none for those who do
not believe in Christ's divinity, nor in the divinity of the Third
Person of the blessed Trinity. The essentials of the Christian
faith are incorporated in our formularies from the Bible and the
Apostles' Creed—explained and enlarged on, but not added to :
the liberty of thought which is consistent with loyalty to our
Church is therefore hedged in by these essentials.

" And then, on the other hand, since the Church of England
is not only Catholic as holding the old faith, but also Protestant,
there are essentials, not of the Christian faith, but of our charter
as reformed from Roman error, which it is equally vain for any
man to hope that he can with a safe conscience ignore. 'The
Bishop of Rome hath no jurisdiction in this realm of England'
(Art. xxxvii.). 'The sacrifices of masses, in the which it was commonly said that the Priest did offer Christ for the quick and the
dead to have remission of pain or guilt, were blasphemous fables
and dangerous deceits' (Art. xxxi.). 'The body of Christ is
given, taken, and received in the [Lord's] Supper only after an
heavenly and spiritual manner. And the mean whereby the
body of Christ is received and eaten in the Supper is faith' (Art.
xxviii.). These and such like solemn protests against Rome,
giving their colour to the whole body of our Articles, close on
this side the liberty of all who would be loyal to our Church."[1]

Like many other Churchmen in those days, Bishop
Tait's personal experience of the loss of dear and trusted
friends led him to have a special dislike and fear of any

---

[1] Charge of 1866, pp. 6-9.

Romeward leanings. The question of some possible corporate Reunion of the Roman, the Anglican, and the Eastern Churches had become prominent in 1865, by means of a published correspondence between Cardinal Patrizi, as representing the Roman Church, and a body of clergy of the Church of England, said to be 198 in number. The Cardinal had somewhat contemptuously declined to reciprocate the friendly " feeling of good-will " which was expressed by his Anglican correspondents, and Archbishop Manning, in a Pastoral Letter published early in 1866, had dealt with the subject at full length, and rejected in a tone of uncompromising sternness the advances which had been made.[1]

Bishop Tait referred thus to the matter in his Charge:—

" We do not forget how desirable it is that Christendom should be one and at peace with itself. We long and pray for this peace and union ; but we want no hollow peace, still less a peace which shall be purchased by sacrificing our liberty and God's truth. Thus we feel ashamed when told of members of our noble Reformed Church going, cap in hand, to seek for some slight recognition from that old usurping power—so unlike the gentle, truth-loving Church of the Apostles, of which it vaunts itself the sole representative—which slew Latimer and Ridley and Cranmer and Hooper in the old time, because they would not surrender God's truth, and which certainly values the pure Gospel now at as low a rate as of old. And we feel some satisfaction in learning how these advances were coldly rejected by the old haughty spirit which they seek in vain to propitiate.

" It pains me also deeply to find men labouring, as I noted above, to show that the Church of the Reformation has, after all, by some felicitous accident, escaped from being reformed ; that, if we could only see it, there is nothing really Protestant in the Thirty-nine Articles, and nothing really Romish in the Decrees of Trent. If this were so, language must be a still more uncertain vehicle of men's thoughts than all acknowledge it to be.

" But, indeed, there is no sign that this mode of making peace

---

[1] *The Reunion of Christendom : A Pastoral Letter.* 1866.

with Rome is possible. Rome is too wise, and I think I may say for at least ninety-nine out of every hundred of English Churchmen, that they are too wise also. Archbishop Laud's saying holds true still : that there can be no thought of union with Rome till she becomes other than she is.

" . . . And then as to schemes of union with the Oriental Churches : I am sure I wish they could come to anything. It would be satisfactory indeed to see the Churches of the early centuries, the venerable Patriarchates, the nurseries of great Fathers, returning to the vigour and earnestness of their youth, and prizing that Gospel which it is the great privilege of some of them to possess, written in the beautiful clearness of their own ancient tongue. When we think what blessings the West has received from the East, both of secular and religious civilisation, no educated European but will desire to repay part of the debt, and concur in any schemes by which the Christian East may be benefited.

" But when we come to projects of reuniting Christendom, we are not to be hurried on by mere feelings of romance. Of course we are not such children as to suppose that the real unity of Christendom is to be secured by the clergy in Rome, Constantinople, and London wearing similarly coloured stoles. We must ask calmly, but very seriously, how far these Churches are exerting themselves to escape from that idolatrous worship of the Lord's mother which for centuries has made Christianity in those regions despicable in the eyes both of Jews and Mahometans. We must ask, also, what symptoms they are showing of a returning desire to teach the people out of the Holy Scriptures. There can be no union on our part which overlooks the deadly sin of idolatry and the concealment of the Scriptures." [1]

A subsequent Chapter will show that in later years, when he was in frequent intercourse, as Primate, with the Oriental Churches, he was led to modify this rather hopeless view of their relation to ourselves, and that he came to entertain for some of their Bishops a genuine and sympathetic friendship, which found repeated expression in his public utterances.[2]

[1] Charge of 1866, pp. 55-61.
[2] See, e.g. *The Church of the Future*, pp. 5-8.

While his Charges were thus concerned with the larger questions of the hour, they were characterised also by careful and detailed suggestions as to practical ways of meeting some of the difficulties of London parishes. One point on which he was fond of dwelling in those years, as a means of giving greater effectiveness to parish work, was the week-day opening of churches, both for short services and for private prayer. The custom was far less common then than it is now, and it is probable that his repeated exhortations did not a little to promote the change. In his private journal, when abroad, in the autumn of 1861, he writes :—

"BRUSSELS, *August* 23, 1861.—How little hope there is of Romanism reforming itself ! . . . I wish indeed we Protestants could have its outward helps to religion in use among us—short services on week-days well attended ; churches used as houses of prayer by the poor. And why should we not? Our friends who revived daily services some twenty years ago committed a mistake—unless perhaps they could not do otherwise with the then feeling of the Bishops—when they established the long daily service at inconvenient hours. What we want are short litanies and hymns and expositions, to catch people as they go to and from their work. How good it would be if we could have the outward appearance and outward helps of religion which Romish countries afford, and a pure reasonable 'Gospel' service, and real religious life promoted by them ! Well, there is good hope for these things in England, and I may perhaps, God willing, do somewhat to stir the clergy in these matters."

He did "do somewhat" in his public Charge of the following year, when he spoke as follows :—

"And why should not our churches be open habitually, to give the poor a quiet place for private prayer? How great is the disadvantage under which they labour, deprived of the power of retirement, exposed to ridicule or other interruptions in their crowded lodgings ! . . . There is everything to encourage us in beginning from this point a renewed effort."[1]

[1] Page 72.

Another subject on which he laid great stress was the need of helping the younger clergy to attain a better style of preaching.   He used frequently to say that young men in their first years in Holy Orders, were almost forced into acquiring a dull and unimpressive style, which never left them.

" One thing I would specially deprecate," he said in his Charge of 1862, " namely, the setting of a young curate to preach every Sunday at some ill-frequented afternoon service, the very sight of the congregation at which is enough to chill him into awkwardness.   It is cruelty to him to undertake, as his chief duty, what is either the most useless or the most difficult part of our parochial work ; . . . and certainly if we set our curates to learn how to preach by addressing empty benches, they will probably learn their work so badly as to be likely to preach to empty benches as long as they live." [1]

One question dealt with in his London Charges demands a somewhat fuller notice.   It used to be said, both by friends and foes, and probably with truth, that it was due to the words of Bishop Tait in charging his clergy from the pulpit of St. Paul's that a change was peaceably effected in the form and manner of clerical subscription to the Church's formularies ; and the story, now almost forgotten, ought therefore to be told.

It will be remembered how keenly he had contended in his earlier days for perfect honesty and straightforwardness in the matter of subscription, of whatever kind. First as a candidate for the Greek Professorship at Glasgow, secondly as one of the four tutors who protested against Tract XC., and thirdly as a member of the Oxford University Commission, he had given proof of his strong opinion upon this subject.   The subscription difficulty now reappeared in another form.   An earnest appeal was made for some relaxation of the law requiring from all

<hr>

[1] Page 87.

clergy at their Ordination certain tests and subscriptions to the Church's formularies. The formal subscription, it was urged, had become both harassing and ineffectual, and if its total abolition was undesirable, it might at least, said the reformers, be redrafted and curtailed.

But the proposal, as was to be expected, met with strenuous opposition. August 24, 1862, was the bicentenary of the 'Black Bartholomew's Day,' when Charles II.'s Act of Uniformity became law. The occasion was naturally seized by Nonconformists and their friends, and by many of the liberal clergy, to call attention to the whole subject of exclusive and protective tests, and, as usual in such controversies, the language used by the hot promoters of reform served to aggravate the indignation and alarm of their Conservative opponents. In the House of Lords Lord Ebury became the mouthpiece of those who desired to modify the form of clerical subscription, but the Bill he introduced was withdrawn for further consideration upon the urgent appeal of Bishop Tait, who, to the wrath of some of his Episcopal colleagues, and especially of Bishop Wilberforce, expressed his general concurrence in Lord Ebury's endeavour to simplify and reduce the formidable array of compulsory clerical declarations.[1] Though custom had made men familiar with the burden, it was certainly 'formidable' enough when plainly stated. Every man ordained to an ordinary curacy had to make seven— or, as some expressed it, ten—distinct declarations of assent, or promises of obedience ; while an incumbent, on institution to a benefice, added four more, making, as it was sometimes put, fourteen separate subscriptions.[2] Many of these were of course mere repetitions, but they were none the less burdensome and cumbrous.

---

[1] *Hansard*, May 27, 1862, p. 18.

[2] For a precise list of these and their history see Report of the Royal Commission of 1864-5, p. 9.

A few months after the House of Lords debate, Bishop Tait delivered in St. Paul's Cathedral his second Diocesan Charge, and referred, as was indeed inevitable, to the prevailing agitation.

"As to the declarations which the law of the land requires to to be made at ordination," he said, "I should be ready myself, even now, in spite of all temporary alarm as to unsound opinions, to relax rather than to tighten the bond. I hold that in this question of guarding the threshold of the ministry, as elsewhere in dealing with the difficulties of an inquisitive age, the generous confiding policy is the best and the most Christian. . . . If there be reason for the revision of the terms of subscription, the subject certainly demands most grave consideration, and I doubt not will—I trust, soon—receive it, both from the Bishops and from other members of the Legislature."[1]

It was on the strength of the support thus given that Lord Ebury, on the very opening day of the Parliament of 1863, reintroduced, in a somewhat different shape, his dreaded Bill. He proposed to limit the clerical declaration for the future to a simple promise "to conform to the liturgy of the Church of England as it is now by law established." With an historical sentiment unusual in Acts of Parliament, his Bill provided that the relaxation should begin to operate "upon the next ensuing Feast of St. Bartholomew." When the Bill came up for second reading, its rejection was moved by Archbishop Longley, who objected in the strongest terms to any interference with the detailed and definite promise of "unfeigned assent and consent to all and everything contained and prescribed in and by the Book of Common Prayer." Bishop Tait, on the other hand, approved Lord Ebury's proposal.

"He had," he said, "carefully and anxiously pondered the question, and it was only common honesty to avow the conclusion to which he had been led—that the declaration which the

<hr>

[1] Charge of 1862, pp. 25 and 47.

noble lord wished to expunge was unnecessary, and, being unnecessary, was more or less mischievous. It gave him considerable pain to differ in a matter of this kind from the most Reverend Primate and from others of his Episcopal brethren, but there was no difference of principle. They were all equally anxious to maintain that eternal truth of which the Bible was the depository: they were all equally anxious to maintain that form of sacred words in which that eternal truth had been handed down by the Church. . . . But it was inevitable for persons of different ages, and moving in different circumstances, that to some more than to others were different forms of opinion and feeling presented, and if it had been his lot to be thrown more than his brethren in the way of those who felt the difficulties in question, he thought himself bound, for the information of public opinion and for the information of their lordships, to state what was the result of his own observation in the matter."

After describing various forms in which the difficulties had arisen, he continued :—

"'There was no doubt therefore that with respect even to clergymen of mature years these words caused scruples and uneasiness of mind ; and with regard to young men who were called to minister in holy things, they ought to be very cautious how they trifled with their consciences. He knew the unwillingness on the part of young men of the highest abilities to bind themselves more than was absolutely necessary. This might or might not be a healthy state of things, but it was eminently desirable to tell such men exactly what was required of them, and the form of words should be such as to stand in no need of casuistry to explain their meaning. Of course the great mass were not troubled with any such scruples, but the most earnest men were often the most troubled, and if any such persons were prevented from approaching or remaining in the ministry of the Church, that of itself constituted a strong argument for the reconsideration or removal of the words. He was glad to think that in such a matter as this they were able to quote the authority of Burnet and of his great master, Leighton,—that by expunging these words they would be acting in the spirit of Tillotson, Secker, and Porteous. These were men of calm minds, who entered very considerately into the people's scruples and feelings ;

and he believed the longer we lived the more we should become
sensible that the Church of England owed a great debt of
gratitude to the moderation and piety with which these men presided over her counsels. . . . He would add his own deep and
solemn conviction that if the Church of England was to live in
the affections of this great country, and hold the place which it
ought to hold in Christendom, it must ever be distinguished by
that spirit of comprehensive love which enabled it to be really the
National Church, and to secure the esteem even of those who
were separated from its pale." [1]

Most of the Bishops, however, and a large majority of
the lay Peers, took an opposite line, and the bill was rejected
by 90 votes against 50.[2]   Then a pamphlet war began, and
the question was fiercely debated in Convocation.   Arthur
Stanley published a copious and brilliant " Letter to the
Bishop of London " upon one side, and Professor Ogilvie
replied upon the other.   Many of the London clergy were
indignant at their Diocesan's readiness, as was said, to
" tamper with the time-hallowed safeguards of the
Church," and an address was forwarded to Bishop Tait
by his two Archdeacons, in which 446 of the clergy of
the diocese recorded their solemn "judgment that the
attempts now made to abolish subscription are fraught
with present danger and future evil to the Church, and
as such are to be deprecated and opposed."

A curious, it may be almost said an amusing, correspondence followed.   The Bishop, on receipt of this somewhat warlike document, asked his Archdeacons, " in order
that he might better understand their address," to send
him a copy of the printed circular letter, not enclosed to
him in the first instance, in which the signatures of the
clergy had been invited.   This letter had been rendered
necessary by the reluctance of some of the clergy to sign

---

[1] *Hansard*, May 19, 1863, pp. 1935-38.

[2] The two Archbishops and eleven Bishops voted in the majority ; four
Bishops (London, St. David's, Llandaff, and Derry) in the minority.

so strong a remonstrance. With the gloss contained in the explanatory letter, the address came to mean very little. The Bishop drafted a reply, and half-maliciously showed it when in proof to one of his Archdeacons, who at once besought him not to publish it. The Bishop however insisted, and this "Address," the "Explanatory Letter," and the "Episcopal Reply," appeared together in pamphlet form. The following sentences contain the gist of the Bishop's reply :—

"FULHAM PALACE, 11*th July* 1863.

"MY DEAR ARCHDEACONS,—I have with great care perused the important Address on the subject of Subscription which you presented to me on the 9th of the month. I have also carefully considered the printed explanation which you were kind enough to forward to me this morning, . . . without which explanation indeed I should have found it difficult to understand the full scope and real intention of the Address.

"In this document of explanation sent round by the promoters of the Address to all the Clergy of the Diocese, with the request that they would append their names, it is stated, as I interpret the words :—

"1st. That those who sign the Address are not to be understood as being unprepared to accept any future revision of the existing clerical subscriptions if undertaken by the Church itself.

"2d. That what is protested against in the first paragraph of the Address is, some supposed intention of abolishing all subscriptions to the Church's formularies by an Act of Parliament.

"3d. That those who sign the Address record their conviction that the Church must have some doctrinal standards.

"It is a great satisfaction to me to feel that not only can I, as might be expected, cordially assent to the principles thus enunciated, but that there can scarcely be any amongst us who, when they fully consider the subject, will not find themselves to be in these points of the same opinion with the subscribers to the Address.

"There are some, perhaps, who believe that all the existing clerical subscriptions ought to be maintained under all circumstances and at all hazards. I agree, however, with those who have prepared the Address, that it is better to leave their maintenance or alteration an open question.

". . . The subscribers to the Address declare, as I understand them, that in their opinion it is hopeless to expect that in these difficult times any improvement can be made in our present declarations. Here the subscribers are no doubt aware that many of their brethren take a different view. For myself, personally, I have stated in the House of Lords that on one point at least I agree with those who are more hopeful. . . . I am reminded, my dear Archdeacons, by words which you have used in your letter to me, that it is our duty to 'banish and drive away all erroneous and strange doctrines contrary to God's word.' It cannot be doubted that all of us, Bishops and Clergy, have much cause in these days to ponder the full meaning of these words in our Ordination vow. The hearts of all good men in England have of late been made very anxious lest the authority of Christ's truth should be shaken amongst our people. . . . I will only say that as our Church has come out of dangerous crises in the past history unscathed and strengthened, so I have full confidence that by God's blessing we are safe now. Are the times dangerous? Every age has had its peculiar trial. I am far from thinking that our state is worse than that of our fathers. Indeed we ought thankfully to acknowledge that we have much better ground for confidence than they. Are there differences of opinion amongst us as to what is best for the Church? My experience now for seven years of the Clergy of this Diocese convinces me that, amidst their natural differences of opinion, there never was a time when they were more heartily and zealously agreed to do their Master's work, or more reverentially alive to the promised blessings of His aid."

It was not to be expected that Convocation would acquiesce quietly in the proposal for this sort of reform. Vehement speeches were made in favour of leaving things alone.

"The effect of relaxing subscription," it was said, "must be disastrous. The faith of the people in the honesty of the clergy will be disturbed. The laity will think the clergy read prayers in which they do not believe, and the moment that occurs all honest and right-minded men will, if they have any sense of Christian morality, leave the Church." "These subscriptions," said Archdeacon Wordsworth, "are a protection to the conscience against the arbitrary, the tyrannical usurpation of the popedom of private judgment installed in the 17,000 pulpits of the Church of England."[1]

A Committee of the Lower House made a report upon the matter,[2] but it was felt that the laymen who were interested ought also to have a voice in any changes which might be proposed, and the Government consented, on the solicitation of Bishop Tait and others, to the appointment of a Royal Commission[3] to inquire into the whole subject of Clerical Subscription and to report whether any changes were desirable. It was a Commission of no less than twenty-seven members, eleven of whom were laymen, and, strange to say, notwithstanding the heat of the previous controversy, the Commissioners were able to agree upon a unanimous recommendation that the relief which had been asked for should be granted, and the subscription reduced to a simpler and much less stringent form. Their unanimity took the Church and the country by surprise, but it made the issue very easy. On May 19, 1865, Lord Granville introduced a Government Bill to give legislative effect to the proposals, and, though debated at some length in the House of Commons, it became law before the close of the session.[4] In lieu of expressing in several successive sets of words his "unfeigned assent and consent to all and everything" within

---

[1] *Chronicle of Convocation*, 1863, pp. 1211, 1359.

[2] *Ibid.*, 1864, p. 1433.

[3] Among the Commissioners were the four Archbishops, the Bishops of London, Winchester, St. David's, and Oxford ; Lords Stanhope, Harrowby, Lyttelton, Cranworth, and Ebury ; the Dean of Ely, and the Rev. H. Venn.

[4] 28 and 29 Victoria, cap. 122.

the covers of the Prayer Book, and to an acknowledgment that "all and every one of the Articles, being in number nine and thirty, besides the Ratification, are agreeable to the Word of God," a clergyman has now on his ordination to declare once for all as follows :—

"I assent to the Thirty-Nine Articles of Religion and to the Book of Common Prayer, and of Ordering of Bishops, Priests, and Deacons ; I believe the doctrine of the Church of England as therein set forth to be agreeable to the Word of God ; and in public prayer and administration of the Sacraments I will use the form in the said book prescribed and none other, except so far as shall be ordered by lawful authority."

To give legal effect to the new subscription it was necessary to make certain changes, not in Acts of Parliament only, but in the Canons ; and Convocation obtained leave from the Crown to formulate the alterations. Long debates took place upon the constitutional questions thus raised, but although the English Church Union petitioned against the change, there was practically no difference of opinion in either House upon that subject, and the necessary alterations were unanimously carried.

Seldom has there been a more conspicuous example of the advantage of grasping the irritating nettle with firmness and determination. The controversy is now long over, and it is difficult to understand either the vehemence of opposition to the suggested change, or the wrathful surprise excited when Bishop Tait declared himself to be in favour of the relaxation.

CHAPTER XVIII.

MEMORANDA AND CORRESPONDENCE—FATHER IGNATIUS—REV. F.
D. MAURICE—THE SPEAKER'S COMMENTARY—ARCHDEACON
WORDSWORTH—RELIGIOUS EDUCATION—PURCHASE OF STONE-
HOUSE—OFFER OF THE PRIMACY.

1863-1867.

IT was the Bishop's occasional habit, as has been already
said, to jot down in a disjointed form—usually when he
was on a holiday—a few sheets of memoranda about the
general progress of whatever work he had in hand. Such
memoranda are the following, which, with four years' interval between them, show how the work described in the
foregoing Chapters presented itself to his own view :—

"LLANFAIRFECHAN, *Sept.* 12, 1863.—These times of rest
are indispensable for enabling me to see on calm reflection what
is necessary for my Episcopal work. This week will see the
close of seven years since Lord Palmerston's letter arrived at
Hallsteads offering me the Bishopric of London. And really it
has taken pretty nearly those seven years to get fairly into the
whole work of this complicated Diocese. I therefore can have
no regret that it was not interrupted by my going to York. Now,
if God spares my life a little longer, I may hope to see schemes
matured, and by God's grace bearing fruit. My main object has
been to endeavour so to present the Church of England, as that,
fully maintaining the truth of Christ, it shall become more and
more rooted in the affections of the people. For this purpose my
attention has been specially directed to those who seemed in
danger of being alienated from the Church: (1.) The middle
class, whom the High Church development seemed fast alienat-

ing. To say nothing of the danger of false doctrine, and the
substitution of sacerdotalism in the place of the simple real
Christianity, it has appeared to me that, on grounds of policy,
the growth of this party must be steadily guided and gently
restrained, lest it alienate from our Churches the vast body of the
religious in the middle class. I am free to confess that late
experience has convinced me of the very great influence which
the clergy of this school gain over the young men who form
their choirs, etc.   And I gladly recognise their self-denying zeal ;
but still, looking to the faults of their religious system, and the
horror in which it is held by the great body of religious persons,
in the middle class especially, I feel convinced that its prevalence
would end in the denationalising of the Church of England.
As one element amongst several, 'it no doubt does good, and
some of the best people in the world belong to this school ; but
it must be restrained, otherwise its faults will prevail over the
good within it.

"(2.) Still more, the poor. To them especially the Gospel
requires to be preached in London. The great efforts of Bishop
Blomfield to build Churches and found new parishes have done
much. But somehow there was something wanting in the work
as he left it. Incomplete of course it must be in its extent as
long as the population grows at its present alarming rate ; but
there seemed to me something wanting too in the spirit of these
efforts. Hence it appeared to be my chief call during the earlier
part of my Episcopate, by preaching myself to the poor wherever
they could be found, and stirring up a missionary spirit amongst
the clergy, to endeavour to bring life into the existing machinery,
and add an expansive power to all our Church movements.   I
think by God's blessing a good deal has been done in this way,
and the example has spread in the kingdom. The preaching
under the dome of St. Paul's is an outward symbol of what is
wanted. The Diocesan Home Mission has been the centre of
this work, as the Diocesan Church Building Society is the centre
of the more regular and 'business' operations of the Church in
the London Diocese. When Palmerston wished to withdraw me
to the Archdiocese of York last year, I felt the danger of the
Diocesan Home Mission perishing, perhaps more than any other
consideration, as an inducement to remain where I am.

"(3.) And then, besides, I have felt and tried to meet the
great danger of the more thoughtful and inquisitive spirits being

alienated from the Church—I mean the great body of the reading public, especially young men. Circumstances have always made me alive to this danger, and from the first I have striven to do what I could to avert it. The vast body of thoughtful and somewhat religious persons in the upper classes, who are influenced neither by the *Record* nor the *Guardian*—after all, if these are alienated from the Church, its nationality is surely gone. I have always thought it was a special part of my mission to endeavour to prevent the alienation of these, and have done what I could all along in this direction."

And again, a few years later :—

" *20th January* 1867.—Now to look back along the years. The first part of my Episcopate was marked by my taking more share than I have done lately in direct missionary work in the diocese—preaching continually in the east of London, often preaching where necessary in the open air. I think this was wise. It gave the impetus to the clergy and encouraged them to break through the old routine rules which cramped their energy, and to put an end to that fear, which was at one time real, that the Church of England might die of its dignity. I helped, I think, to let it be understood that its true dignity consisted in its doing in every proper way, after Christ's example, Christ's work. I may consider this period of my work as marked by the establishment of the Diocesan Home Mission—a great movement, raising up what is indispensable as supplementary to the parochial system in such a place as London. But our efforts were long difficult to bring to pass. It was a good idea to send missionary clergy from the bishop to all sorts of work in London which the parochial clergy could not undertake—the care of navvies, the densely peopled lanes of huge parishes, etc. All that we were able to do at first was to impress on the public mind that this was a legitimate Church of England work. I bore my own part in such work, preaching, for example, to the half gypsy population of the Potteries, Kensington, in the open air almost by moonlight, to the omnibus men in their yard at Islington by night, to the people assembled by Covent Garden Market on a Sunday afternoon in summer, and once to a great assemblage in the quadrangle here at Fulham, while our church was closed. I was not neglectful, I hope, of my other work, preaching steadily at St. James's, Piccadilly, in the spring, and in the various churches in the diocese; attending the House of Lords and speaking on all fit occasions; and I did my best in Convocation. My first Visitation and Charge belongs to this period (1858). My second Visitation and Charge (1862) marks a second stage. The endeavour to evangelise this vast metropolis soon showed that an organisation far more systematic than anything hitherto tried was necessary. Hence, from my second Charge, and the instigation of the Diocesan Church Building Society, sprang the Bishop of London's Fund. Had I accepted Lord Palmerston's offer of York in 1862, I could not have brought this work to pass, and any one coming fresh to the diocese would have found a difficulty in organising it. What I personally have been able to do in it is, I think, especially by the impression of fairness, to keep people of very dissimilar opinions working together. To those who have thus worked, I, and the Church of England, owe the deepest debt of gratitude. Their exertions have enabled a thorough system of organisation to be matured. And now my two great illnesses of this year seem to point to that sort of work which a Bishop can do in old age, if his life is spared and his intellect preserved. To be sure I am only fifty-five, but at present, for my health's sake, I must act as if I was old, quietly directing rather than actively interfering."

In the following letter he sets forth in more detail the comprehensive principle of action alluded to above. An earnest and influential layman, who had actively co-operated in inaugurating the ' Bishop of London's Fund,' wrote, after a short experience, to announce his withdrawal from the Council on account of the Bishop's readiness to avail himself of the sympathy and help of every sort of fellow-labourer. The Bishop replied :—

"I assure you that we are truly sorry to lose you from the Council. Of course you must act according to your conscientious convictions, however mistaken they may be. . . . You think, I gather, that those in authority ought to have taken steps to clear the Church of persons who do not agree with you, or, rather, with the section of the Church with which you find yourself in harmony. Now I grant that the National Church must partake of the fallible condition in which all outward institutions find themselves. It must more or less always be like the net cast into the sea and filled with fishes bad and good. But this characteristic belongs to all Churches, established and un-established. I know that you would not hold a hypocritical profession of the great Gospel doctrines to be of any value without a renewed heart and a godly life, but I know not how any outward body, however small and merely sectional, can free itself from the admixture of bad characters with the good. There are hypocrites everywhere. The National Church, then, like all other churches and denominations, must be contented in this imperfect state of things to be imperfect. But then, perhaps, you think that the authorities of the Church regard some things as not evil which you regard as evil. I know they must, and usually do, take an enlarged and comprehensive view such as many individual Christians without their responsibility do not take. I know also that they must take a more enlarged and comprehensive view of the differences amongst Christians than many ministers of small bodies take, or than Roman Catholics may take who think that the human intellect and feelings can be forced into a narrow groove. I grant also that the whole spirit of the formularies of the Church of England is on the side of this comprehensive charitable view of the comparative unimportance of lesser differences, while men adhere to the grand essentials of the faith ; and I grant that we are also convinced that these essentials may be held with the power of a saving faith by High Churchmen, Low Churchmen, and Broad Churchmen. There is a point beyond which we believe that diversity of opinion must destroy unity ; and where there is denial of the great Christian doctrines, there we hold that men cannot with any propriety continue in our Communion, whether they be expelled from it or leave it of their own accord. But till we see this point reached, we are great believers in the power of the unity of the Faith held even amongst great diversities of opinion ; also we consider it a sacred duty not to push men to extreme conclusions, however logically deducible from their premisses. We do not separate even from a very strong Calvinist, because we think that logically he ought to be a believer in the doctrine of a necessity destroying freedom of will, and therefore destroying also the distinction between right and wrong ; nor from a man who holds very high views of the Sacraments, because logically he ought to be a Roman Catholic.

Provided men do not carry out their peculiar doctrines to these logical consequences, we rejoice that they should be able to act with us in the spirit of the Gospel with the love of the Lord Jesus Christ in their hearts. This is the principle on which the Church of England is comprehensive, and in the truest sense catholic, as a real representative of the Church of Christ.

" I have written at length, not with a hope of altering your opinion, but that you may understand our principles. I have long thought that each man will best serve God by acting as in God's sight on his own strong convictions, and I rejoice and trust that there are many ways in which you will still be able to co-operate with us, even though you cannot follow the course which we believe to be right, doing what we can in the midst of weakness and fallibility for the souls for which Christ died, and leaving results to God."

At a time when the possibility or advantage of reviving some system of lay Brotherhoods in the Church of England is under general discussion, it is not without interest to notice that such a proposal was definitely made in the Diocese of London so long ago as 1861. A thoughtful lay Churchman wrote to the Bishop of London upon the subject, enclosing for his consideration a series of extracts from the opinions which he had privately elicited from London clergymen of all schools. These written opinions were couched for the most part in general terms, and the names of the writers were not given. It might have been supposed that in face of the almost universal dislike at that period to any suggestion of the kind, the Bishop would at once have announced his disapproval of such a plan. His answer, however, was as follows :—

" 17th October 1861.

" MY DEAR SIR,—I beg to acknowledge your letter of the 15th, accompanied by extracts from various letters written by clergy of the diocese on the subject of your proposed plan for a better organisation of voluntary lay assistance in aid of the efforts of the parochial clergy. I feel greatly indebted to you for the trouble you have taken, as well as for all your other efforts for the good of our poor parishes in London. It is difficult to estimate the amount of weight which belongs to the various communications you have received, without knowing how far the writers have been themselves successful under God's blessing in the management of their parishes; and this, of course, the confidential nature of their letters, and the consequent suppression of their names, prevents me from knowing.

"I was last night, *e.g.*, in a very poor parish in the East of London, containing a very large population, where I met between 100 and 200 of the laity, all actively engaged, under the superintendence of the clergyman, in the work of his parish. The opinion of a clergyman who has experience of such a parish would be peculiarly valuable.

"I have carefully examined the extracts you have sent to me, and have been much struck with the suggestions made as to the importance of maintaining the integrity of parochial organisation. I confess I agree also in the difficulties expressed as to the formation of any body which should bear the name and have the organisation of an 'Order,' in the sense usually attributed to that word. . . . You rightly interpret my wishes in saying that I do not desire myself to suggest such a combined movement in my diocese. But you are right also in adding that I am ready to recognise any well-considered plan which receives the sanction of a considerable body of the clergy. . . .—Again thanking you for the trouble you are taking, I am, my dear Sir, yours faithfully,

"A. C. LONDON."

It is impossible in this connection to omit all reference to a subject which brought upon the Bishop for many years an amount of correspondence out of all proportion to its actual importance. The Rev. J. L. Lyne, who was ordained Deacon in the Diocese of Exeter in 1860, and who soon afterwards took the name of 'Father Ignatius,' came after some years to London, where his powers as a religious speaker, together with the peculiarities of his doctrine and dress, attracted great attention. At least one London clergyman was for a short time associated with the so-called 'Order of St. Benedict,' under Mr. Lyne's governance. A small monastic house was established, first at Norwich, and then at Laleham, near Staines; and the extraordinary behaviour of its inmates brought upon the Bishop a series of appeals, both from High and Low Churchmen, that he would inhibit Mr. Lyne from officiating or preaching in the diocese. The Bishop however declined to do so, and Mr. Lyne preached in more than one London church, drawing immense congregations, especially to his week-day addresses in St. Edmund's, Lombard Street, when the street was blocked by the crowds who vainly tried to get into the church. The Bishop remonstrated again and again with him for the extravagance of his proceedings, and repeatedly declined to admit him to Priest's Orders, or to give him any general licence. In one of his letters to Mr. Lyne the Bishop says :—

" Independently of the rules I have mentioned [as to the need of a University degree and other certificates] there are further difficulties in your case. I have always intimated that, considering the strange things which you did, and the book of devotion which you issued in the Diocese of Norwich, I could not entertain the idea of your being accepted as a candidate in my diocese till I was satisfied that you had publicly retracted the book in question, and were resolved not again to encourage the practices which disturbed the Diocese of Norwich. . . . I have no reason to suppose that if you were in Priest's Orders to-morrow you would not follow the same course which you pursued at Norwich, and indeed reports have reached me as to what is going on in a house under your direction [at Laleham], that make me very anxious as to what you are doing in my own diocese. From these considerations—I mention no others—you will see that it is impossible for me to accede to the request contained in your letter. I must urge upon you the duty of conforming to the rules of the Church in which God's providence has placed you. That God has given you powers whereby you are able greatly to influence those whom you address in your pastoral character I am assured by many. Let me earnestly beg you to be contented with such means of influence, and to give up the attempt to engraft on the Church of England parts of the Roman system which are disapproved by the whole body of our Church governors. I am greatly interested in what I hear of your zeal and of the earnestness of your preaching, but you must suffer me to remind you, as set over you in the Lord, that the course which you pursued at Norwich, and which I fear you are anxious to pursue again, seemed to have so much self-will in it that it cannot be expected to be followed by God's blessing. It is my earnest prayer that God may guide you aright, develop by His Holy Spirit all that is good in you, and restrain and regulate all that is amiss."

To those who remonstrated with him for not taking sterner measures, the Bishop answered :—

"Mr. Lyne is only in Deacon's Orders, and the opinion of myself, as well as of the Archbishop of Canterbury and the Bishop of Norwich, respecting him is shown by the refusal to admit him to Priest's Orders. It must be now above ten years since he was ordained Deacon, I believe by the Bishop of Exeter, and from that time to this he has never been able to persuade any Bishop that he was a fit person to be intrusted with the responsibilities of the Priesthood. He has not received any licence, or written permission of any kind, from me to officiate in my diocese. When requested, first by Mr. D——, and afterwards by Mr. H——, to allow him to officiate, after making inquiries respecting the style and substance of his sermons, I have not as yet been convinced that it was my duty to interfere and put a stop to his preaching. It has appeared to me better to allow him, on the responsibility of the Incumbents who have applied to me, to exercise his gift under such control over the doctrine to which he gives utterance as the general law of the Church of England imposes. The alternative would be to remove from him all restraint, and send him forth to exercise greater influence over the young and inexperienced without any check. I am quite aware that it may become my duty to do so, but I have never been able as yet to find, from any of the complaints made to me as to his sermons, that I ought to take this step. The general impression conveyed to me respecting his sermons has been that

they are confined to earnest appeals to the conscience, especially
of the unconverted, and fervid expositions of the love of Christ
for souls. Whether they would assume another character if all
restraint were removed, I am not able as yet to decide. But it
will easily be understood that I am unwilling to run the risk,
without necessity, of turning the eccentric, and I hope passing,
excitement of certain persons who attach themselves at present to
the peculiarities of his system into a life-long slavery to the
Church of Rome. . . . In the whole treatment of this case, feeling that the responsibility, which is great, rests entirely with me,
I must, while thanking Mr. —— and his friends for any information they are able to communicate, request them to rest contented
with the assurance that I am quite alive to the gravity of the
circumstances which have been brought under my notice."

It would be for every reason undesirable to enter into
the particulars of the controversies that ensued. Enough
to say that at length, owing in part to the action taken by
Mr. Lyne in respect to a lady whom he proposed to
" solemnly excommunicate from our Holy Congregation,"
the Bishop found it necessary to issue the inhibition which
had long been asked for. Such importance as the matter
may have consists in the evidence of the Bishop's patient
and considerate treatment of a problem which created at
the time a very wide-spread controversy and excitement.

The following letter has reference to the Bishop's views
upon the subject of Confession. A clergyman holding a
Continental chaplaincy had been requested by a young lady
to receive her to confession, " as she had not had an opportunity of going to confession for some months past." The
clergyman informed the Bishop that he had declined to
receive her :—

" I told her," he wrote, " that I was not conscious of possessing authority from my Church to comply with her request,
as I considered that our Church only contemplated private confession in the case of extreme sickness, or of a conscience troubled
with the sense of some special sin. But as I did not gather from

her that she came under either of the above heads, I said I must decline doing that which I believed would be a transgression of the discipline of our Church."

He asked the Bishop, however, to direct him, as he might see fit. The Bishop replied as follows :—

The Bishop of London to the Rev. —— ——.

"LONDON HOUSE, *March* 1864.

"MY DEAR MR. ——, —I am afraid it would not be possible for me to undertake to give any positive advice as to the particular case which you have brought before me, since the dealing with individual consciences must necessarily be left to the responsibility of each clergyman.

"There are, however, undoubtedly cases in which the Church directs her ministers to invite those who are in spiritual distress to unburden their consciences. . . . I do not think that it is intended to restrict the benefit of 'absolution together with ghostly counsel and advice' to cases of consciences troubled with great and marked sin, since some of the sins specified as disqualifying for the reception of the Holy Communion are such as require spiritual discernment to detect them, and may manifest themselves in the conscience rather by a feeling of general disquietude than by the apprehension of a particular fault. Great care is, however, needed to prevent the use of the privilege given by the Church to her weaker members from acquiring a merely superstitious value, a tendency to the increase of weakness rather than the recovery of strength, which is the danger when confession grows into a system, and when a person is in any way induced to lean unduly upon the minister instead of being raised by the minister's assistance to a trust in God's mercy through Christ.

"I think that, bearing these general principles in view, you will not err in receiving the person who has applied to you to such consolation as confession and absolution may confer.—I remain, yours very truly,   A. C. LONDON."

The following letter to a young clergyman, from whom the Bishop had received several pamphlets, explains itself :—

"My dear Sir,—Some little time ago I received 'from the author' your pamphlet called ——. Probably with my many engagements it might have remained unread, had not my attention been within the last few days pointedly called to its contents. I regret for your sake that you should have written it. I regret also that any necessity should have arisen for calling my attention to it. . . . As I have been asked to read the pamphlet I have done so, and I should not be acting consistently with the respect and regard which I entertain for you if I did not address to you a few words of advice. These will I trust be as kindly received by you as they are kindly intended by me.

"The style of your pamphlet is, as you appear to acknowledge, somewhat rhetorical ; and this makes it difficult to ascertain what the exact doctrinal statements are on which you wish to insist.   I gather, however, from the pamphlet two things :—

"I. That you are not satisfied with that reverent silence which the Church of England, following the example of Holy Scripture, has observed respecting the state of the souls departed, while they are waiting between death and judgment ; that you consider what you call ' the duty of prayers for the dead ' to be ' one of the duties most incumbent on the Christian heart and mind.'   Indeed you seem almost to say that that man can scarcely be called a Christian who differs from you in this matter.   Now it must, I think, strike every one that if this view of yours were correct, the formularies of the Church of England would be a very poor production, and very unfaithful to the truth, from the way in which they have treated this subject.   You have shown by a few very strained interpretations that our Prayer Book might possibly in some prayers, by a perverse ingenuity, be understood as praying for the dead.   But your reasoning on this point will, I think, satisfy no candid person.   I can scarcely conceive that they fully satisfy yourself.   If the view you take of this doctrine be correct, it follows as a necessary consequence that you are right in circulating amongst your people a form of prayer for the dead, and equally that the Church of England has been very unfaithful in providing no such form.   Our Prayer Book has indeed pointed out, in the prayer for the Church Militant, how we may keep alive the thought of our fellowship with those who have gone to the unseen world by ' blessing God's Holy Name for all His servants departed this life in His faith and fear.'   You will act rightly in directing the minds of your people to the full meaning of these important words. It is granted also that the Church of England, preserving the reverent silence I have spoken of above, and never venturing beyond Holy Scripture, has left great liberty to the feelings and imagination of our people in all matters connected with the mysterious subject of the condition of the dead. But it is one thing to feel ourselves at liberty to form uncertain conjectures, and quite another for a clergyman to avail himself of the authority of his office to supply his people with forms of prayer for the souls of their departed relatives, and to teach them (as I understand you to mean) that they are bound as a solemn duty, 'to ask God for the prayers of the blessed saints departed.' Let me earnestly press upon you that you will commit a grave error if, imitating and exaggerating the private opinions of any individual teachers whom you esteem, you go thus far beyond the boundaries which your Church has marked. I fear you will not conciliate those whose longings you wish to satisfy ; for certainly, if they are clear-sighted, you will never convince them that you have with you the authority of your Church. Rather, by encouraging the state of mind which yearns on this mysterious subject for explicit teaching beyond what God has been pleased to give, you will minister to feelings that have led many to be deluded by a Church which has no scruple in speaking dogmatically where God is silent.

"II. I gather further from your pamphlet that you hold some exaggerated view of our blessed Lord's presence in the Holy Communion, from which you think it follows as a necessary inference that our Church's rule—'there shall be no communion except four, or three at the least (even in our smallest parishes), communicate with the priest '—needs to be 'extirpated, as greatly objectionable in mind and intention.' Indeed, I gather that you almost feel yourself called upon to act in direct contradiction to this rule, lest by obeying the law of your Church you should injure your people's souls, who may, you seem to think, derive a much greater blessing from being present while you communicate without communicating themselves, than is attainable either through hearing the Word of God preached, or joining in the prayers. Now I will not undertake to say whether there is that really sound logical connection which you suppose between your speculative belief on the subject of the Holy Eucharist and this practical violation of the Church's law ; but I do very earnestly beg you to pause before you proceed in

practice to the lengths which you indicate.   If you are convinced
of the necessary connection between your peculiar doctrine of the
Eucharist, whatever it may prove to be when stripped of its
rhetorical disguise, and this practical conclusion, I beg you, asking God's good guidance, to reconsider, and if possible modify,
your view of the doctrine, rather than deliberately set at naught
the commands of the Church of which you are a minister—commands not only given in our formularies, in laws which you might
possibly suppose had fallen into desuetude, but enjoined also by
the living authorities to whom you owe personal obedience.

"These are the two points which seem the most important
for me to bring before you. I would urge them on your attention,
not only with the authority which belongs to my office, but with
all the respect and regard of one who feels much interested in
your work, and who is anxious for your own as well as for your
people's welfare. I trust God may guide you, when revising your
pamphlet, greatly to alter both its statements and its general tone.
Indeed, I feel convinced you will do well to leave speculations,
with which I cannot think your habit of mind fits you to deal
satisfactorily, and apply yourself with increasing diligence to the
great work of ministering to your people in the form and in the
spirit which your Church enjoins. Believe me, I have good
reason for a conviction, grounded on what I have seen and heard
of you, that if you do not listen to this warning, you will be yielding to the temptation of that peculiar weakness in your character
through which those who do not wish you well would rejoice to
see you fall. In your present sphere you have great and difficult
duties. I believe you are labouring to fulfil them heartily and
prayerfully. Do not be misled by any fancy that you have a peculiar
mission to bring back the Church of England to what she was before the Reformation. I cannot doubt, from many passages in
your pamphlet, that you love and honour our Church. Depend
upon it, under your peculiar circumstances, with your peculiar
feelings and temperament, your wisdom as a minister of Christ is,
avoiding notoriety, to serve Him faithfully and reverently in that
course which authority prescribes to you, and which has been
traced by the long list of our most honoured Divines.—Believe
me to be, my dear Sir, your faithful brother and servant,

"A. C. LONDON."

To a clergyman holding a curacy in his diocese who

had suddenly joined the Church of Rome, he wrote as follows :—

                              "LONDON HOUSE, S.W.

"REV. AND DEAR SIR,—I heard on Saturday from Mr. C—— that you had ceased to officiate as his curate, and the lamentable cause. From what he tells me, I feel that in this matter you have acted, either with sad precipitation or with want of straightforwardness, as you ministered in the Church of England within a very short time of your avowing yourself a convert to Romanism. The vows of God which were upon you ought to have made you act differently. Your ecclesiastical superiors were entitled to be informed of the state in which you found your mind, and it is right I should tell you that, quite independently of the fatal errors to which you have given yourself, you cannot expect God's blessing on a step taken in a manner so unworthy of its seriousness, and of the position which you occupied as trusted with grave responsibility by Mr. C—— and myself. I pray that God may open your eyes to make you see the impropriety of your conduct in this respect, as well as the dangerous errors to which you expose your soul. Had you opened your mind to me, as you were in duty bound, I should have done my best to direct you ; and if I had failed to satisfy your conscience, you would then at least have felt that you had taken the right course in consulting me.—Believe me, Rev. and dear Sir, your faithful servant,   A. C. LONDON."

The facts to which the following letters refer have been made public in the biography of Frederick Maurice.[1] It was not easy for ordinary men to understand the delicate sensitiveness which made him think it right, as he explained in the printed letter prepared for publication, to resign his incumbency, lest the strong opposition which he wished to offer to some of the theories of Bishop Colenso and the Essayists should be supposed to be dictated by a craven fear lest he should sacrifice his emoluments if he announced his liberal opinions.

----

[1] Vol. ii. pp. 426-434.

The Rev. F. D. Maurice to the Bishop of London.

" *Private.*

" 5 RUSSELL SQUARE, *Oct.* 13, 1862.

" MY DEAR LORD,—A fortnight ago I had determined to write to your Lordship on the subject of this letter : fearing that the diocese was about to be deprived of your services,[1] and wishing, even at the risk of troubling you at such a time, to communicate my intentions to one who has treated me with so much kindness rather than to any successor. As that calamity has, by your Lordship's decision, been averted from London, I venture, though not without regret and hesitation, to disturb you in your retreat with business chiefly, though not altogether, personal.

" I will not exhaust your Lordship's eyesight and patience with pages of manuscript describing processes and conflicts of mind. You will suppose I must have passed through these if you are kind enough to read the proof which I enclose of a letter shortly to go forth to my congregation. The first part of it relates to circumstances which your Lordship will understand better than most of its readers. I did not wish to dwell upon them more than I could help. The duty of acting as I have acted, when I must have been identified with statements which I utterly dislike and repudiate, seemed to me imperative. The other reason I have assigned for my act may commend itself less to your Lordship's approval. At least I trust you will see that I have parted with no conviction which I expressed, and violated no pledge which I gave, when you kindly granted me institution.

" I have to thank your Lordship for many undeserved acts of kindness during the time that I have been allowed to claim you as my spiritual father. I hope you will not consider me unworthy, hereafter, to do any ministerial work in your diocese to which my brother clergymen may invite me. At all events I shall not forget the benefits I have received from you in these last years. I could not, of course, send forth my letter without communicating it first to your Lordship and to Mr. Cowper. I wish that it should appear not much after the appearance of the book, already advertised, of the Bishop of Natal, and somewhat before the next hearing of the causes of Williams and Wilson in the Court of Arches.—Believe me, my dear Lord, very gratefully and respectfully yours,   F. D. MAURICE."

<hr>

[1] See page 270.

The Bishop of London to the Rev. F. D. Maurice.

"*Private and confidential.*

"CROMER, 14*th Oct.* 1862.

"MY DEAR MR. MAURICE,—I have read with great sorrow your letter received this morning, and should be glad indeed if the decision were one in which you were likely to be shaken.

"Two points I ought to press upon you—

"1*st.* That I think many men of ardent spirit who look up to you and share your opinions will, rightly or wrongly, find it difficult to avoid following your example. They will certainly be liable to be pressed as to why they do not adopt the same course as you, and to have unworthy motives attributed to them.

"2*d.* That you seem to me somewhat hasty in regarding Dr. Lushington's judgment, which will probably be appealed against to a higher Court, as a decision of authority in the Church of England, before it has been confirmed.

"I am sure that in reference to a step so important to others far more than to yourself, you have earnestly sought, and will still further seek, the Divine guidance, and to that guidance I can only commend you.

"Be assured that nothing is abated of that deep respect with which I regard your Christian character, and that (as indeed the whole of this letter implies) much as I should myself differ from you in many statements, I am not aware of anything in your opinions, so far as I know them, which should disqualify you from officiating whether you resign or retain your charge.—Ever yours sincerely,　　　　　　A. C. LONDON."

The Bishop wrote by the same post to Arthur Stanley, begging him to call upon Mr. Maurice without delay and to endeavour to dissuade him from the proposed step. The answer was as follows :—

Canon A. P. Stanley to the Bishop of London.

"6 GROSVENOR CRESCENT, *Oct.* 17, 1862.

"MY DEAR BISHOP,— . . . Maurice's affair is very lamentable : the more so as it is so certain to be misunderstood. I have been to see him to-day, but I find (and all his family and his friends say) that, in spite of all their arguments, his decision is irrevocable. The condemnation of his view of the Atonement, and the judgment on Heath in the Privy Council was the first cause of his uneasiness. The condemnation of Wilson's hope of a final restoration by Dr. Lushington was the second. And a taunt from Colenso gave the finishing stroke. His notion is that, like St. Paul (the comparison is mine, not his) he will be able to preach the Gospel better if not suspected of worldly motives. He felt very much the kindness of your letter. You ask what more you can do. Nothing, it seems to me, except this which, if you can do, would be of great importance, both as a support to him, and as preventing the disastrous consequences which are likely to flow from his step, viz., to allow him, or to take means yourself, to publish your letter. This may, indeed, be rendered impossible by the necessity of observing a dead silence on all that relates to the questions which may be coming before the Privy Council. But for this objection (of the force of which I cannot judge) I see no harm and much good that would ensue from its publication.— Yours affectionately,

"A. P. STANLEY."

The Bishop of London to the Rev. F. D. Maurice.

"CROMER, *October* 24, 1862.

" MY DEAR MR. MAURICE,—Since I wrote to you on receiving the first intimation of your intention to resign St. Peter's, Vere Street, I have thought often of the subject. It has not been till to-day that what had at first escaped my attention has distinctly occurred to me, viz., that (unless your position in your chapel is different from what I suppose it to be), if your purpose is to be carried into effect, I must legally be more a party to it than I should wish to be, as the resignation cannot release you without my accepting it. In intimating your intention to resign, you expressed your hope that I would not hereafter consider you unworthy of doing any ministerial work in my diocese to which any brother clergyman might invite you. In answer, assuring you that nothing is abated of that deep respect with which I regard your Christian character, I added that, much as I should myself differ from you in many statements, I am not aware of

2 K

anything in your opinions, so far as I know them, which should disqualify you from officiating, whether you resign or retain your charge. I expressed also my conviction that the step you meditate might be very injurious to others. I feel indeed that it is fraught with very momentous consequences to the whole Church, which may greatly suffer thereby.

"Under these circumstances it is only due to you that I should at once state to you that, in the event of your adhering to your present intention, I may be obliged to consider very carefully whether I shall be justified in accepting your resignation out of deference to your private feeling, or whether I ought on public grounds to refuse to accept it.

"It is of course possible that further explanation on your part may make me view the matter differently ; but as it at present stands, I feel that, if you continue in your resolve, I shall be called by you to consent to what I think a very undesirable step. My former letter was private and confidential, but I do not know why this need be so, if in consulting your friends or otherwise you wish to make use of it. I earnestly pray that we may both be guided aright from above in this matter.—Believe me to be, my dear Mr. Maurice, yours most truly,

"A. C. LONDON."

The Rev. F. D. Maurice to the Bishop of London.

"5 RUSSELL SQUARE, W.C.,
Oct. 25, 1862.

"MY DEAR LORD,—I thank your Lordship most gratefully for your very kind letter, and for the generous permission which you give me to make it known as a reason for changing the resolution which I have formed, certainly not without the most serious and painful deliberation.

"I do not wonder that the paper which I first sent to your Lordship should have left you in doubt whether I sufficiently understood my own purpose, or, at all events, could make it intelligible to others. The one which I enclose, and which is already printed with a view to circulation among my flock, will, I trust, be more satisfactory to you. It will remove, I am almost sure, the impression that my act is meant to be, or is likely to be, an example to other clergymen. My earnest hope and strong conviction is that many who would have been utterly shaken by the publication of the book of the Bishop of Natal will feel that they have a ground to stand upon, in the Old Testament and in the Creeds of the Church, which they had supposed was untenable. I do not mean that the expression of my belief will, in itself, have that effect; but that expression, accompanied by an act which will be some evidence of its sincerity, may lead them to reflect, and may fix them in the Church far more firmly than they are fixed now.

"I know that my kind and dear friend Stanley has a great dread of the effect which my retirement from Vere St. may produce, though, at the same time, he has given me some good reasons for thinking that the effect will be very slight. I cannot, as I have told him, approve in the least of his suggestion that I should announce my intention, and then suspend it, to see what the Courts will do. Such a proceeding would, it seems to me, be ignominious, and yet presumptuous; involving a kind of feeble threat which the Courts and every Churchman would feel, from a person in my position, to be ridiculous. It would also destroy the whole effect of the testimony which I desire to bear on the subject of Bishop Colenso's book, and which, from our past relations with each other, I could not bear, if I had had the slightest personal interest in disclaiming him.

"But, most of all should I be unwilling to mix your Lordship's name in my proceedings, or to let the clergy of your diocese suppose that you had committed yourself to me more than you have already committed yourself, by granting me a licence and by not withdrawing it. I know how much discredit I might bring upon you by such an association with me, as would be implied in the act of your Lordship's desiring me not to resign.

"Forgive me, my dear Lord, if I commit what I hope will be a solitary act of disobedience to your authority by refusing to accept your generous permission to let your letter be made public, and if I respectfully ask you to put no hindrance in the way of my taking a step which I feel in my inmost conscience is right for myself, and which, I trust in God, will prove to be good for His Church.—I have the honour to be, my dear Lord, very gratefully and respectfully yours,   F. D. MAURICE."

The Rev. F. D. Maurice to the Bishop of London.

"THE ATHENÆUM, *Oct.* 29, 1862.

"MY DEAR LORD,—I have received from the Bishop of Natal a strong assurance that the book which he is about to publish is not the book from which I drew my inferences. He protests strongly against my right to speak of the forthcoming work till I have read it. I yield to these remonstrances. I shall be exceedingly sorry to do anything which would be unjust or unkind to an old friend.

"I have, therefore, suspended the issuing of my letter, and will submit to your Lordship's judgment about the course I should pursue hereafter.—I have the honour to be, my dear Lord, your very obliged servant,   F. D. MAURICE."

The Bishop of London to the Rev. F. D. Maurice.

"FULHAM PALACE, *Oct.* 30, 1862.

"MY DEAR MR. MAURICE,—I am most thankful for your note of yesterday, announcing your attention to suspend the issuing of your letter to the congregation of St. Peter's, Vere St., and your willingness to submit to my judgment as to the course you should pursue hereafter.

"I believe that the best members of the Church of England will thank God, as I do, for this resolve.—Ever yours sincerely,
      "A. C. LONDON."

On the nomination of Arthur Stanley to the Deanery of Westminster, in the autumn of 1863, Dr. Christopher Wordsworth, as Canon in residence, published in pamphlet form a long and vehement protest against the installation of one whose opinions, especially on the Old Testament, were, in his view, so unorthodox.[1]   Dr. Stanley, he said,

---

[1] *Remarks on the Proposed Admission of the Rev. Dr. Stanley to the place of Dean, &c.*   The pamphlet contains the quotations on which the virtual charge of heresy is based.   They are such as these—"The history of Israel is not the history of an inspired book, but of an inspired people."   "Deborah was enlightened only with a very small portion of that Divine Light which was to go on ever more brightening to the perfect day."   "The Books of Moses are probably so-called because he is the chief subject of them."

had caused "much grief and trouble of conscience to many faithful members of the Church," by his lectures on the Jewish Church, and he more than implied that the author of these lectures could not honestly subscribe the articles and formularies of the Church of England. A copy of this pamphlet he sent to the Bishop of London with the following letter :—

The Rev. Dr. Wordsworth to the Bishop of London.

"CLOISTERS, WESTMINSTER, 12 *Dec.* 1863.

"MY DEAR LORD,—Since the time when your Lordship invited me to preach at St. Paul's on the evening of Jan. 10th, I have published the remarks of which I beg leave to forward you a copy.

"I should be very reluctant, indeed, even to seem to involve any one, however remotely, in any responsibility for my own acts, and I therefore feel it due to your Lordship to express my hope that you would consider yourself entirely at liberty to make any other arrangement for the sermon on that day at St. Paul's.—I have the honour to be, my dear Lord, your dutiful servant,

"CHRISTOPHER WORDSWORTH."

The Bishop of London to the Rev. Dr. Wordsworth.

"FULHAM PALACE.
Tuesday, Dec. 15, 1863.

"DEAR DR. WORDSWORTH,—I received on Saturday morning your note accompanying your published 'Remarks,' on Dr. Stanley's admission to the Deanery of Westminster. The pressing business of the Ordination week has prevented me from answering till now.

"Adverting to my having requested you to preach at St. Paul's on the 10th of Jan., you say that you would be very reluctant even to seem to involve any one, however remotely, in any responsibility for your acts, and that you therefore feel it due to me to express your hope that I may consider myself entirely at liberty to make any other arrangements for the sermon at St. Paul's on Jan. 10th. As your preaching turn was settled before the publication of your 'Remarks,' no approval of them on my part can be legitimately inferred, and I do not consider it necessary now to reconsider the arrangement. But your note seems to invite me to read your 'Remarks,' and, I suppose, to express some opinion upon them. I regret, for your own sake, as for the Church, the publication of this pamphlet, and, since you wish me to write, I dare not shrink from the disagreeable task of setting before you what you have done, in the light in which, I believe, it will appear to many of the best and most attached members of the Church.

"Of course it is not because you disapprove of some of Dr. Stanley's writings that you have taken the unusual step of publishing this protest. You would allow that in a great National Church like ours, necessarily and rightly including men of very various sentiments, what is written by eminent and good men of one school of theology often gives 'grief,' and even trouble of conscience, to many faithful members of the Church, who have deeply-rooted convictions on the other side of the question at issue. I suppose both you and I have often been pained, if we have not been troubled in conscience, by the published words of good men, both of the high sacerdotal and of other schools within our Church—nay, persons even of opinions like your own often give great pain and trouble by their statements of doctrine.

"It is not therefore in your own disapproval of Dr. Stanley's writings that you seek the justification of your pamphlet. You are understood as coming forward publicly to charge your future Dean with unfaithfulness to the Church in which he has ministered for twenty years, and in which he has long held eminent and most influential offices.

"Now, I suppose no one doubts that you have acted conscientiously, but very many do feel that your conscience is not well instructed in this matter. What you have done will, I think, appear to most good men in this light—that, if you have not distinctly stated, you have used words which imply some of the gravest possible charges against a brother clergyman, that you have endeavoured to support these charges by extracts from his writings which, being separated from the context, are greatly distorted from their real meaning ; and, as to several of the premisses which you attribute to Dr. Stanley, you have sought to load them with conclusions which, even taken as you have given them, they will not bear. Good men will say that this might perhaps be expected in some unknown and irresponsible writer attempting to inflame the passions of the ignorant, but is unworthy of a scholar and a divine, who must know the difficulty of the subject on which he is writing, which is indeed none other than the intricate question as to the line to be drawn between the Divine and human elements in the Scriptures of truth—a subject which, if it is to be entered on at all, requires almost above all others to be treated by theologians with calm exactness, and with a scrupulous regard to well-weighed and explicit arguments.

"Perhaps, however, it will be even more difficult for those who wish you well to defend the latter part of your pamphlet. The words in which you have insinuated, respecting a man of the highest character, that he cannot consistently or conscientiously sign the declarations which he has already made repeatedly at each successive step of his honourable career, and in virtue of adherence to which the office which he is about to vacate, as well as that to which he is promoted, is held,—these words are, I think, sure to be looked upon as unsuitable to the high Christian character which you have hitherto maintained.

"You will, I trust, my dear Dr. Wordsworth, excuse me for speaking thus plainly. It is often the misfortune of good men, highly respected, that when they make a great mistake, they have no one about them to point out their error. Your note gives me an opportunity, of which perhaps few but myself could appropriately avail themselves, of telling you what is in the minds of a great body both of your brother clergy and of the laity. You will not suppose because I speak plainly that I fail in the personal esteem and respect with which I have ever regarded you.— Believe me, yours very truly,   A. C. LONDON"

In his letters to Dr. Stanley himself the Bishop makes no allusion whatever to Dr. Wordsworth's pamphlet, but he takes occasion to impress upon the new Dean some of his more strictly ecclesiastical responsibilities.

"I hope we may have full time next week," he says, "to talk over the future, and I daresay you will let me advise you as to the nature of your new post. The distinctly clerical, as distinguished from the literary, life is somewhat new to you. Milman has much less influence than he ought to have, from ignoring this distinctly clerical side. The Ecclesiastical Commission, the great

Societies of the Church, National Education, the Westminster Spiritual Aid Fund, besides the continual opportunities of preaching—shall we add Convocation?—these give the mitred Abbot of Westminster an influence almost as directly episcopal as that of any Bishop."

The line taken by the Bishop in the *Essays and Reviews* controversy, and in his utterances generally, had the result of bringing upon him quite a flood of correspondence with clergy and others whose faith had been unsettled, and who wished to consult "the only Bishop," as one writer expressed it, "who seems to feel the slightest respect or sympathy for men in our position." Most of these letters, entering as they do into detailed theological inquiry, are unsuited for publication in this book, and the Bishop's usual course was to invite his correspondent to talk the matter over with him. A single specimen instance may perhaps be given. The Bishop had in this case no previous knowledge of his correspondent, who lived in a distant part of England, and had been ordained some twelve years before.

[After a long biographical *apologia*, the writer states his position thus:—] "I thus found at last that my faith in the propitiatory view of the Atonement had left me, as a natural consequence of my having ceased to believe in anything miraculous. Upon this I resigned my living, on the alleged ground that I could no longer yield an unfeigned assent and consent to all and everything contained in the Book of Common Prayer. It seemed to me unnecessary, and in every way undesirable, to publish the extent of that scepticism which had assuredly brought me no peace or happiness. . . . [After long vacillation] the urgent and only too flattering invitations of some of my kind friends among the Unitarians induced me to re-examine the question of our Saviour's alleged mere humanity, and this led me to the conclusion that either Jesus was properly Divine, or the New Testament was an unworthy text-book for a truthful preacher. Still, though the moral beauties of Christianity prevented my assenting to the latter

alternative, I was not then prepared to re-accept the former. . . .
I began to question with myself how and to what extent the
Prayer Book, which my friends and I desired (as a matter of
taste) to alter as little as possible, must be dealt with. I soon
found that either the Prayer Book must be wholly re-written, or
we must retain the doctrine of the Trinity, prayers to Christ,
references to miracles, and a belief in the Atonement. I had no
doubt which way the Bible, if appealed to, would decide these
questions; but the miracles recorded in Scripture bore to my
mind a character of *a priori* incredibility, which prevented (or
disabled) me from referring my difficulties to the arbitrament of
the sacred penmen. I was thus still in my scepticism of a year
ago ; only the option had become more distinctly marked, so that I
must either confirm my disbelief or accept the teachings of orthodoxy. At this crisis an old recollection of the late Dr. Chalmers'
unbelief, and of its being relieved by his studies preparatory to
writing on the Evidences, induced me to read his volume.
The first few pages just brought back to my mind the missing
link. . . . It seems strange to my own mind that so simple a
reflection should avail with me now after several years of growing
scepticism ; but we all read books differently according to the
different states of mind in which we approach them. As has been
said, we find in books what we bring to them. Be that as it may,
however, this volume of Chalmers has, under God's blessing,
been the means of removing my *a priori* difficulty as to miracles.
That removed, I am open to the overwhelming influence of St.
Paul's unquestionably contemporaneous evidence. Christ's wondrous personality speaks to me through the Gospels. The prediction of a seed of Abraham, in whom all the nations should be
blest, convinces me. The Gospels become wholly credible. I
assent alike to the Miraculous Conception, the Resurrection, the
Ascension, and all the other marvels of the Gospel. Difficulties
there are, and I feel them ; but I am satisfied with the substantial
truth of the inspired volume. . . . In a word, I have regained
my belief in the Bible ; I retain my old attachment for the Church
of England and the Prayer Book. . . .

"As to the question, what I am to do with my life and
energies, will your Lordship kindly take the trouble to counsel
me ? Shall I best serve God and man by remaining in idleness ?
or by working at some lay occupation ? or by seeking to resume
the functions of a curate in the Church ? If, as seems to me,

this last be the line of my duty, under whose auspices and in what manner may I best begin? If your Lordship has the patience and sympathy to read thus far, I will only add that any advice you may be pleased to give me will be much esteemed. . . . I ought to add that I have never attached myself to any Nonconformist body; but, as I urged my old friends, on leaving them, to abide in the Church of England, so my family and I have been worshippers therein throughout the year."

The Bishop of London to the Rev. —— ——.

"CROMER, NORFOLK, *9th Oct.* 1862.

"MY DEAR SIR,—Your important letter of the 2d has followed me. It reached me two days ago, and very pressing business has since so engrossed my attention that I have not been able to sit down to answer till now.

"First, let me express my thankfulness to God for having so far guided you. This is a fresh confirmation of the promise, that they who will do God's will shall know of the doctrine whether it be of God. And indeed, seeing what our minds are, there is an unspeakable satisfaction in thinking that He is near and ready to guide in such great difficulties.

"As I understand your letter, that scepticism which was the real cause of your resigning your functions in the ministry, and which went much deeper than those amongst whom you ministered were aware, has passed away, and a peaceful acceptance of the fundamental doctrines of the Gospel has succeeded to that great trial of doubt or disbelief.

"You see no reason now why you should not with a good conscience declare your acceptance of the formularies of our Church, return to its ministrations, and preach the doctrines, your belief in which had before given way, but is now happily by God's guidance re-established. If this be a true account of your state, I cannot doubt that you will do well to seek to return to ministerial duty, and I should not hesitate (while adopting of course all due caution) to sanction your entering on a sphere of duty in my diocese.

"'Two things, however, strike me :—

"*1st.* That as it was in the Bishop of ——'s diocese that you felt yourself constrained publicly to lay down your ministerial functions, you ought to state the whole case to him, that you may ascertain his views respecting your return to ministerial duty. Unless there is some good reason to the contrary, it seems natural to seek to be re-admitted by your former diocesan ; and at all events, if you were nominated to any sphere in my diocese, I should think it my duty to refer to him.

" 2*d*. It would, I grant, be undesirable to provoke any public discussion of your grounds for abandoning and for re-assuming your ministerial functions, which grounds, as I have said, I learn from your letter are not fully understood by those with whom you have acted in their real depth, and in connection with the painful private struggles of doubt and disbelief through which you have passed.

" But I think it is certainly your duty to see that, so far as you can, any who have by your example been unsettled in their allegiance to the Church or fortified in their already formed objections to it, should learn that you have been convinced of your error and that you now earnestly desire that they should be guided by your present and not by your former views of truth.

" I would again add further, that under the peculiar circumstances of your case, I should think that for a time some quiet sphere of ministering amongst the poor would be better for your own soul and more conducive to your ultimate usefulness in the ministry than any prominent post.

" That God by His Holy Spirit may be your guide and stay, for the Lord Jesus Christ's sake, is my hearty prayer.—Believe me to be, my dear Sir, faithfully yours,   A. C. LONDON.

" *P.S.*—On my return home I shall be ready to see you any day by appointment."

Several interviews took place, and the clergyman returned to active ministry in the Church of England.

Among the Bishop's papers is a large amount of correspondence about the origin of the 'Speaker's Commentary.' Valuable as, in some respects, he felt the book to be, and indefatigable as were the pains taken by its publishers, it was always to Bishop Tait a source of keen disappointment that so great an enterprise had not been carried out by its learned editors upon somewhat bolder and more liberal lines. The facts, so far as Bishop Tait was concerned, were as follows :—On December 30, 1862, he received a letter from the Speaker,[1] propounding a plan for the publication of a first-rate Commentary, to be edited, at whatever cost, "by the foremost living scholars, with every appliance of modern culture and research." He had as yet consulted, he said, no one else. The idea was his own, and "I would myself," he added, "take a great deal of trouble about it, in any way in which I could be useful, and I think I could undertake to provide funds almost to any amount for such a work undertaken by good hands." The Bishop at once communicated with Mr. John Murray, who threw himself actively into the scheme, and, after considerable correspondence, it was publicly announced that the book would be published "under the sanction of a Committee of ten members," of whom Bishop Tait was one.[2] The general editorship was intrusted to the Rev. F. C. Cook, and the prospectus added that the Archbishop of York, in consultation with the Regius Professors of Divinity at Oxford and Cambridge, would "advise with the general editor upon any questions arising during the progress of the work."

Several months passed, and Bishop Tait learned that although his name still stood on the published list of the Committee, the arrangements as to authorship and line of treatment had been virtually settled without his having had any opportunity of discussing them. He remonstrated, and the Archbishop of York replied that it had been decided not to invite him to co-operate more closely.

---

[1] The Right Hon. J. Evelyn Denison.

[2] The Committee was as follows :—Archbishop of York, Bishops of London, Lichfield, Llandaff, and Gloucester ; Lord Lyttelton, The Speaker, Mr. Spencer Walpole, Professor Jacobson, and Professor Jeremie.

"I am free to say," he added, "that I thought it better not to ask you, for you would have wished Stanley to be in the undertaking, and I could not have made the attempt with Stanley's name upon our scheme.   I need not say that in other respects I value your candour and courage too much to think of slighting you."

Further correspondence ensued, the most important letter being as follows :—

The Bishop of London to the Speaker of the House of Commons.

"LLANFAIRFECHAN, NR. BANGOR,
Sept. 7th, 1863.

"MY DEAR MR. SPEAKER,   . . . I am afraid I have given you some trouble already, and that this letter will give you more in the reading of it ; but I must beg you to attribute this to the right motive, viz., the very earnest desire which I have, that the great work you have set in motion should be so conducted as to be a real benefit to the Church. . . . Consulted as I had been privately all through, it never occurred to me, till the idea was forced upon me, that there was any intention of arranging everything so as to make my adhesion to the scheme a mere formality.

"I do not know whether you can quite understand the position in which I should be placed unless this matter is cleared up.

"I entirely concur in what the Dean of St. Paul's has said, that this Commentary, to be of real service to the Church, ought to be at once free and critical enough to satisfy inquiring minds, yet so religious as not to disturb the more devotional.   Ever since the present unhappy phase of controversy began to disturb the Church, I have felt most strongly that the only safety lay in the growth of a liberal yet deeply religious party, and that, in handling Scripture especially, the greatest care was needed that nothing should be advanced which would not bear thorough sifting. Now, in the *Aids to Faith*—that answer to the *Essays and Reviews* which the Archbishop of York edited, and to which Mr. Cook was a contributor—the chief writer, whom I find intrusted with a very important share in this Commentary, has, as I understand him, advanced opinions, and argued that they are indispensable to the faith, which are in my judgment dangerous as being untenable and quite inconsistent with a wise and true criticism of the Old Testament.   I feel no objection (quite the reverse) to the great learning and goodness of this author being employed in our work, but I desire that neither he nor any one else shall be allowed to commit us and the Church to dangerous and untenable statements.   Now I must freely confess that I do not think the Archbishop of York is awake to this danger.   I scarcely think that if he had been, he would have admitted such passages as I refer to into the *Aids to Faith*. . . . I should stultify myself if I quietly acquiesced in such statements coming forth under my name.   I incline to think that the knowledge that I was likely to overhaul such statements would prevent them from being made ; or, if they were made at first, I feel confident that in a fair discussion I could convince any Committee or Board of which I was a member, that such statements ought to be guarded or cancelled.   But I do not think it would be consistent with my position, either official or personal, to make objections in a vague way without an opportunity of discussing them, and to be liable to have my objections overruled by the arbitrary decision of the Archbishop of York and my two amiable friends, Drs. Jacobson and Jeremie.   You must remember that the difficulties I apprehend—to be rightly dealt with—require (1st), That those who have to deal with them shall from circumstances have been made fully aware of the force of the difficulties in question, and (2ndly), That they shall have no dread whatsoever of the clamour of so-called religious newspapers or any other blind public opinion. Now I say it with the deepest respect, but you have not at present any such Board or final appeal, unless (as seems implied in their very office) the Committee is intrusted with this function in the last resort.   I am sure that Mr. Cook, with all his learning and judgment, has not strength to deal with such a difficulty as I suppose, and would naturally leave it alone, and, if by any means it found its way to the Archbishop of York and his assessors, unaided, they would let it drop also.

"'To explain more clearly what I mean—this Commentary must be greatly judged of at the very first by the way in which it treats the early Chapters of Genesis—including the account of the Flood—by the notes on the history of Balaam and on the book of Jonah—and difficulties similar to those contained in those passages will be occurring all through the Old Testament. What I think indispensable is that the questions thus raised be dealt with in a calm, candid spirit, and that any rash statements—which are made in accordance with an unthinking public opinion, but are sure to alienate and shock the very persons who most need our instruction and guidance—shall be reviewed and restrained.

"You have been very fortunate in securing the zealous co-operation of the Archbishop of York and Mr. Cook, but neither they nor any other two men, even assisted by such able coadjutors as Drs. Jacobson and Jeremie, can, in the present state of the Church, command such confidence as this work ought to secure if it is to fulfil the end you desire. This confidence will be largely conciliated by the other names on the Committee, but I think it would at once cease to be given if it were thought that those names are simply ornamental.—Believe me to be, my dear Mr. Speaker, yours very truly.

" A. C. LONDON."

It is not necessary to recount all that followed upon this letter. In deference to the earnest request of the Speaker, Bishop Tait abandoned his intention of withdrawing his name from the Committee, but he gave strong expression, in his Diary and elsewhere, to an opinion that a great opportunity had been missed, and that a more courageous course on the part of the Editors would have been justified by the ultimate result.

Little as the Bishop usually concerned himself in the precise details of a ceremonial or procession, he was a stiff upholder of the rights of his office in such matters. It fell to him afterwards, as Archbishop, to settle more than one doubtful point as to his official privilege,[1] and such questions arose occasionally with regard to the Bishop of London. When Archbishop Longley, on December 12, 1862, was enthroned in Canterbury Cathedral as Primate, Bishop Tait insisted, with a pertinacity which both surprised

---

[1] See *e.g.* vol. ii. p. 287.

and amused his friends, upon the due recognition of his own position as ' Provincial Dean.' His friend Dean Alford, in a private letter, invited him to the ceremony. He replied that he could only attend as Dean of the Province, and must receive an official invitation with due assignment of his part in the proceedings. The programme was already issued, however, without any mention of him, and the officials, among whom his letter created quite a little storm, while they admitted that an error had been made, fell back upon the haziness of the precedents, and begged him to attend informally. This he declined to do, and wrote to his legal secretary as follows :—

The Bishop of London to Mr. J. B. Lee.

" FULHAM PALACE, S.W.,
Dec. 8th, 1862.

" MY DEAR MR. LEE,—The Dean of Canterbury has sent to me the enclosed, with two papers—one, the printed programme for Friday ; the other, the official record of what took place in 1848. I have called his attention to an important point which must be submitted to Dr. Twiss.[1] The mistake of the printed programme appears to be this (as compared with 1848), that it ignores the Provincial College and its offices as such, classing them all under the name of ' attendant Bishops '—a phrase which does not occur in the precedent of 1848 ; and this becomes really important in that part of the proceedings in which the Archbishop takes possession of the Marble Chair. The printed programme states that the same form is then repeated as when he takes possession of the Throne. The precedent of 1848 gives a different form, referring to the Metropolitical dignity, and not that of the See, and makes the members of the Provincial College officially to take part in the latter act. A question indeed arises, whether this part of the ceremony, viz., the second enthroning in the Marble Chair, ought not to be entirely transacted by the officers of the Provincial College, and whether the idea of the second enthroning

---

[1] The Bishop's law officer.

is not entirely that of taking possession of the Metropolitical
dignity, and whether the part assigned in this second enthroning
to the Archdeacon of Canterbury, does belong to some officer of
the Provincial College, having been given to the Archdeacon in
days when the whole thing was done without ceremonial, no
Bishop being present, and the smallest number of deputies
employed, and, therefore, the Archdeacon appearing in more than
one capacity.   It is no easy matter to disentomb a mediæval
ceremonial without making great mistakes, and it is rather important that when the Bishops of the Province are summoned to
be present on a State occasion, they should not be ignored in
their official capacity.   Probably the so-called 'attendant Bishops'
may be a mixture of Bishops from York, the Colonies, and Scotland,
the Provincial College and its officers being quite another matter.

"You will be amused at my new-born zeal in such matters,
but if a thing is to be done, it ought to be done properly.—Ever
yours,   A. C. LONDON."

In the end, within a few hours of the ceremonial, the
programme was re-issued in an amended form, and the
Provincial Dean took his anciently appointed place.

The popular dislike in those years of anything approaching to Ritualism led to many irregular attempts
being made, especially in suburban parishes, to open a
rival place of worship, where the old-fashioned doctrine
and ritual should be retained, and the Bishop had many
extremely troublesome quarrels of this kind to deal with,
the dissentients sometimes including the bulk of the former
congregation of the parent church.   A single example
of the advice he gave in such cases will be enough.   The
letter is written to the vicar of a suburban parish who
had applied to him for counsel :—

The Bishop of London to the Rev. —— ——.

"LONDON HOUSE, S.W., *6th March* 1865.

"MY DEAR MR. ——,—Much business and the difficulty of
the subject have made me delay longer than I could have wished
my answer to your recent letter.

"I am sorry to say there are in various parts of England chapels erected under the name of Free Churches, and registered as dissenting meeting-houses. They have generally sprung from certain persons being dissatisfied with the teaching of the Parochial clergy, and adhering so slightly to the law and order of the Church of England, that they prefer to separate themselves from its duly constituted authority rather than worship in their own parish church, of which they dislike the teaching, or take the trouble of going, as they usually might do, to some other neighbouring church, the ritual and teaching of which may be more consonant with their feelings and convictions. That in a national church so tolerant as the Church of England is of diversities of sentiment and teaching in non-essentials, and which, at the same time, rightly concedes so much individual liberty to all its members, this state of things should have grown up, is more to be deplored than wondered at. It requires great discretion in the clergy, and a very tender care for the feelings of those of their people who differ from themselves, to check that sort of undisciplined zeal which often makes good and pious men overlook the evil consequences likely to flow from the rupture caused in the parish by the erection of such an irregular place of worship as you complain of. How far it would have been possible for you by greater tact to avert the rupture which has ensued, I have not the means of deciding, but I know that, looking to the contrast and the not unnatural collision between your own deep convictions and the equally deep convictions of some of your parishioners, you have had a very difficult task, and I am bound to say that you have made various efforts to conciliate those who differ from you. . . . The result [of all that has passed] has been the erection of the dissenting chapel in question. I call it a dissenting chapel because the only way in which it can be legally protected is by its being registered as a dissenting chapel, and I presume it has been so registered. My advice to other clergymen who have applied to me under similar circumstances has usually been not to trouble themselves as to such chapels. The quiet performance of their own duty is far more likely to win their people from such irregularities than any direct interference. . . . It is only in very exceptional cases that I think it is wise to invoke the law in order to prevent members of the Church of England from being deceived by mistaking dissenting ministers and their worship for the clergy and worship of the Church of England ; and even in such a case the law is only invoked to compel registration. If, therefore, the persons by whom you feel yourself aggrieved have registered their building as a dissenting meeting-house, your wise course is to leave them alone as much as possible, merely using your private influence with those whom you can reach to point out to them the great irregularity of the course pursued. No clergyman of this diocese will think of officiating in the building in question.

"If you desire more specific advice, I shall be glad to give it. I have contented myself with recommending that general course of quiet forbearance which, I think, is right in itself, and most likely to keep your people attached to yourself and to the Church. —Believe me to remain, my dear Mr. ——, yours very truly,

"A. C. LONDON."

Irvingism was in those years attracting more attention than now. In August 1862, the Bishop writes to a friend :—

". . . I have read the greater part of the second volume of Irving's life. He was plainly mad, and so for the time were all the people who prophesied to him, though one of them—Baxter, the solicitor—is a shrewd man of business, whom I often see in London. I was struck, however, this morning, in reading the 2nd Lesson from the Acts, with the thought how completely they lived as St. Paul and his company, looking for distinct guidance at every turn. The Apostle had good grounds, and they had not ; but the frame of mind in both was much the same—a waiting upon God for guidance at every step. I suppose we all may have this guidance if we will look for it, but we have no right to look for it otherwise than in the common indications of God's will. The scene of Mr. Baxter, a quiet solicitor, going to the Court of Chancery, and waiting there four hours in expectation of a message from heaven to deliver to the Chancellor, is painfully strange. . . ."

Important efforts were made during these years, under the Bishop's guidance, to promote a better system of middle-class education in London, and the religious difficulty came, as always, to the front. The Bishop's known sympathy with the liberal school in educational matters led some of his friends to suppose that he would agree with them in deciding to cut the troublesome knot by making the education in the proposed schools secular only, and leaving the religious teaching to be given at home or elsewhere. The Bishop hastened to assure them that such was not his view :—

The Bishop of London to the Rev. W. Rogers.

"LONDON HOUSE, S.W.,
April 3, 1866.

"MY DEAR ROGERS,—I have read an article in the *Times* of to-day on your scheme of middle-class education. Some remarks in this article make it necessary for me to remind you that, when I consented to connect my name with your scheme, I stated as distinctly as I could that you must adopt a system of *religious* instruction. . . . I am as distinctly convinced as I ever was in my life of the following axioms, which I inherited from Dr. Arnold, if I did not receive them long before I came under the influence of his great authority :—

" 1*st*. That a system of mere secular instruction is not education.

" 2*dly*. That there can be no real education without religious teaching, and that such religious teaching must be based on doctrine, in the highest and purest sense of that word.

" 3*dly*. That when circumstances make people rest satisfied with a system of mere secular instruction in any educational institution, they consent to act under a great disadvantage, to which they ought not to subject those whom they would instruct without a proved necessity, and without taking other means to fill up the deficiency.   .

" 4*thly*. That it is quite possible to give a sound Christian education and instruction, based on the great Gospel verities, which shall include the mass of English children, even those who do not belong to the Church.

"Now I do not see any necessity for so great a sacrifice as a purely secular system implies in the case of those for whom you wish to provide. The large number of Jewish children can well be provided for by an authorised exemption.

"I understood at our meeting that the intention was to appoint a clergyman of the Church of England head-master, and to leave him free to arrange the system with the Council.   But everything which has been published in the newspapers appears to me to be written with a different view, and I feel that the time has come when the real state of the case must be put forward.   I do not think it is fair to the public to leave any further doubt on the subject, and I am sure you would not wish my name to be used either as approving principles which I disapprove, or to conciliate to the scheme persons who are good enough to trust me, while it is not intended that the views I can alone approve shall prevail.

"I leave it to yourself to determine how this difficulty is to be met, but met I am sure it must be, or the scheme will fail from not being honestly brought before the public in its true colours.   What you want is such a system for the middle class as Rugby has long offered for the higher, with the exceptions which the fact of your institution being a day school for London boys necessitates.   And I am sure the sooner you make this distinctly known, either by the publication of this letter or otherwise, the better. . . .—Yours sincerely,   A. C. LONDON."

And again, a few weeks later :—

"I have no belief in a system which, whenever education comes athwart direct religious teaching, as it must do continually, tries to evade difficulties by an unworthy compromise."

Such extracts as this Chapter has exhibited from the voluminous and varied correspondence of the Bishop's London years might easily be multiplied.   But a sufficient picture has probably been presented of what were, during those twelve years, his public life and policy.   It would be inappropriate, even if it were possible, to depict in like manner the home-life of London House and Fulham during his Episcopate.   Some glimpses of that remarkable home-life he has himself given to the world in the Memoirs of his wife and son.   In the spring of 1868 he purchased, by means of a bequest which had been left him by a distant relative, the small estate of Stonehouse, in the Isle of Thanet.

"This home," he writes, "was intended as a refuge from the almost overwhelming work and anxieties of the diocese of London. It had been an established and necessary rule that the Bishop of London should escape from his labours and out of his diocese for a considerable vacation every year; without this alleviation, no human constitution could stand the pressure of the constant work. Hitherto we had wandered in our vacations from one spot to another. It seemed better now, as an opportunity presented itself, to secure a fixed vacation-home to which our children and ourselves might always together turn, and where we might all together carry on our home pursuits without the interruption of seeking a new residence each season. We had no thought then in entering on 1868 that it was to be the last year of our connection with the See of London, and that the place in which we settled our private home was in the new diocese to which I was so soon to be called."[1]

Diary.

"Stonehouse, *Sunday,* 1*st Novr.* (*All Saints' Day*) 1868.— Preached at Broadstairs. What events in so short a time! Tuesday evening I learned from Mr. Hodgson how ill the Archbishop of Canterbury was, . . . and by Wednesday (Oct. 28th) at noon, the flags half-mast high and the tolling bells announced to the Thanet part of his diocese that he had gone to his rest. . . .

"Stonehouse, *Sunday,* 8*th Novr.*—On Tuesday (Nov. 3) I attended the dear Archbishop's funeral at Addington, returning here at night. A sad sight, that large family party following his coffin to the little church. . . . To-day I preached at Ramsgate. The newspapers and all letters full of speculations as to the Archbishopric. . . . We are very quiet down here, away from all the turmoil. God will guide those who have to act for the Church. . . . With the decease of the second Archbishop with whom I have served on the Bench, I seem to enter on a third stage of my Episcopate. Whether it be short or long, O Lord, grant that it may be spent with a single eye to Thy glory and to

---

[1] *Catharine and Craufurd Tait,* pp. 60, 61.

the good of souls.   The calm of this seaside retreat is very grateful.   We are having a new honeymoon after twenty-five years of married life.

"*Tuesday, Novr.* 17, 1868.—The days passed quietly at Stonehouse after the good Archbishop's funeral, and I and Catharine remained very little if at all anxious.   I felt almost certain that the Archbishop of York would be appointed to Canterbury and the Bishop of Oxford to York.   When friends came down they introduced a little of the anxiety which, it appeared, was growing in London, and on Sunday when Henry Selfe and A. came, they were so much excited that it was impossible not to feel a little of it.   They went away on Wednesday, and we fell again into our quiet state. . . . On Friday morning (Nov. 13th) Fisher entered and gave Disraeli's letter into my hand.   In the afternoon he returned to London with my answer."

The letters in question were as follows :—

The Right Hon. B. Disraeli to the Bishop of London.

"GROSVENOR GATE, *Nov.* 12, 1868.

"MY DEAR LORD,—It is my desire, if it meet your own wishes, to recommend Her Majesty to elevate you to the Primacy.

"I can assure you, in so doing, I feel a responsibility as grave as any your Lordship can experience if you accept this paramount trust ; but I believe that I am taking a course which will be the most serviceable to the Church, especially at this critical moment in its history.—I have the honour to remain, my dear Lord, faithfully yours,   B. DISRAELI."

The Bishop of London to the Right Hon. B. Disraeli.

"STONEHOUSE, THANET, 13 *Nov.* 1868.

"MY DEAR SIR,—I have this morning received your letter of yesterday.   I accept with a deep feeling of responsibility the offer which you make in terms so kind and considerate, and I pray that, by the Divine blessing, I may be guided aright in these difficult days. , Grateful for your kindly feeling towards myself, I remain, my dear Sir, yours very faithfully,   A. C. LONDON."

Diary.

"On Saturday, Catharine and I went up to London, that I might be ready for the consecration of the Bishop of Peterborough in Whitehall Chapel on Sunday. I thought it necessary to send a line to the Archbishop of York and the Bishops of Oxford and Ripon, who were to assist at the consecration.

"That [Sunday] was a solemn day. The circumstances were peculiar indeed. The public did not know of my appointment. There was a great solemnity in going through that remarkable service, just as I was closing the Episcopate which began in the same chapel exactly twelve years before. . . .

"Next morning the *Times* announced the appointment, and I had an interview with Disraeli, the details of which were curious. . . . The servant announced me as Archbishop of Canterbury, on which I said that was not *my* mode of announcing myself. This led him to say that he had hoped to keep the matter secret till all his appointments were ready. Then he harangued me on the state of the Church ; spoke of rationalists, explained that those now so called did not follow Paulus. He spoke at large of his desire to rally a Church party, which, omitting the extremes of rationalism and ritualism, should unite all other sections of the Church ; alluded to his Church appointments as aiming at this— Champneys, Merivale, Wordsworth, Gregory, Leighton, myself, Jackson. He promised to support a Church Discipline Bill, but deprecated its being brought in by Lord Shaftesbury. Remarked that, whether in office or out, he had a large Church party. . . . I stated my views shortly, and we separated. I have only seen him once since. Within a very short time he had resigned office."

A few extracts may perhaps be given from the letters of congratulation which he received.

Bishop Thirlwall, of St. David's, wrote :—

"Rejoicing as I do in your elevation to the Primacy, when I consider how enormously the ordinary cares and anxieties of the office are increased by the present circumstances of the Church, I could hardly have treated your appointment as matter for personal congratulation, if it were not that to be generally recognised as the fittest person to fill such a place at such a juncture is itself an honour higher than the dignity itself. I believe you are so recognised by all who do not belong to the party of those whom it will not be the lightest part of your task to keep within due bounds; and this well-earned confidence will be one element of your strength. I am myself persuaded that the helm could not have been placed in hands better able to steer our vessel through the straits in which she is now entangled, and most heartily do I hope that you will be blessed with a long continuance of health and vigour for the labour and heat of the day, and that a main part of the reward of your evening may consist in the prosperity of your work."

" Looking to the future of the English Church," wrote Professor Lightfoot, " at a great crisis in her history, I cannot but feel most deeply thankful for the appointment. . . . Alas ! there is one sad thought connected with an event which otherwise would have given unmingled joy : the pleasant associations connected with Fulham must now become memories. ὡς δεινὸν ἡ φιλοχωρία. But, if I feel this, the wrench to yourself must be very far greater."

Dean Stanley wrote :—

" It is indeed a solemn, almost an awful, thought to think that you are in the place where, of all others, you can do most good to the Church and country—the place which of all others had most need of you in this most critical juncture. A thousand thoughts of the past and future rush into my mind. In no common sense I do indeed trust and pray that grace and strength may be given to you in the years that—so we cannot help hoping and believing—may be prolonged, in a sphere, if more arduous, yet less laborious, than that which you will leave.

The Rev. F. D. Maurice wrote :—

" It can scarcely have satisfied any of us to join in general addresses of regret at the loss we have suffered, and of thankfulness for the blessing which has been granted to the Church. Each of us has had special experience of your care of us, which cannot be forgotten, and which has done much to teach us what a 'father in God' means. I am sure your Grace does not wish for congratulations on the burdens of new responsibility which it has pleased God to lay upon you. But it may be one of the means by which He enables you to sustain them, to know how much clergymen of all opinions, popular and unpopular, have looked up to you and trusted you. May your Grace be a witness to the whole Church, as you have been to us in this diocese, that there is a unity in Christ which no differences can destroy or even impair."

Dean Hook wrote from Chichester :—

"I remember, though you may have forgotten, that when the late Dean of Carlisle was nominated to the See of London, I took the liberty of predicting the success of your labours, from my acquaintance with the peculiar talent you possess for 'ruling without showing that you rule' the most unruly of men, the clergy. My prediction has been fulfilled, for I believe that no Bishop of London has accomplished so much as you have done. . . . In my old age I again assume the character of a prophet, and I foretell that the historian who shall succeed me will, when he records your administration of the Province of Canterbury, have to place the name of Tait among the most distinguished of the many eminent men who have sat in the throne of Augustine. I only hope that you will not forget that a Metropolitan is more than a Diocesan, and that the weight of your character will be felt throughout the Province. . . . I am still devoted to the Church's cause, and, having three sons and two sons-in-law, I have the pleasure of knowing that they have inherited my loyalty. . . . Perhaps they may be doomed to martyrdom, for I think in the predicted falling-away there will be a persecution of the clergy of all denominations. . . . I am so near the end that I hope it will not come in my time, for I am terribly sensitive, and should not like to burn. The burning of a fat man would be awful! I will not congratulate you on having incurred fresh responsibilities, but I may be permitted to congratulate Mrs. Tait on the tribute paid to her husband's merits with an approbation, I may say, all but universal. . . . If our friend Stanley is appointed to London, I shall turn Red Republican, and go in for Disestablishment."

His old Oxford friend and tutor, Mr. Frederick Oakeley,

who had now for many years been working as a Roman Catholic priest in Islington, wrote in terms of the warmest affection, adding—

"I remember it was what your friends predicted long, long ago at Balliol, and it is an evidence of our prescience. . . . What a curious fact it is that one like myself should have been a pupil of the Bishop of Winchester and the tutor of the Archbishop of Canterbury."[1]

Diary.

"STONEHOUSE, *Novr.* 22, 1868.—I have been almost overwhelmed by letters of congratulation and good-will. . . . To-day I have preached at St. Peter's. I intended to have had the day quiet for prayer and reading. I do feel, I think, in this great change, the nearness of the final change, and the nothingness of earthly honours. Such things come to a man of my age, and in my state of health, with a very softened feeling. O Lord, keep me day by day waiting upon Thee, day by day striving simply to do Thy will, through Jesus Christ. Give me the will and the power to fulfil the duties of this awful post in quiet dependence upon Thee.

"23 *November* 1868.—We have sent off to-day about 160 letters. This is the anniversary of my consecration in Whitehall Chapel twelve years ago. . . . How greatly have I been blessed during these years! . . . Great has been the assistance I have received from the laity rallying round me, especially in the matter of the ' Bishop of London's Fund.' . . . The principle on which I have gone all these twelve years has been not to repress, and always, if possible, to encourage every zealous effort to advance Christ's cause. . . . Amid many mistakes and abundant failures on my own part, God has watched over the work. Lord, I pray Thee to grant that in this new post I may be sustained by Thee. Teach me to live a quieter, a more calm, a holier life. I thank Thee, O Lord, for the great help I have received from my dear wife. Spare her to me, I beseech Thee, for Jesus Christ's sake. . . .

"FULHAM, *Christmas Day*, 1868.—The ordination week passed, full of work and solemn interest. My last address to the

---

[1] See above, p. 44.

candidates in this chapel. And now our last Christmas Day. Preached in Fulham Church, extempore. An excellent sermon by Fisher in the chapel, which was full of the parish, in the afternoon. Lighted up, it looked beautiful. The Choir of Fulham Church came, and we had carols and hymns in the hall, and all our old people, and the orphans who had roused us in early morning by their Christmas hymns. A happy, holy Christmas to end our Fulham time.

"FULHAM, 31*st December*, 11.30 P.M.—I have seen the sun of 1868 go down over the Thames, as I have watched the last sun of many years back. . . . Year has succeeded year, and time has healed our wounds, and Craufurd has become a man, and Edith and Agnes have been added to our family, and much happiness has, by God's mercy, been ours in this home. And now we have come to the end of our connection with Fulham, and, before long, we shall, for the short remainder of our life, be launched on a new home. O Lord, forgive my many shortcomings for the past; O strengthen me for the time to come. Yesterday, as my last act, I published my letter to Mr. Mackonochie.[1] I trust it may do good. Grant, Lord, that all good men may be united in mutual forbearance, and work each according to his own way in saving souls, but avoiding foolish contentions from mere obstinacy, whereby the Church of Christ is rent asunder. O Lord, this year will close in a few minutes. We shall hear the bells from many spires announcing its death. Raise us to hopes of a bright immortality with Thee for ever. Amen."

[1] See above, p. 435.

END OF VOL. I.

Printed by T. and A. CONSTABLE, Printers to Her Majesty, at the Edinburgh University Press.